A Southern Family

Also by Gail Godwin

The Perfectionists
Glass People
The Odd Woman
Dream Children
Violet Clay
A Mother and Two Daughters
Mr Bedford and the Muses
The Finishing School

A Southern Family

GAIL GODWIN

Heinemann: London

William Heinemann Ltd
10 Upper Grosvenor Street, London W1X 9PA

LONDON   MELBOURNE
JOHANNESBURG   AUCKLAND

First published 1987
Copyright © Gail Godwin 1987

British Library Cataloguing in Publication Data

Godwin, Gail
  A southern family.
  I. Title
  813'.54[F]   PS3557.0315

  ISBN 0 434 29753 4

Printed in Great Britain by
Richard Clay Ltd, Bungay, Suffolk

for Tommy

PART ONE

Clare and Julia,
Julia and Clare,
One was dark,
The other fair.
The dark one fled
As soon as she could;
The fair one returned
To home's deep wood.
Old faces haunted
The one who fled;
The other sought answers
Among the dead.
And in the end
They both turned gray;
And their star spun on
To its own dying day.

—*from* Julia's doggerel book

I: OLD FRIENDSHIPS

Going to see Clare's family on the isolated hilltop where Ralph Quick had built his domestic fortress was an ordeal for Julia. She went no more than she could help, and only on those occasions, once or twice a year, when her oldest friend was in residence. Clare, who now lived in New York, always flew down to Mountain City, was met by her mother and stepfather and half brothers at the airport, and was borne away to Quick's Hill in one of their numerous cars. Once there, Clare had explained to Julia, she lost all capacity for independent mobility. She relied on Lily or Ralph or one of the boys to take her anywhere she needed to go. Several times Ralph Quick had offered Clare the keys to a car, but when the hour came to get in it by herself and go where she was supposed to go, something was always wrong: the gearshift was mysteriously locked, or the heater was jammed on High, or the tank was empty and none of the men was at home to unlock the gas pump down by the dogs' kennels. When Julia had asked Clare why she didn't just rent herself a car, she could surely afford it, Clare had laughed brusquely and said, "You know yourself, Julia, that it wouldn't work. It would be interpreted by them as my making a kind of statement, and Ralph would resent it and take it out on Lily, and then my visit would be spoiled for her, and where would the triumph be in *that*?"

That was the kind of atmosphere prevailing up there: layer

upon layer of debilitating resentments and intrigues that over the years had sapped the family members of their individual strengths, and yet bathed them, as a unit, in a certain sinister charm. Clare, the only one who could be said to have "escaped," was still under the family spell. When she came back, she willingly reentered the noxious enclosure and let herself be sucked back into the old games. Julia had once been under the spell, but that was years ago when she was fourteen and had a crush on the blooming, dynamic, unconventional Lily and was attracted to the sexy, penniless younger man Lily had shocked Julia's parents by marrying. But Lily Quick in her present incarnation saddened Julia, and she had become wary of Ralph Quick's insinuating manner. As for Clare's two half brothers, Julia really knew only the elder, Theo. She had danced him around when he was an infant, pretending he was hers by the boy she had then loved. And a decade ago, when Julia had made her decision to return home and take the job at North State College, she had taught Theo briefly in her Western Civ section, but he had angered her, and wounded her pride, by dropping the course.

The only vital connection Julia had to the Quicks now was Clare—who had kept her own father's name, Campion. The two of them had been friends since a day in second grade at St. Clothilde's, when Julia had come upon Clare in near-hysteria over her leggings; they had been all tangled up and the school bus was about to leave. Clare sat on the floor of the cloakroom, a passionate, panicked heap of despair, the wrong foot jammed into the wrong leg. What had both annoyed and enamored Julia was the other child's single-minded rapt air of doom: in her mind, the school bus had departed without her; she was experiencing in her imagination whatever consequences went with her having missed it. Feeling powerful and generous, Julia had knelt down and pulled off the leggings and reasoned Clare out of her fantasy of defeat. Running, the two girls had made the bus—which, Julia realized later, would surely have waited for them anyway. Aboard the bus, Mother von Blücher, in an ill temper, had helped Clare with the leggings. But Mother von Blücher was famous for her ill temper. "Boy, she really *hates* us!" the little girls would exclaim, fascinated by her perpetual wrath. Now, as an adult, Julia realized that the Prussian nun's anger had been more complicated: probably it had a lot to do with the fact that the war had just ended and the Germans had lost and Leipzig, the city of her girlhood, had been given away by our president to the Russians.

The self-centeredness of childhood—and beyond. How long it took to learn that others saw the world from the center of themselves just as thoroughly as you saw it from yours. If the Prussian nun had still been alive, Julia would have gone out to the convent and spent the afternoon talking with her about Leipzig. "I'm a professor of history now, Mother" (only they were all called "Sister" since Vatican II had revised so many things for the Catholics) and I can better comprehend the irreplaceable loss of certain continuities. That the city where Luther argued and Goethe studied and Bach and Mendelssohn wrote music ... not to mention the personal achievements of your own family ... should have come to such an end, well, I would have been ill-tempered too; perhaps even with God. Were you descended by any chance from the General Blücher who defeated Napoleon's forces at the Battle of Leipzig? Was that where your family got its "von"? I would have asked you these things years ago, except I didn't know about General Blücher, and I probably didn't believe, in those days, that nuns had histories. Besides, I was far too busy thinking about myself!"

Clare, at forty-two, still had her rapt air of doom. Despite all the good things that had happened to her, she continued to rely on Julia to reason her out of her expectations of failure and convince her of her own worth. She had become the writer she had wanted to be since she was twelve, she had achieved an enviable combination of artistic and popular success, yet she was still tensed—you could see it in the line of her shoulders—for a crushing defeat. That wasn't all of her, of course. She was also funny, wickedly acute about people, and, when not plotting scenarios of misfortune for herself, had a large capacity for enjoying life. At her best, there was no one in the world Julia got more out of talking to; and even at her worst she would sometimes produce the most surprising and penetrating insights. She had a mind that never stopped questioning and an insatiable craving for things of the spirit; her example, on many occasions, had provided Julia with much-needed doses of confidence and courage. Yet Julia recognized as often as ever in Clare that child on the floor of the cloakroom, sealed away in a private ecstasy of failure that no proofs to the contrary could ever dispel.

Their friendship had lasted thirty-five years, surviving some lengthy periods of dormancy: after Clare at sixteen fled Mountain City to live with some Campion relatives; while Julia was trying to be Mrs. Starkweather Lowndes; and during the years Clare spent in England. It had also survived the novel Clare had published a few years ago, one based rather closely on Julia's family, but in which Clare had taken considerable creative liberties—some more disquieting, or annoying, to Julia than the actual truths from which these fictions had been derived.

On this crisp Saturday evening, the first day of October, Julia was headed to Quick's Hill because it was Lily's birthday, and Clare, whom she had talked to on the phone but not yet seen, had told her it would please Lily if her old admirer "dropped up" for some cake and champagne. "You don't have to come for the whole dinner," Clare had said, "I know they get on your nerves as a group. But Lily has always liked you specially, and then tomorrow you and I can go off and have our picnic alone." The unsaid reverberated, as it so often did between them, beneath her actual words. Julia knew that her friend always felt she had to barter emotionally with her family for the time spent with other people during her visits home. Julia's "dropping up" to Lily's birthday festivities tonight would "pay" for Clare's guilt-free outing tomorrow.

To get to Ralph Quick's Hill, you drove out through Spook's Branch Valley, which once had been the enclave of Mountain City's horsey families. But now the Castleberry estate, where Julia as a child had eaten cold oatmeal out of a silver bowl when she spent the night with the Castleberry twins, had been torn down, and its rolling pastures leveled and divided into one-acre housing tracts. Farther out, the Van Camps' vast meadowland, where their show horses used to romp and graze, had become a private golf course for a community of mansard-roofed dwellings called "Townhouse Acres."

Recently, she had taken her father on an inspection tour of this and several other condominiums going up in town; he was seventy-nine years old, with emphysema, and she had hoped to convince him that he might last longer without the burden of an eight-room house and two acres of lawn and garden in a neighborhood going down fast. Neville Richardson had enjoyed the outing, turning up his nose at the nailed-down shag carpeting, the democratically identical balconies overlooking the picture-postcard views. He was never more lively than when he had things to sneer at, and here, in the space of one afternoon, she had given him cupids in a fountain surrounded by too many colors of impatiens, ornamental shrubberies—some still bearing the price tag from the nursery—languishing sadly in their beds of wood chips, and "color-coordinated" bathrooms and kitchens. Going home in the car, he had sucked at his unfiltered cigarette unrepentantly, cutting his eyes at her like a wizened naughty boy, preparing his riposte. "If it's all the same to you, Cordelia," he'd said at last, "I'd prefer to finish out my days in that old-fashioned thing called a *house,* even if I do have a stroke while mowing my lawn or get my throat cut by a darky neighbor who's decided he needs my wallet. Either death would suit me better than living as a prisoner in one of those Shangri-las of tasteless uniformity. Besides"—he triumphantly waggled his glowing Lucky Strike at her between yellowed thumb and fore-finger—"*this* is what is going to kill me."

"It's your funeral, Father," Julia had said cheerfully.

"Quite so. And now, for matters germane to the living. Shall we have chicken livers boiled in red wine, with saffron rice, for our supper, or maybe some smoked salmon, if the Fresh Market's got any—with white toast and butter and a sprinkling of watercress?"

This evening, they'd had another of his specialities: grilled tomatoes, mushrooms, and sausages, which he prepared. Years of cooking in the stead of his alcoholic wife—who never ate—had made him epicurean when it came to treats for himself. Tonight he had been at his most entertaining, doing cruel imitations of different television newscasters: Bruce Morton's one-sided leer as he signed off, Bob Schieffer's good-natured puns that sometimes fell flat, Tom Brokaw's inability to pronounce his *l*'s, a certain wide-eyed look of relish Dan Rather betrayed when about to report a disaster. Julia had felt relaxed and amused and wished she didn't have to cut him short to go up to Quick's Hill for Lily's birthday. She had found herself looking around at her father's things, the way he lived—finicky, self-satisfied, and scholarly—and comparing it with what she knew awaited her on Quick's Hill. The contrast evoked a surprising, relieved loyalty in her towards her own upbringing, whereas when she was growing up, she had writhed under the narrow assumptions of the Richardsons and couldn't wait to be with the "free" Quicks again. Maybe I am getting old and complacent, she thought, picking up her father's current library book from the table next to his reclining chair, *Sir George Otto Trevelyan, A Memoir,* by his son, the historian. She opened to the first page. "The Trevelyans are a very old family," she read, imagining how her father would have savored those opening chords of superiority. "All families, we must suppose, are equally old, whether we adopt the Darwinian or the Fundamentalist view of human origins; but 'an old family,' I take it, can trace an ascent far back in the catalogue of gentry."

"Don't mind me," Neville Richardson had told her gaily, "I'll be quite content with my book. I know you have to get on up there to see Clare." Sensing her reluctance to go, he was perversely enjoying rushing her off. "So it's Lily Quick's birthday. She must be hitting Senior Citizenhood by now, though she's still a handsome gal. Give her my felicitations. Tell her I said she adds spice to our Library Board. I can't stand him; he's got an impertinence that sets my teeth on edge. And now look at that older son. Gone and made a strikingly bad marriage himself. I hear the girl can't read or write."

"No, it's the girl's father who can't read or write," Julia said. "And the marriage is over. Snow is in Georgia, working in a mill, and she's signed over complete custody of the little boy to Theo. Theo and Jason are living up on Quick's Hill with Lily and Ralph."

"More fun and games," said her father. "And now we wait for the little boy to grow up and make his own unsuitable marriage. Well, give Clare my best. Tell her I am trying to live up to her flattering portrait of me, but there will always be serious lapses, I'm afraid."

In her novel based on the Richardsons, Clare had made Julia's father into a saintly Southern schoolmaster. The rampant and ultimately tragic alcoholism of Julia's late mother had been tempered to a fey, quaint, picturesque tipsiness. Then Clare had taken parts of herself and appropriated parts of Freddy Stratton and made the composite character into Julia's younger sister. And they had all lived amusingly and revealingly together in the English timbered house out at the Belvedere School, and Clare's book had been very popular because everyone wanted to believe that was how a certain kind of Southern family lived.

The turnoff to Ralph Quick's came just beyond the Spook's

Branch Fire Station and the big Baptist cemetery, before the valley narrowed abruptly into a cove whose rough, unpaved roads and inhospitable mountain families, many of whom still lived without plumbing, had so far deterred even the most avaricious of developers.

Turning left, you crossed a wooden bridge over Spook's Branch, the creek that had given the valley its name, and traveled up an access road, recently blacktopped since the land on either side had been sprouting tract houses. Ralph Quick's private hill, announced by a carved wooden sign hanging from an old beech tree, was ascended by a driveway whose hairpin curves were set at a tilt that made your engine gasp and your tires spit gravel. Littering the grassy banks along the steep road were abandoned materials from Ralph Quick's building trade, destroying the otherwise rugged serenity of the rise. There were piles of rotting lumber which looked as if they had been dumped hurriedly from a truck and allowed to lie where they fell, like pickup sticks. There was a rusted wheelbarrow with cement dried to its sides, and an untidy stack of corrugated-tin sheets, also rusted, and even a portable toilet unit tipped at a precarious angle, with weeds and autumn wild flowers growing profusely out of its open door.

That someone would buy a hill of virgin forest, cut a road to the top, build a hundred-thousand-dollar house there, and then leave all this mess along the approach route caused much speculation among the Quicks' acquaintances. Ralph Quick maintained that he "might need" this stuff at some time in the future, but even his own foreman went around saying that the materials were too far gone after being exposed to the elements for so many years. Clare had told Julia that the mess, at first *perhaps* left there by her stepfather until he could find uses for it in other construction jobs, had gradually become a weapon, a sort of ugly *message* from Ralph to Lily Quick when their once-passionate marriage had deteriorated into a holding pattern of outward appearances. "It's his way of saying to Lily, 'I'll be damned if you can cover up *all* our rot with manners'" was Clare's interpretation. As Julia's VW Rabbit sputtered gamely up the unsightly curves on this lovely October evening, the historian in her hypothesized that maybe Ralph's upward climb had proved finally too exhausting and he had collapsed at the summit of his aspirations, like Toynbee's "arrested civilizations," which, after responding magnificently to a severe challenge, had no energies left over for further development. Or, in Ralph's case, even to clean up the evidence of his rise.

The house, of rough-hewn, golden-gray local stones set by a mason who knew his craft, was an example of the way Ralph used to preach houses should be built, back when he had just married Lily, to everyone's amazement, and was working summers on a construction crew to supplement Lily's income as a newspaper reporter. "None of this damn pretentious bric-a-brac," Ralph would say. "A house, if it's designed right, should fit into its landscape like it grew there. I intend to get to the place in life where I can tell potential customers to go to hell if they won't build with taste. I may be a mountain boy with one-eighth Cherokee blood, but I can tell you what taste is. It's not bric-a-brac or imitating the Greeks and the Victorians. It's finding your ideal site and extending it with the finest kind of simplicity."

The setting and proportions of this rambling, warm-stoned house, backed by National Park forest to the top of the ridge and commanding a wide view of Spook's Branch Valley, a scoop of downtown Mountain City on the other side of the local hills, and all of this encircled by the distant blue unfoldings of the Great Smokies, certainly lived up to Ralph's young dream. But paradoxically, thought Julia, the house could never realize its best potential while its builder lived inside it with his family. Its rugged, open-to-air-and-light design was seriously compromised by the life (or, rather, lives: all of them were usually at cross-purposes) that went on inside. For as long as they had lived here, it seemed to Julia, they had shut themselves up inside, closed all the windows, turned on the heat or the air-conditioning, depending on the season, and continued to provoke and intrigue and smolder, oblivious to the peace and beauty of their immediate surroundings. Their agitations spilled out, eventually, infecting the appearance and character of the landscape, just as Ralph's symbolic clutter had marred the approach.

As she searched for a parking spot among the assorted vehicles jammed into the slovenly carport and clustered around the pool (clogged with fallen leaves), she was bracing herself—and losing her temper in advance—for the traditional onslaught of the Quicks' badly behaved German shepherds. It was a bit much that you had to take such pains to avoid hitting them, when they hurled themselves slavering at your car and clawed the paint off your fenders and looked as though they could hardly

wait to rip you to pieces. One of the brutes actually *had* met its
untimely end during just such a confrontation with a car, laden
with visitors, arriving to celebrate Theo's little boy's christening
three years ago. Clare had related the story to Julia, making it,
with her narrative instincts, into a little masterpiece of comic
horror: how the dog hadn't gotten out of the way quickly enough
as the driver, flustered by frontal attacks from the other dogs,
had tried to wedge his car into the only space available, over at
the far side of the pool, between Ralph's two jettisoned
antiques—a 1954 salmon-and-cream Lincoln that once had been
the pride of a now-deceased doctor in town, and a saucy yellow
1960 Corvair with two bashed fenders, belonging to the doctor's
surviving maiden sister, whom Ralph had "adopted," as he liked
to say, though there were others, including Lily Quick, who
maintained that the arrogant old lady knew a good thing when
she saw it and had bewitched Ralph with her aristocratic ways
into becoming her unpaid personal servant, driver, and
handyman. Ralph kept these cars, he said, because one of these
days, when he had a spare moment to himself, he planned to fix
them up and sell them to a garage that leased old cars to film
productions; but Clare told Julia he kept them partly for sen-
timental reasons (the elegant Dr. Anthony Gallant had sewn
Ralph's face up after a teenage wreck and afterwards became a
sort of ideal father figure to him) and partly as another of his
passive weapons against Lily in the cold war into which their
marriage had degenerated. Anyway, Clare said, the dog got its
head squashed between the visitor's car's back bumper and
Alicia Gallant's old Corvair's bashed fender, and the poor
driver—who happened to be one of Ralph's former clients, a
lawyer for whom Ralph had built exactly the kind of house he
swore he never would build when he had reached a certain
place in life—was so upset he didn't even want to go into the
house with his family. To make matters worse, the dog hadn't
died at once and Ralph had to go and get his old Belgian semi-
automatic and fire two shots to put it out of its agony. The
shots echoed all over the mountain, said Clare, as if there had
been twice as many. "And then," she continued, "just please,
Julia, imagine *this* scene: Lily, inside the house with her party
manners, trying to console the poor lawyer and his wife, whom
she had coaxed to come in: 'You mustn't feel bad, you really
mustn't, Vixen wasn't a young dog anymore, she was getting a
bit slow and clumsy, and I don't think she could hear well. You

mustn't blame yourself, it could have happened to anybody, it could have happened to *me*, and that would have been terrible. Wouldn't it have been terrible? Yes, look at it that way, what if I had run over one of my own dogs? So, I mean, actually you have spared me, in a sense. . . .'

"Meanwhile, outside, in full view of the refreshment table in the dining room, in full view of anyone who couldn't help watching surreptitiously while nibbling a watercress sandwich and sipping champagne, are Ralph and Theo and Rafe, and the lawyer's two small children, who are fascinated by the whole thing, and they're solemnly digging this big grave on the lily bank above the pool. And beside them, on the white gravel, is a large mound covered with a bloody bedspread.

"Snow, of course, had abdicated, taking little Jason to a bedroom and lying down. After a bit, Lily sends me to get the baby so that the lawyer and his wife can see him. I go in to Snow, who is languishing under a satin comforter, the baby lying wide-eyed beside her. When I tell her Lily wants to show him around, she looks up at me as though I belong to some alien race she'll never understand. 'How can you all go on with that party?' she asks. 'How can she stay in there and pretend? If it was my dog, I'd be sick over it, not in there pouring alcohol and trying to make them feel good.' 'Well, Snow,' I said, 'it's called keeping up appearances.' 'Appearances!' she lashed out at me like a ferret. Then she sits up in bed and those cunning lavender eyes of hers are shining with triumph because she thinks she's finally pinned down an important contradiction that will show even me how absurd we all are and why she can never be one of us. 'If you all are so interested in keeping up appearances,' she says, slowly letting out her words as if she's measuring out a nice draft of poison for me to take, 'how come you invited that old nigger to my baby's christening?' 'Snow,' I said, 'that old nigger, as you call her, baby-sat with Lily when she was a little girl. And she baby-sat with Theo and Rafe. I missed out on her because she was living in Detroit when I was a child. Matty is our friend, Snow, she's like a member of the family; why, she must be in her nineties by now.' 'Well, she's not going to baby-sit with my child, and I don't care if she's a hundred,' retorts Snow. 'My momma liked to have a heart attack when that old nigger walked right up to the front of the church after the christening and took my baby out of Theo's arms. And that's just being hypocritical, saying she's like a member of the family.

You don't really mean it. You all just talk like that because it makes you seem better. Oh, the air up here always gives me a headache. Will you please go tell Theo when he gets done burying that dog I want to go home?'

"And that," Clare had concluded to Julia, "was the memorable occasion of Jason Quick's christening party on Quick's Hill. Or a few of the highlights, anyway. Of course, after all the guests had left, and Theo and Jason and Snow had gone back to their apartment, and Ralph had driven down to town to see if Alicia Gallant needed anything before nightfall, poor Lily went to her room and cried her eyes out. You see, Vixen was her very favorite dog."

That was Clare: maintaining a heedful balance between satire and loyalty whenever she described the ongoing theatricals of the family.

This evening, Julia's prepared anger towards the dogs seemed in excess for the diminished pack of creatures who surged wearily out of the shadows and dutifully surrounded her car with halfhearted barks. They're getting old, she realized, and then Clare rushed out through the carport, as she always did, to "defend" her friend. She chided them with mock sternness and flipped her fingers to disperse them. Watching her enact the old ritual, Julia was grateful, because it gave them both time to assess each other's changes during the year that had passed since their last meeting.

Julia sucked her stomach in and got out of the car as the dogs, seemingly relieved at Clare's orders, skulked away. The two women hugged awkwardly—Clare had always been restrained in her physical contacts—and then Clare said, with a little too much enthusiasm in her voice, "You're looking great!" Julia knew she was not looking great, at least not so great as she had always taken for granted it was her right to look. The past year had been particularly hard; a stranger had begun usurping her mirror, a stranger like an aunt one had resembled all one's life, but a fuller-figured lady with opinions notched distinctly into her forehead and a self-satisfied little collar of flesh beneath the once-cleancut chin. She had rushed out and written a check for three hundred and fifty dollars to the new Health Club in town, and faithfully swam and did aerobics, panting beside the twenty-five-year-old secretaries. She had become vigilant of her posture and had, to some degree, *willed* the niece, or a pretty good memory of the niece, back into the mirror. But it was an effort, and a tiring day at the college or the least lapse in vigilance was enough to summon back the matronly double.

"You're looking wonderful yourself," she told Clare, which, in a different way, was also a glossing of what she saw. As Clare had bent down to push away gently the dog that was dragging its legs, explaining as she did so that this was Liebchen, who now had arthritis, Julia was surprised to see how extensively rooted the silver hairs had become in Clare's buoyant canopy of dark curls. She was using more makeup, too, and the heavy half-moons of dark-gray eye shadow exacerbated her old doom-laden look. She had gained no additional pounds, however, which must have taken some vigilance on *her* part, because Clare dearly loved good food. But what reassured Julia most about Clare's appearance, and endeared her old friend to her afresh, was how well it had resisted that hardening sheen of visibility people often got when they'd made a name for themselves and expected to be looked at a great deal. Clare was still the old Clare. Emotions still moved, automatic and unguarded, across her face, conflicting and changing like light and clouds in an unsure sky. And it was touching, though bewildering to Julia, how completely Clare had held on to her uncertainty, manifest—especially when she was here on Quick's Hill—in the tense curve of her shoulders and the wary, edgewise slant of her otherwise graceful movements.

"You're sweet, Julia, but it's not the truth," she said, overcoming her reticence about touching, and slipping her arm around Julia's waist. "My physical disintegration is proceeding at a shocking pace. Every month that passes adds a new crack to the façade or a dangerous droop to the whole foundation." She chuckled approvingly at her own choice of words, even though she had been using them as weapons against herself. "That's why I fit right in, up here. *Everything* is falling apart. Appliances, bathroom fixtures, *people*. Theo is in terrible shape, more difficult than ever, if you can imagine that. He completely destroyed me before dinner tonight, demolished my entire *œuvre* with a single phrase. And dear Rafe is already plastered, and Lily has not looked at Ralph once all day." As she led Julia towards the house, she pointed out like a tour guide the squalid areas of the carport: the rusted tools and old tires, the empty motor-oil cans, the broken bicycles, the leaking plastic bag full of garbage the dogs had managed to extricate from an overturned can and drag wetly across the cement. "A few weeks ago, he asked her what she wanted for her birthday, and she said, 'If you'll just clean up the carport and tow away those two sacred jalopies of the Gallants, I'll think I'm in Heaven.' But instead he buys her a two-thousand-dollar Japanese ceremonial robe and she put it on this morning and has been trailing around in it all day in the heat, even though it weighs ten pounds and drags the floor. And she has not looked at him once. Oh, come in, Julia, you friendly ray of sanity and light, and cheer Lily up and talk some sense into poor Theo, and make me remember I'm not crazy, just home for a few days in the bosom of my family."

They went inside. Usually, when Julia came to the hill, she found them gathered around the kitchen table, projecting their self-dramatizations onto one another. This evening, in honor of Lily's birthday, they'd moved their act into the dining room. As Julia entered and all of them turned their faces towards her, she fought down a surge of claustrophobia. It was much too hot and stuffy in here; she could not understand why people would build a house on top of a hill and then shut out the fresh mountain air. Also, she could read, from a single sweeping glance at their expressions, what each of them expected from her. There was Theo, her old problem student, fixing her with that daunting combination of insolence and *need* she recalled all too well from the two weeks he'd suffered her history course. He was sporting a rakish new Mississippi gambler's mustache that conflicted uneasily with the other new addition to his face, a pair of over-sized gold-rimmed spectacles of the style all the young businessmen in town were wearing. Standing beside Theo's chair and nestling into the crook of his arm was a very blond and delicate-featured little boy with sad eyes: the child of Theo's marriage with the decamped Snow. Julia knew she would be expected to admire the child, and, in so doing, compensate Theo for thinking she believed him a failure because he had once dropped her course.

Then there was Rafe, two years younger than Theo. At twenty-six, Rafe was still sheltering beneath the umbrella of college life at Chapel Hill. He was indulged by the entire family for reasons Julia did not know him well enough to understand. He possessed a beachboy sort of good looks and was said to be "the smart brother," but his arrogance seemed to Julia to exceed the justifications for the epithet. Perhaps she was prejudiced, since it was obvious that Rafe saw her as a flat character, a "schoolteacher" who happened to be a friend of Clare's; to Rafe, she existed in eternal middle age, without the enrichments of the history that contained her arrogant youth. As she came into the room with Clare, Rafe granted her a brusque, polite nod, holding her attention long enough with his bloodshot blue eyes to extract from her, against her will, a silent acknowledgment of his animal appeal.

Equally disturbing in another way, Ralph Quick hunched like a cunning cat at his end of the table, his dark eyes shining at her presumptuously, waiting for her to meet *his* glance— which, for the moment, she avoided doing, as she greeted them all. He was waiting (her father had been right: "impertinent" was a good word for Ralph Quick) for her to acknowledge that he might be dangerous: that their relationship to each other might not be so simple as it had been when Julia was fourteen and could tell Clare she thought her new stepfather was sexy and feel perfectly safe from repercussions.

Even though discomfited by the hot room, the mess of dinner plates that Clare hurried to clear away, and the almost painful thrust of Quick personalities into the stronghold of her composure, Julia did not fail to notice that, except for the little boy, who was already standing, not one of the male Quicks had risen to greet her. But their social lapse made her all the more determined to be courtly herself—indeed, behaving well might be her only solace this evening—and she went straight to Lily, at the far end of the table from Ralph, and kissed her enthusiastically on the cheek. "Happy birthday," she said, extracting her drugstore-wrapped gift from the interior of her purse. "My father also sends his felicitations and says to tell you he thinks you add spice to the Library Board."

"Dear Julia," murmured Lily, looking remote and smaller in the stiff scarlet-and-blue Japanese ceremonial robe. "How thoughtful you are. But then you always were. Tell your father I think he's pretty spicy himself . . . that pungent wit." A dainty hand, fingers crooked slightly with arthritis, poked out of the voluminous folds of an ornately embroidered sleeve and swept elegantly through the air, designating with a studied carelessness the circle of seated men. "You see, you're still so much part of the family that nobody even bothers to get up," she drawled humorously, with just a touch of bite. "Here, sit beside me while I open your present."

She still misses nothing, thought Julia, sitting down as instructed beside her old heroine. I was right to love her, she thought, watching Lily tear open the drugstore tissue with childlike dispatch. She was so bold and radiant. She challenged the conventions. Lily had wanted it all, and for a while there it had looked as though she would get it. She had provided a healthy alternative to Julia's mother, who suffered from "nerves" and lived for the approval of a society that had been in flower a hundred years before. Knowing robust, frank, chestnut-haired Lily (who, somewhere during the years, had been absorbed by this fey, frailer, platinum-haired lady) had made it possible for Julia, at fourteen, to say to herself, Well, maybe I can grow up and be a woman in this society and still have some fun.

"My old perfume!" Lily was holding up the long, slender bottle for them to see. "Look Ralph, look Clare, Julia's remembered my old perfume from the Everly Apartment days." She hauled back one of the cumbersome sleeves of the two-thousand-dollar robe and sprayed her wrist prodigally with the scent, almost as if she were trying to spray herself back into the past.

There was a charged hiatus as the fragrance permeated the dining room like a haunting tune only four people there were old enough to remember. For a moment, it was only the four of them again: the young married couple and the two adolescent best friends. Handsome Rafe and his older brother, Theo, who was having some kind of teasing, repetitive dialogue with the little boy, hadn't even been born yet.

"Good old L'Heure Bleue," said Ralph from his end of the table, cocking his head significantly at Lily, who, Julia noticed, did not look directly at him.

"It's only just the cologne," Julia told her. "They didn't have the perfume."

"Well, that's fine," said Lily. "The cologne was all I could afford in the old days, anyway." She hauled up the other heavy sleeve and sprayed the other wrist.

"Angel, I don't *like* that smell!" cried the little boy.

"Jason, that's rude," said Theo, giving Julia a sly grin over the top of the child's head.

"Rafe"—Lily turned to her younger son, who had been sipping regularly from a tumbler of something with melting ice and a sprig of mint—"why don't you open the champagne, now that Julia's here."

"Now that the lady's come, can we bring in the cake?" demanded the child.

Everyone laughed indulgently, and Rafe and Theo and Jason went away to the kitchen. Clare, who was obsessive about cleaning up, was wiping away crumbs from the tablecloth before spreading the dessert plates.

"My grandson calls me Angel," Lily told Julia, "because one day I took him to Altar Guild with me and one of the women said I was an angel because I just went ahead and mended the altar cloth without making a big fuss. Jason heard her, and I've been Angel ever since. Which actually suits me fine, because he calls Snow's mother 'Grandma' and the less I have in common with the Mullinses the better." She picked up one of Julia's hands and studied it possessively. "Do you know that Ralph offered Snow five hundred dollars if she would learn her multiplication tables? She got as far as the threes and lost interest. That's Snow."

"Lily," warned Ralph, "little pitchers have big ears." He jerked his head towards the kitchen.

"Your hands are just as pretty and smooth as they always were," Lily told Julia, as though Ralph Quick had not spoken.

There was the loud pop of a champagne cork.

"Clare, are the glasses out there?" Rafe shouted from the kitchen.

"I'm just getting them, wait a minute." Clare, her tense hunch particularly noticeable as she went about playing the Martha of the household, rushed to a tall black lacquered cabinet and took out champagne glasses. They were the out-of-fashion kind: flat, open bowls of glass set on stems.

"'Just getting them'?" came an angry falsetto imitation of his sister's voice. "Holy shit, nobody can organize anything around here. All the fizz will be gone."

"Watch your language in there," Ralph Quick called from his seat.

Clare set the glasses before each person. Julia noticed that they had a thin layer of dust on them.

"All right, Rafe," called Clare, "bring on the bubbles." She shot Julia a look of humorous exasperation: *See what I mean about this place?*

Julia saw. Already, she had the beginnings of a headache from all their exhibitions and undercurrents knocking against one another like wild molecules in an airless jar. She longed to get up and swivel open one of those casement windows; she would have liked to take her napkin and wipe the layer of dust from her champagne glass.

Little Jason proudly carried in the cake, his father hovering close behind in case he tipped it. There was the requisite off-key singing of "Happy Birthday," followed by Ralph's playful singing of an extra verse: "How O-old are you?" Lily coyly blew out the three candles and said, still not looking anywhere near her husband, that women like herself had only three ages: young, none-of-your-business, and extraordinary. "And I am approaching the extraordinary." The child said, "My other grandma is sixty-five." Lily rolled her eyes back in her head and said with mock exasperation, "Your other grandma *would* tell everyone her age."

"Lily, that's just not —" Ralph began warningly.

Rafe, carelessly sloshing champagne into everyone's dusty glass, muttered angrily, "All the damn fizz is gone now."

After everybody had a piece of cake, Ralph Quick asked, "Julia, did you hear about that nun who was walking through Central Park?"

"No," said Julia innocently, thinking he was referring to something she must have missed in the newspapers. She never bothered to read the local paper; her father was a champion gossip, and he provided historical background with his local news items, as well. Sometimes, when she had a free hour out at North State College, she would go over to the library and skim through the latest issues of *The New York Times*, usually a week or more old by the time they arrived via fourth-class mail. But she performed this exercise less to keep abreast of what was happening in the world at large—her father provided her with satirical up-dates on that, too, when she dropped by after college, several evenings a week—than to remind herself that New York City had been *her* stamping ground for a few heady years after her divorce, when she was in graduate school at Columbia, and then teaching, and also managing to have some fun. Just leafing through the inky pages of the *Times*—the art scene, the ads, even the want ads—brought back those gloriously invigorating days when she had dared to live purely for herself, before Duty to Family called her back to Mountain City.

"Well, this nun, you see, was walking through Central Park late one afternoon, just about dusk," Ralph Quick was saying, "when, all of a sudden, this fellow leaps out of the bushes and rapes her."

Only at this point did Julia realize she was in for one of Ralph's "naughty jokes," as Lily called them. How could she have been caught so unawares? Telling "naughty jokes," pouncing on people with sexual puns and double entendres, was one of Ralph's conversational signatures. It was, Julia also realized, his way of flirting with her this evening.

"Well, anyway, after it was over," continued Ralph in his sing-song mountain twang, "and the nun is straightening out her clothes, the rapist says, 'Hey listen, Sister, what are you going to tell the priest the next time you go to confession?' Well, the nun thinks for a minute"—Ralph cocked his head to one side, pretending to be the nun, his black eyes dancing with the punchline he was about to spring on them—"and then she answers"—pitching his voice up to a shy female octave—"'Well, I'm going to tell him I was raped *twice*, if you have the time'."

Julia heard herself laughing with the rest of them. But except for Ralph, and Rafe, who seemed to derive intemperate glee from his father's rendition of the randy nun, there was something forced about their laughter. Julia and every one of Lily's children had gone to St. Clothilde's or La Fosse Hall, the boys' division of the convent school, and images of real nuns, particular nuns, were rising reproachfully in each of their memories as they laughed to please Ralph, and also out of the all-too-human maliciousness that delights in reversals of predictable virtue and order. Julia saw Clare flush and at the same time glower (although she was laughing, too) and she knew Clare was thinking of her beloved Sister Patrick, the woman Clare had idolized while Julia had been idolizing Lily. Clare always went out to see Sister Patrick on her visits home, and last year Clare and Julia had taken the nun to a popular new restaurant in town, and they'd ordered champagne to go with their tacos and salad, and Sister Patrick, always a delightful raconteur, with the sharp tongue of the Irish rebel, had surpassed herself.

When the laughter had died down, Lily took a long, meditative sip of champagne. Her face was very pink; she looked as if she were stifling in that robe; but her eyes were a faraway sapphire-blue. "I've often thought it would be nice to be a nun," she said with an air of bemusement. "I remember how I used to enjoy visiting those Carmelites when we lived out in Dogwood Hills, in that first house Ralph built for us. I used to bake them pound cakes, just so I would have an excuse to go over and visit. The summer I was expecting you, Rafe, I'd go see those nuns at least once a week. I looked forward to it. Of course, I only spoke to one of them, and she was always behind the grille. But it gave me such a sense of timelessness and peace to go there, and even though that was one of the hottest summers on record, I always felt cool as I walked home. I remember thinking, How lucky we are, to have all these nuns in Mountain City, watching and praying for us." Her light, dreamy eyes lit fondly on Julia, and then on her children and grandchild, and then slid on down to Ralph's end of the table. For the first time since Julia had arrived, Lily looked at Ralph Quick head-on. "You know that old joke, 'When one of us dies, maybe I'll move to Arizona'? Well, when one of us dies, maybe I'll become a nun."

Ralph merely raised his eyebrows and did not reply. Then he ducked his head and began rubbing his right eye with his fist; Julia could hear the unpleasant squinchy sound from where she sat. When he had finished, he said to Julia, "I've got a damn cataract in there, and it's like trying to see through glue."

Before Julia could say, "I'm sorry," or ask if he planned to have surgery anytime soon, Theo spoke out suddenly.

"Women rape men, too," he said.

"Do what?" inquired Ralph, perking up a little.

Theo smiled mysteriously, looking around the table to be sure he had everyone's attention. His little boy, sated with cake, lolled in his lap. Julia remembered that cunning *pause* of Theo's from the classroom: he would raise his hand, ask an ostensibly innocent question, then let the grin spread slowly across his face (as it did now) while he waited for her and the rest of the class to awaken to the question's defiant or subversive undertones.

When everyone was looking at him, he said, still grinning, "Women can use your body in a certain way. Especially if you're a good lover. They can suck what they want out of you without ever giving anything of themselves. They can leave you hating all the parts of yourself they don't want. Women, if you ask me have become terrible."

"Darling, what an awful thing to say." Lily tried to keep her voice amused and light.

Theo shrugged. He crossed his arms protectively over the front of his child and blinked at his mother from behind the gold-rimmed glasses. "Well, Mom, it's true. Women don't want to give anymore, they just want to take. And, in my opinion, when they take a man in the way I'm talking about, it is a kind of rape."

There followed a stupefied silence, during which everyone seemed to be searching for a response to the gauntlet Theo had flung down. His wife had just run out on him, which might account for this outburst of misogyny, but Julia sensed he was trying to articulate something that had been bothering her, too, lately: women, especially young women, did seem different these days. Self-sacrifice, for instance, had become a ridiculously outmoded concept. The practitioner of it tended to be laughed at or pitied rather than held up as an example of goodness. Where, then, did that leave her, who ten years ago had given up all the hard-won accoutrements of the liberated life in order to come back to Mountain City and provide moral support for her father during the ordeal of her mother's extended and humili- ating mental disintegration. Julia had known there was never any other choice for her but to come home. Honoring the ties of birth, however critical she might feel about a parent, took precedence over any "freedom" or "happiness" she might steal for herself by choosing to turn away from them in their lowest hour. She was simply constructed that way. Her history had programmed her to make the choice she had made. But times had changed; perhaps women were being built according to a new model now, a model that had dispensed with such obsolete and incapacitating features as "duty" and "selflessness."

Rafe slammed down his vodka tonic, or whatever it was he had stealthily managed to refill in the kitchen. "Oh, bullshit," he said. "That's just bullshit, Theo. Rape is taking someone against their will. You weren't taken against your will if you say yourself that you were a good lover. You've got to define your terms." He spoke fast and arrogantly. His bloodshot eyes were the same sapphire-blue as Lily's, only smaller and closer to- gether.

"You're wrong, Rafe. If I think I am giving all of myself, and it turns out that someone only wants the pleasure my body can give them, then that *is* against my will. You're too literal-minded, Rafe. I'm talking about the rape of someone's spirit."

"Ha!" Rafe cut his eyes eagerly around the table for cor- roboration. "Can't you all just hear Theo telling the police, 'Officer, this woman has raped my *spirit*!'"

"Bullshit," pronounced the child happily. "Bullshit, bullshit, bullshit!"

"Now are you satisfied son?" Ralph said to Theo.

"Me?" cried Theo, incredulous. "I didn't say bullshit, Rafe did."

"Well, you've said it now," Rafe shot back triumphantly.

Theo looked sadly and reproachfully at his brother. (Or, thought Julia, who had noted this not-quite-authentic behavior in Theo before, he looked like an actor trying to affect sad reproach.) "You always cut corners in your arguments, Rafe. And it's cheap. It's not worthy of your intelligence. You do it to impress others, and most people let you get away with it, but I'm not impressed."

"Well, what were *you* trying to do, if not 'impress others,' announcing to everybody what a good lover you are."

"I am a good lover, Rafe, and I'll tell you why —"

"No, you won't," said Ralph Quick. "Not at this table."

"Oh, dear," said flushed Lily with a crooked smile. "Boys, do try to love each other on my birthday."

"I do love Rafe," Theo told her unctuously. "I just hate to see my brilliant brother ruin his mind with sloppy arguments everyone lets him get away with."

"Phew!" cried Rafe, lifting his long legs high off the floor. "You-know-what is rising in here! In a minute we'll all be drowning in it!"

Little Jason, animated by his uncle's strange antics, threw his head back and laughed hysterically.

By this time, Julia's head was pounding. She still had twenty-one freshman themes (topic: "What Is Civilization?") to grade. She felt a sudden fierce rapport with the absent Snow Mullins, who had told Clare, "The air up here always gives me a headache." Putting on a convincing listener's mask, she tried to distance herself, to let the Quicks' emotional crosscurrents flow around her without penetrating her. She reminded herself that in this house she had no filial or sisterly responsibilities; her only remaining vital tie with this family was to her friend Clare. And even Clare, at the moment, seemed unpleasantly infected with "Quick-ness" as she began relating a high-flown, boastful account of brother Rafe's latest visit to her in New York, when she had taken him shopping for his fall wardrobe in the Ralph Lauren department of Saks, pretending to be his mother. ("But all the salesmen took us for an older woman with her handsome young paramour.") And afterwards, Clare went on, she had taken her little brother to his first literary cocktail party, at a famous writer's Park Avenue apartment, where Rafe had charmed everybody with his Southern accent and bowled over the guest of honor, the German writer Günter Grass, "by explaining to Grass quite intelligently why it was absolutely necessary for us to deploy our MX missiles in his country." There was some irony in Clare's tone when she spoke of the missiles, but not nearly enough. Julia could just imagine how bowled over Günter Grass had been. She had a strong suspicion, from the way the other members of the family were watching *her* as they listened, that they had already heard the story and it was being told again simply for her benefit. Rafe sat with eyes "modestly" downcast, a little smirk on his face, twirling his drink around slowly, as his sister narrated this hyperbolic tale of his easy conquests. He did not seem too concerned with the irony in Clare's voice; perhaps he missed it altogether.

Clare's most troubling aspect, as far as Julia was concerned, was this habit all the Quicks had of shortchanging reality. They didn't give life a chance to express itself, they were so busy making it over into what they'd rather see, what presented them in a more intriguing light, what felt or sounded better. Now, this tendency may have served Clare's fiction (but how *well* had it served it? Julia had some reservations about this), but what did it do to a real, live person when he or she became Quick material—or, in Clare's case, Campion material? How, for instance, could this story Clare was telling contribute anything to Rafe's authentic vision of himself? Assuming he might be interested in one now, or sometime in the future. Julia herself had been Campionized in *The Headmaster's Daughters,* and as a result had undergone moments of subsequent perplexity as to exactly where "Caroline Taylor's" clear fictional presence and motives parted company with Julia Richardson Lowndes's blurrier outlines and problematic desires.

That's enough for tonight, she thought as Clare wound down her New York story. She rose from their table. "Please, don't anybody get up," she said, meaning it fervently. "I've got a bunch of freshman history themes lying in wait for me at home. You all go on with the fun, and thank you for including me." She bent down and kissed Lily. "Happy birthday." Then, because she no longer worshiped her old heroine, she added guiltily, "I love you."

"Thank you," replied Lily with dignity. "And I you. And I love the perfume. I mean cologne. I think"—she raised one eyebrow mischievously—"I am going to start wearing it again." She remained seated, however, in an abstracted, queenly bubble of her own, while everyone else scraped back their chairs and accompanied Julia to the kitchen door.

"Take care," said Rafe, flashing his pretty teeth at her before heading to the ice machine to begin rebuilding his drink.

Clare hugged her, clinging a second too long, the way people do when they are uncertain of your goodwill. "Thanks so much for coming," she murmured. Her smoky-rimmed, light-irised eyes sought Julia's. Thanks for putting up with us . . . with me, they beseeched. You know I'm not always my best self in this house.

"I'm taking you to a wonderful place for our picnic tomorrow," said Julia, relenting and hugging her back.

"I'll walk her to her car," said Theo, whose little boy straddled his hip and clung to his neck like a drowning soul.

"You don't want to take him outside without a sweater," Ralph told his son.

"It won't be for long," said Theo, already holding the door for Julia.

"Suit yourself, then." Ralph Quick shrugged. "That's what everybody in this house does anyway." He puckered his lips at Julia, mimicking a kiss, and then sat down at the round Formica table in the kitchen, cleared himself a space amid the clutter of dishes and papers, and began dealing himself a hand of solitaire. He had obviously been planning to walk her to her car himself, but wouldn't make an issue of it before his sons.

I escaped *that,* thought Julia, as she and her headache followed Theo and his clinging child into the brisk October night permeated with stars. In the decade since she'd come back to Mountain City, at least a dozen married men, including a few with grown grandchildren and one former teaching colleague of her father's, had phoned Julia and, with that telltale innocence in their voices, suggested they'd like to drop by some afternoon or evening to talk about life in general. But she had been thoroughly surprised when Ralph Quick had shown up at her door one evening about six months ago. "Do you have a moment?" he'd asked quietly from the other side of the screen. She hadn't realized he even knew where she lived. Her first thought was that something bad had happened to Clare—perhaps she had been stabbed in New York, or had had some accident—and Ralph thought it would be kinder to break the news in person. Even as she was inviting him in, she was already testing, with a curious distance, her reactions to the potential news of Clare's death. Ralph Quick plunked himself down in the middle of her sofa, as if he had made himself at home in her apartment a hundred times before. From an inside crevice of his windbreaker he extracted a square brown envelope. His bright, Cherokee-black eyes glistened at her (she was still standing) with meaning as he began unwinding the string on the back of the envelope.

"Remember these?" he asked her, handing over a sheaf of five-by-seven-inch black-and-white matte-finish photographs.

She had only to glance at the top one, of herself at fourteen, to remember the whole thing. "Oh God," she said, sitting down, not on the sofa but on a straight-backed chair some distance from Ralph.

"I was going through some old boxes down in the basement," he said, "and I found them. They brought back so much . . . a whole lost world. To tell you the truth, they brought tears to my eyes. We were all so young. Do you realize that when I took those portraits of you and Clare I was only about the age Rafe is? You used to tell Clare you thought I was sexy."

Julia kept her eyes down on the photos, shuffling through them slowly, as though her attention were riveted by memories she found there. Memory was there, of course: she could feel again the heat of those bright floodlamps under which she and Clare had posed tirelessly, against the backdrop of a dark-red-and-gold-brocade bedspread that Ralph had tacked up over the picture window; Ralph was going to make them glamorous. The girls had taken turns gazing seductively over one bare shoulder (they had each draped a swath of gauzy net across their strapless bras) while Ralph, black eyes dancing, tiptoed ecstatically around, caressing the air in front of them with his light meter. But what Julia was more intent on, as she looked at these slightly out-of-focus relics, was how she could get Ralph Quick to leave, with grace on her part, if it could be managed, and without his losing face.

Julia squared the pictures on her lap. "What wonderful foolish old relics," she said. "We thought we were so glamorous." She looked up at Ralph. "Do you know what I think we ought to do? Let's call Clare and ask her if she remembers them. We'll all have a good laugh. Let's phone her in New York. I'll tell her you just dropped by with these pictures, and we'll ask her if she remembers them." Julia stood up energetically. "I'll go get her number. Or wait, you probably know it by heart."

"Well, no," said Ralph, raising himself slowly from the sofa and passing his hand over the crown of his head in a gesture that made him look suddenly tired and old. "I mean, yes, I do know the number, but she might misunderstand. In fact, maybe you'd better not mention it at all to Clare. I seem to be getting misunderstood more and more these days. To tell the truth, I was just on my way over to see if Miss Alicia Gallant needs anything. Sometimes I drive by, about this time of evening, and if the light's still on in her den, I stop in and make us some cocoa and we watch TV for a while."

The picture he conjured up made her relent a little towards him. How lonely he must be, to be driving around at night hoping the lights were still on in an old lady's house so he could go in and make them cocoa! It was touching, in its bizarre way. "You're good to your old friends, Ralph, and I'm sure they all appreciate it." She handed him back the pictures of her lovely, hubristic youth. God, hadn't she thought she was something. (Though she had never told her parents about those photography sessions over at Clare's.)

"Well, I do what I can," said Ralph. "It's not easy to be alone in this world. People who live with people can be alone, too, maybe sometimes even more so. Didn't you feel alone, coming back here all by yourself to the town where you grew up? You must have found everything so much changed."

"They keep me so busy at the college that I don't have a lot of time to think about it, Ralph. And there's Father, you know. I see a good deal of him. And, of course, I do go out with people, middle-aged schoolteacher though I am."

"I think you're still very —" His prominent Adam's apple bobbed up and down as he swallowed. "Well, I'd better be running along." He glanced down at the sheaf of pictures. "I'd be happy to give you some of these."

"Thanks, Ralph, but I think I'd rather remember the good old days without visual aids."

He slid the pictures back into their envelope, carefully rewinding the string. "You both were lovely young girls," he said. "And you're still a very attractive woman."

"Thank you, Ralph."

"Well . . ." He danced his coal-bright eyes at her one last

time, puckered his lips at her as a man does when he's rushing from a woman who just might cling to him when he's ready to be off somewhere else, and exited with his pride intact.

She had leaned against her doorframe and listened until she heard his car roar away into the night.

"I hope I didn't cause you to leave early because of what I said about rape," Theo was saying as they walked across the gravel, powdery white in the starlight, to Julia's car. One of the dogs came blundering out of the shadows and thrust its wet muzzle into Julia's hand. She wondered whether it was Lieb-chen, the one Clare said had arthritis. Just as she couldn't censor Ralph in the way he probably deserved, because he had a cataract over one of those feisty eyes and went around at night making cocoa for old ladies, she took pity on the animal who had lunged and snarled at her in its heyday; reaching down, she stroked its matted, gritty old pelt.

"That had nothing to do with it," Julia told Theo. "I've got a bad headache and I still have all those papers to grade. Actually, some of what you were saying was quite provocative. I've had some thoughts on the changing nature of womanhood myself, but I'm too beat to go into them now."

"This place can give you a headache," he said. "But I wish you would tell me those thoughts sometime. I'm losing my faith in womanhood. Maybe I've already lost it. . . ." They had reached her car. She could feel Theo *pulsing* at her, behind his words, with his need to talk, to confide. Give him another minute and *he* would be inviting himself over to her apartment . . . or simply materializing at her door one night. She didn't have it in her to involve herself further with Quick personalities tonight. She decided to head him off by praising the child riding his hip, head laid sleepily against Theo's shoulder.

"He's a beautiful boy. And its obvious you're the center of his universe."

"I have to be, don't I? If it weren't for him, I'd be long gone from this town. Don't get me wrong, I wouldn't take anything for him. He's my *life*. It's just that I sometimes wonder how I'm going to go on. One thing's for sure. I'll have to keep on living up here for a while. Snow wiped me out with all her charging. I'll be paying off Belk's and Sears and MasterCard for the next three years. And I've just taken a leave of absence from my accounting firm so I can study for the CPA exam."

"But I thought . . . Clare told me you'd already taken that."

"I failed half of it. I wish I could get more excited about double-entry bookkeeping and cost/profit ratios." As his lips stretched over his teeth in the wary smile that habitually ended in a smirk, she remembered that same smile, some of those same words, in her office ten years ago, when he'd come in to have a conference. She recalled the identical apologetic-challenging way he had said, that other day, "I wish I could get more excited about boundaries and treaties and who was on top of the heap when." His description of history had angered her, had wounded her vanity, because she prided herself on *not* stressing those nationalistic aspects. Her forte, she liked to think, was the human essence: the way, through the study of other lives, however remote in time and place and circumstance, you could locate (and then better understand) aspects of the self. Not just the personal self, but the vast, extended Self that used history to become conscious of what it was . . . and could be.

Maddening boy! He had dropped her course, hadn't he? What did he expect her to do for him now? She could feel his attention straining toward her, fully expecting her, his "old teacher," the family friend who had once danced with him in her arms, to lift him with some glib wisdom out of the dreary slough of his present predicament. But what could she say? He *was* in a far from enviable situation. Sole parent and supporter of this little boy, still living under the parental roof (and what a roof!), and not in love with the work he was doing. Whatever she had lost, or missed, in her life, she knew she could count on her work always to interest her.

"What does excite you, then, Theo?" Her bare arms had goosebumps from the chill October air. She could feel shards of the rough gravel shredding the leather off the heels of her best shoes. (She had dressed up tonight, in honour of Lily.)

"I can't think of anything that excites me anymore. I used to want to be a highway patrolman. But Mom and Dad felt that wouldn't be appropriate. They wanted me to go to college and be somebody. Is a CPA somebody? I'm not even that yet."

"Daddy, I'm cold," whined the child. "Let's go *in*!"

"Just a minute, son. I'm talking to the lady. Look up there at all those stars, Jason. Some of them are so far away that they stopped burning thousands of years ago, only we don't know it yet." The weird smile returned. "I reckon that's not the proper way to talk to a child about the stars, is it? I'll tell you something that excites me. The idea of all this being over. Of me, as far away as those stars, looking down on it and not feeling involved anymore. What excites you?"

Confounded by his sudden, cavalier leap into despair, she faltered. What of her own passions could compete with the soothing distance of his cosmic wastes? Damn him, damn this whole confusing hill. She looked back at the house and saw Ralph's shadow against the light of the kitchen window. Spying on them complacently.

"Trying to understand excites me." But the words rushed out too quickly, and, though true—perhaps her truest—sounded cheap.

"To understand what?" he pressed.

"Everything," she said impatiently, frustrated at herself for not being more eloquent, at him for wanting too much from her. "All the patterns and the meanings. The mysteries of people. How it all adds up."

She knew exactly what he would answer, and he did. "What if it doesn't add up to anything? What if there are no patterns or meanings? What if there's nothing to understand?"

"Daddy, let's go *in!*" whimpered the child.

Seizing on this as the cue for her release, Julia stood on tiptoe and kissed Theo quickly on the cheek. (With Ralph watching it all from the window.) She was surprised that his flesh still smelled as sweet as a child's. How strange! "You can understand *that*," she said, smoothing Jason's silky head.

Before he could summon another rebuttal, she slid into her car, slammed the door, and, without taking the time to buckle her seat belt, turned on the engine. Safe behind its protective racket, she cranked down the window. "It's all going to work out," she told him. "Just . . . have faith in yourself. And don't go giving up on women quite yet."

"I'm trying not to," came back the unconvincing answer. He stood, holding the child and shifting his feet, while she struggled behind the steering wheel to extricate herself from the tight spot between the cars. Why was it so damn *dark?*

"Hey, why don't you try turning on your lights?" Theo called in friendly mockery.

As her lights swept him in the quick arc of her getaway, he waved the little boy's hand at her.

All the way down Quick's Hill, and at intervals as she sped

through the dark valley, the picture of the benighted young father and the clinging child remained as an afterimage.

She slammed around in her apartment, usually her sanctuary of peace and self-esteem. She swallowed aspirin and made herself a pot of amaretto tea. She flung herself down on the sofa with a stack of freshman themes.

Three out of the first five began identically: "According to Webster's New World Dictionary, civilization is a social organization of a high order, marked by advances in the arts, sciences," etc. But then, three out of five kids at North State were the first in their families ever to go to college. They couldn't risk being original. With a sigh, she stuffed the themes back in her briefcase. Who would benefit if she vented her exasperation with the Quicks on these first, fragile attempts at disciplined thinking? Better to stay up late tomorrow night, when her head would be clear.

She put on a clean cotton nightgown, taking pleasure in its fresh-laundered smell. Opening a window wide, she took satisfied gulps of Mountain City air. As she climbed into bed, she thought of them up there on Quick's Hill, moiling about with the windows closed in their oxygen-deprived pressure chamber of family life, and blessed her luck in having only one remaining blood tie: her neat, persnickety old father, who needed attention but loved his solitude just as much as she did hers. Then she recalled Clare's startling new crop of gray hairs, wondering if she would dye them or brave it out, and, for some reason, all this sparked a vivid memory of Lily Quick as she had been one afternoon twenty-eight years before, when she had worn her rich chestnut hair in a pageboy. As the girls came in from school, Lily, very pregnant, sat sideways at her typewriter because she could no longer face front. She had that special, elated radiance people get sometimes after they have expended a burst of mental energy. "Oh, girls," she had cried, "if this is ever published, it will blow the lid off this town!" The paper in Lily's typewriter was a page of the novel Julia had been waiting to read ever since; the roundness under Lily's maternity smock was Theo.

Julia reached for a little notebook she kept in the drawer of her bedside table. Pencil poised above a clean page, she frowned and licked her lips; then she rapidly scribbled a series of lines that rose into her mind with the malevolent ease of those old jump-rope chants she used to invent for the other girls on the playground of St. Clothilde's—until Mother von Blücher had overheard one and she'd almost been expelled. (*"Skinny Vinnie got the minnie,"* it had gone. *"Raged and screamed and cried. | She flushed and flashed | Then trickled and pickled | Until she got so mad she died."*)

Since her return to Mountain City, Julia had committed more than a hundred or so of her adult jump-rope chants, or jingles, or whatever they were—she refused to call them poems—to her little notebooks. Slowly she had come to understand that these vehement, satirical, angry, or mournful outbursts, usually dashed off just before she fell asleep, were a balancing stratagem, a private and necessary outlet for her mixed feelings about being home again and all that it might augur.

There, she thought, stabbing in the last period and scanning over the lines with a morose relish: so much for friendships and civilization and human possibilities. Theo's dead stars win tonight.

She snapped shut the doggerel book and switched off the lamp.

II: OLYMPIANS

"*H*ow did you ever find this place, Julia? A meadow on top of a mountain! The air up here is like champagne. Why didn't we know about this spot when we were growing up?"

"It's called Pinnacle Old Bald by the locals, but it still goes by its unpronounceable Indian name on the maps. So when people come asking for it, of course, the locals can't—or won't—tell them where it is. And you know as well as I do that there are a whole lot of things we didn't know about when we were growing up."

"You said a mouthful there, honey." Clare clapped her friend jovially on the arm as the two of them, Julia in front, hiked up a wide path in noon sunshine towards a dome-shaped golden meadow sticking right up into the blue sky. Clare was lighter of heart since Julia had driven her away from Quick's Hill this morning. The frown lines between her brows had disappeared and her shoulders had sprung back, as if released from an invisible load. She grew more confident and relaxed with every breath she took of the invigorating air.

"The spirits are pretty friendly up here," Julia said, "if you come with the right attitude. It's supposed to have been an Indian burial ground once. A retired Navy officer owns it now. But he allows hikers and picnickers, as long as they clean up after themselves and don't bring guns. Anyway, he's not here very much. I think it's just an 'investment' for him. That's a

Christmas tree farm, all those little spruces in rows on that sunny slope. The caretaker was one of my students, that's how I know about it."

"Well, I love it. There's something . . . sacred about it. I wouldn't mind being buried up here."

"I think you'll enjoy it much more by being alive, dear." But Julia was pleased with Clare's enthusiasm. She liked to show her new places, places in these mountains they had never dreamed existed when they were growing up. It had become a self-imposed commission for Julia to be able to produce a different hiking and picnic spot every year when Clare visited. It was Julia's way of reminding her old friend that there were rewards for those who returned to live in the place where they were born. Perhaps it was also, Julia thought, a way of reassuring herself that the old and familiar harbored special revelations for those who hung around faithfully and stayed alert. "I was going to take you up to Mount Mitchell, but George and I drove up there in August for a hike, and when we got there and saw what had happened to it, we just turned the car around and went somewhere else."

"God! It's terrible. I saw a picture of it; it made the front page of the *Times*. All those noble red spruce woods where we used to camp out as Girl Scouts look like some blasted peak in Hell. Acid rain. All the way from Ohio, the article said. From smokestacks of coal-burning furnaces. I got very depressed when I read it. One more old landmark gone. Just like the old St. Clothilde's getting torn down board by board when I was away in England. But Mount Mitchell, you would have thought, was inviolable. Do you remember that year, when we were camping out and everybody started blowing on the fire, only the air was so thin we couldn't get our breaths properly and Freddy Stratton just sank in a heap all of a sudden and that good-looking forest ranger had to pick her up in his arms and carry her to the station wagon so they could get her back down to the camp infirmary?"

Julia laughed. "I'll bet she wasn't so far gone that she couldn't enjoy it."

"You know, I've about got up my courage to phone Freddy. I've been working up to it for years. I want to test whether I'm over that terrible sense of inferiority she could make me feel just by looking at me. It's been over twenty years since I last saw her."

"I wish you *would* call her. It's time you realized she's not the arch-rival you always made her into. I saw her a couple of weeks ago, out at that new crafts center they've made out of the old railway depot. At first I didn't recognize her; I thought it was just one more tense society matron in her Talbots catalogue clothes. She nursed her mother at home through the last stages of lung cancer, you know. Yet, the whole time we talked, Freddy was chain-smoking."

"What did you talk about?" Clare's voice, suddenly regressing to its anxious, adolescent pitch, reminded Julia how jealous Clare had been of Freddy Stratton's sudden courting of Julia when they had reached the age when it was time to meet the right kind of boys and there was Julia's family conveniently living on the Belvedere School grounds.

"Well, her mother, of course. I said, 'It must have been awful for you,' and she said, 'No, I was really *glad* to be able to do it.' And she asked about you. I told her you'd be coming down to visit your family."

"What did she say about me?"

"Well, she asked how I felt about your using my family in your novel."

"What did you say?"

"I said that I had known you were doing it, that we had even corresponded about it, but that, really, it wasn't my family when you got through with us. I explained to her that was the way writers work. You made up your own Richardson family and called them the Taylors. You idealized us into a sort of generic genteel Southern family."

"Oh, do you think so?" Clare sounded annoyed.

"More or less. But what does it matter? It's a fine book. And it's given my father's ego a boost. Not that my father's ego exactly *needs* a boost, but —"

"So how is George?" Clare changed the subject abruptly. "Is that still on, then?"

"I'm not sure 'on' is the word for it—I mean, we were never on fire, or anything—but we're not altogether *off*, so I guess it'll do. We both like to walk, and eat good food, and complain about how they overwork us at North State. We make love once a week, on Friday nights, when I stay over at his house. He's very . . . punctilious. And on Saturday morning we have a big celebratory breakfast because we've acquitted ourselves like a normal couple, and then he starts looking wistfully towards his

study—he's doing a book on medieval French monasteries—
and I rinse the dishes and put them in his dishwasher and go
home and do my own laundry. Actually we suit each other very
well. He would have made a perfect Jesuit if God hadn't been
so inconsiderate as to cause him to be born into a Protestant
family, and I . . . well, I've had the feeling lately that I'm just
marking time until I reach the age when I can dispense with the
social necessity of having a boyfriend."

"Julia, do you really feel that way?"

"I'm exaggerating a little, but I *can* imagine how it would be.
It wouldn't be so different from our early adolescence, when we
were just . . . ourselves. Before we got infected with the notion
that we'd better go hide in our closets if we didn't have a man
to go out with on Saturday night. You know, I counted it up
the other night: it's been fifteen years since I was a married
person, and I was married only four years. Even counting live-
in lovers, by far the greatest portion of my adult life has been
spent alone. It may well be that solitude is my most natural
state."

"I used to think that, before I met Felix. Now I don't know. I
think my talent for living alone may have atrophied. Funny,
isn't it, you're the one who's been married and you're talking
like a spinster; whereas I'm the real spinster. I'll probably never
marry, but I can't imagine life without Felix." She laughed
dryly. "I can't even imagine life without *Lizzie* anymore. It's as
if, over the years, I've become dependent on her for my regular
doses of aggravation. I keep a careful mental list of all her
offenses, the way some people collect stamps or little figurines,
and it's become a down-right pleasure to add a new offense to
the list and then sit down and gloat over my collection and
compare old offenses to new ones. Let me see, I'll say, smacking
my lips over my list, which was worse? The time Lizzie came
forty-five minutes late to the restaurant—you know how Felix
feels about punctuality—and threw her wet umbrella down on
the banquette on top of my suede coat, or the time she was
packing to go back to college and I said, trying to be helpful,
'Here's a book you forgot, Lizzie,' and she tossed her red hair at
me and said airily, 'Oh, you can stand there and hold it for me
until I'm ready for it'? She actually said that! Or I'll ask myself,
which gets the grand prize? The time we came back from a play
and found Lizzie in our bed surrounded by magazines and
snacks, making herself quite at home? 'I felt like I might be

coming down with flu up at school,' she says, 'and our nurse is such a nerd, so I decided to come home and nurse myself, and the TV in your room is better.' Or this past summer when we got back from Europe and she had made a big thing about not being able to meet us at the airport because she wanted to have dinner prepared for us? So we come in the door, half-dead from jet lag, and there's not a sign of dinner. We follow the sound of the TV to Lizzie's room, and when she sees it's us, she puts up a hand of warning—she hasn't seen her beloved father in six weeks, mind you—and says, 'Shh! I have to see this. It's my favorite ice skater and I've been waiting for her to come on for almost an hour.'"

"At least this time she was in her own bedroom, looking at her own TV," said Julia, smiling.

"Exactly! See? Awarding the grand prize becomes progressively more difficult because there are so many shadings and variations to her rudeness. I keep thinking, well, maybe she's improving—I mean, she did *think* about preparing dinner, even if she didn't get around to doing it—and then she drops the next stunner on me. But what I'm saying is, I've come to expect it, I almost look forward to it. Also, there's the superstitious element, and you know how superstitious I am: maybe, I tell myself, putting up with Lizzie is the penalty I have to pay in order to be allowed to keep Felix. Then, at other times, I think Lizzie has been sent to show me how life feels from Ralph Quick's side, to show me what I put *him* through as a stepdaughter. And being able to be on everybody's side is good for a writer. Theo was faulting me on that last night, when he more or less demolished my work."

"Theo was being very provoking last night. He got *me* when he walked me to my car."

"Oh, what did he say?"

"No, you tell me first. How he demolished your work."

"Well, I was sitting in the kitchen late yesterday afternoon, polishing the silver for Lily's birthday dinner, and Theo shuffled in, with his hands in his pockets, and stood watching me for a while, not saying anything in that pregnant way he has which forces you to fill up the silence with harmless, frivolous chatter, if you're in one mood, or not-so-harmless monologue, bordering on diatribe, if you're in another. I was in the latter, I'm afraid, and, taking the tarnished silver as a starting point, I was grumbling in a superior way about the mess on Quick's Hill, how even the soap dish had fallen off in the blue bathroom, over the tub, and, after the hole had stood gaping for weeks, according to Lily, and nobody had done anything to fix it, she had finally cut out an illustration of two Japanese women having tea and rubber-cemented it over the hole. Meanwhile, Theo just kept hovering, making me more and more edgy because he wouldn't sit down, and he had his strange little smile, you know, the one that says, I know something you don't know . . . or maybe it's saying, I want you to *think* I know something you don't know and beg me to tell you —"

"I know that smile exactly."

"Well, there he stood, with his hands in his pockets, with that infuriating smile, and I rose to the bait. 'Theo,' I said, 'what are you thinking right this minute?' Felix and I often ask each other that, and sometimes the answer is funny, or unexpected, or enlightening, but never demolishing."

"So what did Theo answer?"

"He said, 'I was thinking how nice it would be to be a character in one of your novels.'"

"That doesn't sound very demolishing to me."

"Wait, I haven't finished. I thought he meant it as a compliment too, at first. 'Oh? Why is that?' I asked him. 'Because,' he said, 'you take care of them so nicely. You let them suffer a little, just enough to improve their characters, but you always rescue them from the abyss at the last minute and reward them with love or money or the perfect job—or sometimes all three.'"

"Hmm," murmured Julia noncommittally. It was not entirely untrue, she thought. In *The Headmaster's Daughters*, the bereaved widower had been ultimately consoled by remarriage to a gracious, intelligent widow; the older daughter, Caroline, the historian, had at last brought out her groundbreaking volume on the family life of American slaves; and the younger daughter, Tracy, after enduring an arid society marriage for the sake of raising two children, had freed herself at forty from domestic fetters, gone to law school, and, in the epilogue, was becoming an influential figure in local politics.

"I said, 'Theo, that's just not true. I mean, things end up going well for some of my characters, but that's the way life is— life *does* work out well for some people, through a combination of luck and energy and talent and all sorts of individual factors. But, Theo, lots of my characters die, or contract terrible illnesses, or become alcoholics or suicides. You're not being fair,' I said.

'Yes, but those are just secondary characters,' he said. 'The ones you use as a background for your winners. I meant I'd like to be one of your *main* characters. Then I could be sure all this stupid suffering would turn out to the good. But maybe I'm coming to realize I could never be a main character in your kind of world. Maybe I don't even want to be anymore.' Well! This hurt me, and then it made me so mad I wanted to hurt him right back by saying, 'What have you done to make you a main character in *anybody's* book?' But I stopped myself because he's had more than his share of bad innings lately: first Snow, the whole *phenomenon* of Snow, and then failing part of his exam, and having to move back in with his parents at twenty-eight because there's the child to consider, and then he had this girl-friend he liked—Lily says she was the perfect antidote to Snow: a hardworking, cheerful nurse with a little boy Jason's age— and *she's* just broken off with him because she says he's like a roller coaster and she needs steadiness in her life. And Theo's beginning to fall apart, like everything else on Quick's Hill. Physically, I mean. His eyes are going because of all that close accounting work, and he's got two new gold crowns on his teeth—the most perfect teeth of any of us—and also, when he walked into the kitchen, I noticed a slight heaviness around his beltline and a defeatist slump about his shoulders, and it struck me for the first time that my little brother would soon be middle-aged and might have to cope with being a middle-aged failure, as well. So, instead of lashing back, I asked him, 'What kind of world do you think my world is, Theo?' And he said, 'Well, in your books, it's where everything gets wrapped up at the end.' Then he leaned forward towards me over the back of a kitchen chair, gripping the top with his hands till the knuckles went white, and said, 'Why don't you write a book about something that can *never* be wrapped up? What if you came across some-thing like that in life? Would you want to write about it?' 'If it was interesting to me,' I said, 'I might. But frankly, Theo, a lot of the unwrappable chaos and meaninglessness and dreariness that goes on in the world doesn't excite my curiosity at all. What kind of thing do you have in mind?'"

"And what did he say?"

"He wiggled out of it. He said, 'I'll let you know more about it when I know more myself.' Or something to that effect. And then he drifted out of the kitchen in his aery-faery way, leaving me to question the very foundations of my work."

"How so?" inquired Julia, interested.

"Well, I asked myself, *did* I prettify things up too much? Was my work characterized by a sort of Olympian disdain for losers? I had a real bout of soul-searching after Theo left the kitchen. I even questioned whether I had any special gift for perception and expression, or whether I wasn't just a docile, clever product of 'The Southern Way of Life' and of a European-style convent education in which the nuns themselves had been brainwashed by the late Romantic and Victorian traditions. I mean, God, Julia, what if my effects, such as they are, have been achieved simply by learning to satisfy the tastes of the culture that shaped me, rather than trying to sniff out its rotten spots or going beyond it in my imagination? If that's all I've done, what use does that make me to the present or the future?"

"I think," began Julia, treading carefully, "that your temperament *is* one that requires a lot of things to be the way they aren't. That's why you're a fiction writer. Just as something in me needs to understand how things have gotten to be the way they are. That's why I'm a historian. Unless you want to take a more fatalistic or deterministic view, which I sometimes do, and say that each of us is simply living out a parent's thwarted dream. My father always wanted to get his doctorate in English or history; and Lily wanted to publish novels. I think it's good that you question yourself the way you do, but you and I both know you tend to be your worst critic. Maybe you have needed to tell the kinds of stories that you say please the culture that shaped you. There's nothing wrong in that: lots of great writers have worked in that tradition. If it's any consolation to you, Theo sent me home last night questioning the effectiveness of everything from my profession to civilization. I couldn't even grade my papers."

"Boy, it really must have been his evil day if he was able to do that to *you*, Julia. What did he say?"

"It's not what he said so much as the kind of despair he managed to evoke in me. When he walked me out to the car, I felt he needed something from me, a kind of philosophical cheering-up, and I couldn't give it to him. I was too glib. I was tired and I had a headache and I just didn't rise to the occasion. And the way he was acting made me remember how he'd dropped my Western Civ course, so there was my hurt pride to contend with, as well."

"But he must have said *something* to prompt all this."

"First, that nothing excited him, and then he was showing little Jason the stars and he said that the only thing that excited him was being as far away as those stars, with everything over and his not being involved anymore."

"Is that all? Theo's always talked like that, Julia."

"Well, it was the first time I'd ever heard it, and it depressed me. I wrote one of my little jingles about it before I went to sleep."

"Some of those 'little jingles,' as you call them, are really good, Julia. I wish you'd try to publish them."

"That's not the point of them," replied Julia, bristling a little. Clare was always trying to rush her into publication of some kind or another. "They're like a child's poems. They form in my head and I write them down at certain ripe times and they tell me things I need to know. It would be like publishing my diary."

"People have been known to do that, too. But, okay, never mind. I understand. It's one of the things I admire most about you, Julia. You aren't always quivering from head to foot with ambition, the way I am. Why don't you let me carry that backpack for a while. I mean, I'm going to be eating that lunch, too."

"No way. I'm the hostess, remember? Besides, carrying a few extra pounds will help me burn off more calories. We're just going to the top of that sunny hill, where the old oak tree is standing all by itself."

"You always know such good places. It's as if you've discovered a whole other world existing inside the place we grew up in."

"Oh, well . . . I consider it a point of honor to find secret new places to show off to you when you come back. So you won't think I'm down here vegetating, or something."

The more I contemplate it, thought Clare, the more astonishing it seems: I have liked this other person, not a member of my family, and exactly my own age (plus one week), for almost my whole lifetime. I have known her walk—an idiosyncratic stride unlike anyone else's, head thrust back as though she's about to burst into song, pelvis tilted forward, toes pointed out, arms swinging freely, almost dangerously, as if she were cutting through superfluities like so much brush in her way: it is a heroic walk. I wonder if she thinks *I* have a characteristic walk. And I know her laugh—a short, sharp "Ha!" like an enlightened bark—and her sneezes always occur in a series of five. Never four or two. And over so many years I've learned to read between the lines of her tact, too: her noncommittal "Hmm's" and her thoughtful "How so's," which signal, very often, the way she balances her reservations about me with her determination to protect me from hating myself.

And now, lying beside her on the dry grass after her wonderful picnic, while a hawk, curious about our presence in his aerie, circles over us against the bright blue sky as we resume—with some relish—our annual dialogue on the subject of aging, I turn my head sideways in the grass and look over at her and try to *squint through* the blond skin and the wispy, butterscotch-colored hair without a thread of gray yet, and catch the way she looked at seven, or thirteen. But I can't do it. It seems as though she has always looked the way she does now. And yet I know that she has gained twenty or thirty pounds since her "glorious years," as she just called them; I know that in the company of today's thirteen-year-olds we would definitely be identified as women their mothers' ages. Come to think of it, I can't look in the mirror and see how I used to look, either. I can only see what is there, and even when I see visible signs of aging—the gray hairs, the shifting contours, I see the self I have communed with all my life. Perhaps there would not be this failure on my part to see ourselves as the world sees us if we each had lived proper, consecutive married years and now had teenaged children. But is it really an advantage to see yourself as the world sees you?

When Julia and I talk of becoming old, we always end by agreeing that one has to take a position on it. One has to prepare, ahead of time, an image of oneself that can be lived with. Today, for the first time, the theme of *witches* has come up. "I look forward," Julia has just said, "to reaching the age when I don't care what people think, when I will say what I damn please and live how I like. But you have to have a power base to do that from. To be the kind of witch that is feared or admired—perhaps even loved—rather than shunned or burned at the stake."

Then we talk about kinds of power. There is the power base of money, and I tell her about one of Lily's cousins, Cousin Demaris, who married the poor man of her heart and helped him become a millionaire, and how, when I went to visit her when she was widowed and old and living in a suite on the top floor of The Parliament House hotel in Birmingham, she greeted me wearing a brocade dressing gown and asked me whether I was hungry after my train ride. I said I could use a little something, and she said so could she, and I had visions of an appealing room-service table on wheels, with a white cloth and some club sandwiches stabbed with frilly toothpicks and a pile of sweet pickles and potato chips on the side; but instead of picking up the telephone, she went to the stove in her little kitchen, turned the burner on high, and when the electric coils were red she asked me to open a can of Campbell's vegetable beef soup, because it pained her to open cans with her arthritis, and then she put the can right down on the burner, without bothering to transfer the contents into a pan, and we ate it as a sort of lukewarm stew, out of our soup bowls, sitting on her Louis Quatorze furniture, which she's had her decorator do the suite in. "Isn't this fun?" she said to me. "Just you and me, all on our own, Clare. Without having to have anybody lurking around *waiting* on us." And she winked at me and looked so happy, with all her millions, to be eating her own home-cooked glop in her hotel suite. *And I admired her for it*. Whereas, if she had been poor, I would have felt pity.

"Exactly!" says Julia. "And then, of course, there's the power base of fame, especially a fame based on art or wit, or a combination of both, if possible." And we talk about witchy old artists majestically and wittily flaunting their bags and sags and wrinkles, as Cousin Demaris flaunted her soup, because they can afford to. Julia brings up Georgia O'Keeffe, whom I also admire; she mentions Gertrude Stein, whom I don't. Then I tell about seeing Bill Moyers interview Dame Rebecca West at ninety, and how she lunged at him, like a shaggy old lioness wearing a too-tight pearl leash, whenever she got intellectually fired up by her own replies.

"Well, you can be one of those," says Julia generously. "It's not going to matter how old you get or what you look like, because people will be able to connect it with being you, and with the work you've done. But I'm going to have to work out something else for myself, since I'm not known to the public. Because I'm too vain to tolerate becoming invisible, even to strangers. All my life, until very recently, I was used to walking down a street or into a room and having people snap to attention. Now a lot of them just don't see me. When I go to the health spa, the young people don't look at me. I mean, they nod and say hello respectfully, but what they're seeing is a middle-aged lady dropping by to firm up her thighs. And that's not enough for me. I want to be seen as myself, whatever age I am."

"But wait," I say—it's not often I can find a hole in one of Julia's arguments—"they weren't seeing you as yourself in your 'glorious years,' either: they were seeing you as 'a pretty young girl,' just as people snap to attention at the sight of a really pretty tulip in this year's garden. And no matter how famous I get—and it would have to be a lot more famous than I am for even one stranger aboard an airplane to connect my face with my books—there's always going to be a majority who see me as just a woman, then just an older woman, then just an old woman." And to clinch my rebuttal, which I can see is reassuring her, I tell how I was flying back to New York after my book tour last spring, feeling oh so conspicuously notorious after all my interviews, and I sat next to a man who asked me if I was a nun.

She explodes into her bark-laugh and rolls her head from side to side on the grass. "Nuns again! But why would he have thought that?"

"I worked it out afterwards. I was wearing black slacks, a black turtleneck sweater, and a nondescript blue blazer. Also a little pendant on my gold chain; it's just a bunch of gold grapes with a pearl in the middle, but it could be mistaken for a cross. And my makeup had worn off. And I was reading *Framley Parsonage,* which he may have thought was a religious book. And I hadn't spoken until he initiated the conversation, and I didn't volunteer any information about myself."

"Did you, afterwards?"

"Oh, yes. Our plane was delayed in Pittsburgh and we had dinner together. And I could see him slowly become attracted to me. We had a very good talk. He turned out to be a serious man who had thought a lot about the proper way to fulfill his responsibilities to others. For instance, he told me he had been brought up an atheist, but when he had children he decided they should at least know about some formal religion, and after he researched them all and concluded that the Dutch Reformed Church was the most sensible, the whole family joined the Dutch Reformed Church. And he was very unhappy that his daughter had just divorced; he said he couldn't help thinking he had

failed her in some way. That's the kind of man he was. And
after we landed at LaGuardia, and he had already said goodbye
and gone off and I was calling Felix from a pay phone, he came
all the way back from the taxi rank to tell me that he just
wanted me to know that he couldn't imagine a better person
then me to take around the world with him on his boat. That's
a dream he's had for years, to go around the world on a boat,
but his wife's some sort of invalid; he didn't specify, but she
sounded like a whiner to me, though he did say she was going to
be so pleased when he bought her my book and told her he had
met the author on the plane. But the point is, I think he finally
was attracted to something in me that had nothing to do with
how I looked or how old I was or even the fact that I had
written and published several books. Our encounter made me
feel good for days afterwards: if a stranger who started off
thinking I was a nun could come around in two or three hours
to seeing me as the ideal companion for a round-the-world boat
trip, then there's hope, don't you see? Only, we'll have to rely
more on our *essences,* whatever they are, than on sticking up like
the showiest tulips of the season and making a smashing first
impression.''

"Hmm," Julia murmurs, her face tipped up and drinking in
the sun. I can track the mental life going on in her even when
her eyes are closed. Presently she says thoughtfully, "There is
always, I suppose, the power base of a secret, inviolate spiritual
life." She opens her eyes and smiles at me, and then reaches
across and touches my arm. "So maybe your man wasn't so far
wrong when he mistook your occupation, after all."

I've just thought of another power base, that of knowing yourself a Beloved Local Person. She's already got a good start on
that one: her students drop by her house; her friends are devoted,
leave little gifts for her when she's out, put steaks in the refrigerator, think up ways to please her. But I'm afraid to say
this to her because she's still touchy about having come home
again. She's afraid it might mean she's given up, that she's used
Duty as an excuse to abandon the struggle for Self. I think this
about her sometimes. I mean, why doesn't she expand her dis-
sertation into a book? She acknowledges it's about an aspect of
the subject nobody's gone into yet. But if she doesn't hurry up,
someone else is going to beat her to it. That would just kill me.
The trouble with her is, it *wouldn't* kill her. I can hear her saying
(and *almost* completely meaning it): "Actually, I'm really glad

X has published that book on how black slave culture influenced the landowners and, consequently, the culture of the South; I'm not sure I could have done it any better, even if that son-of-a-bitch adviser of mine at Columbia hadn't thrown me off the track with his insistent Marxist proddings until I felt I, as a Southerner, and as the former wife of a descendant of famous slaveholders, had no right even to think about black history. Of course, he was wrong. A few years of reflection convinced me that not only did I have a right, I had a duty, precisely because of the familiarity with the subject my personal history gave me; anyhow, now someone's tackled it, and what difference does it *ultimately* make whether it was Julia Richardson Lowndes, or X, as long as it's finally been done?"

Yet—something else I can't tell her—it's this very attitude of hers that gives me comfort. It's such a healthy contrast to my consuming ambition. The arc of her life has supplied me with more than material for a novel; it has illustrated to me that there are moral natures *outside* of books that are inherently superior to mine. Could I have walked out on all that Lowndes money, and the Virginia plantation, just because I woke up one morning and realized the people I was living among—including my husband—were incurious bigots who were never going to change? And would I, later, out of loyalty to these same bigots, have told my Marxist thesis director, "No, thank you," when he invited me to write a paper exposing some typical inhumane practices of slaveholders, using as documentation some of the entries in the Lowndes family's old diaries, which were already available to the public in a library, anyway? Told him no, even though I knew that my paper would be included in a festschrift for a well-known historian and would advance my career? And even though I myself had been incensed to the point of enlightenment after I had first read those old family records of my in-laws' predecessors, who had written calmly, in their all-in-a-day's-work sort of way, of selling off members of their slaves' families, and forbidding the Negroes to learn to read, calling these "disciplinary tactics"?

Would I have given up the job I'd just gotten at a good college within commuting distance of New York, and a *rent-controlled* Greenwich Village apartment, and a hard-won independence, to come home to nurse a mother I never even liked? Would I be able to do the same for my mother, whom I both love *and* like? Please, God, don't put me to the test.

And here comes the murky paradox: I need Julia in my life, I need to know that people like her exist. But I don't want to be put to her tests. I don't want to trade places with her, or be like her. I just want her to go on being herself so I can watch her fine moral nature in action, and sprinkle a little of her integrity, here and there, upon the personalities of my sturdier fictional heroines.

I say to her now, as the curious hawk, circling back after a short absence to have another look, swoops so low he actually makes a shadow over us, "There is also the power base, Julia, that comes from having been oneself all along. In your case, all your years and years of stubborn integrity are going to add up to nothing short of bewitchingness."

She laughs and says I'm sweet but I always did tend to idealize her.

Then we hear some rifle shots echoing around the valley below, and the hawk abruptly ceases his hospitable swoops, and flaps off, an affronted endangered creature.

"Goddamn rednecks," says Julia, sitting up on the grass. "They've scared away our mascot."

"Do you think the absentee Navy landowner would mind if I irrigated his Christmas trees?" asked Clare as they started down the mountain to Julia's car. "My bladder isn't going to make it even to the nearest filling station."

"Neither is mine. I'll join you."

The two women left the path and descended the sunny embankment into the neat rows of small spruces, where each chose a tree and modestly squatted behind it, out of the other's full view. Now if we had been men, thought Julia, watching her own golden water make a curvy runnel down through the dusty soil, we would have just unzipped our flies up there on the path and stood side by side, continuing our conversation and amicably comparing to ourselves the forces of our individual streams and, perhaps, covertly contrasting the differences in shape and size and hue of our separate penises.

As she stood and zipped up her own fly, she affectionately noted the familiar head of the still-crouched Clare; the abundant hair spiraled up, like curly hot wires, in the sunlight, creating a sort of burning-bush effect. Julia felt contented with her lot and cherished by her oldest friend. Today had been a success. As long as I have Clare to compare notes with at least once a year, she thought, nothing's going to be unbearable. Not even obscure old age.

On the country road leading back to town, they spotted a large turtle, about to cross.

"Oh, no, look!" moaned Clare. "He's sure to get squashed."

Julia braked and pulled over onto the shoulder of the road. The two of them got out of the car and crossed over to the turtle, which, surprisingly fast, already had completed the first quarter of its journey across the asphalt. At their approach, it withdrew into its shell. Clare picked it up and balanced it carefully in her palms. It had a handsome shell, with orange spots. They escorted it to the other side of the road and Clare deposited it in the tall grasses, setting its face towards the woods ahead.

"Well, brother," said Clare, "it sure is lucky for you that we drove by when we did."

It was not a heavily traveled road. The turtle and its ancestors probably had crossed at this spot for generations, with only the rare casualty. This particular turtle would have made it on its own today. But, nevertheless, Julia shared Clare's elation as they walked back to the car, and Clare, happily brushing her hands off, said, "Well, one more catastrophe averted."

"Yes, it's a good omen," said Julia.

There was no one home at the Quicks'. All the cars were gone except for the two relics belonging to the late Dr. Anthony Gallant and his sister, Alicia. Only one dog bothered to raise itself from a puddle of motor oil on the floor of the carport and limp out to meet them.

"But there has to be someone here," said Clare. "I don't have a key. Lily must be at home. Come in a minute and say hello."

The door from the carport into the kitchen was unlocked. "Lily?" Clare called. "She must be here," she said to Julia, "because the door was unlocked. They keep this place locked up like a fortress when they all go out."

But Lily wasn't in the house. "How odd," said Clare. "Where could they all have gone? Rafe probably left for Chapel Hill early. Theo's out somewhere with Jason. Or, no, I think he said he was going to drop over to see that nurse he likes."

"The one who said he was like a roller coaster and she needed stability?"

"Yes. He thought he might see if she'd changed her mind, he said this morning. So Ralph probably has Jason with him, they've gone over to watch the golf or tennis or something on Alicia Gallant's TV. But Lily's car is gone, too. Where has Lily gone? And why was the door unlocked?"

"Do you want me to stay for a while?"

"No, of course not. I'm being silly. It's just that it's never happened before, that I came home and there was nobody here." Clare uttered a grim laugh. "You'd think I was six years old, and not forty-two. Please go on, Julia. I know your father's expecting you, and he likes to eat early."

"I don't know how I'm going to eat anything, after that picnic."

"It was a wonderful picnic. Oh, Julia, I'm so glad I have you."

"I was thinking the same thing, when we were up there squatting behind our separate trees."

"God, I loved that place. So high up, and with the sun and the hawk. Just you and I, on top of the world."

"Olympians on Olympus?"

They both laughed. Julia embraced Clare, and they promised to talk on the phone tomorrow and contrive at least one more meeting before Clare left Mountain City. Julia was not sorry to get out of the Quick atmosphere, which made such a disturbing contrast with the bright, high meadow on top of the mountain where they had been eating lovely food and drinking wine and plotting their witchy old age. But she did feel guilty about leaving Clare alone on Quick's Hill.

"I had a right pleasant Sunday afternoon, myself," Neville Richardson told his daughter as they sat on his screened back porch, sipping their gin-and-tonics. "I took a short stroll down to the end of the block, and there was my new neighbor, Mrs. Evans, quite distraught because she had ordered all these bulbs and hadn't the slightest idea how to go about putting them in the ground. In fact, she was in the process of planting one of them upside down as I made my fortuitous approach."

"Mrs. Evans? Which new neighbor is she?" Julia asked.

"The wife of the black doctor who's just bought the old Tuttle house. A very civilized woman. Only she didn't know which end of a bulb was up. That's not her fault. Nobody ever taught her. I came back here and fetched my little Swiss bulb planter,

and did the first few for her, and she caught on right away, but
without my ever having to explain, in so many words, that she
had mistaken the roots for the crown. I also made her a map, so
she'd know where she'd put everything. There must have been
at least a hundred and fifty dollars' worth of plants. Every color
of the rainbow. *Too* many colors for my taste, but I helped her
organize things so all the reds wouldn't be together and she'd
have some Copper Kings and Black Dragons coming up symmetric-
ally after the Enchantments and Julianas were past their peak."

"I hope you didn't get tired, Father."

"Of course I got tired. You're supposed to get tired, planting
bulbs. But it's an agreeable tiredness. I enjoyed myself. It took
me back to my boyhood, when I'd go and spend a month with
my granny in Culpeper, Virginia, and help her in the garden.
She had a splendid garden. And now Mrs. Evans will be able to
show off her horticultural prowess when she has a grandchild,
and that grandchild will grow up knowing the tail end of a bulb
without anyone having to tell him. I consider my afternoon well
spent, to have assisted at such progress."

They lapsed into a companionable silence, sitting side by side
in their wicker chairs and nursing their drinks. After the day in
the sun, Julia felt a glow radiating from just below the surface of
her skin. She was in a mellow, hopeful mood. Her father's story
seemed to her an emblematic anecdote of how the human race
could renew itself without losing its past: the Tuttles went down
and the Evanses came up, but as long as there survived the
friendly link, strolling by and willing to share from his fund of
memory, precious time and valuable arts could be saved. Out of
such exchanges came bonuses of enlightenment for the old guard
as well, for it had not been lost on Julia that her father had, for
the first time in her hearing, used the word "black" when describing his neighbors, rather than his usual graded epithets of
"darky," "Negro," or "colored," depending on that dark-skinned
person's social status. Mrs. Evans, who yesterday would have
been called "the wife of the colored doctor who's just bought the
old Tuttle house," must have been very civilized, or pleasant,
indeed, to have effected such a welcome change. Julia's spirits
were so improved that she even had hopes of finding at least one
interesting description of civilization among her freshman
papers.

"I've asked my students to write a theme defining civilization," she told her father. "I hope some of them will be original

and not just go to the dictionary or encyclopedia. How would you define it?"

"Oh, don't expect anything original from *me,* Cordelia. I've been far too steeped in schoolmongering to have anything like an original mind left. I can only quote others. Now, who was the fellow who said civilization was a thin crust over the volcano of revolution?"

"It sounds like Mangione, my Marxist adviser at Columbia," Julia said, laughing.

"No, no, it was long before his time. I doubt if he could come up with anything as witty as that. It may have been Havelock Ellis. I think it was. However, I do know an excellent definition of a civilized man."

"What?"

Her father lit a cigarette and, inhaling smoke deeply into his damaged lungs, twinkled at her as he recited: 'We may live without poetry, music and art; We may live without conscience, and live without heart; We may live without friends; We may live without books; But civilized man cannot live without cooks. He may live without books,—what is knowledge but grieving? He may live without hope,—what is hope but deceiving? He may live without love,—what is passion but pining? But where is the man that can live without dining?" Apropos of which, I have a treat for us tonight. A new recipe."

"Your ability to memorize is amazing, Father. How do you do it?"

"Oh, that's nothing. Why, that little ditty is just a drop in the bucket to what Clare had me do. In her novel, I recite the entire 'Shropshire Lad' by heart and make the graduating boys weep. Let me tell you about the new recipe and whet your appetite. It's a foolproof soufflé Margaret York gave me when I played bridge with her last week. You can make it up the night before and stick it in the refrigerator. It's based on the English bread pudding principle. You layer in slices of white bread with the crusts cut off, and then shredded Cheddar cheese, then more bread, and when you get to the top you pour an egg-and-milk mixture over the whole thing. No beating of egg whites necessary. Then, the next day, you just pop it in the oven an hour before you want to eat. You'll have your appetite back in an hour, won't you? If so, I'll go and put it in."

Julia remained sitting on the porch, gazing out over the fences and backyards of her father's neighbors, and feeling the agreeable effects of the gin-and-tonic working its way through her system. In about 1910, this section of town had been *the* place to live. It was close to the center of business, and the lots were large, and the three or four old houses already there—such as the first Dr. Gallant's eighteen-room Victorian edifice with its interesting turrets and cupola—set a standard of lofty graciousness. Then the automobile established itself, people moved farther from town, families got smaller, and most of the old mansions were broken up into apartments. The less lucky ones stood empty and vulnerable atop their slopes, inviting derelicts, who built fires in the wrong places to keep themselves warm, or vandals, who destroyed for the sake of destruction, until the desolate, bare structures were condemned as public hazards and razed to the ground. Her father's house was one of the smaller, newer ones; it had belonged to his parents and he had grown up in it. After his retirement from the Belvedere School, he and Julia's mother had moved here. He had been anticipating the move for years, making little improvements on the house and trying to keep responsible tenants in it until he could return. He did not seem to mind that the neighborhood had deteriorated. Or maybe the image of how it had been in his boyhood was so strong that it mitigated the reality. But Julia's mother had had no image of past graciousness to superimpose on what she called "a budding slum." Being considerably younger than her husband, Marie Richardson could barely remember the days when this street had been elegant. When she was at last forced to live here, she never failed to mention to people that, after all, old Dr. Gallant had lived out *his* last days on the block, and the younger Gallants were still rattling around in the same eighteen rooms they had grown up in. But, within a year, that solace was taken away from her: the "young" Dr. Gallant, who was seventy-four, died of a stroke, and his sister, Alicia, sold the property to the state and moved across town to a safer neighborhood. The Gallant home was now a halfway house for paroled prisoners.

Julia's mother had never forgiven her for leaving Starkie Lowndes. "And there was I, coming to live with you all and be a doting mother-in-law after Daddy died," she had said. "I had it all planned out. I was going to move into that cute little carriage house and invite you all over for tea—or maybe something stronger—once a week. But you had to throw everything out the window, and for what? To go up North and live in a rabbit warren and study under some Italian Communist who tells you you ought to feel guilty about some long-dead slaves you never even owned. It seems to me we would do much better to show a little more guilt and compassion for the people closest to home, who are still among the living."

Well, I did, Mother, I did.

Julia heard the telephone ring inside the house. Her father's social life amazed her, it was far more active than hers. He was always off to somebody's house to play bridge, or to the symphony or a new restaurant with friends . . . and all his various board meetings.

I came back, didn't I, Mother, Julia mused on, chewing the ice from her drink and watching the shadows swallow up the light on the lawn that her father kept weedless and flat as a golf course green. I sat with you on many an evening, after teaching all day at North State, and listened to you tell me what an adorable daughter I was for letting you come and live with me and Starkie (only, you'd forgotten his name and, for some reason known only to you, kept calling him "James"). You and I were alone on the old plantation, at last. You had your chintzes and the carriage house and your dutiful daughter. Father no longer existed. "Who *is* that old man?" you kept asking. "But he seems so concerned. I had better be polite." Only, once you attacked him with a letter opener.

Neville Richardson came out, wearing his chef's apron. "It's Freddy Stratton on the phone for you, Julia."

"Freddy Stratton? Freddy Stratton hasn't phoned me since we were teenagers. How odd. How did she even know I was here?"

Julia put down her glass and went inside. The downstairs phone was in the hallway, on a console table below a mirror. "Freddy?"

"Julia, I didn't want to upset your father, but the most terrible thing has happened. . . ."

Julia stood staring at her slightly sunburned face in the mirror while Freddy Stratton—actually Freddy Stanfield for the last twenty years—relayed her incredible news in the same confidential nasal drawl of her girlhood. Behind Julia's reflection was the reflection of a small oval oil painting of Julia's mother, done the spring she had been crowned Rhododendron Queen. Young enough in that portrait to have been her daughter's daughter today, the young queen with her borrowed scepter and ermine robes gazed serenely over her daughter's shoulder at her own unchallenged expectations.

"I always liked Freddy," said Neville Richardson, who was just getting ready to put the soufflé dish in the oven as Julia appeared in the kitchen. "I think I liked her best of all the little girls who came out to spend the night. She was the only one who treated me like a man, and not just somebody's dried-up old daddy. Is anything the matter?"

"Yes. Yes, it is. Freddy was speaking to Clare—Clare had just phoned her, she said—when an operator broke in with an emergency call for Clare. Freddy made Clare promise to call her back and tell her what it was." Julia sat down on the top of a stepladder beside the pantry.

"And what was it?"

"It was Lily, calling from the emergency room at Memorial Mission. Theo is dead, and the girl is dead. It looks as if Theo shot this nurse and then . . . killed himself."

"A nurse? What was he doing with a nurse?"

"She was someone Theo had been seeing after Snow left him. Clare mentioned it today. The nurse had a little boy exactly Jason's age, and apparently Theo liked her a lot, but she thought he was too moody."

Julia's father put the soufflé dish down on the kitchen counter. He leaned back against the sink and reached beneath his chef's apron bib and extracted his pack of Luckies from his shirt pocket. As he lit a cigarette, his hand was trembling. He took a deep drag of smoke and then coughed it out again. "Poor, poor Lily. She will never be able to put this out of her mind. It's unbelievable. It's awful. For all of them. Of course you must go up to Clare. I've never been as close to them as you have . . . but I do wish I had something to send. If only I had baked my banana-and-dill bread today, but I got sidetracked by Mrs. Evans and her bulbs. But wait, I can send the soufflé, Margaret York's soufflé. . . ." He was already tearing off a sheet of aluminium foil. "It's lucky I was waiting for the oven to preheat and hadn't put it in. I'll just write the directions on a piece of paper and then they will have something to stick in the oven when they need it. Ah, poor Lily. That night when your mother plunged the letter opener into my leg when I was reading aloud her favorite passage from *Idylls of the King*, I thought as a family we had hit bottom, but this! This is in another league altogether."

At night she stood at the window, looking down at the separate, scattered lights that lay at her feet like so many fallen stars. To Honoria, in her unimpeachable darkness, they flashed their lonely semaphores of all the griefs, delusions, and follies that impelled the inhabitants of those houses.

—*from* "Honoria Knows," a destroyed, unfinished novel by Lily Buchel Campion Quick

III: HOUSEHOLD RUINS

*C*lare remained transfixed in the kitchen, listening to the diminishing crackle of gravel as Julia's car descended the curves of Quick's Hill. Just as she always felt compelled to watch Felix out of sight to guarantee seeing him again, she now entertained the superstition that the effects of the power and elation shared with Julia on the mountaintop could be preserved only if she remained completely still until the last sounds of her friend's departure had faded into the Sunday-afternoon quietness of the valley below.

That quietness achieved, she moved slowly to the messy kitchen table and tried to read from the evidence there what the family had been doing since she had gone away with Julia at nine o'clock that morning. Somebody, probably Rafe while nursing his hangover, had been reading the funny papers. Lily had scribbled a note to Ralph in her cryptic, feathery script on the back of a bill: "That Mr. Green phoned again about your building his house." Jason had eaten most of the whipped cream and several spoonfuls from his little glass cup of instant chocolate pudding. Ralph had gone to the ten o'clock service at First Presbyterian, and Lily to the eleven o'clock at St. Dunstan's Episcopal, because there were the programs. Theo and Jason usually went wherever Lily did: she divided her attendance, according to her mood, between St. Dunstan's, with its cheerful, terrestrial rector who counseled and joked his parishioners out of their miseries, and Our Lady of the Mountains, in the neighborhood where she had lived with her mother and small daughter after coming back to Mountain City as a widow. At Our Lady's, there was an interesting new rector who, everybody said, really did look like Jesus Christ, even down to the reddish beard. And he had voluntarily taken a vow of celibacy, and was very young, only about Theo's age.

But where were they all?

Clare wandered into the living room, which faced west and was, at this hour, the brightest place in the house. Furnished in Lily's favorite blues and beiges, and relatively uncluttered—except for Jason's Hot Wheels City strewn across the Chinese carpet—it was the serenest room. But as Clare stood at the picture window, trying to keep faith with the weakening sunshine, she was overcome by a sudden sadness. Nothing was ever perfect for long. Her mountaintop effervescence was draining out of her, and she felt the return of her heavier, dreading, super-critical earthbound self. Why didn't Ralph keep the trees topped? You could hardly see the valley anymore. It was like looking through bars to watch the sunset or the lights of town at night. There was a haunting passage in Lily's old novel, the one she never finished and later repudiated, in which a wise old woman, a sort of town sibyl who lived on a hill high above anyone else, would look down every night and read the secrets of the town through its lonely winking lights. Clare still had dreams that Lily had finished that novel and become very famous and aloof, and would always be leaving a hotel just as Clare checked in. In one dream, Clare had just come in from a swim in the vast hotel pool, when whom should she see coming out but Lily, who put up a hand in gracious acknowledgment (or was it dismissal?) and, smiling distantly, went on to the pool for her own swim. Clare yearned to go back and swim with her, but for some reason couldn't.

What if Lily had suffered a heart attack and been taken to the hospital and that's where they all were? She'd had something fifteen years ago, when they'd first moved into this house. She had told Clare about it long after the event, "because you're such a little worrier." Fortunately, Dr. Anthony Gallant had been dining with Ralph and Lily on that particular night, and had made Lily lie down on her right side and think pleasant thoughts and breathe deeply. The next day he had arranged for tests that showed "not much of anything," according to Lily, and she had changed her diet and taken up swimming and had already outlived Dr. Gallant by some years without further alarm.

Clare considered phoning Alicia Gallant, just to settle her mind. But Ralph got miffed when family members tried to track him down at the old lady's, even though she was ever the sole of graciousness and humour when they did. However, Clare was always daunted by Miss Alicia's sprightly give-and-take in social discourse, and her reluctance to match herself against that fast-paced, impeccably courteous banter outweighed her fantasy-fears of Lily's having been rushed to the hospital while she and Julia were enjoying themselves on the mountain. It was, after all, a fine October day, and why should Lily not be out in it, too? It was just that the door had been left unlocked. . . . Well, that could happen. The wonder was that it had never happened before.

At loose ends, she went from room to room, opening windows. When they came home, someone would immediately close them tight again. Meanwhile, let the house breathe. The room Theo and Jason shared looked as though a tornado had hit it: little socks, toys, Theo's accounting books all over the unmade bed. She went into the blue bathroom across the hall, and while she was studying herself from various angles in the long, wide mirror, she looked up at the ceiling and noticed a new, ugly stain the size of a large puddle. Something had leaked. Was it still leaking? Would anybody do anything about it, any more than had been done about the soap-dish hole in the wall, pasted over with Lily's Japanese women having tea? This had been such a shining, handsome house when Ralph built it, the finest house the Quicks had ever lived in. She had just come back to this country after several years in England, and had been so pleased for Lily, for all of them, that they had at last attained all the required items of the American Dream. The little boys, adolescents, screamed and splashed in their own swimming pool. Lily had a steam cabinet in her bathroom, and someone had to show Clare how to turn on the ultramodern bathroom taps. The blond oak floors smelled of varnish, and the walls of fresh paint. From the living-room window, and from the deck off Ralph and Lily's room, you had an unobstructed view of valley, hills, town, and mountain ranges all the way to the Tennessee border. On that first visit, she and Ralph had gone together in Ralph's truck to choose a shepherd puppy. The litter belonged to an old mountain woman who lived in a cove beyond the paved part of Spook's Branch Road. She and Ralph and the old woman had sat in the kitchen, around the old-fashioned wood stove, which had a fire in it even though it was August, and watched the six black puppies snuggling or playing around their mother. They waited for a sign to tell them which was "their" puppy. After about ten minutes, they had narrowed it down to two of the four females—it had to be a female because Ralph wanted to start his own clan of dogs to protect their house on the lonely hill. One of the two they liked because she was so playful and independent; she was a joy to watch. But finally they had chosen the one that seemed to like *them* best; she kept approaching Ralph curiously, cocking her head; she licked Clare's hand. "Better take love where you can find it," Ralph had said as they drove back to Quick's Hill with the friendly puppy, which was to be named Fritzi and become the mother of the pack of dogs who terrorized so many guests. That afternoon, some of Clare's appreciation of Ralph had returned. It had been like the old days, in her adolescence, before their relationship turned poisonous, when they were always off together somewhere like cronies, almost like a young boy and his older brother. Every Friday evening, Ralph would take her along to see a man he called "Uncle Don," who collected and sold rare guns. She would drive with Ralph in his truck, rattling with his toolbox and the other implements of his trade out the Old Catawba Highway to the gun dealer's house, and sit in his fusty bachelor's room, lit with blue light bulbs because Uncle Don said strong light hurt his eyes. The two men would examine one strange and elegant firearm after another under that eerie blue light, breathing reverently over their sleek barrels and sometimes stroking their carved handles before Uncle Don re-wrapped them in chamois cloths and put them back in their drawers. In those days, Ralph had been too poor to buy the kinds of guns Uncle Don sold, but had established this mostly mute Friday-evening friendship based on their shared admiration for those guns. Watching them, Clare felt as though she had been permitted entrance into some male sanctum; she always wore jeans and a plaid shirt and kept her mouth shut so that she, a feminine intruder, would not disturb their almost religious concentration on the weapons.

But it depressed her to think about Ralph for very long. Their ruined affinity aroused in her an uneasy mixture of sorrow and repugnance. He still tried to get her to talk about it, to "analyze" with him where it had gone so wrong. "Why open a can of worms?" she would say, rebuffing him with one of his own expressions. One day, they had been friends, singing hillbilly songs together, planting grass, and making slingshots; the next day he had become violent and suspicious and unreasonable. Or that was how it seemed at the time, when she had been so miserable and had written that secret letter to her father's people, the letter that had caused Lily so much pain but had secured Clare's teenage escape from Ralph and from the further ignominy of having to drop out of St. Clothilde's and go to public high school because Ralph couldn't pay her tuition.

Where *was* everybody?

She went downstairs, to the basement TV room, where everything was in an advanced state of disintegration. Along one wall, moldering on their shelves, were outgrown books belonging to various members of the household. She recognized St. Clothilde's textbooks from her own and her half brothers' schooldays, and a whole row of books she had bought while in college, mainly to impress herself and others with her eclectic sophistication. Rollo May's *Existence,* mildewing in its black-and-orange dust jacket next to Rafe's or Theo's *Intermediate French Grammar:* she remembered plunking down sixteen dollars—a fortune for a book back then—for it at the Intimate Bookshop in Chapel Hill, but had she ever actually *read* even a page of it from the day she bought it until the day, several years later, when she brought it back to Mountain City in a box of books to be stored with Lily and Ralph while she went off to live in England on Cousin Demaris's legacy to try to become a writer?

In the middle of the basement room—once also handsome and shining with its light pine-paneled walls and long tile floor—was the Ping-Pong table. But the net had been taken down after all the balls had been broken by Rafe's or Theo's smashing them against the table with their paddles when one or the other angrily lost a game, and after the paddles themselves had been misplaced. Now the table was covered with bills addressed to Ralph Quick, stacked in piles which either had no system or represented some mysterious order only Ralph understood. Recently—Lily had told Clare this story—a creditor had phoned Ralph and asked when he could expect to receive his money, and Ralph had laughed ruefully and said, "Once a month I take all the bills and throw them down the stairs. The ones that land on the highest stair I pay right away. The rest have to wait until the next month, when I repeat the procedure all over again." The interesting thing was, Lily had gone on to report, the man had laughed too and said well, he sure hoped his bill landed on the highest step next month, because if it didn't he was going to have to try Ralph's method on his own bills. "And," concluded Lily, smiling in that old way she still could when her husband amused her, "that man's bill *did* land on the highest step the next month."

Clare stepped over some foam stuffing one of the dogs—or perhaps Jason—had been pulling out of an old chair that faced the TV, and sat down at Ralph's office desk in the dark corner. She switched on the gooseneck lamp, but of course the bulb had burned out. However, there was still light from the sunset coming through the western windows. She had descended into this most desolate of rooms, "the family room," knowing it always depressed her with its moldy smell and abandoned items but wanting to make some constructive use of this strange wasteland of time until they all came home again. The type-writer, such as it was, was kept here, on a metal stand adjacent to Ralph's desk, and, after rummaging through drawers that were surprisingly neat compared to the desk's surface, she found a clean sheet of bond paper and a prestamped envelope and proceeded to type a short letter (the ribbon was so worn that the sentences came out a barely readable pale gray) to her editor in New York. He had sent her bound galleys of a book he was publishing, a first novel "by a fellow Southerner," which she had read with absorption on the plane coming down. The language was evocative, the characters worthy of concern, and the insights profound enough to arouse respect in Clare, along with a twinge of envious regret that she had not formulated these particular insights herself. The book examined the lives of half a dozen Southerners—still relatively young—who were trapped, in seemingly inextricable ways, in a shared net of sadness.

On the plane, Clare had been impatient at times with the characters, despite her attraction to the book. Come on, now, she had thought, still thousands of feet above and some hundreds of miles from her own familial net, why don't you people snap out of it? There are solutions for all of you; the first thing you have to do is give up your stubborn loyalty to your *sadness*.

But now, down to the same latitude where these characters

walked, haunted at this sunset hour by kindred ghosts, she understood that their particular sadness—a sort of elegiac mourning for the loss of a world that never had been—was the thing they were least willing to part with. They were *in love* with their sadness more than with one another. Their sadness had become their religion and their art: it provided, as music to a dance, the tempo and structure of their lives.

She looked over what she had written in the faint type. (Tomorrow, she would get Lily to stop downtown at the office supply store and would go in herself and purchase a new ribbon for this machine. Yet, even as she resolved, in this small way, to break the spell of disintegration enveloping this hill like a cloud, she also knew she probably wouldn't: something would come up, something would intervene. That was the nature of the sadness-spell: it enervated you with the enchantment of its ruins until you become—oh, God—like Lily, an abstracted priestess of them, dragging your robes through the temple and smiling enigmatically to yourself as you pasted an elegant picture of a tea ceremony over a gaping hole.)

> Dear Adam
>
> Thank you for sending me the galleys of Olivia Hutchinson's first novel, *Fools of Loss*. You are right: it is special. She's caught something here: that quality of longing in certain people that makes them crave what's found in pain and loss so intensely that, as one of her characters puts it, "they'll give up dreams for it." In a way, it's helped me to understand myself and members of my family better since I've been back down here among them for a week. This last, of course, for your eyes only; the rest, please feel free to use for the greater glory of Miss (Mrs.?) (Ms.?) Hutchinson. Tell her, by the way, I was jealous of how well she pulled off that duck-hunting scene with the two men. I would love to know if she researched it or if someone took her hunting. Speaking of men's demesnes, I haven't forgotten your promise to wine and dine me at the Century sometime this fall.
>
> As ever,
> Clare

Seldom, if ever, could she reread a letter she had written without feeling uncomfortable: there was always an element of *posing*, a disturbing gap between what she said and what she really felt, a masquerading quality. In this letter she was masquerading as the successful writer who graciously took time out from a family visit to patronize a new entrant to the Court of Literature. At the same time, braided all through the message was the recognizable tone of the good girl trying to please Daddy and archly flirt a little. She was just about to crumple the letter into a ball and forget the whole endeavor, when, out of her side vision, she saw a serpentine shape eddying across the floor space between the bookshelf and the old horsehair sofa.

Then she remembered Lily's telling her they had found a snake down here, a small king snake, two Sundays ago. Theo had found it on that morning when he had come down to the adjoining laundry room to iron a shirt for church. He had coaxed the snake, which was just a baby, into a jar, and come upstairs with it, smiling his wicked smile and announcing to everyone that he and Jason were going to take it to Father Zachary's annual Blessing of the Animals at St. Dunstan's, which, it just so happened, was scheduled for that very afternoon. This was a much-looked-forward-to social event that gave the parishioners a chance to show off their dogs and cats and parakeets and hamsters and monkeys, etc. A few of the residents of the exclusive community of St. Dunstan's Forest always contributed style to the occasion by riding their horses over for the Blessing. Anyway, Lily had said, everyone had gone along with Theo, never dreaming he really intended to do it. But that afternoon, just as Ralph was hosing off the dogs' muddy feet before herding them into the back end of the station wagon, Theo and Jason had come out with the little king snake in its tall pickle jar with the perforated lid. "Son," Ralph had said, "sometimes I wonder who is the biggest baby, you or Jason. Can't you see it's out of the question for you all to take that snake?"

"I don't see why," said Theo. "A snake has as much a right to a blessing as any other animal. Maybe even more, considering that his species has been so maligned by the Church."

"Oh, darling, it would set the wrong tone," Lily had pleaded. "And some people are mortally afraid of snakes. There's a special phobia they suffer from, it even has a name, herpe— herpeto—or something. And it might scare one of the horses. That could be very dangerous in a crowd."

"Well," countered Theo, "those snobs from St. Dunstan's Forest who come posting over on their horses, have they ever considered that their *horses* are dangerous in a crowd. But they love to show off their English riding clothes. That's what the whole disgusting ceremony is about, if you ask me. One more chance to flaunt your snobbery. This snake would be a healthy counterbalance."

"That snake is not going to the Blessing," said Ralph. "Now, take it back in the house or, better yet, set it mercifully free to join its own kind in the woods, and let's go if we're going. Damn it, Lily, can't you keep your dog from lying down in the filth when I just hosed her off?"

"It's not filth. It's only your own carport. And my poor baby can't help it if her back legs won't hold her up anymore. Poor Liebchen really *needs* her blessing. Please, Theo, don't let's spoil the day over a snake."

"Okay, I won't," Theo told Lily, surprising her by his easy capitulation. "Jason, go get in my car. I won't be a minute." He disappeared into the house, carrying the snake jar.

And then, Lily told Clare, they had waited for Theo to come out again, she and Ralph standing by the station wagon with the dogs, little Jason obediently opening the door of his father's car and crawling up onto the seat and trying to buckle his own seat belt.

A pistol shot rang out from somewhere in the woods just below the house. Soon after, Theo, smiling, came out the kitchen door.

"Son, what was that all about?" asked Ralph, who had gone very grim after the shot and before Theo's reappearance.

"Oh," said Theo, "I took him down to the basement and let him out of his jar at the same door he probably came in by. And then"—he paused for greater effect—"I *freed* him. An unblessed snake is better off that way."

Ralph Quick looked at his son steadily. "One of these days you are going to go too far," he said. "And that thing is not a toy."

"I never said it was," replied Theo.

They had gone on to the Blessing of the Animals in their two cars, Lily said, because Jason would have been disappointed otherwise. But, "not surprisingly," she had added, the joy had gone out of the day.

"Did Theo really kill that poor snake?" Clare had asked. She had no affection for snakes, but wanton killing upset her.

"Of course not," said Lily. "That evening, I asked him, when just the two of us were alone, and he put his arm around me and said, 'Mother, you know me. What do you think I did when I went into the house?' And I said, 'Well, I think you went to your room and got your gun and then you went down to the basement and let the snake out of the door and then you shot into the air to scare us all, to make us think . . . I don't know what. And your daddy went quite pale. And then you put the gun back and came out to us, and made your ambiguous statement so we'd be punished for not letting you take the snake.' And he smiled, his sweet smile, not that other one, and said, 'Mother you know me so well.'"

So, thought Clare, picking up her letter and envelope and gingerly making her way across the basement, keeping her eyes sharply focused for the least shadowy movement, either Lily does know him so well, and the snake found its way back inside . . . or another snake did. Or: Theo was *really* perverse and let the snake out of the jar inside the house, where he had found it in the first place, and then misled Lily into thinking she knew him "so well."

I really am going to try to talk to Theo again before I leave, she resolved. He's worse than ever. Maybe I'll invite him to come to New York, as I did Rafe, and I'll shower him with little attentions. Felix can help. Young men look up to Felix and his old-fashioned masculine self-confidence. Theo could sure benefit from some of *that*.

She felt relieved to be climbing the stairs—the stairs where Ralph's apocryphal monthly bill-tossing procedure took place—with no further glimpse of the snake. Let them evict or shelter the unblessed creature according to their needs and moods. She could not replace the soap dish in the bathroom or decide the fate of their snake. In household matters it was not for her to interfere. At least she had written her letter. And it occurred to her that there was one more thing she could accomplish while waiting for them to come home again: she could telephone the arch-rival of her childhood and see if she still remained under the spell of Freddy Stratton's powers to make her doubt herself. It would be an interesting test, and if, at forty-two, Clare was not ready to make it, then when? She had not spoken to Freddy, who was now Skip Stanfield's wife and the mother of college-age girls, since leaving St. Clothilde's after tenth grade. She had not laid eyes on Freddy since that incredible night in Chapel Hill when the two of them, both twenty then, had gazed at each other in fierce hatred and misunderstanding across a fraternity bonfire. The true cause of that baleful evening was still a mystery to Clare. It was one of those events that leave a bad taste in your mouth for years afterwards.

What had happened was this: Clare, in her junior year at Chapel Hill, had been dating a member of the Dekes, the fraternity of which Skip Stanfield was then president. Clare had known Skip since the days when he served as acolyte at Our Lady's and she had played hopscotch with Skip's younger sister Beverly. She knew he was pinned to Freddy Stratton, who had gone for two years to a junior college in Virginia and was living at home again in Mountain City, waiting for Skip to graduate so they could get married. Whenever Clare saw Skip on campus, or when she and her date were over at the fraternity house (though Skip usually went to Mountain City on weekends to spend the time with Freddy), she would always ask after Freddy and tell him to be sure to say hello; and several times Skip had returned with the message "Freddy says hello *back*!" "When is Freddy going to come down to Chapel Hill?" Clare kept asking, wondering how the two of them would regard each other after four years. While Clare had been living with her father's people, she had thought a lot about Freddy, and imagined the day when they might meet again. She was both nervous and curious to see if Freddy still had that amazing self-assurance.

And then came that bewildering phone call from Clare's Deke boyfriend, on the afternoon of a fraternity wienie roast to which he had invited her. "Listen," he had begun nervously, "there's a problem. I believe you all knew each other back in Mountain City." "Freddy's here?" Clare had said, not understanding why there should be a problem. "Well, that's fine. I look forward to seeing her again." Though she had been counting on a simple, happy evening when she could enjoy herself with no competition, and especially not that of her old Mountain City nemesis. But it turned out to be worse than that. With mounting embarrassment, her date went on to explain that . . . well, it was an awkward situation. Skip's fiancée had said she wished Clare weren't coming to the wienie roast because it would be distressing for her to see Clare again. Distressing! What did he mean? What had Freddy meant? Well, said the Deke, according to Skip, who had taken him aside in the hope they might work something out, Freddy had told him that stories about Clare's "reputation" had gotten back to Mountain City and Freddy just wouldn't feel comfortable meeting her on the old terms. Skip had thought it might be more congenial for everyone at the wienie roast if Clare's date took her somewhere else for the evening. Clare, at first incredulous, then furious, had told him that staying away would be tantamount to acknowledging Freddy's slander, and the boy had at last reluctantly agreed. They had gone to the wienie roast. All evening long, the nervous fraternity brothers and their dates had watched the two Mountain City girls darting killing glances at each other across the bonfire. After that night, Clare never dated her Deke, or anyone else from that fraternity again. Freddy Stratton married Skip Stanfield, and in the ensuing years, whenever she saw Lily at church, Freddy would ask about Clare. Where *was* Clare, and what was she doing? As friendly as you please.

"I will never understand it," Clare once said to Julia. "I mean, did I dream it, or what? But I have a very clear memory of us on either side of that bonfire; we never once spoke!"

"Oh, come on," said Julia. "Don't be thick. It makes perfect sense to me. Don't you understand what Freddy was afraid of?"

"No!"

"Well, that you were down at Chapel Hill, and Skip was down at Chapel Hill . . . is it starting to dawn in there?"

"You're way off track, Julia. Skip and I never thought of each other that way. We weren't each other's type. It was something much more complex. Maybe somebody *had* told Freddy something awful about me. Or maybe that boy, that Deke, had designs of his own: maybe he was looking for an excuse to get out of our date. Who knows?"

"Have it your own way," said Julia. "I know that sinister intrigues and obscure wounds are a lot more fun for you to contemplate than plain old down-home Southern bitchery."

And maybe Julia was right. For Clare had carefully preserved the venomous evening in a special corner of her memory, where she went to visit it, along with some similar incidents kept in this small shrine to indignation, whenever she needed to stoke her sense of having been *wronged:* a sense that, through some curious psychological alchemy, seemed to revitalize her instincts for self-preservation and, sometimes, even to feed her art.

Clare cleared a space for herself at the cluttered kitchen table, then hauled out the Mountain City phone book from the shelf beneath the kitchen counter and looked up "Stanfield, Sanford K." Her heart beating ridiculously, she dialed the number.

A man answered on the fifth ring. He sounded short of breath and annoyed. Clare considered hanging up but knew that, if she did, she might never have the courage to dial this number again.

"Hello," she said, trying to sound jaunty and assured. "This is Clare Campion. Is this Skip?"

"Well, hello, Clare Campion." Now the man's voice was teasing, jocular. "How've you've been?" He did not seem surprised that she was calling.

"Oh, I've been *fine*. And what about yourself?"

"I can't complain, thank you. Freddy and I just this minute got back from Sapphire Valley. We went up for the weekend with some friends to play a little bridge and golf, and just walked in the door. Freddy's right here and wants to talk to you."

"Clare?" The same voice. Conspiratorial, intimate. "Where *are* you?" A just-us-girls voice.

"Here. In Mountain City, visiting the family. I was with Julia this afternoon and she said she'd seen you, and I decided it was high time I called you up after all these years and said hello." Did that sound casual enough? To this person from the past who had managed to install herself in Clare's adult dream-life, appearing year after year as a sometimes malicious, sometimes helpful and loving figure whom Clare must appease or come to terms with?

"I'm real glad you did, because you want to know something? Last week I was looking through my old scrapbook and I found a picture of us when we were nine. It was at my birthday party and I was sitting on top of you. And ever since then I've had this real strong feeling I would see you again very soon. How long are you staying?"

"I fly back to New York on Friday."

"Oh, good. It wouldn't have been very nice of you if you'd phoned to say hello and then told me you have to leave tomorrow. Now, when can you have lunch? I can't tomorrow, because Monday's my house-cleaning day. And Tuesday I do volunteer work."

"I can't Tuesday, either," said Clare, despising herself for needing to let Freddy know she had a few plans herself. "I think

Lily and I are having lunch with Father Weir and his wife on Tuesday."

"Oh, Father Weir. Skip always loved him. We have this new *young* priest at Our Lady's now. Has Lily described him? He looks exactly like those pictures of Jesus we used to get on our holy cards at St. Clothilde's. He's not much older than my girls, but they say he's taken a vow of celibacy, like the Catholic priests have to."

"Yes, Lily likes Father Devereaux."

"I'm still making up my mind. What about Wednesday? Come over here and I'll fix us something simple and we can drink lots of wine and talk."

"Wednesday's fine. Listen, I was really sorry to hear about your mother. Julia told me."

"Thank you. It hurt me to see her suffer like that, but I'm glad we were able to have her here with us. She remembered you, Clare. I was reading your new book aloud to her, the one about Julia's family, and she said she would never forget how you were over at our house that time, and then Lily and Ralph came to get you and they told you they'd just gotten married and you cried and cried."

"Are you sure I was over at your house that day?" It wasn't true. Clare remembered very well where she had been that memorable afternoon, but she couldn't bring herself to contradict Freddy's late mother. Clare had been left with Ralph's mother, whose house smelled of dogs and Lifebuoy soap and cooking. The woman wore her long gray hair in a single thick braid—like her Cherokee ancestors, she told Clare. "I reckon your mother and Ralph have finally gone off to get themselves married in the church," Mrs. Quick had said in her matter-of-fact monotone. "Oh, no," the nine-year-old Clare had replied haughtily. "They're just good friends, that's all." "They're more than good friends." Something in the older woman's tone had sent Clare into a bedroom, where she threw herself down crosswise on the chenille bedspread and lay in a motionless, despairing trance. Then Lily and Ralph had returned in Ralph's car, Lily smiling guiltily, a white orchid pinned to her suit, and Clare had known it was true. But how had it come about that Freddy's mother had appropriated that afternoon for herself and had assigned Clare all the angry tears she had, in reality, kept back?

"Oh, yes. Mamma said she felt so sad for you she almost

broke down and cried herself, only it would have seemed rude when your mother and Ralph were so happy."

There was a funny mechanical twittering on the line. Then an operator's voice broke in on their conversation. "I have an emergency call for anyone at 555-7090. Will you give up your call?"

"Yes, of course," said Clare, stunned.

"Clare!" cried Freddy. "You have got to call me right back and tell me what this *was*."

"Okay."

"Promise, now. Or I'll worry."

"I promise."

They both hung up. Clare snatched up the receiver as soon as the ring began.

Lily said, "Hel*lo*. You're back." She sounded enigmatic, faintly amused.

"I've been back almost an hour," Clare said accusingly. "There was nobody here. The door was unlocked. Where are you?"

"Memorial Mission Hospital." There was a cat-and-mouse quality to Lily's voice that was positively ominous.

"Oh, my God. Are you okay?"

"I'm *fine*. It's Theo."

"*Theo?* What's Theo done? What's the matter with Theo?"

"Theo is gone," said Lily, with a faraway lilt.

"Gone! Wait a minute. You can't mean —"

"Yes. And so is Jeanette, that nice nurse he was dating. They are both gone."

"What *happened?*"

"Well, what they're all *saying* is that he shot her and then himself. But people always assume the man did it. Nobody actually saw it. They were found in Jeanette's car, right in the middle of Fairfield Road, not far from her house. She had two bullets through her head, and he had one through his. They couldn't do anything for her, but they've had him on one of those machines for the last hour. The doctor told us, 'Your son is still alive, but his brain is dead.' I said, 'If his brain is dead, then *he* is dead.' Now he is off the machine."

"I can't take this in!" Clare yelled.

"Don't try to. I'm not trying. I'm just . . . floating. This nice Negro orderly has been walking me up and down the hall outside the emergency room. He even held my head, and I let him. We said some prayers together. Some of his prayers, then some of mine. And Father Zachary is here. He's with Ralph now. They're doing all those things you have to do. And then there are the *detectives*. . . ."

"But where's Jason? Oh, God, poor Jason!"

"Yes. I don't want to even begin thinking about that yet. Alicia Gallant has taken him off to the hospital drugstore to get a sundae. They were over at her place watching television, Ralph and Jason, when the hospital called our house. I phoned Alicia and told them to meet me at the emergency room. None of us knew . . . I mean, over the phone they only said, 'Are you his mother?' and could I come right away."

"Did you see him?"

"No. I prefer to remember him as he was when he left the house this afternoon. He was going to see Jeanette. He told me, 'I'm going over to see if she'll have me back, and it'll be settled one way or another by three-thirty.' He seemed very optimistic. He even ironed himself a clean shirt. Why don't you get something out of Ralph's liquor cabinet and pour yourself a stiff one?"

"That's the last thing in the world I want."

"Well, whatever. We'll all be home presently, I mean, not all, but . . . Ralph has the State Police trying to intercept Rafe's car on I-40. He got a late start back to Chapel Hill, so we ought to be able —" Lily broke off abruptly.

"I'll be here," Clare said. Then she repeated, "I'll be right here."

"Bye," said Lily in a little-girl's voice.

Clare replaced the receiver but kept her hand on the telephone. The kitchen was already swarming with half-formed thoughts and realizations that, any second, would swell into terrible articulateness and pounce. She couldn't call Felix, because he was in Vienna, trying to persuade an exiled Czech poet to write a play about Kafka for his World Theater. Or, she *could* call him, but it would be almost midnight, he would probably be back at the Kaiserin Elisabeth, asleep. Why wake him with such news? He might feel he had to cut short his trip and fly to her—and what could he do when he got there? He had met Theo only once, at the beach last summer; had started off by "discovering" Theo: "I *like* that boy. Why is it you rarely speak of him? It's always Rafe. This brother is a mensch. He feels things. He makes such provocative and original observations. I

like the way he sees into things. And he has a *sweetness*." But by
the same evening, the bloom was off Theo's rose. He had barged
into their bedroom, to borrow Clare's hair dryer, and caught
Felix napping in his undershorts. He had come down to dinner
without a shirt, and, for some reason nobody could understand,
had brought Jason, whom he had just bathed, wrapped in
nothing but a towel. "I'm sorry, Theo," Lily had said, embarrassed, "but all the men who eat at the table with me have to
have on their shirts *and* pants." "Come on, Jason," Theo had
said, "we're not wanted here." And both Lily and Clare had to
go upstairs and soothe his feelings and beg him to come back
and not to ruin dinner. Which was ruined anyway, because
Clare's corn muffins had burned while they were coaxing Theo
back. "Rafe is easier," Felix had admitted to Clare that night in
bed. "He drinks far too much and uses up all the ice and tonic,
but he's easier."

That night, both brothers had fallen from grace. Rafe had
persuaded Theo to leave Jason with Lily and go girl-chasing in
Myrtle Beach, and they had come back raving drunk at three in
the morning and turned on the porch lights and had a loud
argument on the windwalk, right outside Clare and Felix's bedroom window. "What do you think this is, a flophouse?" Felix,
enraged, swung his feet to the floor, to go to tell them off. "No,
no, let me go, they're my brothers," she had said, and had rushed
out in her raggedy, too-sheer nightgown; her hair flying about
wildly in the wind, she had shouted how ashamed she was of
them, how they had done nothing but abuse her hospitality. For
this was Clare and Felix's vacation cottage; the two of them had
hit on the workable plan of renting it for one month every
summer and then inviting Clare's family down to the South
Carolina island for a week, so that she could see her family in
the South, where they preferred to stay, but on her own terms,
her own territory. When she had finished excoriating her
brothers for their thoughtless behaviour, Rafe had suddenly
burst out laughing and looked down the front of her nightgown.
"Okay, okay, you've made your point," he had said. "Now stop
being such a harpy and go back to bed and get your beauty
sleep." But Theo had looked stricken and, without a word, had
slunk off to the room he was sharing with Jason. Snow had left
him back in April, and Theo had wanted to bring a new girlfriend, who was a nurse, and her little boy. "He's just Jason's
age and they'll keep each other company," he had told Clare

on the phone, the night before he was to drive down to the island. "No, that will be too many in the house," said Clare, feeling mean but determined to preserve her rights as hostess. "If I were still with Snow, you'd have let her come," Theo pointed out. "Snow was your wife and Jason's mother. I don't even know this person. I tell you what, Theo. Let's just be family this year, and if you're still seeing her next year, you can bring them." "Well, I guess that's fair enough," Theo had replied mildly.

Foreclosed possibilities were beginning to take shape. There, in the kitchen, Clare saw scenes that would now never take place, people who could never, or never again, get together. And certain wrongs could never be righted, certain reparations—however keenly intended—could not be made. The faraway lilt of Lily's voice, as it rose on the word "gone," had been like hope taking off on wings into the mists of unknowable places: Lily's announcement of Theo's end, the exact pitch and cadence of it, would dwell in Clare's inner ear for the rest of her life.

As she looked up Freddy's number for the second time that afternoon, her earlier panic at dialling this number belonged to another plane of existence altogether, where disaster was defined by social failure, the degree of ostracism made apparent to the outcast by the temperature of a voice, the finely calibrated measure of censure in a word or a phrase. Ten minutes ago, the worst thing that could have happened was that Freddy would make Clare feel she had been foolish or presumptuous to call.

The news about Theo had released her—temporarily—from this level of preoccupation, but how ironic (or was it something more fateful and mysterious than mere irony?) that, because of the bizarre meshing of the two phone calls, the first human being whom she would personally inform of her brother's death was not one of the people she knew and loved best in the world, Felix or Julia, but Freddy Stratton Stanfield, who had glared venomously across the bonfire at her twenty-two years before. Because Freddy had made her *promise* to call back.

Yet, as she was dialing Freddy's number, she felt it was faithless and wrong of her not to call Julia first. She and Freddy would be linked even more profoundly than in the long-deadlocked rivalry of their childhood and youth. Freddy's mother had claimed to be present at an earlier juncture with sorrow in Clare's history: now the dead woman's fiction seemed prescient of the bond with Clare's family that Freddy would always have as a result of this call.

"Clare? What was it?" Freddy must have been sitting by the phone.

"Oh, Freddy —" Clare could hardly stand to listen to her own voice. She, who had been training herself for years to manipulate words for the greatest dramatic effect, could find no way in her personal voice to convey this material—even the simple facts, which were all she knew—without hearing a spurious note. Every phrase that came from her lips, from "you know I have two brothers . . . I mean, oh, God, I *had* two brothers" to "shot her and then himself, they are saying," sounded like a deliberate attempt on her part to sentimentalize or corrupt the truth, thus destroying the real meaning of Theo's last afternoon and permanently obscuring the essence of what Theo—who could never explain himself again—had been. She listened to herself as Theo himself might have listened, standing above her as he had yesterday, at almost this same hour, his knuckles whitening as he gripped the back of a kitchen chair, challenging her to deal with something that resisted shapely or logical exposition.

"Oh, Lord, this is not the father of the little boy," Freddy was saying. "The one that comes to church with your mother sometimes. Oh, Clare, this is awful. Were they taking drugs or something? What can I do? Do you want me to come to you? I don't even know where your family lives."

"No, no, it's all right," said Clare, sounding even more phony to herself, "I just need . . . I need to do something."

"Is there anyone you ought to call?" suggested Freddy. "Does Julia know yet?"

"No, you're the first person I called. I hate to ruin Julia's evening with this. She's having supper at her father's."

"But Clare, Julia would *want* to know. If something bad happened to her, wouldn't *you* want to know as soon as possible?" Freddy sounded as though she were reasoning with someone much younger than herself—a daughter, perhaps. "Would you like me to call her for you? I could do that."

"Would you?"

"I'd be glad to. Now, listen, I've just thought of something for you to do while you're still alone."

Clare felt totally dependent on whatever this sensible and compassionate voice was about to suggest. Could this be the same Freddy who had narrowed her green eyes to little slits of hatred for Clare across that bonfire? No; marriage, motherhood, caring for a dying mother must have changed her. And Clare resolved that, even if they should become friends, she would never pin Freddy down about what had really happened that time at Chapel Hill.

"You must clean out the refrigerator. Throw out everything you can and make lots of space. You won't believe the amounts of food people will bring. I've just been through this, Clare, and it's going to be worse in your case. Everyone knew my mother was going to die, but this is going to be a shock to the community. Lots of people you all hardly know are going to be coming to the house. Oh, and the other thing you've got to do is get a pad of paper and put it somewhere handy. When people come, write down their names and what they brought, so your mother will be able to mention it when she writes them later. She isn't going to be able to think of these things now."

"I would never have thought of them either," said Clare.

"Well, as I said, I've just been through a death. Not like this one, but . . . I'm going to telephone Julia at her father's now. And I'll phone you again later and get directions to your house and I'll plan to come anytime you want me tomorrow and help you out. Can you think of anyone else you would like me to phone?"

Clare said no and thanked this unexpected source of comfort. But as soon as she hung up, she began dialing Julia's number; what had she been thinking of, letting Freddy do it? Oh, God, that high clear air of Olympus! And the turtle they had saved coming home. She had felt so smug about saving the turtle: one more doom averted. "Yes, it's a good omen," Julia had said.

But Julia's father's line was already busy.

Lily came first, followed almost bumper-to-bumper by Father Zachary, who had been with them at the hospital. Clare had just finished filling a thirty-gallon plastic bag with rotting and dispensable items from the refrigerator and carrying it out to the garbage can and then hosing off the cans. Wiping her hands on the sides of her jeans, she walked across the gravel and opened her arms to Lily as she stepped from her car. But Lily, smiling strangely, lifted both her own arms above her head and did a half-pirouette away from Clare. "Please," she said, "don't anybody hug me." Also denying Father Zachary's offer of a black-sleeved arm, she walked quickly into the house alone.

Father Zachary, an outgoing man, at home in most situations, stepped over to Clare and easily offered himself for the embrace her mother had evaded. If the new rector at Our Lady's looked like Christ, Father Zachary might be said to look like Daumier's Don Quixote, or one of El Greco's counts or cardinals—but with a homely American touch, say, of Ichabod Crane. He was tall and gaunt, with a stiff, well-trimmed gray beard and the elongated facial features of someone from another century. "I'm glad to see you again, Clare, though this is a sad occasion." His hug was genuine, and he seemed truly delighted to see her. She felt a litle ashamed for having so often described him as "the society priest."

"You must have gotten to the hospital awfully fast," she said, walking beside him towards the house.

"I was already there, fortunately. I had taken Communion to a parishioner who's just had serious surgery, and she and I were having a little talk when they paged me on the intercom. It was pretty staggering. I had spoken to him only a few hours before. He and Jason came to the eleven o'clock with your mother."

"This is awful to ask, but . . . did you see him?"

"It's not awful to ask. You want to know. Yes, I did. He was unconscious and you could tell he'd been through something pretty traumatic, but he was Theo. I gave him extreme unction while he was still breathing, or while the machine was helping him breathe."

"I'm glad you saw him. And, of course, that you gave him extreme unction, too."

"Oh, Theo's all right now," he said, laying his large comforting hand on her back as she went first into the kitchen. "It's the rest of you who've got to get through this."

"Can I make you a cup of coffee?"

"Do you have some Sanka, by any chance?"

"No, but I have some excellent decaffeinated that I brought down with me."

"That sounds wonderful," said the priest, rubbing his hands together and folding his long, black-clad body into one of the kitchen chairs. "Mind if I open this window?" His fingers were already resting on the crank.

Clare told him by all means; she put the kettle on and got out the portable plastic filter and filter papers she had learned to bring for herself from New York, along with the special ground beans, so as not to have to endure Ralph's instant coffee. Excusing herself for a minute, she went down to the hall to look in on Lily. The door to the room was open, but before Clare could go in she saw the upturned soles of Lily's shoes, and the lower halves of her legs aligned with the bare floor beside the bed. Lily was on her knees, praying. The priest was waiting in the kitchen, ready to offer sympathy and counsel, but Lily never had been one to show her sorrow to others. Nevertheless, Clare had not imagined she herself could have been hurt so much by her mother's turning away from her embrace.

Back in the kitchen, she told Father Zachary, "I think Lily is . . . resting." She thought his feelings might be hurt if she told him Lily had gone straight to God without him.

"Your mother has remarkable inner resources," he said, his intelligent eyes meeting hers with a frankness that led her to believe he knew exactly what Lily was doing in the bedroom. "I have always admired her for them."

Clare busied herself as long as possible with the filtering of the coffee, making herself a cup as well. She tried to construct an etiquette for such an occasion. When Lily's mother died, Father Zachary had come up to Quick's Hill after the funeral and had sat exactly where he was sitting. But all of them had been gathered around the table then—Lily, Ralph, herself, and Theo and Rafe wandering in and out of the kitchen, helping themselves to things from the refrigerator and listening to anything of interest that someone might be saying. That had been a different kind of death: an orderly completion of a proud old lady's life. Everything had transpired without violence or mystification, from her ultimate—one might almost say *willed*—cessation of breath until the moment when Father Zachary threw the clod of earth on her casket as it was lowered into the ground. There had been a humorous moment, even, which she would have enjoyed: Father Zachary's car had had a flat tire on the way to the cemetery, and he had simply pulled off to the side of the highway and stood there with his thumb out, his long black skirts whipping around the bottom of his coat in the January winds, until one of the mourners' cars picked him up. A perfect illustration of one of Clare's grandmother's pet beliefs: that a gentleman, or lady, never got ruffled by things beyond one's control.

"Do you take anything in your coffee, Father Zachary?"

"No, thanks, just black. And please call me Ned."

She was glad he didn't take milk; she had just thrown out

half a quart because it didn't smell quite right. But she knew she would never feel comfortable calling him "Ned." It would be unthinkable to call Father Weir "Mark." Father Weir, although retired for many years, thought of *himself* as "Father Weir." The only person she had ever heard call him anything else was his wife, who referred to him as "Poppa Weir."

"What good coffee," said Father Zachary. "And it's really decaf?"

"Well, ninety-seven percent or so. It's Swiss water-processed," said Clare, thinking of Theo ironing a shirt. Did you iron a shirt and go out and murder somebody and then kill yourself?

"You know," said Father Zachary, "Theo was joking with me this morning after church."

"Oh, God, what did he say to you?" asked Clare. He must be a first-rate face-watcher, she thought admiringly of the priest. It's part of the secret of his success. That, combined with his disarming absence of any kind of priestly pomposity. He waits, he's easy, and he watches. He makes himself available to people according to what they need, not what he thinks they *ought* to need. That's not a bad lesson for a writer to learn. She felt annoyed with herself for thinking of ways to improve her writing at such a time.

Father Zachary laughed. "He asked me if Christ were to come and live in Mountain City today, which church did I think He'd feel most at home in? I knew if I said St. Dunstan's, he'd pounce. Theo, as you know, was a pouncer. And I knew from several discussions we'd had that Theo felt strongly about what he called 'the snob element' in society. Jesus Himself would have had a few things to say on that subject, and it would have been a fascinating discussion if Theo and I had been alone. But behind him and Jason were all these other people, waiting to shake my hand and say hello. So I had to be briefer than I would have liked." He clasped his long fingers around the small coffee cup, as though he were protecting it from harm.

"What did you answer?"

"I said that if it were simply a question of feeling *at home*, then He'd probably go to Temple Beth Israel, over on Charlton Place. He'd know where they were coming from, I said, even though they've come a long way from the Invisible God themselves. But I knew that wasn't what Theo really meant. He was really asking something else, and I wish I'd had a chance to answer him properly. That's one of the hardest aspects we have to deal with, when somebody leaves us suddenly, as Theo has done. We keep torturing ourselves with all the things we left unsaid, or only partially said. It's as though that person's life has become a question addressed to us, and now we want to answer it more than ever because he no longer can."

"The question I can't answer," said Clare, "is how Theo could have gone out and done what they are saying he did. I mean, he had Jason to think of. He loved Jason more than anything. I can't believe that the person I knew would have done that to Jason, let alone all the rest of us."

"I know. I feel the same," said Father Zachary. "And there was the other little boy, too."

"You mean her child? Jeanette's child? Yes, now *he's* lost his mother."

"No, I mean the rest of it," said the priest. "Do you know about that? He was with them when it happened. He was in the backseat of his mother's car."

"My *God*! But Lily said nobody saw it. Are you telling me that the child actually saw his mother —"

"Nobody knows exactly what he saw," said Father Zachary. "That's probably what your mother meant. When the paramedics got there, the people who had heard the shots and called the police had already taken the child to their house. Afterwards a social worker came and got the child and located the father. I met the father at the hospital. He was making arrangements about his wife; they were separated but not yet divorced. Like Theo and Snow."

Clare covered her face with her hands. "I mean, I can't—nothing *connects,* nothing makes *sense.* . . ." The Theo of this time yesterday had stood grinning down at her, his knuckles gone white as he gripped the kitchen chair. "Why don't you write a book about something to can *never* be wrapped up?" he had said. "What if you came across something like that in life? Would you want to write about it?" "If it was interesting to me, I might," she had said, polishing the silver for Lily's birthday dinner. "But frankly, Theo, a lot of the unwrappable chaos and meaninglessness and dreariness that goes on in the world doesn't excite my curiosity at all. What kind of thing do you have in mind?" And he had said, "I'll let you know more about it when I know more myself." Or something to that effect. And turned his back and drifted out of the kitchen, a man-boy of twenty-eight, thickening slightly around his beltline already, a provoking shuffle of resignation in the careless slap of his loafers upon the tiles. And, for a second, she had hated him—no, she had hated the potential for failure he seemed to be courting. And then she had turned the full power of her vexation upon herself and upon the foundations of her work and of all she had accomplished in the world. . . .

"Oh, god*damn*it, Theo. You asshole! I'd like to *kill* you!" she blurted, the words pouring forth with a rightness and natural-ness, linking her frustration with him yesterday to her fury at what he had since done to the boy—to two little boys—and to the woman and to himself. And then she came to herself and realized she had said these words in the presence of Father Zachary. "I'm sorry," she apologized to the priest. "I didn't mean it."

"I know," he said kindly.

"And yet—oh, God, I did mean it, too. I could just *kill* him for throwing his life away and causing all this horrible pain for all of us."

"I know," he said, just as kindly, "I know that, too."

Uncertainties and uglinesses compounded as the evening wore on. General horrors grew specific details, testing each family member's capacity for acknowledging unsavory realities. But the mystery was in no way diminished. Everyone seemed to know something that undermined someone else's provisional ex-planation. New facts kept being presented that refused to fit into any construct that could offer the consolation of at least knowing *why*, or exactly *how*, such a thing had happened.

Ralph and the child came home, Ralph moving inside a whirlwind of perpetual activity. He did not stop to exchange even a sentence with Father Zachary, only greeted him with a disconsolate raising of his eyebrows and hurried on through the house, down the hall to the bedroom. Clare heard a brief murmured exchange between him and Lily, and then he came back. "Ned, I'm going to have to move you over one chair," he said, "so I can reach the telephone."

"Certainly, Ralph," said the priest, sliding his cup and saucer down one place at the round Formica table, still cluttered with the family's morning debris, which Clare began to clear away, in between pouring Father Zachary more coffee and getting Jason a plastic cup of crushed ice, which he had demanded.

"I saw you at church this morning," said the child to Father

Zachary, "and then I saw you at the hospital, and now you're up here. Don't you have a home?"

Father Zachary laughed and said yes, indeed, he had a nice home, the big brick house next to the church, and he hoped Jason would visit him there sometime.

"I might come one day," said the child, slurping crushed ice. "I'll get Theo to bring me."

"Jason," said Ralph, in the middle of dialing a number, "go and get your Crayonmobile and show Father Ned how well you can ride."

The child slipped from his chair and ran out of the room. Ralph finished dialing the number. "Mr. Moore? This is Ralph Quick. You took care of my mother a few years back, and my father before that. Well, my son's over at Memorial Mission and I'd like you to handle that, too. Yes. An accident. Okay. I see. Okay. I'll get them over to your place as soon as I can."

He hung up and, looking at no one, riffled through the pages of the phone book and dialed again. "Baxter Brown, please. Ralph Quick. Tell him this is a matter of urgency. Hello, Baxter —"

The child rolled back into the kitchen astride his Crayonmobile. "Get him out of here," said Ralph to Clare. "Jason, show Clare and Father Ned how you can ride in the living room. Baxter, I'm sorry, just a moment —"

Clare and Father Zachary went into the living room and sat together on the sofa while the child, pleased to have an audience, showed off before them. Clare heard Ralph asking the newspaper editor, for whom he had built a house in St. Dunstan's Forest, to please do what he could about at least keeping it off the front page. They heard him go down the hall a second time. Coat hangers scraped against a metal rod. Ralph came back and stood in the doorway to the living room. "Tell your mother I've gone out for a while. I've got to take these over to Moore's place."

"Why have you got Theo's three-piece suit?" demanded the child.

"I'm taking it somewhere, son."

"I'm going with you," said Jason.

"No, not this time," said Ralph.

The Child began to shriek.

Father Zachary got up. "Ralph, let me take those. I'm driving right past Moore's. I know all of them over there."

"Well —" said Ralph reluctantly, torn between the needs of

the screaming child and his own need to keep moving to out-distance his pain.

"I'll see you people later in the evening," said the priest. To the child, he said, "Jason I must say goodbye for now. My wife will be expecting me home for dinner."

"I'm not going to eat any dinner," said Jason. "I had a sundae at the hospital. Where are you taking Theo's suit?"

"I'm taking it to a place called Moore's on Merrimont Avenue," said Father Zachary, standing above the child.

"Will Theo be there?"

Father Zachary and Ralph exchanged a look.

"Not just yet," said the priest. "But he needs it to be there."

"Oh," said the child, for some reason satisfied with this answer. He sat down on Lily's pretty blue-and-beige Chinese carpet and began playing with his Hot Wheels City.

Julia arrived soon after. She went wordlessly to Clare and put her arms around her. She did the same to Ralph, who, for the first time, looked close to tears. She put some kind of casserole in the refrigerator, explaining directions which nobody listened to about how to cook it; she then made them all some amaretto tea that she had brought with her. Ralph hated hot tea, but he drank this gratefully. Julia took a cup down the hall to Lily's room, even though they warned her that Lily probably wouldn't drink it, but Julia returned empty-handed, so maybe she had. The three of them sat around the kitchen table and spoke in an oblique way of what had happened; Ralph told what he knew. They were careful not to mention names or say certain words, so that the child in the next room could continue in his blessed ignorance for as long as possible. "Baxter says he'll take care of the paper," said Ralph, "but he has no power over the six o'clock news."

The phone rang. "Yes sir," Ralph said. "No, it's okay, Doctor. I understand perfectly. No, on the whole it was excellent. He took after me in that respect. But he'd started having a little trouble recently, because of the close work he had to do. Accounting. He'd just had some soft lens contacts fitted a few weeks ago, but they hurt him and he didn't wear them much. No, that's okay. Perfectly all right. I understand. Goodbye."

"What was that all about?" asked Clare.

Ralph passed a hand slowly over the crown of his close-cut, grizzly head. "That was a doctor over at the hospital who's getting ready to do a corneal transplant. We gave permission for them to have Theo's eyes. There wasn't much else they could use, everything else had been too traumatized. But Theo would have wanted them to have what they could."

Clare rose unsteadily from the table and made her way outside to the swimming pool. She sat down on the diving board and inhaled deep breaths of evening air. The nausea passed. Julia was coming towards her in the dusk. She sat down next to Clare on the diving board, which smelled of rotting hemp.

"What I can't get over," said Clare, "is, there we were, up on that mountain, on top of the world, planning our old age. And, at about the same time, he was driving across town to make sure he wouldn't have one."

"Do you really think he knew what he was going to do beforehand?"

"Hell, who knows? All we can do is guess. Each of us will take what we knew about Theo and create our own speculations, and, knowing this family, each theory will serve that family member's particular, necessary myth."

"Well," said Julia gently, "what theory will serve your myth?"

"Theo liked to mystify people. He even liked to mystify himself, I think. Once he told me—this was when he was only six or seven—that he was from another world and had been sent here to do something, only he had forgotten what it was. I remember that conversation because the whole setting was so eerie. I had come home from college to visit Lily and Ralph, and they didn't have a guest room in that house, so the little boys had to give up their room to me. Rafe had taken his blanket and pillow and sneaked back into the room and was sleeping with me. Then I woke, in the middle of the night, and heard someone talking very softly. It was so spooky, this soft little voice reasoning with someone, having a dialogue with someone, only you could hear just one voice. So I got up, being very careful not to wake Rafe, and went in search of the voice. It was Theo, lying on the sofa in the dark living room. It was a clear winter night and there was enough light in the sky coming through the picture window for me to see Theo's face. He was staring straight ahead, at some waving branches outside the window, and saying things, at intervals, like 'I will if you want me to' or 'Can't you tell me any *more* than that?' I stood there for a few minutes, listening, until—I don't know exactly how—I realized that the whole thing was being done for my benefit. But it was *still* uncanny. Because the things he was saying sounded as if he really were having a dialogue with someone a lot older than himself."

"How do you mean it was being done for your benefit?"

"To impress me! To win me away from his little brother. You remember, I left home when I was sixteen and went to live in the eastern part of the state with an aunt and uncle and finished high school there?"

"Yes, I remember that. Your Great Escape, you called it."

"Well, when I left Lily and Ralph, Theo was just two, and when things kind of smoothed over again between Lily and me, and I began coming back again for visits, Rafe had been born. And Rafe was a completely different kind of child, so certain, right from the beginning, that everybody had to love him. Once, when I was leaving him—he was only about three at the time— he shook his head sadly and said, 'Boy, you sure are going to miss me, aren't you?' That kind of thing. Whereas, Theo . . . Theo was always *less* sure. He wouldn't bring all his rubber animals and come and jump in the tub with you, or be sure you would welcome him in your bed . . . so he invented this weirdness in himself, to be different. Only I think the weirdness was already there: he just gave it plenty of room to grow. He fertilized it, for God's sake! Anyway, that night I am speaking of, he pretended to be startled when I made a noise, announcing I was there, and when I sat down on the sofa with him and rubbed his back, he told me all this stuff about hearing voices and seeing faces in the bare branches and how these people from another world were sending him messages, telling him what his mission on earth was, only he could never really hear that part, or they would convey it to him in a language he didn't understand. As you can imagine, I was fascinated, old Clare with her trademark on everything imaginative, and I stayed with him until it got light. Which is what he had wanted all the time."

"And so, what do *you* think he did when he drove away from here today?" asked Julia.

"I think he ironed his shirt and got his gun and drove down the hill in his car, smiling that weird smile and . . . just *decided* something was going to happen to put him out of his misery. He told Lily that he was going over to see if Jeanette would have him back and that 'it'll be settled one way or another by three-thirty'. I don't know why they were in her car, or where they were going, or why on earth they had the child with them . . . no, wait, he had to be with them, his mother couldn't go off with Theo and leave a three-year-old by himself. But anyway, you heard Ralph say the thing happened around three-thirty, because that's when the people in that house heard the shot and the squeal of tires. I suppose they might have been arguing, maybe Theo was asking her to come back and she was saying no, and then—oh, I'm just making this up as I go along—maybe Theo took his gun out of the glove compartment, or maybe he had it under the seat, but . . . oh shit, wait a minute, they were in *her* car."

"He could have had the gun inside his jacket or something," suggested Julia.

"Oh, God, Julia, that would make it even worse. Don't you see? If he had it hidden in his jacket, then maybe it *was* premeditated."

"It's horrible," said Julia. "It refutes the whole idea of a comprehending, connecting life." There was anger in her voice.

"But I can't," began Clare, choked up suddenly by the image of the little boy she had just finished describing to Julia, "I refuse to believe that Theo was diabolic enough to do something like this just to . . . win a *point* for the forces of chaos and meaninglessness. Basically he was a sweet, insecure boy trying to win his share of attention from a world with too much competition in it, not some kind of . . . *devil*. You don't think he was a devil, do you."

"No," said Julia more charitably, but with bitterness, "I think he was a troubled young man growing up in a society that wasn't much help to him. And surrounded by people who weren't a whole hell of a lot of help to him, either. Among them I prominently include myself. Last night he asked me for help, but I had a headache and wanted to get home and grade my papers."

By nightfall, a steady procession of cars labored up the steep curves of Quick's Hill, popping gravel under their tires as they passed the kitchen window and then idling behind the beams of their headlights while the drivers scanned the vehicle-cluttered space around the pool, searching for an available parking spot. The old dogs, either discouraged by the constant traffic flow or possessing some animal sense of the sad occasion, did not so much as struggle up the grassy bank and shimmy under the electric wire fence, as their late mother, Fritzi, had taught them.

They only barked, less and less convincingly, from their kennel, as the evening wore on—just as Jason, inside the house, would cock his head at a fresh new crackle of gravel and say, less convincingly each time, "I'll bet you anything *that's* Theo."

Clare, following Freddy's advice, had placed a yellow legal pad between the toaster and the telephone. She wrote down calls that would have to be answered (that Mr. Green phoned again, about Ralph's building him a house; the police department called, saying that Theo's car could be picked up anytime the family wished), and she wrote down what food each visitor brought. The first dishes to arrive tended to be chilly— banana breads and casseroles snatched out of well-stocked deep freezers; later comers brought freshly iced cakes, still-warm platters of fried chicken, a newly baked ham. As she diligently recorded the items, she asked herself which expressed the finer shade of condolence: rushing off at once to the bereaved with an unthawed offering, or arriving later with your sympathies baked especially for the occasion into your proudest recipe. That was the kind of subtle folkway measurement that someone like Freddy would excel at.

When the first visitors arrived, Lily emerged from the bedroom with glittering eyes and fresh makeup. She stood talking to Baxter Brown, the newspaper editor, and his wife. "It" had been on the six o'clock news, but Lily waved away offers of details; Baxter Brown was saying there would be several small paragraphs on the upper-right-hand corner of the obit page— that was the best he could do. The police had listed it as an apparent murder–suicide and it would have to be described as such, but without going into details. Lily smiled tautly, as though she had just noticed a bad smell coming from somewhere, and motioned Clare over. "You must remember Baxter and Ann Brown," she said. "They almost lost their own son three years ago in a hang-gliding accident."

Clare was left talking to the Browns as Lily wafted off to another group of people, clustered by the fireplace, speaking in subdued voices and sipping the tea, coffee, or mixed drinks efficiently provided by Julia. "How did you manage to get here so quickly from New York?" Ann Brown wanted to know. Clare explained, for the fourth or fifth time that evening, that she had been there several days already. "Oh, how lucky," said Ann Brown. And then, as the others had done, quickly amended that she meant lucky only in the sense that Clare could be so soon available to Lily, who was really going to need her.

Julia called Clare to the telephone. It was Sister Patrick, phoning from St. Clothilde's. "I've been trying to get through to you for some time," she said in the intimate, musical brogue that had struck a flame of adoration in Clare's adolescent heart almost thirty years ago, "but the line has been busy. The whole community here is praying for Theo . . . and for your family."

"How did you hear?" Clare asked. Had Freddy called St. Clothilde's?

"Ah, it was on the news, I didn't see it, I was taking a walk. Such a beautiful orange sky and the town spread so peacefully in the valley and there I was thinking, All's right with the world. Then I came back to the convent and Sister Jouret told me. She had Theo in first grade, you know, at La Fosse Hall. She was beside herself with distress, Clare. She's deaf as a post now, and she and Sister Davis, who's as good as blind, have taken to watching the news together so they can be each other's ears and eyes. So Sister Jouret saw it—there wasn't much to see, they only showed the interior of the car and some paramedics working over some people you couldn't see—and she didn't know who it was until Sister Davis started pulling at her sleeve and shouting in her ear, 'Did they say Theo Quick? Surely, Sister, it can't be *our* Theo Quick.' As I said, Sister Jouret couldn't see the faces, and right up until time to go to chapel, she kept repeating, 'I think it must have been *another* Theo Quick.' But Sister Davis finally convinced her she'd heard them say Theo Quick of Spook's Branch Valley, so there we are. I wish I could come out to you, Clare. But you know I don't drive, and Sister Lanier, who's always so good about taking us places, is up in Virginia visiting her family."

"I could come out and get you," Clare said impetuously, then immediately had to retract her offer because she didn't have a car here and felt reluctant about asking Ralph or Lily for one of theirs. They knew how much she liked Sister Patrick, and it might seem as though she were asking for a treat on the night of Theo's death. So she fibbed to Sister Patrick and said all the cars were in use.

"Ah, then, don't bother yourself over it," replied the low, musical voice, riding proudly over the momentary awkwardness, and Clare had a clear memory of Sister Patrick, in the handsome black robes she used to wear, standing in front of the eighth-grade class and dropping her tone to a dramatic, arrogant whisper as she recited, " . . . and I choose Never to stoop." She was reading them Browning's "My Last Duchess" (a strange choice, Clare now reflected, for a nun to be reading to a class of thirteen-year-olds), and with her considerable acting skills had "become" for them the proud, amoral Duke of Ferrara, negotiating for a new wife after having done away with the previous one. But what had been so riveting about her performance of that monologue—and Clare had recognized this at the time—was the way it revealed the nun's own attraction to things proud and superior, a partiality she must have had to fight against in the interests of her vocation.

Sister Patrick asked Clare to tell Lily she would be praying that night for Theo and for all of them. "Tell your mother that I'm on my way back to the chapel right now. And Clare?"

"Yes, Mother?" The nun's particular Irish way of pronouncing her name made her lapse naturally into the pre-Vatican II manner of addressing her old teacher.

"None of us thinks he did it. Despite what those people on the news were saying. Sister Jouret was telling at supper what a sensitive and considerate little boy he was. When Reverend Mother General was visiting from Paris and the first-graders were standing in line to shake her hand, just before Theo's turn came he bolted out of line and dashed off to the bathroom. To wash his hands, he told Sister Jouret, so they'd be clean enough for the Reverend Mother. Sister Jouret translated this into French for Reverend Mother General, who laughed and was very touched. 'That boy is not a murderer, and he's not a suicide either,' Sister Jouret kept repeating at supper. And we all agreed. There's something we don't know, and we may never know. Do you think maybe the girl did it because she was afraid he was going to leave her?"

"I didn't even know her, so I can't say," said Clare, feeling that she had to protect her old mentor, to keep her safe in her bubble of idealism.

"Well . . ." Sister Patrick paused, perhaps sensing Clare's skepticism. "You tell your mother that. And will you let me know about the funeral arrangements? Sister Jouret and Sister Davis will want to go—Sister Davis has to use a walker." She laughed. "There aren't many of us old ladies over here and I'm sure we can find ourselves a ride if we can give a little advance notice."

*　　*　　*

Rafe walked in about nine o'clock. Every inch of parking space was jammed, so he had left his car down at the gas pump, by the dog kennels. Tears were streaming down his face, but he said not to pay any attention, he had been like that for hours. The State Police had pulled him over just before Greensboro. He was prepared to put up an argument, but when the trooper asked him whether his name was Rafe Quick before he even asked for his license, Rafe knew something was wrong. Because, also, the man seemed so *kind*. He said, "Your brother has been in an accident and your parents want you to call home." He followed Rafe to the Kernersville exit and waited while he phoned from a gas station. Rafe came out of the booth and told the trooper, "My brother is dead," and that's when the tears started gushing out, of their own accord, even though the rest of him felt numb. Rafe bought a Coke and filled his tank and even remembered to check the oil because the car had been burning a lot of it lately. When he got back in his car, the trooper, who was old enough to be his father, came and leaned in the window and said, "I'm not going to tell you to keep it down to fifty-five, because I'd be wasting my breath. But drive carefully. Your mother can't afford to lose two of you in one day."

Lily, hearing her son's voice, came into the kitchen. Her eyes were dry but preternaturally bright.

"Mom," said Rafe, his voice breaking.

She stiffened as Rafe flung his arms around her and bowed his head over hers. But she stood obediently while he sobbed and some of his tears fell into her hair. As soon as he released her, she smiled at him crookedly and said, "My baby needs a drink."

"I'm afraid to have a drink. I might lose it completely," he told her.

The child wheeled in on his Crayonmobile. "Why'd you come back?" he asked his uncle.

"Because," said Rafe, picking up the little boy and holding him close, "I missed you."

"Then why are you crying now that I'm here?"

Rafe laughed through his tears. "God, that was worthy of *me* at your age." He shifted the boy on his hip and reached with his free hand for a handkerchief. "You have a pretty high opinion of yourself, don't you?" he teased the boy, blowing his nose and attempting to get control of himself.

"Will you play with me till Theo comes home?"

Rafe had a brief relapse, but pulled himself together. "Sure. What do you want to play?"

"Let's go in my room and play ambulance," said the boy happily. "Theo and I play it all the time. You be hurt real bad, and then I try and see if I can save you."

"It's as if he knew, somehow," Rafe said, later that night, to Clare and Ralph. The visitors had all gone home, but there would be a fresh onslaught tomorrow. Clare, who could not rest, was sponge-mopping the kitchen floor. Ralph and Rafe hunched over their bowls of ice cream, the first food they'd touched since lunch, when Theo had still been with them. "Because we'd be playing in there and sometimes he'd save me and other times he'd say, 'No, he's too far gone, nothing we can do for him anymore.' Could he have overheard someone say that at the hospital? But this is what was interesting. The times when he saved me, he'd always say right afterwards, 'When do you think Theo will be coming home?' But when I was too far gone, he never asked. It was like he was allowing himself to get used to the idea slowly by playing this game."

"I wouldn't put too much confidence in that theory," said Ralph, grimly spooning ice cream. "He and Theo played that game all the time, and they played it just like that."

Lily entered the kitchen. She was still dressed and wearing her high heels. Her hands were behind her back and there was a look of dangerous triumph on her face. "Well, I have a bit of news," she said, eyeing the men's ice-cream dishes with faint disgust—she had touched nothing all evening, except perhaps Julia's tea. "I was just in Theo's room, looking in on Jason —"

"He fell asleep with his clothes on while we were playing," said Rafe apologetically. "I thought it was best to leave him like that."

Lily looked through him as if he hadn't spoken. "While I was in there, I had this sudden . . . intuition. I opened Theo's closet and looked inside his Thom McAn shoebox on the top shelf and there it was." She brought out a shiny black revolver from behind her back.

There was an electric silence in the kitchen.

"Yes," continued Lily, smiling her vindicated smile, "there it was. Exactly where he always kept it. So we have to call the police right away. And, Ralph, you have to call the newspaper, too. Maybe it's not too late to keep it out of the morning edition."

"Lily," said Ralph, looking down at his melting ice cream, "put that thing away."

"What do you mean, put it away. It's evidence. Don't you see? *This is Theo's gun.* That gun they found on the seat between them is somebody else's gun. That throws a whole new light on everything. They just assumed he did it because it was his gun, but if it was somebody else's, then —"

"Hey, Dad, she's right," said Rafe excitedly.

Ralph pushed away his dish, put his face down on his crossed arms, and began to weep.

"Oh, for goodness' sake," said Lily. "I mean, why are you crying *now?* I know it isn't going to bring him back, but at least we can clear his name. We owe him that."

Ralph uttered some muffled sounds into his arms.

"What?" Lily asked.

"I said"—he raised a distorted face to her—"it was my gun."

"Your gun? I don't understand. Will you please explain?" The tone of Lily's voice was like dry ice, capable of searing shut anyone's grief for the time being.

Ralph rubbed his eyes with his fists and sat up straight in his chair. "In the emergency room—I guess it was when you were walking in the hall with that Negro orderly—the police detective came up and showed me the gun they found in Jeanette's car. He asked me if it was Theo's gun, and I told him no, it was my gun. It was my Belgian Browning, the one I got that time at Uncle Don's auction."

"Just a minute," said Lily. "Why would *your* gun be in Jeanette's car?"

"Because," said Ralph, his voice dropping to a whisper, "I gave it to Theo."

"When?"

Ralph, who had slumped forward again, straightened up once more and took an extended, shuddery breath. He looked at his wife as a boy looks when he knows he will probably be punished but must nevertheless tell the whole truth. "A couple of weeks ago, before he and Jeanette had their tiff. A man had broken into her house —"

"I knew about the man, Theo told me. The man who was going to rape her. She woke up and he was standing over her bed saying he wouldn't hurt her if she wouldn't scream and wake the child. Theo told me all about that." Lily sounded rather impatient. "But she did scream, and picked up her child and ran out of the house, and they arrested that man."

"Yes, but he was out on bail," said Ralph. "And Theo came to me and asked if he could lend her my gun. She was afraid because she had to testify at the trial. Theo told me she'd feel more comfortable with a semi-automatic."

"Theo was talking some stuff about that trial today," Rafe put in. "When we were working on my car after lunch, he was saying some kind of strange things. But Theo's always saying strange things, and I didn't think too much about it afterwards."

"Everyone around here seems to know things I don't," said Lily. Her right hand, holding Theo's gun, had dropped limply to her side. She remained standing aloofly above them, but Clare could see she was starting to crumple. "What did Theo say to you, Rafe?"

Rafe, intimidated by her disdainful tone, hesitated. "Aw, Mom," he said uncomfortably, "you know how Theo talks sometimes. When he's trying to get a rise out of you, or just shock you."

"I know," said Lily slowly, "how Theo talked."

"Talked." Rafe corrected his tenses miserably. "Well, I guess this Jeanette had hurt him pretty bad by breaking off with him cold turkey like she did. Anyway, after he phoned her this afternoon, he came outside where I was working on my car and said that he was going over there and see if he could talk some sense into her about going back with him. 'And if I can't,' he told me, 'I've got a good mind to tell her I'm going to show up at that trial myself and testify that she was always asking men home and then crying rape.' I told him. 'You wouldn't really do that, Theo,' and he laughed, and he said, 'Yes I would, if I was mean enough. Just think how it would ruin her. She couldn't hurt any more innocent men in this town. She'd lose her job at the hospital and have to move somewhere else.' 'But you wouldn't do that,' I said to him, 'because you're not mean. And you still care for her, or you wouldn't be going over there asking her to go back with you.' And he smiled and said, 'You're right. You know me so well, little brother.' Then he found the loose wire in my starter and we fixed it, and I didn't think any more about it."

Lily dragged a chair out from the table and sort of toppled

into it. With a lopsided, almost flirtatious smile at Ralph, she said, "I think I would like you to fix me a drink now."

"What would you like, a mai tai?" asked Ralph, springing up at once.

"A mai tai would be fine," she said. "Clare, why don't you put down that mop and join me."

Ralph ended up making an additional mai tai for himself, and even Rafe relented and fixed himself his traditional vodka-and-tonic with crushed ice. "Where the hell's my lime?" he demanded, rummaging in the crisper of the refrigerator.

"I think I threw it out," said Clare. "It was half-rotten. I'm sorry."

Rafe turned to say something scathing, then remembered why he was here and what they were all doing up at this time of the night. "I can live without it," he said. "Look at all the food in here. I wonder who started the custom of bringing food. It's kind of barbaric, when you think of it."

"It's a Southern custom," said Lily, sipping her drink. All the fight had gone out of her. Her usually erect shoulders were rounded like an old lady's.

"But the Irish do it," said Clare. "Or no, maybe they just have it at their wakes."

"The Indians do, too," said Ralph. "At least, the Cherokees do. I remember Mama used to tell stories of the feasts they had when someone died." He looked distraught at having said the word "died," then mused over his mai tai for a moment. "Somebody ought to call Snow," he said.

"I don't see why," said Lily, snapping back into her disdainful posture. "Snow is no longer part of the family."

"She is legally," said Ralph. "They were separated but not divorced. And she's still Jason's mother."

"Oh, *mother!*" Lily pronounced the word with venom. "There are mothers and there are vessels. Snow was just a vessel. Theo said so himself recently, when we were talking. If you call her, she will just want to have everything her way, and scream and carry on like they probably do at funerals, and we'll all be embarrassed."

Ralph started to say something, then apparently thought better of it. He contented himself with shaking his head. "I guess it can wait until tomorrow morning," he said. "I'm not even sure where to call her down in Georgia."

"Exactly," said Lily.

Rafe looked at his watch. "It *is* tomorrow morning."

"Well," said Ralph. "I meant until after all the arrangements are made."

Lily sipped her mai tai thoughtfully. Theo's revolver lay on the table beside her, amid the ice-cream dishes and spoons and glasses, bothering nobody except Clare, who had gotten out of the habit of living with guns hidden in underwear drawers or popping out at you every time you opened the glove compartment in a car. "You know," said Lily, "somebody had better go to the police first thing tomorrow morning and make absolutely *sure* they know about the man who was out on bail. I mean"—her eyes grew brighter—"he will really profit from Jeanette being dead. There will be no one to testify against him now."

"You mean you think *he* could have done it?" Rafe asked his mother incredulously.

"Why not?" asked Lily, smiling slightly, looking from one to another of them. "I mean, it's certainly a possibility. He could have followed them. He might even have been in the backseat of Jeanette's car, hiding all along."

"But Mom, the child was in the backseat. Jeanette's little boy was."

"Maybe he had made friends with the child."

There was a silence. Everybody drank and would not look at Lily.

"Well," she said defensively, "I'm only saying it's possible. Lots of things are possible. Why, even the little *boy* . . . I mean, say the gun was lying on the seat between them and the little boy just reached over, thinking it was a toy, and went 'Bang, bang!'"

"Jesus," said Rafe. He got up and made himself another drink. Then he came over and kissed his mother, and, after a moment of deliberation, went around the table and bestowed an awkward kiss on Ralph's cheek. Ralph was visibly moved. Then Rafe kissed Clare and said, "I'm going to try to get some sleep," and left the kitchen.

Nobody spoke after he was gone until Ralph said, "You're right. It sounds a little fantastic, but what if it was true? Or some other version we might not even be able to imagine? It's terrible, any way you look at it, but not so terrible as not knowing for sure what happened."

"Exactly!" said Lily vehemently. "I mean, of *course* the easiest thing was for them to say Theo did it. Because it's so neat that way, there's so much historical precedent for it—the disappointed lover kills the woman, then himself. But what if it didn't happen that way? Theo can't conduct his own investigation, but he would want us to know what happened. He would want us to find out all we could, at least."

"I'll go down to the station tomorrow," said Ralph, "and speak to that police detective about it. Even if . . . even if it's true that Theo did do what they're saying he probably did, they would want to be able to say they had covered all other possibilities."

"Exactly," murmured Lily, giving her husband a glance of gratitude and approval.

Clare undressed and went to bed about three, but did not expect to sleep. In Vienna, Felix would be having breakfast in the dining room of the Kaiserin Elisabeth. He always gulped down his first cup of coffee, then looked impatiently around for a waitress to pour him another. But no, in European hotels, they left your coffee in a pot on your table, along with the pitcher of hot milk, and you refilled your own cup. And there were waiters, with towels on their arms, at the Kaiserin Elisabeth. She tried to remember the dining room there, but couldn't picture it. She remembered quite well the huge, chilly bedroom with the heavy red draperies and faded gold tassels on the French windows, and the lumpy eiderdowns and the white-tiled bathroom. She and Felix had been poisoned by duck they'd eaten in a restaurant and had spent the next day with stomach cramps and diarrhea, shuffling between the bedroom and the bathroom. Romantic and fastidious creatures that they were, they had used up several books of Kaiserin Elisabeth matches, clearing the air for each other before emerging from each trip to the bathroom. Then, in midafternoon, they had dragged themselves down the street to the Hofburg, so Felix could show Clare the Emperor's former residence. Climbing the marble staircase, they saw where someone had vomited enormous amounts of pink glop, and Felix had laughed and said, "You see we're not the only ones in Vienna with stomach troubles." And Clare had to lean on the windowsill of the Empress Elisabeth's exercise room during the tour, she felt so faint, but was interested to hear how Elisabeth had a fetish about her weight and her hair. Each day the servants put a sheet on the floor around her when they brushed her hair and afterwards they had to count how many hairs had fallen, and if there had been more than twelve Elisabeth went into a rage. The last part of the tour had been the dining room, where places were set at a banquet table for all the members of the Emperor's family. Each member was described, the guide ending with the titillating story of how the Crown Prince and the woman he loved had gone to the royal hunting lodge at Mayerling, and there they had died together "mysteriously," according to those loyal to the Hapsburg name, or in a joint suicide, according to those who were not so loyal.

There was no such thing as a joint suicide unless each of you had your poison, or your gun, and you kissed each other and said, "One, two, three . . ." Homicide-suicide, Baxter Brown said his paper would have to report about Theo and Jeanette (whose last name Clare still did not know) tomorrow morning.

And then, walking back to the Kaiserin Elisabeth, Clare and Felix, realizing they were hungry after fasting all day, decided to have an early dinner at the Drei Hussars. "We don't have to overdo it," said Felix judiciously. "Just because it is one of the world's great restaurants, we don't have to stuff ourselves. Perhaps just a small piece of fish and a nice bottle of wine." On their ebullient exit from the restaurant, after a four-course meal, two bottles of a wonderful Margaux, and brandies, Felix had left a generous tip for the pianist, who had been playing Viennese waltzes. "Who knows?" he said humorously. "If Hitler had been accepted at the Academy of Art, that might have been me playing 'The Blue Danube' in some elegant restaurant in my hometown. My mother hoped I would become a musician, you know. And then some greedy American couple like us would have staggered by, stuffed with veal paprika and Linzer torte, and dropped their money into my little silver dish."

Was that really her life, too? Did Felix, with his humor and his temper and his languages—and his provoking Lizzie— actually exist? Was there a world outside Mountain City?

Lying in the darkness, hearing the intimate exchange of Ralph's and Lily's voices in the kitchen (grown closer to the way they had sounded in the old days since they had agreed to drink together and to let this sinister new possibility—that the mysterious Man on Bail might, if more were known, absolve Theo of his hideous act—flower between them), Clare had the dismal sensation of never having left home. It was as if, after all, the core of her had never escaped, never traveled or lived in

Europe, or met Felix, or written and published books; this part
of her remained forever stuck in the nightmare of adolescence,
where she would always be thirteen or fourteen, trapped inside
the decisions Lily had made, and subject to the whims and
tyrannies of Ralph. For some reason, yet—or never—to be
discovered, the part of her old life she could not seem to outgrow,
from which no amount of love or distance or success had been
able to free her, was located somewhere within the rise and fall
of those two voices and the world they engendered and per-
petuated between them: a place at once provoking and sorrowful
and treacherous and vengeful and duplicitous and miasmic—
yet perversely compelling.

You can meet them in school, or in lanes
   or at sea,
In church, or in trains, or in shops,
   or at tea,
For the saints of God are folk like me,
And I mean to be one too.

—"Grand Isle"

    This 20 [*sic*] year old white male was found dead
of a gunshot wound to the head in a car with a
female companion who was also shot dead. Death
was due to a close range to contact gunshot wound
to the head entering on the right side just beneath
and posterior to the ear. The investigation suggests
that the wound was self-inflicted.

—Summary of autopsy report on Theodore
   Anthony Quick

IV: MAGNOLIA LEAVES

"*I* won't! I won't sit back there in that little seat like a baby. Theo always lets me sit in front with him and buckle up."

"Jason, it's not a question of your being a baby," Ralph reasoned with the child. "Didn't I let you ride over here to Miss Alicia's in the front seat? But she has to sit someplace if she's going to go with us, and you wouldn't ask a lady to ride in back by herself, would you?"

"I'll sit where I want, or I won't go." Jason folded his arms truculently and stood glaring up at his grandfather in Miss Alicia's driveway. The boy was still wearing the clothes he'd had on at the time of his father's death. He had worn them to bed last night and refused to change them this morning. He had also insisted on wet-combing his hair all by himself and the result, Ralph now saw from above, was as poignant as it was ludicrous. The child was engaged in a desperate game of maintenance: if he could just hold out against letting any grownup but Theo do anything for him, wouldn't that mean that Theo would have to come back? As Ralph stood helplessly by, wondering how to coax his grandson back into the car, he almost envied Jason's three-year-old mind. It did not comprehend death; it still held on to its clear picture of a living Theo, returning home again and walking in the door.

"I know what," suggested Miss Alicia Gallant. "Why don't we *all three* ride in front? Jason and I can strap ourselves in together." She made it sound like an adventure they were going to have. "Unless, of course"—her keen brown eyes challenged the little boy—"Jason wants me to try to squeeze into that car seat of *his* in back. But then people would stare at us as we went by and say, 'I wonder what that old lady thinks she is doing, sitting back there in that little bitty car seat?'"

The boy's contentiousness shattered into wild laughter at the absurd scene she had evoked. He climbed back into the car and made room for her. "You better ride up front with me," he said magnanimously. "We'll strap ourselves in together."

"I guess that would be the best thing," agreed Alicia Gallant, as if it had been Jason's idea in the first place. She slid into the front seat beside the boy. She wore her shapeless navy-blue suit, which was going to be too hot for this sunny October day, and one of those pork-pie-shaped hats she made for herself, one to match each outfit, out of her dressmaker's scraps, and the sturdy brown walking shoes she ordered from her own last in England. Like her late brother, Dr. Anthony, she had to have her custom-made English shoes. As she buckled herself and Jason into the same seat belt, she winked at Ralph over the top of the boy's oddly combed blond head. Ralph blessed her. Her wink said so much: how she was with him and was going to remain with him as long as he needed her, contributing her formidable resources of humor and toughness to help him through his appalling list of chores.

They started off for the florist, who had phoned Ralph's house first thing this morning about the casket spray. This was not a good time of year for outstanding flowers, he had told Ralph, but his staff had come up with several ideas for creating an appropriate effect. He wondered if someone from the family could stop by the shop "to actually see the possibilities we're working with" before they went ahead with the spray.

Well, they were proud of their work; they were craftsmen, too. When Ralph built a house, he always made the owners, even the indiscriminate, impatient ones, take the time to look at choices of lighting fixtures and doorknobs and tiles before he put them in. Often he would try to guide their taste because his loyalty was to the house first; its parts must be true to its totality. He was not primarily concerned with the people who would live in the house when he was finished with it. So why shouldn't the florist care first and foremost about the appearance of his spray? That was his job. Just as Moore's job was to provide the casket and lay out the body. And the job of the people out at the cemetery was to sell the plots and arrange for the holes to be dug. And the job of the priests was to say comforting, sonorous words over the flowers and casket, while the backhoe waited behind the hedge to finish up *its* job.

There were going to be three priests tomorrow: Father Zachary, because it was his church; his assistant, Father Tim; and Father Weir, the retired rector of Our Lady's, because he was Lily's favorite priest and her spiritual adviser. Father Tim had phoned first thing this morning. Organizing everything for tomorrow at St. Dunstan's, that was *his* job. He needed to know, for instance, what hymn the family wanted. Ralph told him that Theo's favorite hymn had been the one the children sang in Sunday School, "I sing a song of the Saints of God, patient and brave and true," or what Father Tim referred to as "Grand Isle." But Father Tim had cautioned him it might break people up too much. Episcopalians did not like to show their feelings in church. Lily had been embarrassed, Ralph remembered, when he had sobbed that time during Dr. Anthony Gallant's funeral. "God's frozen people," Ned Zachary had once jokingly called his own denomination from the pulpit. Ralph had tried Lily's church for a while, when the boys were growing up, but it didn't suit him and he went back to his own. Not that Presbyterians exactly rolled in the aisle and hollered to Christ, but they were less aloof. Still, he had been guided by Father Tim into choosing a less emotional hymn. He did not want to sob at Theo's funeral. He'd already broken down once this morning, calling Theo's boss about being a pallbearer. The man had not yet had time to read the morning paper. He hadn't seen last night's six o'clock news. So Ralph had to start from scratch. "My son Theo," he had begun. Then his throat had closed up on him. "My son Theo," he had choked out. Then couldn't continue. "Wait just a minute," he'd finally been able to get out. "Hold on a second and I'll be okay."

But shortly after, when he called Snow, having finally located her, through a series of phone calls, at a trailer in Georgia, he had been so detached that he might have been standing on the other side of the kitchen and listening to his own voice. "Are you sitting down?" he had asked his daughter-in-law. ("She usually *is* sitting down . . . when she's not *lying* down," Lily would have said. Lily had wanted him to wait until after the funeral to call Snow: "She'll spoil it, she'll do something to ruin it for all of us.")

Snow said no, she was not sitting down, she was just fixing herself some breakfast. "You know me," she had said in that insolent, take-me-or-leave-me tone she frequently used with her father-in-law, "I have to have myself a big breakfast before I can do a thing."

"Well, I'd sit down if I were you. I've got some bad news," Ralph had said coldly, listening to himself from someplace far away.

"What do you mean?" she accused. "Is Jason all right?"

"He's all right. Theo's not. Theo was killed yesterday afternoon."

"Killed!" There was a silence. Then, suspiciously, "I don't believe you."

"It's true."

"How? How was he killed?"

"In a car," said Ralph. "We thought you might like to know that the funeral is tomorrow at eleven, at St. Dunstan's —"

"Wait a minute," said Snow. "Wait just a goddamned minute. You mean to say you are calling me up to tell me Theo's *funeral* is *tomorrow*, when I didn't even know he was dead until just this minute?"

"There's no need to speak to me like that, Snow."

But she had gone on: "You wait until this morning to tell me, when he was killed yesterday afternoon? When I'm his *wife*"?

"There was a lot to do up here, Snow," he said, noting how level his voice sounded against her rising shrillness. "And you're not the easiest person to find these days. I had to phone two of your sisters to get your number at the trailer." He had curbed himself from adding, "Where you're living with some man, though you are still legally Theo's wife."

But she snapped right back, "Theo knew where I lived. He had my number. I was talking to Theo on this phone night before last. I can't believe what you're telling me. I was just talking to him Saturday night."

"We're all having a hard time believing it" was what he'd answered. He had not known Theo had talked to her on Saturday. It occurred to him with pain that he himself had not talked to his son alone as recently as that.

"What time did you say it was, the funeral?"

"Eleven, at St. Dunstan's."

"He hated that snob church."

"He was christened and confirmed there, Snow. And you two were married there."

A silence. Then, "Do you realize I'm in *Georgia*? I can't possibly get there for hours." She had shifted from indignation to whining plaintiveness. "And my folks are all the way out in Granny Squirrel. All of us can't possibly get there that soon." ("Excellent," Lily would have said. "The fewer Mullinses tomorrow, the better.")

"I don't even have a *car* here," Snow went on. "And the only person who could drive me is working first shift. They won't be off till three o'clock."

Catching her shrewd use of the genderless plural, he said, "If things weren't so hectic, I'd come get you myself. As it is, I'm afraid you'll have to get up here on your own steam." ("J.D.'s a nice boy," Snow's older sister, Evelyn, had told Ralph this morning. "They met at the factory, and he took her in when she got sick and had to quit her job." Ralph liked Evelyn best of all the Mullinses because she was responsible. She was loyal to Snow but had sense enough to be disgusted with her for leaving Theo and Jason. "She'll never get another one like Theo," Evelyn had said this morning.)

Ralph had meant it, about being willing to go and get her if he'd had the time. If there had been two of him—one to take care of all the things that had to be taken care of—he would have been glad to set off for Georgia and in about five hours to be at her door. Or J.D.'s door. He'd help her pack, making sure she had something decent for tomorrow, and if not, why, they'd stop somewhere and he would buy her a dress. And then they'd have the long ride back to Mountain City, and maybe he could talk some sense into her. He would have to tell her the real circumstances of Theo's death. That is, as far as anyone knew them yet. That was another thing he had to do, after the florist's and the cemetery: stop by the police station and find that detective and tell him to be sure to check out yesterday's whereabouts of that man out on bail, the one who had tried to rape Jeanette. The thing about Snow that baffled him was that she didn't seem to want to raise herself. He could excuse her humble origins. (Excuse? Who was he to excuse? If social class could be measured on a ruler—and lots of people sure as hell acted as if it could—he would estimate that both he and Snow had married up about four inches, he going from about the five- to the nine-

inch measure on a ruler, Snow from about the three- to the
seven-inch one; he figured he had brought Lily and their
children back down to a seven. He could not forgive Snow's
unfaithfulness to Theo, but he could understand it. Hadn't he
been unfaithful to Lily in a much profounder sense than Snow's
apathetic descent into J.D.'s trailer after losing her job in that
mill? He had loved Hannah with his whole heart, and yet had
gone on living with Lily and sleeping in the same bed. And
then, morally speaking, he guessed he had to count all those
times—how had Jimmy Carter put it in that famous *Playboy*
interview?—when he had lusted in his heart. Clare's childhood
rival and nemesis Freddy Stratton had been up at the house
when he left this morning; still cute as a button in her forties,
with that saucy little twat in the tight corduroy jeans. And there
was Julia, grown into a wise, ample ripeness, though she'd
certainly jumped the gun on his intentions when he stopped by
to show her the pictures. He hadn't meant to *do* anything: a
lonely man could get a lot out of simply talking to an intelligent,
pleasant-looking woman who had once thought he was sexy.
And even when he had been newly married to the woman of his
choice, over thirty years ago, and those adolescent girls spent
the night with Clare, running through the apartment in their
shortie pajamas: the way they teased him in their cunning innocence, even Clare. "Oh, Ralph, Julia, thinks you are *sexy*.
Isn't that hilarious?" Or they'd be riding somewhere together in
his truck and Clare would go all melancholy and self-hating
and make him talk her out of her low opinion of herself. "Ralph,
tell me the truth. Freddy's more attractive to men than I am.
You're a man. I need you to tell me why." "You and Freddy
each have your own way of being attractive." "What is *my* way
like?" "Freddy's way is more obvious," he would say, working it
out as he spoke. "She sends a clear signal she's a female and
expects to be treated like one. Her older sister was like that, too.
Sending out signals, but no handling the merchandise, please,
unless you've got plenty of money and a pedigree and a wedding
ring in your pocket. But your way is more subtle. Part of its
charm is that *you* don't know when it's happening. You don't do
anything. It just comes out of you. It makes people . . . it makes
people want you." "Ha!" the fourteen-year-old Clare had
snorted, oblivious to the terrible things going on in him. "I'd
like to know *what* people." That had been a bad time, all right.
Then she had turned against him, without giving him a chance

to work things out in himself. He would never have done anything, he just had to work the thing out logically in his mind.
She and her friends, who ran around with their little nipples
bobbing under their tissue-thin shortie pajamas . . . He needed
time to play the thing out in his mind enough times until it lost
its dangerous charge. But before he could do that, she had
turned against him. Suddenly he was no longer her sought-after
confidant on every matter from sex appeal to algebra. He would
catch her looking at him with contempt. One night at dinner
Lily criticized her for wearing too much lipstick and she sassed
back, "Well, what about *you*, Lily?" and before he knew what
had happened he had backhanded her across the mouth. Whatever he'd been trying to defuse inside himself had been converted
into violence. He hit her some more after that. Then, stealthily,
she had conducted her correspondence with those Campions
down east, and the uncle who was a judge came to get her. Just
showed up at the front door one day in June, wearing a white
suit. And when Ralph got back from his construction job, Lily,
very pregnant with Rafe, was sitting in the bedroom with the
shades down, weeping quietly over Theo's cot. "It was so embarrassing" Lily had told him. "Zeb thought I knew he was
coming. So I had to pretend I did know, that Clare had told me
all about it and that she was leaving with my permission. Oh,
well. They're eager to have her—Zeb the bachelor and his
childless sister—and they'll cater to her and worship any signs
of her father in her, and maybe in a few months her mood will
improve and she'll come back. Meanwhile, we can have some
peace around here."

The "couple of months," however, had turned into two years.
She had finished school down east, coming home for short visits
on the bus. And then the Campions had sent her to college. She
never lived with Lily and him again. As the years passed, the
hurt that remained was that of losing her as the daughter she
had been, briefly, to him, before all that other mess had begun
swirling around in his fantasies. He missed the talks they'd had.
And the sense of having a crony who would go with him just to
the hardware store or to see his mother. Lily had never cared
much for his mother, though she was always scrupulously polite.

He would have liked to have a daughterly figure in his life. It
struck him with a lamentable irony on this of all mornings that
he had been more of a companion, those few good years with
Clare, to his young stepdaughter than he had been to either of

his sons. By the time they got big enough to talk to, he was too busy making money. And after that the thing with Hannah had eclipsed all family life. . . .

And that was why, probably, he had really meant it when he told Snow he would have gone to Georgia to get her, if he'd had the time. They would talk in the car. Something useful or enlightening was bound to get said during a five-hour drive. She had been his son's wife, after all. Maybe she was still redeemable. Could finish high school and get a job. He would build her a house near them, and they could raise Jason together. Even Lily would discover some merit in this girl that Theo had been so determined to have. When they were first married, he would snatch her off the ground—she was just a little bitty thing, wore a size two dress—and toss her up in the air like you would a child. "You put me down, Theo Quick," she would scream, "and I mean right this goddamn minute!" "God's last name isn't damn," he would say unctuously. And with that perverse grin of his, he would fling her up in the air again.

"You know, Jason," Alicia Gallant was telling the boy, "your saying, 'I'll sit where I *want*,' in that imperious manner puts me in mind of a story about myself. When I was a girl, I was riding home on the streetcar late one afternoon —"

"What kind of car is that?"

"It was what they had instead of a bus in the old days. It looked like a bus, but it ran on rails down the middle of the street. It was attached to a wire above, because, you see, it was operated by electricity instead of gas —"

"So it didn't have to stop at the gas station."

"That's right. I declare, you are a smart boy. Anyway, when I got on the streetcar and paid my fare, I looked around and saw it was real crowded. People were coming home from work and there were only two places left to sit. One place was beside a dirty-looking man in overalls who smelled, and the other place was beside a neat old gentleman in a coat and tie. Without any hesitation I sat down beside *him*, even though he happened to be a colored gentleman. Well, I tell you! No sooner did my body touch that seat than there was this tremendous intake of breath, like a single gasp running through the whole car. There was a silence you could have cut with a knife. Then the streetcar stopped and the conductor came pushing through that crowd towards my seat. 'Excuse me, young lady,' he said, 'but you can't sit there. You cannot sit beside that person.' The poor colored gentleman was very nervous and sat looking straight ahead, trying to make himself invisible, and I knew that he wished like anything I had chosen to sit somewhere else—or to stand, if it came to that! Now, in those days, there was a law that said whites and coloreds couldn't sit together, but I was a stubborn young thing and I wasn't going to let myself be vanquished by a streetcar conductor. So I just tipped up my chin and stared him boldly in the eye and I said to him, 'I can sit wherever I like.' And, do you know, that conductor turned right around and went back to the front of the car and the streetcar started up again and that was the end of that. When I got home, I told my daddy what I'd done and he laughed and laughed and said he would have done the exact same thing. 'Always sit by the cleanest person, Missy,' he said, 'and you'll come out smelling like a rose.'" Alicia Gallant began to laugh herself. She laughed often, a girlish laugh, slightly out of breath and exhausted, as if some one had been tickling her for a long time. "That's what he said, Jason. 'You'll come out smelling like a rose.'"

Miss Alicia often told stories of herself and her family. Ralph enjoyed listening to them, and he suspected this story was told as much for his diversion as for the child's—though Jason, infected by something in it, perhaps the old lady's manner of telling it, her obvious delight in her own easy and assured progress through the decades, was giggling and nuzzling against her scratchy wool suit and repeating the part about smelling like a rose. In all her stories, she and her family came out smelling like roses. They not only had adventures in the great capitals of Europe; they managed to have them at home in Mountain City. They met their illnesses, disappointments, and setbacks with epigrams and aplomb. Through all the funny and awful things that happened to them, they were constantly aware of themselves as *Gallants,* a species unto themselves: a little larger, more defined, longer-lived than ordinary families. Ralph's favorite story of Miss Alicia's was about the time in the not-so-distant past when she and her brother, Dr. Anthony, went to a store to buy their father a smoking jacket for his birthday. The salesman showed them the store's best selection of smoking jackets. "I don't know," said Dr. Anthony, frowning and turning over the dark silken sleeves between his fingers. "They all look a little old for him, don't you think, Sissie?" Finally the salesman ventured to ask, "How old is your father going to be?" "A hundred," said Miss Alicia.

Yet something about the story of Miss Alicia and the Negro on the streetcar had awakened an obscure ache in Ralph. It lay like a bruise on his memory, waiting for him to recall why it hurt—and then add it to the rest of the pain of this cruelly bright October day. But they were at the florist's now, and they all got out and went into the moist, ferny air of the shop, which smelled of the pungent, prickly fall flowers that, when he had left this morning, were already being delivered to the house— arrangements of marigolds and asters and mums and pine cones sprayed a dull gold, with small sympathy cards attached.

The florist met them, looking distraught. There was a crisis. The whole town seemed to be out of magnolia leaves, and he and his staff had counted on having a huge bank of their dark, shiny leaves. "It makes a very *masculine* effect with the colored leaves and yellow spider mums mixed in. But there just aren't any." He actually wrung his hands.

"Oh, that's no problem," said Miss Alicia. "My young cousin has a great big magnolia tree in her front yard in St. Dunstan's Forest. We'll go and raid it. She won't even know the difference, as she spends most of her time down at Hilton Head. You just tell us how many to get."

The florist calculated silently. "If you could maybe fill the trunk of your car with them . . ."

"But wouldn't they get too hot in there?" demanded the old lady.

"They might," agreed the florist, hesitating.

"We'll put them in the backseat," said Miss Alicia. "Won't that be the best, Jason?"

The child nodded solemnly and said it would.

The florist, relieved to have everything settled, lent them two pairs of clippers and they were on their way again.

"We'll have to stop by the Security Police's headquarters when we get to the Forest," said Miss Alicia, "to pick up Sally's gate key. It will be quicker than going all the way back to my house to get my spare. You know where the Security Police are located, don't you Ralph? That ridiculous-looking building got up to resemble a Tudor cottage?"

"Yes, I know it," said Ralph. "I've had to stop by the place for keys when I was building additions for people in the Forest."

"Ralph," Lily had said, "I do wish you would at least call that

*psychiatrist woman back. Just tell her you're too busy, if you don't want
to do it, because otherwise she's going to pester me to death about her
'addition.' And that accent of hers is rather daunting. She sounds like a
spy or something. Every time I promise her you'll call back, I feel her
spying into my mind and seeing how very little influence I have over my
husband.'' And so, finally, to please Lily, who had succeeded in shaming
him about his tendency to procrastinate in saying no to jobs that didn't
interest him, he had called the woman, a Dr. Hannah Ullstein, back. As
soon as he heard that peremptory voice, with its harsh accent, he pictured
the person that would go with it. Thick ankles, steel-gray butch haircut,
beady, super-critical eyes behind thick lenses. She was so insistent, he
decided he would have to go and tell her in person that he was not her
man.*

"I'm going in with you!" cried Jason, struggling to get out of
the seat belt shared with Miss Alicia, as soon as Ralph stopped
the car in front of the St. Dunstan's Forest Security Building.
Bless Miss Alicia for calling a fake a fake when she saw it, even
if her cousin did live out here. The Tudor-style timber-framed
structure looked absurd set in the middle of a parking lot, with
a great big satellite dish on its roof so the men could get all the
TV programs. The vertical timber posts in the construction were
genuine, but what Ralph couldn't forgive was that the decor-
ative diagonal struts on the building's corners were *painted in.*
Those sham struts summed up the whole damn Forest.

"No, Jason, you stay with Miss Alicia. I'll be back before you
can get out of that thing."

"I'm going with you!" shrieked the child.

The adults exchanged a look. "Okay, son," said Ralph
wearily.

The boy, hell-bent on having his way in everything this
morning—as if he already understood that he had suffered a loss
so irreparable that the world would have to spend the rest of his
life repaying him—scrambled out of the car and marched beside
his grandfather towards the Tudor police station. Small children
had been Hannah's specialty. If she had not gone back to
Germany, she would have been able, better than anybody, to
tell him how to explain to Jason that Theo was not going to be
driving up Quick's Hill ever again. She would have been able to
advise whether the boy should be taken to the funeral—although
Ralph's own very clear gut reaction said yes, take him, it would
be one more thing of his father's he might remember later. But
how much had he already seen or heard yesterday in that crazy

short time when they were all wandering around the emergency
room, everyone stunned, not believing, then being made to
believe—Lily going up and down, up and down the hall holding
the hand of that big Negro orderly? Ralph had tried to keep
Jason both isolated from hearing anything and close to him, but
the child had run off for a minute once, just before Miss Alicia
suggested they go for the ice cream. "Get that kid out of here!"
a man's voice had shouted, and Jason had wheeled suddenly
out of a room, his arms spread as if he were pretending to be an
airplane about to take off. It was the room Theo was in. On the
machine. ("Doctor," Lily had said, with that flushed face and
arched-eyebrow look she got when somebody had said something gauche, "if his brain is dead, then *he* is dead.") She had
never gone into the room, she refused to see him again, on the
machine. Ralph himself had not gone beyond the doorway while
Father Ned was getting out his oils from that little briefcase of
his, was putting the thin scarf—Lily would know the official
name of it—around his neck. He hadn't seen much, but it was
too much. Yet he had needed to look, even though there was
nothing conscious in Theo anymore.

On duty this morning was a young policeman Ralph did not
know. Usually he would have been glad of a familiar face—his
own foreman's young brother was on the St. Dunstan's force—
but today he was relieved to be just an unknown petitioner for a
lady's gate key. The morning paper was spread out before the
policeman on his desk. It was opened to the sports page. Young
people seldom looked at the obituary page.

"Howdy," said Ralph. He held on to Jason's warm, slightly
sticky hand.

The young policeman looked up. "Morning, sir. What can I
do for you?"

"I've got Miss Alicia Gallant outside in the car. She wants to
pick up her cousin's gate key to Number Five Gloucester
Road."

The boy consulted a clipboard on the desk. "That's Mrs.
McGrath, right?"

"That's right," said Ralph. "She's down at Hilton Head, and
Miss Gallant wants to cut some of the magnolia leaves off the
tree in the front yard."

The policeman turned his head to look out the window and
get a view of the old lady sitting serenely in Ralph's car.
Everything about her, from her crooked homemade hat to the

way she gazed straight ahead, made it clear that she expected
the young policeman to hand over that key and for Ralph to
come back with it, without any fuss. The boy got up from the
desk and ambled over to an Old Master reproduction in a heavy,
ornate frame. With an air of importance he pressed a discreet
wall button to the right of the "painting," which swung open to
reveal a recessed pegboard hung with rows of keys with different-
colored tags. The colors were for the different roads, which had
English   names—Gloucester,   Surrey,   Coventry,   Corn-
wall . . . Shropshire. Ralph, who had seen the little trick many
times before, showed no surprise, and this increased the policeman's respect. "She want the house key, too?" he asked.

"No, just the gate key," said Ralph. "She only wants to cut
some magnolia leaves for . . . for a floral arrangement." If that
boy had worked for him, he would have given him hell for
offering more than was asked for. Either you had a security
force or you didn't. The pretensions of this place grated on his
nerves; even its security was more show than force. That
"hidden" pegboard behind the "painting," for example: why
was it in the main room so every Tom, Dick, and Harry could
watch him open it? And why didn't the pushbutton have a
locking device? Any fool could come in here and press that
button. It was as if they wanted to be robbed. Well, maybe they
did. Their jewelry was in the bank, and they could collect insurance on their pasteboard imitations. ("You hate them too
much," Lily would say. "They really aren't all that important.")

When he freed his hand to sign for the key, Jason was immediately off, flying about the carpeted, wainscoted room with its
lamps and smaller Old Masters.

"I don't like this place!" he shouted. "It's not a real police
station. Theo took me to the real police station downtown, and
it's not like this!"

"It's a private police station," Ralph said, bowing his head
over the register and writing down his name, then Miss Alicia
Gallant's name, then what time they expected to return the key.
"It's just for the security of the people who live in this area." He
could see them in his head, the "committee" that had designed
this place. Mostly women, maybe one or two retired men, the
kind that liked to play bridge with women and sit on committees
in the afternoons to fill the time. They would pick little iced
cakes and leafy sandwiches from silver trays, popping them into

their mouths with dainty greed, talking about their diets and their next meals all in the same breath with their marvelous plans for their "Old English" police station. It was a wonder they hadn't decided on a thatched roof, though that—far more than the genuine struts they had vetoed—would have run into real money. Some corseted old biddy who had taken art in college would have contributed sketches of the uniform being worn this morning by this raw mountain boy who wouldn't be allowed to drive around here in his own clothes after dark: a uniform that was an inane cross between an elevator man's livery and a chauffeur's, with its gold-braided epaulets and storm trooper boots. The whole thing was enough to make you wonder if even the revolver, snapped into the hip holster—a shiny brown, like the boots—was a fake. ("Hey, Dad, let me borrow your Belgian gun. Someone in Jeanette's situation is just going to feel more comfortable with an automatic.")

"I don't care," retorted Jason, narrowly missing upsetting a lamp as he reeled about the room. "It's a silly station all the same!"

Ralph put down the pen, which was chained to the register, and gave the young policeman an apologetic shrug. "He's a little hyper today," he said. But, to his surprise, the policeman's solemn face had erupted into a wide, delighted grin. His gums were red and swollen, already receding from the upper parts of his teeth. Within a few years he would have all the teeth pulled and be glad for the shiny dentures that would keep him from ever having to go to the dentist again. After Theo married Snow, Ralph had paid more than two thousand dollars to preserve her teeth. Twenty-three fillings, two gold crowns for the ones that were too far gone, and a series of gum treatments. She had never been to the dentist in her life, she had told Theo proudly. Her mother, who was the same age as Lily, had a complete set of dentures, and Evelyn, the sister of Snow's he liked best, already had large gaps on both sides of her mouth.

"Nice boy you got there," the policeman said, in the same mountain accent as Snow's—and, to some extent, Ralph's. For a moment the three of them were united in a silent bond against this enclave of bourgeois pretensions that the child had rightly named silly.

"My son's boy," Ralph said.

He was glad not to have to drive down Shropshire Road in order to get to Gloucester Road. He would not have to look at

Hannah's former house, with "her little study in the sky," as she had called it, that he had built for her. You could not see it from the road; it faced the back garden, with a partial view of the mountains through some topped trees. But it would be bad enough just to have to see the house itself in this morning's unrelenting sunlight, with some doctor's wife's sporty Mercedes in the driveway, some spoiled kid's ten-speed bike toppled carelessly on the lawn.

"It's like this," he had told the foreign woman who wouldn't give up, "I could do the work, I could build your attic addition. But, frankly speaking, you'd do better to set a match to this whole damn thing and start over." Then, seeing by her puzzled frown (she did not wear thick glasses or have the iron-gray butch haircut) that her understanding of English had fallen short of his hyperbole, "What I'm saying is, given the structure we have to work with, you'd end up spending half the price again that you paid for the house. The roof has a sag. We'd have to prop up the rafters with knee walls. The fool who built this attic put in two-by-six floor joists, and he put them in the wrong way, running east to west instead of north to south, so the joists aren't acting as collar beams and the roof is pushing the walls out. We'd have to build in supports and raise the floor a good two inches with some two-by-eights. And if I raise the floor, I've got to raise the roof, otherwise you'll be walking around in a stoop."

She was a psychiatrist with an MD, a real genius with disturbed children—he had asked around some—but, like all women, as soon as he began to talk the specifics of his trade, her eyes glazed over and she didn't listen to a word he said. "All I need," she told him, in her strangely accented, guttural English, trippingly precise, "is a little high place, you know . . . a little study where the view would be so lovely and I could go up and write and think." Her hair was so black it had blue lights in it, like the feathers of crows in sunshine. It dropped to her shoulders in careless, girlish clusters, as if she had forgotten to comb it before he arrived. He could not remember having seen her exact combination of coloring, ever: the black hair and then the very white translucent skin and the light blue, almost gray, eyes. She had a startled, rather than straightforward, way of looking at him when he talked. He would have expected a psychiatrist to have a direct, penetrating gaze. Her air of vagueness threw him off. And it annoyed him, the way she stood there with her arms folded, a blue-black swatch of hair slipping forward on her cheek, waiting with her airy, woman's confidence for him to get done complaining about carpentry problems and name his price for building her "little high place" where "the view would be so lovely." "Hell," he said, "if it was a high place you wanted, why didn't you buy or build you a house on a mountain?

There are plenty of mountains around here, and plenty of land available on top of them. If it was a view you wanted, what possessed you to move into this damp, cramped, overpriced swampful of snobs?"

It was then that she gave him the full force of an honest gaze. She laughed. "Because," she said, "I heard that it was the one place in this town that had an unwritten policy of excluding Jews. So, you see, I had to prove to myself I could defeat that policy. It was important to me, to the little German girl half-mad with fear that her schoolmates would learn she had had a Jewish grandmother and report her to the Gestapo. Yes, I know. I am a grown woman now, a doctor who treats the insecurities of others. But no matter how elevated we become, Mr. Quick, I think we don't quite outgrow our own early insecurities."

He was shocked to hear such an unprofessional admission from a psychiatrist. And the women in his experience didn't tell anyone their weaknesses. His mother, who had certainly felt the burden of prejudice because of her Cherokee blood, would never have confided her grievance even to a close friend—if she had had one. And Lily! She wouldn't tell anybody anything. Formerly, with him, she had been more outgoing with her tears and rages, but now she wouldn't admit to so much as a headache, not even if he caught her swallowing aspirin.

But the woman's story was disarming. It kindled a compassion in him and opened up vistas of more serious and deadly wrongs occurring outside the realm of personal slights. He left her house feeling refreshingly estranged from the routine his life had settled into. As he drove home through the summer heat, seeing the town in which he was born and raised as a stranger might see it, he was already shuffling his crew around in his mind, though he had told her these were his busiest months and he couldn't promise anything. "I will try to hope not too much," she had said in her precise but still vulnerable English. He felt protective of her. That's why he didn't have the heart to tell her that the "unwritten policy" she had "defeated" hadn't ever applied to doctors. Doctors were the unwritten exception in St. Dunstan's Forest: everybody knew that. He remembered having an interesting discussion about it with Dr. Anthony one time. "We need our doctors in Mountain City," Dr. Anthony had said. They had been sipping their drinks on the porch of that old monstrosity on Montrose Hill Avenue where he and Miss Alicia had lived until his death. Crossing one patrician ankle over the other and admiring his English shoes of mud-brown suede, Dr. Anthony had explained to Ralph genially that, frankly, Jews made the best doctors because they had done it so long it was in their genes, "like moneylending and scholarship."

He could probably spare two of his men for the job, one good carpenter and Theo, who would be eighteen this year and had been working for him

*these past three summers. If he raised her roof, they would raise her taxes.
So he might just as well raise it a good ten inches and give her a modified
cathedral ceiling. Then she could stand anywhere in the room without
stooping; she could gaze down on the treetops of her neighbors rotting in
their damp rooms. She could lift her eyes to the mountains. . . .*

He got out and unlocked Miss Alicia's cousin's wrought-iron
gate. Then drove midway around the circular driveway and
parked in the shade of the great magnolia tree they were about
to ravage.

"Why are we stopping here?" asked Jason.

"This is my cousin Sally's house," said Miss Alicia. "We're
going to cut some of those pretty green leaves from that grand
old magnolia tree."

"Won't she mind?" asked the boy, scrambling out of the car
behind Miss Alicia, who, with her clippers and pocketbook,
headed purposefully towards the tree.

"No, darling. She's down at the beach playing golf and enjoying herself with her friends. I'll bet she hasn't given a thought
to this poor old tree in ages. And the tree won't mind, either.
It's had its blooms for the year and our trimming will only
stimulate its growth for next year. I wonder, would *you* mind
holding my purse for me, Jason, while I get at these leaves."

"Can I look in it?"

"No, son, you may not," said his grandfather.

"Oh, it's all right," said Miss Alicia. "Just be sure and put
everything back when you get through," she told the boy. "It'll
keep him occupied," she said quietly to Ralph.

The two grownups began to clip the old tree, piling the clumps
of the glossy dark-green leaves at their feet, while the child sat
with the old lady's open purse between his legs on Cousin Sally's
neglected lawn, defaced with plantain and dandelion weed, and
contentedly pulled out a clean folded handkerchief with violets
embroidered in one corner, a man's soft, worn leather billfold
(with dollars in it), a little round box with a picture painted on
its lid and some white pills and some red pills inside, a comb
with several white hairs in it, a pen, a checkbook, and a key
ring. He put everything back except the billfold and the key
ring, and, mumbling to himself, arranged this pair of items in
various positions on the weedy grass. Frequently he would pick
up the billfold and recount the number of bills lying inside.
Then he would go through the keys on the key ring method-
ically, telling himself something about each key.

What, if anything, would he remember of this later? Ralph wondered. Would a day come when he'd fish in his pocket for his own key ring, or be sitting in the grass, perhaps with *his* children, and look down and notice a certain configuration of dandelion and plantain weeds and have his breath knocked out of him by a sudden, outraged feeling of loss? Would he, perhaps even when he was as old as Ralph, find himself staring at someone's magnolia tree in the sun and wondering what it was about the dark, waxy leaves with their downy, orange undersides that made him queasy and afraid? The memory, Hannah once said, was rigged with thousands of little landmines, waiting for you to step on the right place and blow yourself up on a long-suppressed grief or terror or mortification.

As he got into a rhythm, pulling down a low, heavy branch, then snipping the leaf clusters, looking over from time to time at Miss Alicia, who in her hot wool suit was clipping manfully beside him, Ralph's eye began to bother him. Even after eighteen months, his impulse was to rub it, or to spit on his fingers and attempt to dissolve some of the murky soup in there that was drowning his sight. The knowledge of what was going on in that eye could make him feel faint if he dwelled on it long enough. He and Lily had been at a touring opera company's production of *Carmen* at the Municipal Auditorium when he discovered that the right side of the stage was blurred unless he turned his head sharply so he could watch the singers with his left eye. With compulsive fascination and mounting despair, he swiveled his head back and forth. Then (surreptitiously, because the Talman Flemmings were sitting right behind them), he spit on his fingers and lubricated the eye and tested his sight again. "You're a little fidgety tonight," Lily told him at intermission. "Is it boring you as much as it's boring me?" He said he hadn't had a chance to be bored, that there was something wrong with his right eye. "Then let's go home right now," said Lily. "We'll slip out the side door." "But what about the Talman Flemmings, they're sitting right behind us." "Oh, when the Talman Flemmings see our empty seats, they'll kick themselves for not having had the same idea," Lily had replied with the rock-solid insouciance that could still awe him at times, when he was not infuriated by it.

"You're lucky," the doctor had told him, eighteen months ago. "By the time this fella finishes growing, we'll have perfected our techniques for lens implants." It was another eye doctor, a new man in town, who had phoned yesterday. "We're getting ready to do the cornea transplant, and we need to know if he was having any problems with his vision." A cornea (he had looked it up in Webster's at three this morning, just to make sure) was the transparent tissue forming the outer coat of the eyeball and covering the iris and pupil. So he wouldn't be walking down some street in town and suddenly see his son's eyes looking at him out of a stranger's face. They were taking only the transparent part. No, on the whole, Theo's vision had been excellent, he had told the new doctor. "He took after me in that respect." Neglecting to mention the cataract as he tried to impress the man with his and Theo's superior vision. What had he been afraid of? That the doctor would say, "Sorry, if the family's vision isn't perfect we can't use your son's corneas." Just as those different doctors had apologetically kept coming up to him and Lily, when they were still in the emergency room yesterday, saying they were sorry, but they couldn't use the liver . . . too traumatized . . . couldn't use the kidneys, either. As each organ was rejected, he had felt an irrational disappointment on Theo's behalf, as though Theo had failed another subject in school.

And I thought losing Hannah was the worst thing that could happen to my life.

Theo had been getting nearsighted. Ralph had admitted that to the doctor. Anybody could get nearsighted. It was the close accounting work. First he'd bought those gold-rimmed glasses Lily had said made him look like a bank teller, and then when he'd started going out with the nurse (Ralph hadn't even known her last name—Harris, Jeanette Harris—until he read it in the paper this morning), Theo had gone and had himself fitted for soft contacts. Maybe Jeanette hadn't liked the gold-rimmed glasses, either. But the contacts bothered him, he was always conscious they were in there, he had said, like foreign bodies. He could wear them only an hour or so every day, then put them back in their little dual case. One night last week Ralph had been downstairs at the Ping-Pong table, getting ready to perform his monthly rob-Peter-to-pay-Paul sorting of the bills, when Theo had wandered down in that offhand way of his. He walked around the Ping-Pong table several times, with his hands in his pockets, blinking ostentatiously until Ralph was bound to look up and notice. "Those soft contacts still hurting you, son?" "I guess," Theo had replied. Then added, "Not really hurt. It's just that *I'm* too soft, maybe." Ralph had gone on sorting the bills. "Why don't you let me do that for you?" Theo had asked, after observing Ralph's method for several minutes. "Now that you've got you an accountant in the family, you might as well use him." "Hell," said Ralph, "I wouldn't foist this can of worms on my worst enemy. You have your CPA exam to study for." "Is it that you can't pay them all, Dad, or do you just like to put them off as long as possible, to save interest on your money?" "A little of both," mumbled Ralph inhospitably, wishing Theo would stop blinking at him like a rabbit and go away. He didn't like being cross-examined on the subject of these bills. He hadn't even worked out for himself why attending to these bills had become the most odious chore of his present existence. He could remember when he had loved paying bills. Not parting with the money, of which there was a whole lot less then, but the whole agreeable ritual, the organizing in piles, the writing and re- cording of the checks, the pride, as he stacked the freshly stamped envelopes to the right of his ledger, that he was at last a man in charge of a family, in charge of a business, in charge of the men who worked for him and had to have their retirement provided for and their well-being on the job assured, even though these sums must come out of his own pocket. In those days, his desk had been neat, like a little altar waiting for his monthly celebration of the security and self-esteem he had succeeded in winning for himself.

Now Theo, blinking and squinting through his contacts, exuding an expectation of intimacy that was ill timed and downright oppressive, hovered beside him over the Ping-Pong table that Ralph knew was a disgrace, with its three-, four-, and five-month backlog of bills. With Theo, he couldn't get away with the joke about tossing them downstairs once a month and paying the ones that landed highest. No, Theo was waiting for him to *confide* something.

("It's like one of those bad fairy tales, son, where you ask for your three wishes and get them, but then it all falls on your head because those wishes had conditions or sinister properties attached. I wished for a wife I could admire, who would do me credit, and some children, and material success, and respect from the community. I got those things. The year we moved into this house was the pinnacle for me. Clare came home from England and saw you two diving into the new pool and said, 'Well, I see you all have achieved the American Dream.' And then a few

years passed, and Mama died, and Lily's mother died. That
brought us closer, in a way, because Lily had never really
warmed to Mama and it was a sore point between us, and when
Ellen Buchel was alive, she and Lily had an exclusive sort of
sisterhood between them that I couldn't penetrate, even though
I think the old lady had finally come to approve of me in her
last years. And then, when you were eighteen and Rafe was
sixteen, Hannah happened. And when I emerged from that
dream, the decay around home was already making inroads.
Rafe had been expelled from Belvedere for throwing his famous
party and had lost his chance for a Morehead Scholarship, and
then a few years later you and Rafe found your way into that
ill-fated dance down at the Teen Center, where Rafe took it
into his head to dance with a little piece of pure trouble named
Snow Mullins and managed to insult her, and then you, going
too far as always, had to set things right by doing nothing less
than marrying her. And Lily had gone cold on me after I tried
to tell her how I had felt about Hannah. It was all finished by
then anyway, Hannah had gone back to Germany to marry her
rich kraut, throwing over everything her intelligence and
common sense and psychiatric training told her, in order to
compensate herself for a childhood of fear and deprivation. I
wanted to make a clean breast of it to Lily, and with her help
try to understand just how and why it had happened, and then
to try and go on from there: who knows, maybe even build a
stronger marriage, one without so many illusions. But I reckoned
without Lily's pride. Her absolute and total disdain for people
who, as she said, with a contemptuous curl of her lip, 'have to
spill the beans.' We were sitting together on the sofa—I hadn't
been able to sleep and she had come looking for me. 'There's
something I want to tell you about Hannah,' I said. 'Oh, that's
not necessary,' she said, picking up a book on netsukes and
leafing through the glossy pages. 'She was a nice woman, an
interesting woman in many ways, and she and I had several
very good talks in the pool, when she came over to swim on
Sundays. And I will always be grateful for her teaching me how
to make rouladen; whenever we have it, I'll think kindly of her.'
'But Lily, you must know . . . I want to tell you what happened.'
'As far as I'm concerned, nothing did.' She paused at a double-
page spread of animal netsukes. 'Just look at the detail on that
rabbit's foot, and it's the underside, too; don't you think it's
wonderful, the care these people took, even for a belt buckle or

a purse clasp?' 'Will you put down that damn book and listen?'
She closed the book on netsukes, which had been my birthday
present to her the year before, but hugged it against her as if to
protect herself. 'When things happen, they happen for a reason,'
I said. 'They happen because of the things that went before.
Why won't you let me tell you how it happened? I need to
understand it myself. And then maybe we can sweep the decks
clean and make a new beginning.' 'Like housekeeping,' she said
dryly, 'only we're not on a ship.' She sat erect, her shoulders not
touching the back of the sofa, but she was taking such deep
breaths that the silk material of her robe, where it crossed in
front, pulled taut each time she breathed in. I remembered that
thing with her heart that happened when Dr. Anthony was up
here for dinner that time. I didn't want to kill her, I just wanted
to talk to her, really talk to her, the way Hannah had let me
talk. The way we had talked to each other on those Sunday
mornings, God forgive me, when I was supposed to be at the
Presbyterian service. 'She's gone back to Germany,' Lily said
slowly, taking the deep breaths and holding her book on
netsukes, 'and married herself a rich man who can give her lots
of houses and vacations, and make it up to her for his people
kicking her people out of Europe. He will give her the security
she was always telling me in the pool she needed. I think we
were pretty good friends to her while she was here in Mountain
City, and we tried to make her feel at home. Goodness, all those
dinners she cooked up here!' She laughed, still hugging the book
and looking straight ahead, out the picture window at the stars
and, below, the lights of town. 'I was always so jubilant when
she would call around noon on Sunday and say, "Oh, hello,
Lily, it is so hot today, don't you think?" because I knew if I
asked her to come up and swim with us, she'd end up staying
and fixing dinner. Do you remember how, after the first few
times, she always brought along her own spices because mine
were all dried out? I think we all made her feel like a member of
the family. I hope she has that child she wants before too long.
It gets dangerous at her age. And I hope she won't regret giving
up her career. I think a woman always has some qualms when
she has been out in the world earning money for herself and
then agrees to sit down and fold her hands and let some man
take over. I know what. Why don't you fix us both a drink? It
will make us nice and sleepy.'"

"After that, I decided to throw myself into my business. I was offered a chance to build a motel for a Greek, out on the Old Catawba Highway, near where Uncle Don's house used to stand. I'm sorry you never knew Uncle Don. He had a fine collection of guns. After he died, there was an auction, and I'd made a little money by then and was able to pick up a few nice ones . . . that Belgian semiautomatic is a genuine antique now. Well, I'd never done business with anybody like that Greek, and he took my balls. That's when I went to court and my own friend Hal DuPre, we were in basic training together, represented that crook and soaked me for every cent I had at the time. They put a hold on my bank accounts to pay off the subcontractors. You remember that. I was fit to be tied. But what hurt the most was Hal DuPre representing the Greek, when we had been friends. I can't count the number of times he and his wife—ex-wife, now—were over to our house to play bridge. I built their house. After it was all over, I picked up the phone one night and called him at home. 'Hal,' I said, 'how could you have done it? It was bad enough, you representing him, but you know the man was lying, he perjured himself every time he took a breath. And you know I was telling the truth. You know I never would have gone ahead with that extra work on my own if he hadn't specified it.' 'Ralph, I know you wouldn't have,' Hal said. 'I know you're as honest as they come. But you weren't smart. You ought to have got everything down in writing from that son of a bitch.' 'If he was a son of a bitch and you knew it, why did you represent him instead of me, Hal?' 'Now, Ralph, you're being naïve. Because he asked me first.' 'Damn it, Hal, I was the one who brought the suit. How the hell could he have asked you first?' 'Ralph, we've been through this before. I was doing some other business for him at the time, regarding other aspects of that motel, and when you called me I told you I couldn't very well sue my own client.' 'But I was your client for twenty-five years, Hal. That crook hadn't blown into town more than twenty-five *minutes* ago.' 'Look here, Ralph. You're in business. I'm in business, right? You took Zouvlakis on as a client, I took Zouvlakis on as a client. You got burned because you didn't take precautions.' Then I said, 'Is that what it all comes down to in the end, Hal? After twenty-five years of friendship and doing business together? That you could sit there in the courtroom and listen to him perjure himself and know they would put a lien on my bank account and my savings account until

I'd discharged all his debts? It that your idea of loyalty, Hal?'
And you know what he answered? 'My first loyalty is to make
sure that my client wins his case.' And hung up on me.

"And now, son, you stand breathing down my neck, wanting
to know whether I can't pay them all or whether I'm just
holding out on my creditors short of court and bankruptcy in
order to let my own interest accumulate. A little of both, son, a
little of both. And a little of something else, too. What the hell's
the rush? Those bills aren't going anywhere. Neither are the
creditors. You want to know something funny? Some of them
speak friendlier to me now than they did when I paid their bills
on time. I reckon they feel I've come to my senses, got over my
'naïve' gratitude at being allowed to earn my share of the American Dream. I've come to the sad conclusion that in today's
world a successful crook who knows how to let his interest accumulate is admired a hell of a lot more than an honest fool who pays
his bills by return mail. Why, I had one man laughing on the
telephone when I told him I'd throw his bill downstairs with all
the others and if he was lucky this month it would land on the
top step. I'll bet now he's on the phone telling his creditors the
same story.

"So what else do you want to know, son? My philosophy of
life? Well these days my philosophy of life about everything
from bills to cleaning up the carport to sticking fallen soap
dishes back into the wall is, most things will wait another
day.")

He hadn't said any of this to Theo, of course, hadn't even
thought it out for himself until now, the hot sun baking his
back, the clumps of magnolia leaves falling around his feet like
small bodies. Theo had stood a few minutes longer at his father's
side, blinking in protest against the alien contact lenses and
waiting for the father-son confidences they would never have,
and then, sensing Ralph's impatience to be left alone in his self-
made prison of unconfided secrets and unpaid bills, had
shrugged and said, well, he guessed he'd go study in the guest
room awhile, so as not to wake up Jason, who was sleeping in
his bed.

Most things will wait another day. He hadn't said that to Theo,
of course. But Theo hadn't waited, either.

There was another scene with Jason when they got to the
cemetery. He screamed and refused to stay with Miss Alicia

while Ralph went inside to see the sexton about purchasing the plot.

So they all four had to walk in the cemetery, the two men doing their business in a kind of code so that the boy would not understand what they were discussing. The plot next to Lily's mother's was available. And so was the one next to that.

The sexton advised Ralph to purchase both plots. "That way, it'll be just your people all the way to the treeline," he said, at the same time managing to convey to Ralph's mind the picture of a stranger sealing in Lily's mother and Theo, when, if Ralph had only been more prudent, they could have had all the way to the trees.

Ralph looked down at Lily's mother's stone.

Ellen Harshaw Buchel
January 20, 1972

Like mother, like daughter. She had stipulated there be no birthdate over her dead body, it was none of anybody's business. Neither he nor Lily had known how old she was until, going through her things after her death, they had found a copy of the 1890 census entry for the Harshaw family, which listed the baby, Ellen, as two years old. Now why, he had often wondered since, had she kept the incriminating evidence?

It was awkward, just the one plot next to Theo's. Which one of them would go there? He played a grim game of musical chairs with the possibilities. If Lily went first, then he and Rafe would have to find themselves places in the new section, beyond the mature shade trees, where the recently plowed earth still showed red and raw under its seeding of grass. If he went first, then Lily would be separated from her mother. If Rafe went first . . .

Here his imagination recoiled. Enough was enough for one day. In his agitated state, it seemed to him that buying an extra plot along with Theo's incurred some responsibility to him to kill off mentally the family member who would most suitably complete the row.

What about Clare? She would have to be buried somewhere, too. Nobody in their right mind would want to be hidden away in one of those crowded cemeteries in New York. Would Clare be the best candidate to lie next to Theo, at the end of the row? She had doted on Theo when he was born, was always picking him up and kissing his tummy and dancing him around in her room to Nat King Cole. But then Rafe had become her favorite. That had hurt Theo, but Rafe had been so many people's favorite, from the moment he was born. Even Dr. Anthony, who was godfather to Theo, had admired the way Rafe slid into the world, after Theo's tortuous birth. "Here comes a winner," Dr. Anthony had said, hurrying into the delivery room, still wearing his golf shoes, just in time to smack Rafe's bottom and tie up his little belly button. Theo, two years before, had tried to come out feet first, choking himself blue on his own umbilical cord. All the world loved an easy winner.

Ralph told the sexton he guessed he'd go ahead and take both the plots. Not because he'd decided who ought to lie there (maybe it would be best left undug forever, belonging to the family as a restful greensward between Theo and the treeline) but because he was afraid the man would think him cheap if he bought only the one.

"I think you've made the right decision," the sexton said. "Now, what time did you say your son's funeral—" He had forgotten the boy's presence and lapsed from their indirect manner of speaking.

But Alicia Gallant, alert as a fox, perhaps anticipating just such a misdemeanor, stole away Jason's attention with a sudden, weird cry: "My goodness me, I'd completely forgotten. My poor brother's lost lady is over there under that tree!"

"Where?" asked the child. "I don't see any lady."

"That's right, darling, you can't see her. But all the same, I ought to go over and pay my respects. It's such a terrible story, I wonder if you're too young to hear it." Already she had started walking buoyant as a cloud in her brown English shoes, towards a large, upright gravestone in the oldest part of the cemetery.

"No, I'm not too young," cried the boy, hurrying after her.

Ralph and the sexton stood in front of Ellen Buchel's grave, finishing up their business. Ralph knew the story about Dr. Anthony Gallant's lost lady; he had heard it several times from the doctor himself, and several more times, in increasingly elaborate versions, from Miss Alicia after her brother had died. A single time in his life, when he was already in his late forties, Dr. Gallant had found himself in love. The lady, a beautiful young widow who lived in Florida, without a relative left in the world, had been prevailed upon by Dr. Gallant to pack up her worldly goods in her automobile and follow the doctor back to Mountain City. He was to drive in front, up old Highway 1, she to follow safely behind him. In Dr. Anthony's tellings, it was never quite clear just what he was going to do with the lovely lady when he got her home. In Miss Alicia's versions, they were always to have married. Just before the Georgia line, the lady, perhaps because Dr. Gallant was driving too slowly for her taste, or perhaps just because she felt like having a bit of a high-spirited flirt with him, began passing him and waving gaily. Then, of course, he was obliged to pass her. They passed and repassed, until Dr. Gallant began to tire of the game, to become a little bit angry with her lack of restraint. This time, when passing her, he blew his horn and looked sternly over, motioning her to stop this frolic. But she had to have the last word, so to speak, and, blowing *her* horn, imitating his formidable frown, sailed past him one more time. A truck was coming, but she miscalculated the power of her automobile. She forgot she had it packed tight with her worldly goods. Since she had no people of her own left in the world, Dr. Gallant brought her body back to Mountain City and buried her in this cemetery when it was fairly new. He could not bury her over in Riverside, because his family's section there was all filled up, except for the places waiting for himself and Miss Alicia, and she certainly couldn't have either of those.

The sexton told Ralph he could pay by check or by credit card. Ralph gave him his MasterCard and stood waiting beside Ellen Buchel's grave and the space beside it where Theo would go. He heard the confident rise and fall of the old lady's voice as she and his grandson made their way to the lost lady's gravestone. Which of her versions was she telling him? What would she do when she came to the crash? Slide quickly past and get on to the cemetery? Or describe how Dr. Anthony had to wait around in that little Georgia town for two days, seeing to the gruesome details? Jason was not one for letting you skim past the gruesome details.

Neither had Theo been.

The sexton came back, making his way agilely down the grassy bank, weaving between the upright stones, with Ralph's yellow cardholder's duplicate sales slip fluttering from his hand. The spaces for two more bodies purchased. Next month, the MasterCard bill would join the others on the basement Ping-Pong table, but the sexton wouldn't have to worry, he would have been paid in full already.

In a way, Ralph hoped Miss Alicia would not be euphemistic

in her telling. But she would know best. She was wise in the ways of people. From what he knew of her—and, these past few years, she had been pretty much his best and only friend—he suspected she would not avoid details if the boy asked. Let the boy ask. Let him hear. Let him see pictures in his mind and remember later that these gruesome specifics belonged to the lives of other people as well, and that he wasn't some awful exception.

The florist got excited when he saw the leaves. "These are better than anything our supplier sends us," he exclaimed, rubbing a glossy leaf between his thumb and forefinger the way Ralph had seen Lily's mother finger wedding invitations, to determine whether they were engraved. "Just look at this texture. They're going to make a perfect backdrop for those colored leaves and the spider mums."

Miss Alicia, cocking her head judiciously at the effusive florist, said, "They are all handpicked."

They stopped for lunch at the Red Lobster because Jason liked the popcorn shrimp there. Ralph phoned the house to see how Lily was getting along. Freddy Stratton answered from the kitchen. "She's in there with two ladies who have talked too much and stayed too long," said Freddy in a confidential undertone. "I'm fixing to go in and give them the nudge as soon as we hang up. Then Clare and I are going to make her eat something. Did you get the plot you wanted?" Freddy had arrived at the house at nine o'clock that morning. She stepped out of her car looking as fresh as the flowers she brought with her, "handpicked," as Miss Alicia would have said, with the dew from her garden still on them. Except for her hair, which was short and curly and tinted the color of an Irish setter, she was the same old Freddy who had caused the adolescent Clare so many hours of jealous anguish. Slim-hipped and satisfied with herself, she picked her way across the gravel with the sultry, mincing step Clare used to parody in anger and despair ("And they go for it, all the boys go for it, and it's so affected!"). She shook her bunch of flowers playfully at the dogs to distract them from attacking her white corduroy jeans. "I can stay here all day," she had told Ralph. "It was only my house-cleaning day, anyway. You go on out there and get your plot. Do you know what I gave Skip for his last birthday? You're going to laugh, but I gave us both plots. Our family ran out of room over in Riverside, so I went out to this little cemetery in the country,

near where my grandmother had her farm, and there's still lots
of room and lots of *trees*. Skip didn't like it one bit, when I gave
him the deed to our two plots, but I told him, 'I want to know
where *I'm* going.'" He had left the three women arranging
Freddy's flowers, Freddy amusing Lily and Clare with a story
about the time, during her senior year at St. Clothilde's ("long
after you had left, Clare"), when Mother Patton had sent her
home from a dance because her dress was too low in back. ("She
didn't send me home, exactly, but she sent over her little stooge,
Nanny Sawyer—the one who later became a nun—to tell me I
could stay if I let her pin a handkerchief across my back. I just
turned to my date and said, 'Let's go home and dance on my
porch.' And that's exactly what we went and did." "I don't
blame you," said Lily, animated by Freddy's presence. "I would
have done the exact same thing myself.")

After lunch, in the parking lot of the Red Lobster, Jason began
to whimper. "When are we going *home*?"

"Why don't you stretch out in the backseat?" suggested Miss
Alicia. "My brother was always a great believer in stretching
out after a big lunch. The Latin countries, he always said, were
so much more sensible in that respect."

"There's one more stop I'd like to make," Ralph told the old
lady as they started off again.

"You make as many as you like," she replied.

"You're sure you're not too hot in that suit?"

"I'm just fine, Ralph. That air-conditioning in the restaurant
cooled me down to the right temperature."

"I wish we had it for you in the car, but the damn thing's
leaking coolant. I've been meaning to get it fixed, but what
with one thing and another . . ."

"Will somebody tell me when Theo's coming back?" piped
the child's petulant voice from the backseat.

"Lord," murmured Alicia Gallant, "my heart is breaking for
him."

"Will it be today?" Jason persisted, kicking at his car seat,
which had been moved to one side so he could lie down.

"No, son," said Ralph.

"But I *want* him!" The child kicked viciously against the back
of Ralph's seat.

"I want him, too," said Ralph. He concentrated with his one
clear eye, which was not too clear at the moment, on the road
ahead. Out of the corner of his blurred one, he discerned the
shape of Miss Alicia, jerking her hat down sharply towards her

face. She turned away and looked out of the window on her side. He heard the snap and re-snap of her pocketbook. A whiff of lavender filled the car. She blew her nose twice into her handkerchief.

Mercifully, Jason was asleep by the time Ralph parked by a tree-shaded meter in front of the police station, which shared its building with the fire department. Awake, Jason would have raised holy hell if Ralph had tried to go in alone. This was one of Jason's favorite places. Theo was always taking him by to visit the firemen, who showed him how they slid down their pole when the alarm went off. Theo must have been taking him by the police station, too, judging from Jason's outburst at the St. Dunstan's Forest Security Building that morning. Theo had always been drawn to the rescue professions; he had carried a fully equipped first-aid kit in his car, and even had one of those blue flashers on his car in his late teens. Ever since he'd been a little boy he'd wanted to be a highway patrolman. Still wanted it, after they thought it was time he outgrew the notion. A highway patrolman was the nearest you could get to a knight in the modern world, he had said. Knights of the road, he called them to their faces, grinning, hanging around their headquarters, making friends with them. One of them, who'd almost killed himself in a car chase, lay for weeks in the hospital in a body cast, and Theo went to visit him almost every day after school. It was he, more than Ralph and Lily, who had talked Theo into trying college first. "You can always come over to us later," he said.

"This shouldn't take long," Ralph told Miss Alicia. "I want to have a word with that detective who came to the hospital yesterday." He felt in his pocket. "But I ought to leave you a couple of nickels so you can feed the meter if I'm delayed."

"You take your time, Ralph," said Miss Alicia, accepting the nickels. "I'm always glad of a chance to sit and watch the world go by."

He did not relish his task, but he had promised Lily. The whole thing about the man out on bail would probably sound farfetched to the detective. The desperate straw clutched by grieving parents. The idea had sounded that way to Ralph when Lily had first voiced it. But it could be true that the man had been in some way involved, and, if he was, time would be of the essence in the detective's investigation.

The last thing Ralph expected was to be told at the window that Detective Robbins was off duty that day.

"You mean he's out working on a case," Ralph corrected the girl. She was young, she probably didn't understand the difference between off duty and out in the field.

"No sir, this is his regular day off."

"I think that's hardly possible," said Ralph. "He was on a special case. That . . . accident out on Fairfield Road yesterday afternoon. Where the man and woman were shot."

"Oh, the homicide-suicide. You'll probably find the report on that down the hall, in the Records Department."

"The *report?* Already?"

"Uh-huh. It should be in the files." From the way she almost smiled at him, he realized she thought he was praising the efficiency of the department.

He thanked her and went down the hall to the Records Department. An older woman, with a great many moles on her face and arms, manned its window. He tried not to look at the moles, some of which were as large as grapes; he felt she might hold it against him and not help him. "I was told I could find a report here. On the shooting yesterday of that young man and woman."

"What was the name on the one you wanted to see?"

"Theodore Quick, for the young man. And Jeanette Harris for the woman. But couldn't I see both of them?"

"You can see as many as you like. These are public records. But you said *report.* You would like to see the two reports, then?"

"Please, ma'am." Hideous bitch. Still, he did not look directly at the brown grapes that clung to her cheeks and neck, and the sides of her nose, and her arms. She wore a thin wedding band. Some man had to look at those moles across the dinner table every night. Perhaps do more than that. Why didn't she go to the doctor and have them removed? Maybe she hadn't realized how big or how many they were. Or maybe she liked them because they intimidated people.

He stood next to an open window, his back to the woman, scanning the reports. Little bits of information rose up off the pages and struck him in unexpected ways. The girl's middle name had been Corinne—a beautiful name, he'd always thought. Jeanette Corinne Harris. Some French antecedents, no doubt. He had seen her only a couple of times, when she'd brought her child up to the house to play in the pool with Jason. A tall, full-figured woman, blond, with one of those healthy, unsecretive faces. Good teeth, frank eyes, lots of bustle and energy as she played in the pool with Theo and the two boys. The very opposite of languid, pale Snow, with her impossibly small waist and furtive lavender eyes. Had Theo loved this unseductive, buxom nurse (Ralph was surprised to see, on the report, that she was only twenty-three) so desperately that he had been capable of shooting her for not loving him? Ralph hadn't really taken her seriously, figuring she was Theo's antidote to the five years with sly, ungiving Snow. Ralph had merely waved across at them in the pool, not stopping to be introduced, and gone off in his truck. But last night, when he and Lily had sat up talking, Lily had told him that Theo had been thinking of marrying Jeanette, that one night after Jason was asleep, she had found Theo in the living room, making out a little budget for them on his accounting paper. ("He showed it to me. It had everything on it. Rent, electricity, telephone, food, day-care center . . .")

There was a roughly drawn diagram of how the car, travelling east on Fairfield Road (that meant they had been returning to Jeanette's house, in her car, with Theo driving), had skidded and then stopped directly in line with a utility pole, in front of a house. The people who lived in the house heard the skid, then what they thought was a loud blowout, and had gone out to look, seen the bloody occupants in the front seat and the little boy crying in the back. The car engine was still running. They called the police and the ambulance. The ambulance team worked on the victims for almost an hour before transferring them to the emergency room. ("Brought to E.R. flaccid, no pupil response—brain-dead.") The investigating officer, who was taking his normal day off today, had found only one of the shells from the gun inside the car. Where were the others, then? There should have been three of them. Two for her, for Jeanette, and one for him. The gun was described accurately: a handgun, .25 caliber, "old Belgian semiautomatic, 5″ barrel," but Detective Robbins, who had seen fit to go on and take his day off today, had listed it as the property of "Alfred Quick, father of Theodore Quick."

How the hell had he come up with *Alfred?* Ralph, Alfred. Maybe the two names sounded similar when there was a lot of confusion going on. But the man should have checked, goddamnit. This was a report. There shouldn't be confusion in a report.

With rising indignation, Ralph read over Theo's report again. And found his age listed as twenty. Twenty! Had the detective been so eager to get to his day off that he couldn't even be bothered to look at Theo's driver's license. Twenty! Alfred Quick! What else, then? "Suicide" had a check in the box beside it, under "manner of death." (On Jeanette's report, the "homicide" box was checked.)

Just like that, then. Looks like a typical homicide-suicide, looks like a twenty-year-old male, father's name sounds like Alfred Quick. Scribble it all down any which way and take the next day off.

"Hey," the woman with the moles called after him, "those reports aren't supposed to leave this room!"

But he was already back up the hall, at the front counter window. "Look here," he said to the girl on duty (why the hell didn't they have a desk sergeant on duty, the way they used to? The whole world, it seemed, was being run now by little girls who didn't know anything and didn't want to learn), "look here, I want to see somebody. I want to see somebody in charge." His voice was shaking. "You go and get that Detective Robbins's superior. And don't tell me *he* is taking the day off."

"No, sir. The detective sergeant's here. Just a minute." She picked up the phone calmly. Didn't anyone have emotions anymore? His anger hadn't even fazed her. "Detective Sergeant McFall will be right out," she said.

McFall. Could that be his old buddy Mark McFall? Used to have the beat over in Niggertown, when people still called it by that name. Whenever his stonemason would get blind drunk and go on a cutting rampage with his razor, McFall would always phone Ralph as soon as he'd thrown old Ed in the drunk tank. That way, Ralph could be downtown with the bail money the first thing next morning, Ed would have had time to sleep it off, and Ralph could get maybe a half day's work out of him.

The mole woman came panting up the hall. "Didn't you hear me? I said the reports were not to go out of that room. I could have you arrested for —"

"It's all right, Mrs. Darlington. I'll take care of this."

It was his old buddy McFall. Filled out some, and with three stripes on his sleeve. "Come on in my office, Ralph."

"But he's got two of my reports, Sergeant."

"I'll see that you get them back unharmed, Mrs. Darlington."

When he had closed the door to his air-conditioned office behind them, McFall said, "She's a real guard dog about those reports."

He asked Ralph to sit down. "First, let me say how sorry I am about your boy. It was a bad business." He ambled around to his side of the desk, sat down, and handed Ralph a framed color photo of two ordinary-looking children, a boy and a girl, flanking a pretty woman with her hair piled too high on top of her head. "I've branched out myself, since we last met," he said. "Kevin's six, Anna's nine. Anna wasn't even born yet when old Ed was still the cutting terror of Valley Street. He's been dead about ten years now, hasn't he?"

"You've got a good memory," said Ralph, sitting forward with the reports dangling from his fingers.

"I guess you had a hard time replacing him."

"He couldn't be replaced. Nobody does work like that anymore, Mark. Honest to Christ, it seems to me nobody gives a damn about anything they do. My son's report here"—he slapped the paper with the back of his hand—"has got about as many mistakes in it as . . . as that Mrs. Darlington has moles."

The detective sergeant could not restrain an appreciative snort of laughter at Ralph's comparison. Then he got serious. "What kind of mistakes, Ralph?"

"Look for yourself. First off, it has his age down as twenty. Now, there's a hell of a lot of difference between twenty and twenty-eight."

"Your oldest son was already twenty-eight," mused the detective sergeant. "Time really does fly, doesn't it? We'll get that corrected, Ralph. This is only the preliminary report. We've got to have something in the files or the media would drive us all crazy. What else? You said there was more."

"Hell, he's got my name down as Alfred Quick. I don't know how he made Alfred out of Ralph."

"Hmm. Good question. You two met over the E.R., right? He went there to ask you about the gun."

"My Belgian gun, right." Ralph wanted to ask if he would ever get the gun back, but thought it would be wrong on this occasion.

"Could have been that it was so noisy there that he misheard your Christian name."

"I thought along those lines myself, but . . . damn it, Mark, this is a report. Not an approximation of a report. And then he goes on his day off today. I just have a hard time understanding the logic of that."

The detective sergeant made a steeple with the tips of his fingers and looked levelly at Ralph above them. "There wasn't a whole hell of a lot more to be done," he said gently. "There they were. Two bullets in her head, fired from a distance of several feet. One in his, fired close range to contact, aimed at just the right place, as if he sure knew exactly what he was about —"

"But listen," Ralph interrupted, "the reason I came over here . . . before I got distracted by hearing the detective was off duty, and then seeing these misinformed *reports* —"

"What else is wrong? Did you find more mistakes?"

"Well, Mark, the biggest mistake of all might be that fast checkmark in the box next to 'suicide.' I may have some information for you that will turn this case on its ear."

"I'd better hear it, then." The detective sergeant leaned back in his chair.

As Ralph related the story about the Man on Bail—how Theo had come to him several weeks ago and asked to borrow his Belgian Browning because "someone in Jeanette's situation is just going to feel more comfortable with an automatic"—McFall took some notes on a pad. "My son preferred a revolver, himself," Ralph added, encouraged. "He always used a revolver when we went target-practicing. He said the pause was cleaner between shots."

"That's an interesting way of putting it," said the detective sergeant. His pencil was poised above the pad. "Look," he said, "I'll mention this to the D.A. When does this man's trial come up?"

"Pretty soon. It may even be this week," said Ralph. "So you see, he would have benefited more than anyone from having her out of the way. Now there's nobody to testify against him."

"True," said McFall, "but don't you think he'd have had a pretty hard time getting in and out of there without anybody seeing him? The people in the house were outside within seconds of the noise. There was no one else around. No cars, even. It was a quiet road on a Sunday."

Ralph could see the skepticism in the other man's face. His voice had grown progressively gentler, the way people—smart people in authority—talk to sick or crazy people who might cause them trouble.

"I know it's a long shot, Mark. But if you were in my position . . . if it was Kevin . . . you'd want to grab at any lead you had —" He stopped. It sounded, even to him, as though he was undermining his own argument. Desperation made him add, "Hell, my wife and I . . . we even considered the possibility that the child . . . you know, the woman's child was in the backseat. He might have seen the gun lying there and thought it was a toy and picked it up and gone 'Bang, bang.' Has anyone talked to the child yet? If that Robbins hadn't taken the day off, he might have found something out from that child."

"Detective Robbins did talk to the child," said McFall, his voice growing a little colder. "He did yesterday. The child was upset, he didn't know what he saw, and his father was upset. To put it mildly. Even when you're separated, it can't be fun to see the mother of your child with her brains blown out. Look here, Ralph. You and I go back a ways. I'll tell the D.A. about this because it's his business to know, but frankly, looking at things from our side, it's a pretty wild notion. But the case isn't closed yet. As I said, this is only a preliminary report. Robbins went on and had his day off because I told him to have it off. There wasn't any more to be done. I'm going to call him at home and tell him what you've told me, and I'm sure he'll be on it first thing tomorrow morning. He knows his procedure. And we'll take care of those little mistakes about your name and your son's age. Twenty-eight." He shook his head. "It doesn't seem possible. That little tyke who used to ride around with you in your truck . . ."

He blessed Miss Alicia for her tact as he drove her home. Any other woman would have asked, "Well, what happened in there? Did you see your detective? What did you say to him? What did he say?" She just sat there, anchored straight as a plumbline to her own deep certainty of what was most comfortable for any occasion. And Lily professed not to understand why he had turned down a chance to "restore" an old house, full of dry rot, so that he could drive Miss Alicia leisurely to New England for her eighty-fifth birthday, because he had heard her say wistfully once that she would like to hear the Boston Pops before she died.

He felt bruised in his ego and his manhood by the encounter

with McFall. He had failed both in presenting his son's case effectively and in holding on to the detective sergeant's respect. His son's case. What case? He blamed Lily for egging him on in this wild-goose chase. He amazed himself in the middle of the awful thought that it would have been so much easier if there had been no man on bail. Or, for that matter, no Jeanette and no child in the backseat. Why couldn't Theo, if that's what he had to do ("aimed at just the right place," McFall had said, "as if he sure knew exactly what he was about"), have just gone up in the woods with his own revolver and aimed at the right place? As he drove Miss Alicia home, through the streets he had known all his life, he realized he was angry with Theo for leaving him with all these loose ends.

A twelve-year-old Pontiac that Ralph himself had purchased, on Miss Alicia's behalf, for her maid, and had spray-painted a cherry-red, was parked in Miss Alicia's driveway.

"But Susie was just here on Friday," he said.

"She saw the news last night and called me," said Alicia Gallant. "She wanted to come over and use my skillets to make your family some of her special fried chicken. I expect it'll be done by now and you can take it on home. She would have been hurt if I hadn't let her do something."

As Ralph drove back to his hill, the platter of fried chicken, wrapped in silver foil, on the front seat beside him, Jason asleep in the back, the obscure ache occasioned by Miss Alicia's story about her triumph over the streetcar conductor uncoiled itself and became a clear and perfect recollection.

Every spring, when Ralph was a boy, his father and a few cronies would take off for Santeetlah Lake, up in the gorge country of Graham County. They rented a cabin on the lake and took a Negro man with them to clean and cook the fish they caught. Every year they took a different cook with them, no Negro would go twice, and Ralph hadn't understood the reason why his father and the other men laughed about this until the year he was ten and his father said he was old enough to go along. That year it was his father's turn to take the Negro, who rode in the back of their truck. Before they reached Cherokee, it started to rain. The Negro, whose name was Ben, hunched forward stoically. The rain began to fall harder, so hard that Ralph, turning his head to look through the back window, could see the drops ricochet like large silver marbles off the shoulders of the man's sodden shirt and off his bullet-shaped, kinky head. It seemed strange to Ralph that the Negro had taken off his baseball cap, but after thinking about it for a minute it dawned on him that he valued the cap and wanted to protect it from the rain.

"What you keep on looking at back there?" his father asked.

"At Ben. I mean, he's getting so wet. Shouldn't we . . . stop or something?" He knew, and accepted the fact, that you didn't ever ask them to ride beside you in a vehicle.

"You just turn your head on round where it belongs and stop worrying," said his father gently. "They don't feel the rain like we do."

At the end of the fishing trip, when they broke camp, the Negro, who had spoken hardly a word the whole week, climbed into the back of the truck and settled himself in for the long ride home.

"That's right, you get comfortable back there, Ben," said Ralph's father, exchanging significant glances with his cronies, who were gathered around their trucks and cars, packed for leaving. "We just have one stop to make, at the courthouse, and then we'll be on our way home." Ralph heard one of the men snicker.

His father's truck led the convoy away from the shimmering morning lake, where Ralph had been treated like a friend and an equal by these men for the first time in his life, and into the sleepy little country town. Everybody parked in a row in front of the old brick courthouse.

"Wait here, son," said Ralph's father. "I got a little business to take care of." Then he winked at his son. "We're going to have ourselves some fun, like we do every year."

Ralph watched his father saunter confidently into the courthouse, hands in his pockets. One by one, his father's friends climbed slowly out of their vehicles, stretching themselves ostentatiously and cutting mirthful glances towards the back of the truck where Ben sat quietly, almost in a doze, his baseball cap tipped forward over his eyes. It was going to be a hot day's riding in full sunshine, but at least, Ralph thought, it wouldn't be raining on Ben.

His father came back with a large man wearing a big silver star on his chest and hip holsters with pistols. Both men were chortling, but when they got closer to the truck they adopted a serious demeanor.

"This here's my boy, Sheriff. Ralph Junior. He come up with us this year. It's his first time."

The sheriff stuck a beefy hand into the cab and shook Ralph's hand and asked him what was the biggest fish he had caught. Ralph, feeling important, was telling him about the fifteen-inch trout and how he'd almost lost it, when the man suddenly seemed to lose interest. His eyes narrowed to slits and he looked hard at the back of their truck.

"Lord God, Mr. Quick, please tell me my eyes are deceiving me. Please tell me I'm not seeing what I think I'm seeing in the back of your truck."

"There ain't nothing wrong with the back of my truck that I know of, Sheriff," said Ralph's father in a surprised voice.

"I didn't say there was something wrong *with* it, Mr. Quick. I'm saying there's something wrong *in* it."

"I don't rightly follow your meaning, Sheriff," replied Ralph's father, with a puzzled look on his face.

"Look here, fella," said the sheriff gruffly, and Ralph watched anxiously as the big man took his father by the elbow and led him a few feet away from the truck. "Didn't you know about the law we passed in Graham County?" he heard the sheriff ask his father in an undertone.

"What law is that?" asked his father innocently.

"The one about niggers," said the sheriff, still in an undertone, but loud enough, Ralph was sure, for Ben to hear. Ralph began to be afraid. Then he noticed that his father's cronies, glancing at one another with barely suppressed glee, had drifted closer to the truck, and his fear was replaced by complex emotions of a vastly more troubling nature.

"Didn't you know we don't allow no niggers in Graham County?" the sheriff was saying, incredulous now, not even bothering to keep his voice down anymore. "Lord God, I can't believe you boys was up here for a whole week fishing and not knowing about that law. We had to pass it for their own good. A nigger's life isn't worth diddley-squat once he crosses our county line. We got folks up here so mean they shoot 'em like rabbits or squirrels. As recently as three weeks ago, one tried to sneak through in the back of a logger's truck. The fella that was driving the truck said he heard a shot ring out when he was passing through the gorge, but he didn't pay it no mind because people are always shooting around up there. But when he got over the line into Tennessee, he stopped for a cup of coffee and happened to notice some of his logs weren't laying exactly right, and when he got up closer he found that poor nigger who'd been sneaking a ride, and his head was shot clean off."

"Lord, that's terrible," said Ralph's father. "That's a terrible story."

"I know it's terrible," the sheriff said. "That's why we had to pass the law. For their own safety. I just can't be responsible for the life of any nigger who's fool enough to enter Graham County."

"Well," said Ralph's father, "I'm going to try and get my nigger home as fast as I can, Sheriff. I didn't know about that law."

"Well," replied the sheriff, looking around at the other men, one of whom was bent double in a paroxysm of silent laughter, "I'm not going to fine you this time, Mr. Quick, but if I was you I'd tell him to keep his head down all the way, especially when you all go through the gorge."

Another of the men, who had kept an eye on Ben's reaction during Ralph's father's dialogue with the sheriff, pointed in silence to the back of their truck. Ralph turned around and looked through the rear window of the cab. Already the Negro had flattened himself against the truck bed. This time, Ralph noticed, he had left on his baseball cap. Rain was one thing, but bullets were another.

"Sure do 'preciate you fellas coming to say hello," the sheriff said, winking at Ralph. "You bring that young man back to see me again next year," he told Ralph's father. Swaying slightly from the heft of his pistols, he swaggered off towards the court-house, and all the men, waving and guffawing covertly to one another, got back in their cars and trucks and began the long trip home.

"What you so quiet for, son?" Ralph's father asked good-humoredly after they had driven in silence for about half an hour.

"I guess I don't feel too good," Ralph said.

"How come? You eat too many of Ben's hotcakes for break-fast?"

"No, sir, I just —"

"You just what?"

"I don't know. Nothing."

"Maybe the trip was too much for you. Your mother said you were still too young to go."

"Oh, no, *sir*."

"Well, then," said his father gently, "I expect you'll digest whatever it is that's sticking in there before too long."

And his father had begun to sing. He had a powerful baritone voice and people were always asking him to perform at weddings and parties. He had sung for the men every evening in front of the campfire, accompanying himself on the banjo.

> "On a hill far away
> Stood an old rugged cross
> The emblem of suffering and shame . . ."

Ralph had felt like a piece of wood cracking down the middle. He was pretty sure there was no such law. You could keep them from sitting beside you on the bus, but you couldn't keep them out of entire counties. Yet if he admitted the men had been cruel and wrong in "having themselves some fun," then he would have to acknowledge that his father was not a good man. Meanwhile, his father's appealing voice, gaining resonance and fervor in the second verse (for this was his favorite song), filled the cab with its rich, prepossessing sound.

> "And I love that old cross
> Where the dearest and best
> For a world of lost sinners was slain."

The Negro had lain face down, flat against the truck bed, all the way back to Mountain City. He wouldn't raise his head until Ralph's father drove him right up into his own dirt yard and his children came running out of the tar-paper shack and he heard their voices. He had climbed down, stony proud, but trembling visibly all over.

"Come on back with us again next year, Ben," Ralph's father called after him generously. "Don't pay no mind to that bigoted old sheriff."

The man did not turn around, just walked, with his children on either side of him, into the tar-paper shack.

On the way home, Ralph's father had laughed. "Didn't it beat everything, the way he hugged the bottom of that truck right down to the last minute? He's a hardworker, that Ben, but the one we took last year had more ginger in him. As soon as we got past Cherokee, he bounced up like a golliwog and ate himself a fish sandwich. I wouldn't mention any of this to your mother, if I was you."

"No, sir," said Ralph. After a few moments, he had added, "I wonder what the one we take next year will do."

My father and Miss Alicia Gallant, thought Ralph, adjusting his gears for the steep ascent of his hill, his private hill, were both born and raised in this town. If my father had lived, he would be almost Miss Alicia's age. They are of the same generation. My father would have stood on that streetcar rather than sit down by a Negro. He wouldn't have questioned it. He might even have gone to the conductor and had him make the Negro get up so he could sit down. And the law would have been on his side. Yet Miss Alicia, even as a young girl, had been so wondrously sure of her place in the world as to know she was a law unto herself and could sit down anywhere she wanted and come out smelling like a rose.

And there is the difference, thought Ralph. A difference I can never overcome, no matter how high a hill I build on or how much money I make. I come from people who were glad to have somebody between them and the bottom, from people who were too new to society to go about defying it or helping to change it. It's no good, my looking down on my father or pitying him for being what we now call a "racist redneck." He was just an ordinary man living squarely in the middle of his times and holding on to what he had and hating anything that threatened it from above or below. There is no cause to congratulate myself, or feel I've surpassed him because I treat all my construction crew the same, whether they're black or white, and because I don't balk at sitting down to the dinner table with Theo's black friend LeRoy: every middling member of society, which is what I am, does that now, because it's what everybody *does*.

Speaking of which . . . That was one more thing Ralph had to do before his long day was over: get word to LeRoy, who was still serving his sentence for armed robbery, that Theo was dead.

Lily did not view bodies. She hadn't even gone to see her own mother. So Ralph went down Quick's Hill around nine o'clock, after the guests had left and he and Lily had at last persuaded Jason to take off his clothes and put on pajamas and let Lily read to him. Clare and Rafe had gone to the funeral home earlier and were still not back. Probably gone for a drink at Gatsby's, Rafe's hangout when he was home.

Viewing the body of a loved one was not new to Ralph. He'd done it all his life. First his uncle Charlie, who had died under the anesthetic during a routine operation; then a friend in high school who'd driven off a bridge; then his mother's mother, that strange, yellow-skinned old woman who told stories of their Cherokee ancestors and whose occasional obscenities shocked everybody; then his father; then his mother.

He knew what to expect and did not find it barbaric or ghoulish to want to have one last look at the body of someone you loved, even though you knew their hands, if you touched them, would feel like hard wax, and that they would never have combed their hair quite that way themselves.

The parking lot at Moore's was full, and Ralph had to remind himself that other viewings besides his son's were in progress. Moore's was an old establishment. The large viewing room, just to the right of the entrance—the room Lily's mother had been in—had a flag-draped casket with an old man inside who looked at least a hundred. Several family members, some of them in their teens, were sitting at a respectful distance in metal chairs, gazing at the white-bearded profile with a dutiful blankness.

The door to Moore's office was shut, which meant he was engaged in business. Ralph was glad to slip by unobserved. He could find his way to Theo alone; it would be more like a stolen meeting between the two of them. As Ralph passed the funeral director's closed door, he heard agitated voices, the twangy protests of mountain people, all trying to speak at the same time. It surprised him. Moore was just not the kind of man you would need to raise your voice at. But grief did strange things to people, affected individuals in different ways.

Theo's room was to the rear of the building, its windows facing Pisgah. That was nice; Theo liked sunsets. If Ralph had been able to get away earlier and come here, he could have watched the sunset beside Theo's body.

He saw the magnolia leaves first. You couldn't miss them. A blanket of them, piled high and dark and glossy upon the entire lower half of the casket. The florist had been right, they made an impressive backdrop for the lemon-colored spider mums and the colored leaves.

He hadn't realized his son had been so handsome. Why was that? Was it the more formal way they'd combed his hair, parted on the side and revealing his high forehead? He looked older this way, more his real age. But it was something else, something

about the composure of the face. You could appreciate the
features. The fine, big nose, high-bridged and hawklike, the
legacy of an Indian ancestor, but with Ellen Buchel's arrogant
nostrils. The long, almond shapes of the eyes. Or eyelids, rather.
(Though you couldn't tell the eyes were gone, the way Moore
had fixed them.) The full, sensitive mouth. Maybe all these were
noticeable because so much of the time Theo had had his face
screwed up in some joke of a face, or been tormented by suc-
cessive jumbles of emotions. Now it was just . . . his face, as it
had been born to be in some better existence. As it might have
become, had he lived long enough to gain more confidence in
his powers, and to discover where those powers lay.

Ralph felt he was looking on Theo as a man for the first time.
And damnit, son, you were a fine-looking man. What were you always
in such a turmoil for? What made your life so unbearable?

And the large, beautiful hands.

He'd had nice feet, too. Both the boys had nice feet. Clare
and Lily were always saying it was so unfair for men to have
such beautiful feet.

Of course he could not see Theo's feet. They were below the
closed part of the casket, under the wood and its bank of
magnolia leaves. Undertakers never asked you to bring over
shoes and socks, which meant Theo's feet were white and bare.

*That summer, Ralph had worked with the men on Hannah's attic study
in St. Dunstan's Forest until they'd extended the rafters on the south side
for the raised roof, cutting out the old rafters on the north side and framing
the dormer with its complicated angled rafters. That was the kind of work
he never left unsupervised if he could possibly help it. Then he left Theo
and his good carpenter on their own, to start putting in the two-by-eight
floor joists and to build the knee wall. He was digging the foundation for
a house across town, plus replacing the slate roof on the Presbyterian
church, and he couldn't be everywhere at once. So he got into the habit of
stopping by Hannah's around four-thirty, checking on the progress of the
work, then hanging around to say hello when she got home. Already he
knew he was in love—that hadn't taken long—but he was still hoping
that if he conducted himself with scrupulous care he might love her, maybe
even let her know that he loved her, but not deceive Lily with his body.
That part was important to him. He was still in love with the ideal of his
long physical faithfulness to his wife.*

*They were putting in the floor joists the day it all shifted. He'd stopped
by as usual, around four-thirty, only to have Theo climb down the ladder
and approach him with woeful smirk. "I'm afraid that I played hell today,*

Dad, but Grantly helped me patch it. She'll never know if we don't tell her."

By the time Hannah got back from the hospital—he never stopped feeling that little catch in his chest when he saw her in her white doctor's coat—he had pretty much set things to rights in her bedroom: Theo had carelessly stepped through the Sheetrock ceiling. He and Grantly had patched the ceiling and painted it over so you could hardly notice, but they had neglected to clean off the rug and the dresser, where a thin layer of telltale white dust had sifted down upon Hannah's family pictures and her perfume bottles. Ralph had just put away her vacuum cleaner when she arrived. He took her to the room himself and explained what had happened. Theo and Grantly continued to hammer away upstairs, working late to compensate for the time lost cleaning up Theo's mishap.

Ralph showed her the patched-over ceiling. "I wanted to point this out to you before you were lying in bed and suddenly wondered what the hell had happened to your ceiling. We'll fix it up better when we do the other paintwork."

She had shown the most concern for Theo. "Poor boy. It must be so easy to slip. But didn't it hurt his foot?" He had explained that Sheetrock isn't very strong. "Truly? Why don't you build with something stronger, then?" He had explained that they did build with stronger Sheetrock now—he himself always used five-eighths-inch, but whoever built this house had got by with the old three-eighths-inch. Nothing, he said, could beat the plaster and wood lath. In the old days, he went on, knowing they were doing more than just discussing ceilings now, what made the wood lath so strong was that people mixed the hairs of their horses and dogs into it.

Then, suddenly, she was climbing up on her bed, using his shoulder to steady herself. "I am so curious about these things," she said, standing on her bed and poking a finger experimentally at her ceiling. "Yes, you are right. It is not very strong." She knocked it with her fist. "Yes, you are right. Do you hear how hollow it is sounding?"

He reached out an arm to help her down from the bed. She was smiling, her head cocked, an unspoken question in the blue-gray eyes. He realized that she had stood on the bed because she wanted an excuse to touch him. She saw him realize it. It was then that he would have taken her in his arms for the first time, had Theo's foot not come crashing through the Sheetrock, in almost the identical spot as before, the second time that day. "Oh shit!" came the agonized wail from above them. "He's going to kill me for this!"

Ralph bowed his head above his son's face. He reached out, preparing for the cold, waxen touch, and covered Theo's hand—

the one that lay on top of the other in repose—with his own. He wished he could touch the feet one more time, those feet that would never again see daylight.

"Mr. Quick? Excuse me, I'm so sorry. But it seems we've got a problem."

Ralph, deep in his grief, hadn't heard the funeral director come up behind him. The dignified man seemed shaken. "Would you mind stepping into my office just a minute?"

Ralph, not even trying to imagine what further unwelcome surprises this day could spring on him, followed Moore to his office.

For a minute he couldn't understand why he had been summoned to meet such an ill-looking set of people, no doubt the very ones he had heard squabbling as he passed Moore's closed door.

Then he heard himself addressed by a familiar voice. When he swiveled his good eye to the right, his diminutive daughter-in-law materialized before him in all her sharp, purple-eyed fury. She had seated herself at the funeral director's desk, and her indignant, unrestrained voice, he realized, was the one he'd heard rising above the others as he passed Moore's closed door earlier. Now she was laying down the law to him and Moore.

Moore stood beside him, distressed almost beyond bearing that this scene should be occurring in his hallowed place of business, and Ralph, too, remained frozen and without speech while Snow, surrounded by whatever members of her clan she had been able to gather on such short notice (he recognized one brother, who had been at Jason's christening, and the sister who had married the boy with the welding shop in Mountain City, and the boy himself, a red-fisted giant of a hillbilly who looked as if he'd love to start punching somebody), screamed at him that Theo was not going to be buried in that goddamned pin-striped suit, he had hated it; and he was not having any funeral in that snob church; and that as soon as Theo was in the ground where *she* chose to put him, Ralph and Lily Quick had better have Jason's things packed because she was leaving town with him. "He is my child," she concluded triumphantly. "And whether you all like it or not, I am still Theo's wife."

By that time, Moore had collected himself enough to say with his customary quiet dignity, "Excuse me, young woman, you mean you are his widow."

Ralph Quick, twenty-two, who served with the 101st Airborne Division, is working for Reynolds Construction and going to night school at Mountain City Tech for engineering courses. "What I'd like ideally," he says, "is to have my own construction company one day. I'm the kind of person who works best for myself. And of course I hope to meet my ideal woman and marry her and maybe have a couple of nice kids, and, when I've made my pile, build us all a dream house on top of a mountain with a view of the town where I was born and raised."

—*from* "What's Happening to Our GIs Now: Their Dreams and Plans," a feature article by staff reporter Lily B. Campion in *The Mountain City Citizen,* September 19, 1948

V: BETRAYALS

"*T*halia, I've missed you."

"I missed you, too, Lily, honey. Not an hour went by this past week that I wasn't praying for you."

"I need to be in somebody's prayers. I've been so busy hating that girl for all the trouble she's caused us that I haven't even had time to mourn Theo. And I hate her all the more for that."

"She sure didn't do right, making that scene at the funeral home."

"Do you know, the funeral director, Mr. Moore, was so scared her family might sue him that he told Ralph he couldn't go ahead with the funeral until Ralph saw his lawyer. And so, on top of everything else Ralph had to do, he had to meet Mr. Moore's lawyer at eight in the morning. Of course, as soon as he showed the man Theo's separation papers, where she had relinquished custody of her own child and everything, the lawyer said it was okay, we could go ahead. But he advised Ralph to give in to her about riding in the head car to the church. Oh, she was big on that. That's the sort of thing that's important to the Mullinses. I gave up my place so that she could have her *ride* in Moore's big blue limousine. Rafe and I rode to the church and cemetery in his car. But the most disgraceful thing . . . well, you saw it, didn't you, Thalia? Parked right smack in front of the church where everybody could see it?"

"I'm not sure what you mean, honey. You're not talking about the limousine now, are you?"

"No. *Their* . . . conveyance. Or 'vehicle,' as they would call it. I don't see how you could have missed it. That awful black *van*? It actually had a picture of a naked man painted on it, a naked man running, and the word 'streaker' painted underneath him."

"Lord, you don't mean it."

"I don't see how you could have missed it. They pulled up right in front of the walkway, where anybody going into the church had to see them. And when they began piling out, it was like one of those movie cartoons. You know, the ones where too many animals suddenly come out of a small house or truck or something and that's why it's funny: because you *know* there are too many. Only it wasn't very funny last Tuesday, all those Mullinses clambering out of that van with their weasel faces, looking like they were on their way to a free barbecue. . . . Oh, help me, Thalia, I know I'm being awful, I can't help myself, but they ruined Theo's funeral."

"Okay, honey, I'm going to help you. First thing, nobody ruined that funeral. It was a beautiful funeral. I never saw a church so packed. All your friends were there, and Theo's friends, and the three ministers. And the picture on that black van couldn't have been very big or I would have noticed it. Now that I think of it, I did notice a black van, but I didn't see no picture of a naked man on it, and I didn't pay all that much attention to any people with faces like weasels climbing out of it. So they must have blended right in. Second thing is, I want you to take everything out of that head of yours and hand it over to me for an hour."

"Gladly. Take it all, Thalia. Only be careful you don't get scalded from the acid or defiled by the pitch."

The masseuse chuckled low in her throat. "You're too much," she crooned in the teasing tone, bordering on a scold, that she permitted herself to use on Lily in the darkness of this room, the room that had served as a sort of incubator for their delicate friendship. "Too much," she repeated lyrically, as though she might burst into song, which she often did when they were alone in here. She would try out on Lily whatever she was going to sing in church the next Sunday. ("I'm going to stay on the battlefield . . .": her voice, rich and dark and strong, had its own built-in beats and counterpoints, so that, when she really got going, she seemed to be providing her own accompaniment.)

Lying face down on the table, the warm sheet over her naked body, Lily listened to Thalia move softly away on foam-rubber soles to the counter, lit by a single rod of blue light, where she kept her mysterious unguents in their unmarked jars. Substances that smelled of eucalyptus or almonds or cool, rotting moss: oils or salves that could make you tingle or dissolve or simply fall asleep, as Lily had done once or twice on this table. She heard Thalia running water hard into the sink, smelled and felt the steam rise. Ah, she was getting the hot towels today, a special treat of Thalia's when she decided you needed something extra.

Well, I need something extra, my son is dead.

The words, incredible and still impersonal, even after ten days, produced the predictable gush of wetness from the corner of each eye. It was quickly absorbed into the sheet beneath her. These easy, mechanical tears never lasted long because she repudiated them as soon as they surged. They derived, she believed, from the shallower source of self-pity, from what people expected of her, rather than from the real grief that lodged deeper down in the bedrock hollows of a place in herself she had yet to explore. "Why doesn't she go ahead and break down?" She had heard many people muttering this and similar sentiments outside doors, across rooms (but always, somehow, just within her hearing). "She needs to let go. She can't keep up this brave façade." Brave? Was that what they called it? Did they really believe grief was a soft, warm "letting-go"? So many words had turned completely around for her, into their exact opposites, had become parodies of themselves, these past ten days. Words like "love," "mother," "family," "grief." Even . . . God forgive her . . . "God." Coming out of the church after the funeral, she had shocked a woman—the mother of one of Theo's friends, she couldn't even remember her name—by saying, in reply to some well-meaning remark about how dangerous guns were, "Well, if guns don't kill you, families will." The woman had uttered a forced, nervous giggle, patted her on the arm, and, after urging Lily not to hesitate to phone if ever she needed to talk, walked swiftly away to her car.

No, when her grief came . . . but that, too, was putting things the wrong way around: when she came to her grief, it would be like keeping an appointment on a moonless night in a cold, deep lake. And she would have to steel herself (the very opposite of "letting go" or "breaking down") and strip to the bone and descend into its inhospitable element (how she hated cold water, and not knowing what was beneath her—she had always refused to swim in lakes), and the contact would be merciless. There would be no consolations or insulations between her and that dark swim. No hot towels or invigorating hatred of Mullinses to assuage the terrible realities that would come groaning and lapping around her ears and shrivel her heart.

Thalia tiptoed over, flung back the lower part of the sheet covering Lily, and slapped the hot towels down on her feet and calves. Lily uttered a cry of surprise—that was part of the deal, you were supposed to act surprised, it was Thalia's gift to you— and gave herself up to an absorbing review of Snow Mullins's latest outrages while the masseuse hummed and shaped the towels into a hot, wet cocoon around her legs and toes. Just summoning up the image of that contemptuous face will provide me with weeks' worth of insulation, Lily thought. I will *use* my anger to get me through the custody hearing, the appointments with the court psychiatrist—all the indignities of strangers poking and peering into my private life because this girl in her resentment of us has decided to use a three-year-old child as her weapon. Theo would not want me to "break down," as they insist on calling it. He would expect me to postpone my despair until his son is safe from the clutches of those people.

Her legs and feet swaddled in the hot towels, Lily felt like Thalia's baby. But though she had agreed to "hand over" all her thoughts for an hour, she couldn't stop the private movie from unfolding in her head while the masseuse kneaded the soft flesh of her shoulders. There was Snow with her cold, complacent face, playing at grief on the morning of the funeral as the funeral director (playing *his* part well out of fear of litigation) respectfully handed the bereaved young widow, in her dark satiny dress and spike heel sandals, into the limousine. Fifteen minutes earlier, the family had all been inside the house; they were running late, some of them still dressing, and Father Zachary was already waiting for them in the living room, when Rafe had cried furiously, "Here come the bastards!" and they had all gathered at a window to watch the odious black van chug victoriously up the final steep grade of Quick's Hill. It drew up close to Father Zachary's car, as though recognizing a friend among many enemies, and regurgitated Snow, followed by a phalanx of Mullinses of assorted ages and sizes. The parents were not among them—a small blessing. Lily had recognized one of the more presentable brothers, the one who had attended Jason's christening, and the older sister, Evelyn, whom Ralph liked because she had a real job and because she helped him keep tabs on Snow. The disembarked tribe huddled in a defiant knot beside the swimming pool, casting apprehensive glances towards the house. "My God, what is that painted on the side of that horrible van?" said Clare. "It looks like a naked man. There's something written underneath, but I can't see it without my glasses." "What a damn pity we shut up the dogs!" cried Rafe, still knotting his tie. "I'd like to go out there and lash every damn one of them to a tree and not let them go until the funeral's over."

"Darling," Lily had admonished him gently. But only because Father Zachary had come into the kitchen, whose window had afforded the best view of the arrival of the interlopers. The priest had been talking to the child in the living room, waiting for them all to finish dressing so he could lead them in a family prayer to get them in the right spirit for the funeral. Then Jason, following Father Zachary, had seen Snow through the window. "There's my momma!" he said incredulously. And bolted out the door before anybody could stop him. How could they stop him? Snow was his mother, after all. His "mother." "I'll just go out and speak to them for a moment," Father Zachary had said, and followed the child. And then *that* scene through the window: Jason running across the pale gravel to her, she stooping down and opening her arms, and all the Mullinses gloating over the great reunion between Mother and Child. And then Father Zachary striding over and taking in the whole clan with his giant embrace, like a huge, skinny, all-forgiving scarecrow in his loose-fitting black clothes. The hugging priest. Not like Father Weir, who left the hugging to his wife while he looked on, smiling distantly, reminding you by his musing forbearance that there were places in you that could never be solaced by the mere clasp of flesh upon flesh.

After Father Zachary had pacified the Mullinses, who had delivered their Princess Snow to Quick's Hill good and early so she would not be cheated out of her ride to the church in the limousine, the priest had returned to the house. "Jason's just fine out there for now," he told them. "I'd like to have you all together in the living room for the few minutes we have left." They had filed in obediently, Rafe still red-faced with outrage over the scene outside, Ralph in his dark-gray cashmere suit (Lily had to hand it to Hannah Ullstein, she had certainly instilled an awareness in Ralph about his clothes), and Clare in the new dark-plum dress with thin black stripes she had brought with her from New York. On Friday, the day before Lily's birthday, she and Clare had gone shopping and Clare had bought a pair of shoes that went perfectly with the new dress. But when she was getting ready for the funeral, she tried on the shoes and decided not to wear them. "They pinch," she had told Lily. "No use to be uncomfortable." "They look awfully nice, though," Lily had said. But Clare had put the new shoes, pretty oxblood-color heels with a shapely narrow toe, back in their box and strapped on the beige platform-soled sandals she had been wearing when she got off the plane. They were too light against her dark stockings and looked shabby with the new dress. "Ah, these feel much better," Clare had said, wiggling her toes. "Mmm," Lily had murmured noncommittally, thinking it wouldn't have killed Clare to suffer a little pinching on this day. What was it? A couple of dozen steps in and out of the church, a few dozen steps more across the soft cemetery grass.

When the family was seated in the living room, Father Zachary, standing with his back to the picture window, which looked out over mountains and town, began to speak. Telling them how a funeral was for the benefit of the living, how it was the celebration of a completed life. But Lily, discomfited by something not quite right in the room, somebody missing, had held up a hand to make him stop. "Wait," she had said, "where's Theo?" Even before the words were out of her mouth, she had realized her mistake. It was the first of those little disjunctures between the taken-for-granted past and the unbelievable present. Theo was always the tardy one at family meetings. She had even felt, as she was asking the question, a brief annoyance with her older son for being out of the room when Father Zachary had come here to talk specifically about him.

"Try and relax, Lily, honey. I might as well be massaging a telephone pole."

"I wish I were as thin as one."

"You don't any such thing. A telephone ain't got no *shape*."

Lily giggled, it simply erupted out of her, and Thalia, removing the cocoon of towels that had gone cold, joined in with her feisty, collusive chuckle. There were layers, thought Lily, beneath even their flip and superficial exchanges. That was because, at bottom, each was still courting the mysteries and potential dangers in the other. It was a new thing for both of them, this friendship, and they nourished it warily, with tender regard for sore spots and much studying of nuances, even as they bantered and teased. And there remained so much to learn! Thalia, for instance, Lily knew, was sometimes threatened by Lily's frequent resort to irony and dryness: to Thalia it implied a subtle criticism, signaled a sudden cooling off. Whereas Lily was still trying to pinpoint Thalia's motives for switching deliberately into her black idiom in the midst of a dialogue. Sometimes she seemed to do it to disarm Lily in order to make her listen; other times to deflect an adverse judgment of herself; and sometimes, Lily believed, she did it out of sheer wickedness, to punish Lily simply for being a member of the race that had brought her people so much indignity.

Yet it was Thalia who had made the first overture. A year ago, Lily had been lying on this table, Thalia doing the backs of her legs; she remembered it well. They'd been talking about education, and Thalia mentioned that her daughter, Claudine, had gone to Mountain City Catholic for her last two years of high school. "It cost more, but I'm sure glad we did it. My Claudine was always a good girl but when it came to studying she was no great shakes. But there was this nun there that sure did straighten her out. Lord, honey, Claudine would do anything for that woman, and, first thing you know, she was bringing home A's and B's." "What was the nun's name?" Lily had asked, believing she already knew. "Sister Patrick," said the masseuse, working her strong thumbs into Lily's calves. Sometimes, the day after a massage, Lily would notice green bruises the size of pennies dotted around the backs of her legs; once she had asked Thalia to go more gently, but the masseuse had replied, "Does *that* hurt, just that little bit of pressure? Then you ain't doing enough walking, honey." "Oh, Sister Patrick," Lily said. "Clare had her for the eighth grade. That's when she was principal of the grammar school at St. Clothilde's. She had the same effect on Clare, though Clare always liked to study." Then Lily had sighed, trying to remember the gossip surrounding Sister Patrick's transfer from St. Clothilde's to Mountain City Catholic. It had occurred sometime back in the

mid-sixties. One of the stories was that Sister Patrick had gone
to the Bishop and told him she was losing the battle against her
own arrogance and it would do her good to work with children
who were less privileged. Another story had it that the Bishop
himself, during that time of social ferment and upheaval, had
found himself under attack for favoring the "elitist" schools of
St. Clothilde's and the boys' division of La Fosse Hall at the
expense of the more integrated and less expensive Catholic High,
and had sacrificed Sister Patrick—possibly his best-educated and
most charismatic nun—to disprove the allegations. It would
have been interesting to relate the two stories to Thalia and
then discuss which, if either, was probably the truth. But Lily
had been afraid Thalia might be hurt or offended by the inferior
status cast on Mountain City Catholic by both stories. She was
about to end the conversation with something safe and neutral
from what Ralph called her "limitless fund of door-closing
niceties," to say something like "But education *is* so important,
isn't it? Aren't we thankful both our girls got such good foundations?" when Thalia ceased her rhythmic implanting of the
next day's little green bruises on Lily's leg, leaned down close to
Lily's ear, and asked in a confiding, mischief-making whisper,
"Tell me something, honey. Were you ever just the least little
bit *jealous* of that darling Sister Patrick?" A jolt of astonishment
had rippled through Lily as she lay face down on the table. For
a split second she heard her mother's voice warning, "Watch it,
that Thalia is getting too familiar." It was as if the black woman
had heard it, too, because she quickly added in her switched-on
dialect, "But that ain't none of my business, is it?" and resumed
her kneading with a vengeance. Lily did not answer for a
minute, letting herself be mauled in the tense silence. Thalia's
question had shocked her with its keen perception, but it also
had sliced through decades and brought Lily face-to-face with
that bewildering *molting* period of her life, which had lasted from
the time when, after two years of furtive courtship, she had given
in and married Ralph, until Clare's sullen, undercover escape
from them, seven years later: years during which Lily had
presided in a nightmarish languor over her gradual loss of power.
She had watched herself metamorphose from a woman used to
earning a living and making decisions for herself and others into
a female "dependent" in thrall to an increasing number of small,
debasing tyrannies that had succeeded at last in sapping all her
ambition to overcome them. "Yes, I guess I *was* jealous of Sister

Patrick," Lily heard herself admitting to the masseuse. When she had mastered her normal dry voice, she continued: "She was Clare's 'role model,' as they call it today, and I was pretty superfluous for several years. Not that I gave it a lot of thought at the time." She laughed curtly. "I mean, when you're pregnant and sick every morning, and then caring for a tiny baby and trying to please a husband and write a book, and then pregnant again, there isn't too much point in wasting precious energy worrying that your teenage daughter finds another woman more interesting than you." "That's the truth," Thalia had replied, "but it sure can hurt, all the same. I remember I'd be working afternoons in our store—that's after my husband had his first heart attack—and waiting for Claudine to come back from Catholic High and help out, and it got later and later, as that first year wore on. Then, about five or so, she'd saunter in—the school was near enough for her to walk—and she'd have this look in her eyes, so *cool*, you know, like she was already judging us and getting ready to leave us, and she'd open herself a Dr. Pepper and lean against the counter and say how she was so late because she'd waited for Sister Patrick to go to chapel and come back, so they could have a talk. And, honey, it was Sister Patrick this and Sister Patrick that right on till suppertime, and sometimes bed. 'Sister Patrick thinks I should start preparing for college, Sister Patrick thinks I should major in science,' and on and on. And I'd listen, but I'd get to feeling real low, though I didn't let on to Claudine. I'd think, I wish I had me some of that education. Then I wouldn't have to clean people's houses and be stuck in this store. But then I'd remind myself that it was the law of life. You work hard so your children can do better than you did. You get so far and then hope your child gets farther. Now turn over and let me do your front side."

Lily had raised herself to a sitting position on the table and faced the masseuse. They were on the same level, only Lily was naked and Thalia was wearing her starched white uniform. She picked up one of Thalia's strong brown hands, softened by the constant use of oils. She felt very close to this woman about ten years her junior; she felt almost weepy, if she had been the sort who cried easily. "But aren't we glad it worked out so well for them both?" she said. "I mean, Clare is a writer and your Claudine is a scientist. They are both successes at what they want to be doing. And you and I are proud of them." Words that could certainly qualify as what Ralph would call one of her door-closing niceties, but this time they had been meant as a door-opener, and Thalia understood this.

Several weeks later, when Lily was again on the table at the Health Club, Thalia had asked, "What ever happened to that book you were writing? The one while you were having those babies?" "Oh, that book. I put it away for a while after Clare went off to live with her father's people. And then when we were getting ready to move into our new house, I was cleaning out some old stuff and I found it and read a few pages and threw it out in disgust." "Now, why would you want to do a thing like that?" "Because I hated what I read. I couldn't stand it. All those self-consciously lovely words trying to cover up my lack of experience about anything true in the world." "I don't believe that, honey. You're being too hard on yourself." "No, I'm not, it was really embarrassing," persisted Lily vehemently, "all those hothouse-variety sentiments about people and things that never existed, that *couldn't* exist. Why, I wouldn't even want them to, though I must have thought I did when I wrote them." "Well, I don't care, I bet it was still good," said Thalia loyally. She had stepped over to the counter and opened one of her mystery jars and rubbed something between her hands. After massaging a few minutes, Thalia asked, "Would you ever come speak to my writing class? It would mean so much to us if you'd come. I've been getting up my nerve to ask you." "I didn't know you were in a writing class," said Lily, surprised. "Yes, honey. We meet once a week at the Adult Education Center. It's an accredited course, too. It counts towards my degree, if I decide to go on for one." "You mean you're thinking of getting a college degree, Thalia?" "Sure," said the masseuse. "Why not? Better than sitting around home moping. I got the time, what with my husband dead and my father in a nursing home. I want to make something of myself if I still can." "What would you want me to talk about at the writing class?" "Anything you want, honey. Anything from you would be of value to us."

So Lily had agreed to speak to Thalia's writing class at the Adult Education Center. She put a lot of thought into what she would say to them, and when she was dressing on the evening of the class, she realized she was nervous. She took off the tweed suit and Shetland sweater she had been going to wear and put on her more elegant forest-green Ultrasuede dress, with her late mother's sunburst-shaped diamond brooch pinned at the neck.

In this outfit she felt sleek, impervious, and more formidable. She had worn it the night she and Ralph had driven beyond the paved part of Spook's Branch Road to meet with Snow's parents and persuade them to talk their daughter out of marrying Theo. Not that the dress had done much good that night. Snow's father sat in the corner chewing something, and let Mrs. Mullins, who kept calling Lily "ma'am" and Ralph "sir," do all the negotiating. Ralph, who could be persuasive when he remembered to keep the preachiness out of his voice, had been low-key and respectful to the Mullinses as he presented his argument about how the two backgrounds would be incompatible. She had sat straight-backed on the edge of a chair upholstered in a horrible salmon-colored fake velvet and tried not to feel superior to Mrs. Mullins, with her slumped shoulders and sly mountain twang, in which she subsequently vanquished Lily. "Whatever Snow wants is all right with me, ma'am," she had whined, not daring to meet Lily's eyes, "and the two young people, they's purty well set on it." A month later, Snow and Theo were married.

Lily had expected there would be several other black people in Thalia's writing class, but she was surprised when she got there and found herself being introduced by the instructor to an entire roomful of black women. She was glad of her last-minute change to the Ultrasuede, because most of them had dressed for the occasion. Thalia wore a lavender suit with a matching high-necked silk blouse and a bunch of cloth violets pinned to her collar. The instructor, an elderly white man, earned Lily's immediate dislike by allying himself with her as a former journalist who had "published some," and then belittling the accomplishments of the class and telling her not to expect too much of them. It seemed he already had their act planned for the evening: they were to be a team of two educated white people, not above a bit of cavalier flirting and exchanging of compliments, who would perform together, noblesse oblige, a soft-shoe dance of literacy in front of these benighted blacks. But she also saw, after a very few minutes, that she would have to exercise considerable tact in eluding his plan because, though the majority of the women saw through him, they also respected him because he was their teacher. It would not do to put him down too obviously because he was all they had: he would be back next week and she would not. So, to get him to sit down and shut up, she defused his plan by disqualifying herself from his professional esteem. She began speaking directly to the women, making herself just another one of them, saying she had been so honored when her friend Thalia had asked her to speak to this class, but really, not to expect too much, because she hadn't written seriously for years and years. "What happened, you see, was, I was working as a reporter on the *Citizen*, back in the late forties, and one day I was assigned to do a feature story on local GIs, and I guess one of the men I interviewed liked what I wrote about him, because he kept after me for two years until I finally married him." The women laughed appreciatively, and the instructor drifted over to a classroom window and sat down on the edge of the radiator. By the time Lily finished telling them about her abandoned novel and the babies ("You have just so much energy . . ." "That's *right*, that's *right*," came back the chorus of women), the instructor had fixed a polite smile on his face and was looking out the window, beyond the cloying confines of what was obviously going to be a female "rap session." Then Lily quickly got down to business and said she wanted each of them to write something for her. "It can only be a page or so, because I want there to be time for me to read them all aloud and comment on them." "But what do you want us to write on?" asked a tall, skinny woman, very dark, with her gray hair done in corn rows. "I want you to give me one specific picture of something you have done," said Lily, "so that I can see some of the things you saw, and feel some of the things you felt. It doesn't have to be anything out of the ordinary, maybe just going shopping, or something that happened at work. But I want you to write it the way you saw and felt it, not the way you think you *ought* to have seen or felt it. I think, if I had it all to do over again, I'd know now that one sharp picture, in writing, about how I really perceived something, would be worth more to me and others than volumes of fancy prose on exalted topics." "Does it have to be something that happened recently?" asked the woman with the corn rows. "Oh, no," Lily said. "Just so it stands out in your memory. That's what's important."

That woman had written the piece that still stood out in Lily's memory. It was entitled, simply, "Shopping," and told about what it was like for a black girl in the forties and early fifties to buy clothes in Mountain City. "'We were not allowed to try anything on,'" Lily had read aloud from the woman's paper, trying to keep her voice steady and cool, "'so Momma just had to guess our sizes the best she could, and pray when we got them home they'd fit. You couldn't return things, either. In those days also there was no hose to match our legs, just this one mud-color brand they called Red Fox that they felt ought to suit us fine enough. So we bought Red Fox and took them on home and soaked them overnight in strong tea or leftover coffee, or both, depending on how dark we wanted to go.'"

"Now that," said Lily, when she had finished reading, "was exactly what I had in mind. You made me see things," she told the woman with the corn rows, "and know things I wouldn't have if I hadn't read this piece."

"Gladys, why didn't you ever write anything like that for me?" asked the instructor from his radiator seat.

"Because you never asked me," the woman replied, and the class broke into enthusiastic laughter.

After the writing class, Lily and Thalia had gone to the Adult Education Center's cafeteria for some tea and grilled-cheese sandwiches. It was Thalia's treat. "They all loved you, honey. I'm telling you the truth, it was the best class we ever had. I hope Gladys didn't offend you." "Offend me how?" asked Lily, puzzled. "Well, by what she wrote. I was worried you might have taken it personally. You know, as a kind of criticism." "Oh, no, not at all. I thought it was marvelous. It was one of the best pieces." It had been by far the best, but Lily hadn't wanted to hurt Thalia's feelings. Thalia's effort had been disappointing. She had described going to visit her father in the nursing home and had done exactly what Lily had warned against: written what she thought she should have seen and felt rather than what she actually did. As Lily had read the prosaic, euphemistic piece aloud to the class, trying to make her voice register mild approval for her friend's sake, she had pictured Thalia in her dark room at the Health Club, ministering hour after hour to fleshy white women who drawled on and on about the world as it never was and never would be. She is already being corrupted by us, Lily had thought.

But Gladys's "Shopping" had its lasting effect on Lily. A few months after the writing class, Lily had gone into a drugstore to buy a congratulations card for Thalia's Claudine, who had just had her first baby. After browsing among the possibilities for a few minutes, she became angry. She was just about to summon the druggist and say, "You need to update your stock. I've been looking for a card to send to a new mother and I can't find anything suitable." And when he apologized and asked her what she had in mind, she would say, "Why aren't there any cards with black babies on them?" But then she had realized that even if there had been such cards, she wouldn't have chosen one: Claudine might have been offended. And it had struck Lily for the first time what a no-win situation these people were still in because they had internalized white people's devaluations of them.

Lily woke to hear Thalia speaking softly with another woman outside the massage room. She was lying face up, with the sheet over her, and could not remember turning over. She must have fallen asleep less than halfway through her massage. She raised up to look at the big electric clock on the wall and saw to her embarrassment that she had slept into Thalia's next appointment. Why hadn't Thalia wakened her? Then it all came back. That was one of the worst aspects: losing consciousness and forgetting and then having to remember again. It would be better not to sleep, not to let down one's guard. Gathering the sheet around her, she slid off the high table and hastened, barefoot and blinking, into the brightly lit dressing room.

"There you are, honey," said Thalia cheerfully from behind her desk. "I owe you half a massage, but you look rested. Doesn't she, Mrs. Jamison?"

"You should have wakened me, Thalia." To the young woman patiently sitting across from Thalia with nothing but a towel wrapped around her, Lily said, "I'm so sorry I used up some of your time."

"Oh, that's all right, I don't mind," said the young woman, one of the newest members, to whom Lily always nodded pleasantly without feeling the necessity to learn her name. "I'm glad you were able to rest." Then her face lost its bland composure and she blurted, "I can't tell you how sorry I am about—we read it in the paper —"

Lily acknowledged her speech with a grave nod, holding herself aloof as a Roman matron in her sheet.

"What you going to do today, honey?" Thalia quickly put in.

"Well, as soon as I make myself presentable," said Lily, "I think I'll go and visit a few of my old ladies. I had to neglect them this past week, and I don't want them to worry I've forgotten them."

"Bless you, darling. If you go by Hickory Haven, just poke

your head into my daddy's room and say I'll be there on Thursday. Just like always."

"I certainly will," said Lily. "Enjoy your massage," she added cordially to Mrs. Jamison. Then she went to her locker and got her makeup, and, still wearing her sheet, stood in front of the mirror next to Hilda Sewell, a quiet woman of her own age who swam from eight-thirty to nine-thirty every morning. None of their social circles overlapped and they probably hadn't spoken more than several dozen words to each other over the years, yet there was a mutual regard. The two of them stood side by side, putting on their faces for the day ahead. As Lily was pinning on her hairpiece, a plump circle of braids, she said, "My grandson calls this my 'muffin'; I guess he thinks it looks like one." Hilda Sewell laughed softly. Before she left the mirror, she put her hand briefly on Lily's shoulder—the first time she had ever touched her—and that was all.

Eleven years before, Lily's mother had accomplished her death in the same fastidious style in which she had lived her life. There had been no fuss, no blood, no loss of dignity. She had simply run down and the doctor had put her in the hospital for tests, which showed nothing but a disintegrating spine (not unusual at eighty-six, the doctor had informed her ungallantly), a little anemia, and her old friend angina, which she had been using for decades to blackmail others into concessions. She was not sick enough for the hospital or strong enough to go back to her apartment, so the doctor suggested an interim stay at Brenthaven Rehabilitation Center, one of the better places of its kind, where you could still have a private room—if you could pay for it. Exactly one week from her date of admission, she died. Members of the family had been to see her every day, sometimes twice a day. She had welcomed their visits and attentions—indeed, she expected them—but she had seemed preoccupied, even to Lily, with whom she had always been close. At three o'clock one morning, she had rung for the night nurse and told her she couldn't sleep. The nurse gave her a pill; she swallowed it with some water, leaned back with a sigh, then had given a little yip of surprise and was gone.

Lily had admitted to herself that she was grateful for her mother's neat and timely exit. It could have been so much worse. Everyone with parents and the capacity to imagine the future has seen the specter: that costly and protracted leaking away of a body and its personality until everyone concerned is poisoned with impatience and guilt. Examples abounded. The disintegration of Marie Richardson, Julia's mother, for instance. Lily had never liked her; she had been a silly woman and a self-destructive drinker behind her languid, snobbish façade. But then the shell had begun to crack in a manner Lily would not have wished on her worst enemy. She remembered the day she had met Marie Richardson coming out of the bank, stuffing packets of crisp bills into her purse with an odd little smile. "Oh, hello there, Lucy," she had called to Lily, who had said hello back without being concerned about the "Lucy." She knew Marie had no love for her, looked down on her for marrying Ralph Quick, and still smarted under the knowledge that her daughter, Julia, had once admired Lily excessively. But then Marie had beckoned her over and withdrawn a packet of the bills from her purse. "You poor thing," Marie had said, "I want you to have this. I am trying to divest myself. I have so much, you see." Lily had noticed the peculiar blankness in her eyes and understood there was more going on here besides alcohol and snottiness. Gently she pushed away the sheaf of bills that Marie was shoving, rather forcefully, at her. "I'm just going into the bank to get a little shopping money myself," said Lily. "Why don't you come on back in with me, Marie, and let's phone Neville. I don't think you're well." "Oh, go to hell, you uppity bitch," said Marie Richardson. Turning away from Lily, she began importuning a passing white-haired man to relieve her of some of her wealth. Fortunately, a bank officer, who must have spotted something out of the ordinary about Marie's behaviour inside, had now followed her out to the sidewalk. He succeeded in coaxing her to return to the bank with him, though not without a price. "Didn't my daughter fuck you once?" Lily heard Marie Richardson ask the astonished man as he steered her by the elbow up the stairs and out of sight. Lily subsequently learned from Julia, who, not long after this episode, had quit her teaching job in New York and come home, that this had not been Marie's first foray into divestiture. Before her heavy cash withdrawals and aberrant ways had become apparent, she had succeeded in making Neville Richardson twelve thousand dollars poorer. And she was to put him and Julia through a worse and more prolonged ordeal before she was finished.

After her mother's death, Lily began visiting nursing homes. She started with one or two old ladies she had met during that week her mother was at Brenthaven. Then one of them died, and the other ran out of money and had to be transferred to Sunshine Hill, which was supported by Medicaid. So Lily started dropping by Sunshine Hill when she was over in that end of town. Then someone at church told her that an older woman she had always admired had been incapacitated by a stroke and was out at Foxwood, the Episcopal nursing home, and she widened her territory. Now, eleven years later, Lily had an itinerary that took her from edge to edge of the spreading city and included Brenthaven, Sunshine Hill, Foxwood, Autumn Fields, Hickory Haven, Mount Gilead, and Tina's. "Aren't you carrying this thing a bit far?" Ralph had once asked her. "You must cover close to seventy-five miles some days. You could at least get that Domiciliary Care Committee to pay your gas mileage." "I don't want to be paid. That's not why I do it." "Why do you do it, then? We were lucky enough that none of *our* parents had to go to one of those places." "That," Lily had replied, "is exactly the point. We were spared that awful ordeal, and I want to pay back." "Well, pay back by going to a couple of them, but you're making it into a full-time job." "No more than you are," she had countered. "It's just that I spread out my time among lots of little old ladies and you spend all your time with one." "Alicia Gallant is not 'a little old lady' to me," he had bristled sanctimoniously. "She is one of the most intelligent and worthwhile people I've ever had the honor of knowing. And she's Dr. Anthony's own sister. You don't even know these old people, and some of them can't remember you from week to week. You've told me so yourself. I just don't see what you get out of it, that's all." "No, I guess you wouldn't," Lily had said. Then, unable to resist turning the knife once she had it in, she had added, "I suppose I also do it as a sort of investment." He had perked up a little: "What kind of investment?" "I figure," she had replied airily, "that maybe if I visit all these old people now, then God will remember when I'm old and you put me away in a nursing home, and He'll make sure that someone comes to visit me." "It's just irresponsible of you, Lily, to say things like that. In the first place, my body at fifty-seven has aged much worse than yours at —" "Never mind my age," she had interrupted. "— than yours at twenty-nine, I was about to say. I've got this cataract, I have back problems, I had that skin cancer on the side of my forehead. And in the second place, even if I were the terrible ogre you seem to think I am, your children would certainly come to visit you." "They would, but they wouldn't enjoy it. Clare would fly down twice a year, take a cab from the airport, sit on the edge of her chair at the nursing home, and try not to let it show in her face how much I'd disintegrated. Rafe would have a stiff drink before he came. Theo would . . . actually, Theo would be the only one who might enjoy it. He sometimes went to see Mother three times a day when she was at Brenthaven, and he wasn't even her favorite. . . ."

Oh, dear God, thought Lily, stuck in traffic as she headed from the Health Club to Mount Gilead, every mother of more than one child has a secret favorite, so secret that she might go through her whole life and never admit to herself which one it was. Sometimes it takes a crisis, something out of the ordinary, to make her realize her preference. Clare hurt me the most, but she is always interesting; Rafe is the most beautiful, and, from his birth, has been, on the whole, a sunny, effortless joy. Theo was the most trouble, but he was also the most loving. It was Theo I was saving, Theo I was counting on, to protect me from the humiliations of old age. It was Theo, I realize, now that it is too late to lay my head against his neck and whisper it to him (and how happy it would have made him!) . . . it was Theo whom I trusted most to always love me.

The Reverend Floyd had his horse tethered to a long rope in the front yard of Mount Gilead because it saved on the expense of cutting grass. The Reverend himself, attired in jeans and a plaid shirt, was putting in the storm windows on the front of the building when Lily drove into the parking lot. As soon as he saw who it was, he climbed down from his stepladder and ambled over, in his best cowboy manner, to waylay her at the front entrance. From the way he was arranging his face, Lily guessed he had read the papers or heard from somebody, and she prepared herself to endure his condolences interlaced with a few home-spun pieties of the kind he preached on horseback at revivals around the state. But he only wanted to preach her a little sermon about not giving Miss Holly any more cookies in her room because she got crumbs all over the floor and the nurses complained. Lily was so relieved to escape his sympathy—he obviously was not aware of her loss—that she accepted his rebuke with good grace and said she had thought of it herself and was bringing only hard candies or gum from now on. He could not entirely hide his disappointment at her sweet reasonableness. He must have been storing up this grievance ever since her last visit; he must have felt so pleased when those crumbs gave him an opportunity to pay her back for asking him whether he could possibly lower the volume of those taped sermons over the public address system so that the old ladies could hear their soap operas. Of course, she had done it because they had asked her to ("He never listens to us . . . he says the Word of God will make us feel better"), but he probably thought she'd stirred them up because she herself didn't like his style of religion. She had nothing against his dressing up like a cowboy and prancing back and forth on his horse while preaching to a crowd—some people needed God's message glamorized by a bit of showmanship—but she had never liked or quite trusted the man, and that, she suspected, was what rankled in Reverend Floyd's heart whenever he saw her car pull into his parking lot. To patch up things between them, after his lecture on the crumbs, she praised him for getting his storm windows up so early. "I only wish my husband would follow your example!" They didn't have storm windows in their present house, but the Reverend—who seemed pleased that she thought he was doing something right—would never have to know that.

She found Miss Holly in the dayroom with the others. Feeling in her suit pocket, she counted the cellophane-wrapped butterscotch candies to see if she had enough to go around. She didn't. She'd have to sneak Miss Holly hers when the others weren't looking.

As always, there was that disconcerting moment before they became aware of her, when she saw them as they existed hour after hour in this sunlit waiting room between neglect and death. They didn't look unhappy, only far away, dozing or dreaming in their circle of wheelchairs. The television was on, but nobody was watching it. Miss Holly's face was a study in angelic detachment, even with her whiskers. Was it kind or was it cruel to rouse her from her trance just so Lady Bountiful could plant a few sweets in her pocket, bring her scraps of news from a world that had forgotten her, and then be off again?

Now Miss Holly had seen her. Her mouth, full of gaps and the blackened shards of teeth, stretched into a delighted smile. She held out her knobbly old hand and caught Lily's gently: they both suffered from arthritis. "I dreamed about you last night," Miss Holly told her. "So I knew you would come today."

"What did you dream?" Lily asked. There were no chairs in the dayroom, so she bent over Miss Holly's wheelchair. It was not a comfortable position. "I dreamed we went to pick strawberries. My dog went with us, too."

"That sounds like a lovely dream." Lily slipped a few of the candies into the front pocket of Miss Holly's smock.

The black lady in the wheelchair across from them saw her do it, but remarked graciously, "You always look so nice when you come, it cheers me up to see you."

"Thank you," said Lily, wishing she'd thought to bring more candy in case Miss Holly was in the dayroom, "it cheers *me* up, too, to try and look as nice as I can."

"I hope you're taking good care of my dog," Miss Holly whispered to Lily, tugging her sleeve to get her attention back from the black lady.

Lily assured her she was. The dog was a little fiction that had grown up between them; some days, Lily didn't think Miss Holly really believed in the dog herself, but was afraid to say so to Lily, who had promised to keep it until Miss Holly was well enough to go home—another fiction. "Your dog has a good appetite," said Lily, "and she gets along real well with my dogs, though of course she misses you." They discussed the dog awhile; Lily's back began to hurt.

Miss Holly cackled. "My momma is going to be so mad when she finds out I have a dog. We don't have the money to feed a dog, that's what she'll say."

"Well, we won't tell her, then."

There was a silence. Lily straightened up to prepare for her departure.

"I hope you'll bring my sister to see me again," said Miss Holly, sensing she was going to be abandoned. "I enjoyed seeing her so much."

Miss Holly's sister was not a fiction, but the visit Lily had painstakingly arranged and carried out some weeks before, bringing Mrs. Duncan, who had not seen her baby sister in seven years, from Autumn Fields Nursing Home to Mount Gilead, was not an experience she hoped to repeat anytime soon. The awesome mechanics of transportation had been the least of the ordeal. When she had at last wheeled the wispy, scowling ninety-eight-year-old Mrs. Duncan into her sister's room, Miss Holly had smiled broadly and expectantly up at Lily, and then, at the sight of the cranky old wreck in the wheelchair, had frowned in disbelief. Mrs. Duncan had cocked her head critically at her silent sister and, after studying her for a moment, pronounced, "You haven't fell off as much as I have, Holly, but you ain't as purty as I remembered." For the next fifteen minutes, Lily had done all the talking, saying the things the two of them should be saying to each other, while the two sisters sat in their respective wheelchairs in stony, hurt silence. When Lily was pushing Mrs. Duncan out, Miss Holly had snapped to life, pointed at Lily, and said with a smile, "You come back and see me soon, now. I'll always know *you*." Mrs. Duncan had whimpered all the way back to Autumn Fields; her frail body had slipped out of the seat belt twice, and the second time she had hit her head on the dashboard. As far as Lily was concerned, seven years from now would be soon enough for the next visit.

Nevertheless, she heard herself say, as she kissed Miss Holly on the top of her nearly bald head, "I'll see what I can do. Maybe around Christmastime."

"That would be nice," said Miss Holly, bringing out one of the candies from her smock and pulling at the cellophane. She would pop it into her mouth as soon as Lily disappeared from sight and dream on, using the materials of her lost life and God only knew what else.

On to Tina's to see Mamie Van Spruill. If I were old and helpless, thought Lily, would I rather be shut up at Tina's or at Mount Gilead? Tina would respect my dignity more, because she has a soft spot for what she calls "real ladies." But her little house is so dark, and—this is terrible—it depresses me to look at her poor legless husband in his wheelchair, even though he has a Silver Star and a Purple Heart from Vietnam. On the other hand, I don't like the Reverend Floyd. He reminds me of that verse from my childhood: *I do not love thee, Dr. Fell; The reason why I cannot tell; But this alone I know full well, I do not love thee, Dr. Fell.* But the rooms at Mount Gilead are filled with sunshine, and he does keep the windows clean. Light is important, it influences the way you feel. I think I would have to opt for Mount Gilead and just ignore the Reverend as much as possible. And hope there would be a firm person like myself to look in regularly and keep him from playing his sermons too loud on the public address system.

Tina's husband, Dirk, answered the door in his wheelchair. Tina was out buying coats for the children, he said. Lily stood and chatted for a minute, carefully averting her eyes from the two short stumps that lay inert as beanbags beneath his folded trouser legs. Miss Mamie was very angry, he warned her. "She woke up yesterday afternoon and found her new roommate going through her drawers and trying on some of her clothes. Poor old gal didn't mean any harm, but you know how Miss Mamie fancies her privacy. She hasn't spoken a word to any of us since; she wouldn't even notice the children when they came in to tell her goodnight, and she loves those kids. She may not speak to you, either, Mrs. Quick. I thought I'd better warn you." "She doesn't have to if she doesn't feel like it," said Lily. "I've got some embroidery in my purse and I'll just sit with her for a few minutes and at least she'll know I care." "We all care," said Dirk. "She's been with us five years, she's part of the family. It hurt Tina to have to put someone in Miss Mamie's room, but what with costs rising and Medicaid paying only seven hundred and fifty dollars a month, we just couldn't go on treating her like a princess." Lily agreed, making a few clucking noises about rising costs, and went on down the dark little hall to see Miss Mamie in her violated privacy. Dirk had beautiful, sincere gray eyes, guileless and trusting as a dog's. She believed he did care about these old people they took into their home; they were personalities to him, not just a needed income. He was a kind husband and father, Tina had told her so. She had also told Lily Dirk was terrific in bed, which Lily would rather not have heard. Had Dirk always been kind and loving, or had his handicap made him so? *What if I could have Theo back but without his legs?* An awful thought. She squelched it. She did not have to make that choice.

Dirk had been right to warn her. Miss Mamie sat in frozen indignity, her tartan skirt spread modestly around her potty chair, and glared straight ahead at the wall above her new roommate's bed. The roommate, one of those ancient mountain women with a face like a walnut shell and amazing thick white hair down to her waist, lay fully dressed on her bed, singing or moaning a single word that sounded like "oh'm." She also wore a red knitted cap with a pom-pom on top. The furniture in the room had been changed around to make space for the new woman's bed and dresser, and Miss Mamie's potty chair was sandwiched between her bed and her dresser, which blocked her former "throne's view" of the door and the comings and goings outside in the hall. It's one more thing being taken away from her, thought Lily, sitting down in a chair beside Miss Mamie and getting out her crewel. Let her hold on to her anger as long as she needed it; anger was part of personality, part of dignity. Miss Mamie, who was always so glad to see her, had not uttered a word or batted an eye to acknowledge her, but Lily would not insult her by trying to coax her out of her grievance. She threaded some gray yarn and made Eeyore's donkey ears instead: she was doing a Pooh pillow for Thalia's little grandson. If Lily had learned anything these past ten days, it was the foolishness of presuming you could dictate someone else's feelings. The things people had said, the letters she had received . . . Why were some just right and others all wrong? That woman who had actually followed her into the kitchen to say, "But at least we know it was God's will," "Do we know that?" Lily had answered coldly. And that poem Peggy Smith from Altar Guild had written out in her elaborate italic script and sent:

> Do not stand at my grave and weep.
> I am not there, I do not sleep.
> I am a thousand winds that blow
> I am the diamond glints on snow . . .

and on and on about how the dead person wasn't really dead, because he was the sunlight on ripened grain and the gentle autumn rain. Peggy Smith had lost a daughter—the girl was driving home from college and skidded off the road—and this poem, Peggy had said in her letter of sympathy, had been a lot of help to her. But it's no help at all to me, Lily had thought. I want Theo to go on being Theo forever, not subsumed into snow and sunshine.

"Oh'm . . . oh'm . . . oh'm . . ." sang, or moaned, Miss Mamie's new roommate from her bed.

From beneath Miss Mamie's potty chair seat came the brief sound of trickling water, which Lily, as always, pretended not to have heard. In the past, when this happened, Miss Mamie would look straight at Lily and confide some marvelous story about herself, calculated to deflect any pity or disgust Lily might be feeling. The last time the trickling sound became audible, she had told Lily that she was secretly married to a doctor in Virginia who could make new parts for people's bodies, any part you needed, "only you've got to have a strong heart." Today, because of her rage, she had forfeited speech, and with it her powers to distract through storytelling, and although Lily did not raise her head to look, she felt the proud little woman's acute distress and shame.

After Tina's came Foxwood and then Hickory Haven, but since it was almost noon, Lily took an hour's break. Nursing homes didn't like you to interrupt while they were serving lunch, and they were right. Meals were the high point of the day for many of those old people. So Lily went to Bill's Dairy Bar and sat in a back booth and ordered a milkshake and the chicken salad plate. She didn't feel like eating, her throat had been closing up on her lately, but she hated to take up a whole booth during lunch hour and order just a milkshake. While she waited for her lunch, she took a letter from her purse and read it over several times. It had come yesterday from a woman she had never heard of, who had worked with Theo at that first accounting firm he went with, just after college.

> Dear Mr. and Mrs. Quick,
> I was so angry when I learned of Theo's tragic death. He was the most tenderhearted person I've ever known. We worked together for three years at Pollock's and traveled to Greensboro for those week-long seminars. Nobody else in the firm had the integrity that Theo did. He even tried to put the firm before himself by eating cheap when he was on an expense account. He was also the only person at Pollock's who was a team player. People confided in Theo because they knew that he had that rare ability to let secrets stay with him. He never used another's weakness to make himself look better. He wanted to succeed on his own merits and that's very difficult when you're working in an office full of egocentric manipulators.
> I liked Theo very much. We looked forward to having him visit us. He was a good friend to me and I will miss him.
>
> Sincerely,
> Luellen McDonald

It was like reading a new chapter in the biography of someone you very much wanted to understand. She didn't recall his ever mentioning any Luellen McDonald at those seminars in Greensboro. Had there been a romantic attachment? But the letter had been enclosed in a sympathy card signed "Luellen and H.D. McDonald," and besides, she had written, "We looked forward to having him visit us." What kinds of things did people confide to Theo "because they knew that he had that rare ability to let secrets stay with him"? What secrets had he been carrying inside him on Sunday afternoon when he left the house in the shirt he had just ironed, announcing with his mysterious grin, "I'm going over to see if she'll have me back, and it'll be settled one way or another by three-thirty"?

"Probably no one will ever know for sure what happened," Bob Pruitt, Ralph's new lawyer, had told them in his office after he had completed his own little investigation on their behalf, going around to see the police officers on the scene, the people at the hospital, the medical examiner, and the detective Ralph had alienated. "But for what it's worth, I'm going to try to construct a scenario that I think is consistent with all the evidence. However, I want you to keep in mind what we lawyers know about investigations in general. There is no such thing as a perfect investigation, except in detective novels. There are always unanswered questions. There is always some evidence handled inappropriately." He had cleared his throat and rattled his papers importantly, the way those newscasters did on television, even though you knew they had it all printed out for them in huge block letters on a screen.

"Here's what we know. Jeanette Harris worked the seven-to-three shift at the hospital. Theo was waiting for her at her house when she picked up her three-year-old son from the sitters next door. We know that, because while Theo was waiting for her he asked the sitters if they would be willing to keep the boy for another hour so that he and the mother could go for a little drive and have a talk. They couldn't do it, this couple, because they had to go somewhere themselves. But before they went off, they saw Theo and Jeanette and the boy drive away in Jeanette's car.

"The next thing we know is from the people on Fairfield Road who heard the car skid and then what they thought was a blowout. Later one man said he thought he had heard *two* reports and realized they weren't blowouts but shots. There was also a ten-year-old boy who actually saw the car. He was riding his bike in his front yard when the car came around the corner, crossed the median, and skidded. He said he saw a gun waving around inside the car and then heard shots. He ran inside the house to tell his grandmother. Later he said that he thought the woman had shot the man, but after Detective Robbins questioned him some more, he said he was confused and wasn't sure.

"Robbins told me he also questioned Jeanette's little boy, who was in the backseat of the car when it happened. Now, in cases like this, there's a correct way questions should be asked of children, and in my opinion Detective Robbins followed strictly correct procedure. He asked the child, 'What happened?' The child told him, 'Bang, bang, Mommy fell down.' Then he asked, 'did someone shoot Mommy?' and the child said yes. Then he asked him 'Who shot Mommy?' and the child said, 'Theo.'

"As I said, we may not ever know what really happened, but according to the pathologist's report the entry wounds on Jeanette indicate she was shot twice through the left posterior occipital region of the head—that's in the back here"—and he had swiveled in his chair to show them the back of his head, where Lily had noticed that he was going bald, although he wasn't much older than Theo—"whereas Theo's wound was a contact wound, which means"—this addressed to Lily—"the barrel of the gun was actually touching the skin, and it entered on the right side just beneath the ear, which strongly suggests that the wound was self-inflicted. Added to that, Detective Robbins said he found no residue on Jeanette's hands to indicate she had fired a gun, whereas there was inconclusive residue on Theo's hands —"

"But doesn't inconclusive mean they can't prove it?" Lily had asked, determined not to be stifled by the young lawyer's glibness. Bob Pruitt clearly believed Theo had done it, but Ralph and she were his clients, he was going to handle the custody suit for Jason for them, and he had to go through the motions of leaving no stone unturned.

"Very seldom does an investigator see a totally positive result, Mrs. Quick. And in this case, Detective Robbins told me, it was almost impossible to tell anything because there was so much . . . well, there was quite a bit of blood on Theo's hands."

"Oh," Lily had said, quelled.

"Now I will give you my scenario. As I said before, probably nobody will ever know for sure what happened, but I'm drawing on the evidence we have. I'll also take into account the impressions I had of Theo, based on the conversations I had with him when he and I were drawing up his separation and custody papers last spring. Here's what I think could have happened. Please keep in mind I say *could have*, not did.

"Theo went over there, to Jeanette's, to ask her to go back to him. That's what he told you, Mrs. Quick, right? He knew she got off her shift at three, and he told you the whole thing would be settled one way or another by three-thirty. Now, I don't think for a minute that when Theo left your house he had any intention of shooting anybody. As you told me, Mrs. Quick, he'd left his own gun at home in a shoebox, where he always kept it. He may have gone to Jeanette's with some intention of having things out with her, but what I think he had in mind was to take her out for a drive, just the two of them, and use his powers of persuasion to win her back. But then the sitters weren't free, and so I can see her saying, 'Let's take my car because'— what's her little boy's name?"

"Gordon," said Ralph.

'"— because Gordon's car seat is already there,' she might have said, and also there was a bag of laundry in the back, a bag of laundry that hadn't been washed, and maybe she even suggested they could talk at the laundromat. . . . Keep in mind this is just my scenario, based on what evidence we have. Now, maybe they started off for the laundromat and then got into it right away with each other. . . . This is a distinct possibility because, look: it would have been about three-fifteen when she got back from the hospital, they probably didn't drive away from her house till close to three-thirty, and the whole thing was over with by four. That's when the first officer arrived on the scene. So I speculate they got to arguing right away, and she said—or maybe he said—'Let's just go back, we aren't getting anywhere.' And they turned around somewhere, he was driving the car—but Mr. Quick, you said he always liked to drive, so that's not unusual—and they were heading back to her house, in fact they were almost there, when maybe he threatened her in some way. Based on what you've told me, he really cared for her, and maybe he just got desperate and said something like 'I'm not going to let you out of this car until we come to an agreement.' Now, from what Detective Robbins learned from Jeanette's estranged husband, she had quite a temper and was capable of physical altercations. In other words, she did not have a passive personality, and you know she had been in the Armed Forces —"

"I didn't know that," said Lily. "All I knew was that she was a cheerful, ambitious girl who had worked hard for what she had. I told Theo, when they were going together, that she would make him a good wife. It was Snow who broke them up. She had left Theo, but as soon as she found out somebody else wanted him, she threw a monkey wrench into the whole thing —"

"Lily, we don't know that," Ralph said.

"I know it. Theo told me all about it. The two women met, and Snow said things to her."

"When was this?" asked Ralph.

"Theo took Jason down to Georgia to see Snow. And Jeanette rode with them. That's when Snow got to Jeanette. The two of them went into the trailer alone, and Snow told her awful things."

"How do you know what Snow told her?"

"Because Theo told me. Jeanette must have talked to him about it when they were coming back from Georgia. Things were never the same after that, Theo said. And then that man broke into her house and tried to rape her, and there was all *that* fuss —"

"You never told me about this trip to Georgia," said Ralph.

"You never told me you'd lent Theo your Belgian semi-automatic to give to Jeanette after that man broke in."

"I didn't want to worry you."

"And I didn't want to bore *you*. I know you get tired of hearing me on the subject of Snow's malevolence. That's probably why Theo didn't tell you himself."

"Mrs. Quick, Mr. Quick, if you'd just allow me to continue with my scenario. As I was saying, from what we know about Jeanette, she was a likable, responsible girl, but she was strong and she didn't take anything off anyone. Now, if Theo, say, pushed her too far—maybe by saying he wasn't going to let her out of the car until they'd come to an understanding—it would be perfectly feasible for a person of her determination and temperament to pull a gun on him. We know she had one—Mr. Quick's—and she was obviously carrying it in her car at the time. So Theo says, 'I'm not letting you go,' and she opens the glove compartment in front of her and pulls the gun on him and says, 'Oh, yes, you are, take me and Gordon home right this minute, or else.' After all, she had borrowed that gun to protect herself from a man who tried to make her do something against her will. And at that moment, Theo was the enemy. Now, from what I know about Theo, with his pride in his marksmanship and his liking to be the driver of the car, he wouldn't be one to like having a gun pulled on him, especially by a woman. So . . . and this fits in with the kind of skid marks that were found—they were skid marks of a driver in control—Theo may have used the car to create a situation that would disarm her. That's something all those patrolmen he was friends with could have talked about at some time or other; he could have learned it from them. So he may have quickly swerved across the median, to give her a scare, and then stopped exactly one and a half feet short of the utility pole . . . if you'd like to take a look at this diagram. It was done by the first officer on the scene, who was designated as that shift's I.D. It was his job to take Polaroid pictures, make measurements, and secure the vehicle. And, see the skid marks, going perfectly straight for 15.4 feet and stopping directly in line with the pole? He said, in his experience, these were definitely the skid marks of a driver in control of the situation.

"Now, after that, I think they wrestled with the gun. That would be consistent with what the boy on the bicycle saw. You remember I said he told the detective he saw a gun waving around inside the car?"

"Yes," said Lily, "and that he first said he saw the woman shoot the man, but the detective confused him into changing his story. Because everyone believes it's just more typical for a man to shoot a woman than the other way around —"

"Mrs. Quick, please. Most likely the boy didn't see anything concrete. I mean, we have to remember this whole thing occurred within seconds. He saw the gun waving around, he may not even have been sure what it was until he heard the shots. Then he ran inside. When he and his grandmother and the other neighbors reached the car, Jeanette was outside of the car, lying face down on the pavement, with two bullets through the back of her head. Theo was slumped inside the car with one bullet through the right side of his head, just behind the ear. Now, I'm almost done, and then you can ask me any questions you like. I think it is possible that at some point in their struggle Theo managed to wrest that gun away from Jeanette, who then tried to get out of the car . . . and when she did, Theo was so caught up in this battle for control they were having, that fantasy just replaced reality and he fired two shots to stop her. Maybe not even meaning to hit her. But maybe he was a better marksman than he wanted to be. And then, when he saw what he had done, he shot himself. That's what I think could have happened. It makes sense to me in terms of what little I know about the situation of these two people, and it is consistent with the ballistic and forensic evidence. . . . Mr. Quick, you're shaking your head."

"With all due respect for your extensive homework, Bobby, I think the whole thing stinks."

"Oh? In what way?" asked the lawyer with guarded geniality.

"Hell, Bobby, I shouldn't have to tell you. This whole investigation has more holes in it than a damn sieve. That child on the bicycle wasn't questioned right. And let's keep in mind that there were three shots fired and nobody has attested to hearing more than two. Maybe that first shot was fired earlier, have you thought of that?"

"By whom, Mr. Quick?" The young lawyer's lips had gone pale and thin.

"Well, hell. Maybe by someone else who was in that car with them. Maybe by the child in the backseat of the car. It's perfectly possible he could have got hold of that gun."

"Surely you're not saying that a three-year-old child strapped into a car seat could have somehow reached forward over the seat, wrested that heavy gun away from the two adults in front, and placed three accurate and fatal shots?"

"Children younger than that kill people every day. It's in the papers. I"m not saying he did, I'm saying why is it you all won't even look at the other possibilities? Like this fellow who was coming up for trial for breaking into Jeanette's. There can be no trial now, because the only witness is dead. It seems to me he had more to gain than anyone else."

"Mr. Quick, Detective Robbins understood how you felt about that, and he did make some inquiries. The man in question was somewhere else last Sunday, he has witnesses. As for there being any other person in the backseat, the boy on the bicycle would have seen them —"

"That poor kid didn't know what he saw when Detective Robbins finished with him. And another thing, Bobby. You may think this is small, but it's just one more proof of the sloppiness that has characterized this entire process —"

"What is that, Mr. Quick?"

"Take a look here, at the bottom of the pathologist's report on Theo. Just here, where it says 'summary.' Do you notice anything strange?"

The lawyer, visibly annoyed and flushed in the cheeks, stared hard at the place where Ralph's finger tapped accusingly. "I can't say I —"

"You knew Theo," said Ralph. "You drew up his separation papers and Jason's custody papers. You met with him at least three times. I know, because I paid the bill. How old was Theo, Bobby?"

"Oh, I see. There's a typo here. It says 'twenty-year-old white male' instead of —"

"It's not a typo, Bobby. It's pure damn contemptuous carelessness. The day after Theo was killed, I went by the police station and found this same mistake on the report. They didn't even have my name right, I was listed as 'Alfred Quick.' And I brought this to the attention of Mark McFall, and he assured me it would all be corrected."

"Like I tried to tell you earlier, Mr. Quick, there's just no such thing as a perfect investigation. Human beings are fallible. Now, what I think we ought to do in the time we have left—and there isn't much, because, I've got to be over at court again at eleven—is make our plans for the custody hearing. I can see why an error like this would get under your skin, but I really must tell you we've got more serious problems ahead. We're going to need the help and goodwill of everyone we can get, because she, after all, is his mother, and in law courts 'mother' is a sacred word."

"It has become a loathsome word to me," said Lily, "ever since I have heard it applied to Snow Mullins."

"If you'll permit me to offer a little advice, Mrs. Quick, that sort of attitude won't do much to predispose the judge in your favour."

"That's exactly what I keep telling her," put in Ralph righteously, suddenly allying himself with the young lawyer whose "scenario" had not pleased him and about whom he had remarked to Lily on the way to this appointment: "He'll never have one tenth of the fire and brilliance of Hal DuPre, that son of a bitch, but he's hardworking and thorough, and he did do Theo's separation papers, and we need every scrap of continuity we can muster if we plan to walk out of that courtroom with Jason."

*   *   *

Foxwood had the least depressing approach of all the nursing homes Lily visited. Although the buildings were recent, old trees had been spared and the private road wound between them up a gentle curve of hill. The lawns were green and smooth, the shrubberies and flowerbeds planned and maintained by a professional gardener. There were inviting footpaths along the edge of the woods to lure all but the conclusively bedridden to totter forth into the air and sunshine and sustain whatever mobility they still had left to them. Inside, there was a lovely small chapel with an old carved confessional taken from the ruin of a Norman church somewhere in rural England. There was also a beauty shop, a news shop that sold some toiletries and cosmetics, and even a boutique. Foxwood was supported by the Episcopal diocese, but residents still paid twice as much as at the other homes Lily visited, with the exception of Brenthaven.

She went first to little Mrs. Roberts's room and found it empty. A nurse told her the old lady was having a permanent over in the beauty shop. Well, that was just fine, a permanent was as much of an event as a visitor, perhaps more of one; Lily said she would come back the following week. But since she was there anyway, she reluctantly made her way to the room of Mrs. Inez Brewster to see how the haughty widow was settling in, even though that lady had given her such a chilly reception the first time that Lily had vowed never to bother her again. But I might well react like Mrs. Brewster, decided Lily, taking small, careful steps in her high-heeled snakeskin pumps over a wet patch in the freshly mopped linoleum hallway; when Ralph or one of the children finally puts me away, I, too, might be very angry at first, if I still have the pride of my faculties, and then I might snub the first perky do-gooder who flaunts her freedom to dash in and out of my last address.

The blue-haired, angular Mrs. Brewster lay stiffly on top of her bed, her stockinged ankles and narrow flat shoes sticking out from beneath a crocheted throw done in squares of delicate mauves and pinks. Her eyes were closed and her lips set in an expression of faint repugnance.

Relieved, Lily was about to withdraw when the lady's eyes snapped open and gazed up at her accusingly.

"I'm afraid I've wakened you, Mrs. Brewster. I was just passing by."

"It's Kathy, isn't it?" demanded Inez Brewster, sitting bolt up-right and swinging her feet to the floor. She obviously considered it a show of weakness to have been caught napping.

"Kathy?" repeated Lily, puzzled.

"Didn't you say your name was Kathy the last time you were here?"

"No, it's Lily. Lily Quick."

Inez Brewster reached for a pink baby brush on her bedside table and fluffed it through her cloud of fine blue hair. She put the brush back with a sigh. "I don't know any Quicks," she told Lily. "How is it that you know me?"

Lily tried to suppress her pique at the other woman's rudeness. "I don't actually know you, Mrs. Brewster, but your daughter-in-law is on the Library Board with me, and when she found out I visited someone at Foxwood, she said since you were so new here you might appreciate it if I looked in."

"Ha!" barked Inez Brewster. "Anything to keep from coming herself. 'So new here,' eh? I wouldn't be up here at all if it weren't for her. I was doing just fine, thank you, in my own home down in Beaufort. Have you ever been to Beaufort, down in the eastern part of the state?"

"No, but I've heard it's a very beautiful old town."

"Yes, it's 'a very beautiful old town,'" repeated Inez Brewster, managing to sound as if she were making fun of Lily. "And I lived in a very beautiful old house, with all my things around me, and I had a nice girl come in for a few hours every day to tidy up and fix my meals. But my daughter-in-law's a very greedy person, you see. I never trusted her, and I was right. She wanted to get me out of my house so they could sell it and have all that money for themselves. And she won't even tell me what they've done with my things. She's turned my son against me so that he won't tell me anything, either. The last time he came to see me, I asked him what they'd done with my silver, and he said, 'Mamma, Karen's taking wonderful care of everything.' Oh, I bet Karen is! She's either sold my silver or else she's using it on her own table to impress people. 'The Library Board.' She's always been a social climber. But then you and she are probably best friends, aren't you, and you'll go back and tell her everything I've said."

I'll just do one more today and stop, decided Lily, driving wearily away from Foxwood. It'll have to be Hickory Haven, because I promised Thalia I'd say hello to her father, and I'll reward myself by seeing Mrs. Clark last, to make up for that awful Mrs. Brewster. I wonder . . . wouldn't it be terrible if old age simply magnified and intensified your basic nature? But why do I say terrible? I must be afraid of what may become magnified and intensified in me. If good little girls turn into good little old girls, and proud young people age into proud old people, and spiteful and paranoid personalities become more spiteful and paranoid in extremity . . . how will I look to others in that waiting room between uselessness and death? Father Weir told me once that whenever you find yourself really despising a trait in someone, you'd better look carefully to see if it's not your own besetting sin. Is that why I was so incensed by Mrs. Inez Brewster? Oh, please, God, don't let me be an Inez Brewster! And yet I'll have to go back and see her again. And again. "You come back and see me again, Kathy," she said at the last. I provided her with a cat's scratching post. I'll be a stand-in for the hated, social-climbing daughter-in-law. She will patronize me and suspect me of carrying tales to her daughter-in-law (whom I barely know), and she will probably make fun of me behind my back with the nurses.

Now who's being paranoid?

Thalia's father, wearing a handsome maroon bathrobe with a yellow coronet stitched on the breast pocket, was having his daily constitutional up and down the main hall, assisted by his walker. Thalia ironed and starched his pajamas, and their neat trouser creases swayed above his skinny ankles as he shuffled towards Lily, his head and shoulders bent forward in concentration over his slow progress. She was almost abreast of him before he became aware of her.

"Hello, Mr. Thompson. How are you today?"

"I can't complain, thank you, Miss Lily. I eat well, I sleep well. Everybody's real good to me here. How's my gal? You see her today?"

"I did indeed. She said to tell you she'd be here Thursday, just like always."

"Thursday," he pondered aloud respectfully, as though Lily had told him something he didn't know. Thalia always went out to Hickory Haven on Thursday because that was her day off. "Well, thank you. I appreciate it." He was of the old-fashioned generation who still trod with exaggerated deference in the company of whites, even those who he knew were warmly disposed to him. "You been to see poor Miz Clark yet?"

"Oh, dear. Has something happened?" The last time Lily was here, sweet Mrs. Clark had been chipper and full of energy.

"She try to slip off to her nephew's again. Made it all the way through the woods this time, but they say she done fell and got scratched up pretty bad. She was all the way down 'longside the expressway before they could catch up with her."

"All the way to the expressway! That little thing?"

"That's just what I say!" the old man chimed in admiringly. "Beats everything, don't it?"

Mrs. Clark was in bed, with her nightgown on, and one of the nurses was changing the dressing on a sizable gash in her forehead.

"We've been very naughty," the nurse told Lily, swabbing at the gash, while the tiny, docile patient smiled happily up at her visitor and signaled with a rolling of her eyes for Lily to sit down until this less-favored creature left them alone. "We were real lucky we didn't break a hip or a leg, or worse, isn't that right, Mrs. C.?"

Mrs. Clark nodded, but when the nurse was cutting the adhesive for the new bandage, she winked at Lily.

As soon as the nurse had gone, she motioned Lily to move her chair closer. "I almost made it this time," she confided softly. "It was the highway that threw me. It didn't used to be there. There was just a quiet country road. If it hadn't been for all those cars and trucks whizzing past, I could have made it. I had to wait a long time to cross, you see, and that's when they caught up with me."

"But you'd fallen and cut yourself," Lily reminded her.

"My nephew would have given me a bandage. He's a good boy. He's always glad to see me."

"But he's glad to come and see you here. He worries when you try to walk to his house. It's much farther than it seems, Mrs. Clark. And even I wouldn't try to cross the expressway on foot."

"But I was headed in the right direction, wasn't I?" The old lady beamed triumphantly up at Lily, who noticed she also had a whole network of fresh raw scratches on her face and arms. Brambles from the woods, probably. "I know this area. When I was growing up out here, it was all farms. We thought nothing of walking straight as the crow flies when we needed to get to somebody's house. Don't you ever want to go and see somebody real bad, and you know straight as the crow flies where they're located if you can only make it there?"

"But they might not be home when you do," Lily felt she must add, though her heart quivered at the poignant image.

Mrs. Clark stroked Lily's hand, her touch light as gossamer. "But they will be, you see. If you want them to be, more than anything. If you can just make it there, they'll be waiting."

Close to tears, Lily fumbled in her purse for her embroidery.

"I always like it when you bring your sewing," said Mrs. Clark happily. "Then I know you mean to sit awhile."

It was almost five when Lily departed from Hickory Haven and the scratched-up little lady, who had finally fallen asleep, exhausted as a child from her day's adventure. "I'm being rude," she would murmur to Lily, every time she started to doze off, "please don't leave." "No, I won't," Lily would assure her. "You just close your eyes and rest. I feel very content sitting here beside you with my embroidery." And she had been content, pushing her colored yarns through the fine linen, finishing Eeyore's body and then beginning on Pooh, who in his red vest was going to be ascending skyward holding on to his balloon. The calm, slow building up of the stitches had become a kind of alternate breathing that modulated her thoughts and distanced her from her present anguish. Mrs. Clark's evocation of an earlier, simpler terrain, in which hearts' desires could still be counted on to fly straight to their mark, had roused for Lily the landscape of her childhood: that safe, tree-lined street full of rambling porches in a bygone Mountain City that now existed only in her memory. There were lots of other little girls to play with. All of the fathers on that street, it seemed, worked for the railroad, whose motto was "The Southern Serves the South." Her father was night foreman. He saw that the machinists and boilermakers kept the steam engines in repair. In winter he wore a suit with a vest buttoned down the front and a railroad watch in one vest pocket with a chain going across his stomach and attached to the other pocket. In summer he worked with his shirt sleeves rolled up. Winter and summer, he wore a soft gray fedora hat. Every night he left the house at a little before seven and she would wave to him from the porch. Then she would watch him out of sight to the bottom of the hill, which was called Mud Cut, where the streetcar turned around. After that, although she couldn't see him anymore, he would cut across a neighbor's backyard through the blackberry bushes, cross another street, and then go over the long black footbridge that arched over the railroad tracks and ended up at the machine shops. Next to the machine shops was the roundhouse, where the trains could be turned and headed onto whatever track they needed to be on. Once Daddy had taken her there and shown her some men welding a broken engine back together. There were flames and sparks everywhere; the roundhouse looked like Hell itself. It was very exciting. She had been able to lie in her bedroom and hear the trains going back and forth. More than thirty passenger trains stopped every day in Mountain City, not to mention the countless freight trains. She could lie securely in her bed and fall asleep, knowing exactly where her daddy was, "as the crow flies." If she had been an adventurous child, she might have slipped off into the night and walked to the shops herself and surprised him. But she was a good little girl, and besides, she knew he would be home just after seven in the morning, and they would have a big breakfast together before he went to his bedroom and fell asleep.

Every year, about three weeks before Christmas, even before she could write, he would help her print a letter to Santa Claus, in whom she believed just as much as she believed in her father. They would stick the letter on the end of the poker and fly it up the chimney of the fireplace. When the poker came back out of the chimney, the letter was no longer there. It had gone straight to the North Pole. "Straight as the crow flies."

One Christmas she was pushing her beautiful new doll in her new doll carriage down the porch steps to the sidewalk when the carriage tipped and the doll fell out and broke. She started to cry, then made herself stop, because Daddy was rushing out to her, looking as though he expected *her* to break. "It's all right," she told him, "I'm not going to cry." But to her amazement, *he* had started to cry. Then Mother had come out and seen them both crying, and said, "I declare, Theo, I don't know who's the biggest baby sometimes." And Daddy had pulled himself together and laughed and said, "I know it, Ellen, it's just that I can't stand to see the child disappointed."

Now, driving west into the setting sun on the expressway whose fierce traffic had thwarted Mrs. Clark's surprise visit to her nephew, Lily noticed that the red needle on her fuel gauge hovered directly over the empty mark. She had meant to ask Ralph to fill the tank from their own pump this morning, but things had been confused, with both of them chasing Jason around, trying to get him dressed so Ralph could take him to nursery school. All last week, he had refused to go at all, had bitten her and thrown Ralph's car keys down the embankment. The poor child had not been himself since the funeral. It was mainly Snow's doing, putting on her long-lost mother act, sowing seeds of distrust in his little broken heart, telling him how his mommy wanted him to live with her always if only Ralph and Lily would allow her to take him home. Home! When she didn't even have a roof over her head, was living in that J.R.'s or J.D.'s trailer down in Georgia. Father Zachary had hardly finished throwing the clod of earth on Theo's casket when she had taken Ralph to one side and announced her intention of returning with them to Quick's Hill—in the limousine, of course—and packing up all Jason's things and taking him away with her and all those Mullinses in the odious black van that same afternoon. She had stood there arguing with Ralph at the cemetery, many of the mourners still in hearing distance, Theo's grave not even covered yet, and no telling what she might have done if Rafe hadn't smelled trouble and lured Jason away from her and spirited him off in his car with promises of a McDonald's hamburger and a trip to the Nature Center. Snow might have succeeded in kidnapping Jason right away from them; the fact that she later had the nerve to accuse Rafe of trying to kidnap her child showed it was on her mind. And then, Clare had reported to Lily, Snow and Ralph had fought all the way home in the limousine, with Mr. Moore, the funeral director, driving them and hearing every word that was said. Lily, who had been left without her ride when Rafe took Jason away, had remained obstinate in her refusal to share the same car with her daughter-in-law and had begged a ride with Miss Alicia Gallant and her maid, Susie, who had brought the old lady to the cemetery in Susie's cherry-red Pontiac. Oh, the total lack of feeling on Snow's part! Couldn't she have let them at least bury Theo in dignity and sorrow? Before the afternoon was over, Ralph had been forced to threaten her with an injunction if she did not leave Quick's Hill peaceably, without Jason. While all this had been transpiring out in the parking lot by the swimming pool, Lily and Clare and Julia, bless her, and the indispensable Freddy Stratton had been inside taking care of guests. The crowning blow to Lily had come when she was walking Father Weir and his wife out to their car. This lamentable day, a Tuesday, was supposed to have been the day Lily and Clare took the Weirs to lunch; instead of which, Lily was now thanking Father Weir for helping to officiate at the funeral and telling him (he was a little deaf) how beautifully he had read those passages from Romans 8. The awful black van was prominently displayed, but she had noted with relief that all the Mullinses, including Snow, seemed to be packing themselves into it. Ralph stood, frowning and stiff-shouldered, listening to some parting word from Snow. Meanwhile, Lily was grateful that Father Weir did not appear to notice the van or the Mullinses, so intent was he on explaining how, for the sake of the occasion, he had taken a certain liberty in leaving out a few verses in the middle. She had them almost to their car when Mary Weir said to her, "Lily, I think someone over there is trying to get your attention." And "over there" was of course where the black van was, and the someone had been Snow, who waited until they were all three looking her way and then called across the white gravel in her twangiest voice, rich with malice and spite, "I'll see *you* in court!"

Lily got off the expressway at the exit leading to Charlton Street, where she knew there was a Gulf station. But when she pulled into the station, all the full service pumps were in use. As her needle was now registering a little above empty, she drove out again, deciding to risk it. This was the sort of thing that drove Clare mad when she was down visiting and riding around with Lily: "*Please*, Mother, it makes me nervous to ride around on empty. Please pull into that station, for my sake, and let me buy you some gas. So what if we have to go to the self-serve pumps. I pump my own gas all the time. It's cheaper, and besides, refusing to pump gas is just one more way of refusing to take charge of your own life. Let me show you how easy it is. You just flip a little lever and then you stick the nozzle into the tank and pull the trigger. . . ." Poor Clare, the one time she had persuaded Lily to let her pump gas into this car, she hadn't been able to find the gas tank. The attendant had to come over and show her it was beneath the rear license plate (Lily hadn't known where it was, either), and when Clare got back in the car, smelling of gas, she was sputtering obscenities. "Anything *connected* to him seems to have its own sinister power of sapping your independence," she had fumed. "Him" was Ralph, of course. Then they had both laughed and Clare had hastily changed the subject. She had become kinder of late. She no longer milked every opportunity to harangue her mother about how she ought to wrest back control of her life from Ralph. Though Lily knew it still rankled: Clare, after all, was the only one of her children with actual memories of the old Lily who came home from an office smelling of newspaper ink and who wrote all the checks. Yet even then I was never as independent as she would have me be, thought Lily. She wouldn't have been either, if she had been brought up in my time. Neither of us, now that I think about it, has been exactly a revolutionary. She lives openly with a man she's not married to, but women a hundred years ago were getting away with that. Her name may not appear below a man's on a checking account, but since she's made some money she told me herself she has one man who makes all her investments and another who does all her tax work. So what does that leave? The "freedom" to get gasoline all over your hands?

Since she was halfway down Charlton Street, anyway, she drove on to her old neighborhood church, Our Lady of the Mountains, covered her head with a small square of black lace she carried in her purse, and went inside. The new priest, young Father Devereaux, was liberal with incense, as Father Weir had been when he was rector thirty-six years before, and the smell enveloped her with old feelings and associations. Nothing much had changed in here. The water in the little brass font to the right as you entered could have been the same water whose coolness Lily first touched to her forehead in the fervor of her new membership in this parish, hoping its powers of holiness would calm some of the anger and disappointment inside her. She was a twenty-nine-year-old widow living with her mother and her six-year-old daughter. For her, personally, the war years had raced by like a cluttered dream, tipping occasionally into nightmare, during which she had acquired a husband and a baby, lost her father, lost the husband, and then wakened to find herself the mainstay of a little family of females, all her former girlish plans for happiness and solo attainments subsumed in their dependence on her. But the loneliest aspect of her new life was that she could not confide certain feelings to anyone; she had trouble admitting them to herself. For instance, that losing her father had been a far greater sorrow than losing Miles Campion. Her father was the man of her life, the best man she would ever know, the only one who had never let her down. All these years later, she could acknowledge that with defiant pride; whereas, to have admitted such a thing at twenty-nine would have seemed like a deliberate foreclosure of her remaining chances for a normal, fulfilled womanhood.

But she had been lonely and despondent enough to join Our Lady's, in walking distance of the rented house she shared with her mother and little girl, the quaint, English-looking parish whose dynamic rector everyone was talking about: an eloquent and virile man, father, priest, and husband, who possessed a striking combination of worldly charm and spiritual ardor. And what she then thought of as her new religiousness had added a dimension of comfort—and even pleasure—to her existence. The elaborate rituals of the liturgy satisfied her need for beauty and mystery, and the thoughts from Father Weir's well-crafted and provocatively brief sermons, delivered with his appealing sangfroid, resonated upliftingly through her weekday routines. Often on weekday evenings, after she got home from the paper, she would walk to Our Lady's in the violet dusk and escape into its scented, cryptlike coolness, blessing herself with water from the little brass font and slipping with a sigh into a pew. Ah, alone. For a whole half hour. More, if she should need it, for she knew Father Weir left the church unlocked till ten. It wasn't that she didn't love the two who awaited her at home. It was just that their need for her to be their vital center oppressed her; both her widowed mother and her fatherless little girl took it for granted that they were, and always should be, the most important concerns of her life.

Leaving the church after one of these evening escapes, she had met Father Weir and his two children on the sidewalk. They were returning to the rectory after playing baseball in the park, and Father Weir, carrying the bat and glove, greeted her somewhat breathlessly. "They've given me quite a workout," he said, his broad chest still heaving from the exercise. "Thank the Lord, it got too dark to see the ball anymore." He was wearing a pair of old jeans and sneakers, and a loose, faded sweatshirt that said "Princeton" across the front. It was the first time she had seen him without his black clothes and collar. Suddenly, for reasons she knew it would be best not to even think about further, she had felt utterly bereft. It was all she could do to come up with some light greeting in return. (And yet, years later—only last year, in fact—he had surprised and gratified her by remembering, and apparently cherishing, the words she herself had forgotten. "Do you know what you said to me once, when I caught you coming out of Our Lady's one night? You said, 'I've just been for a breath of fresh prayer.'")

In one of her earliest trips to the confessional booth, she had told him, "I know lying is a sin, and yet there is one lie that I go on telling and I know I will continue to tell it. When people ask me about my husband, I say that he was killed in action. But what really happened was that he was driving back to the Naval Reserve Air Base in Memphis after a night on the town, and he was thoroughly drunk, and he smashed into a tree. But how can I ask you or God for absolution when I know I'm going to walk out of here and tell the same lie the next time somebody asks me?" There had been a thoughtful silence behind the screen. At last his voice, sounding both sincere and amused, had replied, "I think we can safely assume that you do your penance by living with the less than ideal facts yourself. What good would be accomplished by offering these painful details to relative strangers?" "That's what I've been trying to tell myself," she answered, "but still, it's officially a lie, isn't it?" "According to the letter of the law, it is, but that's the great relief Christ brought us, when he taught that the spirit of the law is often better served through compassion."

And then, the crucial Saturday morning, several years later, when, driven by conflicting agitations, she had burst upon the Weirs in the thick of their family life. Mary Weir had been ironing in the living room, her hair in pin curls, the children peeping through alternate banister railings at this emotional interloper. Poppa Weir, his wife told Lily wryly, was putting manure on his garden, but was always happy to see a parishioner who needed him.

They sat side by side on a bench in the backyard, in the shade of a blossoming pear tree. The delicate fragrance from the tree mingled in Lily's senses with the pungent smell of the horse manure on Father Weir's shoes. She was trembling, unsure whether she was going to smirk coyly or burst out crying. "There's someone who's been wanting to marry me," she said. "We've been seeing each other for almost two years. Mother and Clare know him, but they think we are just friends. He comes to the house and takes me to dinner sometimes, that's all they think. Neither one of them takes him seriously, because he's . . . well, he's quite a bit younger, and also he's not the sort of person they would ever consider a threat to them. Mother looks on him as a useful appendage to our household . . . you know, a man who's good with tools, who'll drop by at a moment's notice and unstop her sink for her without any charge. And Clare seems to like him—he encourages her to get out and do hardy things. They made a slingshot together, and she goes over to his mother's house and plays with their dogs. But if I were to announce I was thinking of marrying him, Mother would throw a fit and Clare would feel betrayed. And yet, it's not fair to him . . . to keep him dangling like this. I want you to tell me what to do. I'm going crazy trying to decide how to please everybody."

Father Weir had smiled in his wise, detached way. "It might not be possible to please everybody," he said, after a moment.

"That's why I needed to talk to *you*. I'm so embarrassed, barging into your house like this, but what should I do? Should I marry him and upset Mother and break Clare's heart? Or should I send him on his way and devote myself completely to them? I feel like such an oddity. I'm somebody's daughter and somebody's mother, but I have trouble believing I was ever actually somebody's wife. Oh, I wish you would help me decide!"

"But think of the position that puts me in," he said, still smiling. He fished in the pocket of his faded blue shirt with a torn sleeve and pulled out a matchbook and a crumpled pack of cigarettes. He offered her one and leaned forward and lit hers and then his own. "If I tell you, look, if you care for this fellow enough, go ahead and do it, and then it doesn't work out, you're going to come back one miserable day and lay the blame at my feet. On the other hand, if I suggest you prolong the agony awhile longer until the mist clears and you see your true road absolutely, and then he gets tired of waiting and goes away, you're not going to be too well disposed towards a meddlesome priest. You might even stop coming to church."

"That would never happen!" And she had burst into tears, after all. He sat smoking and waited without any apparent impatience for her to recover herself.

When she had, he continued in the same tone of gentle humor. "However, if you do decide to take the almighty risk, I'd be very pleased to perform the ceremony."

Alone in a pew, gazing through the incense-sweetened gloom of Father Weir's old church more than three decades later, she asked herself whether any words of his had made the difference. Hadn't she known all along on that flustered Saturday morning that she would let Ralph prevail on her that very night to drive sixty miles down the mountain to a justice of the peace in South Carolina and marry secretly and drive home again before it got late enough for Mother even to start worrying? Had that desperate descent on the Weirs really been necessary?

Father Weir had married them again in the church several weeks later. She had brought Ralph back to the house as her official husband, and Mother had threatened to have a heart attack on the spot. Ralph had calmed her—he was good with older ladies even then—and the two of them had gone to pick up Clare at Ralph's mother's house. Clare had taken one look at the white orchid pinned to Lily's suit lapel, and narrowed her eyes and looked frighteningly unforgiving for a child of nine. And seven years later, when Clare was leaving for her new life with the Campions and Lily followed her to her room, where she was in the act of slamming shut her suitcase, she had said in a scared but unrepenting quaver, "Well, maybe I *should* have told you I'd written to Uncle Zebulon and he was coming to get me, thinking you knew. But I was afraid you'd find a way to stop me. Just the way you were afraid to tell me about Ralph until it was too late to stop it."

Lily went to the front of the church and lit one of the votive candles in front of the Virgin Mary. There were several flames flickering under the statue already. She had become more popular than the statue of Saint Francis since young Father Devereaux had started making such a fuss over her. The old-timers, who objected to his saying three Hail Marys at the end of the Sunday service, were objecting to other things as well, according to Freddy Stratton, who had confided to Lily, that day she spent at Quick's Hill after Theo's death, that there was gossip about the "celibate priest's" private life. He had had a houseguest at the rectory. A young man. If I could have Theo back, would I mind if he was a pansy? Lily asked the Mother of Jesus, slipping a folded dollar bill into the little wooden box cleverly concealed beneath the folds of her plaster-of-paris robe. Dear Mary, you also had a son who died violently. Help me to keep my temper at the custody hearing and not show disdain for Snow Mullins. And please intercede for us. That child needs to grow up in our home. And please let me live at least fifteen more years until he goes to college.

When she left the church, the last of the sky's orange was fading. In the rectory next door, there was a single light burning in an upstairs bedroom. The Weirs' former bedroom, or one of their children's? Did Father Devereaux sleep there now, or use it for a study? Or maybe it was the guest room, and he was preparing it for another weekend visitor.

She ran out of gas just past the Spook's Branch Fire Station, in front of the Teen Center, where, one fatal Saturday might five years ago, Rafe had persuaded Theo to go to a dance and "cut in on some hillbilly girls." Rafe had danced with her first, said something to make her fly out at him, and Theo had gone over to smooth things over before they both got clobbered by the local rowdies. She cursed at him, too, but just like a gentleman in an old script bent on placating a lady's wounded pride, he had found out where she lived and asked if he could come and see her the next day.

So it's happened at last, thought Lily, not particularly perturbed. She pumped the gas pedal several times, then shut off the headlights, put the key in her purse, and stepped out onto the road. When the car had begun to bump and stutter, she'd angled over to the shoulder, just in case it was what she thought it was. The road was clear but Ralph couldn't miss seeing the car, "his" car, when he came along presently, having picked Jason up from nursery school and dropped by to see Alicia Gallant and been persuaded, as she persuaded him every day, to "at least stay and watch the news." Lily knew she kept ginger ale in her refrigerator for Jason and Jack Daniel's on her shelf for Ralph.

You just can't keep riding around on empty, Mother. One day it's going to catch up with you. Clare said that at least once, every time she came back to Mountain City.

In defiance of them all, Lily squared her shoulders and set off for home, picking her way along the edge of the pavement in her high-heeled snakeskin pumps. A car approached, slowed down as it passed her, then continued on. She was surprised the driver hadn't stopped to ask her if she needed help, but concluded with a certain pride that she had been walking as though she knew exactly where she was going. He probably assumed she was on her way to see somebody in one of the little houses along the road. Then a truck, mounted on wheels much too large for its body, hurtled past, dangerously close, forcing her into the high grass. Teenagers who lived in the cove at the end of the paved road, no doubt; Rafe and Theo had a name for them, the boys who drove trucks like that. Greasers? Something. They hadn't even had their headlights on. Suppose they had killed her. A quick clean swipe, and thud. She wouldn't have felt a thing after that first impact, and they, being the kind of people who could not afford to stop, would have taken one shocked backward look, muttered a few obscenities, and taken off like hellfire into the cove, probably hiding the truck in the woods for a few days.

Then Ralph and Jason would come along and see the car. "Your Angel's had some trouble, it looks like," Ralph would tell the child. "Probably run out of gas. I keep telling her not to use up all her gas on those visits of mercy to old people who can't even remember her from week to week. We'll probably see her walking right along this road, so keep your eyes peeled. . . ."

No, Jason would be asleep. She wouldn't want him to have the sight of his crumpled Angel, in her heather tweed suit, the head turned oddly to one side, the matching snakeskin purse flung an astonishing distance away into a creek because of the impact. They would not find the purse until the next day.

Two funerals in the same family in two weeks. Father Zachary's powers of consolation would be tested to their utmost. He would go around hugging people until his arms ached. Father Weir would read Romans 8 again, remembering how she had praised his eloquence. Clare would be truly desolate and not a little guilty. But she would remind herself that they had been closer these past few years and console herself by recalling details of that closeness. Grief would teach her the value of motherhood and, childless herself, she would mother Rafe: staunch his tears, curb his drinking, and preach to him, using her own success as an example, about how essential it is to have work that fits the contours of your soul. Poor Theo had not had that.

Ralph would clean up the carport. He would have the Gallant jalopies hauled away. He would go out to the cemetery and stand between her stone and Theo's and remember the summer when Theo was eighteen and they had built Hannah Ullstein's upstairs addition in St Dunstan's Forest.

Hannah Ullstein. The predictable phone call every Sunday afternoon that summer. "Oh, hello, Lily, it is so hot today, don't you think?" "Isn't it! Why don't you come up and have a swim?" Her English was fluent, but broken by sudden, comic lapses. She couldn't say "You know," for instance. It came out "Yeaow." "Yeaow, Lily, I have learned this delicious new recipe for chicken tandoori. It is done on an outdoor grill. If you would like me, I could stop by the supermarket and bring the chicken and yogurt, and I have the cumin in my spice rack, I will bring that. . . . Of course, you and Ralph may have other plans for the evening . . . " "No, we don't. I'd be delighted to have you come and cook."

She always brought her swimsuit in a little Pan Am shoulder bag and changed in Lily's bedroom. The ritual never deviated after it was established. The first time, Lily had said, "You can change in the guest room, and I'll just go across into our room." But "Oh, no, I can go to your room as well." So there they would be, the two women, in Ralph and Lily's bedroom. Talking all the time, Hannah would strip in front of Lily. If Lily turned away, to look out the window, Hannah would say something that forced her to look back. Lily was obliged to note Hannah Ullstein's narrow shoulders and full, bouncing breasts, her rather aggressive-looking bush of pubic hair, her long, boyish thighs tapering into geometric-shaped kneecaps; and then the anomaly of the thickish, puckered midriff sloping into what could only be described as a potbelly. Food was clearly one of Hannah Ullstein's weaknesses; food, and what else? Yet she persisted in wearing a bikini; even Clare, still relatively firm, had stopped wearing bikinis after thirty.

Lily would slowly remove her outer garments so as not to seem inhospitable while Hannah was performing her garrulous striptease; but she always finished her own undressing in the bathroom adjoining the bedroom. Not that this deterred Hannah from sometimes poking her head around the door to continue talking. Once she had come in just as Lily was slipping her arms through the straps of her bathing suit. "Yeaow, Lily, I think I am starting my period. May I borrow some of your Tampax?" Then, before Lily could answer, she had slapped her hand over her mouth, as though she had made a great faux pas. "How silly I am! Of course you are finished with all that now." But Lily had been able to poke into the cupboard and offer the German woman all she needed. "Be sure and dust the cobwebs off," she could not resist saying, as she handed the Tampax over. Hannah had frowned and looked briefly as though she were going to hand them back, before she realized it was a joke.

Her English was not yet fully calibrated to irony and figurative speech.

She talked while they swam, as well. She wasn't much of a swimmer. She preferred to paddle around in the shallow end and confide various horrors to Lily. Sometimes the horrors concerned the children she saw as patients (was that quite ethical? Lily always wondered); but mostly they were about her own close shaves, growing up in Nazi Germany in a nervous family who were constantly at one another's throats, so worried were they about the dead Jewish grandmother who might cost them their lives. Hannah paddled and gabbled, intercepting Lily at the shallow end about every other lap. Ralph, looking like a cat who had eaten a nice plump mouse for lunch and had another one stashed away for dinner, floated on his Confederate flag raft and listened benignly to the two women—mostly Hannah— talking about children and life and books. Hannah was reading *The Gulag Archipelago*. "Oh, Lily, it is a must. It will give you a little taste of what it is like to live under a brutal totalitarian government. Americans cannot really empathize."

Ralph, who for years had fallen asleep while reading *US News & World Report* in the evenings, so tired was he from outdoor work, bought *The Gulag Archipelago* and, over the course of several weeks, read every word.

After Hannah's rich German proposed, and she decided to give up her practice and go back to Germany, she had prevailed on Lily to help her get ready. There were so many things to buy. And Lily knew so much about Orientalia. Would she mind helping Hannah find a really nice Coromandel screen, something like the one Lily herself had, if possible? And then, wasn't there this factory, somewhere just outside Mountain City, where you could buy such very good cashmere sweaters for practically nothing? Lily sat on a bench in an overheated dressing room while Hannah pranced back and forth in front of the mirror, tugging herself into a variety of cashmere sweaters. "Yeaow, Lily, I can't decide between the green and the yellow. I must have the gray, I don't need a red . . . but, oh, look how soft and pretty this blue is." "Why not get one of every color?" suggested Lily. And that was just what Hannah had done. Something in her nature—or was it the insecure childhood in a war-torn, malevolent country?—had made her greedy. She felt compelled to stock up on things now that she had money to afford them. She had to *eat*. Sometimes, watching Hannah stick her finger into a sauce to test its flavor, Lily did not know whether she felt pity or disdain for this woman who had insinuated herself into their lives like a . . . what? She was way too old to be Lily's daughter. And they weren't friends, not really. What did Hannah Ullstein, who, after all, was a trained psychiatrist, think of her own behaviour with Ralph Quick's wife?

Yet, after Hannah was safely packed off to Germany with all her *things*, Lily did miss her. She was such an interesting mixture: so transparent in some ways, so puzzling in others. And Hannah had admired her. ("Yeaow, Lily, I envy how you are so complete. And your calmness. I am never sure of myself. Not like you. I think that is why I am so good at my work. I understand what those children are feeling, because I am still like them.") And, Lily believed, Hannah had *liked* her too. She and Ralph sent a cablegram on Hannah's wedding day. She found herself preparing Hannah's recipes: the rouladen, the veal paprika. She even discovered new traits in Ralph to admire.

About half a year after the wedding, Hannah wrote Lily and Ralph a warm letter. Oskar and she were so busy. They were constantly traveling. Oskar had a house in Hamburg, an apartment in Paris, a villa in Lugano, and for her he had just purchased a lovely little chalet near Interlaken, overlooking the Lake of Brienz. "And now, dear Lily and Ralph, please listen to my most wonderful plan and don't think of saying no." Hadn't Lily once said she had cousins near Interlaken, cousins her own age whom she had never seen? Ralph and Lily must make a trip to Switzerland, stay in the chalet ("Oskar wants so much to meet the two people who were so kind to me in Mountain City"), and Lily could visit her cousins. ("I will be happy to go along and provide translation services, if I am not in the way!")

The appealing scene had constructed itself, full-blown, in Lily's imagination. They would go. Why not? They would go and visit Hannah and her rich industrialist, and let her repay their kind hospitality. Lily would buy a German grammar and teach herself phrases of the language her father's parents had spoken when they emigrated from Switzerland. She would drive with Ralph and Hannah, in Hannah's high-powered, expensive car, between the matchless lakes and mountains it had broken Grandfather Buchel's heart to leave. "I remember my father saying how weary it made him, always to be hearing a strange language," Daddy had told her about the grandfather who had died so young and so unhappy he used to beat his head against the wall. "But then, he said, the day came when you heard the foreign phrases coming out of your mouth just as though they were your own. Only he pronounced it 'yust as dough dey vere jure own.' I can still hear him saying those words: 'yust as dough dey vere jure own.'"

"Let's go," Lily had told Ralph. "Neither of us has ever been to Europe. And this way, we can certainly do the Swiss part in style."

And then Ralph had to ruin everything. Oh, men and their "honesty," their "clean breasts," and telling all and spilling the beans and opening their cans of worms and expecting you to thank them for letting you view the writhing, slimy mess inside. ("There's something I want to tell you about Hannah." "Oh, that's not necessary." "But I want to tell you what happened." "As far as I'm concerned, nothing did.") It was already too late by then, even though she had refused to let him spell it out. As if a blind moron couldn't have known what had been going on that summer. Ralph's palpable guilt throbbing through the night hours, alternating with the careful alibis for unscheduled daytime absences. The sudden, feverish flare-ups of poorly suppressed smugness. The new, stylish items in the closet. The ascot worn inside the tan suede shirt costing three hundred dollars. Not to mention *The Gulag Archipelago*. Why couldn't he have carried his sin in silence, done his penance, as Father Weir had once advised her to do, by "living with the less than ideal facts" himself?

Of course she could not go and visit Hannah in Switzerland now. Because, knowing what she knew—or, rather, knowing that Ralph, and maybe even Hannah, knew that she knew—she would have to leave her pride at home.

She would just as soon have gone to Switzerland in her nightgown.

She had never crossed the wooden bridge over Spook's Branch on foot before. Wasn't that amazing. Fifteen years living on the hill beyond it, being transported over it on thick rubber tires at least twice a day, and only now, for the first time, knowing its rough-timbered, uneven feel beneath her soles, hearing for the first time the tinkle of water over the rocks beneath. The sound reminded her of poor, proud Miss Mamie today, her tartan skirts spread modestly around the seat of her potty chair.

It was dark now. Lights were on in most of the tract houses

on the access road leading to their hill. She became conscious of pain in her feet. High dudgeon had carried her on its wings from the Teen Center to here, a good half mile or more, but her corns were protesting against the unnatural pointy shapes that enclosed them, and each step recalled to her the plight of Hans Christian Andersen's Little Mermaid, who for love of a mortal exchanged her comfortable tail for the agony of walking upright on human legs.

She leaned against a rail fence to slip off the snakeskin pumps and rest a minute, and her heart almost leaped out of her body when a wet, furry muzzle probed the back of her hand. It was only the shaggy little Shetland pony she saw grazing in this yard every day; curious and friendly, he had stolen over to greet her in the darkness.

In her stockinged feet, she continued towards Quick's Hill, walking faster. Her heart slowed some. The climb up their own steep road would set it beating again. A heart attack was possible. After all, she had had a little something when they first moved out here fifteen years ago. Dr. Gallant had been there for dinner, and then there were the tests next day. Ralph had been properly scared. Yet angina patients were known frequently to outlive all those around them who had been terrorized by their potential deaths for years. Perhaps she was going to be like her mother: keeping people in line by the threat of beating them to the grave.

But she didn't want to die of a heart attack tonight. Not really. Only to arrive home breathless, with her stockings torn and maybe a little blood seeping through the holes. If Ralph and Jason were already home, it would be quite an entrance. The next best thing would be for them to come up the last curve of driveway just as she managed to complete the hill. ("What are you trying to do? Give yourself a heart attack?") But Ralph's face would be drawn and penitent. He would bring her a cup of tea to bed and resolve silently, as he watched the color steal back into her cheeks, to replace the soap dish in the bathroom and maybe clean up the carport.

During the Hannah Ullstein summer, the carport had been relatively respectable. There had been enough room to set up the charcoal grill. Turning the chicken tandoori with a long fork, licking a little of the yogurt that had spilled on her fingers, Hannah had beamed indulgently on Lily's two sons horsing around on the diving board. "Yeaow, Lily, I know you are anxious for this Vietnam war to be over so that your Theo won't have to go."

> I am a thousand winds that blow
> I am the diamond glints of snow . . .
> I am the swift uplifting rush
> of quiet birds in circled flight;
> I am the soft stars that shine at night.
> Do not stand at my grave and cry.
> I am not there, I did not die.

Never again to hear Theo's car come crackling up the driveway.

Father Weir once preached a sermon about the best way of conquering evil. Let it be smothered within a willing, living human being, he said. When it is absorbed like blood in a sponge or a spear in one's heart, it loses its power and goes no further. And he had gone on to tell the story about Saint Francis walking with a companion on a cold and snowy evening and seeing a castle on a hill, "with its lights glowing warmly out of whatever passed for windows in those times." (That was the sort of touch she had loved in his sermons.)

Understandably, the two men began to talk of happiness. Saint Francis's friend said, "Wouldn't it be a great happiness if we were to be taken into that warm castle, fed royally, treated like long-lost brothers, and put snugly to bed for the night?"

"To me," said Saint Francis, "it would be a great joy if we went up and knocked on the castle door, asked for a little food and shelter in the name of Christ, only to have the door slammed shut in our faces.

"It would be an even greater joy," he continued, "if, emboldened by our cold and hunger, we should knock again and repeat our request, only to be cursed roundly and shoved away, with the great door banged firmly against us.

"It would be the greatest joy," he further said, "if, urged by our sufferings and our needs, we made a third plea, only to be set upon by the servants, beaten and thrown out into the snowy wastes, and, for good measure, had the dogs set upon us."

Lily had been attracted by that sermon, thirty-odd years ago, but only now did she understand it and glimpse the possibilities for joy and comfort inherent in the saint's bleak and strenuous desire.

Suddenly it became her most promising task to walk barefoot on rough shale to the top of Quick's Hill in the dark, letting desolation and hopelessness embrace her like a lover, feeling the ache in her heart swell and swell like a sponge as it absorbed death and betrayal and cowardice and willful, damaging ignorance—her own as well as other people's. If she could make it to the top of the hill carrying her entire and acknowledged load of sorrows and mistakes, as well as all the evils experience had taught her human beings were capable of visiting on one another, it seemed to her she might be granted a kind of spiritual second wind. The certainty spurred her on until she could hardly wait to get to the timbered sign announcing their private road; she could already feel the arches of her feet recoiling from the sharp stones. And somewhere during the ultimate stretch of this honest walk home, after years of "running on empty" inside a protective vehicle, she would be shown how to divest herself of personal grievances (ranging from broken soap dishes to malicious daughters-in-law): how to die to herself without actually dying. What a refreshing atmosphere to live in! As she turned into their road and took her first tentative, agonizing steps to sainthood, she could already breathe the imagined air.

But then came—as something in her had known it would—the inevitable sound of an approaching car. She knew before it was close enough to trap her like a stunned animal in the sweep of its headlights that it would be blue and white, in need of a wash, its interior filled with empty paper cups, half-eaten bags of hard candy, crumpled Kleenexes and the odd screwdriver or pair of pliers, and a child's car seat in which a child refused to sit.

Her darkness was invaded by their bright and noisy approach. A door (in need of some lubricating oil) flung open with a Halloween creak.

"Angel! Why are you out there without your shoes?"

She climbed into the Pontiac beside the child and laid the snakeskin pumps decorously on top of her purse.

"I saw your car," said Ralph. "I figured out what had happened. It's a damn wonder it hasn't happened before now. Better be thankful you didn't run dry in some godforsaken spot between your nursing homes. What's the matter? You don't look very glad to see us. At least we got here in time to save you walking the hill." Then he started laughing. "You were caught between a rock and a hard place, weren't you? I don't know which would have been more impossible, walking barefoot on that rough shale or keeping yourself from breaking both ankles in those high heels."

VI: SNOW

I noticed the brother first. He was drunk and his face was all red and his eyes squinched up like little pig eyes, but there was something about the way he looked you over that put me in mind of Troy. The two brothers stood in the door of the Teen Center. They'd just paid their dollar and had their hands stamped and didn't know what to do next. They both had on those shirts with the polo players on them. The drunk cute one's was in bright green, the other's in a lavender. They stood in the doorway listening to the music with their hands in their pockets. The one in green looked like he'd enjoy starting some trouble; the other one seemed embarrassed.

"Look at them two yonder," my sister Sue's Gary says, "they must of mistook this for the country club."

"Oh, they're just Quick's boys," says Randall, the one I'd been dancing with. "Ralph Quick. Built that big home on top of the ridge. My cousin Clyde did most of the stonework."

The band started playing "Country Road." It was a right good band for what we usually get at the Teen Center. I felt kind of funny being here at all. I felt all turned around. For almost a year, I'd been someone's legal wife, and now here I was starting all over again at the Teen Center. But it sure beat staying home with Daddy. Momma was working second shift and it would of been just me and him and his temper. He didn't like it that I'd come home again, and he didn't make no secret about it.

"Come on, let's dance." said Randall.

We danced. Randall was a good dancer, even if he was just a boy. I never was interested in boys. Troy wasn't no boy. But he was a son of a bitch.

I like country dancing. I do it well and I look good doing it. In country dancing you move as a couple, but you keep yourself to yourself. There's real steps, like the old square dancing they used to do up in Granny Squirrel Hollow. You hold yourself straight and formal-like, and this excites the men more than if you was wriggling and squirming all around like a garter snake that's just been stepped on.

I knew he was watching me, the cute drunk one in the green shirt, and this made me dance better. I felt proud again for the first time in months. I felt lucky to be free. "Just you be thankful you didn't have to pay no more than you did for your lesson," Momma told me when I left Troy and come home, and she was right.

Well, when that song was finished, sure enough he come over to me. Randall didn't like it one bit, but, like I said, Randall was a boy. Sue's Gary is six-four and has his own welding shop and felt like he had to protect the family honor even since he got engaged to Sue, so he was starting over, too, but I gave him a look that said, I can hold my own with this piggy-eyed blond drunk boy from the hill, he don't scare me none. And so Gary slunk on back to Sue, where he belonged.

So we danced the next one. He wasn't much of a dancer, though he acted like he thought he was. He did a kind of a two-step but he would keep changing the pattern so it made it look like I was the clumsy one. Also our heights was wrong. I'm five-one but I can dance real well with people six foot or more. Troy was six-two. This one was only about five-ten and I hit wrong on him.

Also he wanted us to talk the whole time. He was asking me all these questions. About my name and all, why I was called that, and I had to explain about how it had snowed on May first, the day I was born, and then he wanted to know where I was in school, and I told him I wasn't no more. He wanted to know why I quit and I told him it wasn't none of his business. "Oho!" he says, jumping to the wrong conclusion, flashing his teeth at me in a nasty familiar way.

I stopped dead cold, right in the middle of the dance floor. Theo said later that I "flew" at his brother like a bird attacking a cat. He said my feet actually left the floor. But Theo always did exaggerate. The whole family does. The truth is what suits *them*, they have no respect for anything else.

"Just who do you think you are?" I said. "Just what gives you all the right to come in here and make fun of us?"

Because it was also about then that it dawned on me that, all along, he'd been making fun of the way I talked. He would ask me a question and then when I would answer he would repeat it back to me just the way I'd said it. I wish I could give some examples, but it's hard for me to remember just how I talked back then, before the Queen Mother and Theo between them took it on themselves to launder my grammar. I talked like the rest of my family and all the kids I grew up with in Granny Squirrel. Now I talk different. I'm not like I was but I'm not like the Quicks, either. I hope I will never be like them. I can't go back to talking the way I used to talk, but you know what I enjoy? After Jason's been with my folks, he talks like them. Then when it's time for him to go for his visits to the Hill, the Queen Mother almost dies. She has to start her grammar lessons all over again.

As soon as I stopped dancing and started letting him have it, Sue's Gary and Randall was on their way over. It's like they'd been watching. Waiting for it to happen. Some other couples stopped dancing and the girls stood together in a quiet knot and the boys followed Gary and Randall on over to where we were.

"He giving you trouble, Snow?" asks Gary. He's looking at *him,* though. All the other boys are right behind Gary, and slowly they're making a circle around the outsider in the green shirt.

"What's going on here?" he says, all innocent-like. "I was just trying to be friendly and she's saying I made fun of her. I certainly didn't mean to." He's trying to act casual and amused, but at the same time his voice has got higher. He starts to flash his teeth in that superior smile, then suddenly clamps his mouth shut. He's not too drunk to see how close he is to losing some of those pretty teeth. And I'm so mad I've been made a fool of, I wouldn't mind one bit.

Then the brother in the lavender shirt is there. At first, Gary and them think he's come to defend his brother and the circle starts closing in on him. He's real mad, but it turns out he's mad at his own brother. "Damn it, Rafe, I told you!" he says in almost a whisper, sort of hissing it through his teeth. "Didn't I *tell* you we had no business coming in here?"

"For Christ's sake, Theo, I didn't do anything. I was just trying to make conversation."

"Well, you can take your goddamn conversation and stick it you-know-where," I say.

"That's enough, Snow," says Gary, "we'll take care of this." Gary hates it when I curse. He told Sue it was just one more bad thing I had picked up from Troy.

Then there was this silence. The kind just before something's about to happen. The band had finished the song and they was watching, too. I think most everybody in the room, except for the brother in the green shirt, who was looking kind of sick now, was hoping there'd be a fight. Even his brother expected the fight and in some way wanted it, even though he knew he'd get chewed up and spit out. That was the strange part. The way you could see something in Theo wanted it even if they was to kill him. He stood there like he was offering himself to the worst that could happen, like he already had a picture of it in his head, and grinning at Gary and the others like he was ashamed and looking forward to it and daring them to do it, all at the same time.

I was to remember that look, and others a lot like it, the day after he was killed and nobody would tell me anything until I got to Mountain City and Sue and Gary took me to the police station to see the report. The minute I saw the words "self-inflicted," it all clicked. It makes sense, I told the detective, there was always something in him that was fascinated by the worst and he couldn't stop himself from going to meet it. He was always flirting with the idea of his own destruction, and I don't mean just during the five years we was married, neither. His own mother told this story on him, about how she was fixing to whip him when he was a little boy and he crawled under the bed and was trying to choke himself with a belt and she had to beg him to come out and promise she wouldn't whip him.

They said it was my fault the police closed the case so soon. Because I said that about the way he was always flirting with destruction and imagining himself dead in a wreck or in a gunfight with someone. I hated those guns. I mean, it's one thing to have you a rifle and go hunting once or twice a year, but not the way they salt them pistols around in shoeboxes and underwear drawers. The first time we ever went out on a date in his car, he opened up his glove compartment and showed me his gun like he was exposing himself to me or something.

There's not a doubt in my mind there would have been an awful fight that night if Rafe hadn't suddenly changed his tune and stepped forward and apologized to me. He said he'd had one too many down at Gatsby's and they should of just gone straight on home from there like his brother wanted. He said he appreciated me putting up with his terrible dancing, and that if there'd been any kind of misunderstanding during our conversation he was sure it was because he was slurring his words so bad and I had taken it as a sign of disrespect. I noticed he was slurring his words now a lot more than he had on the dance floor, and I knew it was all an act, especially the humility. He just wanted to get them out of there. He must have seen that strange way his brother was *swaying* towards Gary and them, as if he *wanted* them to light into him. And then in some way he would have won. Rafe must have known this tendency in his brother.

And now I wanted them out of there, too. I knew his apology was phony as hell, but I also knew that if there was a fight, somebody'd end up going to the police station, and maybe jail and some people would have to pay some money after it was all over, and it wouldn't be them. They'd have some smart lawyer get them off.

So I say to him, "You're right. You're not much of a dancer, or a talker, neither. I think the best thing for you two boys to do now is to go on up that hill and have your momma tuck you both in out of harm's way."

It was just the right thing to say. Sue's Gary and Randall and the others laughed. Men are right easy to manage sometimes. I'd shamed them two from the hill just bad enough so our side didn't have to go to war.

Rafe cut his eyes at me, then looked away again. He knew what I done and he was thankful. Not that he liked me for it after. He used every chance he got to run me down after that. We two were poison to one another after that night.

"Come on," he says to his brother, taking him by the arm, "let's get out of here."

But Theo shakes his arm free. He's looking at Randall. "Haven't I seen you before?" he says. "Didn't you come up to our house once to pick up Clyde when he was pointing up some of our masonry?" He's looking at Randall like he would some long-lost friend.

"I don't rightly remember," Randall says. He's embarrassed.

This idiot brother in the lavender shirt is messing things up again. "Clyde's my cousin, but —"

"Your cousin! That's right. Of course. Yes, you did come up in a red truck. Was it a Toyota?"

"Jesus *Christ,* Theo, let's go home!" Rafe, no longer bothering to slur or act drunker than he is, grabs his brother and turns him around and kind of pushes him from behind, butting his head between Theo's shoulder blades. They go out the door in this train-fashion, Theo twisting around to call back to Randall, "You tell Clyde I said hello. Tell him he's a real craftsman. . . . It's a dying art, good stonework. . . ."

"I don't know which one I'd of enjoyed whupping most," says Gary after they've gone. "The drunk one who danced with Snow, or that brother with the shit-eating grin."

"It might of been a red truck," says Randall, "but it sure wasn't no damn Toyota."

That's how I met Theo. If you care to ask me. The "official" story, the one out of the Queen Mother's book of family fairy tales, goes like this: Rafe danced with Snow, Snow "flew out" at Rafe, Theo the Peacemaker smoothed things over. Then Snow, that foulmouthed hillbilly girl, cursed Theo, but "just like a gentleman in an old romance" Theo asked Snow where she lived and she told him and then he obtained permission from her to come and see her the next day.

I would never of told him where I lived even if he had asked. And if he had asked, with Sue's Gary and all the others just waiting for an excuse to feather into him, there wouldn't of been nothing left of him to come and see anybody *with* the next day.

I was as surprised as the rest of them when that maroon-and-cream Chevy come up our road Sunday morning. Momma thought it was somebody come to see Cousin Andy, somebody not knowing he was in the rest home and his wife had gone to live with her sister and was renting the place to us now. I hadn't even bothered to look out the window with the rest of them. I was feeling poorly. I was feeling that same old tiredness I had felt two years before, when Daddy was laid off from the lumber mill in Granny Squirrel and we had to move to Mountain City so Momma could get a job in the new furniture factory. I hated Mountain City from the moment I set foot in it. I hated the way the town was all spread out every whichaway so you couldn't never get your bearings right. I hated the school Sue and I had to go to, with its snobs and niggers. In Granny Squirrel everybody knew everybody, most of us was even cousins if you went far back enough; and there was not a single nigger in Granny Squirrel. And I missed my older married sister, Evelyn, and my brothers, Charlie and Dan and Earl. All of them had families and jobs and homes of their own in Granny Squirrel.

So when I heard the car come up the road, I didn't perk up and migrate to the window with the rest of them to see who it was. I knew it wouldn't be Troy ever again, and though I certainly was not waiting for him, it's still hard to forget how it felt when you used to have somebody special to wait for.

"It's that fool from the Teen Center," says Sue's Gary.

"What fool?" asks Daddy, who was the only one besides me who hadn't bothered to get up. But Daddy didn't bother to get up much for anything anymore, excepting meals or to hit somebody.

"One of Snow's fools," says Sue with a little laugh. "All dressed up in a suit." She's leaning into big Gary as the two of them stare out of the window. "I can't believe he has the nerve. How did he know where we even lived?"

"He's a fool, all right," I said, "but he's nothing to do with me. And *I* sure didn't tell him where we lived." I thought they meant it was the other one, Old Stuck-up in the green shirt, the one I danced with.

"He's a right nice-looking boy," says Momma, looking out the window.

Daddy grunted. He let loose a stream of chewing tobacco into the urn he keeps alongside his chair and looked like he was fixing to get up and put an end to all this foolishness.

"I'll go out there," I said, getting up quick. "You all let me handle this."

When I went out into the yard and saw it wasn't the one I thought, but the other one, I was all mixed up for a minute. I don't know why, but I was a little disappointed. What on earth did *this* one want?

He was hesitating beside his car, like he'd got this far but didn't know if he should go any farther. All along, I'd thought he was the younger brother, but in the daylight he looked even younger than the night before.

"How'd you find out where I lived?" I said, making my voice hard. I knew they was all watching and listening.

"I stopped by to see Clyde on the way home from church," he says, that grin spreading over his face, he's so proud of his detective work. "Your friend Randall's cousin Clyde. He did the stonework on our —"

"I know all about that stonework," I said. "I'm sick of hearing about Clyde and your stonework. And for your information, Randall is not my 'friend,' not the way you mean."

"Oh," he said, seeming surprised. He looked down at his shoes, these dark-reddish-brown loafers with little tassels on them, and then lifted up one foot and plucked off a wet leaf that had got stuck onto the side of the sole. That was when I first noticed how graceful he was. He had this grace of body in everything he did, like a deer, or a ballet dancer. I don't think he was even aware of it. Jason has the same grace. Even the delicate way he holds his fork is pure Theo.

Then he said, "It seems all we can manage to do is insult you. First my baby brother and now me. The only reason I wanted to find you was to apologize for ruining your evening. I don't know what Rafe said to you—he doesn't even remember himself. When he drinks too much, he gets arrogant and sarcastic with everyone. I just didn't want you to think it had anything to do with you personally. He's ashamed of himself this morning."

Then why didn't *he* come and apologize? I was thinking. Why are you coming over and trying to act so nice? I was remembering now how he'd tried to play up to Randall last night, like he was a long-lost friend or something, or like . . . yes, that was it . . . like he wanted to convince Randall and Gary and them that he thought they was just as good as he was. He always did want people to like him and think he was nice. Whereas the brother, Mr. Stuck-up with the piggy eyes, didn't care whether people thought he was nice or not. He felt superior and didn't give a damn who knew it . . . only he was willing to back down if it meant saving a few of his pretty teeth from getting knocked out. He would not have gone to the trouble of finding out where we lived and come to apologize.

"It's funny," I said, folding my arms and studying Theo real hard. "I would of thought *you* were the baby brother."

I could see it stung. He swallowed. Then he said, trying to make light of it, "You're not the first person that's ever said that. It must be my innocence." He looked past me, up at the windows of our house. I knew one of them up there must of ruffled the curtain, or shown themselves, and I was ashamed.

I said, "Look, I appreciate you taking the trouble to find out where I lived and coming around to apologize. But there wasn't no need to. None of it meant"—I snapped my fingers—"that much to me."

"That's good," he said in a husky voice, like he suddenly needed to clear his throat. "I'm glad. I mean, I'm glad it didn't hurt you. I guess I'd better get on up the hill. I'm late for lunch already. I'm always late. I'll probably be late for my own funeral."

Then he grinned—what Gary called his shit-eating grin—and got back into the maroon-and-cream Chevy and made an awful racket starting the motor and backed all the way down the road like some daredevil or thief who didn't have time to turn around.

I went back in the house to my family. I should of felt real pleased with myself, but I didn't. I felt he'd won by letting me hurt him. That was a feeling I was going to know real well before it was all over.

"I guess he won't be coming round here and bothering anybody again," I said. I sat back down in my chair. There was all the rest of Sunday to get through. Then Monday and Tuesday and Wednesday and the rest of my life. I'd heard tell of widows and such, whose lives were as good as ended by the age of sixteen. They didn't have nothing more to look forward to. Was I one of those people? The idea brought me so low I even considered going back to that school again. But I'd never catch up now. The snobs would laugh at me, and I'd have to be in a grade with niggers younger than me. It was bad enough to have to be in with them when they was my own age.

"What'd he want?" asks Gary, Mister Family Protector.

"To apologize for his brother's behaviour."

"Why couldn't the brother done that hisself?" says Sue.

"That's what I say," I told her.

"How'd he know where you live?" Gary wants to know, looking at me suspiciously. He's afraid I'll lower myself again and it'll reflect on Sue and him. He told Sue I'd lowered myself by running off and marrying that trash-sorry Troy. Troy may have been a son of a bitch, but he wasn't trash. Not to me he wasn't, anyway.

"He went by and asked Randall's cousin Clyde. Who done that stonework on their house."

"I'm gonna have to speak to Clyde," says big Gary.

"Well," says Momma, going to the kitchen to see about dinner, "I thought he was a right nice-looking boy myself."

Later on that spring I got me a job cleaning rooms at the Pinecrest Motor Court on Merrimont Avenue, just after the stoplight where you turn off for Spook's Branch Road. Gary drove Sue to school every morning—he didn't want her to have to ride the school bus since they'd become engaged—so I got a ride with them as far as the stoplight. Checkout time at the Pinecrest was at noon, but most of the guests was out by nine. It was not the kind of motel you'd want to hang around in, if you could help it. I was usually done with my work by about one, and by that time Momma was up and could come get me in the car. Sometimes, if it was a real nice day, I would hitch a ride up Spook's Branch Road as far as the people was going, and then walk the rest of the way. I never had trouble getting people to stop for me. Nice people, too. The Baptist minister picked me up one time and took me all the way to the end of the paved road. He said he'd love to have me come to his church. Another time a lady with two little boys and a dog stopped for me. Well-dressed and all, in a new station wagon. She lectured me the whole way about how I ought to be careful about who I rode with, and how I ought to sum them up before I got into their car. But she didn't take me all the way to the end of the paved road.

One day it was just beautiful, and I didn't mind when my ride let me off only halfway down Spook's Branch, along about where those pastures was before they turned them into condominiums and a golf course. I still had me a couple of miles to walk, but what was there so wonderful to look forward to when I got home? Daddy in a foul temper becuse nobody needed him no more, and taking it out on me. Momma looking worn out like she never looked when we lived in Granny Squirrel. Going to the stuffy little room I shared with Sue, with all Cousin Andy's wife's knickknacks in boxes piled so high on her sewing machine we couldn't see out of the one window behind it, and taking a nap until Sue come home.

There was this little newborn colt in those pastures, and he was so cute, running around after his mother on those wobbly legs, that I stopped for a while to watch. The air smelled of sweet blossoms and I thought how good it was to be that colt with nothing to do but eat grass and run after his mother and play. And I walked on, thinking about things that happened way back when I was little. I was a late walker, and everybody in the family started worrying that there was something wrong with my legs. Except for Paw Paw, my momma's daddy. "Leave her alone," he says. "There ain't nothing at all wrong with her legs. She just ain't done with crawling yet." Then one day my big sister, Evelyn, carried me into the woods behind our house and put me down by this big tree. She walked towards the stream. I could see the sunshine on the wet rocks and it looked so pretty. I started to cry. "Well, come on, then," she says, turning around. She squatted down and held out her arms to me. "Come on, baby," she says. And I raised myself up against the tree trunk and sort of teetered towards her, not even realizing what I was doing, until she puts the palms of her hands up to her face and screams, "Oh, honey! Oh, God bless you, darlin', you're walking! Just look at you, you're walking!"

I was so proud. That was one of the happiest moments of my life. Walking along Spook's Branch Road, it brought the tears to my eyes just remembering how I took one step after the other into my big sister's arms.

A car slowed down and pulled over. I was so deep in myself that it didn't click for a minute who it was in the maroon-and-cream Chevy.

"Do you want a ride?" he calls out. Then, because I guess I didn't look all that eager, he adds, "Unless you prefer walking."

I didn't want to hurt his feelings again, so I went on and got in. He moved some books over into the backseat. He seemed nervous. "It's a beautiful day, isn't it? Too beautiful to waste in school. I cut my last class."

We started on down the road in his car. "Where are you in school?" I ask, more for something to say than anything else.

"North State College."

"Oh, you go to *college*?"

"I know. I look so young and innocent. Nevertheless, I'm a senior."

"I didn't mean that," I say. "I only meant —" I had only meant, though I decided not to tell him, that I hadn't ever known no one who was going to college.

"That's okay," he said. "It doesn't matter. What about you? Are you playing hooky, too?"

"No, I just come from my job," I said. "I quit school in the ninth grade." Not wanting him to jump to the nasty conclusions his brother had, I added with a laugh, "I ran away with someone and got married."

He hits the brakes and almost sends us both flying through the windshield. That's one thing about Theo I never could stand. The way he used to drive with his emotions. He would let his *car* express whatever he was feeling right then: anger, surprise, even happiness. And that's just as dangerous as drinking and driving, as far as I'm concerned.

"You got *married*? How old were you?"

"Fifteen. You liked to killed us just now, you know that?"

"You let me worry about driving this car," he says. "I haven't killed anybody yet. But fifteen isn't even the age of consent."

"We went to South Carolina. You can get married at fifteen down there."

He looked over at me, curious-like. "You're not still married, are you?"

"My divorce is final this coming September."

"How old are you now? Uh-oh, forget I asked that."

"Why? I was seventeen on May first. What's wrong with you asking how old I am?"

"My mother says no gentleman ever asks a woman her age. And she says a woman who'll tell her age will tell anything." He laughs. "She won't even tell her doctor her age."

"If you ask me, that's a pretty silly attitude," I say. "Your doctor's there to help you. I'm not ashamed of telling anyone my age, but that don't mean I'll tell lots of other things."

"No," he says quietly, "it doesn't mean you would." That's the way Theo always corrected my English. He never said, "No, no, don't say 'don't.'" He'd just say it his way and leave me to pick up on it. The Queen Mother would look like I'd driven a nail through some part of her body on purpose; or when she was trying to be friends, she would give me a powder-puff pat with her fingertips and say, "Snow, I hope you won't take this amiss, it's only because I want you to live up to your potential, but it's better to say either 'I did it' or 'I've done it,' rather than 'I done it.'"

Well, one thing I "done": I made her tell her age in front of the judge and that whole courtroom. I'll never forget the way she looked down at me from that stand. If looks could kill. This was after all her and their friends, and the nuns and priests and niggers, got through testifying what wonderful people the Quicks were, and hinting every chance they got what a no-count piece of trash I was. You should of heard them. Oh, they had it all planned out. The old white-haired priest with the hearing aid who "confirmed Lily" in his church and married "Lily and Ralph" about a hundred years ago. Then Father Zachary, that two-faced hypocrite, who come running out to hug all my family on the morning of the funeral: "Oh, yes, I married Theo and Snow in my church, but I must say I didn't see Snow around much after that. Yes, she came to little Jason's christening, that's about the only other time I recall her at St Dunstan's. Though Theo and the boy came to church regularly." Then, if that wasn't enough, a *third* priest, this pretty fellow with a red beard, *he* gets up there and tells everybody in his soft, sweet voice how the Sundays Theo and Jason aren't at Father Zachary's church with the Queen Mother, they're all at *his* church, Our Lady's Episcopal, on the other side of town. The judge asks him if he's ever seen me there, and he looks down at where I'm sitting and says, "No, Your Honor, I've never laid eyes on this young woman before." Then it was the nuns' turn. Nuns don't mean a thing to me, one way or another; these weren't even dressed like nuns, except the real old one did have on all black and a veil. But you could tell everybody else there was sure impressed by them. My legal-aid lawyer told me that most of these people, including even the judge, had gone to these nuns' school at one time or another. Whether they was Catholics, or Episcopalians like the Quicks, or even Jewish, they went to the nuns' school because it was the place in town to go. The old nun with the veil went up first and told in this quaky little voice with a foreign accent about what a good boy Theo had been in first grade. As if that had anything to do with anything! And how he wouldn't shake hands with some important nun from Paris until he'd gone and washed his hands. She was very deaf and the judge had to shout that her turn was over and she could get down from the stand. Then he called the name of the other one, and she come striding up, stopping to nod to this person and that person, and took the stand like she was preparing to teach a class. She kept twisting this silver band she wore on her wedding finger and talked about how long she had known the Quicks, and how she had taught Theo's older sister, and how the whole family was so committed to "the important values," and how any child lucky enough to grow up in such a family would be set for life. Oh, is that so? I thought. What about Theo? Was he set for life?

After her comes this nigger woman all dolled up in a purple suit, the one that gives massages at the Queen Mother's Health Club and that the Queen Mother always makes a big thing about calling her "friend". She's all dressed up like it's Easter Sunday, and she's nervous, but she says *her* piece: about what a fine person the Queen Mother is, and how she sets such store by her little grandson, and what good physical shape she's in, how she swims a half mile every morning and works out on the hydrogym, and how she's so unselfish and giving of herself to the community. And then comes Jason's pediatrician, saying he's never seen me in his office, that it was always Theo or Jason's grandfather who brought him for his appointments. And then comes some woman named Terry, who it turns out is the person that cuts Jason's hair, and she says, no, she's never laid eyes on me, neither, it was always Theo who brought Jason to her shop for his haircuts. I mean, it was so one-sided it was right funny, if I'd been in the mood to laugh. It was like they was trying to *erase me* so the Queen Mother and Ralph Quick could just shake everybody's hands and go out of that courtroom and raise my child. Sure, none of these people never saw me, because Theo always wanted to be the one to take Jason everywhere and show him off and play the Loving Father. Why, right after Jason was born, and I'd dropped off to sleep, Theo took that baby and was walking up and down the hospital halls, showing him off to strangers, until the nurse caught up with him and made him bring the baby back to the nursery.

"Look here," I says to my legal-aid lawyer when everybody was out for lunch, "why didn't you tell me it was going to be all their show? I could of brought all my family and friends down here, too. There's lots of people I know who could of climbed up on that stand and raved about how nice *I* am."

"Don't you worry, Snow," she says. "We're going to win this thing, but it's going to take a little time. What we're experiencing here is no ordinary custody hearing. It's a class war. But you and me have got our little secret we're saving till after all their depositions, don't we? And, besides that, nine tenths of the time the mother is awarded custody. The judge knows that. Even if he is one of them and has to go through the motions of playing their game."

She was right, though I have to admit I never liked her much. She reminded me of those War on Poverty and VISTA people who was always nosing around Granny Squirrel when I was a

little girl. They'd come down from the North, just out of college
and wanting a little "experience of real life," and they'd follow
us around and study us like we was leftover dinosaurs or something. "What strange food they eat! Why can't they talk so you
can understand them? Why don't they have any *incentive*? That's
the reason why they're all so dirt-poor, of course; they don't
have any *incentive*. But, oh, isn't it all so interesting! Boy, am I
ever going to have me a good time learning interesting things
down here in this Godforsaken place while I take me a year or
two off and let the taxpayers help me find myself."

My legal-aid lawyer was a lot like them. She wasn't from the
South, but she'd come down here to get her law degree, she
said, because it had always been her dream to help poor people
who was being exploited by a society that was reaping all the
benefits of their land and labors. She talked a lot about what a
better world it would be when we had all liberated ourselves
from the class system. She used the word "class" a lot. Now, I
didn't have no quarrel with her dreams and ideals. What kind
of a dingbat would I be if I didn't want the same things myself?
The reason I didn't like her or have much faith in her was that
she acted more interested in my case as an *example* of something
than she was in me. And I have to say, if I'd been able to afford
me a real lawyer, I'd of picked me one like the Quicks had: a
calm, serious-speaking man in a nice suit who treated me kindly
when I was on the stand, even though it was his job to take my
child away from me, and who "respectfully submitted" this and
that to the judge and the courtroom as he spoke, always being
careful to look into the eyes of as many people as he could,
when he wasn't consulting his notes. My woman meant well,
but her voice sounded too loud and harsh after his, and also it
wouldn't of hurt her to have fixed her hair a little neater and
worn a dress or a skirt. She had ideals and she wanted us to
win, but she didn't have no natural common sense how to go
about winning *them* over. I mean, poor ignorant lazy hillbilly
that I am, I knew better than to wear slacks or jeans to that
hearing. I'll bet the Queen Mother rued the day she took me
shopping at Bell's Traditionals, right after Theo and I was
married and she decided to "make me over," when I walked
into the courtroom wearing that gray suit and old-fashioned
white blouse. ("Now, *this* is the sort of thing, Snow . . . you could
wear a suit like this anywhere. It's good material and the heather
tone would go with that unusual touch of lavender in your eyes,

and what would be *really* perfect with it is this pretty high-necked blouse. Aren't you lucky to have such a nice long neck. You know, good dressing is not a thing more than capitalizing on your assets.") That suit was just like new when I took it out of the closet five years later, because I doubt if I'd worn it half a dozen times, that boring old suit with its granny blouse; but it was just ready-made for the custody hearing, and the biggest joke was, the Queen Mother herself wore a gray suit and a white blouse that day! I'll bet she thought killing was too good for me when it come her turn to get up there on that stand and there we was, dressed like sisters, and then it's my lawyer's turn to ask the questions, and she gets up in her pant-suit, with that frizzy hair and Northern accent and, right off, in front of that whole courtroom, asks the one question that the Queen Mother won't even allow her own doctor to ask:

"Mrs. Quick, how old are you?"

When we get to the end of the paved road, Theo says to me, "Do you really have to go right home?"

"I don't have to do nothing," I say. "But where else is there for me to go *except* home?"

"Well, I was thinking we could go up to my house. I could fix us some lunch and we could eat out by the pool, it's such a nice day."

"*Your* house!" I said, starting to get mad.

He picked up real quick on that—Theo was always quick to sense what others was feeling. "There won't be anyone but us," he says. "Rafe's gone back to school—he's at Chapel Hill—and it's Mother's day at The Elephant's Trunk—that's this second-hand-clothing shop run by the Republican women. And Dad's working. It's too pretty a day not to share with someone, and I'd like to share it with you. I'd like to get to know you better, Snow I really would."

It was the way he said it: *I'd like to get to know you better, Snow, I really would.* I don't recollect anyone ever saying those exact same words to me before or since, but it was more than that; it was . . . I don't know . . . his tone of seriousness and respect and the way he made me feel he was really interested in what *I* was . . . the original Snow . . . the me that wasn't like nobody else in the world. It's funny, what attracts you to different men. With Troy, it was just this feeling that made me go all weak in the knees whenever he even looked at me. Though I doubt that

Troy ever gave a single second's thought to what "the original Snow" was like. I didn't give no thought to it myself when I was with him. Not for the first year, anyway. Now, with J.D. it was attraction of another kind. It was because I had power over *him*, I could make *his* knees go weak just from a word or a look. And after all I'd been through with Theo and those Quicks, it was what I needed: to know someone worshiped the ground I walked on and sat listening for me to come back if I so much as went to the grocery store. I don't think J.D. gave much study to "the original Snow," either. When she started coming through, he got violent and jealous. But when he started taking it out on Jason, that was the end of old J.D. He served his purpose, though. I'll always be grateful to him for that.

I said to Theo, "I'll have to let them know at home where I am."

"Do you want me to take you home so you can tell them," he says, "or would you rather go on up to my house and phone from there?"

"Phone, I reckon," I said. "Since Daddy lost his job, he's not always in the friendliest mood. I'll phone and tell Momma, before she goes on second shift, and I'll have her say I'm visiting some girlfriend who works with me at the motel."

"Ashamed of me, huh?" Grinning.

We both knew he didn't mean it.

So he turns the car around—a show-offy, fancy turn he says some friend in the highway patrol taught him—and we drive back along Spook's Branch and cross this little wooden bridge, and pretty soon we get to this private road with a sign that says it's *their* hill, and up we go.

It wasn't like I expected. The house and the grounds, I mean. I had thought from the way Randall was talking that it would look more like, well, something on "Dynasty," except we didn't have "Dynasty" back then, when I met Theo. Oh, they had plenty of land to themselves and all, but it wasn't none of it elegant or luxurious. It was just this long yellowstone house when you got to the top, and a lot of white gravel and a swimming pool. It didn't even look finished; there was still building materials left out where you could see them, alongside the road. But I said, "Oh, what a nice place," anyway, because I thought he would expect it. "Yes, it is, isn't it?" he says. "But I'll tell you something sad, Snow. We were all of us a lot happier in the other houses we lived in, before Dad made money and

could build this." Then he gives this gloomy little laugh and
adds, "Or maybe I just thought we were because I was so young
and didn't know any better."

Theo got out of the car first and calmed all them mean black
dogs swarming around. He called every one of them by name
and really seemed to care about them. I remember how it used
to upset him that the rest of the family neglected the dogs. After
we was married and living in that apartment over on Merrimont
Avenue, he would sometimes get real moody around nine in the
evening. "You know, Snow," he would say, "I have a feeling
the dogs haven't had their dinner yet. Somebody must have
forgot again." And he'd get in the car and drive over there and
feed the dogs. He had a sixth sense about things like that. Even
after we separated and I'd gone to Georgia and had moved in
with J.D., he'd sometimes phone after J.D. had left for his shift
and say, "You were thinking about me and Jason just now,
weren't you, Snow?" And he'd be right. Once he called and
said, "I had the clearest picture of you just now, Snow. You
went to a window and looked out, and then you put your hands
up to your face and gave a little moan and went and flung
yourself down on the bed." Now, that was plain weird. Because
it hadn't been five minutes before that I'd gone and done exactly
like he said. After J.D. had left for his shift, I had stood at the
kitchen window of the trailer, looking at the lights from the cars
and trucks passing on the expressway, and then this feeling of
hopelessness come over me, and I thought to myself, Has
everything in my *life* been a mistake? And the thought was so
terrible, I must of moaned and put my hands to my face like he
said, and then I did go and throw myself down on the unmade
bed J.D. and me had just got up from. But at that time Theo
hadn't never *been* in that trailer, it was *before* he brought Jason
and that nurse-bitch Jeanette down to Georgia, so how could he
have pictured me unless he had a sixth sense?

After he had calmed the dogs, he came around to my side of
the car, real gentleman-like, and helped me out. We went in
their house through the kitchen entrance, and he said, "There's
a phone over there on the counter, Snow, but you'd have more
privacy in Mother and Daddy's bedroom," and he took me
down the hall to their room and showed me the phone on a
little crowded table next to the bed. He said I was welcome to
wash up in their bathroom, and then he went away.

I sat down on the edge of the bed and dialed home. On the

table was a stack of books, most of them religious, and an open tin box full of sewing stuff, and a pale-blue notepad filled with this tiny, spidery handwriting nobody could read. I knew it must be *her* side of the bed, and I suddenly had this feeling she would hate it if she'd of known I was sitting there looking at her things. Their bed wasn't really made, just the satin comforter pulled up to where the pillows was, and there was a faint odor of this person I had never even laid eyes on yet. Some cold cream or perfume, or a mixture of both, and also something not quite fresh, like old flowers. When Momma answered, and I was telling her to tell Daddy I was over at my new make-believe girlfriend's (Momma and I don't keep no secrets from each other, but we've both learned the hard way to protect ourselves from Daddy's temper), I happened to put my fingers down on the side of the table, and when I took them away again I saw my prints, the dust was so thick. After I hung up with Momma, I went into their bathroom and got a Kleenex and wiped off the table where my fingers had been, and it was strange: my heart was beating like a thief's, it was like she was standing behind me, watching me, and any minute would say, "Just what do you think you are doing in my house, with my son, when I'm not home? How dare you sit on my bed and sniff my private smells and touch my things?" I hadn't even met her yet, but I knew that's exactly what she would say.

Theo made us grilled-cheese sandwiches and big glasses of iced tea and he carried everything out to the pool on a little blue tray with Japanese people painted on it. There was even cloth napkins on the side of the tray. We sat at a table under an umbrella and ate the sandwiches. Then he went back to the house with our empty plates on the tray and come back with a fresh pitcher of iced tea and two slices of pound cake on these pretty dishes. As he walked across the white gravel, holding the tray, I noticed again how graceful he was. He was slender and tall and his thick hair, which I'd thought was just plain brown, was the color of honey in the sunshine. I realized Momma was right: he was a nice-looking boy.

"Why are you smiling?" he says. "An hour ago I was washing the whisker stubble of strangers out of the motel's sinks and emptying all kinds of filthy things out of the wastebaskets," I said, "and now here I am sitting on top of this hill, having me a poolside lunch and being waited on by a nice man. I'll take this over the other any day."

He got this real funny look on his face, like he wanted to cry or something, and I could tell I'd touched some deep place in him.

After we'd had our cake, we just set awhile, soaking up the sun. He asked me about my marriage, and I told him a little but not too much. Never tell more than you have to, Momma says. Men may ask, but they really don't want to know. And if you're fool enough to tell them, they'll take it out on you later. I did tell him Troy had once tried to choke me to death—I figured it was all right to say that much. I wanted him to know I had cause to leave. The hitting I didn't so much mind, I told him, but when he left black-and-blue marks all over my throat, I decided it was time to pack up and go. Theo, he got real agitated and said there was a special place in Hell reserved for men who beat up on women. He said he'd rather cut his own hand off before he would strike a woman. And during the whole of our marriage he never did lay a finger on me in violence. Not a single time. Though one time he come close to it. That was the time he ran out of the room and got his Bible, the one his mother had given him when he was confirmed in the church, and he tore it up in my face, ripping out the pages and stamping on them, saying things that were crooked could not be made straight and that I was the woman more bitter than death who had snared him in her net.

"It's hot," he says, after we'd talked and sunned for a while. "Why don't we go for a swim? I could lend you a bathing suit."

I said I'd just as soon not.

"Oh, come on," he says. "The water'll feel wonderful. Why not?"

"I don't think your mother would want me wearing one of her suits," I say, remembering that private smell that come out of her bedsheets and the creeping feeling I got when I was wiping my fingerprints out of the dust on her table.

He laughed and said his mother's suits would swallow six of me, that it was some other suits he had in mind: a whole drawer full of women's suits, some of them never even worn. And he takes me back inside the house and down the hall to another bedroom. Then he opens this drawer and throws maybe ten or fifteen bathing suits on one of the twin beds. A couple of them still have their price tags on. He picks up this one little bikini and says, "This would look real good on you. Don't worry, its clean. She hasn't worn it in years. She thinks she's too fat for bikinis now."

"Just who is this 'she'?" I ask.

"Oh Clare," he says, real nonchalant. And waits, with that grin of his, for me to ask who Clare is, which of course, I do.

"Clare was my wife," he says. He's holding up the panties of the bikini and sort of gazing through them, like he's imagining the body that used to fit inside them.

"Your wife!" I say. I'm getting mad. "You mean to tell me, *you* was married?"

"If I had a wife, I must have been, mustn't I?" he says, looking at me kind of dreamy. "I know I look young and innocent —"

"That's not what I meant, I mean, why didn't you say so after I told you about Troy?"

"I was waiting for the right opportunity, I guess. Anyway, it's all over now. We're divorced."

"Where is she now?"

"Are you jealous?" he asks, with that grin.

"Look here," I says. "I think you'd better take me down that hill. Right now." I had let this family make a fool of me twice, I was thinking, and that was one time too many.

He saw that I meant business, because he wiped that grin clear off his face and he explained that he'd just been teasing, that Clare was his older sister who lived in New York.

"How come you didn't mention her before?" I says.

"I didn't think about it," he says. "To tell the truth, I forget I have a sister sometimes. She's really just a half sister—Mom was married to this other man a long time ago, he was killed in World War Two. Clare only comes down to see us about twice a year, but she leaves things here so she won't have to carry a lot of luggage. She's a lot older than Rafe and me. She left home before I could even remember her."

"Well," I say, "now I don't know which story to believe."

"Wait a minute," he says to me, and he goes out of the room and comes back with this little framed snapshot in color of a woman in slacks and a black turtleneck sweater and a scarf tied around her head, and this cute little towheaded boy of about five, clinging to her legs and laying his head against her. "That's my sister Clare," he says.

"Oh, what a sweet little boy," I say. "Is that you?"

"No, that's Rafe. Rafe's always been her favorite."

I'll never forget the way he said it. There was no resentment or self-pity or nothing. Just "Rafe's always been her favorite." Like he was saying, "Rain falls from the sky." I'm not saying I was a perfect wife to Theo, but I will say this: I come to understand things about him that none of them never did. There come a point when I couldn't *live* with some of them things anymore, but at least I done him the courtesy of seeing who he really was and not what they wanted to make him into or keep him from being. Not that *who he really was* was all that easy to see. Most of the time he was covering it up one way and another, with his grinning and his wild stories or his trying so hard to be what they wanted. That's why I went kind of crazy at the funeral home and made that scene they'll hold against me to my dying day. But what happened was, I walked into that room and looked down into the casket and saw the man Theo was meant to be. I saw the way he would of looked if he could of just been himself and not so intent on pleasing and escaping them, both at the same time. It tied his living face up in knots; even when he was asleep he would twitch and grimace and strain. Now his face was dignified and beautiful. You could see the bones underneath the skin, without the clowning that always hid the beauty. It was like seeing the husband I could have had, only they'd taken him away from me before I ever even met him. I could of loved this one, I thought, looking at Theo's dead face. And then I saw they'd put him into that goddamned gray pin-striped suit, the one he called his "straitjacket." He hated that suit. He wore it like a costume. He'd put it on when he wanted to please them, or to meet with the approval of people who'd already picked their favorites, and he wasn't never going to be one, no matter what he did. The suit he liked best was the one the Queen Mother called his "dancing master's suit" and Rafe referred to as his "pimp suit." It was a kind of rosy-tan, with wide lapels, and it fit him real well in the waist and legs, brought out his natural grace. They all thought I'd made him buy it, and the Queen Mother rolled her eyes and looked as if something was itching her every time he wore it. It got to the point he wore it whenever he wanted to tease them or punish them. Which took away his natural joy in it.

The way they took away his natural joy in himself.

"All families have themselves problems," I told that court-appointed psychiatrist we all had to go and see after the first hearing, when the judge said they could have Jason for four more weeks and then we would meet again in his chambers. "But if you want my opinion, there's something a lot more than that wrong with the Quicks."

"What do you think is wrong?" he asks.

"Well," I says, "it's like they are all acting in a play or something. Each one's got themself a part, and they have to stay in that part as long as they're around the others."

"Did you have a part when you became a member of the family?"

"Ha! I didn't never become a member of that family."

"But after you married Theo, did you ever feel there was a part specially waiting for you?"

"When we was first married, I guess I had a choice of two parts," I says. "I could go on being the ignorant hillbilly girl Theo had raised from the dirt, or I could let the Queen Mother make me over into *her* idea of what I ought to be."

"And what was her idea of what you should be?"

"Not much of nothing, really. Only I should dress like them and talk like them and go to their snob churches and sit around with them in that stuffy house and act like it was the most wonderful thing in the world to be Theo's wife. They just mostly wanted me to *reflect* them. That was to be my part, I guess."

"But you and Theo had your own place to live, didn't you?"

"Oh yes, we had our apartment. But do you think that kept them out? She'd come by . . . you know, just drop in to bring us a pound cake or something, and sure as anything, she'd find something wrong. She never come right out and criticized, she'd just say, 'Oh, now let me see, where should I put this cake? I see your sink area is rather crowded at the moment.' That was her specialty, always picking a time to come when there was some dishes in the sink. She even had the nerve to bring up those dishes in court. When her floors are so dirty that Jason got his Easter outfit completely black crawling across her kitchen. Or she'd come by and ask me if I wanted to go visiting these old people with her. 'It would do you good to get out, Snow,' she'd say, sniffing around. She was always hoping to catch me smoking marijuana or something. 'You need to get more fresh air, Snow,' she'd say. And then when she gave up on that, she tried to get me interested in embroidery. Embroidery!"

"And you had other interests?"

"I had things to do, if that's what you mean. Like our laundry and our shopping and keeping house. I had a *baby*. That's an interest, isn't it? But they wanted me to have *their* interests. I mean, whenever she isn't embroidering or visiting those old people or going to church, she's got her nose in some book. But you'd of thought I was watching pornography every time I watched my programs."

"Programs?"

"My soaps. I'm not ashamed of watching them. But did they ever give me a time about it. 'Why not read a good novel?' they'd say. 'What about Dickens? Well, what about Harold Robbins, then? Oh, Snow, you mean you have never read *Gone with the Wind?* You would just love *Gone with the Wind*!' You know what finally got them all off my back? There's this old lady, Alicia Gallant, that Ralph Quick thinks is the world's most perfect person. He spends more time over at her house than he does with his own wife. And one day, she and I are sitting talking, and it turns out she watches all the same programs as me. Well, the Queen Mother overhears us and she comes over and says, 'Miss Alicia, I'm surprised!' And Alicia Gallant—she can be real funny when she wants—she just laughs and says, 'Well, how else is an old maid like me going to learn anything about domestic strife? And besides, I like to see their clothes.'"

"What was Theo's attitude to all this?"

"Well, Theo, he was so torn. I mean, he didn't like them finding fault with me, but at the same time he was always wanting to go back up there. It was like he was afraid of missing something, even though he knew they was going to hurt him or make him mad the minute he walked in the door. He kept on putting himself in the position where they could tell him what to do, like he'd have to go up there to consult his father about new tires or car insurance. Do you know that even after Theo was a married man and a father, he still didn't own his own car, even though he had paid for it with his own money? Ralph Quick owned everybody's car—he even got that old lady I was telling you about, Alicia Gallant, to put her car in his name, because that way, he said, it could come under his fleet insurance and it would cost everybody less. But, if you ask me, that's just one more way of keeping people from living their own life. Theo was never allowed to live his own life or be his own self. In a sense, it was his own family that killed him, and he let them do it."

"Do you think that was his role, then? The family sacrifice?"

"Well, maybe so," I says. Then I add, "But I'm not a psychiatrist. I'm not even educated." I don't want this man to think I'm getting above myself and start resenting me, because, after all, he's got the power to tell the judge where Jason should go after those four weeks. He's a nice enough man, the psychiatrist, but I don't want to walk into no traps. Like that personality test I had to take for him. If was full of traps. It asked the same questions, in all these different ways, to try to catch you out. Like "Do you ever get the feeling someone is following you?" And then, a few questions down the page: "Have you ever felt the whole world is against you?" Now, nobody but a fool would answer "yes" to either one of them questions. And yet who in the world but a fool hasn't never felt someone was following them or that the whole world *was* against them?

The funny thing was, I was real scared of taking them tests. I told my legal-aid woman, "If who gets Jason is based on taking *tests*, I might as well just give up now." But she said, "Snow, you don't have to be afraid of these tests. You just go over there and be yourself with Dr. Gruber, and answer the questions as straightforward as you can, and you'll be all right. You're going to be all right, anyway. Didn't you hear the judge tell everybody, right there in court, that you would probably get him at the final hearing? That 'probably' was just to let them down easier when the time comes. He's one of them, and it makes him sad to have to go against them, but he's also the judge, and he knows we won our case when you got up there and said you could give Jason a real home because you and J.D. were married."

"I sure did enjoy seeing her face," I said, "when their lawyer asked to see the marriage license and you just whipped it right out and showed him and the judge. I enjoyed that almost as much as when you and I made her tell her age to the whole courtroom."

Later, when it was all over, and me and Jason and J.D. was back in Georgia, the legal-aid woman sent me this brown envelope with that psychiatrist's report in it, or a copy of it she had made. "It is your legal right to see this," she wrote, "and I thought it might make you feel good to know that you passed all your tests with flying colors."

For my evaluation, the psychiatrist had written: "She seems to be a truthful, sensible young woman who, despite her limited education, is capable of intelligent, occasionally keen perceptions about herself and others."

*   *   *

I picked out one of the bathing suits with a price tag still on it, to wear swimming that day. Theo cut the tag off for me with his pocketknife, but he teased me. "This one's going to swallow you," he says. "She only bought that one last year. Why don't you take an earlier one in a smaller size? They've been washed. We're clean people."

"I didn't say you wasn't, but I don't like wearing a suit that's been on somebody else. I don't care if she's my own sister."

"I see," he says, grinning. "So, even if we were married, you still wouldn't wear Clare's old suits?"

I got this funny feeling when he said that, I remember. Just come right out and said "even if we were married." As though such a thing might be possible. But I answer right back, "That still wouldn't make her my sister."

"It would by marriage," he says. "Besides, you'd like Clare. She's a writer. She'd be interested in you, she'd ask you lots of questions."

"That don't mean I'd answer them," I says.

"No," he says quietly. "No, it doesn't mean you'd answer them." And he goes and gets me a nice big beach towel that I can drape around me when I come out to the pool. It's like he put himself in my place and knew I'd feel awkward having to prance through their house and out to the pool with nothing on me but that suit.

He was right about the suit being way too big for me, though I managed to fix the straps so it would stay up. And he was right about how Clare would ask me a lot of questions. Oh, she had plenty of questions, all right, when she come down for the wedding and we finally met. She *was* interested in me, but like I was some kind of rare insect Theo'd gone and caught in a jar. I was a specimen for her, not a sister. Not even a sister by marriage. I wasn't never taken in by her like Momma was. After the wedding, she and Momma sat in the kitchen and Momma told me later she'd gone through a whole bottle of champagne all by herself, asking Momma questions as fast as she could get them out. Whenever Momma's Coke got low (Momma don't drink), she would say, "Don't move, Mrs. Mullins," and jump up and get her a refill. "Lord," Momma told me later, "that girl wanted to know everything, from how I caned chairs at the factory to how I met your father. Imagine anybody wanting to know all that! She's a nice girl, though. The most down-to-earth one of 'em, if you ask me. Excepting Theo, I mean."

Down to earth! What a joke. It was just more of their play-
acting. She had herself a nice bottle of champagne and she sat
down and amused herself with Momma. I could just hear her
telling all her friends up in New York about this hillbilly woman
she sat in the kitchen with, and all about the new sister-in-law,
Snow. ("That's right, her real name, her Christian name, is
really Snow. She's only seventeen and she dropped out of school
in the ninth grade. Her poor father never even learned to read
and write. Yes, that's the family my brother has married into.
But he always was the strange brother. He's never done things
the way anybody else does. Mother calls him a knight in modern
times. He's always wanting to befriend the needy, to rescue
people. As soon as he got his driver's license, you know, he got
one of those flashers the rednecks like to put on top of their cars,
and a first-aid kit, and then he would drive around town late at
night, hoping to come across an accident or someone in distress,
so he could turn on his flasher and rush to the rescue. He's
wanted ever since he was little boy to be a highway patrolman,
but we managed to talk him out of it. Even his friends on the
highway patrol, the men he was always bothering, told him,
'Theo, go ahead and get you a college education first.' They
told him they wished *they'd* had an opportunity to go to college.
So when you look at it in that light, it's not surprising he married
Snow. It was right in character. He has always been attracted
to people he could help. And to people who were different and
strange. And I must say myself, there is something fascinating
about these people. I mean, they've been here longer than any
of us, except for the Indians. And look how they've stayed in
the same place for centuries and let modern life pass them right
by. There's something *quaint* about them . . . romantic. Theo was
attracted by that romance. And then their dialect! Some people
may call it ignorant, but some of the things they say go back to
Elizabethan times. Now, Snow's mother is about as pure an
example of what we call an old-fashioned hillbilly as you can
get. Snow's language has improved a lot since she married Theo,
but she still slips into those 'I done's' and 'I come's' and 'pass
me one of them rolls' a lot. But, even there, the language experts
say that back in the sixteenth century Snow's English would
have been perfectly correct.")
    I could just hear her. And I've heard her enough times since
to know I'm right. Turning everything into a little story that
suits herself. In this case, looking down on us, but at the same

time making it all right with her friends, turning it to her advantage that we was so quaint and old and "romantic." It didn't make a bit of difference what the truth was, why Theo really married me, why I married him. Clare is just like the rest of them in that respect. No, she's worse. Because she makes up lies about real people and writes them down in books and makes a lot of money off the lies. She wrote that big, long book about her best and oldest friend, and I heard the Queen Mother laugh once and say she had actually forgot Julia's father's real name at some Library Board meeting. She had called him by the name of the character in the book instead. "But he didn't mind," she said. "He laughed, too. I think he was rather pleased."

Another story. Who knows how pleased he really was?

I would love to know what that psychiatrist wrote for the Queen Mother's evaluation. I'll bet one thing: the word "truthful" wasn't nowhere to be found on her report.

Theo was already out by the pool when I come out of the house. As soon as he was sure I could see him, he did this fancy dive off the board. Showing off. But it was graceful, like everything he did. He made it look like the easiest thing in the world, just spreading his arms and flying out over the water for a second, then plunging down, straight and clean as a knife. It was the first time I ever seen anyone dive like that. How many hours and weeks and months of doing it over and over again, I wondered, did it take somebody before they could do something as perfect as that?

I took off my beach towel and hurried down those steps at the shallow end as quick as I could. I felt self-conscious. But he was nice about it; he didn't stare openly at my body like most men would. He pretended to be having himself a great time floating on his back, though I saw him cutting his eyes over to see what I looked like in a suit. I have a nice enough figure, I guess. I'm the smallest girl in our family—I take after my daddy, who's slight and wiry. Evelyn says I have the finest bones and prettiest legs of any of us. I expect she's right, though I wish I had a little more up front. Troy used to tease me about that. He used to call me his little boy. But not in a kind way. He said when we saved us some money, he was going to send me to a doctor to get some of those silicone implants. I wouldn't never of done it, though, even if we had stayed married. The thought of having something that's not *me* underneath my skin makes me feel sick to my stomach.

Theo saw me hesitating in the shallow end. "You want to swim laps?" he asks. "If you do, I'll stay on this side."

I told him to do whatever he liked, because I was not much of a swimmer.

"How much is not much?" he asks, looking interested. He swims over to me with perfect, easy strokes. Showing off a little again.

"Well, I'm about a million years from being able to do *that*," I say. "I can't even float good. I'm scared I'll go under."

"Anybody can float," he says. "It's the first thing you ever did. You floated inside your mother for nine months. The water was all around you. Don't you remember how good it felt, sloshing around in there, with nothing to do except sleep and dream? You didn't even have to worry about your next meal. You could float and eat at the same time."

"That's disgusting," I say.

"No, it's not." And he grins that grin of his. I still see it in my sleep, sometimes. Just the grin, separate from the rest of him. "Those floating months were the happiest of my life."

"That's silly," I say. "You can't even remember them."

"Oh, yes, I can. I remember everything about them. It's those first years *after* that are blurry. But I can remember exactly how it was in the womb."

"I don't believe you. Nobody remembers back that far."

"Well, I do," he says. "I remember the way it sounded and the way I felt in there. I didn't see much, because it was dark, but I could sense different lights and shadows. And I could tell when she was happy and when she was unhappy. We could communicate without words. It was like being the center of the world, knowing everything, but not having to do anything about it. It was great. Then one day there was all this sickening turbulence and it felt like someone was trying to suck me down into this terrible hole, and I fought and fought to stay where I was, but the force was too much for me. My bubble had burst and I went down choking. I felt like I was going to be torn apart as I went down through that hole. And then I felt something cold and sharp poking and pulling at me, and there were all these things like snakes around my neck and body, trying to choke the life out of me, and then there was this awful white light blinding my eyes and it was cold and the noise was

deafening. All my world was gone. I remember the first thing I
ever thought. It wasn't in words, of course, because I didn't
know what human language was yet, but I remember thinking,
The worst thing that could ever happen to me has just
happened."

And he pointed to this tiny scar on his neck, just this little
dent, in the shape of a triangle, at the base of his neck, right in
the middle, where you can see people swallow. It was hardly no
bigger than my little fingernail. He said that was the mark Dr.
Gallant's forceps had left when they was trying to pull him out
and he was all tangled up in his umbilical cord. "My birthmark," he says. "It's the only mark I've got on my whole body."
And he smiles, suggestive-like, as if he's really saying, "Wouldn't
you like to see my whole body?" "It's my birthmark, but it's
also the Devil's mark. It was the Devil putting his finger on me
and saying, 'Hey, you. Fun's over. Come on out and join *my*
world.'"

It *was* the only mark on his body. There wasn't a single other
mark nowhere, not even a mole, except for that one little dent
at the base of his neck. It was a sweet mark. I never could look
at it without feeling sad after he told that story. What an awful
way to remember the day you was born. Not that I believed he
could really remember. That was just the way Theo liked to
talk. His family encouraged him in it because it suited them to
have someone in their play that was so different and strange.
But I will say this: for Theo, God and the Devil was very real.
That part wasn't no act. He would of made a wonderful
preacher. He would of had them all sitting on the edge of
their seats, though not in that snob church of hers.

"Come on," he says, "I'm going to show you how well you
can float. Don't be scared. I promise, you can trust me." And
he balls himself up and goes underwater, hugging his knees, and
stays like that for at least a minute. "That's called the jellyfish
float," he says. "Just hold your breath and grab your knees and
you can't help but do it."

"I can't," I says. "I'm afraid to put my face in the water."

"Oh," he says. He looks at me like I'm a problem he has to
solve, but not a problem he minds. "Well, we'll have to start
you on the other side, then. What I want you to do is lie down
in the water. You won't sink, because I'm going to keep my
arms under you. You'll be able to feel them, and I promise I
won't trick you and take them away until you ask me to."

And he worked with me I don't know how long, real patient,
until I relaxed some. My arms floated out to the side and my
hair was swirling around in the water, and he stood right there,
his arms kind of curved under me, but not actually holding me.
"How do you feel now?" he asks.

"I feel good," I say. "I feel like I could just lay here on top of
the water and go to sleep in the sun."

And he looks real happy and says, "Go on and do it. I'll be
right here, just like I am now, when you wake up." And he
swallows. I see the scar move a little. My eyes meet his and
that's when I know he's going to fall in love with me. I don't
think I could of stopped him if I'd wanted to. And why should I
of wanted to? I trusted him. I'd had love with Troy, but I'd
never had trust. Not with anyone, except maybe Momma and
Evelyn. I'd never had trust with a man. When their lawyer
asked me in court, "Why did you give up custody of your child
in the separation papers?" I said, "Because Theo and Jason love
each other so much. And I trusted Theo to take good care of
him and to let me see him whenever I could and whenever
Jason wanted. Theo was somebody you could *trust*. But now
that he's gone, that changes everything."

I meant to be a good wife to Theo, and for a while, even with
his family always picking at us, we was happy. There's different
kinds of happiness. My happiness with Theo was like that first
day when I was lying on my back in the sun, with him holding
me up in the water and looking down on me and saying, "I'll
be right here when you wake up." When we was first married, I
would try to get up and fix his breakfast before he went off to
work, but he would grin and pull the covers back over us and
say, "Let me put you back to sleep, and I'll get my own
breakfast." That side of things was good, while it lasted. It was
funny, I didn't expect it to be so good. Because I wasn't never
excited about him like I was with Troy. But he could carry me
right off in his slow and gentle way. He was a well-built man,
too. It kind of shocked me when I first saw how well. But even
though I didn't have no complaints, he was always asking me,
"Do I make you happy? Do I make you happy?" He tried to
get me to tell him if Troy had done anything I liked better,
anything I missed and wished he could do. "That's over and I
don't want to think about it anymore," I said. I said, "It's
wrong to mix these things up. Now is now and then was then."
One time Rafe was coming by our apartment to see Theo about

something, and Theo starts rushing around the bedroom, looking through my underwear drawer. "What's going *on*?" I says. "Let me borrow your Merry Widow," he says, "and do you have any colored stockings? I want to play a joke on Rafe." He ties my Merry Widow around one of the bedposts, and a pair of my pantyhose around the other bedpost, and then takes this one old black lace stocking I have and unmakes the bed and sticks the stocking in, just between the pillows. He made the whole place look like a whorehouse where people do kinky things. Then, when Rafe comes, he closes the door to the bedroom, and after they have a few beers, Rafe has to go to the bathroom, which is through the bedroom, and Theo waits until his brother's just opened the bedroom door, then he jumps up and rushes past Rafe into the bedroom and pretends like he's trying to hide the Merry Widow and the pantyhose and make our bed look respectable before Rafe "saw" anything. Which, of course, he did, which was what Theo wanted. If only Theo could of just trusted what he was in himself; but he always had to clown and fake and shock people. No telling what Rafe went back and told them on the hill. I don't want to know. One more entry on the wrong side of *my* ledger, that's for sure. Leaves her dishes in the sink. Won't even get her high-school-equivalency diploma. Never took her own child to the pediatrician or the barber. Lays around home and watches soaps all afternoon. Drove Theo practically out of his mind making him do kinky things to her, common little hillbilly slut.

I'm not a psychiatrist, like I told that court-appointed doctor. But I have thought about it a lot. I've had *time* to think about it a lot since Theo's been gone and I left J.D. and it's just me and Jason and my family, except when Jason goes for his four days a month to them. I don't think anybody could of given Theo what he needed. It's like he really did come into this world convinced that his best days was over. Once, when he was real depressed and things wasn't so good between us anymore, he said, "Nobody can love me except God. God is the only thing that knows and loves me at my deepest level. But what if he despises me, too?" It was around that time that he started despising *me*, saying the crooked could never be made straight and I didn't care about bettering myself as long as I had a meal ticket. It was like hearing *her* words come out of his mouth. That was around the time when he started that mess about how I was just a "vessel" to give birth to Jason. He went around acting like it was just him and Jason and I didn't count anymore. He took all the respect and tenderness he'd had for me and transferred it to Jason. If I went out with Sue and Gary somewhere, or just visited my family, he'd say he knew I was out with another man. "But I'll never divorce you," he says, "because in the eyes of God there is no divorce." I could of pointed out that I was already divorced when I married *him*, but what would of been the use? He believed what he wanted to believe. He was acting in his play and hearing his own voices. Then Momma lost her job at the furniture factory and her and Daddy moved back to Granny Squirrel to live with Paw Paw and Maw Maw, and I felt so alone. Sue was married to Gary, but I didn't want to be horning in on their life all the time. I got real depressed—I got to where I was sleeping half the day. Theo'd get up in the morning and dress Jason and take him off to nursery school, and it was all I could do just to get up about noon and eat myself some cereal and watch my programs. I thought maybe I was going to go crazy, that's how bad I was. One morning, about ten, I was just lying there, not really asleep or awake, neither, and suddenly I hear footsteps in the bedroom and then there's this cool hand on my forehead. I turn over and there's Evelyn. She'd driven all the way from Granny Squirrel on her day off because she was worried about me. Said I hadn't sounded like myself on the phone and she decided to come over to Mountain City and see for herself. I broke down and cried like a baby and she fixed a pot of coffee and we talked for three hours. "Maybe y'all need to separate for a while," she says. And she tells me about this good friend of hers, Ray-Ann, whose husband's just been transferred to Georgia, and Ray-Ann's found herself a nice job in a rug factory. "She says they're hiring lots of new people. I could call her tonight and ask if maybe you could get a job there, too. She could put you up until you get a place of your own." After Evelyn left, I felt so much better. I remembered I had people of my own. And that same evening, Theo phoned before he left his office and said, "We've been invited for spaghetti up on the hill, do you think you can manage to get out of bed and dressed by five-thirty?" And I pretend not to notice the sarcasm and say, "Why don't you and Jason go on up there? I had me something to eat around three." "Just as you like," he says. And so that night I stay home and wait for Evelyn's call. She says Ray-Ann is sure she can get me on in the doubling-and-twisting section, and that she and her husband will put me up till I'm on my feet and can find a place of my own. When Theo and Jason get home about ten, I'm already finished packing. I help put Jason to bed and then I wait in our room till Theo reads him to sleep and then I tell Theo I'm leaving tomorrow, if he'll drive me to the eight-fifteen bus. He takes it real calm-like, he even grins and says, "Are you sure you can get up that early in the morning?" But then, when he realizes it's for real, he threatens me. "If you walk out of here, it's the end. You don't come back, ever. Is that clear?" And then he does another complete change and goes all depressed and says, "I know I haven't made you happy. I've never been enough for you, have I? Why won't you admit it. We could at least part on an honest basis." "Maybe we could just try it for a while," I say. "I've lost all my self-respect and I won't be good to nobody till I get it back." "No," he says quietly, "you won't be good to anybody till you get it back." Correcting my English the way he always did. "Maybe we both need to take a little breather. But what about Jason? Can you just go off and leave him like that?" "He'll be with you," I says. "He's always with you, anyway. Maybe he'll be able to give you all I can't." "It doesn't *work* that way, damn it," he says, and then he pulls my clothes off and has me in this cold, brutal way like he's never done before. He don't even bother to remove his trousers. When it's over, he keeps holding me down under him and grinning. "Was that the way Troy did it?" he asks. I don't answer. "It was, wasn't it?" he says. "And you enjoyed it for the first time, didn't you? Admit it." I didn't answer.

Then I thought he was going to hit me. He even raised up and had one hand ready. But that was when he gets up and storms out of the room and comes back with his mother's Bible, the one she gave him for confirmation, and tears it up in my face and stomps on the ripped-out pages. And he yells at me that the crooked can never be made straight and that I am the woman more bitter than death. He's *chanting* it, like, the way a crazy person would, or the way someone *acting* crazy would. Then Jason wakes up and starts yelling, and that brings him back to his senses. He looks down at all of them little pieces of Bible on the rug and breaks down completely. Then I have *two* little boys to deal with.

The next morning I left for Georgia. It was the first week of April. In six more months we would of been married five years.

Down in Georgia I had my own problems. Evelyn's friend

Ray-Ann tried to be real nice to me—she'd been through a divorce herself. She was old enough to be my mother, she kept saying, and if it had been just her and me, we'd of got along just fine. But her husband, he wasn't too happy about me eating their food and sleeping every night on their sofa. He'd hardly say a word to me at meals, and since Ray-Ann and I was on different shifts, it was sometimes just him and me alone in the house. One night when Ray-Ann was working the graveyard shift, I woke up and found him kneeling beside the sofa with his hand under my nightgown. I moved in with another girl in doubling-and-twisting the next day.

Aurora Carpet Mills was a terrible place. We didn't make carpets, we made the yarn that went into luxury carpets. My job was to twist the finished yarn onto cones before it was shipped out to the factory that made it into them thick carpets like the executives have on their floors in the ads. A lot of dust and fuzz come off that yarn and got in my eyes and lungs till I could hardly see or breathe. The air hoses they put in to move the dust just made more dust. That's why there was always a job opening for someone in doubling-and-twisting. Because someone else had just got sick and had to quit. And the noise from the machines was awful. Ray-Ann said her hearing was impaired after only a few months. Then you had to meet production every day—the supervisor would come around and check on you. And if you was too slow you got a warning, and after that you was out of a job. I managed to hang in there for two months without taking any of them pep pills a lot of the women took, and without getting fired. But I had a headache the whole two months and the butane gas from the men's tow machines made me so sick I couldn't hold anything but Jell-O and ginger ale in my stomach towards the end. J.D. was one of the men that ran the tow machines, and he said I could move into his trailer and he'd take care of me till I got better and could find me another job. So I turned in my time card and give my last sixty dollars to J.D. and went to his place and slept eighteen hours straight through. He was real kind to me, J.D. Brought me little things to tempt my appetite and told me to take my time about looking for another job. I knew he was already pretty crazy about me, but I didn't have no intention of sponging off him for long. As soon as I felt better, I went out looking for work, but there just wasn't much around there besides Aurora and a few stores, and the stores didn't need nobody. So I tried to do what I could around the trailer, keeping things neat, doing the shopping. I even planted a few flowers.

At the custody hearing, their side made a big thing about how I'd gone off to Georgia and forgot all about little Jason and didn't lose no time finding myself another man to move in with. And the way their lawyer asked the questions, there wasn't no way I could get out of saying "Yes" without committing perjury. But then when I tried to explain the rest, he'd say, "Thank you, Snow, but that's all I need now." In the end it didn't make no difference, because J.D. and me got Jason, but it still made me mad. Because there was so much more to it than just those yeses. For one thing, there wasn't never a week went by that I wasn't in touch with Theo. I talked on the phone to him and Jason at least once a week. Theo wasn't mad at me anymore, it was like now we could be friends. He was real interested in what he called "my adventures" at the mill. He wanted to know what I did and what the people I worked with were like. It was a side of life he said he'd never known. Jason sounded happy when I spoke to him, and sometimes it hurt my feelings that he didn't miss me no more than he did. He sounded like it was a perfectly normal thing for him and his daddy to be living together and talking on the phone sometimes to Snow in Georgia.

The other thing was this. Along about that time I started feeling sick, I gave some thought to asking Theo if maybe we couldn't try again. One night we was talking, and I'd just about got rid of my pride and was going to ask him, when he suddenly announces he and Jason are living up at the hill now. He'd given up our apartment! When he told me that, it liked to knock the wind out of me. I mean, I'd gone on and signed the separation papers he sent down when I was still living with Ray-Ann, but somehow, as long as that apartment was there and I could count on it in my mind, I still felt, well, that maybe there was some chance for us to make it back together. He knew I was shocked, he could hear it in my voice, and he tried to smooth it over by saying how it was so much easier to have his mother and daddy there to help him with Jason, and how much money he was saving on rent and all. It was *after* that phone call that I quit my job and moved in with J.D. Not before. Many a time, after J.D. had left for his shift, I'd sit in that trailer and just fret myself sick over how clever they'd all been in getting rid of me. I could just picture Ralph Quick making one trip after another to our apartment in his truck, hauling away all our things to store in the basement on the hill, packing up Jason's clothes and toys. And then the apartment was rented to new people who moved in all *their* things, and there was Theo back under his mother's roof, only this time with a darling little grandchild she could start ruining for a part in the family play. I was just "the vessel," as Theo enjoyed telling me towards the end. Of course one part of Jason was me, there wasn't nothing they could do about that, they couldn't very well cut it out of him, but they could do a lot to make him be like them. I hated that, even though I knew he was happy with Theo. But I reckoned I'd just have to stand it.

When he informed me about that nurse-bitch Jeanette and had the nerve to bring her down to Georgia with him and Jason, I had to stand for that, too. Oh, he had it all worked out, he even told me his plans on the phone, about how he had met this nice, sensible nurse, separated like him, with a little boy just Jason's age, and how well they got along and that even the Queen Mother approved of her (yes, he was fool enough to tell me that, like he was taunting me or something), and how he was thinking of maybe marrying her when both their divorces come through. And I hadn't been gone three months! "She's different from you, Snow," he says on the phone. "She's ambitious, she's getting her R.N. in September and then going right on for more training. She's not pretty the way you are, but we have a lot in common. We go bowling together and play tennis, and I believe she loves me." He tells me all that. "Do you love her?" I ask. "Yes, I think I do," he says. "Well," I say, "how convenient. Isn't it all just so goddamn convenient." "I wish I could have convinced you after almost five years of marriage," he says, "that God's last name isn't Damn." "I thought you said you wouldn't never get a divorce, when it came right down to it," I say. "I thought you believed in the eyes of God there is no divorce." Then he says, "You've already divorced yourself from me, Snow." "What do you mean?" I say. "We're just barely separated. That divorce don't come through for months." "No," he says, "it *doesn't,* but in God's sight we're divorced because you have fornicated with that man you're living with." "Well, goddamnit, what about you and Jeanette?" I shout. "We haven't," he says, all smug and self-righteous. "You don't expect me to believe no story like that!" I scream. "No," he says, real quiet and calm, because he's in control, "I don't expect you to believe anything, Snow."

And then he actually goes and brings her down to Georgia. Makes an *outing* of it, her and her little boy, Gordon, and him and Jason. Like they was this married couple already, with two children. First they go down to Six Flags in Atlanta and tire out the little boys with all the shows and rides, and then they stop by J.D.'s place on their way back to Mountain City. Doing all that driving in one day to save their precious honor by not having to sleep over in a motel. They get here real late, and I'm already mad because I've been waiting hours. J.D. has gone on to work. He didn't much want to meet Theo, anyway. When they get here it's already dark and the little boys is bad-tempered and exhausted from all the driving. Jason doesn't even hug me, and I can see *her* taking it all in, thinking, My, she must have been a bad mother if her own child doesn't want to hug her. But Jason hadn't seen me in four months, and no telling what kind of lies they've been telling about me on the hill. And he's confused that I'm living in J.D.'s trailer. Children don't understand things like that. I can see Theo's upset for my sake when Jason doesn't hug me, and I like him for that. He's real tired, too. They all are. She asks if she can use the bathroom and stays in there for a long time. When we're alone, just Theo and me, he says, "Well, what do you think of her?" "What do you expect me to think?" I say. "I mean, I don't even know her. She's a big woman, isn't she?" "It's all hard muscle," he says, with his evil grin. "There's no fat. She's great with patients. She can pick up a grown man and carry him to the bathroom." "Well, isn't that convenient," I say, "just what you're looking for in a wife." "Don't be bitter, Snow," he says, "leaving was your choice." And I could see that he really believed that. He had made himself believe it, or *they* had. Come to think of it, I wasn't real sure he believed it, or whether he was *acting* like he believed it. Was he always acting that much, or was it just towards the end? I will never know. It still makes me crazy when I try to sort out the truth from all the lies. Even his death is all cluttered up with mysteries and lies. How am I supposed to explain things to Jason when the time comes? And he's already started asking.

Then she comes out of the bathroom, and I offer them the iced tea I've made, and I've got some Fig Newtons because they're Jason and Theo's favorite. But she won't take anything, not even the tea—which I thought was rude—and her little boy looks at her and says, "Why doesn't the lady have any homemade cookies?" She says, "Hush, Gordon," and

takes him on her lap and puts her chin down on his head, like
she's trying to just hold on to what's hers and keep herself as
separate as possible from this awful place where Theo's brought
her. She hated being there, I could tell. And through her eyes
I saw poor J.D.'s trailer as mean and small, though I'd done
the best I could to clean things up and make them nice. And
I hated Theo for bringing her and shaming me. The only nice
thing about the visit was when Jason finally come up to me
and put his little blond head in my lap and said, "Snow, why
do you want to stay *here*? Why don't you come on back to
Angel's house with us?" I stroked his head and explained I
didn't think Angel, which is what he calls the Queen Mother,
would like that very much. I suddenly felt cheated of everything in my life. Why was I *here*, and "Angel" and this big
Amazon woman, who wouldn't even touch a glass in my
house, getting ready to take over my child? I felt like crying,
or screaming for them all to get out.

It wasn't too long before they did leave, everybody was so
uncomfortable. She hadn't said two words to Theo since she'd
been in the trailer, and what looks she had sent his way certainly
had not been filled with love.

Then, when they had got up to go and the kids had run on
out to the car, Theo said his awful thing. I mean, it wasn't that
awful, it was just pure Theo, the kind of thing he'd say when he
was nervous or wanting to get a rise out of somebody. He's
standing between us, and he looks at me and then he looks at
her, and then the evil grin spreads across his face and he says,
"Why don't we all three become Mormons? Then I could be
married to both of you."

Well, she goes real red in the face and her whole body kind of
puffs up, like she's going to burst out of those tight clothes and
just explode all over the room. I swear to God she looked capable
of killing somebody, and I think she *was* capable. I have my
own ideas about what went on in that car the afternoon Theo
was killed.

Then she makes an effort to get a hold of herself. She looks
around the trailer in pure disgust, like it was full of shit or something, and then she focuses her hard little eyes on Theo and says
to him in this low, dead-like voice, "If you really meant that
you're sicker than I thought, and if you didn't, then it's a stupid
tasteless joke. Why do you have to act like such an ass?" And
she looks down at me—in height I only come about to her big

breasts—and she says, "I'm sorry I can't say 'glad to have met you,' but the words would stick in my throat."

"I know what you mean," I said. "I feel exactly the same."

Then she goes out of the door and down the steps, and Theo looks at me real sheepish-like and says, "I guess I messed up this time." But he's real pale and I feel sorry for him. I feel, somehow, it's us together against her because she's shamed both of us. She's shamed me in my home, which is the only home I have, and she has showed contempt for my husband. Yes, Theo was still my husband, and I hated her for making him seem worthless and crazy. Because it also made *me* seem worthless for being stupid enough to marry him. For making me think, for the first time ever, What if I was a fool to marry him? What if he couldn't of *got* anybody to marry him but someone like me?

So I called her back in. "There is something I want to tell you in private," I call to her. She's already getting in the car. She looks around like she's trapped, like the last thing she wants to do is come back to my trailer, but I say, "Please. This is real important." So Theo waits in the car and she comes back in and I shut the door. She stands practically against it, like the air of the room might kill her this time, and I wish it would. But at least, I remember thinking, I am going to punish her for what she done here. I am going to get back some of my and Theo's pride.

"Let me tell you something," I say. "You don't understand Theo and you don't understand me. And you'd better know something else, too. I could get Theo back any time I wanted. Because I've taken the trouble to study places in him you don't know nothing about. His religious places, for instance. He may joke, and he may make a fool of himself sometimes, but his religion is no joke. All I have to do is get a message from God that He wants us to get back together again, and I pick up that phone and tell Theo what God wants and it would be as easy as snapping my fingers or opening my legs. Easier. Because that's the way Theo is. That's his deepest self. All I need is God to have Theo back in my bed, and God is more powerful than you, and don't you forget it. He wouldn't like to hurt you, Theo wouldn't, but I can tell you this: he'd hurt you like *that*"—and I snap my fingers in her face—"before he'd go against God."

I got to her. You could see her kind of collapse, like all the air went out of her. And her face got real loose and old. "Either you're just an ignorant, spiteful little bitch," she says finally, "or you and he are both nut cases. And after today, I'm not sure I want to stay around long enough to find out which." And she opens the door and lets herself out and slams it so that the whole trailer shakes, and in a few seconds I hear the car door slam, and then the motor starts up and they're gone.

"Okay, bitch," Theo says, when he calls me first thing next morning. "What did you tell her to poison her against me? You just couldn't stand the idea of anybody else being happy, could you?"

"Happy!" I say. "You damn fool. Come out of your dream world or I'll start thinking she's right, you *are* a nut case. *I* didn't poison nobody. The poison come in the door with you all yesterday. That cow isn't about to marry you, she has contempt for you. Can't you see what's as clear as your own hand in front of your face?"

"What did you tell her, Snow?"

"What did she tell you I told her?"

"She wouldn't say. She said it was too ignorant and disgusting to repeat. All she would say was —"

"Well? What?"

"This is going to hurt you, Snow."

"Nothing that broad-butt says can touch me," I tell him.

"Well, then, she said she had a hard time understanding how someone she cared about could ever have picked you for a wife."

"Oh, she did, did she? Well, for your information, she made me feel I was an idiot ever to marry you. If you ask me, it was somebody else doing all the poison-spreading around here yesterday."

"What did you tell her, Snow?"

"Just that I could have you back if I wanted. That I knew places in you that she didn't and I could use them to get you back in my bed."

He was quiet for a minute. I thought I could hear him chuckling under his breath. Then he asks, "Did she really say I was a nut case?"

"She said both of us was, if that makes you feel any better."

"Not a whole lot," he says. Then he lets out this long sigh. "You know, I'm coming to the conclusion that women are truly terrible, Snow."

"Well," I say, "why not join a monastery? It sounds like that would suit you even better than the Mormons."

"It wouldn't be a bad idea," he says, laughing. "If I didn't have Jason, I just might look into the possibility."

After that, they got back together for a while. Then it was off and on. She went out with some man once and Theo got real mad, and she said now they were even, now she'd paid him back for that awful visit to Georgia. And then she's coming home from doing her laundry one afternoon and she's got all these groceries and this guy walking along the street, he offers to help her carry things in. She says thank you and lets him. Then, that night, she wakes up and finds him standing over her bed. "Just be quiet," he says, "and nobody will get hurt. We won't even have to wake your little boy." Well, she rushes into the next room and grabs her little boy and runs out in the street screaming. They put the man in jail for breaking-and-entering and attempted rape. His story was she had given him to understand when he carried her groceries in that afternoon that he would be welcome back that night. His friends bailed him out, but there was going to be a trial and she was going to have to testify. She was real scared, and Theo lent her one of their guns, the ones they keep stockpiled in their shoeboxes and underwear drawers. Even the Queen Mother has her a little pearl-handled pistol, she once told me. I think the reason old broad-butt was scared was maybe she had a guilty conscience. Maybe she had egged that man on, and then, when he got there that night, well, she had second thoughts and rushed out in the street crying rape. And now she was scared him or maybe one of his friends was going to come back and make her pay. Theo couldn't stop thinking about that trial. He'd call me up just to talk about it. On the days when she and him was getting along, he would say it was clear the man was lying and there was plenty of character witnesses, people Jeanette knew at the hospital, who would testify she was a good person. But then there was other days when he was full of doubts and suspicions. "Snow," he would say, "what if she did lead him on and then lie about it? That would make him just another one of her victims." "Like you?" I asked. "In a way," he says. "She led me on to believe she loved me. Just the way she may have led him on to believe she wanted to sleep with him."

It was strange, what good friends Theo and I got to be over the telephone, those last weeks of his life. We would talk almost every night, after J.D.'d left for his shift. We talked about things we never talked about when we was married and living together.

Like his work, for instance. I knew he wasn't happy with accounting, but he never said why. Now he explained to me how most of his work was just finding ways to help the rich keep their money and avoid paying taxes. He said what he'd really like was to find cheats and turn them in to the government. He was even thinking about going to work for the Internal Revenue Service. He'd sent for an application. And I talked to him about things, as well. One night he asked, "Snow, is J.D. treating you good in the sack?" And I just come right out and said, "J.D.'s kind, but he's not a patch on you. For one thing, he just doesn't have your equipment." I come right out and said that. We even talked a little about getting back together. "Maybe we could start over again in California," he said once, "away from all of them, your family and mine. No, maybe we'd better make it Australia." About a week before he died, I remember, my period was late. I was worried and I told him. "Listen, Snow," he says, "if I were to ask you to get rid of it, would you do it for me? If it meant we could get back together?" I thought a minute. "I believe I could do that," I said. It turned out it was just a false alarm, but I'm glad I can look back and know I was able to say that to him and mean it. I think it pleased him.

And then he called me that Saturday night of the Queen Mother's birthday. He sounded tired. "It's the usual circus up here," he said. "Jason's in orbit, and Rafe and I had an argument at the table which he managed to win by cheap shortcuts, and Mother's been mad at Dad all day because he wouldn't clean the carport for her birthday. He's playing solitaire in the kitchen and she and Clare are in Clare's room with the door shut. Clare's old friend Julia was up here for a while—she used to like me when I was little, or so they say. We went outside and talked some, but she had a headache and wanted to get home."

"That place can give you a headache."

He laughed—real tired, though. "That's what I told her. When I said it, I thought of you, how you always got one up here. It's beginning to give me one."

"Why don't you get out, then?" I said.

"I've been giving it some thought," he says.

The next thing I know, it's Monday morning and Ralph Quick's on the phone. "Are you sitting down?" he says. I said no, I was not, I was fixing myself some breakfast. Then he says, "Well, I'd sit down if I were you. I've got some bad news."

The first thing I thought was, They've let my little boy get hurt, maybe they've let him get killed.

Then he says Theo's funeral is going to be at St. Dunstan's at eleven o'clock tomorrow. Just like that. "We thought you might like to know the funeral is at eleven o'clock tomorrow." Like I was some casual acquaintance they was hoping was too far away to come but they had to invite anyway.

COUPLE FOUND SHOT

A Mountain City man and a woman died Sunday in an apparent murder-suicide on Fairfield Road, according to police.

Police say the bodies of Theodore Anthony Quick, 28, of Spooks Branch Valley and Jeanette C. Harris, 23, of 12 Maple Avenue were found about 4 p.m. in a car that was stopped at 623 Fairfield Road. They had received gunshot wounds to the head. Police said they were pronounced dead at 6:30 p.m. after being taken to Memorial Mission Hospital.

Harris's 3-year-old son was in the backseat of the car but was not injured.

Police said a .25-caliber pistol was found between the two bodies.

—*The Mountain City Citizen*, October 3, 1983

VII: NIGHTMARES

"*R*afe? Would you like to come in?"

"Oh. Are you —"

"I'm Dr. Blake."

"Oh, I'm sorry, I thought —"

"You thought —"

"Nothing. It's just that when they said on the phone I'd be seeing Dr. Blake I automatically pictured a man."

"Does it bother you that I'm not?"

"No, of course not. It's just, you know, the remnants of my sexist conditioning. I'm glad you have the time to see me."

Yet it did bother him, he realized, as she sat down behind her desk, a plain woman, not that much older than himself, wearing a yellow sweater that did nothing for her washed-out complexion, and a pleated tartan skirt, the likes of which he hadn't seen since the tea dances La Fosse Hall used to have with the St. Clothilde girls, with always at least two nuns chaperoning from the balcony of the gym. If she had been a pretty, stylish woman, there would have been other problems, but this way it spoiled something from the start. An unbeautiful woman was a person with a handicap: he couldn't help it if he felt that way. But he would have to be careful not to show it, because it would offend her and she might refuse to help him. Not that she was hideous or anything. But there wouldn't have been this problem with a man.

She was leafing through his old folder. From where he sat, he could see Dr. Shapiro's choppy handwriting upside down. Notes on the Rafe of four years ago, who got nauseated in first-year law classes and couldn't carry on a conversation with a girl unless he got drunk first. He still had to sedate himself with vodka tonics before he could perform the conversational struttings demanded of the flirting male, but thanks to Shapiro no one could ever say he had flunked out of law school. Shapiro had helped him see why his stomach pitched and he felt like gagging every time he opened a law book or went to class; the practical, sharp-sighted little doctor had advised him to go to the dean and request a leave of absence *before* his grades fell. Shapiro had written the dean a letter, and Rafe had been told his place would be there whenever he wanted to come back. Not that he would ever want to, but the door had been left open and he had prevented the blot of a failure on his record. Now he was surprisingly at home over at the Business School, working towards his Ph.D. at what his father sarcastically called his "gentlemanly pace," forecasting and manipulating data in the sleek, well-appointed new computer lab. So much of what he did now was like a game, recalling to him his boyhood fantasies of being in command of the control room on a giant spaceship. In law you were always having to look up what somebody else had said. What his stomach had been rebelling against was the fear of being buried alive under a lot of "precedents." He wished Shapiro were here today; they could continue where they had left off. Shapiro would know who Theo and all the others were. But gifted shrinks didn't hang around Student Health as residents forever. By now he must have a big, flourishing practice of his own. His specialty, he had once told Rafe, was going to be impotence in males.

"How can I help you, Rafe?"

The question was asked so placidly. As if it were all the same to her whether he replied "I can't seem to find a girlfriend" or "This morning I contemplated suicide again." And though both complaints could qualify as partial expressions of a larger distress, he nevertheless was so put off by this colorless woman, who'd probably been assigned to him because he'd called up at the last minute this morning and all the good doctors were already booked, that he considered getting up and saying it was all a mistake, he didn't really have a problem, and going back to the computer lab to work on the valuation analysis he was doing for Professor Alcott, who consulted part-time for a famous national insurance company. The valuation analysis was really needed. Whereas, what profitable results could be expected from an hour with Dr. Blake?

But ingrained politeness and an inertia alloyed with something close to despair kept him seated. "It's probably nothing much," he began insincerely, looking out of the window next to his chair. They were having a January thaw and it was a freakish spring morning, with blue sky and long shadows on the grass. A girl in a cherry-colored sweatsuit glided silkily along a jogging path. "It's just that I'm sad and I've been having these dreams. My brother was killed three months ago and I keep dreaming about him. Until last night, or rather early this morning, I've liked having the dreams. Sometimes I've even gone to bed early, hoping to have another one. It's like he's somehow communicating with me. But this last one —" He had to stop and take a deep breath. "It was different. It was awful."

"How was your brother killed?"

He reached in his back pocket for his wallet and extricated a small newspaper clipping wearing thin in its creases. It would be simpler to hand it across the desk than try to explain. He watched her read the three or four inches of cold-blooded police-blotter language, almost every word of which he knew by heart. She bit her lower lip. Probably when she reached the part about the child in the backseat. Most people were grossed out by that.

"This must have been a terrible shock." She handed back the clipping. "But it didn't make it clear whether . . . Was your brother, Theodore, killed by the woman, or . . .?"

"We'll probably never know for sure. Probably some of us don't want to know. My father's been running an ad in the papers, offering a ten-thousand-dollar reward to anyone with information leading to the conviction of the killer. Dad thinks it may have been this guy Jeanette was supposed to testify against for attempted rape. Then he's also got this other theory that the child, Jeanette's little boy, might have picked up the gun, thinking it was a toy, and shot them both from the backseat. But the forensics people say Theo did it."

"What do you think?"

"I think he probably did it. I don't mean premeditated or anything. But when he went over to see her that afternoon, he was going to force the issue in some way. She'd broken off with him, see, and he told me just before he left the house that if she wouldn't go back with him, he was going to threaten to make trouble."

"What kind of trouble?"

"By showing up at the guy's trial and testifying against her. Saying she was always asking men home and then crying rape. He said his testimony would ruin her and she'd have to leave town. Then she couldn't hurt any more men."

"Your brother must have been very angry."

"I guess he was. And he was hurt. It really got to him when they broke up. He'd been planning to ask her to marry him when both their divorces came through. He showed me this budget he'd made out on the graph paper he used in his accounting. It had their combined salaries—she was a nurse—and he'd broken the figures down into rent and food and heat and lights and child care . . . the whole thing. He'd put all his hopes into starting over, having a really good relationship with a woman. It would have been ideal in a lot of ways. They both had custody of little boys the same age."

"Theo had a child? Where is the little boy now?"

"With his mother. She got custody of him. Our family went to court to try and keep him, but she pulled every trick in the book. Married this guy ten days after Theo's death. *Ten days*. So she could tell the judge she had a respectable home for Jason. Now she's already separated from him and taken Jason to this god-awful place worse than Dogpatch where her people have camped out in squalor for about ten generations. Mom and Dad drove up to get him for his visitation days—they have him four days a month—and Mom told me last night when she phoned that the parents and grandparents and some crazy uncle all live together in this shack with bathtubs and old toilets and burned-out radios heaped outside in the yard. They get through with something, or it breaks down, and they just toss it out the door. And Snow—that's *her* name, the bitch—and Jason are living in this trailer belonging to the crazy uncle. It's in the middle of a mudfield, but somehow she's managed to get herself a brand-new color TV. When they don't even have a telephone yet. She's the limit, she really is. You know, you asked me a minute ago who I think killed Theo. Well, in the most important sense, she did. She may not have been there to pull the trigger, but marrying her was like signing his own death warrant."

"Why did he marry her?"

"You'd have had to know Theo to understand that. But it

was perfectly in character. Theo was a pushover for anybody he could help. He never could resist an underdog. But what I could kick myself for, if it hadn't been for my foolishness they never would have met."

"What did you do?"

"Oh, I was home for the weekend and Theo and I had gone out drinking at Gatsby's. That's this bar everybody goes to. We were supposed to meet some girls, but they never showed up, so we went on drinking and drinking till we were both pretty well tanked. At least I was. On the way back to our house, I saw they were having a dance at the Teen Center—that's the place where all the local yokels hang out—and I talked Theo into stopping. I thought we'd find a couple of cute girls and give them a whirl. Cut our losses, so to speak. But Theo was shy, he never even danced, and I made the mistake of picking Snow to dance with. While we were dancing, she said I was making fun of the way she talked, and we almost had hell to pay, Theo and I. Her red-neck friends surrounded us like goons and I had to do some fancy talking to get us out of there. But Theo, he finds out where she lives and goes to see her the next day. To apologize for *me*. And that's when the little spider started spinning her web for him."

"I see." Dr. Blake leaned forward on her elbows and intertwined her fingers. Her nails were clipped short and straight, in a utilitarian fashion, but he noticed they were manicured and painted with clear gloss. She did take some trouble over her appearance. "Do you remember why you picked her to dance with?"

"Because she stood out from the others. She was dancing with this hayseed, but there was something about her."

"I take it you don't mean her underdog qualities now."

"No, it was —" Was she teasing him? Hard to tell, from her facial expression or intonations, such as they were. She was from somewhere different from the people he was used to. Maybe a place where charm was considered suspect, and the inhabitants spoke in flat, nuance-bare accents: perhaps the middle of the country, where the bleached-out cereal crops matched her face and hair. "There was something foxy about her. She's a little thing, only five-foot-one, but she holds herself well. She has this way of coming on, helpless and dangerous at the same time. And reluctant as I am to admit it, after all she's put us through, she's the kind of girl you look at twice. She has these large, deep-set eyes that are almost purple, and nice dark hair with interesting lights in it, and those fine, long-boned features, you know, that a lot of hillbillies have." He had piled it on a bit thick to punish her for the underdog jibe, intentionally leaving out his ex-sister-in-law's unhealthy bluish pallor and what his mother described as her "weasel look".

"The dream you had last night, can you remember it in detail?" The doctor hadn't noticed, or she had been unaffected by his tribute to physical attractions, even when possessed by an enemy. For the first time he glimpsed strengths that might accrue to persons of either sex who had gazed into their mirrors early in life and, either with resignation or a sort of blessed relief, declared themselves exempt from the rat race of beauty and desirability.

"Remember it? There's very little chance I'll ever forget it. It wasn't like any of the others. It went completely against them. It was a first-class nightmare. When I woke out of it, I saw Theo in a sinister light, and I hated myself as well. It was about an hour before I could even convince myself to get up. It was like . . . some end to something. That's when I decided to call up here and ask if I could see somebody."

"Tell me everything you can remember about it, even things that may seem trivial or beside the point."

"Well, somebody told me Theo had come back. 'Hey, guess what?' he said. 'Your brother's back in town.' It wasn't anyone I knew, I don't even remember his face; he was more just a voice. 'Hey, Rafe, your brother's back in town.' We were in a crowded place. Maybe a bar. Like Gatsby's, only it wasn't Gatsby's. I didn't believe him, but I wanted to believe. I wanted to so bad that I could feel it in the pit of my stomach, even in the dream. I went out and got in my car and started driving around. It was night and there weren't any other cars. It was Mountain City, but it looked like one of those frontier towns you see in Westerns. Dust and little pieces of paper were blowing around. Suddenly I was walking, and I saw this figure coming towards me. He looked just like Theo, only there was something different. It wasn't Theo, though he looked exactly like him. He would have fooled most people, but not me. But I wanted it to be him so bad that I called out, 'Theo, is it really you?' and the tears started streaming down my face. And he came towards me, grinning in this exact same way Theo did, except he took it one degree too far, like an actor who's trying to play somebody and exaggerates just that one degree that ruins it. 'Yes, Rafe,' he said 'it's really me.' And it was Theo's voice, but there was a degree of sarcasm, almost a brutality, in it that Theo never had. Then he put out his hand—you know, to shake hands —and I knew if I touched his hand, if I pretended to believe he was Theo, that he would *turn into* Theo for me. I don't mean that the real Theo would have come back, but that this guy, for reasons I might never know, was willing to pose as my brother for the rest of his life and I would accept him as 'Theo,' and we would go places together and talk about our shared past—through some means he would be able to remember everything I remembered—and I wouldn't have to be so lonely. Well, what I did was pull out a gun, which I suddenly seemed to have on me, and I shot him right between the eyes. I remember feeling so astonished with my perfect aim. Because, see, in real life I could never shoot straight. It was Theo who was the marksman, he was in the Rifle Association and had won medals and everything. But then . . . Oh God, this was the worst part . . . When I rolled the dead man over in the dust and looked at him again . . . Oh, shit, don't pay any attention . . . I've become a tear factory these last three months. Give me just a second. . . ." Now he was grateful for her lack of allure. She sat there calmly and professionally and watched him cry with the same attentive imperturbability she might have shown had he been speaking in a cool, steady voice. "Anyway," he continued when he could, "when I turned him over in the dust with my foot, I had this awful feeling it *was* Theo, after all. And I woke up feeling I'd lost Theo not only in life but in some other dimension as well. And I felt it was somehow my fault, for not being brave enough to make the dream come out differently. I felt that, in a real sense, I had murdered him. I lay there in bed and wondered, really, what was the point of going on. But I have to go on, you see. I used to have the option . . . I gave myself the option that if things got too bad I could just . . . well, you know, check out. But he did it first. So I've got to go on. Only it seems so hard."

"I can well understand it must, Rafe. But let's go back to the way you felt when you woke up. You say you felt it was *your fault* for not making the dream come out right. Surely that's expecting an awful lot of yourself. Have you been able to perform such feats in other dreams?"

"Sometimes. I mean, just to give a hypothetical example, I

might be dreaming of making out with a girl. And I can make things happen pretty much as I want."

"But in this hypothetical dream, do you have the feeling you're *solely* in control of what's going to happen next, or do things sometimes happen a little of their own momentum?"

"Some of both, I guess, but with Theo—I mean, this guy who wasn't Theo—I think if I'd had more courage in the dream to accept his sinister side, I might have learned something important. If I could have just touched his hand and said . . . Oh, *shit*, sorry, give me a minute . . ."

She waited until the sobs subsided. "Touched his hand and said . . .?" she prompted.

"Said, 'Okay, I accept you as my brother, *whatever you are*.' If I could have managed that in the dream, then he might have led me to Theo. Or turned into Theo, like, you know, in those fairy tales where a person's been changed into something else and can only become himself again if someone loves him enough. If I could only have accepted this impostor in the *name* of Theo, maybe I could have broken the spell."

She wrote something down on her pad. He wished he knew what it was. "And if you had broken the spell, and it was your brother again, what then?"

"I'll never know now. But it would have been a *sign*, somehow, that we were still in touch. I guess I need to believe that the dead can still reach us, even if it's in a dream. I certainly felt he was trying to reach me in some of the other dreams."

"How was that?"

"Because he comforted me. The night of the day he died, for instance, I dreamed . . . This is going to sound silly, but I dreamed we were in a litter of newborn puppies. We were two of the puppies ourselves, all curled around each other, the way Theo and I used to sleep together when we were real little, before Dad made us separate into bunk beds. Only in the dream, I could feel Theo's fur. It was real soft and lay close to his skin, like puppy fur does, and it was warm and moist. And then he started whimpering and a big hand reached down and took him away and I was cold. Then I heard human voices saying he was real sick, he'd caught distemper and he was going to die. And I started barking in the dream. I barked as loud as I could at them. What I was saying, only I couldn't speak words, was 'He is not going to die, he is not, because I won't let him.' And it worked. The hand put him back in, next to me, and he licked me all over and I heard the human voice say, 'It's a miracle but it seems he's going to live after all.' And I was happy. Until I woke up and heard Dad on the phone in the kitchen, making arrangements for the funeral. And I've been dreaming that kind of dream pretty regularly ever since. That was the only one where we were puppies. In others, he's helping me fix my car, or we're going somewhere together. In one dream we were trying to get to California, only our car turned into two tricycles. But we were still together. And then last night I had to go and kill him. I may have killed off the possibility of his ever coming back to me in a dream."

Dr. Blake looked at her wristwatch. "I think it's fairly certain that you'll dream about your brother many more times in your life, Rafe. I'll even venture to say you'll still be dreaming about Theo when you're an old man. But frankly, and I'm going to be as direct with you as I can in the few minutes we have left, my main concern just now is that you allow yourself the chance to live and grow into that old man." The smile that she gave him, utterly free of female guile, conveyed humor and a sincere regard for his welfare. "You're going to have to treat yourself pretty carefully for a while. You've suffered a very severe loss and you impress me, on the basis of this one session, as someone who needs to understand all you can about the nature of that loss before you'll be able to . . . I won't say get over it, because you never will get over it. I don't think you'd want to get over it, in the sense of forgetting, or feeling less. But you will need to find ways to absorb it into your life. To make a place for it in the meaning of your life as it unfolds. You have real work to do, and I think I can help you if you're willing to work with me. I have some free time Friday afternoon. Would you be able to come back then?"

"I guess I could, but . . . actually I was planning to go home Friday."

"To Mountain City?"

"Yeah. It's a long drive, I know. Four hours each way, but since Theo died, I have this compulsion to go up there every weekend. Even though I'm miserable when I get there, I'm more miserable if I stay away."

"I see. Well, how about early next week, then? Tuesday, at this same hour?"

"That'd be okay, if it's okay with you."

"I'll see you next Tuesday morning, then. And Rafe, I haven't read your last doctor's notes in detail, because there wasn't time before your appointment, but I did scan them, and I noticed there was a drinking problem. Are you still having trouble with that?"

"It's not as bad, because I like what I'm doing better, over in the Business School. But I still need it if I'm going to socialize."

"Maybe we should talk some about that next time. But meanwhile I'd like to suggest that you watch the drinking. Alcohol acts as a depressant when you're already depressed."

"I didn't know that, but I guess I should have figured it out."

"If you're going to be socializing this weekend, try sipping something nonalcoholic and keep track of what you're feeling and noticing about yourself and others *without* alcohol. Do you think you could do that?"

"Ha. I could *try*. It would be an interesting experiment."

"Good. I'll be looking forward to hearing the results on Tuesday. You take care now."

She's worried about me, he thought, trotting back to the Business School through the prematurely springlike morning. Shapiro never wanted to see me twice in one week; she's afraid I'll do myself in and wants to save me. She takes me seriously because I have a real problem, the kind that will be with me the rest of my life, like a huge rock, too big to be excavated, that you just have to accept as part of the landscape; to "make a place for it in the meaning of your life as it unfolds," as she said. Though who looks forward to "unfolding" into an old man, even if he has retained the power to summon his dead brother in dreams? As his healthy young heart and fit legs pumped him effortlessly across the campus his father was worried about his never leaving ("A Ph.D. in Business? Son, *Business* is going out in the world and starting to work"), Rafe imagined Theo watching him wistfully from the realm of the newly dead. Did Theo, if there *was* some sort of consciousness after the death of the body, miss his own muscles, wish he could sprint across a sward of bouncy grass, eat a baked potato with sour cream *and* butter, feel a solid, chunky erection expanding between his thighs? You damn fool, thought Rafe, tears pricking again, why did you have to go and throw it all away?

Why'd you let me? asked his brother's reproachful voice, accompanied by that half-mad grin. What did you do to try and stop me?

*　　*　　*

"How was the weekend?"

"Miserable. Just as I expected. I'd better report straight out that I flunked your test."

"About the drinking?"

"Yeah. Friday night it was okay because I was tired and didn't feel like going out. Mom and I sat around talking. But by Saturday evening I was going stir-crazy, and when I got into Gatsby's and met some friends, I really needed a lift."

"Before you could socialize?"

"It wasn't even that. These were all guys. It was just that it had been so grim up at the house all day that I felt I owed myself more than a Diet Coke for a treat."

"And if there had been women in the group, it would have been different? You would have needed it for more than a treat?"

"I would have needed it to *talk,* if there'd been women."

"You have trouble talking to women?"

"Not all women. I mean, I can talk to you. I can talk to my mother. And my older sister—she's a writer, she lives in New York, my half sister, really, by Mom's earlier marriage. If a girl is just my friend, I can talk fine. It's when . . . you know . . . all that other stuff gets mixed in that I blow it. If I don't have a few drinks first."

"By 'all that other stuff' you mean sexual attraction?"

"Well, yes. Then there's a certain kind of *banter* that you have to engage in if you're going to get anywhere."

"Tell me more about this banter." She leaned forward, clasping her hands with the nice nails. Was she interested for herself as well? Today, in charcoal trousers and a black crewneck sweater with a stark white collar underneath, she looked better. It was more like a uniform and it suited her rinsed-out blondness and genderless features. If she'd been a nun at La Fosse Hall or St. Clothilde's, back when they all wore habits, he would probably have come home from school and told his mother there was an attractive young teacher.

"It's like you have to speak in this code. The code consists of part teasing and part . . . this arrogant skimming along is the best way I can describe it. You have to have ready-made phrases for things, and you have to seem like you don't care too much, while all the time you also have to maintain this physical tension between you."

"That sounds exhausting." She appeared on the verge of

laughter, but restrained herself. She had smallish, deep-set gray-green eyes that practically disappeared into her crinkly eyelids when she smiled.

"That's what I'm telling you. It would drive most people to drink." Though perfectly serious, he attempted a light tone.

"And what would happen if you refused to perform this ritual? What if you just stood there and talked naturally?"

"I probably wouldn't talk. Or else I'd get nervous and say something asinine, and she'd go off with somebody else."

"I see. But when you say 'go off with somebody else,' you make it sound like a one-night stand. Surely that's not the goal for all those conversational efforts you have to fuel yourself up for. Or is it?"

"No, it's not. But I can't seem to strike a happy medium. I've had serious girlfriends, I even shared an apartment with someone for eight months. But all my long-term relationships either disintegrate into something sordid or boring, or she ends up hurting me."

"Does it ever end with you hurting her?"

"Yeah, I guess maybe that's what I meant by sordid or boring. A point of familiarity is reached, and after that I can't ... well, frankly, I can't stay sexually interested. That's what happened with Sharon, the girl I lived with for eight months. At first it seemed such a mystery and a privilege, getting to watch her put on her makeup in the morning. Then it just began to seem nasty. All that mess in the sink. And I couldn't even keep a quart of ice cream in the refrigerator. She'd eat it all while I was away at classes. She gained fifteen pounds during the time we lived together."

"Wasn't she in school, too?"

"No, she was someone I met in Mountain City. She didn't go on to college. We met at Gatsby's, that bar I was telling you about, and I was real attracted to her and asked her if she'd like to come back to Chapel Hill with me. She got a job in a restaurant here for a while. But most of the time she just sat at home making up her face and then stuffing it."

"And how did it finally end?"

"Well, actually she ended up hurting me quite a bit. She started going out with other people behind my back. We'd go home to Mountain City a lot of weekends, and when she was supposed to be visiting her parents, she was seeing other guys.

This one Saturday night, I called her and asked her if she'd like to go out for a while after her parents went to bed—I knew they went to bed early—and she said she had a headache. I got suspicious and drove over to her house and parked a block away and sneaked up on her. I actually caught her in the act of screwing this guy on the screened-in front porch. Her parents were upstairs asleep in bed. I went into a rage. I would probably have killed them both if I'd had a gun."

"What did you do?"

"I tried to open the door to the porch, but it was hooked on the inside. So you know what I did? I rang the doorbell. I just put my thumb on that button and rang hell out of it. She was screaming at me and he was trying to get his pants on before her parents came. The father comes down first, still tying his bathrobe. 'What's going on here?' he shouts at me, because I'm standing where he can see me and the other guy is cringing in the shadows. And Sharon is boo-hooing. Then the mother comes out and she's smarter than the father, she puts two and two together pretty quick. I could tell she was upset with Sharon, because they liked me, the parents did. They thought I was a good catch. Anyway, I called Sharon a few more names through the screen and I said they were all welcome to her and I'd send her things back from Chapel Hill by UPS. Later she married the guy I caught her screwing with and they have a little girl."

"But hadn't you lost interest before she started two-timing you?"

"That's the funny thing. I *had,* but after I found out she'd been screwing around behind my back, when we were still living together, it really hurt. And I missed her when we weren't together anymore. I mean, I know I said that about the makeup and the ice cream, but I mourned the way it was at the beginning, when she was still so attractive to me and such a mystery. I felt I'd lost something valuable."

"Were you ever unfaithful to her when you two were living together?"

"A couple of times. But not at the beginning. It was only later, when things got kind of dull and routine."

"When the sexual interest wore off."

"Yes. But she didn't know I'd been unfaithful. She was still happy with things. At least I thought she was, but I guess she wasn't. The whole trouble with this girl business—Theo and I used to talk about it a lot—you see, Theo and I never went to school with girls and we never grew up with a sister. Clare left home and went to live with some relatives of her real father when Theo was two and I wasn't even born yet; she left when Mom was pregnant with me. So girls were these strange, unpredictable beings we could only know from the outside. We didn't have any practice in how to talk to them or treat them. The only women we saw on a daily basis were Mom and her mother, before she died, and the nuns at La Fosse Hall, which was the boys' division of this Catholic school we went to; the girls' division was St. Clothilde's, and when we got together with them for anything social, there wasn't a chance for any familiarity because the nuns watched over us like prison guards. And when La Fosse decided to discontinue its high school—they were in financial trouble and also a lot of the nuns were leaving—Dad sent us across town to the Belvedere School for Boys, which was another kind of mistake."

"What kind of mistake was that?"

"Theo and I didn't fit in. It's this prep school that think it's in the same league with Groton and Andover and those places, but it's not. But it's academically superior to the public high school and that's why Mom and Dad wanted us there. If it had just been ma, I could have passed for a Belvedere boy. But Theo was determined *not* to pass. Mr. Hardwick—that's the head-master—had his sights trained on us from the very first day. He's a snob and a sadist. He already hated Dad, who'd got his back up when he enrolled us. We were sitting ducks as far as he was concerned. Theo gave him a good fight, though. But it left a mark on his personality. I think it was while he was at Belvedere that he made up his mind to be downwardly mobile for the rest of his life. He wasn't even going to pretend to fit into society anymore. And that bastard Hardwick had the gall to come to Theo's funeral. He patted my arm on the way to the communion rail. I could have puked!"

"Why didn't you and your brother fit in?"

"Oh, Christ, we're opening a whole can of worms. That's one of my father's favorite expressions. How can I begin to explain to you? I mean, you'd have to be from around here to under-stand all our little stratification systems, all our hidden in-struments of social torture. You can't imagine . . . You're *not* from around here, are you?"

"No." She smiled. "But I'm here now and I'm sure you could

teach me a lot about it. For a start, how was Belvedere different from your other school, La Fosse? They were both all-male schools, both private schools . . ."

She was drawing him out. She was good at it, too. Whereas he hadn't even been able to get a hometown out of her. Shapiro hadn't minded talking about himself . . . his Army experiences . . . growing up in the Bronx. Yet hadn't there been just the slightest bit of rueful humor in her voice when she'd said she was here now and he could teach her a lot about it? Was she lonely here? Having difficulties with the language and customs of the natives? Had she already been wounded, perhaps, even within the safety of her professional armor, by some adverse local judgment of her person or her style?

"They were both boys' schools and they were both private schools and they were both snob schools in the sense that the people who sent their kids there were making a statement. I'm not saying Theo and I were blissfully happy at La Fosse, but it was a warmer atmosphere there. Some of the nuns were like doting aunts or grandmothers. Also, what did we have to compare it with: it was the only school we'd ever known. The only bad thing had happened at La Fosse, I guess, was that the headmaster talked Mom and Dad into making Theo repeat fourth grade, even though he wasn't actually failing anything. He said Theo wasn't emotionally ready for fifth grade, whatever that meant. Dad was saying just this past weekend that he wished now he'd never gone along with it. Because it shamed Theo, he said, and after that he always thought of himself as an outcast and a failure. But I don't think it bothered Theo all that much, after he got used to the idea. I think it upset me a lot more at the time."

"Why was that?"

"Because he was my big brother. And there he was, suddenly, only a grade ahead of me. I remember the first morning when we all came back to school in the fall. The grades were lined up for assembly, and this kid right behind me in the third-grade line punched me in the back and said, 'Hey, Quick, what's your brother doing in the fourth-grade line?' I wanted to smash his face in. He knew, but he just wanted to see what I'd say."

"And what did you say?"

"Oh, some arrogant bullshit that shut him up. I was good at that in those days. As a little boy, I thought pretty highly of myself. But it hurt me to see Theo in that next line. It diminished him, even though he took it well; I remember he just stood there grinning as if he had a secret and special reason for being in the line with all those boys a year younger than himself. But I felt sick, as if something I thought I could keep hidden, even from myself, had suddenly become public. You know, it's making me very depressed, talking about this."

"I think we should go on. What was it you had been trying to hide?"

"For some time I'd suspected . . . Oh, this is hard. There just isn't any easy way to say this. When Theo and I were little, I looked up to him. I took it for granted that because he was my big brother, he was the superior one. But then a time came when I started to feel that I had passed him. It wasn't a good feeling. It was like something had been taken away from me. I tried to pretend it wasn't happening."

"When did you first begin to feel this?"

"I can't remember, exactly. I'm not even sure I thought it out in words. It was just that, whereas before I'd looked up to him, I suddenly realized that I had to protect him. I might even have to cover up for him."

"What would he do that would require this of you?"

"It wasn't so much what he did . . . although he *did* do things; it was his particular way of acting. I mean, a lot of times he didn't show good judgment. He courted punishment when there wasn't any reason for it. At home and at school he was always testing people to see how far he could go with them before they got mad or sick of him."

"And how could you protect him?"

"By being scornful of anybody who dared to suggest to my face that my brother was acting like a fool. I had a pretty mean mouth and I could turn it on them in a way that made them wish they'd never opened theirs."

"What about your parents? What was their attitude towards Theo's behavior?"

"Oh, they came in for their share of exasperation. Dad used to take Sam to him on a pretty frequent basis. Sam was what we called Dad's belt. But then, this one time when Theo had driven Mom up the wall, she went to get Sam out of the closet and Theo beat her to it and crawled way under the bed where she couldn't reach him and tried to strangle himself with Sam. He'd looped it through the buckle and had it around his neck, pulling on it like a noose. Mom had to beg and promise not to touch him. She even cried before she finally got him to come out."

"You were there, watching?"

"I think so, I must have been. Theo was only six and I was four and I don't know whether I'm remembering what I actually saw or getting it confused with the story Mom told later. She tells a good story, though she tends to romanticize things. If she were sitting here instead of me, telling you about Theo, you'd probably get a somewhat different picture."

"What would it be like, her picture?"

"Oh, of a dreamer. A mystic. A boy who was never completely of this world. Someone who was tenderhearted and showed uncanny intuition at times and went wandering through an alien world trying to redress wrongs. Someone with lots of imagination. One of her favorite stories is about how she was trying to make Theo read *The Count of Monte Cristo*. He had a book report on it due for class and was way behind. She made him go to his room for an hour before supper every afternoon till he finished it. But he wasn't making much progress. Then, one afternoon, she peeked through the door and saw him just sitting there, the book on his lap, this rapt expression on his face, looking at the wall in front of him. And she realized that the reason he had such a hard time reading was because the images and ideas in a book stimulated his imagination and sent it off on trips of its own. The thing is, she may have been right; but whether she was right or just romanticizing, it was a way around her having to admit a child of hers was a slow reader. She's even able to comfort herself some by romanticizing him in death. I mean, when I went home this weekend, I saw she'd stuck these pictures of Theo up on the refrigerator. I said, 'How can you stand it? Being reminded every time you open the refrigerator? I still can't stand seeing pictures, it hurts too much.' 'It doesn't hurt me,' she said, 'I *like* to be reminded of him as often as I can.' But then, her religion helps her. I mean, I imagine Theo watching me sometimes, and you know about those dreams and all, but she really does believe that Theo's personality goes on existing, that it's immortal and that he's watching over us and laughing sometimes and that . . . well . . . he can even influence things."

"Influence things?"

"Yes. For example, she was telling me about how she and Dad were having this fight in the kitchen the night before I came home, when suddenly there was this loud crash in Theo's bedroom, the one he shared with Jason after he and Snow split up, and the one Jason sleeps in when he comes for his four-day visits once a month. She and Dad rushed into the room to see what the noise was. It was this huge framed collage of photographs she'd hung on the wall beside Jason's bed—all these pictures of him and his father from the time he was born through the last weeks of Theo's life—so he won't forget him, you know. It had come crashing down, but the glass in the frame wasn't even cracked. And Mom said it was perfectly clear to her that it was Theo's way of stopping the fight with Dad and sort of saying a mischievous hello at the same time."

"How did you respond when she told you this story?"

"You mean to her, or inside myself?"

"Both, if there was a difference."

"Well, sure there was. If it helps her to think of Theo still keeping company with her in that house, it would be pretty mean of me to shoot down her balloon, wouldn't it? So I guess I let her think I went along with it. It wasn't hard to do, because I did have a kind of creepy feeling while she and I were sitting there talking, but it was for other reasons."

"Such as . . .?"

"This is going to sound terrible, but for as long as I can remember, I've always known that she loved me kind of specially. She never came right out and said I was her favorite, she would never have done that, but she's often said I was her joy, and she likes to tell the story about how effortless my birth was, and I've always done well in school and she sets great store on intellectual accomplishment. I know this was sometimes a problem for Theo, that so many things came easier for me and that people were drawn to me without any effort on my part. I was my grandmother's favorite, she made no secret about it; she used to spoil and pamper me like a little king, whereas with Theo it was always 'Oh, hello, Theo,' very friendly and all, but like she was having to remind herself that he existed, too. But anyway, when Mom and I were sitting talking Friday night and she was going on about Theo's continued presence in the house and his 'mischievous hello' and all, I got this really queasy sensation. I realized that, since Theo died, she had *switched favorites*. Theo's the one she admires and loves most now. He's become larger than life, a sort of saint. A force capable of communicating his wishes from beyond death. He has power

now, he has the power he never had in life. I could never begin
to compete with such a power, unless —"

"Unless what?"

"Well, Christ! I mean . . . *you* know. Unless I was dead, too."

"Come in, Rafe. I was worried about you, driving back from
your mountains in all this snow."

"It wasn't so bad. I left early Sunday afternoon, before it
really got started good. And I have new radials on my car. But
I appreciate your worrying about me."

She looked and sounded as though she should be a little
worried about herself. Her voice was hardly above a whisper
and it was obvious that she had a bad cold. He considered
offering an expression of concern in return for hers, but despite
her watery eyes and the raw, Kleenex-chafed redness about her
nostrils, she seemed her capable, alert self, ready to accompany
him through whatever terrain their unpredictable dialogue
would lead them. It might alter some balance between them if
he were to commiserate with her, and he decided not to risk it.

"And how did you find things in Mountain City?" Her tone
conveyed a wry but serious acknowledgment that "things in
Mountain City" entailed, for him, degrees of ambivalence that
might easily defy complete comprehension for the remainder of
his life. She was getting to know his people now: Theo and
Mom and Dad . . . Clare . . . Snow; as well as an old double-
crossing girlfriend and unloved headmasters. Yet he still didn't
even know her first name. Shapiro's had been Martin. Had he
asked him, or had the doctor volunteered it somewhere along
the way?

"It was a three-ring circus. More than usual, because Jason
was there. That's one reason I left early and beat the snow. I
mean, he's a cute little boy and I feel sorry for him, but it's total
confusion when he's there."

"This was his four days a month, I take it."

"No, actually it wasn't. Snow and one of her sisters and a
brother-in-law wanted to drive to Atlanta to hear this country
music group they like. So Snow graciously invited Mom and
Dad to drive three hours to Granny Squirrel Mountain and
three hours back to pick him up Thursday, and then have the
privilege of repeating the six-hour drive to get him home. It
wouldn't have been much out of their way to bring him, because
26 out of Mountain City is the quickest way to get on 85 to

Atlanta, but she enjoys tormenting us every chance she can get. If they want to see him, they have to jump when she snaps her fingers. And they jump. They were thrilled to death to have him the extra time. Dad lost a day's work Thursday, and Mom gave up her Republican Women's lunch, and off they went. And then, when they get him to our place, there's what Mom calls his 'little transition period' to go through, which nobody enjoys."

"What happens during it?"

"Well, sometimes he's glad to see them, and sometimes he sulks for a day or so. Either way, when he arrives, he's tired and irritable from the drive. First he goes to his room, the room he shared with Theo, and checks everything out. They've got the placed fixed up like a combination toy store and father-and-son museum. Like I told you, there's this huge framed collage of pictures, all these pictures of him and Theo together —"

"The one that crashed when your mother and father were having the fight."

"Yeah, Theo's mischievous hello. Then there's a big framed picture on the chest of drawers of Theo in his cap and gown graduating from North State College. There are two closets in the room, one for Jason's 'Quick's Hill' clothes, which he leaves at our house, and the other closet is still full of Theo's jackets and suits and scrapbooks and things. A closet for the father and one for the son, just like it used to be. And there's the new quilted bedspread with matching pillows that Clare ordered out of some catalogue, and it has this Father Bear and Little Boy Bear holding hands and ascending into a starry sky together, with this town spread out below. And then there are all his toys, and his cassette player, and his little architect's drawing table and chair, and his firetruck, and his Crayonmobile. And they always have one new piece of loot waiting for him. This time it was a battery-powered robot about a foot high that walked around emitting beeps and siren noises and saying, 'Hi, I'm your atomic-powered robot, please give my best wishes to everybody,' until we were all climbing the walls. But Jason loved it. So his 'little transition period' was minimal. Mom said he didn't even taunt her the first night about how he wasn't going to church with her on Sunday."

"Does he often threaten that?"

"Usually. He knows it gets to her. It's his way of saying he's still allied with his mother. I doubt Snow's set foot inside a church since Theo's funeral. She's too lazy to get up in the morning, for one thing."

"And by Sunday has your mother won him over to going to church?"

"Oh sure. Always. By Sunday, he's one of us again. He's switched back to our kind of English, and he goes off to church with Mom. Which is great for her, but it ruins it for everybody else."

"Everybody else?"

"Well, me, for a start, if I'm home, and all the other people in church. After last Sunday, I swore I'd never go again if he went. 'But I like to have *both* my little boys with me,' she said. I said, 'Look, when *this* little boy was Jason's age, you made him go to the nursery school, and then later he came in with all the other children for the blessing at the communion rail. That's the way everybody else still does it. How many other little kids do you see staying for the whole service?' 'There was that little girl who came with her father,' she says, 'the one who leafed back and forth through the hymnal so incessantly I couldn't hear myself pray.' I pointed out that the little girl was at least ten. 'Compared to her,' she says, 'Jason was an angel.' She sees what she wants to see, Mom does, and she conveniently overlooks the fact that Jason wriggles and fidgets and sometimes speaks right out loud in the middle of the sermon. He makes both of the rectors nervous—Mom alternates between two churches in town—but they both know all about Theo and they're not going to ask her to stop bringing him. They offer it up to God, I guess. Which is more than I can do. I was so uptight after church Sunday that I had to drive around for about an hour before I could go back up the hill. It wasn't that Jason did anything especially awful, but it's sitting there all tensed up, waiting to see what he *might* do. I drove out to the Belvedere School and had a look around. After we talked about it last week, I wanted to see if it still had the power to fill me with rage."

In spite of having to sneeze violently at that moment into a Kleenex, the doctor was all attention. "And how did it affect you?"

"It's changed some since we were there. For one thing, it's coed now. It sort of defused my anger to see girls walking around the grounds. Made it seem like a different place. But some things were still the same."

"You're smiling. Why?"

"Because Theo's rocks were still there. God, he was so self-destructive, but he could be so imaginative about it. Like about the rocks. For a punishment, Hardwick told Theo he wanted him to haul these rocks from one side of the athletic field to the other. They were good-sized rocks and there were about a hundred of them. It would have taken Theo about a week of staying after school afternoons to get them hauled. He would have had ample time to reflect on his sins, which is what Hardwick wanted."

"What was he being punished for?"

"I don't remember. Some infraction. A 'wrong attitude.' Theo was always getting punished out at Belvedere. He and Hardwick were natural enemies from the first day. Hardwick hated the day students, for a start. He had to take a certain number, of course, but unless they were scholarship students and couldn't afford it, he preferred for them to board. When Dad went out to enroll us, Hardwick gave him his spiel about how Theo and I should board because Dad could afford it and because then we'd be totally immersed in the Belvedere Way of Life. That's Hardwick's mania: the Belvedere Way of Life. But Dad had to climb in *his* pulpit and preach Hardwick a sermon about how he was a self-made man and he wanted his sons to be independent and think for themselves and not to be brainwashed by *any* institution's 'total immersion.' They got off to a real fine start, those two. And then Dad capped it all by refusing to buy the tuition-refund insurance for us. At Belvedere tuition is payable in advance for the whole year. And Hardwick always explains to the parents right from the first that if their kids get expelled, or flunk out, or quit, even if it's only a week into semester, there is no refund on tuition. So he's arranged for this special policy they can buy, and they're all glad to have the protection. But not Dad. He came home so pleased with himself for talking some sense into 'that prissy little tyrant' and refusing to throw away hard-earned money on insurance policies. Well, of course, Theo and I became targets of Hardwick's spleen against Dad. He wasn't going to let up until he'd proved Dad wrong. He started off by proving it on Theo, because Theo stuck out more. Theo always loved to test authority and he'd made snob-baiting into one of his personal missions. What I find surprising about the rock incident, even now, is that Hardwick didn't kick him out for it. I mean, boys were expelled for much less. I was expelled for giving a damn party at my own home and serving beer to a few boarders. But it was like Hardwick was *fascinated* by Theo. Theo was like some exotic snake that had infiltrated his school and then, in some weird way, possessed his mind. Hardwick couldn't get Theo off his mind. It was like he was hoping for Theo to commit his next infraction so he could get outraged and punish him. I mean, for a while there they were operating like a goddamned team. I've often thought that if Theo hadn't quit Belvedere and transferred to public high school, I might never have been expelled my senior year. If Theo had stayed on to bait Hardwick, I might have sneaked quietly through on my four-point average and come to Chapel Hill on a Morehead Scholarship. Damn it, I've sometimes wondered if Hardwick didn't expel me to punish *Theo*. You know the ironic thing? Theo's still getting mail from Belvedere. Something came for him last weekend. I saw it on the kitchen table along with some of Dad's bills. It was a notice about an upcoming alumni weekend. I guess the computer hasn't been informed that he's dead. But I'm not counted as an alumnus, even though I was there for four years. If you're expelled from Belvedere, your name is wiped completely off the records. As though you'd never existed."

"I think we have a lot to talk about here, Rafe. I'd like you to tell me about the circumstances of your expulsion; and also"— she smiled and reached inside her desk drawer for another Kleenex—"I'd like to hear more about this rock incident."

"Well, the rock incident came first, so I'll start with that. The afternoon Hardwick told Theo he wanted him to haul those rocks from one side of the field to the other, apparently Theo asked him, 'Sir, do you really *need* those rocks moved over there, or is it just for my punishment?' Well, I guess Hardwick felt kind of ridiculous, or cornered, because he told Theo he really did have a reason for wanting the rocks moved. So then Theo said, 'Well, if it's okay with you, sir, I'll just take my little brother home first, he's not old enough to drive yet, and then I'll come on back out to the school and get started.' Hardwick said fine, and Theo drove me home chuckling like a madman. I asked him what he was going to do. 'I'm going to make a royal horse's ass out of Uncle Percy,' he says. Hardwick's middle initial stood for Percival, and Theo had somehow found it out and he always called him this behind his back. 'How?' I said. 'You just wait,' says Theo. 'If all goes well, you'll be hearing about it at suppertime.' He left me at the house and went right off again.

That was about three o'clock, and by six-thirty we were all sitting around the kitchen table, Mom and Dad and me and Theo, with a big bowl of potato chips and some sour cream-and-onion dip, and Mom and Dad had drinks, and we were all laughing our heads off. What he'd done, see, was go by the construction site where Dad was building and ask to borrow Dad's truck. He also borrowed LeRoy. LeRoy's this black giant who can carry around two-by-sixes like he's bussing a tray of desserts for old ladies. He and Theo later became best friends and were pretty much inseparable till LeRoy went off to prison for armed robbery. Anyway, Theo and LeRoy go out to Belvedere, load all the rocks into the truck, drive around to the other side of the athletic field, and have them almost completely unloaded before Hardwick even realizes Theo's back. When he sees what's going on, he's apoplectic. He comes tearing across the field, and Theo said he was screaming, 'How dare you, Quick! How *dare* you!' He'd completely lost it. And Theo's standing there real calm, he's hardly even worked up a sweat, because LeRoy's loaded about six rocks for every one of his, and he says innocently, 'But I don't understand, sir. I thought you said you really did want these rocks moved, and this was the most efficient way. I mean, you didn't specify *how* you wanted them moved, did you?' And he had Hardwick there, because he *hadn't* specified. Theo had him on a technicality. Just like he was always catching Theo on technicalities. 'Quick,' he says, when he can speak again, 'one of these days, and the day is coming very soon, you are going to go too far. Now, why don't you take your truck and your . . . *helper*'—Theo said it was all Uncle Percy could do to keep from saying 'nigger,' he said he and LeRoy both *saw* the word flashing above the man's head—'and get out of here and leave my school in peace till tomorrow morning.' God, it was so funny. And Theo's rocks are still sitting there in a heap, right where he and LeRoy unloaded them twelve years ago. I guess old Hardwick's thought twice before asking anybody to move them again. Or, you know, maybe—this sounds farfetched, but it crossed my mind when I drove out there last Sunday—maybe Hardwick has left them as a kind of monument to Theo. I mean to Theo's implacable spirit or something. Because he never did get the better of Theo, not really. Theo quit Belvedere the end of the sophomore year."

"You said you all sat around the table laughing. Your parents approved of what Theo had done, then?"

"'Approved' is probably too strong a word. I mean, we all knew Theo was pushing his luck, but he'd already done it, and then the way he told it was so funny, doing Hardwick's high-pitched rage and then his own innocent replies. Dad enjoyed it because he loathes Hardwick and loves stories where people catch each other on technicalities, and Mom laughed, I guess, because it was so typically Theo, just the kind of stunt we'd all come to expect from him. I remember feeling a little scared, even though I was cackling loudest of all. I knew it wasn't over, by a long shot. I knew Hardwick wouldn't rest till he'd evened the score."

"And he evened it on you, from the sound of it. You were expelled in your senior year? For giving a party at home?"

"I was expelled in *April* of my senior year. Graduation was May sixteenth. I had my invitations ordered. I was going to be the *valedictorian,* for Christ's sake. The top guy in my class! I was on the short list for a Morehead Scholarship. And then *Bam!* Out. For throwing a party up on our hill. Hardwick got *me* on a technicality. Somewhere in the rules, see, it says that you can't drink beer or alcohol while you're at Belvedere. For the boarders that means the whole time they're away at school. Of course, all the boarders sneak and do it; guys keep whole damn bars in the rooms. Not to mention the other substances. I mean, guys dealt drugs at Wednesday chapel. The code if you wanted something was 'Holy Eucharist.' But I was expelled because three guys who were boarders came to my party and went back to school plastered. Two of them were expelled along with me. Hardwick's 'technicality' was that day students were under the same obligations when it came to serving alcohol to boarders. If I helped them break a rule, I was breaking the rule, too. Dad wanted to sue, but his lawyer said we couldn't win. The lawyer had graduated from Belvedere. And the damage had already been done. I lost out on the Morehead because I'd been expelled. If Mom hadn't known the president of North State College in Mountain City, I wouldn't have been eligible to enter Chapel Hill as a freshman in the fall. But he let me finish up my last month of trig and English at the college, because the public high school couldn't offer the advanced levels I was in. God, that spring was a bitch! I thought my life was over."

"You said two of the boarders were expelled with you. What about the third boy who came to your party?"

"He turned state's evidence. Hardwick was able to get me

through him. The other guys weren't going to say whose party it was. Hardwick kept at him till he did. He still wasn't allowed to graduate with his class, though. Hardwick made him do the year over to get his diploma. Also, I later heard his parents had given a big donation to the school's new athletic complex."

"After you were expelled, were you angry at Theo?"

"At Theo? For setting me up for Hardwick, you mean? No, I don't think I was. I didn't really make any connection like that at the time. It wasn't till later, when Theo was older, that I began to feel . . . well, that he was pulling me down. That's when I started blaming him for some things and wondering if maybe Hardwick hadn't gone after me to punish Theo. To punish Theo and *Dad*, really. They weren't his kind and he wanted them to know it. He wanted to prove that nobody from the Quick family could make it through the Belvedere system."

"You say they weren't his kind. Were you, then?"

"No, but I know how to fit in when I have to, in order to get what I want. I hated that school every bit as much as Theo. More, probably, because he was so wrapped up in his little game with Hardwick. All I wanted was to get my good grades and get out of there. I never had any real friends at Belvedere. I didn't even like those guys who came to my party."

"When did you start feeling Theo was pulling you down?"

"When he married Snow. I mean, it was embarrassing at the wedding, seeing how Mom's friends tried to keep their faces from showing how horrified they were when the bride's side of the church started filling up. But they were also amused. They could afford to be. It was just a spectacle for them. I hated them. I don't know which ones I hated the most, Snow's awful tribe or all the snobs enjoying themselves at our family's expense."

"And you felt trapped in the middle."

"I was! That's it, exactly. Damn it, I'm not a snob. But neither do I go around advertising the fact I'm one generation removed from a redneck. All I want, all I have wanted for *years* is the opportunity to do my work so I can reach the place in life where I am judged on my own merits."

"And you feel pulled back by your family?"

"Not Mom. Mom could never pull anyone back. She idealizes you *forward*. I mean, sometimes she idealizes too much."

"What about your father?"

"Well, Dad's an admirable person, I guess. Like he's always

telling you, he's created himself from the basement up, but he's got a chip on his shoulder about it and he manages to alienate people. Especially people like Hardwick. Also, I think some part of him clings to his humble origins. For instance, he built us this real nice house on top of a hill with our own private road, but the sides of the road look like a garbage dump. And our carport isn't too many degrees removed from the way Mom described the mess Snow's people keep around their shack in Granny Squirrel. We even have the prerequisite redneck car cemetery— two old cars nobody's driven for years, parked over by the pool, where they block the view of all Mom's irises and lilies. She's been begging him to clean the carport and move those old cars— that's what she really wanted for her last birthday, which was the day before Theo was killed. But he won't do it, and he won't let anyone else do it, either. I was trying to straighten the carport some over Christmas vacation before Mom had her Altar Guild up, and he came home and caught me and said, 'Son, I don't come down to Chapel Hill and rearrange your apartment when you're out. I need my things where they are, and when I have the time, I'll straighten this place up to suit myself.' If you say something back, like 'But it embarrasses Mom, her friends see it when they come to the house,' you play right into his hands. His eyes twinkle the way they always do when he's *won*, and he says, 'That's their problem, not mine.' Theo had the same attitude. He and Dad were alike in a lot of ways. Theo made it his *goal* to shock the bourgeoisie every chance he got. Even when he needed to stay in their good graces. At this accounting firm where Theo worked, they had meetings with the boss once a week, and Theo had this particular suit the guy couldn't stand. None of us could stand it—the only one who liked it was Snow, she picked it out for him. It was sort of an orangy color and the pants had flares. Flares! It was a pimp's suit; Mom called it his dancing master's suit; it was the last suit in the world for a young accountant trying to make his way up the ladder in this firm. So guess which suit Theo faithfully wore to those once-a-week meetings with the boss? And laughed about it afterwards. At the time of his death he was on leave from the firm; the official reason was that he was taking time off to study for the part of his CPA exam he'd failed before. But the afternoon of his death, when he was helping me fix the starter of my car, he suddenly confided to me that the boss had called him in and started telling him how he didn't think he was ever going to be an 'asset' to the firm. He was probably getting around to firing him, but Theo forestalled him by saying he'd been wanting to take time off without pay and pass his CPA once and for all. It let them both off the hook. Theo asked me not to say anything to Mom and Dad, because it would worry them. And of course I never will now. I mean, what good would it do for Mom to know he'd failed in something else? She'd just have to make up another little romantic story to excuse it or hide it from herself. And besides, the man, Theo's boss, was a pallbearer at Theo's funeral, and he and his wife went on and on to Mom about how wonderful Theo was and how well he was working out. Hypocrites! Every time I see that guy in town, walking around in his blue blazer and gray flannels and penny loafers, I want to yell, 'Hypocrites like you helped kill Theo, too,' and punch his face in. Listen, Dr. Blake, my hour's almost over. You don't want to hear any more of this today. You look like . . . well, frankly, you look like you ought to be home in bed with that cold. And to be honest with you, all this stuff's starting to make me a little sick talking about it."

"I'd like us to go on to the end of the hour, Rafe. Don't worry about the time. If it makes you feel any better, you are the last patient I'm seeing today and then I *am* going home." She blew her nose forthrightly into the Kleenex and tossed it into a waste-basket hidden from his view. "Now," she said, fixing him with her intelligent gaze, "why were you starting to feel sick? There's usually a reason for that. Why did you suddenly back off and become conscious of the time and—though I appreciate your concern—start worrying about my health? Go back and think. What is it, in all you've been telling me, that made you start to feel sick?"

His mind froze, the way it always did for the first few seconds at the beginning of an exam. He couldn't even recall what he had been talking about. Yet he owed it to her to try to remember. She really seemed to be on his side, wanting to think things through from his angle and at his pace, not attempting to shove him into some neat category in order to prove herself to whoever still administered *her* exams. She was going to be a valuable shrink to many people, good in a different style from the way Shapiro was good, maybe even better than Shapiro on some levels. Shapiro, from their first session on, simply took it for granted that he was the authority and could help Rafe only so long as the two of them were in agreement about this. Whereas she was more like a sympathetic friend, a woman who listened to you but someone you didn't have to flirt with—like a sister. Clare listened to him and wanted the best for him, too, but her mind was always dashing ahead, completing some of his thoughts aloud—or, rather, the way she assumed his thoughts would express themselves if she hadn't beaten him to it. Clare loved him and was proud of him, he was her adorable baby brother, but she had an ideal vision of the man he was supposed to grow into and she was getting impatient for him to become that man.

"Let's see . . ." He closed his eyes, straining to trace back to where things had begun to make him queasy and he had felt obliged to look at his watch and express concern about her health, even though he had decided earlier this would be inappropriate. "I think it started when I was telling you about Theo and me, working on my car. . . . We were in the famous filthy carport, both of us bent over my engine, and he told me about how his boss said he wasn't an asset. That was also when he told me he was going over to see this nurse Jeanette and ask her to go back with him. And if she refused, he said, he was going to make trouble. He told me those things, about his job and about his plans for the afternoon, while we were fixing my starter. Or rather *he* was fixing it. He was always better at mechanical things, the way he was better at guns. I guess I was having conflicting feelings. I loved him, he was my big brother helping me out, but at the same time I couldn't hide from myself that he was being an ass and was probably going to end up a failure. I wanted . . . I guess I wanted to get away from him. I was impatient for him to finish fixing my car so I could get in it and drive away from that hill and from him and all his problems. I mean, here he was, twenty-eight years old and still acting about fifteen, and he had this kid and was living at home with Mom and Dad, and he'd just as good as lost his job and hated what he was doing, anyway . . . it all seemed so hopeless, and as I was driving back to Chapel Hill I was thinking about him and trying not to think about him, and saying to myself, Well, Rafe, you haven't fucked up *your* life yet, and you're not going to. And I was trying not to think really terrible things."

"Terrible things?"

"Well, like maybe . . . When we were growing up, Theo used to talk about dying a lot. I mean, dying has always been one of his favorite subjects. Vietnam was on everybody's mind—one of

my classmates at La Fosse had an older brother killed there,
and all the guys used to discuss what they were going to do
when they got to be eighteen and their number was called. There
was lots of talk about keeping up grade-point averages so you
could escape into a good college, and some of the guys said
they'd run off to Canada or Sweden. But not Theo. He said he
might not even *wait* till his number came up, that he might
volunteer. He'd get everybody's goat by saying unpopular things,
like 'Do you think it's fair to hide out in college or Sweden and
let all the black boys and the poor boys to do our country's
dirty work for us?' And he was always saying to me how he had
a feeling he would die in Vietnam. I remember one night
we were lying in bed together—it was after we had separate
rooms, but sometimes if I had nightmares I'd go and get in bed
with him; he was always good about being waked up, and we'd
talk some—and I . . . oh, God! I'm just remembering the dream
I had that night. I dreamed Theo had been killed over in
Vietnam and they sent him home wrapped in a flag, but when
the family began unwrapping the flag it started peeling off like
crepe paper, and the colors started coming off on our hands.
And then I woke up and I was so relieved that he was still alive
that I sneaked into his room—Dad didn't like it when we slept
together after we got big, he was afraid we might turn queer or
something—and crawled into bed with him and hugged him
and started crying against his back. And he woke up and he was
so gentle. . . . He was . . . he was really pleased, I think, that
somebody loved him so much. . . . Wait just a minute, Dr. Blake,
I'll get it together in a minute."

"Here. Have a Kleenex."

"Thanks. Christ, I can't even remember why I started to tell
you all this."

"It had something to do with the terrible things you were
thinking on the way back to Chapel Hill that day."

"Right. You see, when I crawled into bed with him that
night—I guess I was about twelve at the time and he would
have been fourteen—he told me that he had a feeling he *was*
going to die in Vietnam, but he promised me he'd always find a
way to contact me after death . . . and . . . and that he would
. . . oh God . . . that he would always find a way to come back
and help me if I was in danger or trouble. And I guess while I
was driving back to Chapel Hill on that afternoon I was remembering how he used to say he was going to be killed in

Vietnam, yet when the time came—it was 'seventy-three and the war was pretty much winding down—Dad talked him into going to North State, which was about the only place his grades would get him into . . . and I was thinking how, if he had died in his prime, maybe as a hero, before he did anything stupid like marrying Snow, or choosing the wrong career . . . that he would have been spared . . . we would all have been spared his awful, humiliating *sinking,* from year to year. And as I was driving along thinking these things, I suddenly see this red flasher behind me and hear the siren and this trooper pulls me over, but he's not stern, the way they are when you've been speeding. And he asks if my name is Rafe Quick, and then he tells me, he says—I'll never forget the exact words—'Your brother has been in an accident and your parents want you to call home.' It was a nightmare. Only this time it was really happening. I think I knew he was dead even before I telephoned at Kernersville. The trooper was real concerned. He went with me, and when I told him my brother was dead, he said he knew I wouldn't keep to fifty-five, but to be careful, Mom couldn't afford to lose two of us. All the way back to Mountain City, I was thinking, If only I'd spent a little more time with him, if maybe I'd said, 'Don't go over to Jeanette's if you feel like that, let's you and me go for a drive somewhere and just talk. Let me talk you out of your misery the way you used to console me after my nightmares.' If only, if only. And yet I hadn't. What I had done instead was drive away from him down that mountain as fast as I could and imagine how it might have been easier if he had been killed in Vietnam. It was almost as if . . . You know what I'm thinking, don't you, Dr. Blake?"

"I think so, Rafe, but I'd rather you told me."

"It was as if I *made it happen.* And how can I live with that? I mean, in my heart I killed him just as surely as when I shot him between the eyes in my dream."

PART TWO

The more one gets to know this great sonata, the more astonishing it seems; astonishing foremost for its originality and then astonishing for its creative force, passion, and organic life. Then even more astonishing when one considers that it was written when Brahms was not quite twenty.

—*from* Claudio Arrau's program notes on Johannes Brahms's Sonata No. 3 in F minor, Op. 5. *Carnegie Hall Stagebill,* February 16, 1984

VIII: ARRAU

*T*he old man bent low over his keyboard and called forth the notes of the sublime slow movement of the sonata with such simplicity and repose that Felix could feel all around him the hushed elation of the packed hall. Here was the reassuring spectacle of the born artist who had lived long enough to fill out his art. No need of fancy postures, of those pregnant pauses between notes that signified egoistic "interpretation." He had known what his purpose was since the age of five, when he played Beethoven, Mozart, and Liszt at a charity concert in his native town, after which the ladies from the audience unhitched his mother's horses and pulled his carriage home themselves. For him life had been one thing. No broken line. Child, man, and artist were the same. Which no doubt accounted for the way childlike absorption and the serenity of age mingled in his playing. His use of the word "astonishing" in the program notes touched Felix. A man of eighty-one getting excited by a sonata written by a young man of twenty. And having the understanding to know why it was astonishing, and the supreme humility to be able to say so.

Felix had first heard the F minor when he was eight. His mother, a devoted musician, had taken him to hear Backhaus play at the Gesellschaft der Musikfreunde in Vienna. The large hall had been filled, just as Carnegie Hall was tonight. Backhaus had seemed to him a very old man, yet he was only fifty-two then. Felix was now fifty-six, but listening to the slow movement, which began like a child's lullaby and blossomed into a moon-scape of passion and eternal longings, he was eight and eighteen and twenty-two as well. The music consolidated all that was permanent in him, whether it flowed through the boy who sat beside his well-dressed mother, pale with intensity because she wished she could play as well as Backhaus, or through the gray-haired man who sat between the two women in his life.

Several rows of metal folding chairs had been set up onstage behind Arrau to accommodate extra people. In the front row, directly behind the keyboard, sat a nice-looking young man with a blond mustache. Felix's attention kept returning to him, with-out his knowing why, until a wistful strain in the music made him aware of how far away Clare was in some private reverie; then her recent family horror was before him afresh. Of course. The young man on the stage resembled, in features, coloring, and build, the dead brother. It was disconcerting. Had Clare noticed him, too? Or was it his illusion? He had seen Theo for those two days only, last summer at the beach. They'd had just one conversation together, a few hours after Theo and the little boy had driven in. His arrival with the child had completed the family circle: all the Quicks were at last under the same roof, with Clare as their hostess. This was the first time she'd been able to capture all of them, which, for complex reasons Felix thought he half understood, was important to her. To Felix, who had lost his family at ten, the Quicks were a new experience. They made him aware of the things he'd missed. And though they caused him to be grateful that he *had* missed some of them, he felt it was an adventure to observe these Quicks. He was seldom bored around them, Impatient, yes. Frequently mys-tified. Occasionally irritated, or incensed (usually with the step-father) on Clare's behalf. But separately and together as an organ-ism they fascinated him. Lily and he got on. He admired her style and thought he understood some of the reasons for her aloofness and love of forms. Whenever they were together, the two of them made a little pageant out of their mutual esteem. He bowed over her hand and planted a Viennese kiss precisely an inch from actual contact and told her how elegant she looked. She in turn told him, often in Clare's presence, that he had made all the difference to her daughter's life. With Rafe, he felt paternal. On the several occasions Clare's younger brother had visited them, he had argued with the boy over politics, corrected his manners, told him he should drink less, and ended up getting

hugged. As for Ralph Quick, his muleheaded insistence on being
right could aggravate a much calmer temper than Felix's; yet
he felt, almost against his will, a compassionate interest in the
man. Their strange, embroiled marriage intrigued him, too.
Why did they make each other so unhappy? What had their
marriage been like at the beginning? And thinking about the
troubling family unit of Quicks, Felix asked himself how each of
them might have been different if, as had happened to himself,
fate had untied the knot of family earlier in life?

It was this last question that was foremost in his mind every
time his eyes returned to Theo's look-alike on the stage behind
Arrau. Although the face and form were remarkably similar,
the young man with the blond mustache was more certain of
himself, less haunted. He was also probably less interesting.
From the way he was watching Arrau's hands, he might have
musical training himself. Just as Lizzie used to walk around on
her toes for several days after they'd been to the ballet, this
young man with his neat mustache and haircut and junior-
executive's clothes might go home and get out his music again
and attempt the beautiful slow movement of the F minor, the
way Felix's mother had done after the Backhaus recital. The
young man who looked like Theo Quick would sit down at the
bench, flex his hands, take a deep breath, and if he was a decent
sight-reader, carry himself through those rapturous passages
with a lift of the spirits. Life would seem a finer, mysterious
thing because of the music. He would not be Arrau, who actually
appeared to draw strength from the notes he was playing so
softly, now at the midpoint of the *andante expressivo,* but he would
be partaking of the same art and be sustained by his participa-
tion.

"Not everyone can be a *Künstler,*" Felix's uncle Hermann used
to say, "but many of us, fortunately, can be *Teilnehmer in Kunst.*
We can be *partners* in art." Felix's mother's twin brothers,
Hermann and Siegfried, had sniffed the wind earlier and left
Austria in 1936, taking all their money with them to New York.
Hermann had set up a carbon factory across the river in Newark
similar to his carbon factory in Schwechat, in the suburbs of
Vienna. With the money from the carbon products, he bought his
brother, Siegfried, who had been a writer and singer of political
cabaret, a furniture warehouse in the Village which Siegfried
turned into a theater. When Felix arrived to live with the uncles
in 1938, they were happily producing musical skits and plays in

German for émigrés homesick for their culture and their language. He had grown up in partnership with them: after school, he would hurry to The Old World Theater and construct scenery, or collect programs from the printer and bring coffee for the actors in rehearsal. When he got older, he did some acting and singing himself. But unlike his mother, or his uncle Siegfried, or the woman he was later to marry, he never aspired to be a *Künstler*. *Teilnehmer,* for him, was occupation enough.

Could art have saved Clare's poor brother? If he had been given the power of expression in some imaginative form, if he had been able to impose unity and coherence on his life through a creative enterprise, would he have been alive today? During the seven and a half years Felix had been together with Clare, he had been struck repeatedly by the way her mental health corresponded to how well she was succeeding in transforming the raw material of experience into unifying shapes. When she was not being successful, she was the unhappiest of creatures; close as they were, he could provide little comfort other than to listen. She hated herself at such times and couldn't understand how anyone could love her. She picked fights with him for not sharing her low opinion of herself. When she lost, even temporarily, the power to sustain an imaginative world, it was as if the real world had no meaning. He had once heard her tell an audience of aspiring writers, "If I hadn't been able to be a writer, I would probably be in jail—or worse." There had been a roar of appreciative laughter. But she means it, he had thought at the time. He couldn't quite picture her behind bars, she who couldn't even kill a mouse or swipe a piece of candy from the open bins at the supermarket, but he had no difficulty accepting the spirit of her remark. If she had not been able to do what she did, she would have done damage. If not to others, then to herself. It was conceivable that by this time her remains might be lying in the same cemetery as her half brother's; she might even have preceded him there through a dramatic burst of violence, nurtured by years of frustration, similar to his. But dismissing these disastrous extremes, he could also imagine . . . No, he didn't wish to imagine; it would make him sad. He did not want to picture too clearly the negative doppelgängers of his Clare. What if the gods had given the boy Arrau a tin ear, or placed him in a family who thought music was for sissies? Or, conversely—though the speculation was becoming cliché by now—the Vienna Academy had raved over

the landscapes of young Adolf and welcomed him with open
arms into the community of Art?

And yet, thought Felix, it is because the artistic fates of these
three people followed exactly the paths they did that I find
myself here tonight, in the center of row E, Orchestra, sitting
between Lizzie and Clare, and listening to this gorgeous sonata.
Claudio, I share your attraction for this English word "astonishing." I am astonished by my own good fortune, despite everything.

"We're too much for you, all of us at once. You've come out
here to escape."

Theo had sauntered out, hands in pockets, to join Felix at the
end of the cottage's long windwalk. He sat down deferentially
on the bench and grinned shyly at the older man beside him.
He had driven in earlier the same afternoon with his little boy,
and after unloading a great deal of beach paraphernalia, most
of it belonging to the child, had taken the boy for his first wild
romp in the surf. Hysterical with excitement, the exhausted
Jason had to be dragged screaming from the beach and was
now taking a nap with his grandmother. Ralph Quick was off
on some errand of his own, and Clare and Rafe had gone to the
new Harris Teeter, or Teeter Harris—Felix always forgot
which—to buy more tonic and crackers.

"Not at all," said Felix. "I like seeing Clare with her family.
She was so pleased you were able to come this time. No, I sit
out here every afternoon about this hour, when the sun is not so
brutal, and I count the pelicans flying back from wherever they
flew off to at six this morning, and I watch Southerners. They're
even more fascinating than the pelicans."

"In what way?"

Felix saw that he had aroused Theo's interest. "Watching
them and listening to them, I get the impression that they're
living inside a country of their own, no matter who happens to
be president in Washington. They fly Confederate flags instead
of American ones from their decks. The teenagers sunbathe on
Confederate towels and the little children splash about on their
tiny Confederate rafts. That war is still their most significant
political fact. It defines their personal style. The way they walk
and move—the very cordial way they greet you on the beach,
and that special *ruminative* slouch the men have when they
wander down to the surf carrying their drinks in the evening—

it's as if they're heavy with history, wearing it like a sort of romantic robe that other Americans aren't entitled to. They're still carrying a grievance, but it makes them feel separate and proud. Clare makes me park the car sideways in front of the cottage, so our New York license plates won't be visible from the road. No use rubbing it in their faces, she says, especially when she's one of them. Not that they would do anything. Southerners are the politest people in America."

"Their politeness is a very effective form of aggression," said Theo Quick, gazing sternly over the railing at the incoming tide.

Surprised by the remark, Felix looked more closely at the young man beside him on the bench. In face and build, he was of finer proportions than his younger brother. Actually handsomer, in the classical sense. Yet something in his attitude had caused Felix to miss this beauty on first meeting. After the swim with his child, he had dressed again in the same rumpled khaki pants and cotton shirt and loafers he had arrived in. His glasses case and a pencil stuck out of his breast pocket, and he wore his watch and belt. Unlike the gleaming Rafe, who went around all day attired only in oil and the briefest of shorts, he was obviously not ready to strip and relax, even in the presence of his own family.

"Why do you say 'their'?" asked Felix. "Don't you count yourself as a Southerner?"

Theo narrowed his eyes at the horizon and appeared to be giving the matter intense consideration. Like an actor, Felix thought. Then, with a slow grin, he turned to Felix. "I don't guess I do," he said, as if it were news to him, too. "At least, not the way you were describing them. I'm glad they lost the war. They deserved to. I don't feel heavy with anybody's history except my own twenty-seven years. Twenty-eight this August. The only thing that weighs me down is their hypocrisy and the way they use 'graciousness' to cover their viciousness. South Carolinians are among the worst, probably. Columbia was burned to the ground and they're still mad. But they enjoy being mad." He waved his hand at the Confederate flags flying from cottages on either side of them. "That way they can keep manufacturing old false memories of having their 'aristocracy' smashed."

"Ah," murmured Felix compatibly. He was enjoying the turn their conversation was taking. He liked to analyze why people, or groups of people, behaved the way they did. It was one of his and Clare's favorite pastimes. He found himself wondering why Clare hadn't spoken more of this brother. In temperament he seemed closer to her than Rafe.

"They still treat black people like half-wits . . . or their personal property," Theo went on. "I know Clare likes coming down here to this particular island because they drive around with their 'Arrogantly Shabby' bumper stickers and condescend to anybody whose grandparents didn't vacation here as children. She loves that kind of thing; it gives her more to write about. And down here she's tracked it to its most pure and virulent strain. But she's not one of them, either. Nobody in our family is or ever was. My mother may think she was once, and what's the point in disillusioning her? What's sad about our family, and why we're probably doomed, is that we haven't been able to be ourselves. Every one of us has wasted too much time being ashamed of the wrong things." He folded his arms and stuck out his chin at the sea, with the air of someone who has delivered an unpopular opinion long on his mind. Then he turned coyly to Felix to assess the effects of his remarks. "I've probably shocked you, talking about my own family like this. I've spoiled your idea of nice Southerners."

"No, you haven't," Felix assured him. Intriguing as the present subject was to Felix, it would put him in the position of listening to things about the family—about Clare and Lily, especially—that they might not want him to hear. The tide had reached the seawall in front of the cottage. Felix gazed down at the active water's swirling patterns and wondered what wrong things the Quicks had been ashamed of. "I couldn't help noticing," he said to Theo, edging them, he hoped, into less compromising territory, "how your Jason clings to you. Watching you play together in the surf was a pleasure. He's a beautiful little boy. You are his world."

Theo sighed. "Yes, I'm his world, all right, And he's mine. But the responsibility boggles my mind sometimes. She signed over complete custody to me. I guess you've heard the sorry tale of my marriage from Clare. It makes a pretty good story, if nothing else."

"She told me a little," admitted Felix. "But, you know, I raised my daughter, Lizzie. Her mother and I separated when she was only two. I was afraid also, but I knew she'd be better off with me. I had more time for her. Her mother was set on an acting career."

"That's better than Jason's mother," said Theo bitterly. "I think she's set on a vegetating career." Then, remembering his manners, "Did your wife make it as an actress?"

"Not the way she had hoped, but she keeps busy. Lizzie goes and visits her in California and the two of them get on very well. Like sisters more than mother and daughter. But if Lizzie had been raised by her, they would have been at each other's throats. But the point I am making is that you can do it if I did it. Others will help you. Your parents will help you. My two uncles helped me with Lizzie. They were wonderful. Only, having three men fluttering over her, anticipating her every whim, has spoiled her a little. Or some would say it has." He scrupulously avoided mentioning that Clare had been one of the most enlightening critics as to the extent of Lizzie's spoiling. "My advice to you is, enjoy him. It goes by so quickly. Their marvelous little brains growing by the hour, absorbing, interpreting everything. The things they say! You reexperience your childhood through them, remember things buried for years. Then it's over. They go to school, make their own friends, find other heroes . . . and before you know it, there is this stranger living in your house, a stranger who reminds you . . . touchingly, at times . . . of your lost child. But this stranger is his own person and you'd better not forget it. He keeps his most interesting thoughts to himself and is capable of regarding you very objectively. Sometimes uncomfortably so. But, for now, there is this bond between you unlike anything else in the world. And if you nurture it, both of you will have the memory of it for the rest of your lives. The memory becomes its own sort of bond. My Lizzie is about your age, almost twenty-six, but however much we may get on each other's nerves, there is that thing between us, forged when she was little, that can never be broken."

"Jason and I have that bond," said Theo, nodding vigorously. He appeared to be drinking in Felix's eulogy to fatherhood. Or, thought Felix, he wants me to believe he's drinking it in. There was a puzzling ambivalence in this boy. One minute, his sharp, antisocial observations. Then the soft gray eyes imploring you like a dog to like him. Ingratiation atoning for aggressiveness. "If it weren't for his sweet little breath and his arms around my neck in the morning, there'd be nothing to get up for."

"But what about your work?" asked Felix, alarmed by this admission. "Doesn't it interest you?"

"Not much," replied Theo, grinning slyly. He seemed pleased to have startled Felix. "I mean, the part of it where I have to deal with people can be interesting, but the rest is just . . . eyestrain. I've been going out with this woman who's a nurse. A good nurse. She really cares about what she does. We get together in the evenings, and when she starts telling me the things she's had to deal with at the hospital, I'm jealous. She's involved in life and death. What she does matters. In my line of work, you go over the same column of figures until you find the mistake, and that's your reward for the day. That and helping rich people get richer while you can barely meet the minimum payments on your credit cards."

"Would you have liked to be a doctor?"

"Oh, sure. I would have loved it. But my grades weren't good enough for me even to consider it. For a real long time I wanted to be a highway patrolman. But it wasn't socially acceptable to my family."

"Hmm, I see," murmured Felix. He was caught up in the boy's problem; he wanted to help him. "Perhaps you could be a paramedic. Lizzie had a boyfriend who was one. He worked the midnight-to-eight ambulance shift in Harlem. Now *he* had stories to tell. He was certainly involved in life and death. He became burned out though. Now he's living up in a quiet village in Maine, teaching other people to be paramedics. I was fond of him—more than my daughter was, unfortunately."

"Paramedics don't make any money," said Theo bluntly, ignoring Felix's attempt at lightness. "I mean, they can probably get to the place where they're making more than I am now—I think anybody can—but they don't get anywhere."

"Ah. You want to make money, and get somewhere, *and* do something that really matters to you. Now that's a big order."

"I'd gladly settle just for something that matters. And I'm not putting in any orders. I'm not in the position to."

Felix felt rebuffed, but determined to continue all the same. "What does your father say? Surely you've discussed it with him."

Theo uttered a short rueful laugh. "A couple of months ago, when I'd had it up to here with the place I work, I asked Dad if I couldn't maybe go into business with him. He just laughed and said, 'What business?'"

"But what did he mean by that? I had gathered from Clare that he's doing quite well as a contractor."

"He was. But he's lost faith. A few years back, this crook he was building a motel for went back on his word and Dad got stuck for a whole lot of money. The thing that hurt him most was that his old friend and lawyer represented the crook. They put a lien on his bank account and completely wiped out his savings. Mother had wanted him to transfer the money into her account—that way they couldn't have touched it—but he wouldn't do it. He's stubborn. He has to be in control. So they took all his money. Since then he's lost interest in building. I've heard him turn down at least four people this spring who phoned the house wanting him to build for them. He doesn't say no, but he just keeps putting them off, and eventually they get sick of chasing after him and call somebody else."

"So how does he make a living?" asked Felix.

"Oh, he still has his crew. They keep busy with additions and renovations. There's a lot of that going on. But he won't let himself think big anymore. I offered to go out and get business for him, so he wouldn't have to deal with personalities; and I could have helped him with his books and his estimates, which he hates, and he could have spent more time outdoors, which is what he's always enjoyed best, anyway. He likes to watch a structure go up, be involved in the physical part. Once, when I was little, he took me out to where they were preparing a site for a house. There was this excavator lifting stumps of hundred-year-old trees out of the earth, then swinging its arm around and dropping them into a pile that reached as high as a two-story building; and at the same time, there was this bulldozer pushing huge piles of dirt around, changing the shape of the land while we watched. It was like these two great big yellow machines were doing some kind of *dance* together, and he was holding me in his arms—I couldn't have been much older than Jason is now—and it was as though an electric current was going from him to me. And his face was so happy. It was full of this power. I said to him, 'Daddy, I like watching this,' and that made him real proud, that I hadn't been scared. And he squeezed me close and said when I grew up I could go into business with him and we could watch stuff like this all the time. When I reminded him of this again a couple of months ago, he got this real sad look on his face and said, 'Well, son, I guess we both kind of forgot about it, didn't we?' 'We could be partners,' I said, 'and then when Jason gets grown, we'll call it Quick, Quick, and Quick. It'll be three generations.' He shook his head and said no, things were different now and we were different people. Then he laughed and reminded me how clumsy I was on construction jobs. Once, when I was eighteen, I fell through the Sheetrock twice in one day and he's never forgotten it."

"But you said you were going to handle the accounting side of things, the personal relations. Not walk around on roofs. So what did falling through Sheetrock have to do with it?"

"Nothing. But Dad's arguments follow their own logic. When he decides it's no, then it's no." The son reported this with a certain pride, even though his hopes had been crushed on the occasion.

"But you ought to have work that you like," Felix insisted. "You spend most of your waking life with your work. It's extremely important for a man." He felt indignant and suddenly sad on Theo's behalf. It was the first time he had heard anyone speak of Ralph Quick with genuine love, with a desire to see him happy, to understand his needs. He imagined, not for the first time, what it would have been like to have a son. If his wife had not insisted on the abortion, he might be sitting here with a son almost Theo's age, dispensing advice. I would have been a good father to a boy, Felix thought, not so indulgent as I've been with Lizzie. And Lizzie would have had a brother only a year younger than herself. Then it wouldn't have been so difficult for her when I met Clare. But of course if Susanne hadn't sneaked off like a guilty housemaid to get our child butchered by a quack, we might still be together. No, we wouldn't be. She was too miserable over her career—or wanting more of a career than her modest talent could bring her. "Work can be extremely important for some women, too," Felix added, thinking of Susanne and Clare. As yet, Lizzie had shown no sign of being one of these work-driven women. Did that please him or not?

"I hope it's not too important," Theo said, "because the way things are looking lately, I'll be lucky to settle for what I have. It's not so bad, really. I have some clients I like, people who really need me. And it pays Jason's and my bills." He leaned back on the bench beside Felix and stretched out his legs, gazing at his brown loafers. "What *you* do must be interesting," he said amiably, shifting into the role of polite boy who has been brought up not to talk about himself too long, and especially not about personal problems. "Having your own theater, working with the actors. Putting on plays that help us understand the rest of the world better."

"Not all of them succeed, unfortunately. We have our share

of flops. And it's the director who works with the actors. I'm what is called Executive Producer. Most of my time is spent raising money to get us through the next season. At least we own our building. That's a great help, with rents being what they are in New York now. And I have to go abroad often, in order to see new plays and arrange for translations and adaptations. When my uncles started the theater, it was for homesick émigrés like themselves who'd had to leave Europe in a hurry. The plays were mostly in German or French; they did experiment with some in Russian and Polish, but for some reason those never filled the house. We called it The Old World Theater in those days. But times change, and now everybody's English, you see, and their children have grown up ignorant of other languages, in the American tradition. So now, although we call it The World Theater—we dropped the 'Old' in the late fifties— all the plays are in English. The only way to get audiences to come and watch what the rest of the world is doing is to translate it for them. And often to adapt it to a locale they can identify with. Having to do this often depresses me, though. Every language has its untranslatable flavor. And changing a setting from, say, a rich Japanese's villa to a rich American's country estate, or an apartment in Moscow to an apartment in Chicago, can have its problems, too."

As he listened to himself talk, Felix was aware that he was stressing the shortcomings and disappointments of his job. But he felt it would be unkind to Theo, trapped as he seemed to be, *faute de mieux,* in his profession, and denied the chance by his father to help rebuild and expand a family business, to exult in his own engrossing work, so compatible with his instincts, which his loving uncles had bequeathed to him—along with the majority of shares in the Newark carbon factory, which went a long way towards allowing Felix to fly around the world in search of new plays. Not infrequently, Felix found himself in the odd position of feeling embarrassed by his good fortune, by his confident and relatively easy passage through life so far. He and Clare often discussed this: how, despite the fact that both his parents had been killed in a London air raid before they could join him in America, he had managed to retain his exuberance and his optimistic temper. "I don't completely understand it myself," he would say, puzzled, as though contemplating a serious flaw in his character. "Sometimes it seems callous on my part that I wasn't damaged for life. Perhaps it has something to

do with my name. Maybe if my parents had named me Ernst or
Aloysius or Tristram, it would have been a different story."

"No, I'll tell you what it is," Clare would say. "They set you
up for life with more than your happy name. They gave you a
happy childhood. You had all the security you needed for those
first ten years before your world flew apart. If a person has a
secure childhood to build on, he's indestructible. That's my
theory. I don't mean he'll never get sick or have a traffic accident, but his inner core will be indestructible, whatever happens
afterwards."

"I think your core is pretty indestructible," Felix would say,
"even if your childhood wasn't as carefree as mine, and despite
your tendency to expect the worst."

"Ah. That's because I have built my rock out of the materials
of insecurity," she would reply.

And then there was Brahms. Being the young show-off now in
the *allegro energetico*. Pouncing and leaping all over the keyboard,
exerting himself for sheer joy in his emerging powers. "Clara,
come quickly," Schumann called to his wife while the unknown
young man, some say, was finishing the sonata under the eyes of
the older composer. "Come and hear something you have never
heard before." And Clara is supposed to have entered the room
exclaiming, "But I thought I heard *two* pianos!" What a moment
that must have been for the twenty-year-old Brahms. It was
very likely the most exciting moment of Brahms's entire life,
thought Felix as he listened to the frolicsome movement. Out of
it came Schumann's public announcement of Brahms's genius in
the *Neue Zeitschrift für Musik,* lavishing superlatives hoarded for
just such an occasion. He anointed Brahms, the chosen one who
would express the exalted spirit of the times. He said Brahms
transformed the piano into an orchestra of mourning and re-
joicing voices. He wrote to Brahms's father assuring him that he
could look forward with complete confidence to the future of his
boy, who was a "darling of the Muses." After that, it was all
music. Brahms the man was to lead a very uneventful life. Wrote
music. Taught a princess at the court of Detmold and had time
to write more music. Sat by his mother's deathbed, which
inspired his *German Requiem.* Became conductor of the Gesellschaft
der Musikfreunde, where Felix's mother took him to hear
Backhaus play Brahms sixty years later. Wrote his large-scale
orchestral works. Never politicked or built monuments to himself

like Wagner, or philandered like Liszt. Took care of Clara Schumann and her children and grandchildren and remained devoted to her, but never married. Was the only well-known musician of his time who steadfastly refused to travel abroad: when Cambridge offered him an honorary degree, he turned it down, not wanting to cross the English Channel. Music was his world, his security, his adventure, his wife. Some hinted at a love affair with Clara after her husband went mad and died, but there was no real evidence. He caught a chill at her funeral, which brought on an attack of jaundice, the first outward sign of the liver cancer that was to kill him eleven months later. But not before he turned death into a rhapsody in his *Four Serious Songs*.

In a sense, thought Felix, Brahms's personal life ended when he played the F minor sonata for the illustrious couple who became his Parents in Art. From that time forward, it was all seriousness. Brahms the youth had to die in order to live up to the great future prophesied by Schumann. From then on, his existence fed his art, and his deepest emotions expressed themselves through his music. Was that a terrible price to pay, or not? How could you answer that question, thought Felix, unless you yourself had been chosen to pay it?

The last year of his life with his parents in Vienna, his mother had been reading a biography of Clara Schumann. He could still see the furniture in the room. The rugs, the piano, the coal-burning *Kachelofen* with its inviting hot white tiles that Felix liked to put meltable things on and watch them change shape. Then the maids had to clean up the mess and Felix's father punished him, but never harshly. Her new reading glasses slipping down her nose, Felix's mother strained forward eagerly over the volume in her lap. "Poor woman!" she exclaimed aloud at one point, then read a long passage to Felix's father. "Poor Clara didn't have an easy life," she concluded, sighing, "despite her great talent." And even at the age of nine, Felix understood why her sigh was one of relief and vindication for herself as well as one of sympathy for Clara Schumann.

Mutti could never have made it through this rambunctious third movement, thought Felix, even if she had lived to practice the sonata many more years. Those octaves, the exertion of it, would have been beyond her. Yet look at how Arrau conserves his strength through those hectic passages. May I have his strength at eighty-one!

*   *   *

"I *like* your brother Theo. Why is it you so rarely speak of him? It's always Rafe. This brother is a mensch. He feels things. He makes such provocative and original observations. But he has troubles. He needs someone to help him."

"Help him how?" asked Clare, frowning at herself in the mirror. They were in their room at the beach cottage with the door shut, and Clare was already showing signs of strain from this family house party she herself had wanted and planned for.

"Show him we're on his side. Give him moral support. We had a very interesting talk while you and Rafe were at the supermarket. He's unhappy with his work. That's not good. Maybe we should invite him to come and stay with us, he's never even been to New York. We could show him the city and I could take him to the theater and you could talk with him. I think he needs the example of people who like what they are doing. It could give him courage to start something else."

"Poor Theo."

"It's not that hopeless, is it? He's a nice-looking fellow, only twenty-seven. I like the way he sees into things. And he has a *sweetness*. He just needs more confidence in himself. Why do you say 'poor Theo'?"

"Oh, I don't know. You're probably right. We could have him visit, but what about Jason? He'd never let his father out of his sight long enough for a trip to New York."

"He could come, too," suggested Felix, less certainly. "Lizzie could always baby-sit."

Clare smiled at Felix as though she were fourteen years his senior and not the other way around. "You really are the eternal optimist, aren't you?" She picked up her brush and fluffed out her hair until it made the sort of bushy tent she liked around her face. "Theo has somehow failed to *mobilize* himself," she said. "And he undercuts himself and plays the fool too much. But you're right, he's extraordinarily perceptive, in a skewed sort of way. He sees angles most people don't care to see. He's got more of a social conscience than any of us, and he's genuinely kind. Not for anything he can get out of people, but because he's made that way. If I end up old and alone and helpless one day, he's the person I can most picture driving up in his car to take over. He'd do it if I were poor and drooling and hideous, and I think he'd still love me. He might love me more than ever, because then I'd need him. Yet he exasperates me, maybe because I see too much of myself in him, the kind of person I might have turned into. If I hadn't got out of there at sixteen, I'd have stayed around and watched Ralph finish turning my independent mother into a helpless wife, and then I'd have offered myself as their battleground. They'd have kept their marriage together by draining my spirit and filling up the empty carcass with the poisons they'd brewed between them. But I ran for my life to my father's people . . . it was like I was creating the plot of my own life when I wrote that letter to my uncle . . . and then I left Theo in charge as the oldest child. My God, that's just what I *did* do, didn't I? He was only two when I left, Rafe wasn't even out of the womb. Poor Theo had to take *my* place as the battleground."

"Don't go sinking into a quagmire of guilt."

She smiled at him. "God, you know me so well. My guilt isn't going to do Theo any good, is it? But you're right about him visiting us. We'll be his champions and exemplars and spoil him a little, as I do Rafe."

But by the day's end, Felix's enthusiasm for Project Theo had begun to wane. Without knocking, Theo had barged into the bedroom to borrow Clare's hair dryer and wakened Felix, clad only in undershorts, from a late-afternoon snooze. After which, Felix had had to humor Ralph Quick at the cocktail hour by sitting "man-to-man" with him in the kitchen, drinking his mint juleps and listening to his Army experiences. Felix, born two years after Clare's stepfather, had just missed being old enough to fight Hitler, a piece of bad timing which had caused him frustration as a youth and still nagged at him periodically. And even though the war had ended before nineteen-year-old Ralph Quick could be shipped overseas, there was a provoking note of patronage in his mountain twang as he boasted of parachute jumps and muddy crawls through simulated war conditions in Texas. Hiding behind the camouflage of mint leaves in his silver julep cup—Ralph had brought both the mint and the cups from Mountain City in his ice chest—Felix sucked the syrupy bourbon mixture through a packed wall of crushed ice and uttered polite "Mmm's" and "Ah's," reminding himself that Ralph had come down only to pick up Lily, who had been staying a week, and that tomorrow at this time he and Clare would be alone again, drinking a nice chilled Riesling or Sancerre, and he would be pleased with himself for having remained what Lily always called him, a hospitable European gentleman, throughout all the tensions and aggravations of Clare's annual family party.

Then the other members began to gather in the air-conditioned kitchen, which was downstairs, under the living quarters, and had its own maid's room—which Rafe had claimed for himself, so he would not wake everybody when he came home from Myrtle Beach at five in the morning, he said. First came Lily, who always dressed for dinner, even at the beach, in a fresh linen skirt and a high-necked blouse the same color as her periwinkle eyes. Felix stood up; Ralph, remaining in his chair, asked her if she would like him to fix her a mint julep. Lily raised her eyebrows, smiling distantly as though something very private had amused her, and said, "No, I don't believe so. Maybe Felix could get me a glass of some of his nice white wine, since he's already up."

Next, Clare came down, changed from her old khaki shorts into white slacks out of deference to her mother's habits, and began rattling skillets and getting out platters and bowls with the worried look of a little girl about to take an exam. She cooked with dash and confidence on her own territory, but had been known to ruin things when her family looked on.

"How about a mint julep?" asked Ralph Quick. This time, his offer was closer to a challenge.

"Or some of Felix's lovely Riesling," drawled Lily, raising her wineglass on high towards her daughter like an exhibit.

"A mint julep, by all means," said Clare with determined enthusiasm, looking at neither of them. Facing them from behind her work counter, she shook cornmeal into a mixing bowl. With a gratified groan, Ralph rose from his chair and began the complicated ritual once more. As he wrapped ice cubes in a dish-towel and solemnly crushed them with a hammer, Lily rolled her eyes to the ceiling and smirked at Felix. Clare chopped an onion, keeping her eyes down. She loved her white wine, liked to get the maximum of alcohol with the minimum of calories; but she would drink several of Ralph's sickly-sweet concoctions, Felix knew, out of loyalty to her heritage and to keep her stepfather in a good mood.

Rafe entered next, showered and dressed for his evening prowl at Myrtle Beach. "Oh, mint juleps," he said sociably, brushing past his father on the way to the refrigerator, where he replenished his own empty glass with vodka from the freezer and a splash of tonic. "Hey, Dad, can I have a little of that crushed ice you're making?"

"If there's any left over," said Ralph Quick, stopping his

labors long enough to give his son a critical once-over. *"Your* cocktail hour seems to begin earlier and earlier," he remarked caustically.

"Forget it," said Rafe, returning to the freezer for two ice cubes.

"Doesn't my baby look gorgeous in white clothes with that tan?" Lily Quick asked Felix, twirling her empty glass by the stem.

Felix replied with a bow that Rafe was indeed a handsome boy and asked if he might pour her more Riesling.

Surprisingly, there followed a half hour or so of harmony and good humor. Clare drank two of Ralph's mint juleps quickly in succession and said he made the best ones in the whole of Dixie, and told a story on herself about how she and another expatriate Southern woman in New York had gotten homesick and tried to make juleps in a blender. "When my back was turned, she threw in the mint. Even I would have known better than to do that. They were a catastrophe. I kept spitting out little flecks of green leaves for days afterwards." "She couldn't have been a real Southerner if she put the *mint* in the blender," said Rafe with triumphant scorn. "Well, actually, you know, she wasn't," Clare suddenly remembered. "She was the wife of a Southerner, this magazine editor who grew up in Winston-Salem. I think she was from California." "That explains it," said Lily, cocking her head playfully and observing her two children with benign merriment. "Well, I'll tell you," said Ralph, "there are lots of secrets to making a good julep, but the only way to experience a perfect one is to drink it out of a silver cup. That's why I carry these with me to the beach." To Felix, he explained, "These were a gift to me from a lovely old lady it's been my privilege to get to know. Miss Alicia Gallant. The set belonged to her brother, Dr. Anthony, who sewed my face back together after I wrapped my first car around a telephone pole." "It is certainly a first experience for me," interjected Felix pleasantly, "to drink whisky out of a silver cup." "I'm going to put the corn muffins in now," said Clare. "Why doesn't Theo come down?" "He and Jason were going to have a bath together," said Lily, nodding subtly to Felix that, yes, she wouldn't mind another glass of Riesling. "I'm sure they'll be down soon."

And at long last, in came Theo. Without his shirt. Carrying his naked boy wrapped in a large bath towel. Felix would never forget the impression their entrance made. Lily's eyebrows shot up briefly at her son's bare, skinny chest, its dark nipples round and glaring against the milk-white pallor. Then she transferred all her attention to the child. "Come here, darling," she crooned, holding out her arms, "and let your Angel finish drying you. Then Daddy can take you back upstairs and you can both get dressed."

"I *am* dressed," said Theo, handing the bundled boy down to Lily. He avoided meeting Felix's eyes, as if he knew the rapport between them had suffered a sea change since he had burst in on Felix's nap. "This is the beach, isn't it?" he gave his mother an uncertain grin, which came out more like a grimace.

"I'm sorry, Theo," said Lily, trying to keep her voice amused as she made a great fuss over rubbing Jason with a corner of the large towel, "but all the men who eat at the table with me have to have on their shirts *and* pants."

"But we're not going to eat yet, are we? I thought Dad was making mint juleps."

"We've been down here for some time, son," said Ralph. "I'm getting ready to close up shop. As usual, your timing is a little off."

"I've already put the muffins in the oven," Clare explained gently to Theo, "but I think there's still time for you to have one isn't there, Ralph?"

With a long-suffering sigh, Ralph shambled once more to the kitchen counter and wrapped ice in a towel and pounded his hammer.

"It's cold in here!" the child accused everybody.

"That's because we've got the air-conditioning on," Rafe told his nephew, winking at the boy between sips of vodka tonic, "and your demented father has brought you down wearing nothing but a wet towel."

Theo snatched up the boy from Lily's lap. "Come on, Jason," he said, "we're not wanted here." And rushed out of the room, leaving them all confounded.

"Oh, *shit*," said Clare, flinging down a potholder. "Now he's hurt. I'll go up and talk to him."

"All the liberated women say those words now, I know," Lily murmured to Felix, "but I still think they sound terrible." She rose from her chair, looking suddenly old. "I'd better go up with you," she said, and followed Clare out of the kitchen.

"Anyone need some crushed ice?" Ralph Quick asked, still holding his hammer.

"I might as well, I guess," said Rafe, handing his glass to his father. "It'll just melt, otherwise."

Ralph sighed and swept the pile of splintered ice into his son's drink. He sought Felix's eye. "Be glad you just had a daughter," he told him with a self-satisfied weariness.

"I probably shouldn't have said what I did," said Rafe, addressing his glass. "Theo can be so sensitive. You never know how he's going to take something."

"He just doesn't think," said Ralph Quick. "He goes and does these things without thinking why, and then he's surprised when they backfire in his face." He delivered these words in an automatic sermonizing singsong, as though he had expressed himself on this subject many times before.

Felix considered saying something on Theo's behalf, but could not quite think what.

They waited awhile longer in silence. Between the pounding of the waves and the shatter of crushed ice against Rafe's teeth, Felix thought he heard the faint sound of Clare's voice on the floor above.

Rafe stretched his neck and sniffed the air like an animal on the alert, "Hey," he said, "I smell something burning."

It was Clare's delicious corn muffins, but they were beyond saving.

That night, after Jason had gone to sleep in his grandparents' room and Theo, persuaded by Rafe, had departed for Myrtle Beach with his brother to pick up girls, Clare and Felix lay side by side in bed, knowing their voices could not be heard over the sound of the ocean.

"Why do I do it?" asked Clare. "What am I hoping to accomplish? They'll never change. Nothing will change. Why do you let me drag you into this and spend good money? It's the same family travesty as always, only in a different setting. I mean, I love it when we have Lily here alone; it's the only time I've had her to myself for years, and she's comfortable down here, she doesn't like it in New York. . . ."

"Then that alone is worth it, isn't it?" put in Felix. "I'm very fond of your mother. You know that. I love her little private rituals, the way she takes her teacup and goes off by herself with her prayer book . . . or puts on her bathing cap and goes down and battles those waves. She bounces up and down like a child. And it's fun to take her out to dinner; she dresses up so prettily and enters a room like visiting royalty. It's not an imposition on me, at all, having her share our vacation."

"Yes, but you can't say that about the rest of them, can you?"

"It's a *different* kind of experience," Felix admitted. "But it isn't for very long. After all, *he* only comes to bring her, and to pick her up afterwards, if she doesn't ride back with Rafe. And Rafe's very little trouble for the two or three days he's here. He sleeps till noon and sunbathes till six and then goes to Myrtle Beach. And this is the first time Theo's ever come. Poor Theo, it hardly seems worth it, arriving so late on a Friday afternoon and having to leave on Sunday."

"Now look who's calling him 'poor Theo.'"

"He is a bit difficult," Felix conceded. "What a strange way he behaved, coming down like that with the boy."

"Yes, and then sulking the whole evening. Instead of just putting it behind him and drinking that brandy you offered and reinstating himself. He's so different from Rafe in that respect. You criticize Rafe, he bounces back."

"Rafe is easier," agreed Felix. "He drinks far too much and uses up all the ice and tonic, but he's easier."

Theo's visit to New York was not mentioned by either of them again.

"Well, my *Mädi*, what did you think of the great Arrau?"

"He was so *teeny*," said Lizzie, spooning into the snowy island that floated in the middle of her hot borscht and guiding just the right mixture of spicy red broth, shredded beets, and cool sour cream to her mouth. "When he came out on the stage, he looked like a beetle walking upright and wearing tails."

"Jesus, Lizzie," said Clare, rolling her eyes at Felix in a kind of exalted indignation, "you have no respect for anything, do you? I bet if God walked out on the stage, you'd find some fault with Him." She was having the cold borscht, purple and creamy.

"No, I wouldn't. I'd avert my eyes. Jews aren't supposed to look at God."

"There would be no one there to look at," Felix corrected his daughter. "There is no physical God in the Jewish religion. That's why Jewish painters have always been forbidden to make images of God."

"Why did you keep all these things from me for so long, Pop?" Lizzie was an old expert at counterattack.

"I didn't keep them from you. You never showed the slightest bit of interest before. Now that you are suddenly so very interested, I want you to at least get it right." Felix had passed over the soup course and was slowly sipping Polish vodka. In the old days, he would have felt disloyal ordering anything but Russian vodka in the Russian Tea Room. But the Russian Tea Room was no longer what it used to be: the old seedy authenticity was gone. When Felix had said *spassivo* to the waiter, who turned out to be from San Juan, the poor fellow thought he was asking for espresso to accompany his vodka.

"I'll probably never get it right now," said Lizzie. "I'm too old."

"I'm doing all that I can to make reparations to you, Liesl. You're off to Israel next week to visit your great-aunt and our long-lost cousins. My father's sister was fervently Orthodox, even back in Vienna."

"So what was my grandfather, then?" asked Lizzie accusingly. "Was he one of those assimilated Jews?"

"He was not. He always went to the synagogue on the High Holidays. My mother was not religious at all. There are degrees of devoutness just as there are degrees of everything else. Nationalism, Zionism, and so on."

"I don't understand why with all your traveling you've visited your aunt in Israel only once. And don't even know my cousins."

"It's very simply explained. I never liked her, even as a boy. Actually, I ought to amend what I said about Jewish artists. There *weren't* any Jewish artists, to speak of, until the Enlightenment. During the age of great religious painting, there would have been nothing for them to paint. But after that came Soutine . . . Max Liebermann . . . Chagall . . . Rothko . . ."

"And *many* artists, regardless of their creed, were *teeny* in stature," put in Clare, unwilling to let Lizzie off the hook for her Arrau remark. "Toulouse-Lautrec . . ." She frowned, obviously trying to come up with more names. "Also, you know, Lizzie, when you get old you shrink. When you are as old as Arrau, you may be two or three inches shorter than you are now. Maybe more than that."

"Not if I take calcium and exercise," retorted Lizzie complacently, relishing her borscht.

The silvery fire of the vodka beginning to light up his insides, Felix privately delighted in the two women sitting side by side on the red banquette: his daughter, with her pert, precise movements as she ate her soup; her freckles and her masses of flaming hair—the same golden ginger as his when he was a boy, only such hair was wasted on a boy; and Clare, trying to be stern and not quite succeeding, because of a propensity she had to preside over herself ironically in all but the most desperate of moods. He was relieved to see them sparring again; in the old days, it had made him nervous, he had wanted them to love each other more. But after Theo's horrible death, Clare had returned to New York subdued and curiously humble. She had abandoned her habitual tone with Lizzie, a sort of teasing exasperation, flashing with bursts of wit and philosophical self-parody. ("Oh, God, here I so triumphantly escaped myself as Impossible Young Girl, only to be confronted with one ten times more impossible than *I* had the chutzpah to be!") Perplexed by Clare's cautious, protective new treatment of her, as if she were an object that might easily break, Lizzie had responded with an uneasy self-restraint. She forfeited her arsenal of provoking remarks and flippant retorts and hung back, respectful of Clare's grief. Felix realized Lizzie *missed* Clare's verbal assaults. It was then he understood that all this time he had been worrying they didn't love each other, the two of them had been building a form of love acceptable to the pride and competitiveness of each. It had been a rough four months for them all. Lizzie had dreamed of the dead Theo, whom she had never met when he was alive. They all had had their dreams. Felix had dreamed of some strange, tall Swiss people, Clare's relatives on her mother's side, people she had never seen, who rang the doorbell of his brownstone. He opened to see them driving off in a sleek car, having abandoned a small blond child on his doorstep. The boy, wearing lederhosen like the ones Felix had worn, smearing butter on them when they were new to make them look old, addressed Felix in pure High German. *"Hier will ich bleiben,"* he said formally, in his clear, childish voice. Here I would like to stay. Felix knew that the child was Jason, Theo's child, but he was also, in the way dreams like to combine things, Felix's son, the one he might have had if Susanne had not run off to the butcher to save her career. "You are welcome to stay with us," Felix had replied. With his heart full, he had reached down and picked up the boy. He felt the exact weight of him in the dream. Clare will not mind, he thought. She was always wary of babies because they stopped her mother's writing, but this will be different. This boy already exists, and he's a beautiful boy, and besides, he has nowhere else to go.

Of course the real child, Theo's Jason, did have somewhere else to go, and now, after a bitter struggle in court, a struggle

Clare had followed almost daily over long-distance telephone with Lily, he was with his mother. Had been with the mother since Christmas. First in a trailer in Georgia, and now, since she had discarded the new husband whose trailer it was, in another trailer back in the mountains of North Carolina, in a place called Granny Squirrel. Tomorrow, as the result of a recent correspondence with Snow—a personage Felix had come to regard as possessing almost mythical degrees of cunning and seductiveness, at least through the medium of Clare's continuing narrative—Clare was actually flying off to visit Theo's widow (ex-widow?) and child. For the first time, Clare would land at the Mountain City airport and be picked up, not by Lily and Ralph and Theo and Rafe, but by Snow and her mother, who would transport Clare seventy miles west and deep into the kingdom of Snow's clan. Felix had also dreamed of Snow, but a man couldn't be held accountable for such dreams. Or, rather, he had dreamed of the sharp-tongued, purple-eyed vixen in Clare's storytelling: who knew what the real Snow was like? For curiosity's sake alone, Felix would have enjoyed accompanying Clare to Granny Squirrel if he himself hadn't had to fly off to Europe tomorrow evening. "Knowing your family has helped me begin to know the real America," he had told Clare this past week. "What do you mean?" she asked, fascinated. "Just that. The real Americans. Not some New Yorkers who came to this country a few years before I did." "But how are we different from them?" she had asked. "Oh, there are so many differences," he had replied vaguely. He couldn't really express what he meant. Pushed for an explanation, he had added after a moment's hesitation: "You carry guns, for one thing." "Ah yes, that," sighed Clare.

"And now we have come to an important crossroads," Felix announced solemnly to Lizzie and Clare.

"Yes, Father," responded Lizzie with equal solemnity, placing her spoon ceremoniously in the center of her empty borscht bowl.

"Yes, Father," echoed Clare, clasping her hands attentively upon the flamingo-pink tablecloth and trying not to smile.

They both had his number by now. He couldn't fool them with this one anymore. Like children who have been read the same story again and again, they knew what was coming next.

So he decided to switch it. Or at least detour around it for a little, if his appetite could hold out. To keep them on their toes. Keep them guessing. Keep them all fresh for one another.

"No, I'm serious," he said. And suddenly he was. "All of us are flying off in our separate directions after this meal together. Clare, at eight tomorrow morning, to the mountains of western North Carolina; then I go in the evening to Vienna on Swissair. And on Monday, Lizzie leaves for Tel Aviv. Remember, Liesl, you have to be there *three* hours ahead of time for El Al."

"I know, Pop. You and El Al have reminded me quite a few times already."

"So we are each going off on our separate missions. Lizzie to meet old relatives and learn more about her Jewish side; Clare to make peace with her nephew's mother and learn more about Snow's people; and myself to give a pep talk to a fine Czech playwright so he will finish what I know will be a wonderful play about Kafka if he'll stop doubting his ability to write it. He is temporarily blocked, that's all. By what he thinks is the magnitude of his subject. That's not unusual for a writer. I'm not one myself, but I do seem to have a certain knack for talking them out of the barricades they set up against themselves."

Clare gave a quiet, despondent groan. "When you get back and I get back, you've got to talk me out of a few new ones of mine."

"It will be my pleasure," said Felix, trying to keep his tremendous relief from showing. This was the first time in four months that Clare had expressed the intention of beginning something new. After Theo's funeral, she had returned to New York and thrown out the rough draft of the book she had been working on for almost a year. "These people don't need to exist," she had told him balefully. "The world doesn't need any more false hope." "What do you mean?" he had asked, really worried. To throw out a whole year's worth of work! She'd never done that before. She took it out to the street herself and dropped it in the garbage, then watched from an upstairs window until she saw the truck come; so there was no question of her secretly wanting him to rescue it—the way Kafka had given his stuff to Max Brod and said, "Be sure and destroy this when I'm dead." "What do you mean, false hope?" he had asked her. "Theo expressed it very well the afternoon before he died. He came into the kitchen and more or less *confronted* me with my work. He said he could never be a main character in my kind of world and he wasn't sure he even wanted to be anymore. He said I wrapped things up. That I rewarded my characters—the main ones—after making them struggle and suffer, and life wasn't like that. Then, the next afternoon, he went out and proved it." "But life *is* like that for some people," Felix contended. "Somebody has to have the courage to write about them, too. That's not giving false hope; that's saying, yes, it can happen. I know it's the fashion to have everything end in a sort of anesthetized angst—it's been the fashion for thirty years; but many people *do* make it, after struggling and suffering. It happened that way for me; it happened for you." "I know. But for the first time it seems . . . shameful to parade it, disrespectful to those millions of others who don't make it."

"*Ja,* Felix vill help you vith dose artistic barricades," Lizzie told Clare. "Not efferyvun kan be a *Künstler,* but many uff us fortunately kan be *Teilnehmer in Kunst.* Ve kan be *partners* in art."

Clare and Felix burst out laughing. "God, Lizzie," said Clare, "nobody is sacred with you. Not even your dear departed old uncle Hermann, who worshiped the ground you walked on."

"To whom you owe your financially independent prolonged American adolescence," put in Felix, lowering his brows as threateningly as he could.

Lizzie bowed her head modestly, her abundant hair striking off the most amazing lights.

One day she is going to return the love of someone else, perhaps even someone who loves her as much as I do, thought Felix. It's a miracle it hasn't happened already. Will I be able to stand him?

Lizzie cleared her throat importantly. "And now," she announced in an officious, rumbly voice a whole octave below her usual one, "we have come to the crossroads and must make some *very* serious decisions." Her accent was perfect: and it was harder to do than poor Uncle Hermann's, which, despite his forty years in America, remained to the end almost a parody of a German-speaking émigré's dialect. The only remaining giveaways of Felix's foreign origins were his vigorously rolled *r*'s and a particular lilting spacing of his words, and Lizzie had gotten it as perfectly as she got the rest of him. She hulked forward over the table (Felix's stiff-shouldered bear hunch) and, as if suddenly she had grown shaggy, unruly eyebrows, lowered her forehead threateningly at them.

"My serious decision," announced Clare, joining in the ritual

and passing out the three menus that, at Felix's request to the
waiter, had been left in a corner of the banquette, "is whether
to have the cotelette Pojarsky or the luli kebab." On relaxed
occasions and in certain restaurants, they liked to make their
decisions course by course, pausing at each "crossroads."

"I could order one and you could order the other and then
we could share," suggested Felix. "If I know Lizzie, she's having
the blini."

"I never pass up the opportunity for good Jewish food," said
Lizzie in her own voice, cocking her head challengingly at her
father.

"This is Russian food, Liesl. How many times do I have to
say it? What people in this country, and I include Jews, call
Jewish food is not Jewish food at all. It's Russian food or German
food or Polish food that the Jews who lived in those countries
happened to grow up eating."

"Well, when I get to Israel, I suppose there'll be Jewish food
there."

"No, it will be Middle Eastern food. And what grows in the
climate. Melons, bananas, citrus fruits . . . tomatoes . . . avocados."

"But, Pop, surely the Jews must have some food that's all
their own. What about matzoh balls?"

"Ah, that's another story. Now you're talking about various
special dishes served at a Seder. Foods eaten to symbolize
hardships the Israelites endured. When they were fleeing the
Egyptians, they didn't take along any yeast to make their bread
rise, so they had to eat unleavened bread. That's what matzoh
is. A matzoh *ball*, however, is just an unleavened *Knödel*. Or
dumpling, in English. It's not that I'm trying to deny Jews a
cuisine, Liesl, but I get very impatient when people insist on
mixing things up."

"All the same, I think you're hard on Jews sometimes."

"If I am, it's for the same reasons I am hard on you sometimes.
Because I feel vulnerable and responsible on their behalf. Because they are part of me."

"I think you are harder on them than you ever were on me"
was Lizzie's complacent comeback. How she loved having the
last word. Nevertheless, she had touched on something tender
that he would have to think about. He remembered asking Theo
Quick, during the only talk they were ever to have, "Why do
you say 'their'? Don't you count yourself as a Southerner?" And

then his startling follow-up: "What's sad about our family, and why we're probably doomed, is that we haven't been able to be ourselves. Every one of us has wasted too much time being ashamed of the wrong things."

Why did I say "they" for Jews? Felix asked himself, raising his hand to summon their waiter, the swarthy young man from San Juan who thought "thank you" in Russian meant espresso. What wrong things have I been ashamed of?

"You do a wicked imitation of your old dad," Clare told Lizzie, after they had all three ordered.

"She probably gets it from her late uncle Siegfried," said Felix. "He could impersonate anybody. And he caught the subtleties of people, it wasn't mere parody. One of his dreams was to start a good political cabaret in America, but it didn't work. His theory was that cabaret wasn't suited to democratic countries. All that freedom took the edge off satire, just as too much permissiveness takes away the mystery of sex."

"I can only impersonate people I know well," remarked Lizzie airily.

"Uh-oh," said Clare. "I wonder who your next victim will be."

"You, maybe," said Lizzie, smiling a demure threat under all her bright hair.

Clare looked down at the napkin in her lap. She thought for a minute. Then she said, with the raised eyebrowns and semi-sarcastic tone she often resorted to with his daughter, "I think, knowing *you* a little by now, Lizzie, I am going to take that as a compliment. Otherwise, why would you go to the trouble? Not that I'm going to be pleased with what you come up with."

Lizzie shrugged nonchalantly. "You may be right," she said. "On *both* counts."

Felix looked away, surveying the other late-evening diners. He took in all the colors, the reds and greens of the waiters' smocks, the crowded paintings in their gilded frames, the samovars and tinseled sconces and chandeliers: the whole, un-predictable-predictable melting pot of cultures and styles and peoples. It was the nearest the two women had come to a verbal exchange of affection. He liked the way they had done it, the style of each.

I can't help it, thought Felix. Despite all the lost people in the world, despite the horrible things I know all too well have happened and can happen again, I seem to be that most un-popular of characters: a happy man.

A woman got on the highway
Left her life behind
Stored her guilt in the family trunk
Went to see what she could find

Put the top down on her car
Put the top down on her mind
Halleluja! Here I come
To see what I shall find

A slim dark car of unknown make
Seduced her with his lights
She let him pass and back she blinked
His license plate said MARS

In the Sheraton as they screwed
He said you've got to teach me
I'm not from here but I'd like to learn:
What do earthlings want?

They screwed all night
They screwed all day
They screwed till her hair
Down there turned gray

You've taught me quite a lot, he said
Rising gleaming from her bed
Tell me, Mother, what's the fee
For your generous hospitality?

I can make you famous
I can make you rich
Shrink you back into a virgin
Swell you into a witch

Just take me to the mirror, she said
And kindly hold my hand
And let me die standing up
Facing what I am.

—*from* Julia's doggerel book

IX: HOSPITALITY

"*Y*our old friend Lily Quick certainly saved the day at our Library Board meeting last Thursday," Neville Richardson told his daughter. He repositioned his bandaged foot on the padded stool in front of him and wriggled deeper into his armchair with a waggish shake of his head. "*Mystifying* gal. You're never quite sure where she's coming from—or do the young still use that expression? That's one thing I miss about teaching, you lose touch with the argot of youth. Anyway, on Thursday Lily Quick was just splendid."

"What did she do?" Julia was curled up on her father's couch, the same couch she had studied on as a schoolgirl at St. Clothilde's. She had a biography of W. J. Cash open on her lap, just as her father had Lord Asa Briggs's *A Social History of England*, which she had given him for Christmas, open on his. Neither of them had very serious intentions of reading, but it was a form they kept up, largely so that her father wouldn't feel he was hindering her from preparing her classes. She had made supper for them, but the menu was at his dictation: bacon sandwiches with melted Cheddar on top, served with a dark English ale he had just discovered, which unfortunately cost eleven dollars for a six-pack. Since he had broken his foot in January, she spent considerably more time with him; not that she had been negligent before. But now she had to run his errands and drive him to the doctor's and to social engagements at the houses of those of his friends who had stopped driving: most of them had, it seemed to Julia. On weekends, she stayed overnight; it was simply easier, since she was going to be with him most of Saturday and Sunday, anyway. This was Sunday night, however, and soon—but not too soon, or he would think she was hurrying to get away from him—she would make his toddy and gather up her books and briefcase and overnight bag and drive to her own apartment. She needed those few hours to herself before meeting her nine o'clock freshmen on Monday morning.

"Well, we had ourselves a ticklish situation. Do you remember the Robert Jones incident back in November?"

"The black man who was caught lying on the floor and peeking through the stacks at the woman's legs? Of course." Did he really think she could possibly forget such a story, or his sprightly telling of it? Or his surprisingly scrupulous use of the man's name, Robert Jones, for a person whom, as recently as six months ago, he would have labeled simply "that brazen darky," or worse, considering he had been caught in the act of looking up a white woman's dress in the public library. But her father's growing respect for Mrs. Evans, the wife of the black doctor who had bought the old Tuttle house at the end of the block, had changed all that. Ever since the October Sunday—*that* Sunday when Freddy Stratton had telephoned here with the news of Theo Quick—when Neville Richardson had found his new neighbor planting her next spring's bulbs upside down and rushed to her aid with his little Swiss bulb planter and tactful advice, the Robert Joneses of the world were allowed to have names and individualities, notwithstanding their crimes, because they had something in common with "that very civilized Mrs. Evans." When her father had fallen off the stepladder in the kitchen, trying to reach some of his peach preserves on a top pantry shelf, it had been Mrs. Evans he had phoned after failing to locate Julia at the college. Mrs. Evans had driven him to the emergency room, where his foot was X-rayed and pronounced broken, and driven him back next morning, after the swelling had gone down, to have it set in a cast. She brought him home-baked cakes and casseroles hot from her oven. They exchanged recipes. She took to "dropping over" to check on him on weekday evenings when Julia could not get over or when Dr. Evans worked late at the hospital, always phoning first to make sure she was not intruding, and he would ask her to make them both toddies and they would sit together for a while. He would tell her stories of the old Mountain City: what this street had been like in the days of its prime, when the Tuttles and the Gallants reigned at either end of the block. She giggled like a delighted child, he said, when he described, what nasty little hellions Dr. Gallant and his sister had been as children; how they used to throw the poor Tuttle girl's shoes over the back fence into the woods and threaten her if she tattled; and how Mrs. Gallant, in whose eyes little Anthony and Alicia were angels, later told his own mother, "You know, I never thought that Tuttle girl was too bright. Every time she came over to play with Tony and Sissie when they were little, she would manage to lose her shoes." Since her father had been laid up with his foot, the existence of staid, appreciative Mrs. Evans had been a great relief for Julia.

"As you may remember, the Board suspended Robert Jones's library privileges for three months. That was all we had the power to do under existing policy because we didn't even have a rule against what he'd done. Those guides to behavior in the library were drawn up around 1915, and the worst crime *that* Board could imagine was disrupting the quiet. Robert Jones had been quieter than a mouse when he arranged himself on the floor and made his little peephole through the loose books on the bottom shelf. Of course, if he had done what he did in 1915, he would have been taken out and lynched, probably. But then, he couldn't have done what he did in 1915, because black people weren't allowed to use the library in those days. So we told him he couldn't use the library for three months, and even though he denied doing anything—he said he was hunting for a book and the woman jumped to the wrong conclusion—he left the library and didn't come back for weeks and weeks, and we thought we were rid of him for good. But on the first Monday after those three months were up, there was Robert Jones in his usual place, over by the newspapers. Some of the older women complained. They said it wasn't safe to come to the library anymore and one of them made a fuss about it to Karen Brewster, the newest member of our Board. She's a hardworking young woman who wants to do the right thing, but she hasn't a shred of grace or humor. Last Thursday, she made a motion that we put into the bylaws that loitering was forbidden on library property. Then, of course, we had to spend an hour or more attempting to *define* 'loitering.' Karen Brewster said it was pretty clear to her what loitering was: if someone showed up when the library opened and stayed there all day until it closed, as Robert Jones did, and if this person wasn't a *student* or doing research of some kind, then he was a loiterer. The trouble is, we've got a dozen or so people who spend their days in the library and who aren't *students*. They are mostly old, and they come to read the newspapers and magazines free, and to keep warm, and to see other human faces. Bruce Denton, our chairman, pointed that out to Karen Brewster. By then it was everybody's suppertime, but she was still determined that we finagle an exclusion clause into the bylaws that would apply to Robert Jones and Robert Jones alone. You see how impossible this was getting. The four men on the Board hung back from telling her she was being ridiculous, as they would certainly have told another man, but you have to be so careful with women on committees these days: the least criticism and they think you're condescending to their sex. But then, praise the Lord, Lily Quick, our only other woman, who'd been sitting there demurely embroidering one of her animal pillows, set everything to rights in a way that no one else could. She rested her needle in the cloth and looked around the table at everybody with those distant blue eyes and said in that whimsical, musing tone she employs when she means business but doesn't want anyone accusing her of earnestness, 'I don't know . . . is it really our place, as members of a library board, to deny the consolations of literature to anyone?' It was just the perfect tone, the exact right thing. Everyone in the room knew about her recent tragedy and I'm sure each one of us had visions of her leafing through some book for consolation in the middle of the night. But she dispelled any awkwardness that might arise from our sympathies by getting this mischievous look on her face and saying, 'I am one of those women who have the most to fear from someone like Robert Jones, because I still wear skirts all the time. Yet I feel perfectly at ease about our coexistence. If he ever looked up *my* skirt, I would just reach into the stacks and push a load of books straight down on his head—quietly, of course.' Everybody burst out laughing, even humorless Karen Brewster, who, by the way, always wears pantsuits. She's in awe of Lily Quick because Lily goes out to visit old Mrs. Brewster, who can't stand her daughter-in-law, at Foxwood Nursing Home. Apparently the old woman is a shrew of the first order, but Lily has added her to her list of senescent orphans and carries euphemistic messages back and forth between mother-in-law and daughter-in-law. Anyway, thanks to Lily, we were able to placate Karen Brewster by voting on a motion that the librarian would issue a *warning* to Robert Jones that if such behavior is ever repeated, out he goes again. Then we adjourned, and Bob Fawcett drove me home. His wife was visiting relatives, so we stopped at the Three Little Pigs and had some very tasty barbecue."

"I saw Lily in the Fresh Market the other day," said Julia. "She's lost weight and looks fifteen years younger. Her makeup was perfect and she was wearing a gray cashmere sweater and a gray tweed suit with little flecks of orange in it. It was bizarre, how well she looked, there was a sort of porcelain sheen laid over her grief like a mask. We talked about the custody hearing; I hadn't seen her since they lost. She said, 'I am going to make every effort to be civil to my ex-daughter-in-law, the Princess Snow, but I will never forgive her for making me tell my age in court. Never. Even if I have to serve time in Purgatory for it.'"

Neville Richardson chuckled with pleasure. "No, Lily Quick would never forgive anyone for that. She's the quintessential Southern woman, in many ways. But, as I said, she's mystifying. There's something . . . how shall I put it? It's the business of Southern women to be mystifying, we all know that, but with Lily Quick you feel she's taken it an extra length, given it another twist."

"I didn't think of her as the typical Southern woman, at all, when I was growing up," said Julia. "She was the most vibrant, sensual woman I knew. She said daring, unconventional things; she mocked the status quo. She was writing a novel that she said was going to blow the lid off this town, only she never finished it. I still dream of reading that novel. Now, whenever I meet her, I feel I'm talking to someone under a spell. It's as if she'd been trapped and transformed into the kind of woman she used to scorn. But she takes some deep, perverse pleasure in acting the part to the hilt. Sometimes I want to shake her; other times she makes me want to go off somewhere and cry."

"Did you ever consider," suggested Neville Richardson, eyeing his daughter slyly, "that the *other* Lily, the one you admired so as a teenager, might have been an act? An act she couldn't sustain?"

Julia was silent for a moment, thinking. Her parents had never approved of her crush on Lily; they thought Clare's mother, in her other incarnation, was a dangerous influence. Yet if Mother had lived to be Lily's age, Julia realized sadly, she would have approved of her now. They might have become friends, visiting nursing homes and going to church together. "No, I don't think it was an act," said Julia. "Or at least if it *was*, I believe she was trying and hoping to become the person she was acting. I see her as a victim of a certain time in history and a certain place, and maybe a certain kind of marriage."

"Oh, now *him*," snorted her father, reaching for one of his two last cigarettes for the day. (He now rationed himself to ten since his doctor, having failed to impress him with gentlemanly, jocular warnings, had described in detail how a person slowly and horribly suffocated to death in the final stage of emphysema.) "She married him for sex, of course. What else could it have been? He hadn't a penny to his name, his mother came from people who were part Cherokee, and his father used to run numbers games in the back of that little tavern he kept, down behind the old Langley Hotel. She was a highly sexed widow and he was an attentive young stud, and chemistry took precedence over good judgment. And look at them today. She goes her way, he goes his. I'm told he spends most of his time with old Alicia Gallant. Neglects his work, turns down jobs, puts his foreman in charge of everything, while he takes Miss Alicia to the Mall and then to the Red Lobster for lunch. Margaret York's maid Lucille's mother, Susie, cooks for Alicia Gallant, and she says he eats with her three or four nights a week, and on some occasions when she's stayed late, she's seen both of them sitting sound asleep in their chairs in front of the TV, like some old married couple. That terrible thing with the son seems to have driven the Quicks farther asunder, if you ask me. What do you hear from Clare?"

"She's been pretty depressed about it all. It didn't hit her fully till she got back to New York. Then she followed the whole custody battle over the telephone with Lily. She isn't writing. She threw out the book she'd been working on for over a year. She's full of guilt for not loving Theo enough and for escaping when he couldn't. The whole bit."

"She hasn't escaped," said Neville Richardson. "You can tell that from the books. Especially the one we're in. I don't care whether she lives in New York or Soviet Russia, she'll spend the rest of her life stuck right here."

"She probably knows that," conceded Julia. "Up to a point, anyway. But this thing with Theo really threw her. They had this talk about her work the day before he died. Since then she's felt a kind of revulsion against her writing, questioning everything."

Her father took a languorous puff on his cigarette and exhaled a shapely plume of its lethal residue. "I'm not too worried," he said dryly. "If I know our Clare—and, after all, I *was* her father for five hundred pages of *The Headmaster's Daughters*—she'll rally and give us another tale about ourselves. And I'll wager that the lamentable episode with the brother will find its way into print before too many moons have waxed and waned. Only she'll make him and everybody else both larger and smaller than they really are, as she did us."

Julia had entertained similar thoughts herself, but felt she owed her friend the loyalty of silence until Clare proved Neville Richardson right, or at least announced her intentions of proving him so. People should be allowed a grace period by their best friends, in which to foil others' predictions of what they were bound to do next. Given his puckish but shrewd aim in these guessing games, Julia was not at all sure she would want to hear her father sum up what was in store for *her* before too many moons had waxed and waned. Or maybe it was because she already saw the outline of what he would see, as well as how he would phrase it, even down to the nickname for her he would use.

"Ah, that was a somber one," said her father, with his uncanny scent for the drift of her thoughts. "Penny for it."

"Oh," she answered with a sigh, "I guess I was worrying, as I always do on Sunday nights, how I am going to make history fresh and exciting for my freshmen on Monday morning. Honestly, with each new crop I feel more and more we're losing our memory of the past. Sometimes their ignorance and their indifference are just stunning." A partial evasion, but with enough truth of her abiding concerns clinging to it to lure him towards a more favorable topic. The decline of others, or of the race in general, was always more comfortable to discuss than the decline of oneself and one's personal hopes.

"That's nothing new, Cordelia. When I began teaching at Belvedere in 1932, I used to give my new history students a little quiz on the first day of each semester. I wanted to find out how much I could take for granted they already knew, and at the same time I wanted to show them we were going to have some fun. I'd ask things like, oh, 'Who was Socrates' most famous student and who was later *his* most famous student, and who was later *his* most famous student?' The association of fame with the word 'student' perked their own ambitions, and the question itself had that cheeky repetition that young people love. Most of them could answer the first part of it and then there were a few smart ones who could work backwards from Alexander the Great and put the rest together, and there I had the Socratic method—well, a version of it, anyway—working for me in class before we had ever opened a book. Well, not to bore you, to make a long story shorter, I saved copies of my little quizzes from year to year so I wouldn't repeat myself. Boarding schools, especially, have a notorious academic grapevine, as you know: the sixth-formers passing down to the fifth-and fourth-formers what Old So-and-So asked on his first quiz last year. I had no intention of becoming Old So-and-So, that's why I kept my records. Well, my child, the sad time came—I would say it was after I had been at Belvedere about twelve years—when I would look through my folder at those early quizzes and say to myself, 'Good Lord, did I really ask such a sophisticated question of my first-year students? Did some of them actually know the answer?' And then I'd shuffle through the later quizzes and trace how, imperceptibly at the time, I'd been making them easier every year. 'Why did Socrates drink hemlock?' 'What was inside the Trojan horse?' 'Why was the Magna Carta an important step for Democracy?' 'What *was* the Magna Carta?' 'Name the freedoms guaranteed to you by the Bill of Rights.' 'What is your *favorite* freedom guaranteed you by the Bill of Rights?' 'What *is* the Bill of Rights?' "

Laughing, Julia slipped the biography of W. J. Cash into her briefcase and went to the kitchen to make her father's toddy. Please, God, she prayed, setting the kettle on the front burner to boil, let my father keep his wits to the very last. That will make it so much easier for me to be what seems to have been written in the stars that I am destined to be. She unscrewed the little bottle of sugar water she made in batches, and measured a tablespoonful into her father's glass. She took down the Jack Daniel's from its place on the shelf. "One jigger or two?" she called to her father, as she did every Sunday night.

"Just one, Cordelia," came his jaunty answer. "I have to save up *some* vice for when I'm old."

That was a good sign and put her mind to rest for the week ahead. For several Sundays past, it had been "Two, if you don't mind, Cordelia. A man my age is entitled to a little oblivion."

Rather than following the pattern of streets she had known all of her life, she took the expressway between her father's place and hers. It meant doubling back for a mile or so to get to the nearest entrance, but the effort was important for her morale. During those five or six minutes of whizzing along the highroad among cars with out-of-state licenses that might be going anywhere, she refreshed her memory of what it was like to be a stranger rather than someone who belonged. In other times, and not so long ago, she, too, had hurtled past cities and towns that cradled the sleeping and settled lives of their inhabitants; *she* had been the one in transit, her destination still ahead of her somewhere on the vast and diversified map of possibilities. As she drove fast for those few minutes on the expressway above night-time Mountain City, she reminded herself that she had once gone to California and back all by herself on the same interstate highway that fed through this town. She had made her home for five years in the most stimulating and dangerous city in America, riding home after dark on a subway crammed with the descendants of the black slave families she had intended to make her academic specialty. She had been other things besides what she was now. She had been a wife. She had been a divorced woman lighting out for the promised land of adventure and self-fulfillment. She had had some adventures and some self-fulfillment. And then she had come home to be a daughter again. She didn't resent being a daughter. She didn't see, under the circumstances, how she could have done anything else without hating herself. And she was not unhappy. She was not just a daughter, either. She was a force and an influence in the lives of her students, even if one of them, and not a stupid boy, had asked her last week, "Dr. Lowndes, why are people always saying 'the Second World War? I mean, for there to be a second, there has to have been a first, doesn't there?' The worst part of it was, he had been so proud of figuring out this flow in historical logic all by himself. But what good were deductive powers when the premises were based on rampant ignorance? At such times she would ask herself, "What am I doing here?" But looking at it another way, didn't a student who had gone through twelve years of schooling without ever hearing of World War I need her more than the student who had? Yes and no. The student at North State needed her, but he needed so much less of her than she had to give. Wasn't this the crux of her frustration: that there were whole areas of herself nobody was using? Lately, even her sexual fantasies had changed. She could no longer imagine real men, but had to fancy consorting with extraterrestrial ones, because she simply could not think of anyone in her local world who would be able to see her for all she still was and not just how she appeared: as a plump, fortyish, overworked schoolteacher.

If areas weren't used, they stopped developing or went to seed. Her own mother, who had spent a lifetime refusing to think, ended up being unable to think. And that awful story Freddy Stratton had told her when they met at the cheese counter in the Fresh Market last week about a former classmate at St. Clothilde's. "Do you remember Myra Jenkins?" Freddy had asked, shrewd little green eyes glittering with relish at the bizarre news she was about to relate. "One day she just stopped going out of her house. It had been building up for a long time, apparently. First, she wouldn't fly, then she wouldn't drive. She was real clever about getting friends to take her places. Even her husband didn't suspect for the longest time. Then in December Janey Smith came by to take her out—they were going to do some Christmas shopping—and she said that Myra came to the front door all ready to go and when she started to cross the threshold she began to cry and shake and hold on to the doorframe. She couldn't make herself walk out of her house and down to Janey's car. They had to hospitalize her for a couple of weeks, but now she's back home. A volunteer comes, from some organization of people who've all suffered from the same thing, and she works with Myra. She holds her hand and they take little walks around the yard; then when Myra gets so she can handle that, they'll try to get her in a car again."

"How terrible," Julia had said, really disturbed, though she hadn't seen or thought about Myra Jenkins in years, didn't even know whom she had married. But she saw in her mind the flighty, vivacious girl who amazed everybody on the playground by the way she could run intrepidly into the arc of the fast-swinging jump rope and start jumping without ever missing a beat. What series of diminishments had transformed that bold little dynamo into a cringing housewife tottering around her own lawn and holding the hand of a volunteer?

"I know," agreed Freddy complacently. "It's called agoraphobia. And she's just our age. When I heard about it, I told

Skip he was going to have to let me go off by myself on an airplane at least once a month so it wouldn't creep up on me. Oh, I had the nicest letter from Clare. I think it was the first letter I ever got from her in my life. A real *long* letter. I've been intending to write her back, but I was always a hopeless correspondent. She said the family was real upset about losing the custody of the little boy, but you know, Julia, Ralph and Lily are really too old to bring up that child. Small children require an enormous amount of energy."

"I know," Julia had responded automatically, and had earned the briefest of supercilious glances from her old classmate, enviably slim in her neat suburban clothes, leaning on a cocked elbow against the cheese display case in an easy Chaplinesque pose. How, after all, would *Julia* know what prodigious amounts of energy small children required?

As she unlocked her front door, she heard the phone ringing inside her apartment. Oh, God, what if he's stumbled in his cast and fallen and broken something else, she thought, hurrying through the darkness and almost tripping over a lamp cord: a broken hip that will never heal right—he has dragged himself to the phone; or a final coughing fit—he will barely be able to choke my name, and before I can phone the ambulance and get back there myself he will be dead . . .

"Julia?"

"Oh, *Clare*."

"You sound out of breath. Was this a bad time to call?"

"No, I just got back from Father's. Wait a minute, let me turn on a light." The glow of lamplight over her own things, waiting for her just as she had left them on Friday, reassured her. She took a deep breath, thankful to be back in these surroundings she had made for herself. Clare wanted something; Julia could tell from the anxious edge to her voice. Clare always sounded on the defensive when she needed something from somebody, even if it was her best friend. With a curious reluctance Julia returned to the phone. Ordinarily she loved Clare's calls, prodigal in length, rich in anecdotes, and disarmingly laced with confessions of her latest fears and failures, so incongruous in the midst of her lovely abundance. And the way the two of them could strip down to the current essentials of their inner lives in a matter of minutes. But tonight Julia would have liked more time alone to replenish her well of selfhood before having to rise to

Clare's insistently idealistic image of her as Wise and Inspiring Friend and Admirable Human Being. "Hi, I'm back." She was aware of the effort to pump energy into her voice.

"I called several times last night, but you were out. I figured you were probably with George."

"No, George is in France, living in a Benedictine abbey. He took half a semester without pay, he was so thrilled when the abbot wrote he could come and do research on his medieval monastery book and live the way the monks live. I spent the weekend over at Father's. Since he broke his foot, it's easier to stay there on weekends rather than drive back and forth half a dozen times."

"Ah," said Clare, with some misgiving mixed in with her respect. She admired Julia for being the good daughter, but had frequently taken it upon herself to warn Julia of the temptations of "burying herself" in such a role. "How *is* his foot?"

"On the mend. He was feisty as ever tonight. What's up?"

"I'm coming down there next Friday. But there's kind of a ticklish situation. You see, Lily and Ralph don't know I'm going to be there."

"What do you mean?"

"I'm going to visit Snow and Jason up in Granny Squirrel. She and her mother will pick me up at the airport. I'll stay with Snow in her trailer Friday and Saturday nights, and then on Sunday I've got to fly to Columbia to do a week of workshops for the South Carolina Arts Council. What I was hoping, if you feel like doing a little driving, was that you might come and pick me up in Granny Squirrel on Sunday morning and drive me back to Mountain City to the airport. Then we'd at least have some time to talk in the car. My flight isn't until late Sunday afternoon; I have to change planes in Charlotte. The reason I decided not to tell Lily was so it wouldn't mix things up. She and Snow aren't exactly in love with each other after the custody battle. I mean, Ralph and Lily drive back and forth between Mountain City and Granny Squirrel to get Jason for his weekends with them, but I want to try to get along with Snow, and I thought any rapport we did achieve from my going to visit her might be spoiled if, at the end of the visit, Ralph and Lily came to pick me up. Snow would think we were running her down as soon as we drove away. And they probably would be, and, if I know me, I'd slip right into it with them. I want to keep my impressions separate from theirs, if I can. I want to go and see Snow in her own territory and understand her on her own terms. She offered to drive me back to the airport on Sunday, but, if you're willing, it would be so much more fun with you."

"Of course I'm willing. But I was just thinking —"

"You don't want to leave your father." Clare interjected, leaping ahead, in her typical fashion, to embrace disappointment before it was even offered to her.

"No, Father's fine. He's got plenty of friends and a nice neighbor lady who comes and sits with him in the evenings anytime he wants. She laps up his stories and the bygone snobs that used to live on their street. Father could certainly survive without me for a *day*, Clare. I don't go over there every night of the week. No, what I was thinking was, why don't I drive you on down to Columbia myself next Sunday?"

"Oh, *no* Julia! That's too far. I couldn't let you."

"It's not so far. The slowest part of it is that stretch through the gorge between Cherokee and Granny Squirrel. The Columbia part will be a breeze, straight down 26. We could be in Columbia in just about three hours longer than it would take to get you to the airport."

"Yes, but you forget you have to drive the three hours back as well."

"I haven't forgotten. It'll do me good. I need to go somewhere. I drove home on the expressway tonight just to remember how it felt to whiz by other people's settled lives. I saw Freddy Stratton in the Fresh Market the other day, and she told me Myra Jenkins has agoraphobia. I don't want to catch *that*. You remember Myra Jenkins."

"I wrote to Freddy the nicest letter, but she never answered it. Sure, I remember Myra. The jump-rope queen. She told such big lies. Like the one about her father being a famous tennis star. Only it turned out he was just a pro at some hotel in Florida in the winter. And remember that awful birthday party she gave where her mother tried to make us play Charades, only no one wanted to? And then you and I were walking to the bus stop afterwards, talking about what a creepy party it had been, and she suddenly jumped out of the bushes and started screaming at us?"

"Oh, God, of course! She had followed us all the way from her house and listened to everything we'd said about her. Clare, how can you *remember* all that stuff?"

Clare groaned. "How can I *forget* it?" But there was a definite note of smugness in her complaint. Clare's memory for long-ago incidents and dramatic details—even those connected to the peripheral figures of their past—had served her well in her writing. "Nevertheless, I'm sorry to hear poor Myra has agoraphobia. It seems to be a popular disease right now. I was just reading the galleys of a new novel where this woman who is married to a film star slowly loses confidence in herself and gets it. Then she's cured over a long period of time by a psychiatrist specializing in agoraphobia because his *own* wife had it, and she flies off to Europe to surprise her famous film-star husband on location and she gets killed by a car just as she's crossing the street to run into his arms."

Julia started laughing. "You mean that was the end of the book?" She felt her energy returning and was glad, after all, that Clare had called.

"That was it. The book's sure to be a success. Hopeless endings are very popular right now. I guess the feeling is, why should people in novels live happily ever after when real people are dropping like flies? It's been that kind of year, hasn't it? Those two hundred Marines killed in their sleep in Beirut by a car bomb. All those high-school boys who hanged themselves. Or am I just looking for dark patterns because of what happened to Theo?"

"It's understandable that you would be more likely to pick up on them under the circumstances. But tell me how it came about that you're going to go see Snow in Granny Squirrel?"

"It started when I was sending Jason and her a Christmas card and I decided to write a note to Jason so he wouldn't forget me. But then I thought, If I write him a note and don't write her one, she'll bear a grudge and 'poison his mind' against me. I remember when I was a child and threatened to go and live with my father's mother if Lily wouldn't do something I wanted, Lily would just say very casually, 'If you feel you have to, then of course we'll be glad to send you down on the train, but, you know, if you do anything to offend her, she'll make you sleep in the chicken house, like she made your father and his brother do when they were growing up.' It wasn't till years later, after that grandmother was dead—she died without my ever seeing her—when I went down there to stay with Uncle Zeb and Aunt Mamie, that I found out she was a humorous, loving woman who had kept pictures of me in her Bible and wondered why I never wanted to go and see her. And the chicken house was a myth. Or, rather, Lily had reconstructed it to meet her needs. My grandmother had *kept* chickens, but the room she'd banished my father and Uncle Zeb to was a room off the garage, with a little bathroom in it, which she called 'The Drunk Room.' She made them sleep there, Aunt Mamie told me, whenever they came home drunk so they wouldn't smell up the house. I figured if Lily could tell stories like that about my father's mother just because her marriage had disappointed her and she wanted to be finished with the Campions, then Snow would have a lot more reason to turn Jason against his father's half sister, especially after our family tried to discredit her in court."

"But *you* weren't there. You didn't come down to testify."

"That's what I told myself when I started writing my note to Snow. At first I felt all defensive, and then I thought, Wait a minute! Maybe I still have a chance with her. Maybe she doesn't hate me yet. I mean, I gave them a wedding present and I was nice to Snow's mother and I am Jason's official godmother, I swore all those things on his behalf in church. And I ended up writing her a long letter, saying I wanted to know her better as *herself*, not just because she was the girl my brother married or my nephew's mother. It was a good letter, if I do say so myself. I really got into it. I sent it off to Georgia, where she was living with that husband she married ten days after Theo died, and a few weeks after Christmas I got this long letter back from Granny Squirrel, where my letter was forwarded to. She's already left husband number three and is back with her clan. She and Jason are living in a trailer belonging to some uncle who bought it before he went off to Vietnam and came back not quite right in the head. So now he lives with his parents in the house down the road. Anyway, she wrote me this remarkably literate letter—there wasn't a single word misspelled, and that's more than I can say for a lot of college students I've had in creative-writing workshops. It was really a very winning letter. It was confiding and yet it had dignity and it was written . . . well, it was written better than Snow *talks*, in this plain, straightforward style, without any mistakes in grammar."

"Maybe someone wrote it for her?"

"I considered that at first, but after I'd gone over it a few times, I decided not. The *rhythms* were somehow hers and actually the punctuation left something to be desired. And besides, who up there could have helped her? She's probably the most literate person in the family. She did get through the ninth grade."

"Hmm. True. Now that I think of it, I've had students who were raised in Granny Squirrel, and their reading and writing were pretty fair—a lot better than the average city high-school graduate's."

"Maybe they still use the good old hickory stick method of education up there," Clare answered, laughing. "Anyway, her letter really gave me a whole new impression of her and I pounced on her invitation to come and see them anytime I could. I knew I had the South Carolina thing coming up, and Felix had already planned to go to Vienna next Friday, so this coming weekend seemed the perfect time. I wrote her back and asked if I could come then, and she answered right away and said she would meet me, which means a considerable drive for her and her mother, and she said she had things to tell me about Theo."

"What kinds of things?"

"The things they discussed the last time they talked on the phone. Listen, Julia, there's an aspect to all this that makes me feel pretty rotten. I feel I'm poking into Theo's privacy just like those detectives who read his love poems to Jeanette and then tried to fob off copies to Lily and Ralph because they wanted to test the originals for 'substances.'"

"But you're not the detectives, you're his sister. Did they really keep the poems? I didn't know Theo wrote poetry."

"He never did, to anyone's knowledge, till he and Jeanette broke up. Then he apparently stuffed her mailbox with them."

"Have you read them? Are they any good? I know one shouldn't ask that."

"They're . . . better than you would expect. Parts of some of them are very strong, especially in the ones where he's complaining about the world and not just pining over Jeanette. Lily sent me Xeroxes. She insisted that the detectives give her back the originals. Oh, Julia, do you really feel like driving me all the way to Columbia?"

"I really and truly do, Clare. As I told you, I need to go somewhere. I *like* driving."

"The prospect of spending five or six hours with you in the car is a wonderful thought. I need to talk to you about so many things, Julia. You know there was a place in Snow's last letter where she said Theo loved me, and when I read those words I felt like a fraud. Of course, maybe she was just saying it because she knew I would expect to hear it, but if it was *true* . . ."

"But why shouldn't it be true?"

"Because I paid so little attention to him. God, Julia, this is a terrible thing to admit, but whole months of my life went by without my thinking of him. Maybe some whole *years*, except for when Lily would mention him on the phone or in a letter. And, you know, he wrote to me, too. Not often, but I've gone through my old boxes and found letters from him. One from when he was fourteen, which has an odd little fantasy in it—at least I'm pretty sure it was a fantasy—about how someone shot at him from a passing car when he was walking on the golf course. And then several thanking me for gifts, graduation and so on. And then there's this touching 'Godmother's Report,' on that graph paper accountants use—he must have spent hours on it—it's made out like a financial report, only it has entries like 'Jason eats his first real banana' and 'First tooth—left bottom.' But the thing that killed me when I read all the letters was that he had obviously worked hard to make them interesting and witty and entertaining. He was trying to impress me. And Jesus, Julia, I'm trying to remember, I'm not sure I even answered some of them. And there was one letter that I re- member, but I couldn't find. He wrote it after *The Headmaster's Daughters* came out. It was about how all the people in his office were reading it. He described each person by name and, by what they said about the book, you had a sharp little charac- ter sketch of that person. I looked all over for that letter the other night and couldn't find it. Then I had an inspiration. Maybe I filed it in my fan-letter folder at the time, because it was such a good letter about the book. But when it wasn't in that folder I started to cry. Because I realized what must have happened. You see, I don't keep all my fan letters. Just the ones that strike a particularly interesting note or are especially intelligent or engaging. It seemed too much to bear that I had appreciated him so little when he was alive that I wouldn't even let him into my *fan* folder! I must have thrown that letter away, Julia, because it didn't quite make the grade. What's really awful is, I've thought about Theo more since he's been dead than I ever did when he was alive. It's like he had to *die* to get my complete attention. Only, my complete attention can't do him the least bit of good now. And yet, if Snow wasn't just flattering me, he must have told her he loved me. How *could* he have, when I gave so little of myself?"

"In the first place," said Julia, "love doesn't work that way, and you know it. We don't always love people because they love us, or even because they're worthy of love. But in the second place—and I think this must be the one-millionth time I have said this to you—you are too hard on yourself. You like to dwell on your negative aspects. I'm sure you gave Theo lots of reasons to love and admire you. And didn't you ever consider that it was nice for him to have someone to want to impress? Look at the people in your own life. Didn't you often love the same people you tried hardest to impress?"

"Yes, but I was usually able to make them pay attention to me. I made them love me back. I was luckier than Theo."

"Ah, poor Clare. How are you ever going to punish yourself enough for having all your good luck? What time do you want me to arrive in Granny Squirrel?"

One day, thought Julia, as she passed through Cherokee on U.S. 19, I'm going to have to think about the Indians. I wonder how many Americans say that to themselves: One day I am going to have to think about the Indians. But it will have to wait until I get through thinking about the South.

Like all the other children she knew, she had been taken to the Cherokee Indian Reservation and the Oconaluftee Indian Village, where the descendants of the tribe that once owned much of Tennessee, the Carolinas, Georgia, and Alabama dressed in feathers and moccasins and acted busy practicing their crafts for the descendants of the whites who had driven their own ancestors out. In college, she'd had a boyfriend who had acted in *Unto These Hills*. She had visited him backstage and watched him and the other college actors smearing red Pan Cake makeup all over their white bodies for the evening performance. But she had managed never to think much about what any of it meant until a fellow graduate assistant at Columbia University told her how he'd had a nervous breakdown working with Pueblo Indians in New Mexico. "I got infected with their death wish," he had said. "They knew they were anachronisms and they wanted to die. And one day when I was trying to enlighten them about something, I don't remember what . . . one of our superior ways of doing something . . . it occurred to me that I was just as much of an anachronism as they were. The days of the conquistadores and the missionaries were just as much over as the days of the Indians. We were all ghosts together, wandering around that pueblo. Only, I was the outcast ghost, I had no business being there. I left and was completely disoriented for a year. I had to go home and live with my parents. My mother was sure the Indians had done it to me with some drug. Even after I was able to go back to graduate school and function again, I could never regain that wonderful blind faith in myself I'd had before I went to the pueblo. It was that faith that had made me want to go to the pueblo and help the Indians. But I could never again feel superior because I was a white American male. Because I also realized, after my breakdown, that the superior male in our society is also an illusion. He's an extinct animal who thinks he's still walking around. When he wakes up and realizes he doesn't exist, there's going to be an epidemic of nervous breakdowns all over the country."

Poor Nelson. He had not been a very prepossessing specimen of the arrogant white male. He'd been one of those soft men, all sensibility and no command, the kind of man you could talk to as you would to another woman because you weren't interested in seducing him. She suspected he'd been the same before his breakdown among the Indians. But let him think it was the Indians. At least it had given him an interesting subject, something to specialize in and gain a reputation with. In that sense, he had done far better than she had. She often came across his articles when she leafed through historical quarterlies in the college library. The titles of some of them were like little giveaways to his own psychic struggles: "Loss of Identity in the Southwest Patrilineal Clans of the Eastern Pueblo Indian"; "The Relationship of Magic to Potency in the Fertility Ceremonies of the Hopi."

And what would my reputation have been like, she wondered, entering the deep, sunless gorge of Nantahala, if I had gone on with my research into black slave family life instead of rushing home to the family's call of distress? What would my titles have revealed about me? "The Consolations of Family Life for Slaves"? "Family Freedoms in Slavery," by A Family Slave in Freedom? Now, Julia, don't get cynical or you're lost. And don't complain to Clare about feeling closed in or she'll jump on her bandwagon of self-determination and say I owe it to myself to get on with my own life. But what does she expect me to do? Leave Father to die alone? It's easy for her to preach independence from family: *her* only living parent is married to a younger man who will take care of her regardless of whether they can stand each other or not; Ralph Quick is that kind of man. Whatever happens, he will be faithful to his image of himself as a dutiful husband. And there's Rafe, too. Rafe is his mother's sweetheart. I'll never forget that scene when he walked into the kitchen with the tears pouring down his cheeks and the way Lily, who had been standoffish all evening with the people wanting to get close to her and console her, let Rafe put his head down over hers and drop his tears into her carefully sprayed hairdo. From the little I have seen of Rafe, and from what Clare tells me, Rafe will always be coming home again. He might end up a male version of me someday, giving up a promising job to come back to Mountain City and live the Family Romance to its dregs. He will slip out at night and screw barmaids that get younger and younger. The way I scribble erotic fantasies into my doggerel book. Oh, God, *stop* it, Julia. Stop predicting other people's fates as your father does. You don't have his style. When you do it, you sound bitter and mean. Whatever kind of old woman you become, don't become a bitter and mean one.

But as she left the wild beauty of the gorge behind her and descended into the region inhabited by Snow's people, her personal dilemma was replaced by her historian's awareness of the striking aesthetic deterioration. As soon as she entered the land at the farthest corner of her state, a stretch that lay outside the protection of national forest or reservation, evidences of greed and sloth and abuse and bad planning began to assault her eye. The lumber mills had raped and pillaged, mining operations had heaped gigantic gray and yellow piles of the earth's innards along the road; new roads crisscrossed indiscriminately, trapping solitary old buildings, or parts of towns, in culs-de-sac; sleek modern brick-and-glass factories with turf lawns and nursery trees shared the same hills with tar-papered shacks and dirt yards. The people in the tar-papered shacks probably worked in the factories. Come South, said the old advertisements in Northeastern newspapers and trade journals, and take advantage of the "cheap and contented, 99 percent pure Anglo-Saxon labor." W.J. Cash had quoted such advertisements. And who had put them in those Northern papers? Who had invited the Yankee mill owners down, offering them inducements of free sites and tax exemptions? Impoverished Southerners who were too hungry

to realize, or to care, about the irony: Yankees went to war with
the South to free the enslaved blacks; then the conquered South
invited them back down to enslave the "cheap, contented, 99
percent pure Anglo-Saxons." Cash had been brilliant; one of
the few Southerners able to live at home and see it, historically
and objectively, for what it was, and still love it. But five months
after the publication of *The Mind of the South* he hanged himself,
at age forty-one, in a hotel bathroom in Mexico.

"After you pass the town, such as it is," Clare had told her
yesterday on the phone, "you will see a sign that says 'To Granny
Squirrel Mountain.' Just beyond that sign, on the left, there's a
road that goes up to the mountain. But you want the road across
from it that leads down into the valley. You follow this road—
it's pretty awful, be prepared—along the creek, and you cross
two bridges, and they're in a sort of cluster almost at the end.
The grandparents' house is covered in asphalt shingles, a kind
of grayish-green, and there are a lot of old stoves and re-
frigerators and just about everything in the front yard. Snow's is
the trailer in the field after you pass the house. According to
Snow, her grandfather used to own all the land along the creek,
all the way up to the highway. But he's been selling it off until
now there's only the bottomland and one little hill. He gave the
hill to his favorite granddaughter, Evelyn, the only one of Snow's
generation he likes. Snow and he don't get along. She asked
him to give her some land to build a house on and he refused.
But he's crazy about Jason and is always wanting him to come
over and spend the night in his bed. He's an impressive old
geezer. Eighty-three years old and I came across him hammering
in a fence post this morning. I was taking a walk around the
edge of the field to keep from going stir-crazy. He wouldn't talk
to me at first, when I said I was visiting Snow, but when I told
him I was Theo's sister, he opened up some. He said Theo was
the best husband any of the girls had brought home and Snow
would never get so lucky again. Then he smelled the air and
told me it was going to rain in about fifteen minutes and I'd
better finish my walk. I finished my walk and in fifteen minutes
it rained."

"How are you getting along with Snow? Are you phoning
from her place?"

"No, they don't have a phone yet. I'm at the Seven-Eleven in
town. Snow's outside in the car, getting gas. We're getting along,

I guess. I haven't had a chance to be alone with her much. Oh, Julia, I need you to help me interpret all this. It's so grim and underprivileged . . . and yet they're so complacent, even proud. Don't get me wrong, they're being very hospitable, but everything is sort of . . . moment to moment. They mostly sit around and watch children and pass the time of day. There's lots of talking but no real conversation. Last night I couldn't sleep, the trailer was so hot, so I read the local phone book."

It's already *been* interpreted, thought Julia, as she felt her Rabbit, which she had just washed yesterday, sink to its hubcaps in the red mud of Snow's grandfather's road. As she labored and coughed along in low gear, an old mountaineer in overalls, carrying a crooked stick, emerged from a sideroad and, moving at an uncanny clip for his bent shape and advanced years, soon overtook her, lifting his arm in a sly wave as he passed her struggling machine. She was in the heartland of the people John C. Campbell had named "our contemporary ancestors" when he came to these parts seventy years ago to study "the peculiar character of Southern mountain life." She was in the mud ruts of Cash's Peasant at the Center (which he tactfully changed in a later draft to "The Man at the Center"): the simplest of the simple men in this part of the world, the fellow who was content to let his more energetic and successful brothers push him farther and farther up the creeks and into obscure coves and valleys; who was inclined, through lack of ambition or because he had little capacity for any extended exercise of will, to accept what each day brought: to plow a little, fish a little, hunt a little— and sell off a little more land to buy another day's respite from striving. One of Julia's reasons for reluctantly abandoning the idea of using Cash's unique book in her Southern History seminar for seniors was that he had been too cruelly succinct in his description of the type from which many of them sprang. The other reason was that his dense and resonant rhetoric, so rich in classical allusions, was simply beyond them. They would skim—and resent; and retreat deeper into the backwoods of their ignorance and illusions.

Some of the houses along the road were new: frame bungalows, painted in pastel shades, with light, shiny fiberglass roofs and wrought-iron trim around the porches, standing proudly in their naked clearings where red soil still predominated over grass. She passed only one old-time log cabin of the type you always saw on calendars and in picture books idealizing the scenic quaintness of Appalachia, but the grounds around it were too neat and it had a suspiciously "restored" aura about it, from the recently cedar-shingled roof to the shiny red Jeep Cherokee parked in front. Then she crossed the second of the two bridges Clare had told her about, and descended a mud-slick stretch into a wasted and deforested cul-de-sac dotted with several forlorn specimens of human habitation, about which there was not the slightest sign of aspiration, restoration, or attempts at maintenance. She recognized the grandfather's house with its greeny-gray siding of asphalt shingles, but Clare, usually inclined to hyperbole rather than understatement when describing something bad, had not prepared her for the demoralizing impression of the junkyard radiating out from the center of the patriarchal compound. There must have been at least half a dozen cast-offs of every kind of household appliance, implement, and utensil, including bathtubs and toilets. In several spots the mound of debris rose higher than the house. Julia's chest constricted from the sheer insolent ugliness of it. There was nothing funny about it. It could only be laughable to someone who had no connection to it or who was insensible to its implications. It could only be "interesting," without pain, to the sociologist types or rural snoops in search of picturesque proof to substantiate the "orneriness of the hillbilly" or the horrors of poverty. But this wasn't just orneriness or poverty. It was something much worse; it was visible and tangible evidence of a cluster of attitudes that, if shared by enough people, could bring down civilization: apathy, blindness to beauty, a refusal to be responsible even for your immediate surroundings. Oh, poor Clare, thought Julia. No, Clare would find some way to use it, to turn it into a story or anecdote before it could hit too hard. Poor *Lily*, who was obliged to come down this road every month if she wanted to see her only grandchild. No, Lily—the Lily of today, of the porcelain mask and the distant blue gaze— would make whatever adjustments necessary to protect herself from truly seeing what was in front of her eyes. As Ralph Quick drove them by this scene, she would look inward, at something else. Later, if you asked her, she would not remember, unless the occasion might profit from her remembrance—if she and Ralph should go back to court, for instance. And what about Ralph Quick, when he came to the end of this road, as Julia was doing now, and surveyed this kingdom of neglect his dead son's marriage forced him to revisit every month? Was it a nightmare of regression for Ralph, who had so recently achieved Quick's Hill? And yet it was only four months ago that Julia had driven up Ralph's hard-won hill, wondering at the piles of rotting lumber that lined the road, the rusted sheets of corrugated metal, the overturned Johnny on the Spot with wild flowers bursting from its open door. When Theo had first driven his bride up the steep curves of Quick's Hill, had Snow recoiled at Ralph's unsightly cast-offs? Or had she thought, Oh, well. More of the same. Or had she failed to see it totally, just taking it for granted, as Julia, no doubt, had missed countless landscaping effects the first time Starkie drove her ceremoniously up the oaklined drive of the Lowndes plantation in his little yellow Thunderbird?

The road through the field to the trailer was not exactly a road, but grass flattened by many tire tracks provided a sort of mat above the ooze. Two unsmiling little boys, both towheads, stood just inside the trailer's storm door, watching her approach. She checked her watch: eleven-ten. Not bad. "If you can get here around eleven," Clare had calculated on the phone, "we can sit and be sociable for half an hour—they'd be hurt, otherwise—and then be on our way."

In her Coleman picnic cooler on the backseat were a bottle of Vouvray, sliced turkey sandwiches, carrot sticks, and green pepper slices, along with the last of a moist coconut cake baked by Mrs. Evans that Julia's father had insisted she must have. It was an overcast February Sunday, but not too cold, and her plan was to find a nice lookout spot in Maggie Valley, or somewhere along the shore of Lake Junaluska, where they could have lunch in the car before beginning the unscenic trek down 26 to Columbia.

Clare, wearing jeans and a red sweater, edged out of the door past the little boys and made her way warily down the makeshift wooden steps and around the cars and pickup truck parked close to the trailer. She was frowning and her shoulders curved anxiously forward in their doom-expectant hunch. Somebody had laid down black plastic garbage bags and anchored them with large stones to provide a mud-free walkway. Clare hugged Julia and murmured in her ear, "The grandfather has just sent word he wants us to go down there for lunch. They eat early, so it won't delay us but about an hour. Is that okay? I said it was up to you, but they seem to think it's an invitation no one in her right mind would turn down."

"Sure, why not?" said Julia gamely, with a brief passing regret for the cold turkey meat in its nest of mayonnaise and crisp lettuce, the chilled Vouvray. She had even packed real wine-glasses, which would be frosted white when she removed them from the cooler. But she was here, after all, in the role of Sup-porting Friend, and it was clear from Clare's tone that she either wanted to go or thought they ought to go.

"This is Michael, Snow's nephew," said Clare, introducing a tough-looking, square-shaped little boy who was staring up at Julia as if she had just landed from Mars, "and you remember Jason, don't you, from last October?"

She remembered. The stars and Theo. The clinging child riding his hip. And how she had slid into her car, slamming the door and cranking down the window to offer her cheap comfort. "It's all going to work out. Just . . . have faith in yourself." How her bright lights had swept over the father, waving the child's hand at her, as she made her getaway. Jason had changed. He had lost the trancelike air of the clinging child as well as his baby softness; he was more like a chary young animal, angular and sinewy-tense.

"Jason, this is my oldest friend," Clare told him. "We weren't very much older than you and Mike when we became friends. And Julia was Theo's teacher. She taught him history."

It was too much for him. Julia could see him trying to work it out: how one person could have been both a child and his father's teacher. He studied her openly, keeping his distance.

A large young woman in tight pants and a bright lavender velour top came out. "Hey, come on in," she called cheerfully to Julia from the top step. "Jason and Mike, you two get back inside or I'll whip your butts good!" The little boys raced up the steps and ducked beneath her arm that held the door. The three of them disappeared inside the trailer.

"That wasn't Snow," said Julia, who definitely recalled de-scriptions of Snow's smallness.

"No, that's her sister Sue, They share the trailer. Sue just separated from her husband. She's little Mike's mother. There are more inside, but don't try to keep them all straight. It's taken me forty-eight hours to get it right. Snow's gone to town for some cigarettes. She's peeved about having to go to the grand-father's but won't go against the consensus of her mother and sisters. You sure you don't mind about the lunch? I saw your picnic cooler in the car."

"If I know us, we'll get to it, too, before the day's over."

"God, Julia, I'm so glad you're here. I'm sorry about the muddy road. Your poor car."

"It'll wash," said Julia, following Clare into the first trailer she had ever entered in her life.

It was more spacious than it appeared from the outside. She had expected it to be narrow, with things built into the walls, like the sleeping quarters on a cabin cruiser. But the living room had about the same proportions as that of any small house. It contained more furniture than her apartment, and had curtains that matched the covering on the sofas, and a TV with a screen twice the size of her father's. On this screen a perspiring Sunday prophet in a powder-blue suit and Western string tie was preaching his sermon with the sound turned off. The interested faces of Snow's family, seated on the two sofas placed at right angles to each other, tilted up towards Julia as Clare, assisted by the hearty Sue, performed introductions. Snow's mother, a worn mountain woman who looked vaguely frightened. Snow's oldest sister, Evelyn, of a fading blond prettiness, who held herself with calm self-respect. She must be the one the Quicks called "responsible" because she had a good job and had stayed married to the same man. Next to her was her son, Trevor, a circumspect boy of about ten with wistful eyes; and in a playpen set up as the focal centerpiece between the sofas was Tiffany Ann, Evelyn's granddaughter, a smiling baby dressed in several pounds of pink and white ruffles. Tiffany Ann's mother, Sue explained to Julia, had gone to Knoxville the night before to hear her favorite group and wouldn't be back till evening. "Luellen's just nutty about Alabama. If they're playing anywhere this side of the country, she hops in her vehicle and goes. She's got to where she knows 'em all and gets free passes to their shows. Then she comes home and spends hours looking at the picture of her favorite one on the front of the album and fantasizing about what she'd like to be doing with him. Jason and Mike, if you don't stop opening and closing that door and letting the heat out, I'm going to get out my hickory stick and tan your little butts."

A place was made for Julia on one sofa, next to the solemn Trevor. Evelyn, the older sister, smiled encouragingly at Julia and asked her if she'd had much trouble getting down the road.

She was somewhere in her late thirties, Julia calculated, and already a grandmother. Several back teeth, on either side, were missing. Julia felt sad about this. When the first front one gave out, she would probably go to one of those clinics where they pulled all your teeth and fitted you with dentures the same day.

There was an embarrassed silence. No one knew what to say to the newcomer. Everyone, including Clare, perched stiffly on the edge of an armchair, focused intently on baby Tiffany Ann, who was banging a rattle happily against the bars of her playpen, drinking up the attention.

Beside Julia, the boy Trevor nervously cleared his throat. When he had her attention, he asked in a pure, sweet voice, "Is it true you taught Theo in school once?"

"Yes, I did. He was in my history class at North State when he was a freshman." She understood that this was not the place to say that he had dropped out of her class after two weeks. Clare had already billed her as "Theo's teacher," and so as not to disappoint or disillusion anyone, she added, "Theo could certainly ask some of the most provoking questions. He kept me on my toes when he was in my class."

"We all thought a heap of Theo," said Evelyn with quiet enthusiasm. Julia saw her hand brush gratefully against Trevor's arm. She was proud of her son for saying the right thing to break the ice.

"Oh, Theo was something, all right," said Sue, collapsing vigorously beside her mother on the other sofa. "There wasn't nobody in the world like him. Mike, why don't you and Jason go get your video dashboard, and maybe Trevor will play it with you."

The little boys ran off down a hall. A heating system came on, making the walls shake. "I wonder what's taking Snow so long," said her mother plaintively. Nobody answered. "I wish she hadn't started smoking again," the mother went on. "She smokes too much." She leaned over to Julia on the adjoining sofa and confided, "She's always been nervous, but lately it's been worse. She studies over Theo a lot."

Julia nodded sympathetically. She felt, rather than saw, Clare's glance at her. Clare wanted to be sure she had picked up on Mrs. Mullins's quaint Anglo-Saxon usage of the verb "to study." "What grade are you in?" she asked Trevor, who had been gazing hopefully in her direction, waiting for her to notice him again.

"I'm in fifth. I was held back a year because my birthday was in October."

"But he's only ten," Clare interrupted on his behalf. "When he finally *got* to school, he was so smart they let him skip a grade."

"Now he's right where he should be for his age," put in his mother softly. "*Whurr*" for "where." They all spoke with such marked mountain accents. If this had been a movie, Julia would have said, "No, the actors have gone too far. They're making *fun* of these people."

"I was in an accelerated class for a while this year," Trevor told Julia. "They said I was bright enough to go on to sixth if I wanted. But I was always having to take these tests and I missed being with my friends." His wistful eyes sought her continued sanction. "So I decided to go on back to the regular classes."

"It was his decision," his mother said. "We left it completely up to him. They worked him *so* hard."

"But Trevor," Clare said, looking fondly across the room at the boy, "I'm sure you'd be able to get back into those classes, as we were discussing yesterday. I mean, if you found things were going too slowly for you in the ordinary classes and you were *bored*." Dear Clare, so determined that everybody should excel. Her voice had taken on the same testy tone she used on Julia when nagging her about her abandoned project on slave family life or exhorting her to send off her private doggerel to poetry magazines.

"No, I probably —" Trevor began, then was cut off by outraged shrieks. Two little boys ripped through the room, Jason screaming and holding the side of his head, Mike in furious pursuit, pummeling him with fists from behind. They sideswiped the playpen, causing Tiffany Ann to collapse in an undignified heap on top of her ruffles.

"*Hey*, you two!" The ready Sue sprang into the fray. Wedging a hefty hip between them, she separated the fighting cousins.

The humiliated Tiffany Ann set up an eardrum-penetrating protest.

"What's going on here?" demanded Sue, handcuffing Jason's angry fist midway to his cousin's face.

"He hit me!" screamed Jason, trying unsuccessfully to free his fist. "First he called me a cuss-word name and then he hit me!"

"He called me a cuss-word name, too!" Mike counteraccused.

"Okay, boys, who did what to who first? I want the truth or I'll beat your butts raw."

Evelyn had risen and plucked her screaming granddaughter from the pen. With coaxings and strokings of the head she quieted the baby.

"He called me an asshole," said Jason.

"He left the video dashboard over at Paw Paw's," cried Mike, "and I was the one got it for Christmas. And then he called *me* a cuss-word name. He called me a igor-nut hillbilly."

"That's not a cuss word, stupid!" said Jason contemptuously. "It's what you are."

Sue's eyebrow shot up and her mouth narrowed to a grim slit. Her grip tightened on Jason's small wrist.

"Ow! You're hurting me! Let me go!"

"Let him go," said a new voice. A small, unsmiling young woman in jeans and cowboy boots, coat collar turned up around her delicate, moon-pale face, stood just inside the door. She had come in during the commotion without anyone's hearing her.

"Honey, what took you so long?" asked Mrs. Mullins plaintively. Sue dropped her nephew's wrist as if she had been caught stealing, but her eyes flashed with indignation.

"They were out of my brand," said the young woman, not bothering to look at her mother. "I had to go to three places." She advanced towards her child. The room might as well have been empty, except for the two of them. "Jason," she said, gazing down at the boy with a hypnotic single-mindedness, "you will apologize for your rudeness."

Jason shifted his feet and pressed his lips together obstinately. But he remained transfixed by the inexorable gaze.

"Say it to Mike and then it'll be over," she said almost gently. " 'I apologize for my rudeness.' "

He looked down at his feet and mumbled, "I-pol-gize-f'-m'-rudeness," running the sentence together as if it were one word.

"Look at Mike and say it slowly, so he can understand it." Did Julia imagine it, or was there a subversive hint of contempt for her sister's child's powers of understanding?

Jason looked at Mike, who had sidled into Sue's crotch to await his due. "I . . . apologize . . . for . . . my rudeness," he said clearly, with exaggerated slowness.

"Thank you," said Snow. "Now, go wash your face, because we're going to eat with Paw Paw and Maw Maw. If Paw Paw sees you've been crying, he'll find a way to blame it on me like he does everything else these days."

A flicker of solidarity with his mother was momentarily visible on Jason's face. Then, apparently motivated by the reasoning behind her request, he spun around and cantered off.

Satisfied, Snow stood with her hands thrust deep into the pockets of her coat and let her glance move slowly around the room as if she were somewhat reluctantly bestowing existence on the rest of them. There was a restiveness about her and, at the same time, an irritable resignation. In form and feature she was much finer than either of her sisters, but she lacked Evelyn's sweet, self-respecting serenity and Sue's forceful vitality. She seemed permanently offended by something but not cowed by it: only determined to maintain a languid separateness from it all. As she sighed and extracted her Marlboros from one pocket and a lighter from another and proceeded to light up with an insouciance any deb would have envied (back in the days when smoking was still de rigueur for debs), you could almost hear her thinking, Let's see, I've disciplined my child and pacified my sister and my nephew. Now, what do I still have to do before going to Paw Paw's and getting blamed for everything there? Oh, yes; greet the visitor, say something nice to Clare's friend and Theo's old teacher. The violet eyes rolled ceilingward for a moment in a savoring accompaniment to the first gratifying puff, then singled out Julia for the recognition due her. "Hello. I've certainly heard a lot about you," Snow said in a flat, rather oblique tone that guaranteed no assurance that she had liked all she had heard.

Julia reciprocated graciously, though permitting himself the slightest shade of irony, which was either lost on Snow or ignored by her.

Mrs. Mullins rose from her place on the sofa with a little groan. "Reckon I'd better get on down to Daddy's and start the bread. He don't like his dinner to be late."

"Someone'll drive you, Momma," said Evelyn, rising at once with her granddaughter in her arms. "You can't go walking out in all that mud." To Julia she explained, "The county's getting ready to pave the road because of all the children down here that have to get to Headstart. Their bus is always getting stuck. But we've had this spell of rain and they can't finish the grading till it dries out." It seemed important to her that Julia understand the mud was part of a

process that was going to improve things, not a permanent
factor in their lives.

"I'm not going to Headstart tomorrow," said little Mike to
his mother. He glared at his cousin, who was being helped into
his coat by Snow. "Not with *him* I'm not."

Sue took down a similar little coat, down-filled, with a hood,
from a hook near the door. "You're not?" she repeated cheerfully, squatting down to bundle him up. "That'll make
everybody real sad. If *you* don't go to Headstart, who is going to
put the pins in the weather map? Who is going to put on the
little doctor's uniform? You and Jason make up, now. You and
him have lots of good times together and you'll always be close
because you got the same blood running through your veins.
What one is, the other is, so you might as well love one another.
Go hug Jason and make up before we go to Paw Paw's." Though
Sue's words were addressed to Mike, Julia felt there was also a
message being sent to her remote sister.

The two little boys clumsily embraced in their layers of down.
A murmur of adult approval accompanied the reconciliation.

"They usually play together real well," Evelyn told Julia.
"All children fight, it's in their nature. But when they make up,
it's so sweet to watch, isn't it? They don't hold grudges."

Snow stood thinking her own thoughts, communing with
her cigarette. Against her better judgment, Julia was
fascinated.

Clare said, "I think I'll put my bag in Julia's car now. Because
we really do have to be on the road pretty soon. I mean, after
lunch, of course."

Nothing could be said in Julia's car as they drove to the
patriarch's, because Clare had invited young Trevor to ride with
them, much to his pleasure and his mother's pride.

"I'm not going to forget you, Trevor," said Clare.

"I won't forget you, either," the boy replied.

"I'm going to write to you," Clare told him, rather portentously. "It may not be a long letter, maybe just a few sentences
to find out how you're getting along. Will you answer?"

"I might. I mean, I'll try."

"Good. I want to hear that you're doing well in school, that
you aren't *bored*. If you get bored, that's usually a sign that
you're not living up to your capabilities. Then you might want
to join that accelerated class again."

"Well, I'll see," said Trevor ambivalently, not wanting to offend his new friend.

Julia parked in a relatively unsquishy spot at the edge of the junk heap. Backing in so she could get out fast, she heard and felt her tire crush something that sounded like an ominous combination of glass and metal. Family members disembarked from vehicles turned to gape. A man, not bad-looking, who was splitting firewood in the dirt yard put down his ax and watched Julia in what seemed to be almost rapture as she flung herself out of the car with a groan and marched to the rear of her poor mudspattered car to assess the damage. But it turned out to be only a very dirty aluminum-foil roasting pan that had either fallen from the heap or had been thrown short of its goal in the first place. "Thank you, Lord," breathed Clare fervently, also rushing around to inspect. She laid a hand on her heart in exaggerated, self-mocking relief. Once more, reality had spared her the dire scenario her imagination had leaped ahead to provide: in this case, a flat tire, maybe even a bent wheel rim—in any event, delays and complications that could trap them here for a few hours . . . or a few days.

Snow hung back to wait for them. Was she deciding to be friendly, or was she just not in a big hurry to see the grandfather? Her small mouth turned up in a wintry little smile. "That's my uncle Cratis over there splitting logs," she informed them in her languid nasal twang. "Don't be offended if he don't speak to you or if his answers don't make sense. He fell out of a plane in Vietnam and his parachute didn't open right away and he came back home a little strange. It's his trailer me and Sue are living in. He bought it before he went to Vietnam, completely furnished with curtains and carpets, wall-to-wall carpet—everything—and never even got to live in it."

"That's really sad," said Julia sympathetically.

"Well, like I was telling Clare, I'm sorry it had to happen, but it's worked out real well for us. Jason and I'd probably be living in a *tent* if it wasn't for Cratis's trailer." Rising on this grievance-note, her voice implied much: certain people who should have risen to the occasion (her grandfather with land still to give away, her father-in-law in Mountain City with funds) had not treated Snow with the munificence and respect to which she believed herself entitled. "My ex-daughter-in-law, the Princess Snow," Lily Quick had called her in the Fresh Market. But the two of them are *alike*, Julia thought, in a sudden, curious burst of clarity, as she walked between Clare and Snow to the grandfather's house. Dirty brownish smoke curled weakly from the cinder-block chimney and bled like a bad watercolor into the low, overcast sky. Lily Quick and Snow were alike; they shared the same Remote Princess quality. Even in the midst of the family life that had molded them, contained them, ensnared them, they preserved a secretive separateness: they *bestowed* themselves. They chose what to be aware of, and when. Both used their enchanted-evening eyes to communicate their wishes or shut you out. Snow in her borrowed trailer in Granny Squirrel, and Lily, incarcerated by choice (or default) on her husband's hard-won hilltop, possessed the same patrician aloofness that made you worry about pleasing them and kept you guessing about who they really were.

Neither of them, however, she thought, saying hello anyway to the damaged uncle, though she had been warned he might not respond (he didn't, only attended to her passing with the rapturous stare; his otherworldly scrutiny reminded her uncomfortably, now that she knew its cause, of the shining, detached faces she sometimes gave to the extraterrestrial men in her erotic fantasies)—neither Snow nor Lily would thank her for such a comparison. Both would feel insulted. Even Clare, who claimed to be so dependent on Julia's "interpretations," probably would not welcome this one.

They went into the house. An old woman in a print dress and cardigan lay on a sofa next to the wood stove. She had a small oxygen mask strapped across her mouth.

"Maw Maw's had emphysema real bad this winter," Snow said. "She has to take her treatments six times a day."

They stopped to pay their respects to Maw Maw. "This is Theo's sister, Clare, who's been staying with me, and this is her friend Julia, who was Theo's teacher." A cajoling note perked up Snow's languid voice: she was trying to impress the old grandmother with her guests and win points for herself in this house where, for some reason, her stock was low. Blinking dolefully at the newcomers from behind her oxygen mask, Maw Maw extended a doughy invalid's handshake to each. Should I say my father also suffers from emphysema? wondered Julia. No, better forgo that conversational offering. She looks like the type of invalid who wouldn't relish sharing her limelight with a fellow sufferer.

The others were gathered in the kitchen at the rear of the

house. There was no intervening door. Mrs. Mullins was mixing something in a bowl, holding it close to her chest. There was an attentive stirring of family life around an old man in a plaid shirt, already seated at the table. His back was to the main room and he had Jason clasped between his knees, murmuring something to the boy.

But first Julia and Clare had to be treated to an exhibition of family pictures. The grandmother indicated this by grunting at Snow insistently from behind the oxygen mask and waving her hand at the surrounding walls, which were covered with snapshots and studio portraits of children. Julia had never seen so many pictures per square inch on walls; some were framed, some simply nailed and curling around the edges, some Scotch-taped at the corners. The three of them moved respectfully around the patterned linoleum floor, Snow reciting, still in her I'm Being Nice voice, the names of children and whom they belonged to, accompanied by various scraps of family news. Those were the children of the brother who lived in the eastern part of the state. "You remember Danny"—to Clare—"he stood up as Jason's godfather with you at the christening. My daddy's down with Danny and his wife right now. And here's Evelyn's Luellen when she wasn't much older than her own baby, Tiffany Ann, is now. And that's my momma when she was about ten, with a fish she caught. Wasn't she a cute little girl? And here's Mike and Jason in their little baseball caps, we just had those made about three weeks ago. And here's my uncle Cratis on his pony when he was little . . ."

The cutoff point in age seemed to be ten or eleven. Why was that? Perhaps Maw Maw and Paw Paw found adolescent children, grandchildren, and great-grandchildren less reward-ing than the young ones. Why waste wall space on pimpled and gangly souls beginning to assert their independence when there was a constant supply of fresh-faced babies waiting their turn to shine like little stars in the prolific family's gallery?

From behind came the grandmother's sudden imperious yip beneath the oxygen mask. She flashed five fingers at Snow, who, after a moment's incomprehension, said, "Oh! Maw Maw wants you all to know that before *her* momma passed on, twelve years ago, there was five generations of us alive at the same time."

"My goodness, how wonderful!" exclaimed Clare, making a little bow towards the grandmother. But her eyebrows rose superciliously, and her mouth wore that bunched look it got when she was being insincere. The grandmother, apparently satisfied, closed her eyes and sank back on her pillows.

They passed under the moth-eaten head of a small, sad-eyed deer. "Uncle Cratis shot a deer before he went off to Vietnam," Snow said, "but it had this fawn, so he caught it and brought it home and Maw Maw raised it. After it died of pneumonia, they had it mounted."

At that moment the deer shooter himself shambled through the room, his head held a little to one side; he showed no sign of having heard his name.

It was interesting to see how Snow faded into the background as soon as they entered the kitchen. Evelyn introduced Clare and Julia to Paw Paw, who made no attempt to get up from his chair. Their credentials for this family were always the same: "Theo's sister and Theo's sister's friend, who taught Theo in school."

"We already met yesterday," Clare said to the grandfather affably. "And you were certainly right about the rain. It did come down exactly fifteen minutes later, just like you said it would."

The grandfather narrowed his eyes at her as if she were demented. "What's she saying?" he asked nobody in particular.

"She said it rained, Daddy," Mrs. Mullins replied, emptying a can of sauerkraut into a sizzling-hot black skillet.

"It rained? When?"

"Yesterday," said Mrs. Mullins. "Just like you said it would." To Julia's alarm, she spooned a huge glob of Crisco into a pot of otherwise appetizing-looking green beans.

"Well, of course it rained yesterday," said the old man, baring sharp little brown teeth in a strange, one-note laugh. "Any fool and his brother knows that."

Clare retreated to the far end of the long table, which was covered with a white plastic cloth, and sat down next to Snow under a picture showing Christ knocking by night at the door of a house. She had the abashed demeanor of the good student who has been unfairly flunked. Christ looked anxious, as though he were being pursued.

"Why don't you sit here?" Evelyn said to Julia. "Next to Paw Paw, so he can hear you."

As soon as Julia sat down, the old man reached out and turned on a dusty radio that sat in the middle of the table. A ghoulish-spritely organ tune blared forth. "This is the Ivy Funeral Home's

Noonday Funeral Column," announced an unctuous voice over
the music.

Uncle Cratis, sitting directly across the table from Julia,
suddenly looked her straight in the eye and said in a tender,
drawling mountain baritone, "We have applesauce." He pushed
towards her a giant-sized jar of Johnny Appleseed's Superfine.
"You want applesauce?"

"Thank you. That would be very nice." He seemed very
intent on her having applesauce. She spooned some onto her
empty plate, not wanting to upset him. His dreamy, wide-set
eyes followed her movements. Uncle Cratis must be about her
own age, she guessed. His thick hair, lovingly barbered by
someone, was beginning to go gray, but his face and brow were
unlined.

"I'll have some applesauce, too," cried Jason, who was playing
the video dashboard at the other end of the table with his cousin
Mike.

"Me, too!" shouted Mike.

Uncle Cratis picked up the jar of Johnny Appleseed and
carried it personally to the little boys. He stood watching
carefully while Sue spooned a little onto their plates. "Now you
have some," he said to her.

She laughed. "We'll all have some of your applesauce, Uncle
Cratis. Don't we always?" She helped herself and passed the jar
on to Snow and Clare. Clare was saying something about Snow
and Jason visiting during the coming summer at the beach.
"Well, I'd like that," Snow said without much enthusiasm. "But
without any car, getting places is kind of hard." "Oh, we'll
think of something," pressed Clare. "If you'd like to come, we'll
find some way to get you there. *That's* no problem."

Mrs. Mullins set steaming platters on the table: the sauerkraut, the green beans (into which the Crisco had mercifully
dissolved without visible trace), and some kind of hash or stew.
The good daughter, Evelyn, helped the old grandmother into
the kitchen, where she was arranged, with much solicitousness,
in a chair backed with pillows at the head of the table. She at
once devoted all her attention to the "Noonday Funeral
Column." She seemed a different person without her oxygen
mask. Her complacent old face danced with spiteful energy as
the oily radio voice, backed by the manic organ, intoned the
names, addresses, and ages of those already fallen, and announced the hours for their viewings and services. Mrs. Mullins

set down a huge platter of hot biscuits and Evelyn brought glass pitchers of milk. The old grandparents had their plates served for them, their milk poured out; then all the rest helped themselves.

They ate silently, listening to the "Noonday Funeral Column." The biscuits were out of this world: Julia wondered if she could get the recipe for her father. Good Evelyn spooned mush from a small jar into her granddaughter Tiffany Ann's mouth, then took alternative bites from her own plate. Uncle Cratis reminded everyone there was applesauce and encouraged them to take some. Mrs. Mullins, who nibbled one biscuit almost guiltily by the stove, never sat down; she fluttered nervously above the eaters, checking plates, refilling the milk pitchers. "Daddy, have you another biscuit . . . Snow, honey, don't you want no beans?"

"Elbert Floyd Crisp, of Sweetgum Hollow, age ninety-two," crooned the radio voice, "Ora Lee Madrigal of Panther Creek, age eighty-nine . . . "

"I knew it!" screamed the grandmother triumphantly, giving Paw Paw a hefty slap on his arm. "I always knew she was older than she said!"

"These are delicious biscuits," Julia told Mrs. Mullins the next time that lady peered anxiously over her shoulder to see how she was doing. "I'd love to get your recipe. And this is such a tasty stew."

"Oh, that's just Campbell's vegetable beef soup," protested Snow's mother modestly. "Instead of adding the water, you just fry it up by itself. And there ain't nothing to the biscuits. I've been making biscuits since I could walk. Momma used to stand me in a chair and let me mix 'em. All in the world they are is a little milk and some flour and Crisco."

"No baking powder?"

"No, ma'am."

"And . . ." Julia tried to hide her discomposure at this puzzling "ma'am." "I mean, you don't even use buttermilk? Just ordinary milk?"

"It don't signify. Just whatever you have in the house."

"Mike, if you don't quit messin' that food round your plate, you know what's waitin' for you when we get home," warned the ever-watchful Sue.

"There's applesauce," said Uncle Cratis, nudging the jar towards Julia like a shy boy's gift. "You have some more."

She took some more. A sudden, entirely inappropriate vision of Uncle Cratis as a lover passed through her mind. Did he have women, or was that function impaired, too?

The gleeful-morbid radio voice said, against a swell of organ volume, "Tune in tomorrow at this same time for the Ivy Fu —"

Paw Paw snapped off the sound. He accepted another biscuit from the hovering Mrs. Mullins. He chewed, surrounded by respectful silence. Then he turned slowly to Julia and looked her up and down like a farmer assessing an animal of dubious quality at a cattle show. "I thought right much of that brother of yours," he said. "If your folks hadn't been in such a big hurry about that funeral, I would have gone. But you didn't give none of us time to make any plans."

"Actually, I'm not —" Julia began. She pointed down to Clare in her red sweater at the other end of the table, hoping to re-direct his attention.

Without so much as a waver in his glance, the old man went on: "He was the best son-in-law May and Monroe got out of their whole bunch, and they ain't going to get any more like him. They keep trying to say about a shooting, but I don't want to hear none of it. He was a good boy and I miss him. There's some around here, not mentioning no names, who might ought to have set more store by him when it would of done some good. Not carrying on after it was too late. If they had set more store by him, he might of been setting right here with us today."

Julia nodded thoughtfully. She did not see what else she could do. Clare sent her a look of combined condolence and com-plicity: Thank you for taking my rap; we'll be out of here soon and then we can *talk*! All around the table there was a strained, embarrassed attentiveness. She was their guest and entitled to consideration, but nobody dared correct the grandfather's mistake. Actually, what did it matter? Julia accepted her share of guilt for failing to set store by Theo when "it would of done some good"; what did it matter whether she failed him in the role of teacher or of sister? He didn't know the difference now, any more than the grandfather. Everyone, even the children, seemed pensive and sorrowful in the soft gray-white gloom of the kitchen. Heads were bowed, eyes cast down, as in the echoing aftermath of a sermon. No, there was one impenitent face, one who resisted: Snow, sucking deeply on a freshly lit Marlboro, gazed sullenly out the window at a hillock of dried grasses, spotted with a few green bottles and old cans.

"Oh, that Theo, he could be so funny! You know what he did once?" Sue's robust twang, rescuing them. "Paw Paw, he was in the woods, having himself a little siesta, and here comes Theo, going to the crick to fish. Well, he seen Paw Paw lyin' there and he thinks he's had a stroke or something, and he rushes over and starts layin' him out. He was fixin' to give him artificial respiration, when Paw Paw wakes up and he can't understand why Theo's tryin' to sit on top of him."

Laughter. A moment of relief for everyone. Clare, who had laughed too hard, then looked close to tears, tried to catch the grandfather's eye. "Theo was always trying to save people," she said. "He would drive around at night when he was a teenager, with this first-aid kit he had, hoping to find an accident."

The grandfather looked her way briefly. "What's that they're all saying?" he asked Julia. "Is it about that shooting?"

"No, Sue was telling about that time Theo found you asleep in the woods," she told him, the others nodding her on, "and he tried to give you artificial respiration. And then *Clare*"—she pointed once again towards the red sweater—"who is Theo's sister—I was just his teacher for a while—Clare was telling how —"

"I can't hear well," the grandfather interrupted her. "I can hear some men's voices pretty well, but I can't hear women. Women's voices, they're too fine or something. I was talking on the phone to my sister over in Ivy yesterday and she begun to fade. I told her, 'You're fading, so we might just as well hang up and save the money.' "

"Oh, God, I'm so depressed," said Clare, as soon as they were on the main road. "It was like a bad dream. I don't mean the nightmare variety, I mean one of those dreary, pointless dreams that trap you in drabness the whole time you're in them, the kind that aren't even in color, just shades of gray. I don't know what I expected. What did I expect? Less mud, for one thing. I never dreamed it would be so ugly. Lily said it was ugly, but I guess some upbeat part of my imagination held on to an element of the picturesque. That junk pile! It leaves me speechless, that junk pile. I couldn't begin to speculate what that junk pile means to them, and I won't try. At least not today. God, Julia, I expected the visit would have some kind of *focus*. I thought I would come away understanding these people. But I don't know any more about who they are than I did when

I arrived. Maybe I know *less*, in some ways. I mean, you get certain *outlines* of things from a distance, like in painting. In some ways, I might have done better to stay in New York and imagine Snow and Jason down here. I believe I was getting to know Snow much better from her two letters to me than I know her after spending two nights under her roof—or whatever the top of a trailer is called. When we were leaving and she gave me that limpid hug, I honestly couldn't decide whether she was glad I came or was relieved to get rid of me. I don't know if she likes me or hates me."

"But you all must have talked. Weren't you alone together any?"

"We were, at *night*. Sue and little Mike went to sleep up at Evelyn's house so Snow and Jason and I could have the trailer to ourselves. Evelyn and Sue were very nice to me, but then they're both nicer to everyone than Snow is. Evelyn invited me up to see her new house yesterday. She's a supervisor at this factory that makes jeans and was so sorry I came on the weekend because she had wanted to show me how the assembly line works. Her husband runs a sawmill and between them they put every penny into this house they've built all by themselves, with some help from friends in raising the walls and things. It was really touching, the pride she showed in that house. It's not quite finished, it's just sitting up there on the top of this muddy hill that the grandfather gave her, but she's already got her wall-to-wall carpeting down, and there are plastic liners everywhere to keep people from tracking in mud. We sat in the living room and looked through her daughter Luellen's wedding album—she was married only three months—and then we went down to the basement to see the room they're putting in for Luellen and little Tiffany Ann. The flooring wasn't finished yet, but they had already put up this scenic wallpaper on one wall, a view of some Vermont woods with birches, even though there were *real* woods right outside the window we were looking through. Snow was with me, Snow and Sue both. Sue was being her usual ebullient self. Being in her older sister's dream house inspired her, you could tell; she started planning ways she was going to improve Uncle Cratis's trailer. She wanted to buy a fish tank with tropical fish and she said she was going to learn to make silk flower arrangements. Snow didn't say much, she just smoked and followed along on Evelyn's house tour. We went upstairs and saw Trevor's room with its bunk beds and his desk and the Atari he got for Christmas, and then right next to it is his parents' room with this fancy bedroom suite Evelyn ordered out of a catalogue. Only there'd just been a tragedy. The bed, which was an ornate four-poster job, wasn't made well and the wood frame had cracked clear down the middle. Evelyn and her husband had been sleeping on the floor while they were fighting with the factory to either give them a new bed or take this one back and repair it. Evelyn was bewildered and upset by this; it was like a crack in her hard-earned dream. She kept asking us, 'They have to fix it or give us a new one, don't they? they have to stand by their product, don't they? If I catch a girl cutting corners on my assembly line, I come down on her right hard, because we stand behind our product.' Sue finally boomed out, 'Damn *right*, they better come get that bed and fix it. If they don't, you've got Roper to go down there and beat their butts.' That didn't cheer Evelyn up very much and then Snow cheered her up even less. She blew out a languid trail of smoke and narrowed her eyes at the broken bed and said, 'I wouldn't count on anybody doing anything they can get out of doing. Not unless you take them to court.' Then there was an awkward silence, because I guess everybody was remembering that Snow went to court with *us*—and won. Then Evelyn said in a faint, embarrassed voice, 'Oh, Roper and I don't want to go to law over this. That would cost more than just buying us another bed.' Snow shrugged and said, 'Suit yourself,' and smiled in her frosty way and drew back into herself. But then last night, when we were alone in the trailer, she got pretty eloquent on the subject of Evelyn's house. Snow maybe comes closest to eloquence— and energy—when she's cataloguing the wrongs done to her by others. The grandfather had given Evelyn land, the last decent hill on the place, but he wouldn't even give *her* a dinky little piece of bottomland so she could build a house for herself and Jason. When she asked him for the land, she said, he just laughed in her face and asked her who was going to build the house for her when she couldn't even hold on to a man. He told her she'd lost two men in one year. She said that wasn't fair, that one of them had been killed and that the one after that had beat up on Jason. When she reminded him that Jason was his favorite great-grandson, he said in that case maybe he would leave the land to Jason for when he got old enough to build *himself* a house, but he wasn't about to throw away his last remaining acres on a no-count woman who hadn't had the sense to know when she had a good man and a good life. That old tyrant. You got a taste of him. 'Ah cain't hear wimmen.' I have to sympathize with Snow, even if she didn't exactly cry her eyes out when we were leaving."

"Mountain people are undemonstrative," Julia reminded her. "They're not your typical Southern gushers. But look. When you all were alone, didn't she tell you any of the things she promised in that last letter?"

Clare sighed vehemently. "She did . . . up to a point. But there again she seemed to come across much friendlier and more intimate in her letters to me than when we were sitting alone talking in that trailer in the middle of the field at night. Isn't that strange? That a person who hasn't gone past the ninth grade could say more in writing than in talking? But maybe Snow is like me in that way. I remember my first editor saying to me when we finally met, 'Gosh, you sound so much better in writing.' It wasn't very tactful, but I understood what he meant. I *do* express my soul better in worked-out prose than when I'm just bumbling along, pulling phrases out of the air. And maybe Snow does, too. Oh, God, maybe I should have stayed up in New York and gone on *corresponding* with her. I mean, she did tell me some things about the last time she and Theo talked on the phone—apparently he asked her to go back with him, or so she says—but somehow . . . oh, I don't know, maybe it was just in my imagination . . . I expected some startling revelation that would explain everything, that would clear up the whole mystery, not just of Theo's death but of his character. She just said he wanted them to get back together and try again and there was some uncertainty about whether or not she might be pregnant by that guy she was living with down there in Georgia at the time, the one she married ten days after Theo's death. She said Theo asked her whether she would be willing to get rid of it if it meant they could get back together, and she said, yes, she would do that for him. As it turned out, it wasn't necessary, her period was just late. Then she went into a diatribe over poor Jeanette and described this terrible visit when Theo brought Jeanette to the trailer in Georgia . . . God, all these trailers in our lives suddenly! I was lying in bed Friday night, my first night in Granny Squirrel, and the heating system was going full blast, shaking the partitions . . . it was too hot to sleep and I had drunk too much coffee, Snow's family doesn't touch alcohol, and I read through the phone book for a while . . . it was the only book I could find . . . I had deliberately *not* brought a book because I was afraid I might be tempted to escape into it and I wanted to devote my full attention to Snow . . . and it was while I was running my eye down the yellow pages, trying to construct some sort of concept about where I was from the listings . . . abortion clinic, adoption agencies, denture centers, feed stores, gun shops, lots of beauty shops with names like Billie's Beauty Box and Norma's Cut and Curl, and lots and *lots* of 'mobile home' suppliers . . . that I suddenly thought, Is God sending our family a *message* through Theo, through the way Theo lived and the woman he chose to marry? Is God saying, 'Okay, Ralph Quick, you've made it to the top of your hill and sent your sons to the best private schools, but I don't like human beings to forget their humble origins so quickly, so your grandson must go back and start over at Headstart. And you, Miss Clare'—I often imagine God speaking to me in the voice of old Dr. Anthony Gallant, who called me 'Miss Clare'—'And *you*, Miss Clare,' God would say, 'Don't you think it's time, after your determined, breathless climb up the hill to national prominence as loving chronicler of the complacent middle class, to take an astringent little descent into the land of the have-nots and come to some compassionate understanding of why not everyone can make it?' Then I heard this roaring sound outside the trailer and I looked out my window and there was this huge transport truck coming slowly down the muddy road in the moonlight. It went right to the dead end and after a lot of groaning and shifting of gears used our field to turn around in. Then its headlights went off. It was sinister. I was sure the trucker was on his way down to break into our trailer and rape Snow and me. I turned off my light and tried to see a figure approach, but nobody seemed to get out of the truck. I just lay there for a long time, looking out the window, till my shoulders got stiff. Then I fell asleep and had two terrible dreams. In the first one, I was living with Lily and Ralph again. I was a teenager, but I was also the person I am now. And the place was a mess. All these dirty clothes and lots of *children*. I was carrying one of the children to wash him off—he had snot all over his face, and it had dried so he couldn't even open his eyes. I got him to this very inadequate bathroom—it was a mess, too, all the fixtures were coming out of the walls and ceilings—and I managed to find a relatively clean corner of a filthy washcloth and start cleaning his face. I suddenly saw his blond bangs and his big, trusting eyes and his pink cheeks. It was Theo, of course, but it was also Jason. It was officially Jason. Then Lily came into the bathroom, a much younger Lily, and she said, 'You can take care of things now. I have to go do my assignment.' Her assignment was that she wrote features about her children for some syndicated column and did little drawings of them as well. She showed me one of Theo in a fireman's hat. Then the dream shifted. I had managed to get parts of Theo from the mortuary and was going to bring him back to life. First I had to pour some fluid out of a plastic bag and retain the bones, like meat bones. I put these to one side, on a windowsill, where they immediately started eating some plant. But this was encouraging in the dream. It meant I was succeeding in my revival of Theo. Then I 'fried' some other pieces of Theo in a pan, and when they were done I drained them on a paper towel on a platter. Then, somehow, it was accomplished and there he was, a man in a coat whom I had to help escape, because of course since he was alive again he could be arrested for murder. I was hurrying him into a car when I realized no one would probably recognize him because he was a blind man now. As Theo would be, because, as you remember, Ralph donated his eyes." Clare's voice broke. She writhed in the harness of her seat belt and turned her face away to the window on her side. Julia heard her weeping quietly.

"Would you like to stop for a minute?" They had entered the gorge. A faint mist was rising from the rushing stream that paralleled the road. Julia herself was close to tears.

"No, it's okay. It's just that everything has been so intense, even though nothing really happened the way I hoped it would. I used to love this gorge, I thought it was so mysterious and romantic. Then Ralph told me a horrible story. It was about this trick his father and his fishing buddies used to play on their Negro cook every year. The men would fish for a week up here at Santeetlah Lake, and on the way home they'd stop at the local courthouse and one of them would go in and get the sheriff and he'd come out and go into this big spiel about how Negroes were forbidden in the county because it wasn't safe for them, that they were always getting their heads shot off, especially when they went through this gorge. And the Negro man would get so scared that he would lie face down in the back of the truck all the way home. No cook ever came back a second year."

"God," said Julia with disgust. And she had just been feeling sorry for Ralph, remembering that phone call from the eye doctor at the hospital, a few hours after Theo's death; how she and Clare, sitting in the Quicks' kitchen, had listened as Ralph donated Theo's eyes.

"Ralph wasn't condoning it," said Clare, picking up on Julia's line of thought. "He was using it as an example of how race relations had changed since he was a boy. He was congratulating himself because he used to sit down at the same table with LeRoy, this black boy who worked for him and who was Theo's friend. In fact, that's how the subject came up: Ralph was saying how he ought to get word to LeRoy, who's in jail, about Theo's death. But while Ralph was telling me the story about his father, I suddenly remembered an incident from years back. I was about ten, it wasn't long after Lily and Ralph had married, and Ralph and I were going downtown on the bus. I don't know where Lily was. Anyway, all the front seats were already filled with white people and the only seat beyond this point where we could have sat together had this one black woman in it. She was pretty far front for those days, but she was within her rights, as there weren't any whites *behind* her. I remember her just as clear as anything. She was a big, smooth-faced woman with her bags spread around her on the double seat, and she looked tired. She was probably somebody's maid going home at noon on Saturday. Ralph went up to her and asked her to move to the back of the bus, where the rest of the colored people were crowded in, and she refused. So he went to the bus driver, who stopped the bus and came back himself and told the woman to move. She was really indignant, but you could see her starting to shake. She stood her ground for a few minutes while the two men shouted at her; then she picked up her bags and left the bus rather than give in. I remember worrying because she would lose the money she had spent on her bus ticket. As she was going down the last step of the bus, Ralph called after her, 'Black bitch!' And he was shaking all over with hatred in a way I had never seen. Well, after he had finished the story about his father and given a little sermon about how we all loved black people now, I asked him—I know it wasn't very tactful of me— if he remembered that day. I didn't have the heart to remind him about the 'black bitch' part, but I just said, 'Do you remember that time when we went downtown on the bus and you made that Negro woman move and she left the bus?' And he

looked perfectly blank and said, 'No, when was that?' And I
added a few more details . . . I still left out the 'black bitch'
part—I mean, after all, Theo wasn't even buried yet when we
were having this conversation—and, you know, Julia, he didn't
remember it. He really didn't. I was watching him closely and
he did not remember that day."

"I can believe it," Julia said dully. There was a congestion
around the area of her breastbone. Briefly she retasted Uncle
Cratis's applesauce, mixed with the sauerkraut and Mrs.
Mullins's thrifty stew. She felt temporarily overwhelmed in spirit
by the convoluted lives of the Quicks. What truly worthwhile
"interpretation" could she contribute? Maybe in some cases
narrative was as far as you could go; and that was Clare's department, narrative.

"I guess you've seen those embarrassing black-bordered ads
Ralph has been putting in the newspaper," Clare went on. "The
ten-thousand-dollar-reward ads for information leading to the
arrest and conviction of Theo's murderer."

"Yes."

"Lily sent me a couple. It's so strange. She got him started on
this 'outsider' theory, the night of Theo's death. He took it up
for her sake. But now he's the one who believes in it, and she's
gone on to other detective work. What she wants to solve now is
the mystery of the afterlife. She told me last week on the phone,
she was quoting from a hymn Theo loved, about the saints of
God—there are these lines, 'and one was a doctor, and one was
a priest, and one was slain by a fierce wild beast'—and she said
to me over the phone, 'A wild beast killed Theo, *whoever* it was.'
But she believes his personality's still around—or she wants to
believe it, and she's collecting all the evidence she can find. In
books and poems . . . and discussions with her priests. I think
Lily has accepted that Theo—or the beast in Theo—might have
pulled the trigger, but Ralph can't. Of all of us, Ralph is the
only one who's clinging to the outsider theory. He even thinks it
may have been Jeanette's little boy, who was riding in a car seat
in the back."

"I've been reading Morrison's biography of W.J. Cash," said
Julia. "You know, he hanged himself in Mexico soon after he
published *The Mind of the South*. He and his wife had gone there
on his Guggenheim, and they hadn't even been there for a
month when he started hearing voices of 'Nazi agents' plotting
his death because of the editorials he had written in North

Carolina papers against Hitler and Mussolini. His wife got him
to a doctor, who gave him an injection of vitamin B, but Cash
was sure he was trying to poison him. They changed hotels four
times in one afternoon, and at the final one Cash just cowered in a
corner and waited for the 'killers' to close in. His wife went for
help, but when she got back he had fled the hotel. They didn't
find him until ten o'clock that night. He had registered at another hotel and hanged himself by his necktie from the bathroom
door. The biographer lists all the theories people have put
forward about his death. There's the brain-tumor theory. There's
the 'success-suicide' theory—you know, like Ross Lockridge
killing himself after *Raintree County* was published. There was the
acute-hyperthyroid-attack theory—paranoid delusions are apparently consistent with such attacks. And then there were others
who said Cash was so depressed over the South's future that he
couldn't stand to live with the contradictions he had uncovered
in his book. But Cash's father, to the very end of his life—and
he lived to be ninety-one—believed his son's death had been
caused by foul play: that Nazi agents, or whoever, had hanged
Cash from the bathroom door in Mexico."

Clare was silent for a minute. "What kind of relationship did
Cash have with his father, did the book say?"

"Sort of a love-hate one. The father was a puritanical Baptist
of the most straitlaced sect, a plain man who had worked his
way up in the mill system, and a white supremacist. Cash wanted
to please him and make him proud, but at the same time he'd
go out of his way to irritate him. He was christened J.W. Cash,
but he reversed the initials to differentiate himself from his
father, who had the same ones. His father insisted he go to Wake
Forest because it was a good Baptist college, so Cash went, and
got on the school paper and proceeded to write editorials poking
fun at the puritanical Baptists and the Fundamentalists. When
it came time to pick a mentor, he chose H.L. Mencken. He
wrote these devoted letters to his father, trying to justify his
views and explain himself, and yet there are some people who
believe the intensity and the eloquence of *The Mind of the South*
stems from its being *underneath* a kind of schizophrenic attempt to
condemn and praise the father at the same time. A love letter
and a hate letter all wrapped up and concealed in a book about
'the South'."

Clare groaned. "Some of this sounds disturbingly familiar. I
want to reread that book. Or, to be honest, read it. I must have

owned at least three copies over the years since college. I remember underlining it, and getting excited about certain paragraphs, and carrying it with me on long plane rides, but I never actually finished it. It's one of those books like . . . I don't know . . . *The Decline of the West,* maybe. You think, One day I'll really read this and then I'll understand what went wrong and what to do next. Oh, God, I wonder what kind of book Theo would have produced if he had been a writer. Even in those teenage letters of his I was telling you about, there was this *tone.* Like someone laughing at us all, including himself, but deeply sad and, in places, disgusted. But this is all just remorse on my part. Theo a writer? He wasn't even much of a reader. I don't think he ever read my books . . . He just picked up on reviews in the local papers and what other people said about them, and then he wove together his own 'critique,' the one he devastated me with in the kitchen the afternoon before his death."

"Mmm. You could be right. But in that case, you can stop being so hard on yourself about the work you've done if he didn't have any real basis for his criticism."

"No, that has nothing to do with it. Theo taught me something, whether he had read my books or not. He was speaking out of his knowledge of *me* that afternoon. In his quirky way he put his finger on . . . I haven't decided whether it's more a flaw or a shortcoming, but, whichever, it limits my writing. I won't let things be themselves. I arrange things around me the way I want them . . . the way I need them to be . . . and shut the rest out. I shut Theo out all of his life because he didn't fit into the life I intended to have for myself. At sixteen I didn't want a baby brother whose love for me would hold me back from fleeing the family caldron, and at thirty-two I was so busy building my career that I couldn't stop to answer his letter thanking me for his graduation present. Money. I dashed off a check and bought a card with a mortarboard cap and diploma on it, and put him out of my mind. And back came this shy, charming letter . . . the charm had been carefully worked up . . . with just the tiniest reproach in the P.S., which said, 'Write me a letter sometime, when you have nothing better to do, and tell me what a sister's day is like. Any old day will do.' Now I've lost that opportunity forever, just as it may also be too late for me to train myself to see things as they are . . . even when they're ambiguous or just disappointingly dull, like the real visit to Granny Squirrel compared with how I imagined it would be beforehand. You know, Theo went out *looking* in a way I never did. Nobody else in our family did."

"But art *is* moving things around." put in Julia, somewhat impatiently. The air in the car was thick with déjà vu. They had had this dialogue before and before and before. "I don't think you should confuse the shortcomings of your writing . . . or what you conceive them to be now . . . with your guilt over being negligent towards Theo. The qualifications for being a good sister might not be the same as the ones for making art, you know. And if you want my opinion, I don't think it's too late to answer that letter. I think when you get back to New York, or take one of your weeks alone in the country, you should sit down and describe to Theo what a sister's day is like. Just any old day."

"You mean as a form of therapy for me," Clare said bitterly.

"Call it what you like. But write it to Theo and see what happens. Maybe nothing will. But don't count on it."

"But it won't do him any good. It will just be a form of self-indulgence."

"If you look at it that way, aren't prayers for the dead self-indulgence for the living? Yet I often pray for my mother, even though I don't have a picture of God in my head anymore. I make a few requests for her peace of soul and then I slip into conversations—*arguments*, a lot of the time—with her. 'You were so wrong,' I'll tell her, or 'Didn't it ever occur to you that blah, blah, blah,' or 'Why didn't you ever . . . ?' That kind of thing. And though my rational mind tells me I'm talking to myself, I also feel there's the distinct possibility I'm . . . well . . . I'm continuing my mother's education."

"Do you ever feel she answers you?"

"Sure she does. When I do her side of the conversation as well as my own. Like Edgar Bergen used to do Charlie McCarthy's. But sometimes her answers surprise me, even as they come out of my mouth. It's as though she were really speaking and we had become closer. She's become a more thoughtful person—in the sense of thinking things out for herself. And, you know, thinking was not one of her favorite activities in life. Looking good was her chief occupation, and when that became an effort she drank and went crazy. But there was a lot more to her than that. She just didn't get to develop it in her lifetime."

"God, Julia. If I die before you, will you promise to have those conversations with me?"

Julia burst out laughing. The request was so typically Clare. Striving for self-improvement to the very end . . . beyond.

"I absolutely promise," she said. "And if I die first, you have to write me long letters about what is going on in the world. Put in lots of details. What you ate and what was on the evening news. Don't feel obligated always to be dramatic or significant. Because you never can tell what I'll need when I'm on the other side."

"I promise, absolutely. I may also have conversations, if that's okay. I mean, in addition to the letters. And you might want to do a letter occasionally yourself."

"I might indeed. Listen, whatever *did* happen about that mysterious trucker? The one who parked outside Snow's trailer . . . or Uncle Cratis's trailer, rather . . . and switched off his lights?"

"Oh, right. He was gone the next morning. I told Snow about it and she said it was a cousin of hers. He drives a moving van for a big company in Florida, and when he's anywhere near the area he likes to pull into the old family road and snooze there rather than at some truckers' stop. It makes him feel safe, she said."

"Ah, yes, safe," said Julia, sounding more caustic than she had intended. "Buried up to the hubcaps in familiar old family ooze. It's a wonder he got out in the morning."

"Isn't it the truth!" exclaimed Clare delightedly, picking up on all the levels, as usual.

June 17, 1974

My dearest Clare,

I'm sorry I haven't written sooner, but I live such an exciting life that I really have to look for time. I have been gathering a whole lot of material for a bestseller novel titled "Teenage Rookie" with the main character a young man who learns more about life in his eighteenth year than he has ever learned or could hope to learn in the future. Maybe we can collaborate and make a million dollars.

I am deeply grateful for your graduation gift. Nothing could be of more use to a young graduate going off into the cruel world.

I would tell you about all my romances, but the last three girls I have dated are married now and all of them to other Leos. I just sit around and watch television these days. It doesn't talk back—most of the time—and it surely can't run out on me.

Love always,
Theo

P.S. Write me a letter sometime, when you have nothing better to do, and tell me what a sister's day is like. Any old day will do.

X: DEAR THEO

Thursday, March 29, 1984

Dear Theo,

I am up here alone in the country, and there is a real blizzard raging outside, gale winds, shifting mounds of snow, the poor little birds flying slant against the heavy winds to and from the bird feeder. Felix was supposed to fly back from Toronto, where he's been at a Chekhov festival, but our nearest airport is closed, so he'll stay another day and night at the Harbour Castle and try to get here tomorrow. I came up here yesterday, bought food, watched the Democratic hopefuls sit around a table and take turns telling how each would run the country if he was president. I had already sent money to Gary Hart, but ended up being more impressed by Jesse Jackson, the only candidate at that table who talked in larger realities. I feel sure, if you had been watching it with me, that you would have felt the same. But maybe it's because he knows he could never win that he is the only one who can afford to speak in a language of bold ideals. The others have a chance; therefore, they must be cautious, compromising. Afterwards, I called Julia, who had also watched the debate, and asked her if it bothered her that as girls we hadn't seen such obvious realities as racial prejudice, that we had had to wait until braver people came along and pointed these things out to us. And she said no use going into a tailspin of guilt, that it was just that certain realities were now inescapable. "Well, what do you think are the current in-escapable ones that only brave people can see? That you and I haven't recognized yet?" I asked. She laughed and said, "You expect a lot of me, don't you? For a start, let's take the planet itself. What irrevocable damage have we already perpetrated on it?" (I am right to expect a lot of Julia: she says smart things. You would have done better not to drop her Western Civ course, Theo.)

Then I made myself a hot milk and rum, with a double-whammy shot of Myer's dark, and dipped into two new novels, both of which I had been looking forward to. I soon saw they were both going to be disappointments, and, after allowing myself a brief surge of writer's gloat, tried to analyze why. One of them, a first novel, was by a young Southerner still in his twenties (younger than you by a year), and the other was by a middle-aged Eastern European, exiled from his country, who has established a following among the intellectuals because of his special brand of mordant philosophical cleverness. The worst thing that happens in the first novel is that the boy narrator discovers his mother is having an affair with a Man Beneath Her; the worst thing that happens to the other narrator is that Russian tanks invade his hometown. Though both novels had that show-offy, peacockish tone to which (*I* think) male writers are more frequently prone (maybe it has something to do with the male of the species having to flaunt his colors and feathers in order to "attract"), I lasted longer with the Russian-tank man, out of a sense of inferiority and pique. The inferiority because, as an American, I have never had the experience of being invaded by a foreign army; pique, because after a few pages the author announces (with a great fanfare of spread feathers) that it would be senseless for him to try to convince the reader that his characters are real people. Well, then, why go to the trouble of writing about them? I thought. The answer, of course, is that he needed them, needed their flatness, the lack of crucial in-formation we are given about them, in order to display to best advantage his own contrasting flesh-and-blood roundness, his greater historical reality. The pleasure to be got from such a book has little to do with your feelings or curiosity about the stick-figure characters being manipulated by the author, and everything to do with how far you are willing, or able, to admire the mind of the manipulator. I put up with his admirableness until my mind grew fuzzy from the rum, and then I turned off the light and lay wondering why finding out something painful about your mother should be considered less "important" than having Russian tanks roll down the streets of your hometown. Both were the incidents the respective narrators had felt most deeply as the betrayals that changed their lives. Yet many people I know, if asked publicly (publicly may be the key word here) which was the more "serious" incident, would answer dutifully, "Oh, the Russian tanks. The other is just, well, after all, one adolescent boy's feelings about his mother." Then I imagined what I would say if I were put on the spot, publicly, and I am happy to report to you that I amazed everyone present, from editors of *The New York Times* to Ivy League Distinguished Professors to big shots in the Reagan administration, with my perspicacity by replying calmly, "How long will it take us to see the connection between the occurrence of wars and the way parents treat their children?" (An idea stolen from a book by a woman psychoanalyst I recently was reading in an effort to find clues to *you*.)

I don't remember falling asleep, but it was already daylight when I woke with my heart pounding from a dream unlike anything I've ever dreamed. There was no action in it, no visuals, I didn't see anything or hear anything in the dream. It was all pure, vivid emotion. I wanted to die . . . or kill somebody . . . or both at the same time . . . because this person didn't, or couldn't love me. The person didn't have a sex. I didn't have a sex. The whole thing was just the giant, unbearable reality of not being loved and wanting to kill/die to avenge myself and put an end to the anguish. When I woke, I was still possessed by the utmost rage and despair. For several seconds I didn't know who I was. Then, slowly, the awfulness drained away and I started counting my blessings and distancing myself from that poor lost soul who had inhabited me in the dream. When I went to the window and pulled the curtain, even the snow was a blessing, though it meant Felix was not going to be able to get here today. But I *had* a Felix: the same person I loved, loved me back. I realized I had an enormous appetite and went to the kitchen and made a real breakfast, a meal I don't normally eat. Then I washed my hair, just in case Felix did make it, though the snow outside the windows wasn't even flakes anymore, just a white sheet. About ten, Felix phoned from Toronto to say the airport at our end was closed, and we were both relieved to have the prospect of his uncertain travel ruled out; much better for him to remain safely in his nice hotel on the harbor, sipping brandy and ordering tasty snacks from room service, even though it meant another day apart. Because of our professional commitments, we have had more of those days than usual this spring. After he hung up, I made some more coffee and walked around the house, feeling self-consciously *spared* from the bad things of life—for the present! But right outside was the howling white storm, driving so hard against the house that I flinched when I passed under the tall expanse of north windows. (This place in the woods, where you have never visited me—I never invited you, did I?—was built about fifty years ago as an artist's studio.) My moment of well-being was, as usual, shadowed by reminders of what could have been . . . what could still be. Only some panes of glass, and insulated walls, and the big oil furnace thrumming away beneath the floor separated me from the impersonal furor of the storm; just as some blessed mental insulation, made up of more-or-less-balanced parts of perception and sanity, had allowed me to look in on madness—the state of that creature in my dream, so utterly bereft and in a fury that it must kill and die in order to stop the pressure—without succumbing to it. But how long will such a balance last? How long can such *luck* last?

I bought this place ten years ago, spent all my savings as a down payment on the mortgage at the same time you were collecting your material for "Teenage Rookie" and sitting in front of the TV wondering why girls preferred other Leos. That was the summer in which I decided the time had come to insure my old age against undignified failure. I was thirty-two years old, unmarried, and making less than five thousand dollars a year from my writing; the savings had come from a three-year teaching stint, winters and summers, at Iowa (where you did pay me a surprise visit in your sixteenth year, when you and LeRoy were fleeing the Law—or believed yourselves to be fleeing the Law.)

My plan for the future, while I was teaching in the Writers Workshop out in Iowa, was that I would be living in New York City before my thirty-fifth birthday, and that I would, by that time, through a combination of that city's legendary energy, which made things happen faster, and of my own obstinate desire for it to happen, have become a successful writer. By which I meant someone who could pay her bills from her writing and who would be more than likely—rather than not at all

likely—to find her books in stores when she went looking under
the "C's" in Fiction. But a crucial access route to this future was
to have been Julia, who in those years had an apartment in
New York and a room in it waiting for me. However, just before
Christmas, after I had told the director I wouldn't be back next
year so he would have plenty of time to get somebody else, Julia
decided her conscience compelled her to move back to Mountain
City to help care for her mother. I could have gone back to the
director and said I was staying after all, but I had a fateful
feeling that if I didn't honor the date in May I had already set
for leaving, I would never cross over into the realm of my desire.
(I'm speaking of Success, now, of which New York was just the
symbol.)

I was terrified, of course, but I went around muttering that
passage from *Julius Caesar* Sister Patrick made us memorize in
eighth grade, the one that went: *There is a tide in the affairs of
men/ Which, taken at the flood, leads on to fortune* . . . and pricked
my courage by recalling the thrilling *ominousness* she put into her
voice when she got to the lines: *Omitted, all the voyage of their life/
Is bound in shallows and in miseries.*

So I gave away my plants, mailed my boxes of books to Ralph
and Lily's latest basement, and drove to New York in May.
(I'm sorry you never had Sister Patrick. At just the time when
she would have been your math and literature teacher at La
Fosse, the Bishop sent her over to Catholic High to salve his
political conscience: so the "less privileged" got her, when who
knows how much influence her attractive, infectious belief in the
pursuit of excellence might have had on your life.)

It took me less than a week in New York to realize I could
not survive there as a writer without Julia's temporary haven
and a lot more money than I was likely to have for years.
Everything cost three times as much, in cash *and* energy, as it
had in Iowa. My savings would pay for about a year's rent on
an apartment it would depress me to live in, and I felt I was
past the point in life when I could share accommodations with
another "girl." If I stayed in New York, I would have to get a
full-time job, or else be in a panic about money all the time,
and neither state of existence would be conducive to the kind of
fiction I was trying to write: deep-breathing, reflective, and with
that patience for detail I admired in those medieval stone carvers
who would lavish their skills on the lowliest gargoyle simply
because . . . that was their job for the day, and every day's work

was done for the glory of God. Running for subways, wearing my purse strapped around my chest like a musketeer to discourage snatchers, toting up desperate budgets in my journal at night, it seemed to me, would be much likelier to produce shallow gulps of prose, fragmented narratives peopled with unfinished beings whose creator was too tired, or too demoralized, to imagine them in loving detail.

I bought a map of New York State and circled the area that lay within a two-hour drive, and then I checked out of my third-rate hotel and, forking over almost as much as I'd paid the hotel in order to ransom my car from a sleazy parking garage, headed north on the West Side Highway towards the George Washington Bridge, narrowly missing getting sideswiped by a speeding junk heap crammed with the most derelict-looking kids I had ever seen . . .

I feel you recoiling. This was the tone you hated, wasn't it? I don't mean the derelict teenagers, you would have been interested in them, would have hoped they'd invite *you* on their wild ride, and ask you home afterwards to have supper with their families in Harlem. No, I mean—how did you put it? "You let them suffer a little, just enough to improve their characters, but you always rescue them from the abyss at the last minute and reward them with love or money or the perfect job—or sometimes all three." For it's clear that, if I were to go on, this would be one of those stories people love to tell after they have made it. "I walked ten miles, each way, to school . . ." "After I lost everything in the stock-market crash, I just rolled up my sleeves and . . ." "Alone, obscure, no longer young, too poor to live in the magic city, the heroine made some astute calculations as to how she might be near enough to partake of its legendary energies without sacrificing her talent or pocketbook, and then drove resolutely across the bridge and two hours north in search of a minimal dwelling that would at least be her own (because, as everyone knows, even the humblest shack with a mortgage on it and some unruly phlox growing around the door can make the difference between a grizzled old girl whom neighbors respect as 'eccentric' and an out-and-out bag lady, empurpled legs tucked under a ragged coat, snoring on a hard bench . . .)"

The tone makes me recoil, too. It embarrasses me, just as the unexpected richness of my present life embarrasses me, especially since you made me aware of it in the kitchen last October, on the afternoon of Lily's birthday. You were referring to my

books—come on, the truth: did you ever actually *read* one of
them?—but I wonder now if you weren't also obliquely passing
judgment on the tone of my life, as you saw it. "Expecting the
worst—a trademark of hers—the heroine forged diligently ahead
and a few years later everything fell into place for her. In her
affordable country retreat, she took deep breaths and chiseled
away at her fiction, treating herself to bimonthly excursions into
the magic city to have lunch with her editor or her agent, or go
to a museum, or see a new play or film; and one September
afternoon, two years later, because she happened to have had
her wallet removed from her purse by an agile thief while she
was hurrying from the Museum of Modern Art to the new
Ingmar Bergman film at a movie house on Third Avenue, and
because she did not become aware of her loss until the moment
she stood in front of the box-office window to pay for her ticket,
and because the man just behind her in line who witnessed her
distress found something about her appealing enough to make
him wish to step out of line and offer his assistance, she ended
up meeting the love of her life; not only that, but getting to live
in Manhattan, after all, in the roomy old brownstone his uncles
had left him, filled with stolid prewar European furniture and
countless pictures of the daughter who was away at college.
('Gee, Pop,' she said reproachfully, upon being informed of the
fait accompli, 'you certainly didn't wait very long to get a new
room-mate.')"

Yes, all this sounds like like the Campion Tone, all right: the
wry, self-deprecating recounting of the fears, the setbacks, so as
to make it acceptable when . . . as you put it that afternoon in
the kitchen (gripping the curved metal top of the chair you
were standing behind till your knuckles went white) . . .
"everything gets wrapped up." And then you leaned forward
towards me, like a grinning prophet behind your pulpit of doom,
and demanded, "Why don't you write a book about something
that can *never* be wrapped up? What if you came across something like that in life? Would you want to write about it?" And
I got on my high horse and more or less said I wouldn't, because
unwrappable chaos and meaninglessness and dreariness "doesn't
excite my curiosity at all," and all the time you were standing
there I was thinking, parallel to our conversation, Theo's beginning to fall apart, like everything else on Quick's Hill, and
congratulating myself for having got out in time.

Oh, dear God. Why didn't I just get up out of my chair and

walk those few inches around the table and hug you? You were nice to hug, you were just the right height and you always smelled good. Unlike Rafe, with his combination of Brut and alcohol, you had retained the sweet, scrubbed smell of a little boy. But you had just announced that maybe you didn't even want to be a main character in my kind of world anymore, and I was hurt and angry. Angry because you were my brother, Lily's child, and yet you were standing there in the late-afternoon October sunlight almost bragging to me that you intended to be a failure. Hurt because in your assessment of me (masked as literary critique?) you had raised some profoundly troubling specters: what ugly truths of human existence had I been regularly avoiding in my life and work in order to maintain my vision of life and my belief in myself?

But I'm dissembling after the fact. I'm trying to pad an experience with more significance, and wisdom on my part, than was there at the time. The same way I did when I was telling you about how, ten years ago in New York, I calmly reasoned that I couldn't write my deep-breathing, reflective, gargoyle-loving fiction while running for subways and foiling purse snatchers. I *couldn't* have thought anything like that during that traumatic week: nothing so sustained or far-seeing. My thoughts that week were little more than exclamatory eruptions of panic or self-hate: I'M NOTHING HERE . . . GOD, I LOOK FIFTY IN THAT PLATE-GLASS WINDOW . . . HOW CAN A CHEESEBURGER COST THAT MUCH? . . . MUST GET OUT OF HERE . . . CUT MY LOSSES . . . REGAIN MY DIGNITY . . . NOBODY KNOWS WHO I AM . . . YET! That carefully constructed endorsement of "full" writing, as opposed to the flimsy kind, was worked out as recently as this morning, inspired in no small measure by the impatience roused in me last night by the close-fisted smugness of the Russian-tank man. In the memory of my New York week, I saw an opportunity to heroinize myself in retrospect and, at the same time, discreetly "puff" my own methods—what I have learned I do best—at the expense of his and some more enemies'/rivals' styles.

No, I was more impatient with you in the kitchen than I was hurt. You didn't mean enough to me at that moment to have the power to hurt me. (Now, *that* admission hurts me, if it would be any consolation to you.) I was much more exasperated with you for being connected to me and making such an obvious mess of your life than I was impressed, or oppressed, by any "profoundly troubling specters" you had evoked. There were maybe some stray, scratchy little filaments of doubt about my work, but I used them to my own advantage the very next day with Julia, on our Olympian picnic. I confessed them, she dispelled them; or, rather, in her valuable way, she pointed out how I should employ them as incitements for new challenges rather than more snags in my hairshirt.

And if I had come home, after that glorious picnic, to find you moping around the house rather than gone from it irrevocably, I would have flown on back to New York in a few days and continued work on a book I was fairly pleased with, not only because I was filling it with the kinds of people and stories that I thought would express my vision of life but because it was to be a departure and an expansion. It was going to *get beyond* family life and the South and independent young-ish women wriggling out of the deadly twin-embrace. There were to have been three *major male characters*: a charming dead diplomat (based on a friend of Felix's, not dead, who loves to regale us with stories of "the service": the fiasco of the portable toilets ordered for Eisenhower's visit in Iran; how, when his family's furniture arrived in Egypt, it included the two full pails of garbage they had thrown out in Washington); a solitary, art-loving financier who, at fifty, falls in love with his niece's fiancé, who returns his love; and the son of the dead diplomat, a young man about your age, who has lived in so many countries he can't take America's value system seriously and is obsessed with the question of how he can live a *useful* spiritual life in a greedy, nonspiritual society. But he falls in love with an utterly ruthless girl, whom I was going to have great fun doing, drawing on the grim go-getter who resides in me, only she wouldn't have my scruples or my timidness: I was looking forward to seeing how far she would go, what awful things she would do to get there, and whether or not she would succeed in corrupting the spiritual young man (who also resides in me). Then there was going to be the Good Girl, the niece who loses her man to her uncle. The Good Girl was to balance out my Bad Girl, as Amelia Sedley balanced out Becky Sharp in *Vanity Fair* (which you probably never read, either); she and the bad girl knew each other years ago in grade school (but not in the South!). It is the Good Girl and her uncle—before he runs off with the fiancé to a cabin in Maine—who give the Bad Girl her toehold in New York—and end up scorned and betrayed by her when she gains the top of the ladder.

When I got back to New York after your funeral, I allowed myself a few days before I dared go into my study in Felix's house (which I was going to bestow, furnished differently, on my bachelor financier); I knew that, after all that had just transpired in Mountain City, the problems of my characters in "Gotham" (that was to be the novel's name: it's a nickname for New York City, and also means "a place known for the folly of its inhabitants") were bound to seem relatively remote and insignificant—at least for a while. But I was not prepared for the total revulsion I experienced when I did at last open that folder and begin to skim the pages. Who *were* these people? What did they have to do with anything that mattered? Whom, for God's sake, had I been trying to impress . . . or fool? Towards what crass market-place had I been trundling my spurious wares, while maintaining a deceptive Jamesian slow-march of prose to keep the critics from thinking I had "gone commercial"? Who *needed* this book, with its shameless derivations from *New Grub Street* and *Vanity Fair,* its pandering to easy dichotomies, to the "hot topics" of the day? Had I actually taken myself seriously, at some point during the previous year, when I had scrawled importantly across the front of the folder, in black ink, "Great social themes vs obsessional private themes"?

Confronting that material in the folder a week after your death was like catching an unexpected glimpse of myself in a mirror and seeing the outlines of a person for whom I—the genuine "I," if there is such a thing; yes, damn my nervous curtsy to fashionable theories, I still believe there exists a bedrock reality of the self—felt contempt. The experience wasn't pleasant. "I don't want to see that fat coming back through our door," a woman at my health club quoted her husband as telling her after she'd slimmed down. Which, I'd thought to myself while she was so proudly quoting him, was an unnecessarily churlish way of putting it. But as I took "Gotham" out to the sidewalk in a twist-tied plastic bag and deposited it in our can, and then subsequently watched from an upstairs window as a young black sanitation worker with Rastafarian locks tossed it cavalierly into the grinding jaws of the garbage truck, I found myself paraphrasing the husband's ungracious admonishment. I don't want to see whoever wrote those pages, I thought, coming back through this door.

And yet, to be fair—which is never, of course, as sharp-edged or dramatic in effect, when one is telling this kind of change-of-heart story—to be fair to that writer who went out with the garbage, I believe she was proceeding in good faith at the time she was composing those pages of "Gotham." She had pretty much completed the chronicle of the questing young woman who goes out into the world in search of self and art; then she had returned to her home turf for a nostalgic rendering of a best friend's family life, and thus managed to make it up to herself for having a family life that had thwarted, angered, and embarrassed her. Now she wanted to try something different, that was all. Un-Southern, unfamilial. (Not a single major character in the New York novel possessed a living mother or father, brother or sister!) And there is nothing in essence wrong with having as your aim "Great social themes vs obsessional private themes" except that, when written down in black ink in resolute convent-girl script, it might strike the critical eye as both naïve and grandiose.

Another thought also has tweaked my conscience in the months following the trashing of "Gotham." Maybe I would have abandoned it sooner or later, anyway. There never was, between it and me, the vital umbilical connection I had with the other books. All the others originated as compelling clusters of feelings seeking the form of a compatible story. Whereas "Gotham" was as willed as a term paper in which I was determined to exceed previous expectations. It was the kind of thing *I thought I ought to be doing next.* Perhaps at its very best it could have been only a contrived and competent, but dead, thing. Perhaps I welcomed the excuse of your violent death—and the kind of rethinking it was bound to engender—to free me from the obligation to go on with it.

Back from an interruption. Phone call from Donald, my accountant. "We're in good shape for April 15." By that he means, thanks to his foresight (state taxes prepaid in December, maximum contribution socked away in Defined Benefit Retirement Plan), I am all paid up for 1983 and can now start worrying about 1984. I have never met Donald Buscaglia (Irish on mother's side, Italian on father's), who came excellently recommended, but over the past few years in our discussions we have established a rapport. There is a peculiar sort of intimacy in a woman's sharing her innermost financial condition with a pleasant-voiced male she's never laid eyes on. I don't want to lay eyes on him: I like him just as he comes across on the phone, from his deferential opening ("Is this a good time for me to call?") to the way he steadfastly browbeats me in his Buffalo accent, employing quaint, old-fashioned words, when necessary, into doing "the prudent thing." Our first battle (which he would pronounce "*bee*atle") was over putting away the legally allowed amount in my retirement fund. "But Donald," I protested, "I won't have the use of all this money till I'm *old*. Wouldn't it be better just to pay a little more tax now and have access to what's left over? I mean, I may not live into my sixties. I might contract a deadly disease or get run over by a truck." "That's possible," he acknowledged patiently, and allowed me to rant on a few minutes longer, at my expense, before striking me down with one of his charmingly unmodern phrases. "But Clare, if you only put in the minimum contribution, you forsake twelve thousand dollars out of pocket." What person of imagination can hold out against such a romance-fraught old word as "forsake"? Or keep from sliding one's fingers into that well-evoked pocket and finding only crumbs, or an old ticket stub, or a paper clip . . . when, if only you had let your accountant transfer a few figures to line 27 under "Adjustments to Income," you could be grasping a roll of bills as fat as a muffin?

Donald is thirty-five. He has been an accountant for twelve years, or, as he put it proudly in a recent conversation, "I've got twelve years, you know, Clare." He works long hours this time of year, but he exercises regularly three times a week ("Racquetball now, jogging when it gets warmer"). "So you're not fat, then," I asked, at the time he told me this. "Oh, *no*. Five-eleven and a hundred and sixty-five pounds." It was endearing to hear someone speak of himself with such satisfaction. He had recently married, he went on, and his wife always had a salad waiting for him when he got home. "Just a salad?" "Oh"—he uttered a low chuckle, bordering on the sexy—"but it's a very *adequate* salad." Pronounced "*e*adequate *se*alad." Several times I was on the verge of telling him, "One of my brothers is an accountant, too," but I was afraid he might ask how you liked it, or if you'd passed your CPA exam yet. These days, when Donald Buscaglia and I talk, I often try to hear how you might have sounded to a female client like me, what irresistible words or phrases, or tone of voice, you would have used to convince her to do what you had already decided was best for her.

But you didn't have sympathy with clients like me. In Granny

Squirrel, Snow told me you had sent for an application to the IRS just before you died. She said you told her in one of your last phone calls that you were sick of helping rich people keep their money. I can see how it might have worked out for you, such a job. You would have been able to combine the excitement of the police work you hankered after with the tedious checking over columns of figures that you despised. You could have nabbed tax cheats on your calculator, if not fugitives and speeders in your patrol car. It would have been a second-best option, but better than no options at all.

And in only seven more years, *you* would have been thirty-five.

There is a picture of you—falling through the air in slow motion—that I can't get out of my mind. A picture of *us*, actually, for I am involved, too: involved yet uninvolved as I watch you silently from a window, utterly transfixed by your baffling behavior. It is a late afternoon in summer. I am on one of my visits back from England, where I am spending the remainder of my youth trying to grow into a writer—that is, when I am not worrying about ending up an old maid. I am in my late twenties by then, so that must make you, let's see, about thirteen. You all were then living in the house before Quick's Hill, the one Ralph built in Huckleberry Woods, where Lily made the first garden in her life, a rock garden on the steep slope of the hill, with blue flowers only. Dr. Anthony Gallant, who always delighted in abetting people in their exclusive tendencies, had ordered her a rare variety of blue tulip from Holland along with a remarkable array of perennials and heaths and heathers, all in shades of blue, from a Connecticut nursery run by English people who put out a haughtily written spring and fall catalogue that Dr. Anthony loved to read aloud from, lingering deliciously over the Latin names and the subtle, malicious pokes at the taste lapses and the impatience of the average American gardener.

The house in Huckleberry Woods on that late afternoon, sixteen, seventeen summers ago, was unusually quiet. Where was everybody? Ralph was undoubtedly out of work. These were his peak years, when he had three or four jobs going at once and was still in love with the building trade. Rafe and you (I thought) were down swimming in the pond shared by the families of Huckleberry Woods. Ralph and his friend the insurance man, Dave Kellogg, and another friend of Kellogg's were in the process of creating the community of Huckleberry Woods out of the hundred wooded acres Kellogg's father had left him. The three men had picked off the best lots for themselves and Ralph's first three houses were up: showpieces for future buyers. It was the first time I had visited you in this particular house, and I remember being pleased by it: the way it sat on its slope, surrounded by trees below so you couldn't see the other houses (only hear the voices of children, which was a reassuring sound), and with a view, from the living room and from Lily and Ralph's bedroom balcony, of some distant low-lying mountains to the east. I think the reason I was by myself rather than out with Lily that afternoon was that I had been painting the view from the balcony. Painting was my great happiness when I was a child. When I was about seven years old, a dignified older man who worked on the newspaper with Lily, a sort of small-town Renaissance man named C.P. Summerall, who taught an evening class in creative writing that Lily went to and who painted landscapes that hung in the local art gallery, had taken me on as his pupil, and he and Lily and I would go out to pretty spots on Saturdays and "Mr. C.P.," as Lily called him affectionately, would help me set up my easel and squeeze out my colors, working counterclockwise around the top of the palette from warms to colds, with an extra-large blob of white, and then I would more or less copy what he did, sketching in my view, putting in the sky first, because however the sky was when you started was going to influence the lights and shadows in the rest of your picture, even though that first sky might change completely before you were done.

Yes, that may have been the afternoon I painted the view from Lily and Ralph's balcony, the same afternoon on which I later watched you fall slowly backwards through the air, clinging to the top rungs of Ralph's tall ladder, with that rapt expression of someone welcoming a long-sought end. When I try to imagine (God knows *why* I try) the expression on your face the moment before your death, it is the look of the boy on the ladder, ecstatic . . . accepting . . . foredoomed.

Although I can't remember for sure which afternoon during that visit I painted the picture (which is now stashed away in the Quick's Hill basement along with some other artworks, including poor C.P. Summerall's defaced oil portrait of Lily as an attractive young widow in a green silk blouse, with distant blue

eyes and a sibyl's half-smile), I have no trouble recalling the
mood I was in. I was contented. I hadn't allowed myself the
luxury of painting since I was living abroad, maybe even longer
ago than that; I don't think I painted in college, either. And I
didn't do oil painting when I lived for those two years with my
father's sister and brother in the eastern part of the state, only
some drawing and watercolors to pass the boring afternoons,
and there were so many of them—yet I loved them precisely for
their boringness and normality and respectability. Hadn't I fled
from Lily and Ralph and you and the impending Rafe because
I longed for the same bourgeois life that most of my school
friends took for granted, with middle-aged adults who acted
middle-aged and didn't moan aloud from erotic pleasure from
behind thin doors or joke like bohemians over suppers of
macaroni and Jell-O about how they would be able to pay the
phone company or the electric company this month, but not,
under any circumstances, both? (And yet, at the same time,
they were filling the house with babies.)

As I squinted at Lily and Ralph's first real view, more than a
decade after my escape ("Squinting's the only way to see the
values in your landscape": a prime piece of advice from my old
teacher, Mr. Summerall), it must have seemed to me that things
might be going to turn out okay for everybody concerned, after
all. Ralph's houses for his family had been getting costlier and
more spacious, but this one in Huckleberry Woods was the first
one I felt did Lily justice, with its acres of privacy and her blue
garden and the lovely new furniture she had chosen for its looks
and not because it would hold up well or was on sale. And
Ralph was so much more bearable now that he and his fleet of
yellow trucks were in such demand; he no longer shuffled around
in the evening with that needy look, listening in on conversations
or poking his head in the door to ask what I was reading; he
was downstairs in his pine-paneled basement office, clicking
away on his adding machine. And you and Rafe each had your
own room, decorated as you wished, shelves stocked with the
latest games and gadgets, walk-in closets, replete with all the
sartorial requirements of La Fosse Hall boys: the little blue
blazers (winter and summer weight) with their red shield-shaped
crests and red neckties; the multicolored selection of Lacoste
shirts for after-school "casual wear" at home, along with the
right brands of jeans and shorts and sneakers. You all were okay.
You were in your proper places, everybody behaving according

to contemporary American society's current specifications for its normal, upwardly mobile families. The giant freezer was stuffed with steaks and ice cream and there were no audible mating cries from behind these solid maple doors. I could stop cringing from the old embarrassments and relax on this vacation; I could at last cease feeling guilty for running out on Lily and concentrate totally on building my own life.

As I painted my vision of the view from Lily and Ralph's first balcony, I remember comparing the American air with the softer English air, the muted, less demanding light, which had depressed me at first, then proved so beneficial to my apprentice nerves because it made me think of time in a different way: not as a straight road with goals to be jumped, one after the other, like hurdles, but more as a soft, swirling atmosphere made up of particles of past, present, and future. It had provided just the right ambience, as well as the inspiration, for *The House on Cheyne Walk*, which several drafts later would allow me to return home from my self-imposed exile, a published writer at last. But this American light, together with its pungent air, was like an elixir; it made me paint fast and boldly, exaggerating the blues of the distant ranges, the purples of the shadows, bestowing lavish quick fixes of white on close-up trees to create the illusion, as "Mr. C.P." had taught me, of leaves moving in sunlight. "She has a sophisticated sense of color for a child," he would murmur to Lily, who often on our outings could not resist snitching a small square of upsom board from his knapsack and, borrowing the brushes no one was just then using, and squeezing out a little circle of colors for herself from my tubes, would dash off in her lap a "miniature" more intriguing than anything we did. I had my "sophisticated sense of color" and a precocious facility for aping technique, Mr. Summerall had his respectful photographic faithfulness to nature, but Lily had the knack of making things look as charming as she wished them to look, and I remember Mr. Summerall's once telling her, a catch in his throat, that she was a downright sorceress when it came to creating her effects.

Of course he was in love with her. Who wouldn't have been? I was in love with her myself. She was not much older than you when she reached her zenith as my heroine. How can I describe her "effects," this shared mother of ours, in her earlier incarnation? So much about her was different then: her hair an earthy auburn rather than the color of Venetian glass, her figure fuller (unlike most women, she has gone from robust to petite); even her smell was different, though it would be decades before I learned the true source of that mysterious, *worldly* scent that clung to her clothes when she came home from the newspaper office or from Mr. Summerall's evening classes in creative writing. Not long ago, she confessed to me that she had been a secret smoker back then; she told me she had always carried a tiny bottle filled with Listerine in her purse, to gargle with in order to keep her mother from finding out. But all those years in between, I had been convinced it was the perfume she had used in those days, one called Tweed, although, sometime during my twenties, longing for a sniff of the past, I bought a bottle of it and was disappointed when I unstoppered it: I thought the manufacturers had changed the formula, because it no longer had that haunting "woodsmoke" essence.

The Lily of my childhood believed in Art the way the Lily you grew up knowing counted on God. It was her resource and her respite, her trusted magic and her trump card. At the time you came to consciousness, Lily was giving up on Art, but as far back as I can remember I was taught by her to believe that special patterns of words, or the resolutions of chords, or inspired slashes of colored pigment on a flat surface could make all the difference between feeling you were an ordinary person, lonely, disappointed, and trapped, and knowing you possessed a pass-key to a kingdom with powers and privileges unlike any other. Lily loved poems with lines like "*To strive, to seek, to find, and not to yield.*" She admired beautiful, tough-minded heroines with names like Dagney Taggart and Eustacia Vye. She had this one piece she played, over and over, on our upright piano, the Chopin Prelude in C minor. She didn't need the music for it, she had worked it up for a college recital years ago, and it was her solace piece, or her cry of defiance, or her snort of triumph, depending on what kind of day she'd had. I would get goose pimples down my legs every time I listened to her *appropriating* the keyboard with those loud opening chords . . . and then suddenly she would get soft . . . the contrast was so dramatic: it was like someone bowing gracefully to fate after making a splendid protest, echoing the bold opening in a sorrowful, wiser voice.

Here I go embellishing the past again. The goose pimples were the truth, and my feeling that it was *her piece*, that the music unfolded in a way that expressed *her*—that I probably felt, too. But the rest is after the fact. I just went and put Arrau playing the Chopin Preludes on the turntable, and lay back on the sofa watching the driving white snowflakes outside in the fading bluish light, and waited for "Lily's piece," which comes at the end of a set of three. And then it came on, the opening passage played less defiantly than Lily played it (but why should Arrau be defiant, when all his long life he has sat serenely isolated in the center of his own blessed gift?), and afterwards came the poignant, restrained restatement, and I thought, The shape of this piece is like the shape of Lily's life. And that end, that mystifying single chord that ends the piece, so full of ambiguity! It could be either a resigned question mark, addressed to the Great Unknown, or a final, defiant "There!" flung back at a lifetime of things that never added up to the Ideal. And I suddenly pictured Lily in her last moment, going out on such a typically ambiguous note, and I wept in advance over her death, and for myself and how betrayed and abandoned I was going to feel.

But back to the balcony in Huckleberry Woods, where I am painting the mountains in the distance and the trees with C.P. Summerall's little flecks of animated white light.

Of course it was the same afternoon that you fell off the ladder. Whom am I trying to kid? It had to be. It was the reason why you were on the ladder. I saw this, I understood this, for the first time—*this is the truth*—while I was listening to the Arrau record and getting myself worked up to cry over Lily's death, though you are the one who is dead. I understood that it was *me* you were climbing through the air to sneak up on, as I painted on the balcony that afternoon. You had plotted it out and made your stealthy preparations in order to see what this thing called a sister would do with her day when there was no one around to watch.

Maybe I had finished my painting by that time. Or maybe I had just taken a break to go to the bathroom. Anyway, I was in the house, and I had gone to my room—the guest room—for something. This was the first of Ralph's houses big enough to have a guest room. In previous ones, you and Rafe always had to give up your shared room to me when I dropped out of the blue, first from college, then from England. I was in the guest room, which was across the hall from Lily and Ralph's master bedroom with the balcony. From the guest room's side window, you could see a corner of the balcony, jutting out over empty space, and then, about twenty feet below, the side lawn sloping down into the woods. Well, I was alone in the silent house, in the guest room, which was still new enough to smell of paint and varnished floors, when I heard an odd metallic *scraping* outside the side window. I looked out just in time to see the ladder arching away from the balcony. You, riding its top rungs, that ghastly rapture on your face, passed within inches of me on the other side of the screened window.

What happened then? Did I put my hands over my eyes so as not to watch you hit the ground? I know I definitely did not see you complete your fall. I remember no sounds. No clanking rattle of aluminum hitting the ground, no cry of pain.

And then what happened? Did you narrowly miss being hurt, and lie there on the ground, massaging an ankle or something? Or were you, the son of a builder, after all, an old adept at ladder play? Had you staged the "fall" for my benefit? Maybe, when you had climbed all the way up to the balcony only to find that I had left it, you made scraping sounds until you glimpsed you had my attention from the guest room, and then pushed off, setting your face in that doomed look ("I'll *really* frighten her!"), and fell to earth as lightly as a cat, and waited to see what I would do next.

But here is the part that bothers me. The next thing I remember—and this is very vague—is seeing you walking slowly around the house, as if you were deep in thought. You were passing in front of Lily's blue garden, so that must mean I was now looking at you out of the guest room's front window, from which the garden would have been visible. And I remember wondering, This strange boy, what was he trying to do on that ladder? Was he trying to spy on something he thought was going on in Lily and Ralph's bedroom, or what? It didn't occur to me then that your behavior had anything to do with my presence in the house.

And then I just put it out of my mind. You hadn't been hurt, and I don't remember either of us ever mentioning it to each other or to anybody else. I never thought about it again until now, when, just as I keep replaying your death that I never saw, trying to fill in the blanks (the way it actually happened, the motives, what you were really up to), I watch you falling, over and over again, past my window, through the air of that summer day, haunted that I'll never know—*because I didn't bother to find out*—whether your fall was accidental or intentional, or the exact circumstances of how you hit the ground.

Haunted also by the realization that the end of that memory should have been as follows: I rush outside, to find you either stunned on the grass or doubled up behind a tree, laughing at the scare you have given me. Either way, I should have rushed out and after saying something sisterly like "You damned jackass!" at least acknowledged your act. And then, after reiterating a few more times how impossible you were, slipped my arm around your waist and given you a relieved kiss or hug because you were still okay.

Felix just checked in again from Toronto. "I took a taxi to the Chinese section and had a nice lunch, and then went to the Art Gallery. The Henry Moore outside was covered with snow, it was a rare sight. Then I came back and took off my wet shoes and socks and ordered a Calvados. I'm having dinner with a woman—don't be alarmed, she's of the other persuasion—who runs a repertory theater in Saskatchewan. How is it there? I just listened to a weather report and it looks as if I'll be able to fly out tomorrow."

Then I drank a glass of red wine and went around the house turning on lamps because it's beginning to get dark. I put on my boots and went outside and refilled the bird feeder, which was almost empty. As I turned to go back inside, hugging the bag of leftover sunflower seeds to my chest, I looked in the window to the left of the door and saw the books, the fireplace, the lamps, the sofa, the plants. For an eerie moment, I was a homeless stranger out in the snowy night, looking in on exactly the kind of life I wanted. And I remembered my dream of last night, and wondered if it could have been a sort of visitation from you: you, showing me in a dream how it felt to be you at the moment when you made the decision to put an end to all the pain that went with being you.

I went back into the warm house and closed the door against the cold and bolted it against strangers, and opened a new bottle of red wine and poured myself another glass and put on the Fauré *Requiem*. When Fischer-Dieskau was singing '*Libera me, Domine, de morta aeterna,*' I turned my face into the chintz pillow and, against the background of the sublime sounds, wept over you.

I have spent most of this day with you. More consecutive

hours than I ever gave to you in your lifetime. More *waking* hours than the one visit you ever paid me, when you and LeRoy arrived on my Iowa doorstep one cold November night, wearing jeans and T-shirts, on the lam (or so you wanted to believe) from the cops in Mountain City.

Ralph had phoned in the late afternoon. I'd just got back from teaching. When I heard his voice, long-distance before the rates went down, I knew the worst had happened: Lily was dead. I stood in the middle of the carpeted kitchen in my rented house and looked through the Thermopane window of the back door, past the bare trees to the embankment where the freight trains went by on the tracks below, and I imprinted the scene on my heart: the landscape I was looking at when I first learned that Lily no longer inhabited the same world.

"Something's wrong," I said into the receiver, going to meet the nightmare halfway.

"We-e-e-ll . . ." Ralph's twangy voice drawled, but with aggravation, not sorrow. Aggravation tinged by the tiniest hint of amusement, of self-importance. My fear drained out, my stepdaughter's hackles started to rise: what inconvenient news was he getting ready to spring? "Theo's run off. We think he's probably on his way to Iowa, to you."

"What do you mean? What happened?"

Even though he was paying prime-time rates, Ralph couldn't resist the opportunity to unreel the story slowly, like a fishline. He didn't have my complete attention, I was still recovering from the scare about Lily. But there was this sexy English teacher at the public high school that you had a crush on, "Babs," and you and LeRoy had gone to her house and rung her doorbell. You had quit the Belvedere School the previous spring, after your famous rock-moving victory over "Uncle Percy" Hardwick. Anyway, this Babs had called the sheriff's department and when the deputy arrives you all are still standing there like fools, ringing her bell. He tells you to go wait by his car, but you and LeRoy run for your car and flee instead. Later in the evening, Ralph gets a phone call from the sheriff himself. "Mr. Quick"— here Ralph really enjoyed mimicking the sheriff's plaintive tone—"Mr. Quick, I know you and you know me. We both got teenage sons. But I'm short-staffed and short-budgeted and I don't have men to waste on car chases for entertainment. I don't know what your boy and that nigger were up to, but you and I both know that fleeing the law is serious. However, I'm wlling to let it go this time if you'll just talk to your boy when he gets home tonight and tell him life isn't a movie." "As soon as he walks in this door," Ralph told the sheriff, "I'm taking his car keys and grounding him for a damn month."

But you didn't walk in the door that night, and at about one in the morning Lily and Ralph are starting to phone the hospitals when they get a hysterical call from Babs, the sexy English teacher. She's weeping and apologizing and saying she didn't realize it was Theo out there, all she saw from the window was this grinning giant Negro standing with his legs apart on her porch and flexing his muscles. And now she's just had a collect call from Theo, who says he's somewhere in Kentucky because she's gotten him in trouble with the law and he can never come back home again.

"That's when we figured out where he was probably heading," Ralph told me. "Only why isn't he there by now? It doesn't take but about sixteen hours to get there. Hell, I could have made it in ten when I was his age."

I said I'd been at the college all day, maybe you'd been trying to reach me.

"Oh," said Ralph. "He's probably trying to phone now. I'll hang up. But the minute you hear from him, I want you to call us right back. And if he walks in your door, you tell him to phone home before he even goes to the bathroom."

Ralph had barely hung up when you called collect. "It's me," you said mysteriously. "I'll pay you back. But this is sort of an emergency." I could feel you grinning with the importance of the adventure you were about to relate. "I'm in a place called Rock Island with my friend LeRoy. Would you be willing to harbor two fugitives from justice?"

"Ralph has just called," I said. Adding, "They're very worried about you," though Ralph hadn't entirely given that impression.

"The police are after us. We had to run."

"Well, they're not after you anymore. The chase has been called off."

"Oh," you said, in a slightly deflated voice. You put your hand over the receiver. Relaying the news to LeRoy, probably. "Did Dad tell you that?"

"Yes. He and the sheriff have settled things. And your teacher, that Babs, called the house crying. She was very upset."

"No kidding?" Your voice picked up a little. "She was really crying?"

"That's what Ralph said. She was upset that she had gotten you in trouble by calling the sheriff. But she only saw LeRoy."

"Yeah, she told me that, too, when I called her. But that's just her prejudice, I told her. Just because a person with dark skin rings your bell, it doesn't mean he's out to rape you or kill you. LeRoy and I were driving around last night and I decided to go by and ask her about my test. I know other students have dropped by to see her. She encourages it. What was I supposed to do, ask LeRoy to wait in the car like some servant I was ashamed of?"

"Listen," I said, "Rock Island is an hour away from Iowa City. We'll talk when you get here." I gave you directions. "I've got some stew meat, I'll make you all a good stew."

"We can sure use it," you said. "I have Dad's Mobil card but no cash. LeRoy only had about five dollars in his wallet, so we've had two stale cheese sandwiches and one Coke between us since we left Mountain City. We'd expected to get to you sooner, but we got lost a couple of times."

Then I called Ralph back. "They're in Rock Island. He'll be here in an hour." Delivering you over.

Ralph had already made his plans. He would arrive at the Louisville, Kentucky, airport at two the next afternoon. If you and LeRoy got on the road early in the morning, you'd be there in plenty of time to meet his plane. "I first thought of flying to Chicago," said Ralph, "there's a direct flight from here. But Chicago's a big place, Theo'd probably never *find* the airport. No, they can pick me up in Louisville at two and I'll have them back to Mountain City by dark. I'll need LeRoy on the job first thing next morning. We've got to finish getting in a foundation before the ground freezes. But I still want Theo to call me the minute he walks in your front door."

"Okay," I said. He's enjoying it, I thought. He gets to buy a plane ticket and fly off to the rescue and then drive you two penitents home, showing you what real driving is when you know how to make time and don't get lost. And in the years after, whenever he told the story, he made it more and more his own. Your part in the narrative dwindled in importance until it became the incidental excuse for the time Ralph Quick had to fly off to Louisville in a hurry and before being allowed to board the plane was singled out by two security guards who took him off to a room and frisked him from head to toe and afterwards apologized. "But I understood their point of view," he would say proudly, enjoying as always the chance to show his solidarity with the tough and powerful. "They didn't know me. They didn't know who I was. All they had to go on, they said, was that I perfectly fit the profile of the potential hijacker. No luggage. No necktie. No fat on my body. Traveling alone. The perfect profile of the potential hijacker."

So I got out my meat and browned it in butter and made the stew. If I'd had something important to do that evening, it might have been different, but as it was I enjoyed the chance it gave me to play the part of the grownup sister able to provide a haven. Despite knowing there was nobody else for you to run to, I couldn't help feeling touched and flattered. And I was curious about LeRoy. I had never had a black person spend the night in my house. I was curious to see how he would behave, and before you two ever arrived I was already dining out on the story.

Your big adventure. Our big night together. Yet you were upstaged on either side by Ralph and LeRoy. When you two arrived in your skimpy white T-shirts, I made a big production out of hugging you because your friend was watching. Then I looked, aghast, from you to him, and playing Concerned Big Sister for all I was worth, I said, "I can't believe you all drove from Mountain City to Iowa in *November* without any more clothes than that."

"Oh, we had the heater in the car," said LeRoy, smiling down on me like a shy giant. I had expected someone older, more hardened. But aside from his towering height and his bulging arm muscles, this boy looked sweet and innocent as any mother's child. "This is some place you got," he said. "I ain't never seen no carpeting on a kitchen floor."

"I haven't, either," I told him. "It was my landlady's idea. When she called and told me she wanted to do it, I thought she was crazy. But she got it in some kind of sale, and now it's my favorite room."

You rolled your eyes in ecstasy. Overdoing it a little. "God! Is that our stew I smell?"

I asked if you all would like to wash up. And would anyone like a glass of wine, or some Scotch. Or orange juice?

You and LeRoy looked at each other, grinning and shrugging. Then LeRoy looked down at himself disparagingly, flashed his beautiful white teeth at me, and asked, "Is there time for me to take a bath before we eat?"

After I had laid out his thick towel on the toilet seat and started his water running, and enjoyed his incredulous wide eyes as I pointed out the generous selection of soaps and bubble baths, you and I must have talked. We had plenty of time. Because you know the story I told and you told . . . and then later Lily and Ralph told to their friends . . . so many times later. LeRoy stayed and stayed and *stayed* in that bathroom. He took his bath, but his mother or somebody must have told him you must always wash the tub out afterwards, and my tub had a slow drain. Since I was the only person who ever used it, I hadn't bothered to ask my landlady to fix it. But it actually took thirty or forty minutes to drain after a good-sized bath. Poor LeRoy stayed in the bathroom for almost an hour. First you went up: "Hey, LeRoy, you about ready to eat?" And then, awhile later, I crept up (the landlady had shag-carpeted the stairs) soundlessly, and knelt down and peeked through the old-fashioned keyhole. LeRoy sat fully dressed on the toilet seat, hands clasped woefully between his knees, staring at the sluggishly sinking level of the bathwater. He was waiting for the water to finish draining so he could be a good guest and wash all traces of himself from the tub.

At last he came down, smiling and shining. Nobody referred to his tardiness. We had our stew. If my memory is correct, I drank wine and you two drank milk or orange juice. Both of you lavishly complimented the stew. At some point you must have called Ralph and coordinated your plans to meet at the Louisville airport.

Then the two of you began yawning like little boys who had stayed up too late. We opened the downstairs sofa bed for LeRoy, and his eyes widened again when I gave him a fake leopardskin throw for a blanket.

You and I shared my queen-sized bed upstairs. I do remember—I wasn't a complete ogre, after all—rubbing your back for a while in the dark. Lily had this game she played with me on my back, we called it "Feathers," where she would stroke in a certain way and I would have to guess what color it was. "You do it just like her!" you kept exclaiming into your pillow, astonished. "That's exactly the way she does gray. That's exactly the way she does purple."

"Well, that's not so surprising," I said. "After all, she used to do it this way on my back. I remember the way it felt."

At some time during the night, I woke up and heard you snoring lightly. I shook you a little and you moaned and turned over and started breathing deeply and regularly again. Then I remembered LeRoy, and couldn't resist creeping down the shag-carpeted stairs to see how he was doing. He was sleeping quietly, scrunched up under the fake leopardskin. It's hard for me to think of him as a convicted criminal serving out his term in our prison system. Does he still sleep curled up so guilelessly? Does he still wash out the tub? I don't even know if they have tubs in prison. Probably not.

Before you all left the next morning, I gave you my L. L. Bean hunting jacket. All the writers in Iowa were wearing them that year. I didn't have anything big enough to fit LeRoy, so I gave him the fake leopardskin throw. He left the house clutching it around his massive shoulders like some sort of African chieftain's shawl.

Later, on one of my visits to Mountain City, Lily returned it to me, sealed in dry cleaner's plastic. Lily always has things I have forgotten, waiting for me there. Old evening dresses with twenty-one-inch waists I couldn't zip around my thigh anymore; books that I bought to impress myself or others, mildewing in the basement. Costume jewelry bought at age fourteen with Julia, in a downtown store that no longer exists. A silver crucifix Sister Patrick sent to me, along with a little green leather pocket edition of Saint Thomas's *Summa*, "Simplified for Everyone," the first Christmas I spent away from Mountain City, after I had gone to live with my father's people. The message on the flyleaf, in the handwriting that was mother to mine, reads: "To Clare, with best Christmas wishes and the hope that this will help your soul find the truth which is its birthright. God love you. I do."

Lily still has the eighteen-by-twenty-four-inch canvas I painted of the view from their balcony in Huckleberry Woods. Unfortunately, because I used too much turpentine, and because that was before I learned that C.P. Summerall's highly re-commended Prussian blue had been on painters' blacklists for years because it loses its color, the picture has gone lifeless and flat. Lily also keeps "Mr. C.P.'s" oil portrait of herself in the same basement closet, but who can bear to look at it anymore? After he died, she got a notion one day that it had never really looked like her, so she dragged out my equipment from his old painting lessons and went to work on the face. She said he hadn't gotten her nose right, he had idealized it into a more Grecian nose than hers. She shortened it and widened the nostrils, then she messed with the lips some (he had made those too thin, she said later), until the picture finally became so grotesquely un-Lily-like, she had to take it down from the wall where it had hung in the undisputed place of honor, over the sofa, during those lean years when it was the only painting Lily and Ralph had. It remains the only family portrait we have ever owned.

A couple of times when I came back for visits, in those years when you and Rafe were still small, I took it out and squinted at it and thought I could still see the outlines of the old Lily. I knew the enraptured "Mr. C.P.'s" faithfully executed vision of Lily could not be restored, but I was arrogant enough to believe *my* skills and *my* memory could bring back its essence. I got out my paints and brushes and turpentine and rags and dabbled and wiped and put in and took out some things. But all I finally succeeded in doing was removing the secret sparkle from the distant blue eyes, the only part of the painting—except for the blouse—Lily herself had wisely refrained from tampering with.

Thursday p.m.—Snow arrives with Jason.

Sunday a.m.—Snow leaves. Jason to stay.

Sunday p.m.—Lily and Ralph arrive.

Tuesday a.m.—Ralph leaves, taking Jason back to Snow.

Tuesday p.m. to Friday—Lily all to myself.

Friday p.m.—Rafe arrives.

Sunday midday—Rafe and Lily leave.

—Clare's plan for the family visit

XI: NO SAINTS

*T*he first night, the sea always kept Felix awake. Or, rather, he would sleep, then be wakened intermittently by the ceaseless drumming and plashing. The sound, both reassuring and impersonal, had a subduing effect on him. One day I will no longer be around to hear this, he would think, but that won't make the slightest difference to *it:* it will continue its rhythms without me. Then he would stretch his legs under the sheet, or arrange his body in a new position, and let his mind seek whatever pictures and thoughts it would, while the sea, not fifty feet from his pillow, made its background music.

The first week at the cottage on the island, before Clare's family began arriving in instalments, he and Clare slept in different bedrooms. This was not from any unfriendliness, but from a habit begun four years ago on the first night they had ever spent in "No Saints." It had been hot, the air still muggy, and the double bed did not accommodate them as well as the queen-size to which they were accustomed. Clare had been snoring gently, and Felix hadn't felt desperate enough about sleeping to shake her by the shoulder, which usually stopped her. So he had gotten up and wandered across the living room to the other seafront bedroom, the one the landlord had told them was his favorite. It was smaller than the room Felix and Clare had chosen, and was connected to another bedroom; this was one reason they had decided against it, even though it was the lightest and breeziest. "Lily will love this room," Clare had said, "and then when Ralph comes to pick her up, he can have the adjoining room, and Rafe can sleep downstairs in the maid's room. That way he'll be nearer to Myrtle Beach *and* the ice in the refrigerator." There had been no mention of Theo's coming the first year. Why was that? Felix tried to remember. Possibly because he and his wife and their one-year-old child would have crowded things? And then, the second year, he had been studying for some accounting examination and couldn't take time off. By the third year, the young wife had fled to Georgia and he and the boy had come down together. Felix could still hear the child's wild shrieks as his father carried him into the surf for the first time. He remembered how Theo had come out to sit with him later on the windwalk. How he had folded his arms and stared out at the rising tide and said about Southerners, "Their politeness is a very effective form of aggression."

But on that first night of the first year, four summers ago, before any of Clare's family had descended, Felix, wandering hot and sleepless, in unresentful retreat from Clare's blocked nasal passages, had been one to discover the amazing properties of the breezy room the landlord had pointed out as his favorite. No sooner had Felix lain down on top of the white cotton bedspread than he had felt the ocean lift him up from both sides. The pale curtains with their splashy country flower designs danced at him in the moonlight like alluring and graceful ghosts. The life and thoughts of Felix Rohr fell away and were replaced by the life and thoughts of . . . whom? Of nobody, really. No, that wasn't true: the Nobody in the breezy room was still a man, very much so. He was acutely aware of his sex and the sensual benefits that went with it, but it was as though his sensuality could roam abroad in this windy darkness loud with sea noise and attach itself to all sorts of things. Fish. Stars. Crabs scuttling boldly across deserted beaches. The thoughts of people all over the world, of people dead for centuries and people not yet born. His loving attention reached out through the night to an immense variety of thoughts and creatures that *were* him, he realized for the first time, even though they were outside him personally. He fought to stay awake to prolong the experience. Had the landlord had it, too? Was that why he had spoken of the room? Was it something to do with so many windows facing the sea on two sides? The way the bed was placed, at an angle between them, so that you felt you were being launched straight into the night tides, the breeze lifting you up from either side?

"That is a wonderful room, you have to try it tonight," Felix had told Clare the next morning. "It is quite an experience."

"How do you mean, an experience?"

"I'll tell you, but first I want you to see for yourself."

"Does that mean you can't sleep in there with me?"

"Maybe we can. We'll start off together . . . see what happens."

So they had put sheets on the bed in the breezy room and that evening they started off together, making a merry time of it. But after Clare had fallen asleep, Felix went back to the other bedroom.

"I see what you mean," Clare told him the following morning. "There is something different about that room."

"Ah. What happened to *you?*"

"Oh, no. First you have to tell me what happened to *you.*"

He had related his quasi-mystical experience. "It was a little like sharing the feelings of God. For the first time I had the idea that if God exists, He isn't just a blind brute force but something that enjoys making new things to love, even if some of them don't turn out well, or get destroyed in the process."

"Now you're making me ashamed. My experience in the room was much more personal and selfish. It was just a dream, actually; but not the sort of dream I usually have. You know. The kind where you wake up feeling you've been told something important."

"What's there to be ashamed of in that?" Felix had asked.

"Well, the content of the dream was a little embarrassing. I mean, to tell aloud." She had proceeded then to tell him how she had dreamed she was aboard a spaceship. "I was climbing these circular stairs. Someone was taking me to meet the captain. 'Now don't go falling in love,' this person said. 'Although everyone does fall in love with the captain. They can't help themselves.' And then I reached the top of the stairs and my guide disappeared and there was this great big metal door. I knew the captain was behind it. I pushed it open—it was very heavy— and inside, sitting in one of those high pilot chairs in front of an instrument panel, was the captain. It was a woman. Oh, no, I thought, this is terrible. If I fall in love with the captain, I'll be falling in love with another woman. But I was already in love, even though I hadn't seen her face. Her back was to me. Then slowly she swiveled around in her chair and held out her arms to me. It was the oddest thing. The captain was myself. I mean, a more powerful self, and also she was a lot older, though it didn't show in a physical way. There was something timeless about her. And I went right into her arms and was filled with such happiness. Then I woke up in the room and the moon was shining in and the curtains were fluttering like live things and I thought, I wish I could find that woman. Maybe I can track her down by following the feelings I had in the dream and trying to match them with a scenario in a novel I will write someday. Anyway, that was my dream. Disgraceful, isn't it? Dreaming about falling in love with myself. Don't you find it disgraceful after your godlike vision embracing everything from unborn souls to creatures of the sea?"

"No, I don't find it disgraceful at all. Don't forget. I'm in love with the captain myself."

"Oh, but she was much better than I am. She was *more* than I am."

"Yes, but you dreamed her," Felix pointed out.

From then on, Clare spent her nights in the breezy room until her mother came. Then she changed the sheets and moved out her books and journal and slept with Felix in the "ordinary" seafront room. The first time Lily arrived at the cottage, she was informed of the room's propensities. "You'll have an important dream the first night," Clare told her. "Or maybe even a vision. You'll understand something you never understood before." "It's a very nice room," Lily had told them after spending the first night. But if the room had revealed any secrets to her, she wasn't telling them. "I slept so well" was all her daughter could get out of her. Lily was not the type who shared dreams or night thoughts. She told what she wanted to tell, and she told it with charm and imagination. She also had an equally charming way of not telling things. Once, when she was visiting them in New York, Felix watched Clare refill Lily's wineglass many times in an effort to pump her for details of her marriage to Clare's father. Lily held forth obligingly with wit and animation, drank her wine, and managed to tell Clare nothing more memorable than how well Campion had played tennis and how handsome he had looked in uniform.

"Don't you want your turn in the breezy room?" Clare asked Felix each summer when they came back to "No Saints." "It seems unfair of me to hog it, when you were the one who discovered it."

"No, you have it till your mother comes. I'll visit you there, if I may."

"You're welcome anytime."

Thus it became established. It was Clare's room for the first week. Then Lily's. Then Lily and Ralph's, when he came to pick her up. It mystified Felix how they carped at each other or let several hours pass without addressing each other directly, then crawled complacently into the same bed and slept side by side through the night. Ralph, ignoring Clare's invitation to "spread out" in the adjoining room, might leave his open suitcase on its bed: that was all. What his nighttime visions had been in the breezy room, no one knew. It could be, thought Felix, lying awake by himself in the "ordinary" room on the first night after their fourth summer, that no one ever asked him.

The only other person who had slept in the breezy room during their occupancy had been Clare's editor, the summer before, after her family had left. An amiable bookish man who never talked about his thoughts or feelings, but who was quite happy to tell you who had sung Mimi in *La Bohème* at the Met in 1948, or refresh your memory about minor characters in nineteenth-century novels, he sat on the beach listening to Gregorian chants on earphones and taking frequent solitary dips in the ocean. There was something lonely and boyish about him, Felix had thought, even though he was a sixty-year-old grandfather and a respected and successful man. Before everyone retired the first night, Clare told him what to expect in the breezy room. "That sounds lovely," he said affably, "but I seldom dream. Or at least I don't remember my dreams." The next morning at breakfast he reported that he had dreamed he was in the middle of a desert, watching an archaeological dig. "I knew the names of all the archaeologists, and I knew that they had just uncovered the tomb of a goddess, but I couldn't manage to get close enough to see what they had found. I was sorry about that." And he had smiled at them wistfully and buttered another piece of toast for himself. "I really did want to see what the artifacts of a goddess would be like." A week later, back in New York, he met a dynamic young woman half his age at a publishing party. Eight months later, he called up all his friends and stunned them by announcing he was putting an end to his forty-year marriage. "It is something I have to do," he told Clare over the phone. "Some people will understand, others won't, and I am going to cause a great deal of pain. But not to do it would be much worse. It would be like refusing a gift from the gods." "Or the goddess?" suggested Clare. From the way he chuckled, Clare told Felix later, she couldn't tell if he remembered his presageful dream in the breezy room at "No Saints," or whether he was just being agreeable, but Clare herself felt that there were interesting connections to be made.

So. Instances accrued of the breezy room's powers. Whether they came from an auspicious positioning of windows and furniture, or from some ancient affinity between the soul and the sea, or, as revelations were reported over breakfast and important dreams guaranteed by Clare to new guests, from the power of suggestion, there was evidence for belief that the room could tell you something if you were ready to listen.

What would it tell Snow, who was arriving on Thursday and bringing the boy? Clare was giving up the room three days early for Snow. She had planned this summer's guest schedule with the meticulousness of a hostess determined to see all the people she wanted to see without subjecting enemies or rivals to unbearable proximity. Snow had not forgiven Ralph and Lily for making her look bad at the custody hearings. So she was to come Thursday, driving the new car that Clare had helped her buy, and they would get to know her, "draw her out," that was Clare's plan, until Sunday morning. Then she would pack up her things and drive away before Ralph and Lily arrived. She would leave the boy behind at the beach so the grandparents could have their monthly visit with him. And two days later Ralph would take Jason back to his mother and leave Lily at the beach to have her time alone with Clare. Then Rafe would arrive the following weekend in his little sports car crammed to the gills with his comforts: the eiderdown, the ice chest, the Walkman and the tapes and the Panama Jack Trophy Oil, the multicolored beach garb and evening wear. Of course there would be one family member who would stay for the whole time, his irrecoverable presence making the silent centerpiece of this year's gathering.

Felix was most curious about Snow. At last he was to meet the diminutive purple-eyed vixen. How would they get on? What would they all talk about? Did she drink wine? Would Clare promise her a night of revelation in the breezy room? Would she tell them if she had one? It interested him very much: Snow, the awaited and treasured guest, coming to sleep in the magic room of the beach house rented to him by the son-in-law of a late governor. The opposite ends of society coming to meet. It was such an American story.

He turned onto his other side. An image of his red-haired daughter flared out at him from the ocean-washed darkness. What was she doing back at the house in New York? What made him so sure she was *at* the house? It was Saturday night. But since she had been back from Israel she appeared to have no boyfriends. At least none that she brought home. And he had always encouraged her to bring them home. Ever since he had accepted the fact that his little Liesl, his *Mädi*, was in every sense a normal, modern girl, he had worked hard at being a good sport about boyfriends. He was too inveterately of the Old World to stand at the stove and cheerfully fry up pancakes for them after they had spent the night in his daughter's bed (as the movie-producer father of Lizzie's college roommate did, according to Lizzie), but he had not been deaf to creaks on the stairs during the tenure of Mike the paramedic, the young man he had liked best of all, and he knew that on nights when he was abroad, or when he and Clare were out of town, that Lizzie might be curled up alone under her satin comforter watching TV—or, equally, she might not be alone. He knew, moreover, that at some unspecified moment during Lizzie's college years he had given her his tacit release: *I accept that you are a woman now, but please stay on in our house till you marry, I can better protect you that way.* They always had been able to let each other know things without words. And, without words, she had seemingly acquiesced: *Okay, Pop, we'll keep our show going for a while longer. It suits my love of comfort and it suits my style.* Her style, pert to the point of impudence, like that of many of her American contemporaries, was nevertheless as Old World as his own when it came to personal pride and demeanor. She thought too much of herself to be vulgar or double-dealing. Those telltale creaks on the stairs had occurred only *after* he had told her how fond he was of her forthright, idealistic paramedic and even hinted shamelessly at what a pleasant son-in-law Mike would make. And she would recoil as much as he from any pancake breakfasts the following morning with everybody shlepping around in pajamas. Even when he and Clare were not in town, he had faith in Lizzie's good sense and discrimination. Since the departure of Mike, there had been no steady young man, but Felix had perfect confidence that his daughter would never bring home anyone dangerous. As far as he knew, she had never gone in for

the dangerous sort. If anything, she had tended towards nebbishes. That was why Felix had been so delighted with Mike.
He had been sweet and let Lizzie control him, but he wasn't
a nebbish.

Yet since she had come back from visiting her cousins in Israel,
she had brought no young men to the house, nebbishes or
otherwise. There was a new solemnity to her. She stayed in her
room a lot, reading books about Judaism, and when the three of
them went out for a Chinese meal, she shunned her old favourite
mu shu pork, and would not order any of the shrimp dishes,
either. At home she refused Clare's veal paprika, ostentatiously
helping herself only to the brown rice and salad, and when Felix
made a few lighthearted queries as to the origin of this sudden
kosher fervor (for none of his aunt's children, or their children,
either, kept kosher kitchens, Lizzie had reported on her return),
she shrugged dolefully and said she didn't want to spoil anyone
else's appetite, but that, once you really thought about it, it *was*
pretty awful to eat pieces of some poor animal in a sauce made
from its mother's milk.

The trip to Israel, which had cost Felix a pretty penny, had
not been an overwhelming success. Except for her climb with
her young cousins to Masada—the only part of the visit that
seemed to meet her expectations—Lizzie told Felix she might as
well have gone to Minnesota. "They all had reddish-blond hair
and tans from being outside all the time, and all the boys *and*
girls seemed to talk about was their military service." "You must
remember they're a new nation," Felix told her. "They've had
to protect themselves. And it's a hot country, Liesl. People are
outdoors more, and they get tans. You yourself have reddish-
blond hair. Why shouldn't your cousins? You didn't really
expect some dark little people wearing heavy black clothes,
sitting inside and squinting over the Torah. Or did you? If so,
maybe I should have bought you a ticket to Crown Heights
instead of Tel Aviv."

To which Lizzie's reproachful reply was "Oh, Pop. Everything is a joke to you, isn't it?"

Clare's diagnosis was that Lizzie might be going through a
religious phase. "I recognize a few of the symptoms from mine.
The first thing you do, you try to muffle the unserious parts of
yourself, the way Lizzie is trying to put a cap on her usual
brightness and sass. I mean, look how she denies herself her
comebacks. She always withdraws from the field and lets me
win now, when we have our little exchanges. I remember when

I was thirteen and decided to dedicate myself to the Virgin Mary, even though I wasn't a Catholic and couldn't join the Sodality with the Catholic girls. I also went around trying not to smile, not that I was ever much of a *smiler,* but it turned out I smiled more times during the day than I'd ever realized. And every time I did, during my religious phase, my face felt as if it were going to crack and I loathed myself for being so trivial when there were so many sorrows and serious matters in the world. You never saw pictures or statutes of the Virgin Mary laughing. Another symptom is you get critical of everybody. I was even critical of my idol, Sister Patrick, who had probably inspired the whole thing: even she smiled . . . and laughed . . . far too much to suit me. And once in the cafeteria, when I saw her butter her roll and bite into it, I remember thinking what a pity it was that nuns had to eat. Of course I was only thirteen and Lizzie's twenty-six. But that doesn't mean she isn't hit just as hard; harder, maybe, because it's come late in life. Just as adults suffer more when they come down with childhood diseases like chickenpox or mumps."

"Yes, but those books she's reading are about Jewish observances more than about any relationship to a God. I don't like to go into her room when she's out, but I must confess I stepped in, just for a minute, the other day, and looked at the titles. Nothing about the ancient mysteries, nothing at all about the Kabbalah, which I was fascinated with as a young man. No it's that hairsplitting stuff about how to set the table and where to hang a mezuzah, all that sixteenth-century codified ritual that neither my father nor my mother could take seriously. Why is she doing this? It hurts me to see her muffle herself. Why should she want to? She's been brought up an American girl, with the whole world open to her. Why should she want to shut herself up in a box of tiresome, outdated old rules? Especially since she didn't even *like* Israel. I don't understand."

"Perhaps it's a form of rebellion," said Clare. "My solemn stint with the Virgin Mary was, though I didn't see it that way at the time, of course. I was seeking to align myself with what I thought of as her coolness, her stoic, statuesque qualities. Mind you, we're talking largely about a certain statue of her in the school chapel. I loved the *statue* largely. I see now it had nothing to do with the deep cosmic mysteries or a genuine religious impulse. She was the lovely, remote antithesis of all the things that made me afraid or uncomfortable at the time. I don't remember giving much thought to what the real person might have been like. For someone like Sister Patrick, I think she had a much bigger significance, to do with intercession and a kind of vast womanly sympathy that the earth needs to keep healing itself. But I just grabbed at the part I needed at the time."

"I wonder what it is that Lizzie needs that is making her grab at kashrut recipes and tefillin procedures."

"Why don't you ask her? Let's ask her down to the beach this year. We never have before. That suddenly strikes me as a strange omission. Why have we never invited Lizzie to the island?"

"Well, because it's your place for being with your family."

"But isn't Lizzie my family, too, in a sense? I mean, Lizzie and I have been together, through *you,* for almost eight years. Under one roof for a lot of that time. Ralph and I were together under one roof, through Lily, for seven years, and, for better or worse, I consider him my family. I can't imagine why we haven't asked Lizzie to the beach. It might be just the change of atmosphere she needs. All those Confederate flags flapping in the breeze. All that good forbidden shellfish. You can take her to Charleston one day and show her the mansions on the Battery and have a heart-to-heart with her. A real Father and Daughter Day, just like old times."

"You know, that might not be a bad idea. Bless you, Clare. But will we have enough room for her? Where will she sleep?"

"She can sleep in that bedroom next to Lily's. After Ralph leaves. She and Lily would get on famously. And she should stay on until the weekend when Rafe comes down. Then he can show her the nightlife at Myrtle Beach."

But Lizzie, with a wan smile, had turned them down. It was sweet of them to want to include her, but, to be honest, she had been counting on having that time alone in the house. To do some serious reading and thinking.

"Sitting inside, in the beautiful June sunshine," lamented the miffed and baffled Felix. "Reading *The Jewish Catalog* and *The Second Jewish Catalog.* I didn't know they had such books now. Sort of how-to books, with lots of photos and little cartoon drawings. A *Whole Earth*-type, do-it-yourself kit for becoming a Jew. I was appalled. I don't like myself in the role of a snooping father, but she leaves them open on her bed. It's almost as if she's chosen the pages that she knows will irritate me the most.

I wish I knew whether this is a rebellion or a conversion. Frankly, I am praying for rebellion. Rebellion from what? Because I didn't bring her up with all those old shibboleths my parents saw fit not to bring me up with? Perhaps. But I don't want my Lizzie to lose her Lizzie-ness."

"Maybe what she's doing is searching through Jewishness to see if she can find any lost parts of herself," Clare had finally suggested. "Maybe she's looking for *more* Lizzie-ness."

"The Good Lord help us all!" Felix had expostulated with a laugh. But the idea had made him feel better again.

Felix turned on his other side and sighed loudly. A fatherly sound of fond exasperation. Then, abdicating that role for the night, he arranged his long legs (knotted now with a few varicose veins inherited from his mother) in a scissorslike position and jiggled the bottom leg in a special, steady rhythm he had employed since early childhood to lull himself to sleep. The loud ocean sang to him out of the Southern darkness and he felt his head draining of responsibilities and thoughts. Would death be anything like this?

Clare had first heard about this island from Dr. Anthony Gallant, whose parents and grandparents had vacationed there as children and, in turn, had brought their children. Dr. Anthony had many pet stories about "The Island," as he and all its aficionados called it, as if there were no other island to distinguish it from, as far as they were concerned. Dr. Anthony had known Clare since she was a little girl; he had removed her tonsils and adenoids and, in a follow-up visit to the hospital room, the tonsils and adenoids of her stuffed bear. In his status as family physician and friend, he had kept watch over her student life at St. Clothilde's, not quite trusting the education of a young girl to women so perverse as to forfeit the chance of marriage to a real man in order to wear the wedding ring of Jesus Christ. Whenever he dropped by to see Clare's grandmother, who suffered from angina, he would question Clare carefully about the school and ask if she had any compositions to show him. He threw his head back and laughed when he read her story about a dog on holiday, from the dog's point of view. She had illustrated it with a drawing of the dog with a pasted pillow feather sticking out of its mouth: the dog had chased a duck. He had drawn his snowy eyebrows together when he read a later essay of hers entitled "A Man's Reach Should Exceed His Grasp," written in the eighth grade under the influence of Sister Patrick's passion for Browning. Then he had taken out his prescription pad and written one long word on it: *megalopsychia.* "You will suffer chronically from this all your life," he told her, tearing off the paper and presenting it to her with a flourish. "But what does it mean?" she had asked, frowning at the strange word that had the sound of a very undesirable condition. "I should have known!" he exclaimed with delighted sarcasm. "You go to school to all those Papists and they don't bother teaching you derivation of *Greek* roots." With obvious relish he had remedied their default. *"Psyche* is the soul, or the human mind. *Megalo* is the prefix meaning large or great. If a patient has megalocardia, he has an abnormal enlargement of the heart. You can die from that. You won't die from megalopsychia, but it will cause you some suffering. High-minded people always suffer. But if you learn to temper your megalopsychia with laughter and feminine charm, you will become an enviable woman."

Enviable in what way, he had not bothered to specify. But he didn't seem at all surprised when she became a published writer; neither did he seem worried as the years passed and she didn't bring home a husband. Yet he had been so hard on the nuns for not wanting husbands. Of course neither he nor his sister had ever married. Miss Alicia was an out-and-out old maid, you could never have imagined her as anything else, even when she was a girl, Clare's grandmother said; whereas Dr. Anthony— and here Ellen Buchel always curled her lip a little—Dr. Anthony had dated a generation of girls, then those girls' daughters, then their granddaughters. For whatever reasons, Dr. Anthony continued to approve of Clare, as if he himself were charting her course—her travels, her growing reputation as a writer, her residence in remote un-Southern places, where surely she did not live the life of a nun. And when she came home to visit, they always found an opportunity to sit together nursing their drinks and telling each other the sorts of stories they knew would most appeal. Clare kept him up to date on her accomplishments, but made sure to temper her recitations with laughter and feminine charm; and he, well, as the years passed by, he was likely to confide the strangest things, sometimes in the middle of a gentlemanly reminiscence of the Romantic Old Days. Once he stopped suddenly in the midst of his description of the Rhododendron Ball of 1925, when he danced all night with a girl who sailed to England the following week to marry a viscount, who was to treat her brutally and send her home years later when her face lift was a failure, and said, looking at Clare significantly from under his bushy white eyebrows, "But you know, I could never *have fun* with the nice girls. For some reason, I just never could. I suppose that's why I never married." Clare nodded understandingly and then transferred her gaze to the depths of her drink. She didn't say a word; he would have been displeased if she had. Nevertheless, she knew exactly what he was telling her, this canny old bachelor, and he knew she had understood his meaning. It had even occurred to her that he might assume she suffered from the same malady: that she could not *have fun* with the nice boys. And naturally she could not bring home one of the other kind. Of course women could fake having fun, whereas it was a more serious problem for men. Dr. Anthony Gallant, the old roué, had probably gone to his grave believing Clare to be a female version of himself. A high-minded one, of course. What would the old doctor have thought of Felix? Hated him, probably. He would have been jealous that she had at last found someone nice to have fun with and consoled himself by crossing an elegant ankle when he was home again and remarking to Miss Alicia caustically, "Well, Sissi, the Chosen People certainly grab a good thing when they see it. I hope Miss Clare will be happy with Mr. Rohr."

An era had died with the passing of Dr. Anthony and his kind—the last generation to believe in their stories and feel no modern self-consciousness or guilt about the reasons for all those self-serving myths and legends, the highly embroidered tapestry of the sacred Old Locale. Many people would say such an era was better off dead. Clare herself thought so, up to a point. She had learned to see the flaws in the fabric. She knew perfectly well that her fate would not have been a happy one if she had been born into the heyday of the society Dr. Anthony loved to describe: a society distrustful of new ideas and strangers, where archaic customs were respected more than living accomplishments, and mediocrity often hid behind grade and style. Dr. Anthony and his sister had been prisoners of it themselves, probably more than either realized. They both spoke far more of the past than of the present and, for all their independent ways, it was their memory of *what their parents and grandparents had been* that gave them their belief in themselves; not their own quick minds and *élan vital* and ability to entertain others. The conundrum was, would they have been their same attractive, superior selves if they *hadn't* felt themselves children of the old privileged myths? Just as, conversely, Clare often wondered if she would have developed into quite a different person—or, rather, failed to develop—if she had been born into one of those families whose belief in the divine right of their clan exempted her from having to strive for anything more. Julia had once told her that she idealized the very institutions that would have kept her down if she hadn't been so diligent, and so *fortunate,* in her escape from them. But Clare had argued back that she *didn't* admire those institutions, she didn't think she idealized them, but she wanted to know about a certain kind of security she felt she had missed out on. She wanted, for reasons she was still discovering, the experience of having had it. So she made reparations to herself the only way she could: through observation and imagination. And when you dwelt on something closely, in great detail, truly trying to apprehend it from the inside out, loving aspects were bound to slip in. *Tout comprendre, c'est tout pardonner.* And then, having understood, having loved through the rendering, no matter how much you might disapprove in principle, you could go on to understand something else.

All of which had something to do with why she had felt the spasm of homesickness for a place she had never been when, four springs ago, looking for a new vacation spot for Felix and herself, she had come across pictures and a brief description of Dr. Anthony's island in a book called *Southern Island Retreats.* There it was, "The Island," where a local cook named Agrippa had a pan of hot gingerbread waiting when the children came in from their morning swim, and sixteen-year-old Alicia Gallant, "walking out" with a young suitor on the dunes, slipped and punctured her bottom on a spiky plant called Spanish bayonet and lost her dignity, and where their father had told them stories of a summer club *his* father had belonged to on "The Island," a club called "The Gallivantin' Fish," for men only, which met each Friday from eleven in the morning until sundown. Each member brought his own wines and prepared dishes and a servant, and everyone played billiards and tenpins and then sat down for hours of feasting and drinking and the discussion of politics and the singing of songs.

> A gentleman came riding home
> As drunk as drunk could be.
> To find a horse within the stall
> Where his horse ought to be . . .

It was the island Dr. Anthony's mother had loved so much she started looking forward to next summer's visit while this summer's visit was still in progress. The summer of her last illness, they had taken her there, her husband carrying her frail body in his arms through three changes of trains, then up the Wacamaw River on a boat, so she could be carried from the house to the thatched-roof lookout and lie on a wicker chaise, watching the sea between naps. "And every summer after that, when my father brought Sissie and me back, we'd all three go up to the lookout first thing, and we could feel her presence there."

"One of the oldest beach resorts in the country," Clare's book said, "the island has been a favorite vacation retreat for Southerners since the late 1700s, when wealthy Carolina planters, discovering that the deadly 'Country Fever' (malaria) would not cross the salt marshes, built ample, sturdy beach houses with gabled roofs and wraparound porches. Here on 'The Island,' as the original cottage owners called it, the families hid from the deadly scourge from early May until the first hard frost."

Clare had phoned the two real-estate brokers on the island and said she would like to rent one of those old cottages for several weeks in early summer. She was told by both brokers that the "old" cottages were still in families and not available, and the newer ones, which were rented, had been booked a year in advance by people who had stayed there before. She detected a note of satisfaction in the deep, low-country accents of both brokers. Which made her all the more determined to breach their exclusive little domain. She would have to get in via an insider. She did not dare phone Miss Alicia Gallant down in Mountain City; she had never been the hit with the wry old sister that she had been with the brother. To get on famously with Alicia Gallant, you had to admire her unreservedly, as Ralph Quick did, or else know yourself, beyond a sliver of doubt, to be her equal. "Oh, everyone *I* knew on 'The Island' is long dead, now," Miss Alicia might feel perfectly justified in telling Clare. Then, hanging up the phone, she would shrug pertly in the direction of her family members, preserved in little gold frames on the piano, and demand of them, "I did the right thing, didn't I? The poor girl wouldn't have enjoyed herself down there even if I were to have remembered Mr. Lachicotte's granddaughter still rents a cottage out, or did the last I heard. Our poor little 'Island' would have been much too plain for Clare and that continental gentleman of hers."

Clare called a magazine editor who had published some of her stories and who, she knew, kept up an extensive Old Boy network down in the Carolinas, where he was born and raised. "Hal, I want to rent one of those old cottages on that island everybody just calls 'The Island,'" she told him, "but I can't get to first base. It seems you have to have been there before they'll allow you to go." "Yeah, I know," he said, laughing. "It's like trying to get a union card. You have to have a job first. But you can't get a job till you've got the card. Give me a couple of days, will you, and I'll see what I can find out." In a couple of days he had called back. "Well, I was able to get you one for the second half of May and the beginning of June. But it was only built in 1936. Is that good enough?" Clare said it was great, but how on earth had he managed it? Oh, an old buddy from Charleston knew a man who owned a cottage on 'The Island.' The three weeks happened to be free because the people who usually rented the cottage then were in China on some kind of exchange program. "The owner's name is Buddy Fauquier," the editor told Clare. "He married the Governor's daughter." He gave her Mr. Fauquier's address and said it was customary to send a check for half the rent in advance.

Clare and Felix arrived too early at the cottage the first year. White-haired, military-looking Mr. Fauquier was vacuuming the rooms, bare-chested and barefoot; his daughter, her hair covered by an old bandanna, was washing a sinkful of dirty dishes. The landlord greeted them politely, but he was clearly put out by their premature arrival. They fled back to the mainland "to do some shopping," and resolved to each other not to return until at least fifteen minutes past three p.m., the arrival time Fauquier had designated in his letter. Clare felt they had gotten off to an awkward start on two counts. Her initial faux pas, though it had been the editor's fault, was to have sent that first check made out to "Buddy Fauquier." How she had cringed when it was returned soon after among her canceled checks, primly endorsed "Philip Waverly Fauquier Jr." on the back. What a familiar, presumptuous woman, he must have thought. And then Felix, tired from the long drive down to New York and feeling inconvenienced because the cottage wasn't ready, had glowered and been rather brusque with Fauquier, who probably thought they were a thoroughly ill-mannered couple. The other unpromising development had been the appearance of the house itself. Even though she had been warned by the

editor that it was not one of the really old cottages and that the
old-timers proudly called their island "Arrogantly Shabby," she
had expected something more *picturesquely* shabby. Not just a
beach shack painted blue with white trim, with dark rooms and
watermarked furniture and lampshades swinging wildly in the
wind and those terrible-looking black skillets with years of grease
burned into them that she had spotted hanging from a cast-iron
ring during her first quick look at the kitchen, where the
Fauquier daughter in her bandanna had been tackling the
dishes. While Felix and she had been marking time on the
mainland, they had bought a whole set of aluminium pans,
mugs, cutlery, scouring pads, and a big red plastic salad bowl.
"We won't touch any of their stuff," Clare said. "We'll make it
habitable somehow. Anyway, remember, it's only three weeks
and it *is* the beach after all." She was much more worried about
everything than Felix seemed to be; she felt she was to blame for
dragging him into this nostalgic excursion. Nostalgia for
someone else's past!

But when they returned to the island at a quarter past three,
they found their landlord and his daughter graciously awaiting
them. Fauquier was wearing a T-shirt now, with a Citadel
bulldog on it, and the daughter had removed the bandanna;
her tawny hair looked freshly washed and curled. An American
flag was flying from a horizontal mast at the front of the cottage,
and Clare wondered if he had done it for their benefit, to make
them feel less alien among all the Confederate flags and Palmetto
State flags flapping from the other cottages. Fauquier, still
barefoot, led them on a tour of the house. He showed particular
pride in the wet bar upstairs, with its plentiful array of glasses
for every kind of drink. Over the counter hung a framed
yellowed page from a newspaper: the complete text of King
Edward VIII's abdication speech. On the kitchen table was a
green cut-glass bowl filled with red and pink oleander, and upstairs in the living room, on the butler's table and a large drop-
leaf table by the window, were little china pitchers filled with
asters, marigolds, and candytuft. "Oh, did you do these?" Clare
asked the daughter. "No, ma'am, that's Pap," said the girl,
nodding proudly at Fauquier, "he likes to do that when people
come." The landlord took them out on the porch, not fifty feet
from the sea, and pointed out the hammock. There was an old-
fashioned tin washbucket, filled with fresh water, where they
could rinse off their feet when they came up from the beach.

The sea breeze whipping his cotton-soft hair, Fauquier stood there telling them stories about the man who had built this cottage, the chief engineer of a famous local bridge. "He used the cypress pilings left over from the job, and then he went around to lumber yards and got what is called pecky cypress, because of all the holes in it. When I bought the cottage in 'fifty-nine, I asked this old colored fellow who'd helped with the construction, I asked him, 'Wasn't it kind of extravagant to put pine paneling throughout an entire beach house?' 'Naw, suh,' he said, 'my boss didn't pay no more than twenty-five cents for every stick of wood in this house.' 'Now, surely he must have paid more than that,' I said. 'Naw, suh,' he told me, 'in those days people done paid you to take *away* their pecky cypress. That was befo' it got its social ability,'" Fauquier laughed. "That's what he called it: 'social ability.' Well, Becky and I'll leave you folks now. We've got to run on down to Charleston." He put a fond hand on the girl's shoulder. "She's got a dance to go to tonight. Anything else you all need to make you comfortable?" "There wouldn't happen to be an Episcopal church around here, would there?" Clare asked him. "My mother is coming down next week and she never misses a Sunday." "There surely is," said Fauquier, looking pleased. "All Saints. Go straight across the causeway and just continue on the same road. You'll see signs. It's my church, too, when I'm down here. As a matter of fact, this cottage is named for it, in a way. We call it '*No* Saints.'" "In that case, we should feel right at home," said Felix, who had been charmed by the entire performance and had recovered his good humor. "I hope so, sir. Hope you will," said Fauquier, shaking Felix's hand.

Several days later, Clare was unwrapping some peaches and tomatoes bought at a local fruit stand. The woman had been out of brown bags and had taped them up in some pages from the Charleston Sunday newspaper. Clare's eye was caught by a cluster of "society" photos taken at a charity auction ball for the Spoleto Festival. ("Among the young crowd were Miss Rebecca Fauquier, who was presented at the St. Cecelia Ball last January, and her escort, Mr. Trey Smyth-Huger...") "Look," Clare had showed Felix, "that girl washed all those dishes and cleaned our cottage and then took off her bandanna and went to the ball like Cinderella. It's from the day after we arrived, this newspaper. That must have been the dance she was going to in Charleston." Back in New York, Clare loved telling this story: only she changed the Spoleto Ball into the St. Cecelia Ball because it made a better story. Many Northerners had heard of the St. Cecelia Ball, but didn't know whether it took place in January or May. And even in Clare's own mind, the Fauquier daughter became "The Cinderella of the St. Cecelia Ball."

Although there were knobs missing from the gas range, and one of the toilets sang until you took off the lid and fiddled with the apparatus, and the fluorescent light in the kitchen went on a half hour after you had flipped the switch, there was nothing vulgar in the cottage. Except for a framed Botticelli reproduction, a close-up of Venus rising from the sea, which Clare took down and hid behind a dresser because the position of Venus's hand on her breast looked too much as though she were checking for lumps, the contents of the place made an appealing ambience. The large carved pelican, the shells, the woven grass baskets hanging from hooks on the walls, the amateur watercolor portraits of two Airedales, the books and magazines provided intimate glimpses into the individual and communal tastes of a family. You could read the people in what they had left behind. Someone knew a good chintz pattern; someone cared about history and not just Southern history. There was Sandburg's *Lincoln,* and biographies of Roosevelt and Kennedy, and the Morgenthau *Diaries,* as well as Bruce Catton's Civil War volumes and mildewed stacks of the *South Carolina Historical Magazine.* When it was too hot at midday to be on the beach, Clare sat cross-legged on the floor of the dark, cool living room upstairs with its paintings of ducks in marshes, and leafed through the old magazines, skimming the correspondence of a Yankee prisoner in Charleston to his parents in Maine ("I am *disgusted* with the Confederacy"), or finding strange bits of information in colonial tax reports and censuses (a free Negro in the parish of St. George had owned nine slaves); from this general historical snooping she proceeded shamelessly to the contents of a certain cupboard beneath the bookshelves and began researching the Fauquiers through the interesting debris they had seen fit to conceal from their paying guests but not remove when they had turned the cottage into a rental property. There were pictures of Negroes with white children. An old hand-tinted photograph of a queenly African woman, long-necked and statuesque, wearing a white turban and a high-necked green blouse with a jeweled brooch and holding a baby in its christening dress. Clare guessed it would be a parent of either Fauquier or his wife, with his or her Mammy. A blown-up photo from the early 1970s, judging from the short skirts of the two girls, one of about nine, the other perhaps fifteen, snuggling up on either side of a severe old lady, black as ebony, wearing rimless spectacles, a white lace dress, white picture hat, white gloves and shoes, and an orchid pinned to her shoulder. Clare recognized the Cinderella of the St. Cecelia Ball in the younger girl. What was the occasion this time? Why was the old woman being celebrated? There was a posed formal portrait of a genial-faced gentleman, his large, smooth hands crossed on the desk in front of him. That must be the landlord's father-in-law, the Governor. An eight-by-ten photo of a white Charleston-style house with piazzas on two floors. Whose home? A photo of what appeared to be an ordinary public school of the 1930s. Whose childhood memories?

What mystery am I trying to solve here? Clare had asked herself, going through the Fauquiers' things. Why should I care what these pictures mean to people I don't know? All of them were enclosed in cheap dime-store frames. Once each must have hung in a specially chosen place on the "pecky cypress" walls of the summer cottage. But she had actually been miffed when she discovered a little black volume of memorial addresses delivered in the U.S. Congress eulogizing the passing of a beloved senator. There was his picture: another portrait of the genial man with the large hands. She read the little book. Not only had he been a governor, but he had been a U.S. senator. Moreover, five of his forebears, one of the eulogies said, also had been governors of the state. Now, that's too much, Clare had thought, oddly discomfited. Why should she be vexed to discover that Fauquier's father-in-law had been more illustrious than the editor had suggested? What did it have to do with her? Why should it threaten her that some people have fathers-in-law or fathers or grand-fathers who had been governors or senators? Was it something to do with power or security or both? What difference would it have made, how would it have affected the things in her life that mattered most, if her grandfather had been a senator with illustrious forebears instead of a railroad man whose father had been a Swiss immigrant? Or her father a governor of his state instead of a dead serviceman? Or was she discomfited because she was afraid different things must have mattered to her if she had had other origins: that *she* might have been different? Different how? Different more, or different less? And by whose standards? Did she, as many people did, subscribe to the notion that you were more if you came from illustrious forebears? But what did their achievements have to do with you? On the other hand, maybe there was something equally spurious in believing yourself to be more than others because you had distinguished yourself in ways they had not. And why had she felt it so very important to distinguish herself in the first place? Had she seized on her most promising skill and diligently whetted it into a weapon to gain power over others? Or would she have become a writer no matter what, because she could not stop herself from imagining the lives of other people? Had her art been born out of her particular circumstances and necessities, or did there exist at her core some pure, writerly essence that would have had to express itself whether she had been a governor's daughter or someone with the background of, say, Snow Mullins?

What of me is singularly *mine*, and would be so regardless of whom I was born to and how or where I grew up? What of anybody's was purely her own or his own, if you took away family and religion and upbringing and social class? Four summers later, in the cottage the Fauquiers called "No Saints," on the island of Dr. Anthony's childhood happiness, Clare was still occupied with the question, though the focus of her research was about to change as she prepared for Snow's visit.

She had more or less satisfied herself as to the lineaments of the Fauquier family. She believed she had discovered the kinds of things that gave meaning to their lives and some of the sources from which they operated. Through knowing them a little and living in their cottage, she had located their essentials by studying the particulars. And once you had the essentials, you could grasp the typical. The Fauquiers were a prize find, really; you couldn't go much further if you were looking for a specimen of a certain kind of Southern family. A specimen that might, moreover, be soon extinct. Mrs. Fauquier, "the Governor's daughter," was a shy, unassuming lady with a stammer. Though she was somewhere in her early sixties, a fey girl looked out on you from oblique green eyes. She had bought a rustic old inn at the other end of "The Island" and ran it successfully by herself, from June to September, yet there was a helpless, otherworldly quality about her. Fauquier drove to "The Island" on weekends, looked over her accounts for her, told charming stories to the guests, and went to the bank for her on Monday morning before returning to his law practice in Charleston. During the week she went about in her vague, bewildered-child manner, quietly stammering orders to cooks and yard boys and maids and repairmen. She was deferential, almost apologetic, seeming to want people to believe the inn ran itself without her—in spite of her, even. She brought a boy over to "No Saints" to mow the lawn, but they couldn't find the lawn mower. "Oh, dear," she said, laughing, shrugging helplessly. She and the boy got back in the car. "I'm sorry to have disturbed you all for nothing," she called shyly to Clare. They drove away. During Felix and Clare's third stay in the cottage, the refrigerator began giving them mild electrical shocks whenever they opened it. They took to using a towel so they wouldn't feel them. "I hate to bother Mrs. Fauquier," Clare said, "she has so much on her mind with that inn." "True," said Felix, "and one eats less this way." But then the shocks got worse; they traveled through the pipes and leaped out at them when they turned on the upstairs faucets; Clare's editor received a nasty jolt when he started to turn on the outdoor shower. Clare tried to phone Mrs. Fauquier at the inn but got a busy signal for an hour. Exasperated and angry at her own reluctance to "bother" the Governor's daughter, Clare flung herself into the car and drove to the other end of the island. The blue-haired lady at the inn's reception desk was on the phone and hardly looked up when she entered from the screened porch. "I'm looking for Mrs. Fauquier," Clare finally interrupted her during a pause. "It's kind of an emergency." The lady waved her to a row of wicker chairs and continued telling someone in an animated drawl how it had rained buckets through a hole in the tent at the wedding and the guests had tracked mud into the house. So this saga, and not inn business, accounted for the busy signal Clare had been getting for the past hour. Hunched in one of the wicker chairs, she swelled with impatience and indignation. This was taking arrogance and shabbiness a little *too* far. To be paying six hundred and fifty dollars a week, plus state tax, for the privilege of being shocked by your refrigerator and faucets and then to be ignored by some antiquated blue-haired belle as if you were an unwelcome peddler . . . Clare prepared and refined several cutting sentences to release on Mrs. Fauquier as soon as this chatterbox bitch got off the phone and located her. The whole world of Southern manners, where you had to put up with this sort of behavior or else make a scene and brand yourself as common, suddenly seemed a crock of shit—and old shit, at that.

Presently Mrs. Fauquier wandered out of another room, looking dazed and bewildered, wiping her hands absently on her green cotton wraparound skirt with little white whales printed on it. "Why, h-h-hello," she stammered, obviously startled to see Clare here. She looked self-effacingly towards the blue-haired bitch, who suddenly saw fit to cut short her telephone chronicle. "This lady wants to see you," she told Mrs. Fauquier brightly, managing to make it seem that Clare had just that minute walked through the door. "Oh, is anything wrong?" asked Mrs. Fauquier in a guilty, frightened tone, as if she already knew there was, and, moreover, that it was all her fault. Clare abandoned her caustic prepared remarks and, as gently and protectively as she could, explained about the shocks. "I really hate to bother you, but it's kind of unpleasant to use the refrigerator, and then my editor from New York almost got knocked down when he touched the outdoor shower." "But that's awful," said Mrs. Fauquier. "I feel just terrible." She stood there, abject and sorrowful, her hands hanging uselessly at her sides; they might all have been electrocuted already and there was nothing more to be done. "I think we need to call a good electrician," suggested Clare. "And probably as soon as possible, since it's Friday afternoon. I think we should do something right away. It might be hard to get someone on the weekend." Mrs. Fauquier remained motionless, as if in a trance. "If you tell me who you use, *I'd* be glad to call," Clare prompted. "Oh, n-no," said Mrs. Fauquier, "I'll c-call. There used to be this nice man. I wonder if he's still on 'The Island.' He did it as a sort of free-lance thing." She turned to the blue-haired bitch. "Mrs. Pettigrew, l-let me use your phone for a minute." The receptionist gave up her seat, but remained in the room, watching Clare suspiciously, while Mrs. Fauquier first spent some time trying to track down the nice free-lance electrician. His named was either Humphrey or Humphries, but his first name, Mrs. Fauquier was fairly sure, was Ted. There were several T. Humphreys or T. Humphrieses in the phone book, but the one Mrs. Fauquier had in mind seemed to have left the area. Then she made a series of calls to electricians, who were not in. She left messages, in her halting, deferential way, for them all, chatting some with the wives or whoever answered the phone.

Then she followed Clare back to "No Saints," where Felix and Clare's editor were beginning to wonder what had happened. Felix had tried phoning the inn several times, but the line was busy. He and the editor were having vodka tonics in the kitchen when Clare returned, trailed by the contrite Mrs. Fauquier. Both men stood up, and Clare introduced her editor, whom Mrs. Fauquier greeted as though he were some rare dignitary. "I am just so s-sorry about this," she said, and wafted dreamily towards the refrigerator with her hand outstretched placatingly, as one would approach a dog with a reputation for biting. "I wouldn't touch it, Mrs. Fauquier," warned Felix. "N-no, I guess not," she said, stopping short and casting an inquiring, reproachful glance at the appliance. "I just don't understand. It's only about seven years old. And I can't imagine how it could have got into the faucets. But the men will tell us. One of them should come soon. But what about all your f-food? And you can't use the faucets either." She stood looking from one to the other of them, in her bewildered-child way. In the soft kitchen gloom, you could see what a lovely girl she had been. They tried their best to console her. "The food's all right," said Felix. "It's cold. We just can't get to it for the moment, that's all." "The faucets on the *other* side of the house are fine," Clare told her. "It's just all the ones on the same side as the kitchen that shock." "I'm taking us all out to dinner this evening, anyway," said the editor, who was proudly wearing the new "Arrogantly Shabby" T-shirt Clare had bought for him. "Well," said Mrs. Fauquier, "I expect I'd better be getting back to the inn, then. But please phone me if none of the men come."

After she left, Clare drank a stiff vodka tonic and began to become unhinged. "Jesus Christ!" she shouted. "I mean, it's too much! Nobody will come and then it will be the weekend and if we try to phone over there to *tell* her nobody came, that blue-haired bitch will be describing society weddings on the phone and we won't get *through*. This woman is unreal. This whole situation is unbelievable." "It's so Southern," said the editor happily, despite having been electrified earlier in the day by the outdoor shower. They went out to a seafood place for an early dinner and came back mellowed. There was a truck parked in front of the cottage. A strikingly good-looking man in jeans and a faded workshirt was kneeling on the windwalk, testing the outdoor shower with his voltameter. In a thick lowland accent even Clare had trouble understanding, he explained to them how the instrument worked. He had already located the source of the shocks: someone had grounded the refrigerator, which had faulty wiring, to a main water pipe. (That nice free-lance electrician? Clare wondered.) Felix, fascinated by his accent, asked the young electrician to stay and have a drink. He couldn't, he said, he had promised Mrs. Fauquier to report to her at the inn as soon as he found the trouble. He unplugged the dangerous refrigerator for them before he left, and in the dusk they carried trays full of perishables upstairs to the small refrigerator in the wet bar. During the evening, the phone rang at least five times; each time it was one of the electricians for whom Mrs. Fauquier had left her distressed messages. None of them seemed put out when Clare told them the problem had been solved. "That's all right, then," every one of them said. "Just so's Mrs. Fauquier's been taken care of."

On Saturday afternoon, Mrs. Fauquier came by the cottage in an abstracted flutter and unloaded covered dishes from a tray. There was an oyster pie, a dish of wild rice, buttermilk biscuits, and a pecan pie. "Our cook made these f-for you . . . since you've been so inconvenienced." Guiltily, she had peeled back the aluminum foil covering the pecan pie and revealed a large wedge of empty space. "It was a wh-whole pie until a few minutes ago, but I'm afraid my little granddaughter got into it," she explained, smiling sadly. Then she reached into the pocket of her skirt and took out a wad of bills. She peeled off four hundred and thirty-nine dollars' worth of twenties, tens, and ones and left them in a pile on the kitchen counter. "A m-man's supposed to bring you a new refrigerator sometime today or tomorrow. If you wouldn't mind giving him these . . . I *think* it's the right amount."

On Saturday evening, just before dark, an elderly man drove up in a truck. He was very thin and stringy, tanned a leathery reddish-brown. He unloaded a refrigerator from the truck while they all watched in amazement. He carried it slowly on his back into the kitchen, slid it down to the floor, and accepted Felix's and the editor's help only in pushing the bad refrigerator out of the way so he could set up the good one in its place. He said he was sorry he couldn't load the old refrigerator in his truck and take it away tonight, because there was no one to help him. "I can load *down* but not *up*." He was seventy-three years old, he told them. He also declined Felix's offer of a drink, but invited them all to come and worship at his church on Sunday if they felt so inclined.

After he was gone, the three of them sat on the porch and drank and discussed Mrs. Fauquier. "The thing is," Clare kept saying in a querulous, puzzled voice, "that, despite all that flaky deference, I'm convinced she really doesn't care. She is above it all, or beyond it all, or something. If things go wrong, it's terrible, of course; if they go right, that's fine. But, either way, she's off in some dream and she's never going to wake from it." "It's probably why she makes a good innkeeper," said Felix. "Something is always going wrong at the inn. If you let it defeat you every time, you'd soon be a mess." "She *acts* defeated," Clare went on, puzzling it out, "but I really think it's because she wouldn't ever want anyone to say she was bossy or haughty. But . . . my God! Her vagueness, the indirect way she goes about things! Peeling off those four hundred and thirty-nine dollars like she did. We could have taken them and gone gambling in Myrtle Beach. I think they have gambling up there, or don't they?" "But she knew we wouldn't," said the editor. He chuckled into his drink; he was enjoying himself enormously. "When you consider," he mused, "that we didn't put in our complaint until late yesterday afternoon, and that it's the *weekend*, that little lady got quite a lot accomplished. I'd like to see anyone in *New York* get an electrician to come on Friday night and five more to call back, and get a new refrigerator delivered on his back on Saturday evening by a seventy-three-year-old man who invites us to worship at his church." "Perhaps we should go," suggested Felix. "What, exactly, is a Pentecostal Holiness church?" "I think he might be embarrassed if we showed up," said Clare. "You're probably right," agreed Felix. He started laughing. "And the slice cut out of the pie, that the little granddaughter ate. I liked that, too. I think I liked that best of all."

"It's so Southern," repeated the editor, shaking his head with dazzled amazement.

There was a Fauquier son, also, and two more daughters besides the Cinderella of the St. Cecelia Ball. Fauquier III was an athletic fellow in his twenties who called Clare "ma'am," to her chagrin, and made polite yet easy conversation. He rode over on his bike from the inn the first summer and demonstrated to them how, by hitting the fluorescent light in the kitchen with the broom handle at a certain spot, you could make it come on without waiting the thirty minutes. He had been living in Spain, he told them, playing soccer on a team, but his mother worried over his injuries so much that he finally decided to stop and come home. The following summer, he was there on a visit from Peru, where he had started a little export business in Christmas tree ornaments of woven straw. The third summer, he was back to stay for a while. His father had suffered a massive heart attack—two heart attacks, actually, one at the office and another in the ambulance on the way to the hospital. His family had reached Fauquier III just as he was about to set out for Machu Picchu—he supposed he'd have to go back and see it one of these days. He pretended to be disgusted with his father, who'd had friends sneak cigarettes to him in the hospital on the bottoms of fruit baskets, but he couldn't keep a tinge of macho pride out of his voice. He apologized for having painted the porch two shades of gray, but it had been almost dark when he did the second half and he hadn't noticed the mistake until the next day. His oldest sister worked as a decorator in Charleston; the new green sofa cover with white piping and the pillows with ducks on them were her doing. Cinderella was now working as a waitress in a new restaurant. The middle sister was the only one of them who was married. She was the mother of the pie-eating granddaughter. Clare and Felix met this sister during the third summer, when the Fauquiers invited them for dinner at the inn. She was a small-boned, pretty girl who habitually deprecated herself as her mother did. To hear her tell it, anything good or clever she had done had been pure accident! For a while, she and her husband had run a home for abused children, Fauquier told them. "They even had little Cara, who was scarcely more than a baby herself, helping to change the diapers of all those poor infants." Now she worked in a maximum-security facility for juvenile offenders. "But what does she do?" asked Clare, really impressed. She watched this small, delicately made girl carry a heavy tray stacked with dirty dishes to the kitchen; one of the maids hadn't shown up for work that evening, so she was filling in. "Oh, she mostly just gets beat up on," said Fauquier wryly, yet with a touch of pride. "But, according to what I hear, they set great store by her when they're not trying to kill her." Then he entertained them with the story of his heart attacks. How the ambulance got stuck in a traffic jam because of a parade and how, when they'd almost reached one hospital, the hospital radioed it was full up, so they had to turn right around and go *back* through the traffic jam to the other hospital on the opposite side of town. "That was when I was having my *second* one," Fauquier told them, twisting his mouth sarcastically to match the absurdity of the occasion. "But since there wasn't much else I could do, I just lay there and looked out the window and watched the tail end of the parade."

Yes, at the beginning of her fourth vacation in "No Saints," Clare felt she at last understood the Fauquiers and what they stood for. They were no longer the intriguing branch of social arcana that had challenged her from the musty shadows of the cupboard crammed with family memorabilia. She had read the entire little black book of Congressional eulogies to Mrs. Fauquier's father, who had died in his prime at his post of duty; to the best of her ability, taking into account her own biases and her heritage, she had separated the rhetorical and euphemistic from the revealing and significant. Certain words were used again and again: "service," "welfare of others," "loyalty"—to family, to friends, to state, to country, *to one's own.* One senator described his late colleague as a representative of the high civilization of America as expressed in the Deep South. Another gave as the definition of a gentleman: "Someone who has never intentionally caused another pain." The *Rubaiyat* of Omar Khayyam was quoted (more than once); Tennyson was quoted; Gray's "Elegy Written in a Country Churchyard" was quoted— all used to point home likenesses to the eulogized man but also taking the opportunity to pay handsome respects to that mysterious equalizer, Death, as well. The little black book, issued by the U.S. Government Printing Office in 1955, already had the quaintness of a relic of a past civilization; even the language of the senators had a bygone flavor. And who in Congress quoted the *Rubaiyat* or dared to praise "old aristocratic families" anymore? A senator who must have been a personal friend actually disclosed the dead man's bequests to his daughters: the family silver went to one; a chair once owned by an American president to the other. Had Mrs. Fauquier gotten the chair or the silver? Which would she rather have had? First Clare decided the silver, because Mrs. Fauquier would value her family more than a president in someone else's family. But then she decided that Mrs. Fauquier would not permit herself to *have* "rathers." Not consciously, anyway. She would accept as her fate whatever her father had seen fit to leave her, and still feel herself unworthy of it. Or go around trying to appear that she did.

Now it was time to move on to something else. It had taken Clare two years and five hundred pages to satisfy herself suf-

ficiently as to what it would have felt like to be a member of
Julia's family, a Richardson, and grow up in her admired
friend's house with the picturesque, exacting little father and
that quirky, haughty mother who could always make you feel
so ill at ease. And it had taken her three summers to understand why people like the Fauquiers (a totally different article
from the Richardsons!) were not interested in impressing
others anymore and why they took a dégagé and fatalistic
attitude towards the inevitable decay all around them, an
attitude extending from refrigerator wires corroded by sea air
to their own deaths, whether eventual or imminent. They had
transcended the personal, in a way. Everything worth pushing
and shoving for had already been won by predecessors. (Fauquier's family's correspondence with the famous figures of their
time were all numbered and catalogued in the *South Carolina
Historical Society's Manuscript Guide,* which Clare had also read,
along with the magazines.) Now one polished the silver for
special occasions, or cherished the president's chair, and while
waiting for individual extinction, did one's loyal best for one's
own family, or served others who were fighting to hang on,
or who did not seem to realize that the best days of civilization
were over. Though she had fewer illusions about them and
realized how temperamentally unsuited she was to their incurious and laissez-faire existence, Clare nevertheless felt a
possessive fondness for the Fauquiers when she raised their
broom for the fourth summer and hit the fluorescent light (she
would never dream of telling young Fauquier his trick didn't
always work) and when she took down the nasty black skillets
with their years of Fauquier grease burned into them and
merely wiped them lightly with a paper towel before frying
her fish in them. She regarded the Fauquiers the way she
regarded characters she had carried through a certain quantity
of pages in her books: she now knew enough about them to
predict what they would probably do next; she had mastered
them through her obstinate empathy, her selective observation,
and her imagination. It was as if she had *been* them for a time,
and the experience of having realized life from inside them
soothed old resentments and insecurities and freed her to go
on to other human mysteries.

Such as Snow Mullins Quick. Or, to be strictly accurate, Snow
Mullins Something-else Quick Something-else, then Quick by
choice again. Or, as Lily would explain it, to get Theo's Social

Security money, even though she had been married to someone else after his death.

Clare really did not know what to expect from Snow's visit to "The Island" with the child. The *idea* of it intrigued her, but when she tried to imagine it from minute to minute, it made her apprehensive. What if Snow just sat around, as she had up in Granny Squirrel? And she would miss her afternoon programs, because the Fauquiers' television set made horrible hissing sounds this summer, and the picture rolled and the set was only a black-and-white one; Snow was used to color. What if Snow bored Felix and he went all surly and glowery? He was a bit on the touchy side anyway because of Lizzie's refusal of their invitation to the beach. His baffled frustration over his daughter's new remoteness, since she had come back from Israel, might make for some very tense hours if compounded by a sullen, uninteresting Snow as a houseguest.

On Tuesday, two days before Snow was to arrive, Clare stood in the doorway of the breezy room and tried to have a first impression from Snow's point of view. It was a pity she would be arriving after dark, because the room showed to best advantage in sunlight. However, there would be the soft, faded blue sheets with scalloped edges turned down neatly over Mrs. Fauquier's white cotton bedspread. That was one advantage of Snow's night arrival: it allowed for the extra welcoming gesture of a turned-down bed. On the dressing table there would be a bowl of fresh flowers (five or six of Mr. Fauquier's pink roses from the front yard, with the aphid-eaten leaves clipped off) and a new bottle of suntan lotion (SP15 for Snow's—and Jason's—vulnerable pale skin) and a new bottle of the aloe vera skin lotion made up specially for "The Island's" apothecary, a silky, rich balm with a lemony-almond fragrance, and some mysterious other scent—didn't all the really desirable perfumes and lotions always have that mysterious "other" ingredient, which was often perhaps no more or less than the smeller's own associations with the place or time or person or cluster of circumstances connected to the scent? For Clare, who took several bottles back to New York each year, the smell of the local lotion represented her victory over her ambivalent feelings about the "Old South." By coming with Felix into one of its last strongholds for these several summers, she had been able to relax her defensiveness against its peculiar brand of snobbery based on its invincible assumption that what had happened yesterday (or what it would like to *think* had happened yesterday) could always cancel out the upstart of today. Looking at these Southerners through Felix's eyes, she saw that yesterday, for them, had happened only *here,* and in this wider context they shrank into harmless, rather touching local anachronisms whose complacence elicited her wry protection more than her resentment or condemnation—they would all be gone so soon anyway!—and whose charms she could partake of and enjoy, just as she enjoyed rubbing the sweet aloe lotion all over her body after a hot bath on a cold Northern night.

And standing in the doorway of the breezy room, which Snow would be occupying in two days, Clare imagined how, when Snow was packing up to leave after her visit, she herself would tuck this bottle of "The Island's" essence into a corner of her sister-in-law's suitcase, saying, "Remember the fun we had when you used this," or "Remember how we got to really know each other here," or "Think of me sometimes when you use this," depending on how the visit turned out.

Then she remembered that, back in the trailer in Granny Squirrel, Snow had put new sheets on the bed she had slept in. She had been touched, though they were stiff and still had the gluey smell of the sizing in them. What if Snow felt offended when she saw there were old sheets on her bed in the breezy room of "No Saints"? ("Here I went out and bought new sheets for *her,* and she won't even . . .")

Clare drove over to the big Belk's in Myrtle Beach on Tuesday afternoon and bought new sheets for Snow's bed and some thick, giant-sized Perry Ellis towels. She and Felix could always use them at home later. But maybe she should make a gift of them to Snow; she was sure Snow had never had such towels in her life. But Snow might think she was trying to "buy" her. Of course, Clare had already helped Snow buy a new car. Back in March, after Clare's visit to Granny Squirrel, when she had been up in the country alone, she had phoned Snow one evening to put forward the idea of the beach trip. "Felix and I rent this place, you know, so I can have my family visit me on my own turf. You and Jason could come down first, before any of them arrive, and we could have a little birthday celebration for him and . . . well, we could get to know each other some more and you could enjoy the beach. It's a lovely beach. The ocean is practically outside the door of this cottage we rent."

There had been a silence at Snow's end. "That would be

nice," she finally said, not very enthusiastically, pronouncing the adjective with her short hillbilly *i*, "but I'll have to see. I never know *what* I can do too far ahead of time on account of I always have to depend on somebody else to drive me."

"Oh," said Clare, ashamed for not have considered this. "Well, maybe you could . . . fly. If your mother or sister could drive you to the airport in Mountain City . . . I mean, I'd be glad to have your tickets waiting for you and all. I don't think there's a direct flight, you'd have to change in Charlotte, but —"

"I can't stand to fly," said Snow. "I hate planes."

"Oh, dear. Well, if you hate to fly, then you shouldn't. I mean, this is supposed to be *fun* for you, not an ordeal. . . ."

"Jason would love it, he adores planes, but I wouldn't," Snow said. "It would make me sick."

And then there was a longer silence before Snow said, "Maybe I'll have me a car by then. I was talking to my brother-in-law. He's friends with this Mercury dealer that might be able to get me a good price. But they always want this down payment. I don't know how I'm going to manage that. I figure I could just about squeeze the monthly payments out of what Jason and I get from Theo's Social Security, but —"

"I'd be happy to help with the down payment," said Clare, jumping in with both feet. Why not? She could afford it. And it made her feel good to offer before actually being asked. Her father's brother, Uncle Zebulon, had been like that: he always jumped in before you had a chance to ask. Are you hungry yet? he would demand. Would you like that hair dryer I saw you looking at in the drugstore? Do you need any money? It wasn't just with her, his dead brother's only child; he was the same with everyone connected with his small-town bachelor existence, from the haughty old lady who frowned from her rocking chair on the porch next door to the clubfooted black boy who raked his leaves and mowed his lawn. "I know you like those first white peaches, Mrs. Carrington," he would boom, loping across her lawn with his giant strides, carrying his little brown sack, "so I took the liberty of picking you out some." "You probably need an advance, don't you, Grady," he'd say, slapping his hand cheerfully on the wallet in his back pocket before the boy even had a chance to pick up the rake. Watching him in action, Clare had seen how his own precipitant generosity galvanized him with self-confidence and elation, and she felt the same current of delight flow through her as she anticipated Snow's request. How much better for their friendship that Snow had not *had* to ask!

"I don't know what to say," said Snow, sounding not quite as genuinely surprised as she might have. "I don't know how I'll ever pay you back, but I'll try."

"You can pay me back by just being happy," Clare said, disgusted by the fulsomeness of her own reply.

"Well, I'll try," said Snow flatly.

"And by coming to visit me with Jason at the beach."

"Oh, I can certainly do *that*," said Snow, with slightly more energy. "Now that I'm going to have a car to get there."

On the way home from Myrtle Beach with her purchases, Clare stopped by the Harris Teeter bakery counter in Litchfield and ordered Jason's birthday cake for Saturday. She had already bought his presents: some little bathing trunks with a rainbow on the pocket and a Confederate flag float like all the other children had for the water. Before returning to Felix, she made a final stop at "The Island's" only laundromat, used almost exclusively by the black population, and stood contentedly dripping sweat and planning menus in the un-air-conditioned enclosure built of cinder blocks while Snow's new sheets and towels undulated in their suds on the other side of the little glass porthole. While black women folded their families' laundry on the long wooden tables, Clare imagined conversations she and Snow would have together during the long beach days. And on that first night, when they arrived, she would tell Snow, showing her into the breezy room with the newly washed and turned-down sheets and the flowers and the lotion, "This is a very special room. Everyone who sleeps in it has an important dream their first night." What would Snow dream? Could she get her to tell it the next morning? At the moment it was easier for Clare to imagine what a Fauquier would be likely to dream than what Snow might. But if this visit went as she hoped, that would change very shortly.

On Wednesday afternoon, Clare said to Felix, "I've just had this feeling. She's not going to come."

"But why shouldn't she?" asked Felix. "I'm sure she's looking forward to it just as much as you are. Perhaps more."

"You don't know Snow," said Clare, chewing her lip.

"No. I'm very interested in meeting her. But why are you worried she won't come? Because she hasn't called? Was she supposed to call?"

"I think we agreed she'd call me a day or so before she left. Or did I say I'd call her? I really don't remember! But the date's certain. That's been set up since March. And we worked it out on the phone that she'd have to leave Granny Squirrel by ten in the morning to get here in the early evening. It's a long drive, but she said she loved to drive, especially since she got her new Mercury Lynx."

"Then what are you worried about?" asked Felix. "Why not go and call her, if you're uncertain who was to call whom."

Clare phoned the trailer in Granny Squirrel. No answer. She tried again a half hour later, then an hour later. No answer.

"It's afternoon," Felix reminded her. "She's probably out doing some last-minute shopping for the beach. Wait till suppertime. She's sure to be at home then. Or perhaps she has already left. Maybe she wanted to get an early start and break the long drive, spend the night along the way."

"Maybe. But oh, I wish I didn't have this feeling!"

"Just tell yourself you can't do any more about it till suppertime, and cheer up. Remember, this is also a day in your life."

But before suppertime, Clare's feeling turned out to be right. Lily phoned from Mountain City. Felix answered. "Hell*o*," said Lily in that playful-yet-remote tone she saved for him, as though they were in league together on some level but she could be depended on to be perfectly discreet about it. "How are you?"

"We're very well," said Felix. "We're looking forward to seeing you this Sunday."

"Actually, we might see you a little earlier than that," said Lily. "Something has suddenly come up for Ralph, so he has to be back in Mountain City by Sunday evening instead of Tuesday. So we were thinking of driving on down *Friday*, now that it seems Snow is backing out. Honestly, that girl!"

"This is the first we've heard anything about it," said Felix. "Wait a minute, I think I'd better put Clare on."

Clare took the phone. He saw she already knew by the look on his face that her carefully made plans were crumbling. "Hi," she said guardedly into the receiver. "Oh, I'm fine. What's up? . . . What? What! . . . Wait a minute, I don't understand. *When* did he talk to her? . . . Oh, of course not, you *never* . . . I'm sorry, but here I had everything minutely set up, and now you're telling me it's all changed and I haven't heard a goddamn thing about it. . . . Well, what did *he* say to make her say that? No, I'm *not* taking her side, but this is all getting messier by the minute. I'm expecting Snow and Jason to drive in tomorrow evening, and I've got new sheets for her bed and his presents already wrapped and now you call to say it's all been rearranged. I mean, who's party *is* this? . . . I know you didn't, but why haven't I been informed? Why didn't she call me? . . . Of course I still want to see Jason, but now the whole thing will be changed. The human logistics will be utterly altered and you know it and I suspect foul play. . . . I'm not accusing you of anything, I'm accusing him. He always manages to get control and mess things up. So *why* does he suddenly have to be back in Mountain City by Sunday evening? . . . Yes, of course I still want you to come, but damn it, I feel it's all been taken out of my hands. I've been trying to call her, but there's no answer. . . . Well, okay. Okay. I'll try again, and then call you back. . . . Of course I want to see Jason, I've got his cake ordered and all, but don't you understand how I feel? The whole thing is insidious, it's *sinister*, the way this family can confuse things. . . . *No*, not you. I know it hasn't. I know it hasn't been easy for you. Look, I'm going to hang up now, I'm very upset, and then I'll try Snow again and I'll phone you back later. Okay? . . . I'm sorry. I know, I'm sorry. . . . I won't. I never do."

Clare hung up, stared at the phone several seconds, went white under the eyes, and screamed. Then she stood very still and inclined her head slightly forward, as if listening for an echo, or for neighbors' reactions. The Fauquiers' noisy airconditioner, which had considerably muted the scream, thrummed crankily on; the steady, impervious surf outside the kitchen's closed windows never missed a beat. Clare slumped against the wall and grimaced apologetically at Felix, who'd been keeping her company while she peeled two pounds of shrimp for the shrimp salad she had planned for Snow's arrival late the next day. "I guess you heard," she said. "You heard my side. And you know them well enough now to fill in the rest. Ralph has gone and *tinkered* with my plans, and Lily's trying to cover up for him and blame Snow. For some mysterious reason, known only to himself, he's decided he has to leave early; therefore, he has to come early. So he calls Snow—not me, the hostess, but Snow—to tell her he won't be able to bring Jason back Tuesday because he has to leave Sunday. And then she says, or rather Lily says she said . . . or, to be perfectly accurate, which this family's lost the ability to be, *Ralph* tells Lily that Snow said she isn't coming to the beach."

"Because they were coming early, or had she decided beforehand?"

"Ah! Now that little fine point will be obscured forever, if it's left to them. But I'm going to find out if I have to keep calling that trailer all night."

"I gathered from your side of the conversation that Jason might still come?"

"Oh, yes. Dear Ralph, so long suffering and put upon and kind, has offered to drive all the way to Granny Squirrel and back tomorrow, to pick up Jason, and then they'll bring him down on Friday and Ralph will return him on Sunday."

"This is not what you wanted," said Felix.

"No," said Clare, "it's what they have decided I should want. Or rather he has, and she colludes. Or she has, and he colludes. That marriage *is* like a can of worms. They've writhed around in there together till you can't tell where one stops and the other begins. And yet, oh poor Lily! She sounded exhausted. Even her voice has changed during this past year. There's a *querulous* note that never used to be there. And I was rougher on her than I should have been. So now, not only is Snow not coming, but the air between Lily and me is poisoned even before she gets here. I mean, why do I set myself up for this, year after year? Why do you let me drag you into it? They're nothing to you."

"As I remind you, year after year, that is not true. At first I wanted to know them because they were your family. And they were an entirely new experience for me. But now I am implicated in a much larger way. Not just on your behalf, or because I see them as 'an interesting American family.' "

"Oh, they're good at implicating people," snorted Clare, picking up her shrimp tool and returning to her task at the sink. "But how do you mean, 'in a much larger way'?"

"It's like being inside a drama in which good influences and bad influences are being played out through the family members. Only it's not as simple as the old morality plays where the saint or the villain was cut out of whole cloth. There aren't clear-cut saints and villains in your family. The good and the bad, the true and the false show up in everybody. What makes

your family so fascinating to me . . . if you'll forgive the way
this sounds . . . is that I am never able to predict which influence is going to manifest itself when, and in which person.
It's impossible for me ever to affix *blame* for very long. Of
course, I have my favorites. I find Lily's style more compatible
than Ralph's. Ralph tries my patience and my temper, but
when I don't have to be around him I find myself thinking
about him, about what kind of individual he is . . . or could
have been. And, as you know, I'm fond of Rafe. I worry
about him the way I'd worry about a boy of my own. I don't
know what I would have felt for poor Theo if I'd had a
chance to know him longer. I suspect he might have succeeded
in irritating me as much as his father can. But what I'm trying
to say is that whenever I'm with them for any length of time,
or hear about them through you, I'm never quite sure who's
telling the truth or even if there is any one truth when it
comes to Quick matters. I'm never able to put my finger on
who starts the trouble. And as an old theater person, I have
to tell you it's not boring. And that's a value for both of us,
isn't it? Your family can infuriate and depress me, but the one
thing they never fail to do is keep me guessing. How many
hundreds of hours have we spent, just the two of us, trying to
anticipate how some particular crisis in Mountain City is
going to turn out? And when have they failed to surprise us?
Either by doing something much better than we gave them
credit for or by behaving much worse than we could have
predicted?"

After trying Snow's number every fifteen or twenty minutes
for the next hour or so, Clare finally reached her. Then Felix
made two stiff vodka tonics and they went out to sit on the
wind-walk. The sun was sinking behind them and the constantly
forming whitecaps in front of them had a warm, pinkish hue. A
lone pelican, an old-timer to judge from his size and apparent
sang-froid, flapped leisurely home from a day's fishing. Felix
had the highest respect and affection for this dignified, funny-
faced survivor, whose species, according to Fauquier's much-
handled bird book, had changed hardly at all in thirty million
years.

"So," he said, "I don't get to meet the interesting sister-in-
law this time."

"No," said Clare with a sigh, "and I doubt if I'll ever know for sure when she decided not to come or if she ever really planned to come at all."

"Which did it sound like on the phone?"

"She was very wary at first, and she seemed guilty when she heard my voice. I don't know whether I was wise, but I decided to pretend I didn't know anything to the contrary and was just innocently calling to confirm what time they'd be likely to arrive tomorrow. So when she said in that deadpan voice of hers, 'I'm not coming,' I acted real surprised and hurt and said, 'You're not coming? But I expected you. I've got everything ready for you and Jason. I've ordered Jason's cake.' And she said, 'Oh, Jason can come, if Ralph wants to drive to Granny Squirrel and pick him up, but I can't come. I've got to go to Georgia and get some things of mine I left down there with this friend of mine to store at her house.' I said, 'You mean, that's why you aren't coming? Because you have to pick up those things? Couldn't they wait another week?' And then she got bristly and defensive and said none of us had really ever understood her, that we thought she was just some ignorant hillbilly, but one day we were going to think different. I said, 'Snow, the reason I wanted you to come to the beach was so I could understand you better. I thought we got on pretty well when I came to Granny Squirrel.' And she said, 'Yes, but that was different. I wouldn't feel comfortable down there with you all.' I asked her why not. I told her how we had been looking forward to her visit. 'And Felix has been so interested in meeting you,' I said."

"What did she reply to that?" asked Felix.

"She sort of snorted, as though I were trying to flatter her or put something over on her. Then she said, 'And I didn't know the rest of them were going to be there. You didn't tell me that.'"

"Ah! Then Ralph and Lily did mess it up," said Felix.

"That's just it. I can't be sure. Don't you see how murky it's all getting. The usual Quick murk. And I was in it, too, now, because I had pretended not to know anything when I called. So I went on with that, I said, 'Snow, it was to be just you and Jason and me and Felix, and they weren't to arrive till after you'd left on Sunday.' And there was a silence on her end, such a lengthy one I thought she might be reconsidering, but then she said, 'How do *I* know what you all would end up doing? But I told you, I can't come now because I've got to go to Georgia and pick up those clothes and things. I need them. I told Ralph he can come pick up Jason if you want him. But I can't come.'

Then I said, 'Snow, are you really not coming because you have to go and get those clothes, or is it that you just don't want to come, or did Ralph and Lily somehow change your mind?' By this time I'd accepted she wasn't going to come, but I wanted to get to the botton of her *reason*."

"And what did she say?"

"She just repeated, 'I wouldn't feel comfortable.' And I said, 'But Snow, I thought you and I had established our own relationship, apart from Lily and Ralph.' And she laughed in her mirthless little way and said, 'Well, I thought so, too, but maybe it's impossible.' And I didn't want to push her any further, I was afraid I'd lose everything, so I just said real sadly, 'Well, Snow, I want you to know I'm extremely disappointed.' Because if I said any more, if I admitted I *knew* about Ralph's call to her, that would make the whole premise of my call a lie. Which it was. Oh, God, Felix, I'm trying so hard to grow up and be a straightforward, responsible adult, but an episode like this sets me back *years*. I don't know *what* the truth is. I don't know *who's* to blame. Just like you were saying in the kitchen: nobody's *clear-cut!* This afternoon I still thought she was coming and now I'm so confused, I'm wondering if, subliminally, I kept her from coming. I mean, why didn't I phone *her* the first of the week? I could so easily have picked up the phone and called her and said, like any sweet Southern hostess, 'Oh, I am *so* looking forward to youah visit, honey.' But I just sat here like a lunk, and probably, when Ralph called her, she thought I was sending a message through him that I didn't want her. Felix, you're still *relatively* outside all this. Can you please tell me: did I help cause her not to come? Or did she ever plan to come in the first place? Or did she use Ralph's call as an excuse to get out of coming? Do you think she said she would come only in order to get me to pay the down payment on her car? And, most important of all, how should I *ideally* have behaved? You have to tell me that! Otherwise, I'll never be able to get outside them enough to be *free!*"

Clare's voice had risen to the pitch of a little girl's. It was true, thought Felix, they could set her back years. After the confusion of the past few hours, he was not entirely clear of "Quick murk" himself. He looked out to sea and used that comfortingly definite line of horizon to steady his thoughts. Below was sea; above was sky. Yet, if one were to row out to that horizon in a boat, the line he saw from here would be nonexistent. . . . No! This was not the time to entertain ideas about relativity. Concentrate on that simple line: the way it looked from where he sat. He owed her all the honesty and steadiness he had, because he loved her and wanted her to be free; she was at her best when she was feeling free.

"It sounded pretty straightforward to me when you told me in March," he said. "I put it down in my little book. Although I have never met her, from the way you spoke I never doubted she would come. You might have been wise to call her earlier in the week and tell her you were looking forward to her visit— you are sometimes too shy about picking up the telephone—but I doubt that your call would have made any difference if it was Ralph's call that put her off. I think she *would* feel uncomfortable if all of them were here; it hasn't been that long since they were trying to discredit her in court. As to how you should have 'behaved ideally,' you acted in good faith, up until the time of Lily's call. You prepared for Snow, you anticipated her comforts, you were sure she was coming . . . until earlier today, when you had your feeling that she wasn't."

"Maybe my 'feeling' was simply my knowledge that they'd screw things up just as they always do. As *we* always do. Because I'm one of them, God help me. When I finally reached Snow this evening, why didn't I just say, 'Snow, up until a few minutes ago, I expected you tomorrow. But now Lily has called and said you might not come. I hope this isn't so, because as far as I'm concerned, nothing has changed here. Felix and I are expecting you and Jason.' Why didn't I say that, Felix? I acted in bad faith by pretending not to know anything, and as for the clothes in Georgia, that was probably her pride. She figures we didn't want her, that we were trying to squeeze her out and get Jason here by himself, so she saved face and said she couldn't come because she had something of her own to do."

Felix, sipping his vodka tonic, acknowledged to himself that all this might be the case. But this was a day in their lives, too— or rather, what was left of the day—and they both needed to replenish their energies for the influx of Quicks on Friday. Also, when Clare decided to be hard on herself, she needed no assistance from anyone else.

"What are you thinking?" she asked suspiciously, as if she knew exactly what he was withholding and was determined to hear the worst about herself at last.

"I was thinking, indirectly, about the Fauquiers," he said, not untruthfully.

"The *Fauquiers?* Why the Fauquiers?"

"I was imagining how pleased with themselves they must have been when they came up with the name for this cottage. Whose idea was it, do you think?"

"Oh, his, probably. Because of the church being *All* Saints and then . . . but no, it might well have been hers, only she would be too modest to be presumptuous enough to name a cottage . . . that's a man's job, after all . . . but she could have planted the idea in his mind so he'd think it was his . . . the good old Southern way. On the other hand, it could have been young Fauquier, he's witty and he seems to have a little distance from it all. . . ."

That's my girl, thought Felix thankfully, watching her climb out of the maelstrom of family cross-purposes via her healthy imagination. Her voice regained its low, slightly humorous, storytelling pitch. After a dose of the Quicks, he thought, a little distance never hurts anybody.

"Angel!"

"Yes, darling."

"When are we going to be at the *beach?*"

"In a little while," said Lily.

"How long is a little while?"

"Not too much longer, darling."

"You know what's wrong with you, Angel?"

"No, what?"

"You never say anything *exact*. You always go *around*."

Ralph, at the wheel, burst out laughing. It was not a friendly laugh. It was a cold cackle forced up from the chest. "Wisdom from the mouths of babes," he said.

Feeling as though she'd received an unexpected blow in the stomach—but why unexpected? this animosity between them was nothing new—Lily glanced down at the flat gold watch, studded with small sapphires and diamonds, that she wore on a chain around her neck. "It is four-oh-four now," she related in an *exact* brittle monotone. "We should have been there by six, but since Grandaddy got a late start because he had to take Miss Alicia for a walk, we won't get there till about . . . till seven, at the earliest."

"More like eight," put in Ralph casually, destroying her edifice of exactness before she'd even finished building it.

"Will eight be dark? Will it be too late to swim at eight?"

demanded Jason. He was sitting between them, unbuckled, because neither of them had had the energy, when they finally left town, to fight his wishes. He had one leg tucked beneath him, and every few minutes the hard little sole of his sneaker jabbed into her left thigh. She would have bruises everybody would see when she wore her bathing suit. She bruised more easily now. One's skin got thinner as one aged. The little green penny-sized bruises from Thalia's massage on Tuesday, and now the crescent-shaped ones from her grandson's thoughtless foot. She would look as if someone had been painting her legs in shades of green and yellow and purple. Of course at her age, one wasn't supposed to worry about being looked at on the beach. Grandmothers, having fulfilled their genetic mission, were expected to cover up as much as possible and fade back into the landscape.

"Angel! Didn't you hear me ask you a question?"

Funny how you could hear a parent speaking through a child. That was Snow's kind of phrase. "You asked me two questions," Lily corrected him. "Will it be dark at eight, and will it be too late to swim at eight. It won't be dark at eight, this time of year, not quite; whether it will be too late to swim will depend on what Clare has planned. She might want to feed us first. Clare likes feeding people."

"But I want to swim!" Jason began to whimper.

"No use to take it out on him," murmured Ralph morosely.

"Take *what* out?" Her turn. Indignantly.

"You know as well as I do, Lily." Sanctimoniously.

"No I'm sorry but I do not." Innocently-indignantly.

His long-suffering sigh as he turns on the car radio. The station he always plays now. The one she hates. Popular tunes from the forties and fifties, but in bland, sound-alike music. He has explained the success of this new station in his proprietary way. They figured there are enough people in their fifties and early sixties who will listen to these tunes because the music makes them nostalgic, and these are the people with the money to respond to all the advertising. He's always smug and proprietary when it comes to explaining the successful schemes of *others* for making money. She remembers tunes, but not their names or what she was doing forty years ago when she first heard this one or that one. There's enough nostalgic debris in life without tuning in to more. Or buying it and bringing it home from Sunday flea markets and antiques fairs. *I don't want my own old things, let alone some complete stranger's.* That's one of her wounding retorts, for when he brings home more junk. Oh, what a charade. Each of them piling up points against the other—for whose benefit? And yet, since they've become their own audience, for the most part, the game's ante seems to have arisen. Wounding retorts are sharpened, their stings savored in advance. Each has become so cunningly vigilant, lying in wait for the other to *act in character.* Knowing someone all too well, without affection or charity, can be a vicious weapon.

"Grandaddy, will *you* take me for a swim? If it's not dark? I'm not even hungry. I don't want any of Clare's old food."

"You're not hungry now, son, but we're talking about several hours from now. But we'll see that you get down to that ocean tonight. Even if it's midnight."

His voice of masculine reason, tempered with kindly indulgence. She could remember, just slightly, how it felt to believe oneself safer for being indulged by such a voice. But now its sound was ugly, because not only was she outside its protection, but it was actually being used against her. He was allying Jason with himself against her petty stickling.

"Ha! Hear that, Angel? I can swim in the ocean even if it's midnight." The triumphant little sneaker dealt Lily's thigh another bruise for the beach.

"Young man, if you kick me one more time, you're moving to the backseat." She couldn't stop herself from adding spitefully, "He didn't actually say you could swim. He only said he'd see that you 'got down' to the ocean tonight. None of us are always paragons of exactness, are we?"

"None of us pretend to be paragons of anything, Lily." The wounded singsong, verging on sermon-time. "But is it really so impossible for you to be pleasant?"

"It is difficult to be pleasant when you gang up against me with a child, yes."

"You're mean, Angel!" The boy kicked her hard, deliberately this time.

Tears flooded her eyes. "You little devil!"

Ralph, exuding righteous authority under severe strain, sighed and pulled off the highway.

An indignantly weeping Jason was transferred to the backseat. "I *won't* go in that car seat! You can't make me! I'll die first!" he screamed.

His consoling grandfather, all reason and kindness, said, "No one's going to make you, son. But Angel doesn't like you kicking her, so you have to stay back here for a while." Ralph made the boy a little nest of beach towels and sheets and Ralph's own special goosedown pillow he always took with him if he was going to be away overnight, carrying it in pompously from the car with that look on his face that proclaimed to his hosts, I know what comfort is and I don't trust anyone but myself to provide it. "You've been riding around in cars all yesterday and today," Ralph crooned to Jason, arranging the boy in his nest. "No wonder you're restless. Those legs need some *room*."

Oh, God, help me, thought Lily, massaging her thigh, I hate this man. But it wasn't the hate that made her feel so bereft. It was a cluster of things, all painfully intertwined, that this episode had presented to her like a terrible package laid in her lap. Inside the package were strands of her life that had got knotted together and probably could never be separated again: what she had made of herself and others out of what others had made of her. The awful cluster or clump was somehow the essence of her life story, condensed with cruel economy into these few moments of Ralph's stopping the car and Ralph's voice consoling the boy and the boy's haunting threat, and of her during it all, sitting in front feeling like both the frozen queen and the isolated, naughty child who had caused the trouble in the first place. There was only one person who could fetch the magic key—she could still see that key—and "unlock" the good girl again, and he had been dead now for forty years. Her father had been able to calm her good-humoredly and restore her to her senses the way Ralph was able to do with Jason. One day, decades from now, when she and Ralph were crumbling in their graves, would Jason, as an elderly man, feeling suddenly ill-tempered or lonesome, recall with a pang of yearning his grandfather's kind and cajoling voice as it had sounded on that long-ago car ride when he had comforted the boy with the magic nest and its special pillow? Just as she yearned now for the lost security of Daddy's voice as he pressed that little key gently against her chest, just above the heart, and said, "Now I'm going to unlock my good girl again, because I've missed her so much and it's time she came back." What had that funny little key really been for? It had been much too small for a door. What had happened to it? Mother had probably thrown it away at some time or other. She had been impatient of their little games. Of the "key" game, she had once remarked sarcastically, "Well, who locked up the 'good girl' in the first place? Who's the one with the key? Not me. Has anyone ever thought *that* out?" Mother was always telling Daddy that he should act more grownup and dignified. He played with children, she said, as if he were still a child himself. And he was too friendly with the men under him at work, and that was why the railroad was never going to promote him to executive status. And it never had.

The key has been thrown away and the good girl is never coming back, thought Lily, as Ralph, with another self-righteous sigh, slid back into the driver's seat. My daddy got the last goodness out of me. After him, I became . . . devious. Why? It somehow seemed necessary. There was nobody I could really trust. And now my heart is a stone, as, I suppose, my mother's heart was a stone. When did hers harden? When did she stop trusting people? She was cold and derisive as far back as my memories go. Yet I got on with her in later years. If she were alive, a woman my age now, I might like to have her as my friend. We could go out to lunch and feel comfortable together. We could tell each other things in her (our) cool, elliptical way and know we were saying much more. She was the wrong woman for Daddy, though they both agreed he "worshiped" her. That may have been the only thing in their marriage they agreed on. Ralph "worshiped" me for a while. Possibly he thought he loved me. Then he met Hannah. Who suited him a thousand times better than I ever did. Why didn't they marry? Why didn't he divorce me and marry her? I'll never give him the satisfaction of asking why not. Besides, I know, anyway. He was too self-righteous. Did Daddy ever find anyone who suited him? No, I don't think so. Those were different times. And if they weren't, I don't care to know about it.

But why are we doomed to repeat? Jason's wild threat, "I'll die first," had curdled her blood. Why those exact words? Why had they come so easily? What kind of hope do any of us have, thought Lily, when we are susceptible to such repetitions? For those were the words, the very same words, Theo had flung at her, from beneath the bed, that time when she had been going to whip him with the belt called Sam; only, he had beaten her to Ralph's closet and whisked it down first and plunged beneath the bed, into a space too narrow for her to crawl after him. "I'll die first!" he yelled triumphantly, and then, just before *she* had started screaming and crying, she had heard the terrible *aaakk* sound as he pulled the leather noose of Ralph's belt tighter and tighter around his neck.

They drove without speaking until Ralph's favorite music station faded. The landscape changed to flat sandy soil, palmettos and leggy pines. Signs advertising pecans and fireworks and palm readers began to proliferate along the edges of tobacco fields. Ralph hunted unsuccessfully for another congenial sation, then grimly switched off the radio. A car full of sunburned young people sped by in the opposite direction; the tanned golden-haired leg and bare foot sticking out of the back window reminded her of Rafe, although she hoped he knew better than to put his leg out of the window of a speeding car. In the backseat, Jason, who had fallen asleep almost immediately, was emitting a surprisingly adult-sounding snore. She turned her face towards her window so Ralph would not catch her in the act of smiling.

But he was getting ready to speak. She could feel it coming from the little truncated sighs and a certain strained congestion building in his throat. When had she first become aware of this annoying mannerism? It dated back, at least, to those first post-Hannah weeks, when he was so eager to tell her things she didn't want to hear. She could sense already that he was going to spring something unpleasant on her now.

"I guess you're wondering," he began significantly, "why I had to bring you down earlier, so I could go back on Sunday."

"I did wonder"—sweetly—"but I figured you would tell me if you wanted me to know. Of course it's changed poor Clare's carefully planned itinerary, but I'm sure you have your good reasons."

"Lily, I have been very accommodating." Patient. Long-suffering. Much of the skill in their deadly game lay in not being the first to express open hostilities. "I drove up to Granny Squirrel to get Jason yesterday. I'll drive him all the way back on Sunday. You'll have your week with your daughter. You'll have two days more than you would have had otherwise."

"Yes, I know, and that's nice, but just between us, don't you think your call to Snow kept her from coming? Clare was looking forward to Snow's visit. I mean, you know how *I* feel about Snow, but this was Clare's party."

"Why should my call have kept Snow from coming if she'd wanted to come? The purpose of my call was to say I'd have to leave the beach Sunday, so I couldn't bring Jason back on Tuesday, like we'd planned. Or like you and Clare had planned for me. I only called to tell Snow she'd have to take Jason back with her on Sunday."

"Yes, but when she realized we would be coming down earlier, she felt betrayed. Clare had promised it would just be her alone, so she wouldn't feel uncomfortable."

"Why should she feel uncomfortable with us? I get along with Snow fine now. We see her twice a month."

"Aren't you being deliberately obtuse? That girl hates us and you know it."

"I know nothing of the kind. What you mean is you hate her. You're projecting."

"I! I suppose you love her and think she was the perfect wife for Theo."

"No, Lily, I don't love her and I don't think anything of the sort. But this is what we *have,* and we might as well make the best of it for his sake." He gave an unctuous nod towards the sleeping child in the backseat. "I don't love her," he repeated slowly, "but I can sympathize, perhaps better than you, with some of the things she's had to put up with."

Now all she had to say was "Oh? For instance?" and have the pleasure of scorning him as he delivered his "privileged vs. non-privileged" sermon. He, of course, a member of the under-privileged team with Snow; she, Lily, cast into irredeemable outer darkness with the arrogant enemy. Oh, wasn't this all tiring and silly! Wasn't there a level of communication, accessible to each of them still, from which they could view this sort of squabble as beneath—far beneath!—the best in them both? Why couldn't they, as fellow human beings, climb there together? What could she, in her traditional role as "inspiring woman," say to him to initiate that climb? They couldn't be lovers again, they couldn't even be good friends, probably, but she knew couples . . . no, she didn't actually, but she could *imagine* couples who, with very little left in common, could still be kind to each other.

But what was the point in just "being kind"? Wasn't that a patronizing form of death blow? So, while she didn't allow herself the satisfaction of provoking his time-worn remarks on the psychology of the scorned, some proud, last-ditch intransigence kept her from offering a number of possible phrases that could have brought them, for the moment, at least, closer together. She chose, instead, out of God only knew which of the precedents that had shaped her, to ride obdurately and silently on in this deadly enclosure until he (who could never last out a silence as long as she) began clearing his throat and uttering tentative, congested little groans.

When at last he announced, his lips trembling with indignant self-pity, "I have to be back Sunday because I'm going into the hospital first thing Monday morning," what shocked her most was how low she had sunk. Because her first response to his words was not "Oh my God, what for?" but "Well, I'm vanquished *this* round. Who can compete with going to the hospital?"

He was asleep; then he was awake.

"Ja-son. Jaaaa-son." Grandaddy singing his name. "Jason, here's the beach."

He didn't want the beach now. He wanted to sleep. He'd been riding around in cars all yesterday and today. Grandaddy said so. But it was just the one car. Grandaddy's car. Which other one did he mean? His mother had a new car. It smelled nicer. But his mother had to take that car to Georgia to pick up some of his toys and his bike. He remembered living in Georgia for a little while; then they had to leave in a hurry. He spilled his milk on the floor and J.D. hit him. Hard, on the side of the face. You lay a finger on him one more time and it'll be the last, his mother said. J.D. hit him another time and he and his mother took a long bus trip in the middle of the night. Now he lived in Granny Squirrel with Sue and Mike and Trevor and Tiffany Ann and the real old people, Paw Paw and Maw Maw. Maw Maw was sick, but Paw Paw gave him candy and told him about the time the bear came down the mountain towards him on two legs. He liked Granny Squirrel a whole lot better than Georgia. There was always somebody to play with, and it never hurt to have your own kin around you. That's what his mother said. Angel didn't like Granny Squirrel, his other grandmother said, because she never took off her fur coat when she came. Angel said on the phone to somebody, Theo would be so sad if he knew Jason was living in Granny Squirrel. But Theo did know he was living in Granny Squirrel, because when he asked Angel if Theo was able to look down on them from Heaven, she said, He certainly is, my darling. Just when I'm in this house, he asked Angel, or wherever I am? And she said, Wherever you

are, my love, wherever you are in the world. So she must have
been fibbing to the lady on the phone. Theo knew where he
was, all right, whether he was in Granny Squirrel or Angel
and Grandaddy's house or even just driving back and forth
between.

They were walking towards a house and he wasn't so sleepy
anymore. The air here made his skin feel sticky.

"Hear the ocean, Jason?" Angel was trying to make her voice
sound happy for him. She wasn't mad at him anymore for
kicking her in the car and calling her mean.

"I hear it," he said. It was a big machine roaring on and on,
like in the factory his aunt Evelyn took him to visit, to show him
where they made his jeans. He walked ahead by himself. A warm
wind came and made his clothes feel damp and soft. It was
almost dark, but there were lights in the house and he pretended
not to see faces looking eagerly down at him from a screened
porch above.

He went up the steps by himself, even though Angel stuck out
her hand. Grandaddy was unloading their stuff from the car. At
the top of the steps, a screen door opened and Clare held her
arms out to him. Clare came to visit him in Granny Squirrel
when it was still cold. She brought him a stuffed lion that felt
soft, like real fur, and she gave his mother a sweater with silver
buttons and lots of colors in it. It was still in his mother's drawer,
in its plastic case. Clare was white in Granny Squirrel, but now
she was brown. She knelt down and hugged him and kissed
him. She smelled of a sweet lotion. The big man beside her
stepped forward and shook his hand. "Hello, Jason. Remember
me from last year?" He had a very deep, funny voice.

"You remember Felix from last year," Clare said. "You
remember last year, when you and Theo came?"

She was looking at him funny. They all were. Angel and Clare
and Felix. They stood above him, wanting something from him.

"Yes, I remember," he said, walking away from them, across
the screened porch and into the house. He went through some
rooms that made him feel sad. Then he opened another door
with a wet screen and the ocean was loud around him. He
crossed a different porch and saw the hammock. He ran to it
and lay down, folding his arms across his chest and closing his
eyes. The hammock swung back and forth. He was happy.

They all came out. "Oh, my God, will you look where he is?"
That was Clare. "The very first place he went to. He does

remember. They lay there together last year. Rafe took that photograph."

"It's more than that. I feel him out here. I think they're together in that hammock right now." That was Angel, using the voice she kept for her special secrets.

He wriggled out of the hammock and raced down a long narrow walkway, with white railings, above the sand. At the end it got wide again, like another porch, and you could look through the railings and the ocean was right underneath you. The railings were slick from the wet spray. He knelt down and traced patterns in the wet with his finger. The ocean came in and went out. Came in and went out. He touched his hair. It felt different, soft and sticky.

"Oh, careful, Jason. Don't fall."

"He re*mem*bers."

They came after him, down the walkway, one following the other because it was too narrow for more than one at a time. The ocean made their voices sound little. Smiling, they surrounded him in the half-light, their faces searching his.

"He's a fine-looking boy," said the big man, Felix, to Grandaddy, who was still wearing his straw hat.

Grandaddy sighed. "Yes, he is. He's a carbon copy of his father at the same age. Even their walk is the same."

Clare knelt down and hugged and kissed him some more. He heard her knees crack. She was a lot older than his mother but not as old as Angel. She turned him this way and that way like he was a doll. She held him by his shoulders and looked into his eyes. "You do remember last year, don't you? You and Theo drove in about five, and the first thing you all did was lie in the hammock together. Then he carried you out here and you looked over the rail, just like you were doing now, and then that goof ball just kicked off his loafers and walked down those steps and went right into the surf with you, with his trousers still on." She was telling it like a story. His mother said that's what she did. Told stories on people and got money for it.

"Of course he remembers," said Angel. She looked sad, but she made her voice sound happy. Clare's face was like people's got when they were trying not to cry.

"I remember!" he shrieked, and before they could stop him, he ran down the steps and down a path with some spiky plants and down some more steps. The ocean swirled around his sneakers, making them heavy. "I remember!" he shrieked

out at the noisy ocean. "I remember! I remember! I remember!"

Strong arms lifted him from the water. Grandaddy carried
him up the steps and down the long walkway into the house.
"You said I could swim! You said I could swim! You promised
even if it was midnight!"

"Well, mercy, son. Not in your clothes. Not in your *shoes.*"

The he was being put into Clare's new bathing suit for him
with a rainbow on the pocket, which was one of his birthday
presents. The other birthday present was a raft with a flag on it,
but Clare said tonight they would just splash in the ocean because the tide was too high and tomorrow morning would be
better for the raft. Grandaddy, looking sad, carried away his
wet pants and sneakers and socks. Angel got her embroidery
scissors out of her suitcase. "I'm going to go out there right now
and cut the points off those Spanish bayonets before someone
gets hurt on them," she said.

"Did Dr. Anthony ever tell you about the time Miss Alicia
was walking out with a suitor and slipped and sat down on a
Spanish bayonet and lost her dignity?" Clare said, laughing.

"I'll bet that's all she ever lost," said Angel.

He and Clare splashed in the ocean. First it was cold; then it
got warm. She made him hold her hand, though he told her he
wasn't afraid. But sometimes a big wave would come and he
was glad to hold on. She still had her shorts on, so he tried to
pull her far enough to get them wet. "Oh, *no,* Jason," she would
scream. "Oh, *yes!*" he would scream back. Way off down the
beach, colors popped and exploded in the sky. "We'll get you
some firecrackers tomorrow," she said, "but Grandaddy will
have to set them off, I'm terrified of them." "How long am I
staying here?" he asked her. "You're staying tonight," she said,
"and all day tomorrow, and part of Sunday." "Can I stay in
the water all day tomorrow?" "Just so you don't get burned,"
she said, "but I got you some SP15 lotion and we'll just keep
rubbing it on." They splashed some more and a big wave came
and wet her shorts. "Oh, now I am *drenched!*" she screamed. But
she wasn't mad. There was a round red moon. It came up big
in front of them and made a line on the water. The line came
straight to them like a path they could walk on.

"You know what I'd like to do?" he said.

"No, precious, what?" Clare bent down to him. She looked like she loved him a lot.

"I'd like to walk across this ocean to that moon," he said.

He was in bed next to Grandaddy, who was already asleep. Outside the windows, the ocean made a washing sound around them. It sounded like his other grandmother throwing buckets of water on the porch in Granny Squirrel to wash it off. It was dark in the room, but he could smell Angel's cold cream, so she would be coming to bed soon. She would lie on his other side and then he would feel Grandaddy's bones and her softer bones pushing him in tight.

The man Felix had also gone to bed in another room somewhere else. He heard Angel and Clare talking softly in the next room, where the lamp was still on. But he could hear when they were talking about him.

"That child is so sensitive . . . it's like having *him* back," Angel said.

"When he ran down to the water with his shoes on, it gave me chills . . ." Clare said.

"I know. Exactly the same. It was uncanny."

"And you know, when he and I were out together . . . God! children are exhausting, aren't they? But he saw the moon come up and he said to me, 'You know what I'd like to do?' and I said, 'No, what?' and he said—I swear to God, in that same faraway, mystical voice Theo had as a child—he said, 'I'd like to walk right across this ocean to that moon.'"

"Oh, that's exactly the kind of thing Theo used to say!"

Ralph no longer loved the beach. Since his bout with skin cancer, he couldn't go in the sun without a hat and shirt. There had been a period in the late sixties when he'd become pretty adept on the surfboard . . . an expensive one he had bought for his sons, only they had both lost interest when they hadn't been able to master it in the first ten minutes. Where was that surfboard? Still in the basement somewhere. He would have to dig it out sometime in a few years and teach Jason how to ride it; start him young; avoid the impatience he had shown with Theo and Rafe. He believed he knew better now how to instill self-confidence in boys. You didn't criticize so much or get angry, you just set the best example you could and tacitly conveyed the message, You can do it, too.

Too bad you didn't learn these skills a bit sooner.

Since when had Lily's voice, in her role as his antagonist, begun to answer him—usually to contradict him—in his head? Her dry, ironic drawl, contemptuous more often than not, could intrude at any time, rupturing the healing processes of his thoughts. It was if he carried his enemy around inside of him.

By this time Tuesday, he might be dead. There was a good chance. His uncle Charlie had died under the anesthetic during a routine operation. The thought of his own death and how it would affect others momentarily invigorated him as he shaved in the tiny front bathroom of "No Saints," the one with the slanting floor. If that laid-back Fauquier didn't replace that rotting front post, the whole ill-designed shack was going to fall on its face within a couple of years. The idea made him almost happy, for the briefest instant, until, inspecting his face for any missed whiskers, his filmed-over right eye reminded him afresh of the ordeal that lay in wait for him on Tuesday morning.

"But isn't it one of the safest operations?" Lily had asked in the car. "There's always a risk with a general anesthetic," he had replied, and reminded her of his uncle Charlie, how his father said afterwards it ran in some families, an intolerance for anesthetics. "Then why not just have a local?" she had said, "that's all Father Weir had. He was awake the whole time. He said they put a sheet over his head, with just the hole cut out for the eye they were doing, and he felt like a one-eyed ghost on Halloween." Now, how could a man reply to that sort of thing, and coming from his own wife?

After such a remark he would be damned if he ever admitted to her, as he had candidly to Miss Alicia, "I couldn't go through with it otherwise. Sometimes just the thought of what they are going to do in there makes me want to pass out."

Lily's well-known disinclination to indulge people's infirmities had been his main reason for deciding to have the surgery while she was away. He had reminded her of this in the car when she accused him of being "underhanded" and not telling her until it was too late. "Would you have liked it better if, when Dr. Nathan phoned me last week and said they could fit me in, I'd asked you to give up your week at the beach? You would have resented it, you would have felt obligated to stay home, and you know how you hate sick people." "I think you should have trusted me enough to tell me," she had said reproachfully, and for a moment he had felt he'd made a mistake, that by not telling her he had unfairly denied her an opportunity to show she still cared for him. "I didn't want you to feel you had to make a choice between me and Clare," he said after a minute. But his remorse had quickly evaporated when she replied with her deadliest offhand sweetness, "Whereas *this* way you've fixed it so I'd have to feel bad whatever I might have chosen."

They had driven on awhile in silence. Replenishing their separate arsenals. "But who will drive you home from the hospital?" she asked finally. "Since you've become such a devoted chauffeur, hasn't Miss Alicia let her license lapse?"

"Her maid, Susie, will drive her," he said. "It's all been arranged. They're coming to pick me up when I get discharged."

"Well, my goodness. You seem to have taken care of everything!"

"Everything under my control. Of course, there could be complications with the surgery. Or with the anesthetic . . ."

"I'm sure there won't be," Lily had said, cutting him off lightly.

Ralph found Felix alone in the kitchen, having himself a leisurely breakfast and obviously relishing his solitude. He was reading a manuscript bound in a black folder and eating a piece of toast heaped with cottage cheese when Ralph ambled in. Though Felix was all cordiality, the Complete European Gentleman, springing up at once to make fresh coffee, reciting choices of juices or fruit, brown bread or English muffins, Ralph found himself wishing he had slipped out on his own and gone to a diner on the mainland. But it was too late. Felix was making the effort and he would have to, too. Ralph had no definite grievance against Felix, he could even see why Felix would be exactly the sort of person Clare could be expected to pick, but he always felt slightly uncomfortable around the man; they had no real affinities, no points of genuine communion. Last summer Ralph had tried to make conversation about the war. With men of a certain age, that was always a safe topic. But as it turned out, he had miscalculated, Felix had just missed being old enough to join up, and he only ended riling the man by putting him on the defensive. And then there was the Jewish thing. Not that Ralph had any anti-Semitism left in himself—how could he, after knowing Hannah? He hadn't even known he had *been* anti-Semitic until Hannah had taken him by the hand and led him back through his past and shown him how very deeply ingrained it had been in him. But the trouble was, once you were aware of how sensitive they actually were about it, then you were more on edge that some perfectly harmless thing you might say to anybody else might be misconstrued as prejudice by one of them. Another strange thing—he had no explanation for it—was that although Hannah frequently talked about the feelings and problems of being Jewish, he had at some point stopped thinking of her as being "Jewish," or indeed as being anything except Hannah. Whereas, whenever he saw Felix, who had never once referred to Jews or being Jewish, a warning signal flashed on in Ralph's head and he thought to himself, I must be careful not to say anything that could be misconstrued.

"Do you prefer de-caf Colombian or Kona Hawaiian?" Felix was asking him. "Clare mixes them together, but since I'm making a new pot, we could have it all caffeinated."

"I'm just a simple coffee man myself," said Ralph, going to the refrigerator and pouring himself a glass of orange juice from a carton while Felix carried out an elaborately fussy ritual involving beans and filters and bottled spring water.

"Wait until you taste this Kona," he told Ralph. "It has a delicious flavor, better than anything I've tasted." The man thought far too much about his palate; he and Clare both did. Ralph had heard them sit down to a meal and start discussing some other meal they had eaten in New York, or one they were planning to eat in the future. Felix was too large, but it didn't seem to bother him. On the contrary, to watch him move about the kitchen—he was exceedingly light on his feet for such a big man—you got the distinct impression he took pleasure in every ounce of himself. "It's going to be a perfect day for the beach," Felix said to him. "Jason had Clare out there by seven o'clock. They've been splashing around like two children ever since. I believe Lily has gone for one of her long walks."

"I can't go in the sun much anymore," said Ralph, wishing he had remembered to bring along a simple loaf of sliced white bread, the old-fashioned, spongy kind that the gourmets and health nuts turned their noses up at. "Not since I had my bout with skin cancer."

"I went through that myself a few years ago," said Felix cheerfully, as though they were talking about some holiday spot each had passed through.

"Which did you have, the basal-cell kind or the squamous?"

"I don't recall. The doctor probably told me, but it slipped past. I had one on my nose and one on the back of my hand. I simply called them my cancerettes at the time. Don't have that supermarket jelly, Ralph, it's something the Fauquiers left behind; have the peach preserves on the table. Clare buys them at the island shop."

Ralph considered returning the grape jelly, which he actually preferred, to the refrigerator, for the sake of affability. But why should he, when Felix had just cut him short on one of the few subjects they had in common? Lily would have done the same if she had been in the room. It was bad manners to talk about illness and disease; was that why Felix, the European Gentleman, had brushed him off? "Cancerettes." Ralph felt his gorge rising. He carried the grape jelly to the table, out of a sense of loyalty to himself. He wasn't even hungry anymore. All he wanted was to get through this "breakfast" without incident and to fortify himself for the long day ahead. He sat down with his juice and an untoasted English muffin and the lowly supermarket jelly, then realized he needed a knife to spread his butter. But there was Felix, the cordial host, suddenly reaching around him like a waiter and placing the needed knife, as well as a folded paper napkin, to the right of Ralph's plate.

"The coffee will be ready in a moment, Ralph. Do you take milk, or sugar? I seem to remember both, from last year."

"If you have them," said Ralph, feeling like a helpless, hulking clod with this confident fellow dancing attendance on him. "But I could have got them myself," he added unconvincingly when Felix presently returned with a little pitcher and a sugar bowl and the famous Kona coffee.

The two men sat across from each other, having their breakfast. Felix had brought himself a fresh piece of brown toast, which he heaped with more cottage cheese and sank his teeth into with relish. The manuscript he had been reading when Ralph entered lay politely closed beside his plate.

"I'm afraid I interrupted your reading," Ralph said, sipping his coffee. It had a show-offy quality of deliciousness. It made you notice it, when all you wanted was a little stimulation for the long day ahead. "You are right," he told his host, "this is very good coffee."

"Isn't it delightful? No, actually, I've already read this. Several times, in fact. I'm in the process of making some painful cuts. It's a play I commissioned for my theater. But as this script stands at the moment, the play would run six hours. That's two hours longer than *Strange Interlude,* which most audiences find rough going; and this isn't O'Neill, but a Czech playwright who is unknown in this country."

"What is the play about?" Ralph tried to sound interested.

Felix laughed. "It was supposed to be a play about Kafka. But as it turned out, it is a play about the playwright's childhood and adolescence in Prague. Kafka simply served as the fusion point. The reason the playwright was so fascinated by Kafka turns out to be that some details in Kafka's life—the father aspect in particular, the ambivalent feelings about Judaism to a lesser degree—provided powerful echoes for Anton. Anton is the playwright."

"That must have been disappointing for you," said Ralph. "Ordering one kind of play and getting another." He was trying to remember what he knew about Kafka. Not very much. To the best of his knowledge, Kafka had been a German. And he didn't recall anyone's ever telling him Kafka had been Jewish. But better to stay off that subject, even though Felix had been the one to say the word "Judaism." Actually, Ralph reflected, he knew more about the word "Kafkaesque" than he did about the man Kafka. When people said, as they frequently did, that something was Kafkaesque, they meant there was a no-win element of nightmarish bureaucracy. It was Kafkaesque the day after Theo was killed, when he had gone to the police station to read the report and so much had been wrong and everybody had given him the runaround.

"No, not at all," said Felix. "This play is actually better than the one I had hoped for. It has caught something that goes beyond national boundaries or the life of a single historical figure. It's captured beautifully the essence of a child's frustration at his own powerlessness. A wonderful thing happened to Anton in the writing of this play. He found his own best material and at the same time broke through to the universal. He calls it *An Apartment in Prague,* but when people see this play, it could be an apartment or a house anywhere a child has ever felt like this. Poor Anton went through a bad time last spring—I had to fly to Vienna and tell him '*Coraggio!*' and let him talk through his misgivings. But the bad time, the misgivings, were simply the prelude to his breakthrough. As soon as he got past Kafka and into the heart of his own material—where Kafka, his idea of Kafka, rather, had been trying to lead him all the time—nothing could stop him. He wrote twenty, thirty pages of dialogue a day, whereas before, he was blocked for weeks. Are you sure you wouldn't like that English muffin toasted, Ralph? Isn't it rather bland . . . and cold?"

"No, it's just fine," said Ralph. "I never have been one for fussing a lot over what I eat," he added, rather testily.

"Well, it shows, Ralph. Look how slim you are." Felix looked ruefully down at his own belly and laughed. "I should follow your example." Yet his tone made it clear he had no intention of doing any such thing.

There was a hiatus in the conversation. Hearing his own jaws crack as he chewed the tasteless muffin to pulp, Ralph wondered if Felix, on his side of the table, was thinking him crude for having said that about fussing over food.

However, Felix apparently hadn't been thinking of Ralph at all. He slapped the Czech's script beside his empty plate with hearty approval and said aloud, as if completing some highly engrossing interior conversation he'd been having with himself while Ralph worried about manners, "An artist has found his true subject, I think, when he dramatizes the truth he can no longer escape rather than the illusions he has been longing to make true."

Ralph nodded thoughtfully—it was the most appropriate response he could make—and carried his plate and cup and saucer to the sink, where he rinsed them carefully and stacked them in a neat row in Fauquier's mildewing rubber drainer. His back to Felix, he allowed himself a brief, gratifying moment of resentment of the man's aggressive celebration of life in all its myriad manifestations: food, art, even "cancerettes."

But as he was fixing to escape from the kitchen, Felix disarmed him against his will by growing serious and saying with what appeared to be genuine fellow-feeling, "Clare told me about the operation you have coming up on Tuesday. I didn't want to bring it up while you were having breakfast, but I do want to wish you good luck. However, from what I've heard, the high level of skill they have now, and those wonderful lens implants, they say it's miraculous, the difference. A literal eye-opener: light after the darkness."

Ralph was tempted to stay awhile longer and chat about his doctor, and the lenses, and confide his fears about Uncle Charlie and the anesthetic. But he didn't want to appear negative, and even though the man seemed sincere, it could have been a form of door-closing nicety. So he simply thanked Felix for his good wishes and said, with his own brand of rueful humor, that he could use some more light, and shut the door on Felix and the Czech playwright.

He went upstairs and used his WaterPik. Then he neatened up his things and made the bed he and Lily and Jason had slept in. Made it properly, the way he had been taught in the Army, with squared corners and no creases. Lily had already made it up her way, the way she had done for years at home, just pulling up the spread and folding the top sheet back over it and leaving the pillows exposed, as if someone planned to crawl back in during the day and didn't want to have to go to the trouble of unmaking the bed. Jason's things were strewn about this room and the one adjoining it. He went around picking up the little pajamas and socks and Jockey shorts and folding and stacking them in a pile beside his own open suitcase on the bed in the spare room. Despite the vigorous ocean breeze that blew the unfastened flowery curtains every whichway, Lily's perfume, Lily's distinctive, pungent female smell, dominated the room. Once upon a time, he had found this smell mysterious and arousing; now it stirred his antipathy: the slightly unhygienic arrogance of it struck him as careless and selfish. His mother had never allowed herself to smell like that, she had scrubbed every day with a hard brush and Lifebuoy soap; perfume had been a luxury she neither wished for nor could afford.

And stacked on the Fauquiers' wobbly little three-legged table beside the bed: Lily's current library for getting through life. *Dreams: A Way to Listen to God,* by Morton Kelsey, a biography of Saint Francis of Assisi and two P. D. James mysteries from the library, along with her old perpetual standbys, the Book of Common Prayer and *The Night and Nothing,* Father Weir's favorite spiritual guide. Once Ralph had taken covert pleasure in regularly checking the titles of Lily's books and seeing how well he could match them up with what he knew of her prevailing concerns. But at some point the exercise had begun to fill him with hopelessness and distaste.

Ralph put on his trunks and a shirt and the straw hat that Miss Alicia had ordered for him from L. L. Bean. He went down to the surf, where Clare was pulling Jason back and forth on the little Confederate float she had bought for him. He stood to the side, watching them for a few minutes. Clare would pull the float out a little way into the gentle waves and help Jason climb on it, facing shorewards. Then they would wait for a wave and Clare would give a push and the boy would go shrieking towards shore, holding on to the sides of his float. They did this over and over again; the waves this close to shore were so gentle they hardly broke.

"Why don't you take him out farther?" Ralph asked Clare. "Give him a better ride."

"Yes! Take me out farther!" demanded the child.

Clare handed the little raft to Ralph by its ropes. "Here," she said, looking provoked, "*you* take him out and give him a better ride."

"Sweetie, I wasn't criticizing." He felt thoroughly misunderstood, like a child who has been rebuffed when he only wanted to join the fun. And here he was the one going to the hospital on Monday.

Clare must have read something on his face, because she softened. "I know, Ralph, I know. You were just trying to suggest how we could do it better. But look, you play with him for a while, okay? I need to go inside and put on some chili. We're having hot dogs for lunch."

"Lunch?" he quipped. "Felix is in there still eating breakfast."

She didn't find this amusing. "A good chili needs to simmer at least two hours," she said, not looking at him but squinting out at the ocean. She had little dry lines, now, radiating from the corners of her eyes. "Jason, you and Grandaddy play for a while," she told the boy, and turned sharply on her heel and headed up the beach. Her legs had aged better than her face, thought Ralph; they were almost the same as they had been when she was fourteen.

"Grandaddy, take me *way* out, now!"

"All right, son. Climb on and I'll take you out to where there's a little more action."

He pushed the boy into more vigorous waves, until he himself stood waist-high in the ocean. Jason's body tensed; he uttered little yips of fright when the waves splashed his face. "It's all right, son, there's nothing to be afraid of. I'm right here beside you."

He turned the child around so he faced shore. "Now, hold on to the sides," he instructed, "and look straight ahead, don't look back. And when I let you go, you stay balanced in the middle."

They waited for a good wave. The boy, trembling all over, clutched the sides of the float. "Here comes one. No, look straight ahead."

The wave came, Ralph launched the float, and the child shot forward with a shriek of terror and elation. The float was ghost-ridden. The white-blond hair of the boy on it, his taut back, the long torso and long, straight, pale legs were Theo's. For a moment it was as if everything in between had been a mixed-up, exhausting dream, some kind of spiritual warning, and here Ralph was, back with his first-born son, watching his triumphant ride on the wave, being granted the chance to do it all over again, and get it right, this time.

After lunch, he sought Clare out and asked her to go for a walk with him. He saw her hesitate, trying to hide her reluctance. She was afraid he was going to go over old things, but was obliged to honor his wishes because he was going into the hospital.

She emerged from the cottage wearing a wide-brimmed hat, dark glasses, and an oversized, long-sleeved cotton shirt that came almost to her knees.

"Why are you bundled up like Garbo?" he joked. "I'm the one that has to be careful of the sun."

"I have to watch it, too, at this time of day," she said matter-of-factly. "Since I've gotten older, it crinkles my skin and I get these unsightly moles. I had ten of them sliced off me this past winter. At twenty bucks apiece. Which way would you like to walk, Ralph?"

"Whichever way you like," he said diffidently. He felt he was here on sufferance. And yet once there had been a time when she would have been happy to go for a walk with him, would have proposed it herself.

"Let's go north; the houses get dinky at the south end. And this way, we'll have our backs to the sun while it's at its worst."

"Fine." He quickened his saunter to match her businesslike march. He could practically hear her thinking, At least I'll be able to burn up a few calories after that big lunch. Clare was a great one for making the best use of her time.

He glanced back at the cottage. The rest of them were inside napping. If he'd eaten and drunk the amounts they had, he would be in a damn stupor. Felix had taken two hot dogs and placed them sideways across his open roll and heaped them with chili, cole slaw, and chopped onions and tucked in with his knife and fork. He had never seen anyone eat hot dogs that way. Lily and Clare and Felix between them had consumed most of a half-gallon bottle of wine. Then Clare had stayed behind in the kitchen after lunch to start preparing *supper*. Boiling potatoes for potato salad. That's when he had suggested the walk.

"Is something the matter?" she asked, slowing down. "Did you forget something?"

"No, I was just looking at Fauquier's roof. He's got him a sagging rafter and half a dozen tiles missing. See there? And this morning when I was shaving, I felt like I was trying to keep my balance on a sinking ship. If the man doesn't do something soon, he's going to have a pile of rubble on his hands instead of a rental property. How much does he charge you for the month, anyway?"

Clare laughed delightedly. Then, as if he couldn't have chosen a topic more to her liking, she plunged with relish into a catalogue of all the things that had gone wrong in "No Saints" during her occupancies. She spoke of the various family members and their foibles with humorous, possessive indulgence. They might have been relatives of hers, but not of his. The topic got them past three breakers, and she became animated and involved, forgetting to maintain her wary standoffishness towards him. She told him that what she had learned through the Fauquiers was priceless, but wouldn't tell him how much rent she paid, even though she'd told him what her dermatologist charged when he hadn't even asked. She could be as evasive as her mother when she chose.

Yet, listening to her hold forth on the Fauquiers made him realize she hadn't changed much, in some ways, since adolescence. She still measured herself constantly against others, studied them to learn any secrets she believed they might have for living better than she did, for being more attractive, making more friends. She had developed an ironic sophistication over the years, but underneath it ran the same raw, tense wistfulness of the girl who once sat high beside him in the truck, agonizing aloud over why Freddy Stratton had more boyfriends, and demanding to know how she could become irresistible.

He was clearing his throat, getting ready to remind her of those old days when she trusted him and sought out his company, but she forestalled his raid on the past by returning him to the unhappier present:

"You must be nervous about your cataract operation on Tuesday. I would be. It's not so much what they're going to do—*that's* almost certain to improve things—but the thinking about it beforehand. The eye calls forth imaginings in a way that most other organs don't. I wonder why that is; I wonder if it's because the eye has been used so often as a symbol. The window of the soul . . . the 'power behind the eye' Emerson said could charm down insanity or wild beasts . . .'if thine eye offend thee . . .' Yuk, I've always hated that passage in the Bible. Too graphic. Maybe that's it: the whole thing's too graphic for comfort. But Ralph, why did you schedule the operation for when Lily was going to be away?"

"Doctors have busy schedules, you know. And I didn't see any reason for her to stay home from the beach. What for? So she could visit me in the hospital? I won't be in but for three days. Monday, they prepare you. Tuesday morning's the surgery. Wednesday, if all goes well, I get discharged. Any one of my men could drive me home. As it happens, Miss Alicia's maid wants to do it. Then I have to be quiet for a few days, and not bend down or cough or anything. I don't see what use your mother could be to me there."

"Ralph, that's not the point and you know it. I know that I would feel terribly hurt if Felix sent me off somewhere to enjoy myself and then told me at the airport or something he was going to check into the hospital for an operation while I was gone. And Felix would be shattered if I did it to him. He'd find it incomprehensible."

"Well . . ." He didn't trust himself to go on. Resentment gathered like a knot of phlegm in his throat. Did she have any idea how callous she was being? First the graphic images . . . "If thine eye offend thee . . ." Not the kind of picture you wanted in your head two days before an eye operation. And then her glib comparison of herself and Felix with him and Lily. Insincere, too. She knew how things were between him and Lily; how could anyone be around them for more than five minutes and not know? And did she think he didn't know she and Lily talked? *He* hadn't mentioned his operation, yet both Clare and Felix knew. And from Clare's reproach, he could hear almost verbatim how Lily had presented it from her side. ("He just sprang it on me in the car when we were halfway here. I know he'd rather have Miss Alicia fussing over him and Susie's cooking, but I think he might have told me. Not that I'd have *forced* myself on his convalescence, but I do think that, after thirty-four years of marriage, I'm entitled to that option!'")

"I don't think it's any secret that your mother and I haven't been compatible for some time," he said. If she wouldn't let him talk about the past, he could at least force her to be candid about what was going on in the present. "To pretend any different would be hypocritical."

She gave an exasperated snort and increased her forced-march pace. "But you're still married, aren't you? If you all are going to give up trying, what's the point of staying married? I mean, Rafe's grown. And —" She didn't go on, but they were both thinking the name she had been going to say. "There must be *some* reason you two choose to stay together, there must be *something* you like about each other. Otherwise, well, God! It would seem like you all stay on together because you enjoy torturing each other."

"I certainly don't want to torture anybody," he said. And then heard himself through Lily's ears as sounding "sanctimonious." The idea came to him then that he might try explaining to Clare as he would to a friend about this antagonist-Lily he carried around inside him, and what a torture *that* was. Clare might find it interesting. In her books she was always mapping the complexities and contradictions of people's inner lives. "People change," he began. "Marriages change. . . ." ("*Oh-oh, warmup for sermontime,*" interjected the dry Lily-drawl inside him.) He forced himself on, in pursuit of the truth he wanted to share with Clare: "Over the course of a long marriage, you incorporate in yourself the image the other person has of you. If the image is good, you become a better person. You change for the good. But if the image turns out to be mostly negative, then you change for the worse. It gets to the place you find it hard to do anything right anymore. You just don't have the energy needed to turn things around —"

Clare stopped in her tracks and flung up her arms at him. "You have no idea the distress this is causing me!" In the hat and dark glasses and long baggy shirt, she looked like a stranger: some minor movie actress in disguise, having a moment of petulance on the beach.

"I don't mean to," he said sorrowfully. "I was just trying to think some things out in the presence of someone who might understand. There was a time when you and I could talk. I remember —"

"Damn it, Ralph —" She stooped suddenly and picked up a shell that had caught her eye. Then saw it was slightly flawed and flung it angrily into the water. "I mean, try to see it from my side. First you come along when I'm nine, and you take my mother. You change her life, you change my life. But it's all for love and passion, and so it's all right; society has to accept it; even I, eventually, accepted it. I was just being a selfish little girl who wanted her mother to herself. I have learned to see it that way. You took away Lily's independence, but that's acceptable, too. As long as she agreed to let you take it away. But now, you all tell me, you don't love each other anymore. You get on each other's nerves. You destroy each other's souls. You 'incorporate' each other's negative images. Well, it *hurts* me to hear this. It's like the whole thing has been for nothing." She gave a bitter laugh and whirled around, starting them back in the direction of the cottage. "It's really quite ironic. First, you two loved each other against my wishes, now you hate each other against my wishes. Now is the time for you all to be good to each other, after all you've been through. That's what *I* would like. That way, I could —" She laughed in a different, embarrassed way, as though she were grudgingly revealing her hand. "That way I could stop being obsessed with the Quick family soap opera and get on with my own life."

Most people would say you're doing pretty well at getting on with your own life. I never said I didn't love your mother, although I'm well aware she may have said that about me. You can't take away someone's independence that they never had. Even when Lily was working, her mother had to balance her checkbook for her. And when we were courting those two long years because she was scared to tell her mother she wanted to leave her, Lily used to lie wrapped around me in the backseat of my car, on top of the mountain, and moan, "I need you to take care of me . . . I need you to take care of me."

Any or all of these things he might have come back with and won his point, shocked her into a long-overdue awareness of who had first come on to whom in this marriage, who had been the more needy at the time. But he hadn't engineered this walk to bellyache about his marriage or to (as Lily would put it) "spill any beans." His object had been to try to put things right between himself and Clare. They had not been right for twenty-seven years, and he wanted that much repaired, if it could be, before he went under the anesthetic Tuesday morning. If he should follow in the footsteps of his uncle Charlie, he would like to think that Clare might one day do him justice when he was no longer around to defend himself.

"There was a time when you liked and trusted me," he began.

Clare hit her head with her fist, almost knocking off the hat. "Oh, why do we have to open up that old can of worms, Ralph?"

"Because," he said, trying to take a reasonable tone, as he would with Jason during one of his tantrums, trying not to be sucked into her anger and panic, "that can of worms has been open for twenty-seven years. The worms are in a looser clump now, but we might as well separate the ones that are still tangled up, let them go on their way . . ."

She could not restrain a laugh at his image of setting free the still-entangled worms.

Encouraged, he went on: "We went for walks . . . we drove around in my old truck . . . we sang songs . . . I taught you the songs my father taught me. We went to see Uncle Don, the gun man, remember? You asked my advice, confided in me. Remember how you used to worry about Freddy Stratton having more sex appeal?"

"Why do we have to go *into* this!" she yelled. Then looked quickly around, from behind the dark glasses, to see if any of the sunbathers lying on the beach had seen her outburst. She veered out towards the surf, began kicking up the spray, making deliberate splashes, like a small child.

"Because"—he pursued her—"maybe if we went into it again, you would realize that I was only trying to do my best for you at the time. The best I knew how. Maybe then we could be friends again."

"We are friends, Ralph . . . but, oh, Christ! What a bad memory you have! Or do you just shut out the parts you don't want to admit?"

"Such as what parts?"

"Well . . . shit, Ralph! The parts, for instance, where you started hitting me in the face and knocking me around all the time."

"It wasn't all the time," he said sadly. "And for those few times, I am very sorry, believe me. I didn't always act wisely. I wasn't old enough to have achieved any wisdom. When I married your mother, I was twenty-four. Three years younger than Rafe is now. Can you imagine Rafe, even now, marrying a thirty-two-year-old widow with a nine-year-old daughter? And in some ways, I was even younger than my age. I'd been in the Army, of course, but I didn't have much experience with women. I did the best I could, but a lot of the time I was wandering around not knowing what had hit me. I hadn't even lived, then suddenly there I was, married, with a nine-year-old daughter. Then I was working all day on construction jobs—for somebody else's construction company—to make ends meet, because Lily had given up her job. After that, there were the miscarriages—Lily had two miscarriages; we kept them from you because you were going through a phase of disgust for everything physical, and Lily thought it might damage your passage into womanhood—and then, suddenly, I wasn't much older than Theo was when he died and I had a small son, and you and all your little friends who spent the night were running around the apartment half-naked, and I became aware of . . . complications in myself . . . of feelings that I knew I shouldn't be having . . ."

"What kind of feelings?" Clare asked. Grimly. Resentfully. Reluctantly knowing.

"Well . . . I mean, damn it, look at Rafe. For ten years he's been a college boy. He's twenty-seven now, a graduate student getting his Ph.D., and every fall he goes to the freshman orientation dance and picks up a new eighteen-year-old girl. Eternally rejuvenating himself. What I'm saying is, I never had a carefree youth like Rafe did. I joined the Army right out of high school, and I worked afternoons and evenings the whole time I was in high school, and then I came back from the Army, got a job, met your mother, and my future was fixed. But there was a period there, when you and Freddy and Julia were running in and out of the bathroom in your shortie pajamas, and Lily was worn out from her pregnancies, that I felt cheated. I felt I'd been done out of my right to have a carefree youth . . . to *dally*, like Rafe seems to be doing forever. I resented you and your friends, and I lusted after you all, and I hated myself. I would never have laid a finger on any of you, but . . . I needed time to come to terms with myself."

"So you just whapped me on the side of the face and knocked me down," said Clare, marching grimly along. "In order to come to terms with yourself. I suppose I should be grateful to have escaped the Lolita syndrome. Oh, Ralph, what good does it do to go over all these old miseries?"

"I wanted things right between us before I got into the hospital. You know, my uncle Charlie —"

"Yes, Uncle Charlie. Who croaked under the anesthetic before they'd even cut him open for his routine gallbladder operation." Clare took a deep breath and burst into song: "The poor old slave/has gone to rest/we know that he is free —"

With aching heart, Ralph nevertheless joined in, because he understood that his message had been received and, in some measure, accepted—otherwise, she would not have initiated one of "their" old songs: the one that had delighted her most as a girl, because of its rapid descent into gibberish. Uncle Charlie had taught that song to his younger brother, who, years later, accompanying himself on the banjo, had taught it to his only child, Ralph. "—his bones they lie/disturb them not/way down in Tennessee —"

They walked on together, singing. "The pe-or eold sle-ave/has ge-one to re-ast/we kne-ow that he-o/is free-o-free-free —"

And on some more, to the sight of Fauquier's ramshackle cottage, "No Saints," with the neighbors' Confederate flags flapping to either side.

"—the pickety-pack-poor old slickety-slack slave/has gickety-gack-gone to rickety-rack-rest/we knickety-knack-know that hickety-hack-he/is frickety-frack-free . . . his bickety-back-bones they lickety-lack-lie/distickety-stack-sturb them knickety-knack-not/way dickety-dack-down in tickety-tack-Tenn-e-see-oh-see-see . . ."

On Tuesday morning, Lily did not come down to have early breakfast with Clare and Felix. It was the first time she had broken the tradition the three of them had begun four years ago. When Lily was visiting "No Saints" and there were no other guests, she prided herself on fitting into their schedule as unobtrusively as possible. Upon learning that Clare and Felix liked to wake up early enough to walk on the beach and watch the sunrise, and then have a light breakfast and use the freshest morning hours for work, and that Felix worked in the kitchen so he could spread out his scripts and budgets and blueprints for stage designs, Lily also rose at sunrise. Her tact and timing were impeccable. As they returned from their walk, they would meet Lily starting out on her shorter one. Then Felix would shave and go into the sea with the lather still on his face—one of his favorite moments of the day—and if the water was the right temperature Clare might join him. Then they would dress and go down to the kitchen and hit the fluorescent light with the broom handle, and by the time the two rods flickered on, the coffee would be made and Lily's tea brewed, and her sweet roll warmed in the oven, and, as if she had been watching from the wings for her cue, Lily would enter with her cordial "Good morning," and sit quietly at her place, drinking her tea and taking small, delicate bites of her sweet roll. If anyone was in the mood to talk, she would join in. But she understood enough of the creative process, she told them, to know how superfluous talk too early in the day could sometimes wreck a promising train of thought. She always took her second cup of tea upstairs and sat on the open porch with it, either reading her prayer book or gazing out at the ocean, and then, as soon as Clare came up—she worked at a long table in the big, dark "pecky cypress" living room, with lamps turned on—Lily would quietly retreat to her room, the "breezy room," and shut the door and nap. "The sound of your typewriter is my lullaby," she told Clare. "It assures me that you are accomplishing something and I can rest. It's only if you *stop* typing that you'll wake me up." And whether it was the power of suggestion or the daughter wanting to prove to the mother she was honoring her wishes, Clare usually typed, more or less steadily, for an hour or two. Then Lily would tiptoe out, wearing her wide-brimmed hat, and take her long walk for the day.

When she got back, Clare would often have done all she could, and say so, and Lily would reply in her dry, amused way, "In that case, I suppose you're allowed to enjoy the beach." And they might go for a swim together. It touched something in Clare, the way Lily bounced up and down in the ocean with the abandon of a child. Some part of her *was* still a child, only Clare had not seen that aspect of her until these visits to "The Island"; the way she came in to breakfast, merged so obediently into their working mornings: she was being their good and petted child, showing them how little trouble she could be, wanting to justify their faith in including her. Yet she was also Lily the hard-driving Mother-Muse, expecting her daughter to keep typing, keep excelling, keep achieving, and, only after she was all typed out, to enjoy the beach. So much did Clare honor this tradition of Lily's expectations for her that, even though she had no work-in-progress this summer, she had brought some notes that could pass for one, in sound, at least, when typed as accompaniment to Lily's morning naps.

On Monday morning, the day after Ralph and Jason had left, she had been at the long table, with the lamps turned on, by half past seven, feeding into the typewriter a dialogue between two women, already sketched in part on a yellow pad. She had no big plans for it; if anything, she wanted to *protect* it from any of her usual big plans. It was just a scene involving two old friends on a mountaintop at high noon, watched over by a friendly hawk; two women comparing notes on the first half of their lives, and plotting strategies and attitudes to meet Part Two. There was to be nothing crafty or grandiose about it. She wanted merely to hover above them like the curious hawk and overhear what they confided in that brief Olympian celebration of themselves-so-far, before shots rang out in the valley below and summoned them out of the sunshine.

But Tuesday morning, on returning from their sunrise walk, Clare and Felix did not encounter Lily starting out on hers. When they got back to the cottage, the door to the breezy room was still shut. "Let her sleep," Felix told Clare as they bathed in the sea together after his shave. "She was up late last night; I saw her sitting out on the windwalk when I went down around midnight to console myself with a nip of brandy. I couldn't sleep for thinking about *him* and his operation this morning. She was probably doing the same thing. After all, they've been married over thirty years."

"I woke up thinking about him," said Clare. "I imagined myself as him in the hospital, waking up and knowing it was time, and getting prepped by the nurses, and the fear . . . Uncle Charlie. You know, I told you. By now they're doing it to him. Whatever they do. I don't think they use a knife anymore. It's a laser beam. Ugh! Well, Ralph, you did a good job making us all feel sorry for you."

"He has that quality," said Felix. "He rubs you the wrong way while you're around him, and as soon as he's gone you find yourself feeling sorry for him."

"He certainly did his number on me on our walk," said Clare. "It will take me at least a year to digest all the new mess he told me."

"The lust he felt for all you little girls, and his guilt for feeling it? Poor man."

"That didn't surprise me as much as it might have," said Clare glumly. "I think I always knew, in that way you know things when you don't want to know. But I was shocked about

Lily's miscarriages. I mean, we were all living jammed together in that small apartment and I didn't even know she had two miscarriages. It seems unforgivable on my part that I could have tuned out like that. Even with the help of the Blessed Virgin. Ralph said Lily wanted to keep it from me because I was going through a period of revulsion against the physical side of life. He said Lily thought it might damage my passage to womanhood."

"You didn't tell me that part."

"No," said Clare, pulling her fingers back and forth through the warm sea. "I wanted to think about it for a while. About whether I had been damaged or not. I don't mean Lily's miscarriages, because I didn't know about them, but by Lily's situation as I saw it then. By her helplessness because she was a prisoner of her body. The way I guess it looked to me was, her body had somehow betrayed her mind. I've been wondering if I didn't make one of those subterranean psychic decisions back then: never to get into Lily's position. And that's why, maybe, I never could bring myself to marry . . . or even get pregnant."

"And what did you conclude?" asked Felix, his face going very still and serious.

"So far, I've concluded that even if I did make such a decision—unbeknownst to myself, of course —"

"Of course."

"That I'm sorry for the way things have turned out. I mean, whatever my deformities or peculiarities, I have to say that I can't imagine a life that would suit me better than the one I am living right now."

"In that case," said Felix, looking very thoughtful for a moment, "it's been well worth the price. Don't you agree?"

"Oh, I agree," said Clare. "The only thing that makes me sad is that Lily paid most of it for me."

When Lily failed to appear after they were halfway through breakfast, Clare made her mother's tea and heated the sweet roll and arranged a breakfast tray. "This isn't like her. I'm going up."

She carried the tray upstairs and was about to knock on Lily's door when she was overcome by a horrible superstition: if she were to open the door of the breezy room while carrying the tray, Lily would be dead. She tiptoed over to the long table in the living room and put down the tray beside her typewriter and the sheaf of notes about the two women on the mountaintop.

She considered turning on a lamp—the room was so dim—but this act, too, seemed to be proscribed by superstition. When she returned to Lily's door, knocking seemed forbidden also. She took a deep breath and turned the knob slowly.

Lily, wearing a summer kimono, was sitting up in bed, scribbling rapidly in a little spiral notebook, one of those she carried to remind herself of things and copy out passages she wanted to remember from books. She gave a guilty jerk when she saw Clare and rearranged her face. "Oh, darling, I didn't hear you knock."

"I didn't knock," said Clare. "I just wanted to see if you were all right. Felix and I got worried when you didn't come down to breakfast at your usual time." She lingered nervously in the doorway, a bit shaken because for a flash of a second she had glimpsed an image of Lily that she had never seen before. She had seen a frail, grim little lady, her face screwed up with a frightening absorption that excluded everyone else in the world. It was as if, on some demonic level Clare had neglected to prepare for, she *had* opened the door to discover her mother was gone.

"I'm sorry," said Lily, smiling up at her daughter and closing the little notebook. "But I overslept and then, just before I woke up, I had this dream and I wanted to write it down. I hope I haven't upset your and Felix's working morning too much."

"No, it's still very early. We just were worried. . . . What kind of a dream? Or, I suppose, you won't tell."

"Of course I'll tell, if you want to hear," Lily replied humorously, as if teasing an overly pessimistic child. "It wasn't much, but I thought it was sort of interesting."

Clare came forward and sat on the edge of the bed with the new sheets on it she had bought and prewashed for Snow.

"I dreamed I was lying on a narrow bed in a convent cell," began Lily, her blue eyes going cool and distant. "Ten or maybe fifteen nuns were crowded around my bed. They were in a kind of . . . awe, and one of them said, 'She's dead.' Another one asked, 'Are you sure?' 'Oh, yes,' said the first nun, 'and she looks so beautiful in her death. You can tell she's a saint.' And another nun asked, 'Shall we begin laying her out?' All this time I was thinking, But I'm *not* dead, yet all the same I continued to lie perfectly still and let them think so. I couldn't bear losing the opportunity of being a saint."

"And that was the whole dream?"

"That was the whole dream. I told you it wasn't much. I doubt if it lasted even a minute."

"I think it's very much," said Clare. "I think it's a very significant dream."

"I don't know," said Lily evasively. "I thought it was worth writing down because it was like a little story. It was *different,* but I don't know if it was significant. I know where it came from. I was reading Father Kelsey on dreams before I dropped off to sleep last night, and then this cottage being called 'No Saints,' and . . . oh yes, I even know where the nuns came from. I also dipped into this biography of Saint Francis some, and there's a nice chapter about his friend Saint Clare. She was determined to be a nun, against the wishes of her rich family, but Francis helped her. She ran off to his monastery and the monks cut off her hair for her and gave her an old brown robe and took her to some Benedictine sisters nearby. You might enjoy reading it; I know you like things about nuns."

"Is that why I was named Clare? After Saint Clare?"

"No, I don't think that was it. I don't think I even knew about her then. I just thought it was a nice name. Short. Clean. Clear. *Clarity.* A name a girl could make whatever she wanted out of. I always felt my own name, though it's perfectly all right, was a little . . . well . . . *flowery.* My mother chose it. Daddy wanted to name me Sophie. Actually, that might have suited me better."

"I can't possibly imagine you as anything but Lily. I think it suits you down to the ground, as the English would say."

"Well," said Lily vaguely. "You've never known me by any other name, have you?" and laughed in her dry way. "*Your* daddy wanted to name you Ophelia. So, you see, I have looked out for your interests, right from the start."

"Ophelia and Sophie," Clare drawled with slow sarcasm, to cover the pang she felt at Lily's last words. Though sheathed in protective irony themselves, they nonetheless contained a plea for a certain assurance: the assurance that she had, despite everything, been a good mother, the *right* mother, for this particular human being called Clare. "You might have creaked through fairly successfully as Sophie," Clare said, "but as an Ophelia I would have been a goner, probably from first grade on, if not sooner. I would never have made it! Thank you for knowing what I needed before I could ask for it myself. But why did he want Ophelia? After Shakespeare?"

"I doubt that very much," said Lily with a trace of scorn. "Probably because it was . . . oh, *beautiful*, you know." With a wickedly eloquent roll of her eyes, she dismissed the fanciful, chimerical needs of men.

She looked levelly across at her daughter. "But I'm glad you like Clare," she finished. Simply and subtly. She knew what had been going on between them.

"Oh, God! Guess what? I forgot your tray. I brought you tea and a sweet roll up, and then left them in the living room to get cold, I was so interested in your dream. I've been telling you for four years to have a dream in this room, but it took the okay of an Episcopal priest before you'd do it. Let me go and warm up everything again and I'll bring you breakfast in bed."

"Please don't," said Lily, getting up hurriedly. "I hate being served in bed. It makes me feel old and infirm." She sat down at the mirror and started pinning up her hair. "If I haven't delayed you all too much, I'd rather come down to the kitchen."

"You haven't delayed us," Clare assured her. "We can't be working all the time."

"I don't see why not," joked Lily archly, studying herself in the mirror. It was as though the lovely intimate exchange had never transpired; only they both knew it had.

While Lily, for once, lingered over her tea with them, the phone on the kitchen wall rang.

Clare answered. "Oh, hello, Miss Alicia." She looked at Lily, who was putting her cup silently down in its saucer. "Yes, she's right here."

As Lily got up and made her way to the telephone, she wore a strange, lofty look, that of someone who knew she was about to hear bad news but was determined not to go to pieces.

She took the receiver from Clare. "Hello." She sounded enigmatic, faintly amused. But her face had gone gray and she held the receiver awkwardly. "Oh," she said, after a minute, and the color began to come back. "Oh, well, it's very sweet of him to worry and very kind of you to let us know. Tell him I'm relieved . . . that we're all relieved, and that I hope he feels better soon." Then she murmured and rolled her eyes while Miss Alicia, on her end, went on about something. "Yes, I know. It must be. . . . Well, it's so kind of you. . . . Yes, I will. Thank you so much . . . Oh, I *know*." At last she hung up. "Well, it's all over," she told Felix and Clare brightly, "and they think the operation was a big success, and he was very sick from the anesthesia when he first woke up, but now everything is going to be all right." She spoke in a singsongy way, as though narrating a tale with a happy ending that she couldn't quite take seriously. "In fact, Miss Alicia has the highest hopes he might even be able to eat a dish of her homemade vanilla ice cream before the day is over."

On Friday, about eleven in the morning, Clare began preparing the maid's room, across from the kitchen, for Rafe, scheduled to arrive in the late afternoon. She was tucking her last set of clean sheets into the mattress, squaring the corners Armystyle, the way Ralph had taught her thirty years ago, and thinking of all the other things she had to do: peel two pounds of shrimp, Rafe's favorite food down here; pick up some more bottles of tonic; get a ten-pound bag of ice cubes . . . oh, and some more limes. She was also musing, in a more essayistic vein, about maids' rooms in general, the few she had seen and the many she had read about in books: it seemed deplorable to her, all of a sudden, that maids always got the worst space in a house. They got the low ceilings, the awkward corners, the poor ventilation, the wobbly or cracked furniture, the absence of view or vista. And yet, more than the others in the house, they needed a good room to escape to, their own place where they could be themselves. But maybe that was the whole point—from the masters' side, that is: they weren't supposed to have a place that encouraged them to think of what their selves were like; if they did, they might want more. They might stop being maids. On the other hand, she knew a man—he had done some typing for her up in the country—who had hand-built himself a little cabin on an acre of land in the woods and fitted up his tiny bedroom to resemble the maid's room he remembered from the house in which he grew up: "I've got the same washbowl and pitcher," he had pointed out to Clare proudly, "and the same little bookcase painted white, and I even managed to find the same yellow chenille bedspread. I always loved that room when I was a boy. It made me so happy to be allowed to go in there."

The maid's room in the Fauquier cottage was deplorable—hardly habitable, really. No screens on the windows. A nasty old air-conditioner. A cement floor covered with a thin, damp, moldy-smelling green carpet. A bathroom the size of a closet, containing the lidless toilet, a half-tub with a rubber hand shower attached by a hose to the tap, and a sink coming loose from the corkboard walls. That the Fauquiers didn't expect anyone to use it anymore—except for the most desperate overflow of guests—was made clear by the junk stored in corners, and the ancient rusted Electrolux parked right inside the door. But Rafe preferred it to being upstairs with the others. That way, he could get in from Myrtle Beach as late as he liked, without disturbing anybody, and he was directly across from the kitchen if he felt like having a snack or a drink.

She believed the past winter and spring had been harder on Rafe than on the rest of them. Theo and he had not been alike—indeed, the very personality of one had been a frequent source of irritation to the other—but they had been deeply entangled with each other: the self-despising brother with the arrogant one; the philosophical and fatalistic with the pleasure-loving. All his life Rafe had maintained a balance with this brother, so close in age, and now that balance had been destroyed. A part of Rafe had been shorn away by Theo's death and he was truly bereft. "I feel robbed," he had wept to her one night over long-distance, "I feel *robbed*."

And there were other shifts, more subtle or sinister, for him to adjust to. The favored son had *not* been killed, which led to some painful soul-searching on all their parts. Why had Rafe been valued more highly than Theo? On what criteria had their standards been based? What had been *Theo's* strong suits, Theo's overlooked virtues? Wasn't it more than likely that he might still be alive if his special qualities had been recognized and appreciated? Rafe tormented himself with these questions, and questioning his right to be alive made it all the more tempting to wish to *avenge* Theo. He had nightmares and daydreams, he confessed to Clare, even though the whole family had pretty much accepted that Theo had probably done it, of tracking down the killer and shooting him through the head. Only, in one of the nightmares, Rafe said, he had mistaken Theo-come-back-from-the-dead as an impersonator of Theo and had killed his brother a second time.

Poor Rafe. What was going to happen to him? How could she help him? It was one thing to tell him "I love you" over the phone and give him a membership of a health spa for Christmas and contribute to the cost of his new Mazda and invite him to the beach, but somehow she couldn't help thinking there were more important things a sister could do—if only she had more experience at being a sister. She wished she could give him some of her . . . what? Her belief in him? What had been the source of that belief? His attitude, a rosy little boy, of being worthy of everyone's love and attention; and later, when he was in school, of expecting to be the best, the first, without much effort; and having proved he could do it, of letting everyone know he intended to maintain this state of affairs for the rest of his life: he would accept nothing less for himself. And nothing had happened to shake his confidence in himself and his future until his expulsion from the Belvedere School, a stunning blow to his self-esteem. To be the valedictorian of your class and then expelled a month before graduation for serving beer to some boarders in your own home! When Lily had written to her about it, Clare had been sick with the injustice of it. That despicable martinet Hardwick: it was so clear to her he had been serving some cause other than that of justice, and she knew what cause: the cause of the "in" crowd against the interlopers. Anguishing over the outrage of it at the time, Clare, up in New York, had written dozens of letters to Hardwick in her head.

But she hadn't sent any. From what she had heard of "Uncle Percy" Hardwick from Theo and Rafe, he could get vicious when backed into a corner; a letter from her might simply have stimulated him to think up more ways to make it rough for Rafe: headmasters maintained influential networks with deans of universities and colleges, and Rafe's expulsion had already caused him to lose out on the Morehead Scholarship.

And yet the hypocrite had dared to show up at Theo's funeral. Had patted Lily on the arm as he passed to go up to the communion rail. He was there for appearance's sake, of course. Theo, who had not been expelled but had quit on his own, would always be listed as a Belvedere boy. Would Hardwick have shown up for the funeral if it had been Rafe's instead of Theo's? Interesting point.

Had the expulsion from Belvedere, on the eve of his first public glory, ended Ralph's charmed existence by puncturing his ebullient belief that between him and the best of everything was a line as easy and straight as an arrow shot from destiny's bowstring on the day of his birth? Sometimes it seemed so. He hadn't the same faith in himself, but maybe that wasn't too bad; maybe it was just more realistic. And though he drank too much sometimes and had self-destructive tastes in women and would have used up a decade to meander through college towards a profession, he was certainly not a failure according to the world's standards or even his own. When he was a little boy and people asked him, "Rafe, what do you want to be when you grow up?" he would answer, to everyone's amusement, "Important." Or sometimes, "A millionaire." And even though, when people now asked Lily, "What is Rafe going to be when he gets out of school?" and she replied in her dry way, "Old," the facts were that he would take his comprehensives at the end of the summer, felt confident that he would pass them, and seemed to have found a corner of the business and academic world no one else had mined: providing accurate data on the most profitable real estate to big insurance companies that had billions of dollars in pension funds to invest. He and his professor, who consulted part-time for one of these companies, had published a paper together recently (Rafe had done all the computer research) under both their names. There was every reason to believe that in his chosen field Rafe would eventually fulfill his childhood prophecy for himself: he would be important; he might even become a millionaire.

So why did Clare's heart clench for him as she smoothed one of Mrs. Fauquier's ubiquitous white cotton bedspreads over Rafe's bed in the maid's room? Because of a forlornness in him—someone who didn't love him might call it an emptiness. But it wasn't emptiness; it was even sadder. There was an untapped level. She was afraid he might never be called upon, or might never call upon himself, to use his intelligence to its fullest. He would simply skim along in his chosen field, and maybe only a handful of people would recognize that on some deeply imaginative level he hadn't lived. But she would be one of that handful, and it would make her ache for him and be angry with him at the same time: just as she had been both disappointed and indignant that, as soon as it was no longer necessary for him to get A's in English courses, he had never shown the slightest interest in opening a novel again. Neither he nor Theo had ever read any of her books. Why, even Snow, back in the days when she was first married to Theo and was trying to get along with the family, had taken the trouble to buy a magazine with one of Clare's stories in it and send word through Theo that "I didn't expect to like it, but I enjoyed it right much."

The phone was ringing in the kitchen. Felix must be out for a swim or a walk, because he usually got it on the first or second ring. She hurried across the breezeway. Possibly it was Ralph with another of his bulletins on the miraculous progress of his vision; already, he had said yesterday, he saw better out of that eye than he ever remembered seeing before. Or, less happily, it could be Rafe, announcing the postponement or cancellation of his visit. The way her careful plans so far had been confounded, it seemed the predictable next event.

But it was Lizzie. "Oh, hi," said Clare. "Your father has been phoning you, but you're always out."

"I know," said Lizzie somewhat portentously. "Is he around?"

"I think he's either gone for a walk or a swim. Shall I go look? Or can he call you back?"

There was a pause. "Actually," said Lizzie, "I'm at Myrtle Beach."

"Myrtle Beach!"

"Well, the Myrtle Beach Airport. I decided to take you up on your invitation." The flippant announcement was undercut by a nervous little giggle, which caused Clare to suppress the corrosive comeback that was springing to her tongue. There might be something wrong, and then Lizzie would never forgive her.

"I guess we'd better come and pick you up," said Clare. "Only it may be a while, because if Felix has gone for one of his thinking walks, there's no telling when he'll be back."

"Couldn't you come and get me by yourself?" Almost pleading.

"Of course I could. I mean . . . sure."

"Actually, I'd prefer it." Back to Lizzie-like insouciance. "I need you to help me prepare Pop for something he isn't going to like one bit."

"Oh, Christ, Lizzie, what? Look, I'm not in the mood for surprises just at the moment. Is it something bad?"

The girl laughed. "*I* don't think so. *I* think it's awesome. But you're going to have to help me with Felix."

"Will *I* think it's awesome?" Clare demanded.

"I'm not really sure. I don't know you that well" was the maddening reply.

"If you don't know me that well, Lizzie, after eight years," said Clare, who couldn't decide whether she was more angry or hurt, "what makes you so sure I can 'help' you with your father?"

"I only meant about whether you'd think it was awesome. Of

course I know you well enough to be sure you can influence my father. That is, if you want to. You can pretty much bring him around to anything you want."

"I could say the same for you," Clare returned dryly.

"In most things, yes," acknowledged the girl, "but this time I'm going to need you on my side." As if it was already assumed Clare had no choice but to be on her side.

"The drive from here takes at least thirty minutes," said Clare.

"That's okay. It's noisy here, they're remodeling or something. But I can entertain myself. I have lots to think about."

"If Felix gets back in the next few minutes, while I'm dressing, he'll want to come, too."

"Couldn't you just leave him a note and come as you are? I could be waiting right outside the front entrance. It's a very small airport. Please, Clare."

"Oh, all right." But she couldn't resist a parting shot. "For someone you don't know very well, you do a pretty good job of bringing me around when it suits you."

Nevertheless, Clare did take time to change clothes. Not even Lizzie's "awesome" urgency was going to entice her to go rushing off in short shorts, a sweaty, too-tight shirt, and beach thongs. And she *would* have to get out of the car: after picking up Lizzie, she would have to stop at Belk's for another new set of sheets (Lizzie could damn well sleep with the sizing on them) and for Rafe's ice and tonic and limes—and, oh shit, something besides shrimp for Lizzie's dinner, in case she was still on her Jewish diet.

She scribbled a note to Felix on a yellow pad:

> Gone to Myrtle Beach Airport to pick up Lizzie, who has some kind of news she thinks you won't like, but she says it's "awesome," which I think means good. I am supposed to help bring you around. . . .

No, that was two-faced; it was also more interested in creating drama than understanding; it betrayed Lizzie, worried Felix, and, in its disingenuous way, made herself the wise and humorous centerpiece. It had definite elements of that she had described as "Quick murk" to Felix a week ago during the family's mis-communications with Snow.

She crumpled up the page and wrote a second note:

> 11:30 a.m.—Gone to Myrtle Beach Airport to pick up Lizzie, who has decided to take us up on our invitation after all. Back as soon as I get her and do some last-minute shopping.
>
> Love,
> Clare

Placing the note on Felix's pillow, she looked out the window behind the bed and saw Lily's blue bathing cap bobbing up and down. Shoulder-high in the ocean, she was doing her aquatic aerobics. Up and down she bounced, like a happy little girl, totally oblivious of the rest of the world. Lizzie would have to sleep in the room adjoining Lily's; Clare could not imagine how they would get on. The whole scenario of this family party had taken on a life of its own.

There was a girl waiting in front of the airport, but it wasn't Lizzie. She was too slight and had very short hair and wore a skirt. Oh, God, it was Lizzie. She had cut off all her gorgeous hair; Felix was going to be sick. But why did she look so small? Then Clare realized it must be because of the missing hair. Lizzie's abundant red hair had given her mass and buoyancy and elevation; the way it had lifted and spread out, rippling and flashing its brilliance, had contributed much to the un-put-downable aura one associated with Lizzie. This girl, with her shorn head (even though it was a fashionable cut) and too-long, crumpled cotton skirt(Lizzie abhorred skirts), standing quietly in a shady corner beside her suitcase, looked like just another girl, wearing what Ralph Lauren or one of his competitors had decided she should wear—though, from what Clare recalled of the girls in the ads, with their Pre-Raphaelites-visiting-in-Newport look, he would never have allowed her to cut her hair that short.

Clare pulled up to the curb. Lizzie put her suitcase on the backseat and slid in front beside Clare. Giving her a casual once-over, she commented, "I knew you'd dress, anyway."

Neither of the went in for kissing, but Clare, moved by how vulnerable and ordinary Lizzie looked without her crowning glory, put her hand on the girl's crumpled skirt. "So did you," she said gently, amazed at her own feelings. "I think the only other time I've seen you in a skirt was at your graduation—and it was under your gown." Then, because she wanted to get it over with, and because Lizzie was so defiantly exhibiting that little bare neck for her observation: "You've cut your hair. I almost didn't recognize you for a minute. It's very . . . chic, but it makes you look so different."

"Yes," said Lizzie, with a toss of her chin (only now no swirling cascade of brightness gave emphasis to this imperious gesture), "but it's so much easier. And I *am* different. And I plan to be more so."

Clare released the brake and pulled away towards the airport exit. "How do you mean?" She felt as if someone had just handed her a script and, when she saw what her lines were, she realized she wasn't the heroine anymore. She had become, all at once, the motherly figure, the middle-aged woman whose part in the drama is to feed the necessary questions to the bright young star in order that she may reveal her intentions.

"By September I will be wearing a wig whenever I go out in public," came Lizzie's sprightly reply, a horrible non sequitur for Clare, thoroughly disorienting her. Her first chilling thought was that the girl had cancer and was trying to put a brave face on things. But that couldn't be: not even Lizzie at her worst would be so cruel as to mislead Clare on the phone that it was good news—no, "awesome," she had said. Cancer could, of course, be construed as awesome. But why, in that case, would Lizzie be smiling now as if to burst with happiness and pride? Oh, no, it was something good—good for Lizzie, at any rate. Something good for Lizzie that Felix was not going to like one bit. Oh, wait; oh, no. The light was beginning to dawn. Lizzie's Jewish phase. It was a man; of course, it was a man. Lizzie was going to marry one of those extreme Jews that Felix detested, the ones who lived medieval lives and couldn't even carry a wallet on the Sabbath, and the wives wore wigs except when they were alone with their husbands. But how . . .? Who . . .? When . . .? Oh, poor Felix!

But "A wig?" seemed to be the appropriate next line of her own script. For the middle-aged woman to put herself forward by cleverly anticipating the young heroine's news would not be good theater. And Lizzie, it was obvious, was intent on making the most theater of her moment. That was why Clare had been wanted alone at the airport. Lizzie must have the full, delicious savoring of her shocking announcement; she must be given the satisfaction of flummoxing and then enlightening, at her own chosen narrative pace, a sympathetic and concerned adult who could be counted upon not to upstage her. Felix in this car might have erupted already in a fusillade of fatherly protests, robbing the heroine of some of her limelight, if not totally stealing the show. And understanding this, Clare was given an unexpected sidelong illumination into the enigma of the Quicks, why it was they coexisted in such an impacted, embattled, fascinated stalemate with one another. Was it because not one of them was willing—or had never learned the modest and subtle art of how—to relinquish center stage for a single episode of their family drama?

But this was not the hour for studying Quicks. She was now supposed to be foil, elicitor of confidences, adjunct to another's destiny; she had become a secondary character at last. It felt strange. It felt like being old, or invisible, yet curiously free. Was that how mothers felt when their daughters succeeded them as heroines in the continuing drama of humankind? If so, Clare had managed to learn one more thing about lives she had not actually lived herself.

As they drove to Belk's for Lizzie's sheets, the young woman had her triumphant monologue. She had met him on the El Al flight to Tel Aviv. His name was David. David Marks. They had sat next to each other. Or, rather, she had been assigned her choice of a window seat and he his choice of an aisle one, and there turned out to be an empty place between them, so they had talked across it. The empty seat had acted like a sort of matchmaker, in a way: they had been close, but not too close; if they'd been squashed together elbow to elbow, one or the other of them might have felt crowded, but this way . . . Was it fate, or wasn't it, that empty seat, the fact that they were both assigned that *row?* And what if Lizzie had taken her father's advice and asked for an aisle seat? Felix was adamant about having space next to him on transatlantic flights so he could stretch his legs. But she'd gone ahead and said window, because she liked to look out, even when there was nothing to see but a floor of clouds. If she'd asked for an aisle seat, she might have been put in front of David and never laid eyes on him; or behind him, where, at sunrise, flying over Greece, he would have been merely one more of those odd males of assorted ages who suddenly stood up at dawn, strapped themselves up with little cords and little boxes, and, oblivious to the appearance they made, began bending rapidly from the waist while flight attendants with trays of wake-up towels edged tactfully around them.

Clare mustn't think he was some fanatic creep, either. David was not some anemic little man in black clothes sitting inside and squinting over the Torah, as Pop had described the Jews in Crown Heights. David was six foot three and played tennis every morning after davening—that meant praying, for Clare's information—and had a terrific bachelor apartment on West End Avenue. His kitchen was completely kosher. The family had a big printing company—they were quite well off; they were rich, if Clare wanted to know the truth. If it hadn't been for the yarmulke David always wore—his sisters embroidered beautiful designs on his yarmulkes; the whole family was so close, and so funny!—and if he were to walk into Pop's house, Pop would probably say something like, "Now there's a healthy specimen of manhood, *Mädi*, why can't you fall for someone like that? *He's* no nebbish, I'll bet." But then, when David turned around and Pop saw the hated little cap, he'd be off on one of his tirades: "I want the world for my Lizzie, not for her to shut herself up in a prison of old shibboleths even my own parents couldn't take seriously." Lizzie's art of mimicry was still wickedly on target: she got Felix's accent, his confident speech rhythm, his pet words. Clare recalled how, that night at the Russian Tea Room, after the Arrau concert, just before Lizzie flew off to Israel, she had semi-threatened to make Clare the next victim of her mimicry; and Clare couldn't help wondering if Lizzie had already "done" her for the entertainment of the Marks family, "so close, and so funny." But at the same time she was guessing what Lizzie's imitation of her might be like, she was also feeling extremely anxious for Felix and thinking of the first things she could say to soften the blow for him. The hair, or lack of it, was going to be bad enough when Lizzie walked into "No Saints"; she only hoped the girl would not rub it in by announcing the coming wig in the first few minutes.

But what Pop had to realize, Lizzie was going on, was that there were people—there were Jews—who *liked* being part of those old shibboleths. They *weren't* shibboleths for them, they were beloved links to a four-thousand-year-old tradition. And observing them gave you a sense of permanency, such a wonderful sense of security . . . and, well, frankly, she was going to tell Clare something odd: living like that was extremely *sexy*. David's mother and father, David's two married sisters: you could see that sexual tension, even with the old couple. The women belonged to their husbands, and all of them belonged to something higher. David's sister Vivian had told Lizzie that today, after ten years of marriage, it gave her the same thrill she'd had as a new bride when she came in from shopping and took off her sheitel—her wig—for her husband. The other sister, Ellen, didn't wear a sheitel—you didn't have to, if you were Orthodox, but Lizzie was going to, because she wanted to go the whole way with David—but it had been Ellen, who was a buyer for Bergdorf's, who had made Lizzie a gift of three designer skirts with coordinated tops. Orthodox women, for Clare's information, were forbidden to wear pants. When Lizzie had had her hair cut off the week before—short hair was so much easier when you went to the mikvah, the ritual bath—she had gift-wrapped the shorn hair and presented it to David, and he had been so moved he had actually cried. And then they had touched hands and it was like being set on fire, it was a million times more passionate than all the times she'd gone to bed with other people. She and David had both sown their share of wild oats. That's why they had decided to observe the strictest code of Jewish law that prohibits premarital sex and allows only holding hands: this time was different for both of them. Not having sex was like having it for the first time and really meaning it, if Clare could see what she meant.

Clare did see, in a way. In fact, she surprised herself by how much she felt the attraction of the thing, from Lizzie's point of view. It was so beautifully extreme, so theatrical; it perfectly satisfied the requirements of someone who thought highly of herself and wanted a gesture equal to the occasion of bestowing that self. At fourteen, Clare had wanted to be a nun; and in her early twenties, before Writing took over, she had vaguely dreamed of giving herself up to a man whose attractions would come down like a sledgehammer on her grim ambition and careful preservation of self, and wake her, sometime later, in a fecund, erotic cave of wife-and-motherhood. Lizzie had found a way, perhaps the one way available in Western civilization, to do both.

"So you plan to get married in September?" Angling Felix's car into a parking space in front of Belk's.

But her sympathetic capitulation apparently fell short of Lizzie's requirements for this occasion. "You're appalled, aren't you?" accused the girl with a superior, knowing look. Her fragile, naked neck reminded Clare of a new-hatched bird's. "You're going to get Pop alone as soon as you can and say what an idiot I am. And you two will come to the wedding and he'll be beside himself taking mental notes of all the *shibboleths,* and then you'll lie in bed together criticizing everything afterwards."

"But you'll be in bed with David by that time," said Clare, "so what will it matter?"

Lizzie flushed under her prep schoolboy's haircut. "True," she acknowledged, smiling slyly.

Beginning to taste the dramatic possibilities in her role as secondary character, Clare decided to give Lizzie the first of her wedding presents, right now, in the car, before they joined the shoppers in Belk's. "If you want to know the truth," she said, speaking slowly not only for emphasis but because she never in her life had expected to say such a thing, "I think I envy you. It's an experience I'll never have: giving myself away like that. When I was your age, I just couldn't afford to. I wanted . . . I guess I wanted to *keep* myself more than anything. And now I'm so solidly what I am, because of that early decision, that anybody who loves me would love me because I *am* that unmistakable single being. And I like it that way, I really do. But all the same, I envy you. It's an experience I once yearned for and it's an experience I would have liked to have." She couldn't prevent herself here, however, from uttering a darkly ironic laugh. "Not permanently, of course, it wouldn't have suited me, but I would have liked to have it for a *while*." Then she went too far by adding, "I guess I only have one more chance and that's when I give myself up completely to Death."

"Oh, Clare!" Lizzie grabbed her hand. The girl had tears in her eyes.

Hell, thought Clare, I'm hopeless. I tried to steal her scene, after all. "Let's go get you some pretty sheets," she said. "You should pick something out that you can take back to . . . David. I don't mean it will be my wedding gift, but, you know, just as a sort of symbol. The sheets you first slept on after you came down to break your good news."

They went into Belk's together. "This way," said Clare, cutting left through the Boys' Department. "I know my way around here. I was in here last week to buy sheets for my sister-in-law, only she never showed."

"I could just sleep on those, couldn't I?" offered Lizzie agreeably.

"No, they're already in use." Clare laughed. "This has been quite a busy house party."

"Clare, you know what I'm really looking forward to?" demanded Lizzie suddenly, stopping them both under the archway leading to Home Furnishings.

"No, what?" replied Clare, supplying the requisite line.

"I look forward," said Lizzie radiantly, "to living a life where I no longer have to think of myself as the most important person in the world."

You little dreamer, thought Clare. But she kept her face straight as she delivered her line according to the script. "That is a very noble ambition," she told Felix's adored daughter solemnly.

He pulled in soundlessly, and the difference between this year and last advanced to meet him like a mocking welcoming committee-of-one before he'd even turned off the engine. He couldn't breathe for a minute. He sat very still inside his gun-metal-blue Mazda RX7, the thing he had desired most in the world this time last year, and waited for the choking sensation to pass. In front of his windshield, the little ragged red and yellow and white flowers sparkled in Fauquier's weedy beds. An American flag hung down from its pole beside the plaque that read "No Saints." From the deck of the cottage next door fluttered the same weatherworn Confederate flag he remembered from last year. The owners must have left it out all winter; several inches of its tip had been eaten away. There was something indecent about letting a flag deteriorate that far; he felt sorry for the flag. The thought occurred to him that after dark tonight he might sneak over and steal it. Give it a decent burial. That was the kind of thing Theo would have enjoyed doing.

He swung open the door and unfolded himself into the sea air. Filled his lungs with it and stretched. The promise of his life was restored to him again. He began unloading his stuff, wondering who would be the first to discover his arrival and come out and greet him.

He made several arm-laden trips from his car to the scummy "maid's room." It was dark, damp, and disgraceful, even with poor Clare's efforts: the dresser scarf on the shabby chest of drawers, the little pitcher of ragged flowers from the garden. If he'd been the maid, he would have pissed in the family's orange juice, just a few drops each morning; then stood respectfully at the stove while they drank up and asked, "*Now* what kin ah git foh y'all folks next?"

He carried his ice chest to the kitchen. Where was everybody? Put his quart of vodka in the freezer. There was already a quart of Absolut in there. Good old Clare; only the best for her little brother. Nobody had told her that Popov was just as good for vodka tonics. But it's the thought that counts. He loaded his sugar-free tonics into the main refrigerator. Clare had antici-pated him here, too; only she'd bought the regular kind. He'd have to tell her about sugar-free; calories added up, as he was discovering for the first time in his life. There was a big glass bowl full of shrimp, covered with a sheet of Saran wrap. He peeled it back and picked out one of the shrimp. Pink, chilled, and thoroughly clean—the way his grandmother Buchel used to do them: not one trace of their little panicked green or black defecations from just before they were swept into the net. He popped the shrimp into his mouth and chewed, feeling cherished. But where were they all? Where was Mom? He opened the crisper drawer: four fresh, plump limes. Good, But where was Clare?

Now where did the Fauquiers stash their tall glasses? Ugh. A dead cricket. Oh, wait. The other cabinet, to the right above the sink. And Clare had stocked up on the ice this year, too. Intelligent woman, to learn from last year's mistakes.

He built himself his first drink, rather defiantly staring down a chimerical suggestion of Dr. Blake's bleached-out furrowed brows just slightly to the left of a hanging strip of flypaper. This is the beach, damn it, he reminded her. But where the hell was everybody? Where was old gregarious Felix? Why had nobody come to greet him, to say how happy they were to see him?

Last year he'd hardly pulled in—of course his Bonneville had been a noisy old clunker; it was easier to hear its arrival above the loud surf—when Clare had run out from the kitchen, wiping her hands on a towel, and Mom had come down from upstairs, where she'd been watching for him, and they'd both kissed and pawed him, and then Felix had been there to shake his hand and hug him and help him carry in his stuff and tease him about how did he ever expect to wear all the outfits he'd brought in just two and a half days at the beach. And later in the afternoon, after he had mellowed out with the sun and a few tonics and was relaxing in a beach chair on the windwalk, listening to his Walkman and sort of pleasantly buzzed, he had suddenly felt a shadow fall over his chair. He had opened his eyes to find Theo standing above him, holding the kid. Theo's mouth moved silently: he was grinning. "What?" Rafe said, removing his earphones. "Hello, little brother," Theo said in his mocking way. "Jason, say hi to your uncle Rafe." Jason, whey-faced, as if he'd been sick in the car, clung tightly to Theo and demanded critically of Rafe, "Why do you have that oil all over you?" "To make me brown and beautiful," Rafe answered sarcastically. Theo was almost as pale as the child. The pair of white faces gazed down at the sun god—Rafe had gotten an earlier start on his tan last year. They had driven in late, because Theo's boss wouldn't give him Friday morning off. Theo's khakis were crumpled and there were perspiration circles in the armpits of his shirt. He had on a pair of new glasses with flashy gold rims that made him look like a salesman, the kind who wore double-knits and carried his samples in an imitation-leather case. Anger, pity, and guilt had surged through Rafe. "Hey, you two, get out of my sunshine," he'd said. Playfully, but meaning it.

A chair scraped on the porch above, and, between the poundings of the waves, he heard the muted exchange of female voices through the kitchen ceiling. That explained it: they had been sitting up there on the ocean side talking and hadn't heard him drive in. Checking his drink, he was surprised to see that its level had fallen several inches during the time he had been standing in the kitchen. He topped it off again with ice and more Popov, and, composing his face nonchalantly, went outside and slowly mounted the stairs that came up through the floor of the long oceanfront porch.

He saw them a moment before they saw him. His mother, in her deep-blue-and-white-patterned cotton kimono, sat embroidering in a wicker chair pulled up close to the hammock; her profile was to him. Her needle moved in and out of the cloth as she listened intently to a strange girl lying in the hammock facing away from him. The girl wore a long white terry-cloth robe and her short bronze hair lay close to her head in wet curls. She must have just come out of the ocean, or a shower. Her slim white feet were crossed at the ankles and she was gesticulating with her hands as she talked. The intimate tension between his mother and the strange girl spooked him: he felt suddenly as if *he* were the stranger, the intruder. " . . . completely changing everything . . ." The girl's excited phrase reached him over the crashing of the surf. Who was she? She looked thoroughly at home in the hammock. His mother had that almost rapturous attention about her she sometimes got in church during a sermon she found interesting. A crazy idea flashed through his mind that the girl was here for *him*—in the same way the Absolut and the wrong kind of tonic and the little raggedy flowers in his room were. But then, quickly following that, a more menacing and likely suspicion: she was someone they had decided he should marry. Perhaps this whole scene had been set up for his benefit: his mother, or Clare, who was hiding somewhere, had heard his car but wanted him to find the pair of them like this as some sort of message. He advanced on them: cautious, resentful, intrigued, rattling his ice as he came. He hadn't seen her face yet. He didn't even know if she was pretty.

"Oh, my baby!" Lily sprang up. She seemed genuinely surprised, or else she was acting the part well. She had taken time out to fix her embroidery needle safely in the cloth before getting up, but she would have done that either way. "We didn't hear you come in," Lily complained contritely.

"I figured that," he said, holding his drink at arm's length while she hugged him. Over his mother's head, he saw the girl in the hammock examining him; but he couldn't be sure whether the animated interest was inspired by him, or whether it was left over on her face from what she'd been telling Mom. She wasn't a world-class beauty, but she definitely had a quality of her own.

"This is Lizzie, Felix's daughter," said Lily, "Or have you already met in New York?"

"No, I —"

"The one time you stayed at our house, I was away skiing," the girl finished for him. "I was sorry to have missed you, after hearing Clare go on for years about her fabulous little brother." She appeared suddenly disconcerted and sat up quickly in the hammock, carefully drawing her robe around her legs as she swung them to the floor. Her face had colored and they both knew why: without meaning to, she had reminded them all of Theo. Rafe felt sorry for her and liked her for her obvious distress. He'd had a totally different picture of Felix's sharp-tongued little daughter, based on what Clare had told *him* over the years. He'd been shown one or two snapshots of a bush-haired little redhead, but in those she had looked like someone's kid sister, bratty and self-absorbed. This girl seemed like a human being, appealing to look at, in her way; someone he might be able to talk to.

Still holding him around the waist, his mother said, "Lizzie flew down and surprised us. She's only just arrived herself. She brought her daddy some unexpected news. Clare's out walking him up and down the beach until he gets used to it a little bit more."

"You make Felix sound like a dog," he said, taking a swig of his vodka tonic.

The girl tossed back her head and laughed mischievously. Her dark, bright eyes shot Rafe an appreciative acknowledgment of camaraderie, of the young against their difficult parents.

"So what's the news?" he asked, smiling down at his mother and the girl.

He didn't know why, but he'd fully expected it to be something about a career. A sudden upheaval in professional plans, as when he threw up law for the Business School; a soul-searching shift from commerce to art, or private sector to Peace Corps— something like that. She seemed that sort of girl. But all they were telling him was that she was going to get married in September. What was so world-shaking about a twenty-six-year-old woman getting married? The reason Felix was being walked up and down the beach by Clare, who had apparently forgotten completely about Rafe in this greater excitement, was that Lizzie was going to marry a different sort of Jew from the kind Felix was.

"Congratulations," he heard himself say, flashing her his Cordial Southern Boy smile. "That's great news. I'm sure you all will be very happy."

"I know we will," Lizzie replied, tucking her terry-cloth robe chastely around her legs and smiling back at him. "We already are. But now we've got to worry about poor Pop. He was completely undone when he heard about it. We've got to get him through it, somehow."

"He'll come around," predicted Lily gaily. "You know what can be counted on to bring him around? That first grandchild."

The first grandchild didn't do a very great job of bringing *you* around, thought Rafe, slipping out of his mother's loose embrace. "I think I'll go in the water," he said.

"Do, darling," said Lily. "You need some sun. You don't have your usual tan this year. Oh, I'm glad my little boy is here. I suppose you'll be going to Myrtle Beach tonight, though."

"It's a distinct possibility," he said lightly. "Well, see you ladies after a while." He turned and went back down the stairs feeling slightly disgusted and somehow cheated. It was as if something had been promised to him and then hastily withdrawn. The strange girl lying with her back to him in the hammock. The white robe and the slim white feet. The excited, gesticulating hands and the mysterious, hopeful phrase coming to him over the crash of the surf: ". . . completely changing everything . . ." Nothing had changed for him. Clare's lover's daughter was going to get married, that was all.

On his way to the maid's room to change into his bathing suit, he stopped off at the refrigerator and made himself a new drink.

He dived into the wave. And then into the next, hurtling his tense, pointed self like a missile under the thundering fall of foam. His timing was perfect for every wave. He experimented with alterations to increase the risk: diving a mini-second too soon or too late. But it didn't seem to make a difference: he cut through clean as a knife against unresisting butter every time. The sea wasn't interested in playing around with him, either. As little boys, he and Theo had practiced this for hours. At first he had been terrified by that threatening curling peak. "Go *on*, Rafe," Theo had called to him. "You can't *hesitate* like that, Just fling yourself in when it looks its worst!"

A woman in a black cap and a low-cut black suit waded purposefully towards him through the surf. It was Clare. They hugged and kissed, both a little shy. It felt weird to him sometimes to have a sister so much older, more like an aunt or a younger friend of his mother's.

"I had planned to be waiting for you when you drove up," Clare said, standing waist-high beside him in the water. Every time a wave approached, she turned her back to it and cringed, "I had planned a lot of things, and not one of them has turned out the way I'd planned. I think I'd better stick to my *books* if I want things to turn out my way. If this had been a house party in my book, the people I wanted to arrive would have arrived when I wanted and they would have behaved according to my plans. Poor Felix is fit to be tied. I gather from Lily you heard the news. Lizzie is wallowing in her great announcement like a cat in a wading pool full of cream, and poor Felix is absolutely heartbroken. When we were taking our walk, he practically cried. She's going to wear a wig and spend all her time and intelligence keeping track of what not to eat with what. I had to buy some chicken for her because she can't eat shrimp, and then, halfway through dredging it in flour, I realized I had soaked it in milk, so I felt honor-bound to wash it all off with water and start again. The only one who seems to be enjoying the whole thing thoroughly is Lily. Lizzie has enough compassion to feel sorry for Felix and let it temper her triumph a little, but Lily . . . well, it's totally captured her imagination."

Felix came out of mourning to join him on the windwalk, where he was sipping his drink and soaking up the last of the afternoon's sun. He was carrying a book and a drink of his own. "I guess you've heard," he said, sitting down on the bench beside Rafe. "My daughter has decided to return to the Middle Ages. It's my fault, of course. It always is the parent's fault. If I had only had the sense to raise her Orthodox, I might now be welcoming a Muslim as my son-in-law." Though he spoke gravely and with a certain bitter irony, he did not appear either "completely undone" or "heartbroken." On the contrary, he seemed very much like Felix, robustly sure of himself and unable to prevent a congenital playfulness from erupting through the disappointed father's tone. Rafe, relaxed and confident in the moment's perfect balance, achieved by exercise and alcohol, put his arm impulsively around the big man's shoulders and gave Felix's arm a bracing, filial slap. The two men sat stiffly in a moment of embarrassed affection before Rafe moved his arm again, greatly relieving them both.

"What are you reading?" Rafe casually asked.

"Manchester's biography of Churchill." Felix laughed. "Actually, I brought it out to show you this passage. Wait, I'll read it aloud, I thought you might like it. Young Churchill is just packing his steamer trunks to go off as a war correspondent to the Boer War, and here is what he takes . . . listen to this: 'In addition to a compass, a new saddle fitted with a pigskin case, and his Ross telescope and Voightlander field glass repaired at

Borthurck's expense, he was taking thirty bottles of 1889 Vin d'Ay Sec, eighteen bottles of St. Emilion, eighteen of ten-year-old Scotch, a dozen bottles of Rose's Cordial Lime Juice, six bottles of light port, six of French vermouth, and six of Very Old Eau de Vie 1866.'"

"God," Rafe said, laughing. "That makes me feel absolutely Spartan."

"I thought you'd like it. But there's a footnote that's even better. The footnote says these amounts may seem extraordinary today, but were much less remarkable then. Look here, it says that in the Sudan campaign Major Haig's personal pack train included 'one camel, laden with claret.'"

And now Mom had replaced Felix on the windwalk. Mom was saying, "Do you know what that precious child did? The minute he got here, the first thing he did was run and lie down in that hammock. And he hugged himself, the same way he did in that picture you took last year of Theo and him, lying there together. And then he ran, with all his clothes on, into the ocean, like Theo did last year, and he screamed, 'I remember! I remember!' It was uncanny. And then Clare was with him in the ocean and he saw the moon rising over the water and he said, 'I'd like to walk right across this ocean to that moon.' Exactly the kind of thing Theo would have said. It makes you wonder, doesn't it?"

He went to the maid's room to dress for dinner, showering in the hateful little maid's bathtub, holding the rubber nozzle above his neck; he put on clean Jockey shorts, white trousers, and a striped navy-and-white polo shirt. He flashed his teeth at himself in the tarnished mirror: "Oh, you handsome devil, you!" No one was in the kitchen yet, though there were promising smells, so he freshened his drink and went back upstairs. Lizzie was out on the windwalk, in a white blouse and long, clinging skirt. He didn't care what he said anymore. "Come with me to Myrtle Beach," he said, sitting down beside her. "You have the rest of your life to be good."

And then there was a blank space, a sort of hiccup in time, and she was talking to him softly, matter-of-factly, conspiratorially. "They are perfect for each other," she was saying, "so I don't have to feel too guilty about abandoning him."

"Who? Who's perfect?"

"Pop and Clare. Clare and Pop. I've been giving it some thought. Inside Clare there's a happy person waiting to get out, and inside my father there's a sad person waiting for the opportunity to express himself, and they make a perfect foursome. I hated her for years, but now I'm so grateful. Now I can go to David without worrying about Pop languishing."

"It's worked out great for you," he heard himself say sarcastically.

"It will for you, too, Rafe. Oh, Rafe, I'm so happy. Please be happy for me. You know, I was always sorry I didn't have a brother. I wish you would let me adopt you as my brother. As my first sisterly act, I am going to get very presumptuous and tell you I think you drink too much. Do yourself a favor and stop. You're killing millions of brain cells."

"Come and dance with me in Myrtle Beach, then."

"Rafe, I can't. It's Friday evening. I wouldn't expect that to mean anything to you. Even if you were my real brother, we couldn't go dancing tonight."

He stood up and kissed her, fast, before she could stop him. "If I were your real brother," he said, "I wouldn't have asked you."

At the long table in the kitchen, they ate Clare's fresh shrimp sautéed in butter; Lizzie, across from him, picked at her chicken-with-the-milk-washed-off and yellow rice. She kept her eyes lowered; she wouldn't look at him. He felt like weeping. Dad had just phoned, and everybody was talking about his miraculous new eyesight.

"He says he's thinking about buying himself a plane and taking flying lessons," said Clare. "Then he'll be able to go and get Jason in Granny Squirrel."

"I can see it now," said Lily wryly, twisting her wineglass around and around by the stem. "Somehow that plane will find its way to our carport and *perch* itself there, with all the other junk."

"Rafe, you look restless," Felix said. "I suppose you're impatient to get to Myrtle Beach."

"Are you sure you're fit to drive?" asked Clare.

But when he rose to go, nobody made any effort to stop him.

A fine young man in his fine new car skims like a bullet up the sunset-washed highway to his pleasures. "*He travels the fastest who travels alone.*" You want them back, you *will* them back, he explained to Dr. Blake, and they don't come. Down at the health spa, when I'm lifting weights, it's like I'm trying to push it *out* . . . the realization he's really gone . . . but I can't. I mean, there doesn't seem to be any shortcut in getting used to the word "never". And so many things I still can't handle. The way the funeral home took liberties with his hair. And everybody was saying, Oh, look how handsome he was, he had such a nice nose and noble forehead, and you can see them so much better with his hair combed back like that. But you know what I thought? I thought, That's what death does to you: gives everybody the right to make you over. And you no longer have the power to do the simplest thing like take out your comb and change the part in your hair back to the way you want it. You know what? I still wake up in a sweat sometimes and think, It was cowardly of me not to have had the guts to take out my pocket comb and fix his hair for him, fix it back to the way *he* liked it. I think of him down in his grave with his hair parted the wrong way. Only—and this is the awful thing—I would probably have changed it around some myself. I mean, without meaning to. It just wouldn't, it *couldn't*, be the same.

Last year they'd gotten a late start to Myrtle Beach because of Jason. He had to be put to bed first. Lily read him about fifteen of his little books, but it was as if he knew that his daddy wanted to go off with his uncle and have fun without him. It had been almost ten before they'd slipped away. They'd taken the longer, alternative route 17 to avoid all the beach traffic and get to North Myrtle Beach, where all the clubs were, more quickly. But on the very darkest and most deserted part of the highway, the radiator of the Bonneville had leaked dry, and there they were, walking fast along a perpendicular stretch of country road in the dark (just as they had since walked such roads together in the country of his dreams and nightmares) towards a single light shining from a house across a field. And he was yelling, "Shit, oh fucking shit! We're *never* going to get to the Quarterdeck at this rate!" And though Theo wanted to get there just as much as he did, he had been perversely amused by the whole episode, it had appealed to his love of danger, of emergency—something: being out alone in the dark on a strange road with just your petulant little brother yelling "Shit!" so you could grin mystically into the darkness and say, "Rafe. Now,

Rafe, just cool it. We'll get there." And chuckling like a madman, enjoying it *all*, when Rafe screamed back like a thwarted child, "But all the good girls will be taken! Fucking damn junk heap!"

The house in the middle of the field had belonged to some Negroes, who had been scared out of their minds to have their front door rapped on by two dressed-up white boys appearing out of nowhere. Nobody would come out, though you could see them rustling the curtains. Then Theo had called out, as if he were a character in some old movie, "We're in distress, can you please help us?" And something, the archaic phrase, the trustworthy ring of his voice, had worked. One of them, a thin boy of about fifteen, had emerged from around the side of the house, making *them* jump, and said huskily, "What you all want?" Theo did the talking, he had a more natural touch with black people, and the boy had gone away and come back with a large metal watering can full of water and they'd all walked across the field and down the country road to where the Bonneville was stranded, and Theo had tried awkwardly to keep a conversation going with the boy: where did he go to school and all that. They'd given him a five-dollar bill for his trouble, and after they were on their way again, to the nearest service station to have the leak checked out, Rafe had said, "He didn't seem very grateful. He acted like it was just a dollar instead of five." And Theo had said, "He probably thought it *was* a dollar. He was too shy to look before he put it in his pocket. And it was dark." "Oh, right." Rafe had been impressed, he remembered, by the way Theo had seen it from the boy's point of view. "Just think how surprised he'll be when he gets home and discovers it's a five," Theo had said.

And that had been the best part of the night, though he hadn't known it then. It was to be, as it turned out, the last adventure they would ever have together.

What was going on here? There were *two* Quarterdecks. A left one and a right one. Both with the identical blinking pink-and-yellow sign. Was he drunker than he'd realized? Now, wait a minute, wait just a minute here. No, wait. No, he was saved. The sign on the left said "Quarterdeck I," and the one on the right said "Quarterdeck II." If he were seeing double, he'd see two "I's" or two "II's". I still have a few healthy brain cells, thank you, Miss Lizzie.

"You've split things up since I was here last year," he told the guy at the door. He'd been going to make a joke about thinking he was seeing double, then thought better of it. They didn't like you arriving drunk; the guy would have the bouncers on his tail all evening.

"Yeah. The college kids like their music, the older crowd wants theirs."

"Which side is which?"

"Sample them both. It won't take you long to find out. Commute between them all you want. The price is the same."

Admission was still five dollars, like last year. And after they'd checked your I.D. just inside the door, you got the same fluorescent green bracelet snapped around your wrist to show you were over twenty-one and could order mixed drinks with the complete grownups as well as just the beer and wine of the eighteen-to-twenty crowd. It was one of those plastic bracelets you couldn't get off again unless you cut it off. "Just like the hospital," Theo had said, flourishing his delightedly. "And we're on our way to the terminal ward at last, grown up and legally able to order our own poison."

The guy was right. It was easy to see which side was which as soon as you looked in. Down the corridor to the left, inside the new partitions, the guys in their white pants or designer jeans and polos, the girls in their jeans or long, swishy skirts and lowcut silk shirts, their gold chains bouncing on perspiring, suntanned breasts as they gyrated, free-form, with their partners to the latest jungle beat on the juke. Down the other corridor to the left, shagging under the whirling strobes to the live band, now playing "Carolina Girl," were the "older crowd," the men in their suits or pressed slacks and polos—it was the men who wore the gold chains on this side—and the women in their cocktail dresses or silk pajama outfits. Oh, nitelife, Southern, U.S.A.

But to which side did he belong?

Last year, scoping out the possibilities, when there was just the one big room, Theo had shaken his head and told him, "I don't even know any of the dances they're doing anymore." And after they'd bought their mixed drinks, to which their hospital bracelets entitled them, he'd given Rafe a nudge forward towards a table where a group of girls were sitting. "Go and conquer, I give you my blessing, little brother," he'd said. "You mean, we finally get here, after all that shit, and you're not even going to dance?" demanded Rafe. "You've got to remember, I've been a married man. Let me sink back into the social whirl slowly." And Theo had stood on the sidelines, leaning against the bar like a sardonic Mississippi riverboat gambler, and grinned benevolently, but always with that sardonic and slightly superior air, on his baby brother as he swaggered up to bimbos, flashed his teeth in invitation, then flapped like a scarecrow and shimmied like a snake for the duration of that number.

He went back to "Quarterdeck I," the "kids' side," and brandishing his iridescent hospital bracelet, ordered a vodka tonic and, after tasting it, slid it back across the bar. "Hey, I think you may have misunderstood me," he told the bartender, who looked like somebody's kid brother. "I ordered a vodka tonic, not a water-and-tonic." The kid started giving him a hard time, and he didn't feel like arguing, so he ordered a shot of straight vodka and paid for it, then in disdainful slow motion poured the extra shot into his old drink and stirred it ostentatiously with the plastic swizzle stick.

Sipping, he stood and watched the writhing dancers, flailing around; watched them with a sardonic smile on his face, like a Mississippi riverboat gambler, like the ghost of his dead brother, and felt no desire . . . absolutely none . . . to intrude upon their ranks.

Sometime later, he found himself standing at the other bar, in "Quarterdeck II," hoisting a better vodka tonic to his lips. The bartender here called a shot a shot. He knew he'd damn well better. The customers on this side got up in the morning and went to work; they paid taxes; they weren't going to meekly accept a glass of watered-down shit and pay three-fifty for it. The dancers in this room made him feel sad. They were already old enough to look back at life—an incredible number of guys were losing their hair—and know they might not get all the things they'd thought were their God-given right when they were the age of the kids in "Quarterdeck I." He felt profoundly sorry for the state of the world. A phrase, from his childhood full of church, intoned itself from deep inside: " . . . all those who, in this transitory life, are in trouble, sorrow, need, sickness, or any other adversity . . ."

A great mood to be in at the Quarterdeck in Myrtle Beach. Whether "I" or "II."

There was a woman sitting at a table with a much younger woman. They looked as if they were arguing. When the young woman took her bag and flounced off, the older woman looked after her, then back at her drink—one of those awful snifters full of pink muck and pieces of fruit—and shrugged. Then she looked straight up and at him. He went over, his heart sinking when he saw how flawed, how definitely flawed she was. She was not from his world at all. It was awful, how easy it was to tell: skin, teeth, hair, clothes, posture, a thousand little giveaways. But, by God, she had worked all day under fluorescent lights in some office and she had the price of admission and the price for two or three of the sad pink concoctions, and she had come out for the evening with a friend, a much younger woman, probably someone who worked in the same office, and here they were, trying to partake of their share of American nitelife, only they weren't having any fun.

Tossing off the rest of his drink, he put the empty glass on the edge of her table and claimed her wordlessly for the dance. He felt like one of those compassionate gents in the Victorian novels he'd been forced to read, or pretend he had read, at La Fosse Hall and out at Belvedere. Her perfume was overpowering: Mom would die if she sniffed a perfume like that. It had an effect just the opposite from the one she had bought it for. He felt like gagging. Luckily the dance was a slow one, because he was a little dizzy. "Blue Velvet," one of those golden oldies he'd danced to at St. Clothilde's, holding his little tartan-skirted chickie at arm's length while the nuns looked on from the balcony above the gym.

The woman in his arms affected a slight lisp as she described herself through moist red lips. She was the personnel manager at Something-and-Something Systems in North Myrtle Beach. Living in Myrtle Beach was a whole different thing from vacationing there. Raising a daughter in Myrtle Beach was no easy thing, either. "Oh, that was your daughter?" "Yes, she's the one who wanted to come out tonight. Now she's mad because I won't sit over in the other part, so she can dance with kids her own age. But they play music so loud over there, and they don't keep the tables clean. I told her, 'You go over there, then, and I'll wait for you here.'" "Good idea," he heard himself say, nodding sagely. "But what about you?" she wanted to know. Before he knew what had hit him, he found himself launched into a preposterous story about himself. He was a professor of economics, he said, a widower. "You look awful young to be a widower," she had put in doubtfully, licking her lips, which seemed to be a habit with her. "We married young," he had said. "She was ... she was an Orthodox Jew. My folks were furious. They wouldn't speak to us. They only began speaking to me again after she died." "Was it cancer?" asked the woman. "How did you know?" he asked. "I just figured that was it. Did it take long?"

Then he was back at the table with a fresh drink the woman had ordered for him. "On me," she had insisted. She was telling him about her ex-husband. "He didn't even send Sheila a birthday card for her last birthday. I had to go out and buy one and fake his signature and say he'd sent it to her care of my office and I'd misplaced the envelope. Sheila didn't believe me for a minute, of course."

Sheila herself stood over them. "This place sucks," she said. "I'm ready to go anytime."

He danced with Sheila, a tarty little number, and found himself being more turned on by her than by the mother. She was fourteen. He remembered his elegant, sneering grandmother Buchel saying once of old Dr. Gallant: "First he dated the daughters, then he dated the granddaughters. But he was a Gallant, you know, so he got away with it."

He was aware he was causing sorrow. The mother, whose name he didn't know, sat bravely on alone at the table, wearing a determined, faraway smile, while he, on the dance floor, wriggled and shook and rolled his eyes at fourteen-year-old Sheila, who was chewing gum.

"Oh, Rafe, I'm so happy. Please be happy for me ... I wish you would let me adopt you as my brother ... Do yourself a favor ... You're killing millions of brain cells ... Even if you were my real brother, we couldn't go dancing tonight."

". . . eighteen bottles of St. Emilion, eighteen of ten-year-old Scotch . . . one camel, laden with claret."

"Theo?"

"Yes, little brother."

"I'm drunk."

"Tell me something else new."

"Can you get me out of here?"

"I did last year, I guess I can again this year."

"I don't know. Is this a good idea?"

"Easiest thing in the word. You wouldn't believe my powers. Just sit back and relax."

"This isn't the Bonneville. It's a Mazda RX7. Mom put in some, Clare put in some . . . Dad put up for the insurance on his fleet policy and provided the lecture on how he'd never been given a car like this in his life. Theo, are you sure you can do this?"

"Rafe, can a man pick up an ant on the tip of his finger and transport it to the other side of the ant heap? Relax. I operate on a cosmic scale now. It drives nice. You always cared more about cars."

"What do you mean? You didn't?"

"Of course I did, but what I really wanted, more than anything . . . oh, Rafe! If I could tell you. If I could only begin to tell you!"

"What? Tell me. I'm listening, tell me!"

"Oh, Rafe, you know what's sad? It's that you are in a state where you can hear me now. Only, when you wake up, you won't remember any of it."

"Theo, you've got to help me. Jesus! My head is going around like those strobe lights and I'm so sick I could die!"

"Listen, Rafe, just relax and keep cool, and don't close your eyes and I'll get you home. Hold on. God! I can't begin to tell you! I know everything but it's too late. I mean, it's too late for me. But I can get you home. Just do as I say. Lean your head back, but not too far back, on that fancy-smelling new vinyl, and let me tell you all I've learned. Let me tell you the secrets of the universe. You won't remember any of it in the morning, but you'll know I at least got you home."

He awoke lying on his side, fully dressed, on a mattress from one of the lounge chairs, with the red sun rising in his face. He remembered dragging himself like a sick dog to the end of the windwalk, spewing his guts into the sand below, then pulling the mattress down off the lounge chair where he'd been sunning yesterday and falling onto it, clutching its sides as if it were a raft while the storm of stars flew around and around his head. Now the tide had gone out and taken his pollutions with it. The blazing star that warmed and lit the planet ascended effortlessly from its bath of night to preside over a rinsed and shining world. He envied the resurrective feats of nature.

Someone had covered him during the night or early morning with his own eiderdown. The one he always brought with him, that Felix had teased him about last year ("I see you have brought all your comforts"). Who, in "No Saints," had his merciful angel been? He lay for some time, gazing with a mounting disgust at the cheap little puke-green plastic bracelet shackling his wrist, trying to decide the likeliest person to have seen him, gone down to his room to get his security blanket, and covered him up. He went over their names in the order of who could be expected to love him most, then next-to-most, then next-to-next-to-most. The one who loved him not at all was the one he wished it had been, but he decided never to ask. He hoped no one volunteered the information. That way, he could at least have the company of his illusions for the rest of this visit.

September 28
  (Wenceslaus, martyr)
Sister Jouret's Profession Day, 1919

September 29
  (Feast of the Archangels Michael,
  Gabriel, and Raphael)

September 30
  (Jerome, priest and doctor)
Ann-Margaret Ferguson (Duvall)
wedding day

October 1
  (Memorial of Theresa of the Child Jesus)
Eamon Patrick's birthday

October 2
  (Memorial of the Guardian Angels)
pray for the soul of Theo Quick, d. 1983

—a page in Sister Patrick's Book of Days

XII: ANNIVERSARY

*T*he nuns were preparing for a feast in the big dining hall of St. Clothilde's. Sister Patrick was arranging centerpieces of pine boughs mingled with summer flowers down the tables covered with white cloths. For once all the sisters were working in harmony. They moved as parts of a celestially choreographed ballet. No one lagged behind or cocked her head critically at another's work. No one was old or bent, or complaining about shakes and aches and afflictions. All at once, great barn doors in the rear of the dining hall, doors that Sister Patrick had never noticed before, swung open without a sound, revealing a square of black night. And Sister Patrick's father, dead these thirty years, stood before them in his mud-spattered riding clothes and checked wool cap. "Fiona," he said, flicking his crop against his leg, "Shadow's come back and she's the same devil as before. They haven't taught her a blessed thing. Just go round and see her, won't you, before she mortally wounds that young man."

Sister Patrick excused herself to the other nuns and, hiking up the skirts of her habit, ran out of the newly revealed barn doors into the moist, moonless night. Her feet flew down the path between the old Victorian building and the stables. How stupid of me, she was thinking, to let all these years pass before I realized Ireland was just to the back of the dining room of St. Clothilde's in Mountain City. She heard Shadow's waggish whinny and could hardly contain her joy at the prospect of seeing her old playmate again. Then there was a thud and a cry and, in a spotlit circle in front of the stables, a handsome young man lay crumpled and dead on the ground. Ah, she had come too late! She knew it was wrong of her, but she was put out with the strange young fellow for going and getting killed. Now they would have to shoot Shadow.

But as if the young man sensed her disapproval, he rose immediately from the ground, brushed himself off, and asked with an ingratiating grin, "Hey, Sister, would it be okay if I went back with you to the school and washed my hands?"

She knew it was her duty to offer him that chance because that was the life she had freely chosen. Even though it meant turning her back on the stables and never seeing her beloved Shadow again. Up they went together to the school, the young man just risen from the dead and the nun. Talk, talk, talk. He was one fine chatterbox, to be sure. Though, without her hearing aids in, she couldn't hear a word he was saying. Mutter, mutter, mutter, he said, flailing his arms for emphasis. Mutter, murmur, murmur, he went on, as they climbed the hill into the sunrise.

. . . *Mutter, mutter, murmur, murmur, mutter:* from the other side of the wall, Sister Marvell, an invalid now, whose mind wandered, was saying her morning prayers in bed. Her rumbly old voice, which she made no effort to keep down, rose and fell, carrying through the thin walls of the new convent, built in 1968, and waking the other nuns before daybreak. If she put her hearing aids in, Sister Patrick would hear what the others were hearing: snatches of French, followed by antiphons chanted in Latin, interspersed with impassioned utterances, often shouted, ranging from the most familiar ejaculations, such as "My Jesus, mercy!" to a more individual type of entreaty that varied from morning to morning and seemed to be composed out of shards of phrases banked deep in her religious memory as she went along. Some were as startling as they were touchingly original: "Mary pure of heart, disinfect my grave!" "Jesus meek and humble, toughen up my soul!" Community members responded to these precipitate predawn rousings according to their natures. Sister Lanier twisted her pointy, acerbic face into what passed for a smile and remarked in her Southern drawl that it was thoughtful of God to save her the price of a new alarm clock, especially in view of the shrinking purchase power of their thirty-dollar-a-month allowance. Sister O'Hare, if present when the others were discussing it, widened her reproachful gray eyes, made enormous by the magnifying lenses worn since her cataract operations, and said nothing—thus very effectively recalling to them the rule of speech that had been drummed into them long ago as novices: nothing should be said that does not glorify or serve God or provide someone with necessary information. A bit self-righteous, Sister O'Hare was. Sister Steinmetz, their resident hypochondriac, brought low since the death of the only other German nun in the community, Sister von Blücher, who scoffed her out of her fears and then turned around and waited on her tenderly, said Sister Marvell ought to be in a retirement home, where she could be sedated by nurses when she carried on like that and wakened the other sisters. If Sister Steinmetz didn't get her full eight hours, she shook worse than ever and was unable to do her share of the work. Sister Jouret, of course, was deaf, but so sweet-natured it wouldn't have occurred to her to complain even if she hadn't been, and Sister Davis, who was almost blind, said Sister Marvell's early-morning performance came as a blessing to her, because it reminded her to be grateful for her unimpaired sense of hearing. Sister Dugan, their youngest nun at fifty-six, said being wakened by those lovely phrases in French and Latin made her nostalgic for the old days when they still had the liturgical hours in the grand old Victorian building, which had housed forty-nine sisters and the boarders and all twelve grades of the school. In those days the nuns had said their first prayer of the day in French, to honor the language of their order, and had sung the Psalms in Latin, and had worn the full-habit. Poor Sister Dugan, a Mountain City girl, had barely been professed before Vatican II took away all her cherished forms. But she had stuck it out, bless her, the only one in her age group to have done so. Now she balanced the convent's accounts, taught art to the dwindling classes at St. Clothilde's— La Fosse Hall, almost completely staffed by lay teachers, and also found time to make wedding books for her many nieces and nephews and favorite old students, baby books for their children, and daybooks for the nuns left at the convent. Custom-made, as she called them, they were individualized love offerings done in her exquisite calligraphy, each one entirely different. The days of Sister Patrick's were illuminated in green and gold paint (the green for her Irishness, Sister Dugan explained, the gold because she had been a nun for fifty years); on the facing pages across from the days were reproductions of paintings or copied-out poems that Sister Dugan knew that person liked. Sister Patrick's Book of Days was rife with Browning quotations and details from Italian Renaissance art. Everyone saved picture postcards from the Louvre and the Uffizi for Sister Dugan, and her room was piled chest-high with glossy art magazines donated by friends in town who knew of her avocation.

Sister Patrick rose from her narrow bed and, as she had done every morning for the past fifty-two years—except on linen-changing days—made it up at once, with the sleep still in her eyes. Then she put on her robe and slippers and took her sponge bag from the dresser and went down the hall to one of the two community bathrooms. As she brushed her teeth briskly, she couldn't help smiling at Sister Dugan's new sign, lettered in Gothic script, taped to the bottom of the mirror.

> Christ—in the next person—thanks you for
> cleaning the sink for Him and taking
> your hair with you.

The sign, which had been up for two weeks to no avail, was for the edification of Sister Marvell's Home Helper, who came three days a week and spent a great deal of time shut up in the bathroom making up her face and combing her hair over the sink.

Carefully rinsing away all signs of her own scrubbings and combings, Sister Patrick returned to her room and laid out her clothes for the day. Sixteen years of dressing as a lay person had not brought her the automatic ease with which she remembered putting on the habit. And yet, if you counted up the actual number of garments and the method of securing them, the old routine had been far more cumbersome and complicated. With lay clothes, it was the grooming details that required the extra foresight and effort. A laddered stocking, a snagged hem, untidy hair, *showed*. Even without vanity, one became increasingly concerned with the duty of sparing others the distractions of your oversights. And then there was the cost of things. Under the old regime, they had been so blissfully protected from all that. Once every six weeks, old Sister Yvonne, from Housekeeping, had come around to collect your shoes with the rundown heels and they were taken to the cobbler's along with everybody else's, and when you next saw them they were standing side by side in your closet again. When a skirt wore out, or, in the case of some, when you grew out of your skirt, you went to Reverend Mother and she put in an order to Sister Hannah, who took out some black serge and ran you up a new one. Soap, toothpaste, and sanitary pads were issued by Sister Irene in the storeroom. Now you got your shoes to town the best you could, paid for their mending out of your monthly allowance, bought your own toothpaste and toiletries. If you needed a new pair of shoes or a suit or a blouse, you had to save up. Of course, one was now allowed cash gifts from one's family or friends. And many well-meaning ladies, fashionable mothers and former students of the school, donated their last season's clothes to the nuns. The contents of these gift boxes offered almost as many occasions for laughter as they provided opportunities for penance and humility. However, there were usually enough wearable items in the boxes for the sisters who needed them. (Sisters Marvell, Jouret, Davis and O'Hare still wore modified versions of the old habit.)

Sister Patrick put on underwear, stockings (she could not abide the airless, twisting pantyhose), drip-dry blouse and skirt (a nice Irish tweed sent from Galway by her nephew's wife), and the stacked-heel Amalfi pumps for which she had saved six months. She skimped on blouses, but was particular about her shoes. She fastened a chain with a small silver cross around her neck and slipped into a cardigan (too snug in the upper arms) from one of the fashionable ladies' boxes. Last of all, she fitted in the two small, square hearing aids, and the generalized muffles and murmurs were amplified into specific household sounds. The clatter of Ruth, downstairs in the kitchen, preparing breakfast; the swish-swish-*bump*, swish-swish-*bump* of Sister Davis and her walker making their slow morning pilgrimage down the linoleum corridor to the elevator. The muted thump of a refrigerator door's closing in Father's quarters below and the clinking of glass: that would be Sister Lanier, who was Sacristan this week, pouring the water and wine into their cruets for morning Mass. *"Leurs bons anges, veillez sur elles!"* cried Sister Marvell on the other side of the thin wall. Her mind might wander, but she had remembered that this was the second of October, the Memorial of the Guardian Angels.

Having turned off the lamp, Sister Patrick opened her bedroom blinds. The sun was just rising, burnishing the tops of the mountains that ridged the western sky. The valley below, in which Mountain City rested, still lay in a deep bowl of shadow.

Oh, morning, and the brown
brink eastward, springs—
Because the Holy Ghost over
the bent
World broods with warm
breast and with ah!
bright wings.

Hopkins had got the dawn better, but on the whole she preferred Browning. Since the old school had been torn down and the hill on which it stood leveled to make an athletic field, the nuns on the new convent's second floor had fallen heir to the best view in town, the same lofty, panoramic sweep one gained in former days by climbing the circular staircase to the Victorian building's tower. As a young nun, Sister Patrick had loved to do her meditations in the tower. Now she had been vouchsafed the identical prospect from her bedroom window, but who knew for how much longer? If the school closed down—which seemed likely—what with progressively lower enrollments, staggering debts, and no new young women suddenly discovering they had vocations to teach for no further recompense than God's reward—the sisters would have to sell off the rest of their land and buildings to Doctors' Park, the proliferating sprawl of specialists' offices that already had gobbled up several of the outbuildings as well as St. Clothilde's majestic former entrance, a long, curving driveway lined with hundred-year-old spruces. When Sister Patrick took her evening walk around the convent's diminished grounds, she sometimes felt as if the expensive stone-and-glass doctors' buildings with their rhododendrons and Japanese maples, had crept a few feet closer during the course of the day without anyone's being the wiser. Sometimes she could swear there was a patch of ground gone, or a sapling or two missing, that had been there the evening before.

She went to the chapel and said the Angelus and made her morning meditation. She was in the second week of Ignatius's *Spiritual Exercises*, following a new contemporary text written by a Jesuit in Missouri. Today she contemplated the Obedience of the Child Jesus to His parents and the Finding of the Child Jesus in the Temple. Which in turn were to lead her towards self-examination, asking to what new call to service or stage of growth God, in His loving Providence, might be leading her. It was a question of particular concern to her and she welcomed the opportunity to sit quietly before morning office and Mass and listen for answers. What "new call to service or stage of growth" did God have in mind for a deaf seventy-year-old retired teaching nun? She still tutored, of course; she had one-to-one sessions with some four or five children a semester. Their parents were glad to pay extra in order that the slow son or the daughter with attention problems could sit side by side with Sister Patrick on the sofa in the visitors' parlor and be drilled in square roots and fractions or coaxed into belated recognition of a poem's invisible subtext so that he or she could be promoted to the next grade. But she could do such teaching with a tenth of her mind. It took greater patience, it was true. It had demanded some pretty stringent curbings of her natural *im*-patience. Yet there were rewards: modest, unceremonious ones, some surprisingly sweet. She witnessed the moment when a young self-hater began to respect himself. She was deeply touched when she glimpsed, purely by chance, a three-column list of "My Most Often Misspelled Words" copied out by a little girl onto one of her notebook dividers. It must have taken her hours to look up all those words and to copy them with such decorous care—without ever having been asked. The emotion these children elicited in her was different from the exalted, ju-bilant pride she'd felt in her old winners, the ones who carried off the prizes in state speech contests, and wrote brilliant, dashing essays, and captured the scholarships to Radcliffe and Bryn Mawr and Duke, and went on to become the teachers and scientists and actors and writers she had predicted all along they would be. These days, Sister Patrick found herself increasingly prey to surges of tender appreciation for the steadfast little underachievers who bent over their notebooks in such proximity that she could identify the flavor of LifeSaver on their breaths and fancied she could often feel the heat of their labored concentra-tion glancing in waves off her own skin. More and more she was coming to believe that they were teaching *her* a lesson, that they were widening her definition of what winning was all about. . . .

Well, Fiona, you've answered your own question, then, haven't you? Or You have begun to answer it in me.

As the rest of the nuns filled the chapel, she made her special devotion to the Holy Spirit, asking guidance in the planning of her day. She had two tutorials, one at ten, one at noon. And then she must do something for Lily Quick on the first anniversary of her son's horrible death. Since Sister Patrick had served as a character witness for the family during the custody hearing for Theo's little boy, she and Lily had gone out to lunch several times. She enjoyed the other woman's company—after having become accustomed to Lily's characteristic coolness of manner, which Sister Patrick at first had mistaken for disdain. Lily Quick said interesting things. The only trouble was, Sister Patrick missed half of them when they went to lunch, because all sounds in a crowded restaurant were amplified equally. Yet she had not mentioned this to her new friend for fear of seeming unwilling to meet. Today, however, lunch would be difficult: the last tutorial ended at half past one. And then there was the added complication of Sister Patrick's dream. The young man who was kicked to death by Shadow and then rose again and was so eager to explain himself as they had started up the hill to the old school had been Theo Quick. She had identified him within moments of waking up—after she had gotten over her disappointment at missing Shadow; she would have liked a glimpse or a touch of her old horse, even in a dream. Would it be helpful to share the dream with Theo's mother, or kinder to withhold it? It was, after all, Sister Patrick's own nighttime scramblings of the Lord knew what combination of stimuli from the previous day. (Yesterday had been her father's birthday— he would have been a hundred and four if he had lived; and there, right below his name in her daybook, had been the name of Theo Quick; and then, of course, there had been so much talk of late among the sisters about the school's possible closing, which had led to much reminiscing about St. Clothilde's at the peak of her operations, when they were still in the romantic old building—a Victorian hotel recently gone out of business when their order purchased it in 1910—with its labyrinthine stairwells and passages, the great dining hall of which she had dreamed last night, its gingerbread trim and the tower, its sun porches made over into classrooms and its ballrooms into study halls.)

To say to Lily Quick, "I had a dream about Theo last night": would that not be presumptuous? Setting herself up as a kind of medium?

On the other hand, what if—and we know so little of how these things work!—the dream had dreamed itself in her because it knew she would be speaking to Lily today, had been reminded several days ago to do so when she had turned the next page of her daybook and had seen the message to herself written on the night of Theo's death one year ago.

Abraham dreamed. Jacob was wounded while wrestling with an angel in a dream. Joseph was freed from prison and placed in Pharaoh's service because he understood dreams. Eli advised Samuel to answer the voice that called to him in dreams, and thus learned the future of himself and his house. The Church Fathers dreamed. Polycarp, on his way to Rome, dreamed he would be killed there, and was. Saint Justin Martyr, a student of philosophy, believed, as did Irenaeus, that dreams were a means of maintaining a direct union with God. Constantine saw "chi" and "rho" written in the sky, and at night Christ appeared to him in a dream carrying these two letters in His hand. The King converted to Christianity, and the letters, worn on the shields of his warriors, became the symbol of the Greek Empire for more than a thousand years to come.

But of course there were spurious dreams, also. Temptations from the other side to set oneself up as self-important. Ignatius, in the Fourth Week of the Exercises, had much to say about the discernment of Good and Evil Spirits. (As always, when doing the Exercises, she had not been able to resist peeking at the difficult chapters ahead.)

I will telephone Lily Quick after breakfast, Sister Patrick decided, and suggest an afternoon drive. It's a fine day for the mountains. And then, if we go, I shall let the Holy Spirit guide me in the matter of the dream.

Sister O'Hare, who was hebdomadary, solemnly opened her prayer book, setting its brightly colored silken markers momentarily aflutter. She spoke the opening line of the office being said by religious communities all over the morning world. "Lord, open my lips."

"And my mouth will proclaim your praise," answered her sisters in unison, the old voices and the soon-to-be-old merging somewhere in the upper range of a composite female contralto. The sound they had made together as younger nuns had been closer to soprano. However, there had been six times as many of them then. Had the marked change in pitch been caused by age or diminishment of numbers or some combination of both? She would have to ask Sister Lanier, their musician, about this.

"Thalia? It's Lily."

"Where are you, honey?"

"I'm afraid I'm still at home."

"You're not coming in?"

"No, I—not today, Thalia. But I didn't want you to worry."

"The swim would do you good, baby. The swim and your massage. Look, do you think I don't know what day this is? But I still think it would do you good."

"You remembered."

"Honey, of course I remembered. I'll remember every year for the rest of my life. The day after your birthday. You got my card, didn't you?"

"Yes, it came on Saturday. It was so sweet of you to remember my birthday. And I especially liked the message on the card. You are my important friend, too, Thalia."

"Thank you, Lily. I can't talk you into changing your mind? Not even if I promise I won't leave my little green bruises on your legs?"

"Oh, dear, there's that infernal call-back thing he had installed. It means there's another call coming in. Can you hold on a moment, Thalia?"

"Listen, honey, I got to run anyway. I got a lady waiting for her massage. You come tomorrow, you hear?"

"Yes, all right, Goodbye. Oh, damn, this *rude* machine. He *would!* Hello?"

"Hello, Lily? This is Sister Patrick. Am I phoning too early?"

"Sister Patrick. How nice to hear from you. I was going to call you sometime later this week and see if we could have lunch again soon."

"I was wondering, would you be free this afternoon? I can't make lunch, but I'd be free from around a quarter to two until evening prayer at five o'clock. I know what day this is, of course, but if you're willing to take a bit of a drive, I know a lovely spot out in Maggie Valley. I went there for a retreat this past summer. It's a very special church on top of a mountain with breathtaking views all around. And today being so fine . . ."

"It sounds lovely, I'd like to very much. I was planning on going out to the cemetery later this morning—you're sure you can't have lunch?"

"No, Lily, but thank you. I've got a tutorial until half past one. But I could make myself a quick cup of tea and a sandwich and be waiting outside the convent at a quarter to two."

"I'll be there then, Sister. I'm so glad you called."

*   *   *

To the florist's for two long-stemmed red roses, still furled, in those little bud vases with pointed tips you could stick in the ground. Then along the traffic-congested single-lane highway out to the cemetery. Memories of other trips along this road. When they were on their way to bury Mother and Father Zachary's car had a flat tire and he pulled off to the side of the highway and hitched a ride. When they were on their way to bury Theo, and she and Rafe rode alone in Rafe's car because Snow had insisted on having her place in the limousine. Rafe sobbing the whole way, and she, trying to say something to keep him from running off the road, had commented on how beautifully Father Weir had read that passage from Romans 8. And Rafe answering bitterly, "I'm sorry, I really wasn't paying a whole hell of a lot of attention." Rafe was going to be all right. He passed his comprehensives and hadn't been able to make it home for her birthday because he had a teaching assistantship and his class met yesterday. But he had phoned and said how much he loved her. Clare had phoned, too, from Switzerland, very excited about having looked up their Swiss relatives at last and discovered them to be attractive people. She offered appealing descriptions of how they lived, the Buchel window in the thirteenth-century church in their little village near Interlaken, what food and drink they served, and how Felix had to translate because the older ones spoke only German. One of the cousins had a whole glass cabinet full of shooting medals. He was the third best marksman in all of Switzerland. "Theo would have loved talking to him; they could have compared their medals."

Last year on her birthday, she had had all her children around her. And had been angry all day because he hadn't cleaned the carport, as she had asked, but instead had chosen to impress everybody (except her) by giving her that Japanese ceremonial robe. The carport had never been cleaned. For this birthday, there was an added obstruction: a trailer with contents of a drugstore in it. He and Alicia Gallant, on one of their "Saturday drives," had passed through a little town Miss Alicia had loved as a girl, and there was the same old drugstore—only with a going-out-of-business sign. He and Miss Alicia had gone in and had Cokes, sitting at the counter, and then to show off to Miss Alicia, he had arranged with the old druggist to buy out his entire stock. Now, every weekend, he and Miss Alicia took a few boxloads of their drugstore items to the flea market, where they

had great fun selling off old apothecary jars and metal hair
curlers of the type Mother had used and Pan Cake makeup that
had been moldering away in cheap pink plastic compacts for
fifteen years; afterwards, they would go back to Miss Alicia's
and he'd make them each a screwdriver—Miss Alicia's favorite
drink—and they'd divide up their profits as gleefully as two
children who had spent the afternoon selling lemonade on the
front lawn.

And around dusk, he would sigh (oh, she could just hear him,
see him) and say, "Well, I guess I'd better be getting on up the
hill," and part sadly from his eighty-seven-year-old playmate
and head home to his cross-on-this-earth, his denigrator, his
confidence-snatcher, his prison matron, his legal and lawful
doom. And they'd begin their nightly rigmarole: she would
resolve to be gracious and receptive despite the hostility that
lurked inside her constantly, like a dog about to snap (all their
real dogs were gone now: the two younger ones carried off by
heartworm last winter, and the last, her sweet Liebchen, who
had lost all control of her back parts, put to sleep in August);
and he, disarmed and lured by her determined sweetness, would
try to rise to some kind of an effort himself, and make them
drinks. She preferred wine, but because her drinking it made
him angry—for some reason, he equated wine drinking in
women with alcoholism—she would accept a mint julep or a
mai tai just to keep the peace.

On most nights be would make popcorn, and they would sit
across from each other at the kitchen table and talk about things
they had in common—mostly Jason, or the latest thing Snow
had done to inconvenience them or postpone the child's visits.
Warily skirting any of the ten thousand and ten bones of con-
tention between them. Gradually he would begin breaking the
rules by relating the funniest thing Alicia Gallant had said that
day, or one more of the charming stories about her family in old
Mountain City, which always led to a rhapsodic panegyric to
Miss Alicia's "wonderful attitude towards life." Or she might
break the rule by sliding the message pad across the table and
reminding him that Mr. X, or Y, or Z, or Mrs. A, or B, or C,
had called back *again* about the new house or the kitchen re-
novation or the garage roof that a tree fell on or when his men
were going to come back and clean up the rubbish from the job
they had finished months ago, and he would utter a long-suffering sigh and say it was too bad a man couldn't come home at

the end of the day and have a drink and some popcorn in peace. In a while he would ask what they were having for dinner, and she would say, What do you feel like having, and he would say, I never have been one for fussing over my food. And this might lead to unkind reminiscences about how Felix and Clare made meals into a sort of religion and about those hot dogs Felix put away; and often, God help her, she betrayed poor Felix and Clare by agreeing they overdid it at times and that Felix was certainly shopping for a heart attack by carrying around that extra weight. By then they would have eaten up the popcorn, and neither of them would be hungry, but if she didn't go through the motions of making some potato soup, or chipped beef on toast, for him to leave most of on his plate, she wouldn't have fulfilled her wifely function.

If they made it till supper without an argument, she would tell him about Altar Guild or her visits to the old ladies, which bored him, or he would start that choking noise in his throat and say he had a good mind to put another of those ads in the paper offering a ten-thousand-dollar reward to anyone with information leading to the conviction of Theo's murderer. And she would ask, Don't you think you ought to let it be, I mean, it won't bring him back; and he would remind her that she—yes, she—had been the one who had put the idea in his head in the first place, did she not remember that night when she had entered the kitchen triumphantly waving the gun, Theo's gun, and suggesting possibilities no one else had even thought of until then. I did not wave it, I would never enter a room waving a gun. I brought it into the kitchen in the shoebox, the Thom McAn shoebox he always kept it in. You had it in your hand, there was no shoebox. There was, he always kept it in that shoebox on the top shelf of his closet, have you forgotten that? I haven't forgotten it, but we're talking about when you walked into the kitchen; you had it in your hand. My God, you distort everything. And *you* remember things the way you want to remember. I *may* have entered the kitchen carrying it, but I certainly did not *wave* it, that isn't my style. And I don't see why you're making such a fuss over that gun, anyway. The whole point of my bringing that gun into the room was to show that it was still in the house. Which meant he didn't do it. And then *you* started crying and told us all that you'd given him your gun, that Belgian one, which was the one that killed him, whoever did the shooting. Theo came to me and asked me for my gun, he wanted it for Jeanette. She was afraid because she had to testify at that trial of the man who tried to rape her, and I'm still not satisfied . . . that man left town right after the deaths; and also, the possibility that the child . . . that the gun might have been lying in the backseat and he picked it up and said, "Bang, bang," and aimed it at Jeanette and Theo in front. Oh, Ralph, that's so *unlikely!* But you, Lily—yes, *you*—were the first one to suggest it. . . . What's the use of all this, Ralph! It won't bring him back, nothing will bring him back!

She had read somewhere recently that fifty-two percent of the married couples who lost a child got a divorce within three years.

Someone had beat her to the cemetery. And left, at the head of Theo's flat stone, a hideous green pot with plastic lilies in it. The color of the lilies wasn't even a color in nature, it was a sort of horrid brownish-pink: like the color of the "flesh" on those cheap rubber dolls. There was no card attached but everything about its physical appearance cried Mullins. Which one of them, or several of them, had made the trip all the way from Granny Squirrel to lay this offering at her son's feet? And lilies, too: the offhand insult was perfect. Of course, they had meant well; the awful thing had probably cost a lot more of money than her two roses. And it was only she, not they, who had seen the irony of the odious flowers just happening to represent the ones she shared a name with. They hadn't thought them odious; they had thought them beautiful.

Yet she was unable to lift a hand to move the pot even an inch from its prominent center space. It was as though her son's own hand prevented it, as though his own voice, with its particular teasing-reproachful quality, defended the tribute of his humble in-laws. Contritely, she got to her knees on the dry, prickly turf and, tears spilling in gratitude for the momentary contact with him, even if it had been to send her a message of filial reproach, pushed the pointed tip of her tasteful bud vase into the ground beside their lilies. Within three days her roses would have withered into unsightliness; whereas the triumphant plastic lilies, barring an act of vandalism, would endure the winter ahead.

The other rose she placed at the foot of her mother's stone. Here, center space was entirely her due.

Ellen Harshaw Buchel
January 20, 1972

She would have no birthdate on her grave, either, when the time came; had already so stipulated to Ralph and her children. But it was not written down anywhere. What if Ralph, who thought she was being silly, went against her wishes after she was dead and had the truth chiseled in stone for the whole world to see, even the Mullinses, when they came to visit Theo?

She took out her embroidery scissors from her purse and trimmed where the grass had invaded her mother's stone. The line was clean-cut around Theo's. Because it was newer, or had someone trimmed it?

Because there was still time before she was due to pick up Sister Patrick at the convent, she stopped by a candy store on the highway and paid a quick visit to Miss Holly at Mount Gilead, passing out the candies to everyone in the dayroom. Miss Holly's sister had died in August, but it didn't seem to bother her. "How's my dog?" she asked Lily. "She's just fine," Lily assured her about her imaginary pet, "and she has a very good appetite."

Mamie Van Spruill, out at Tina's, was dead, too. Lily missed the proud little lady who sat with her skirt spread demurely over her potty chair and covered the sound of her helpless bladder by telling fantastic fibs. Tina's legless husband, Dirk, said the whole family was broken up by the loss of Miss Mamie and Tina was hoping to get another lady who would be like Miss Mamie, just one of the family. When he told Lily that, last month when she dropped by to see how they all were, Lily had had a sudden vision of herself, a few years from now, as somebody's helpless resident "lady." Incapacitated by some errant blood clot or by wasted functions, she would sit banked on pillows or (please God, not) perched over the abyss of her potty chair, maintaining a mysterious little side-smile or utilizing whatever other devices were left to her to proclaim the message poor sweet little Mrs. Clark out at Hickory Haven had written out by hand and taped above her bed:

P B P W M! G I N F W M Y!

(Please be patient with me! God is not finished with me yet!) And after their Saturday drive, or their lunch at the Red Lobster, or on the way to barter their drugstore debris at the flea market, Ralph and Miss Alicia would visit her nursing home and gamely keep her company for a quarter of an hour every week.

Sister Patrick, her large pocketbook beside her, was waiting on a bench outside the convent, on the little knoll overlooking the athletic field where the old St. Clothilde's building used to ramble on its hill. As soon as Lily drove up, she loped down the knoll with alacrity, entered the car, and strapped herself into the passenger seat. Whereupon she began to talk at once, entertaining Lily all the way down to the railroad crossing, where they had to stop for a passing freight train. She told about the students she was tutoring, and how her left hearing aid gurgled in her ear like a brook until she had sent it off to be repaired under warranty for the third time in six months. She talked about tutoring math, how, in the old days, "we just taught mathematics, but now there are names for everything. Sets, for instance." She explained sets lucidly, so for the first time Lily understood they were nothing that she hadn't known already. Sister Patrick said, "And so much of the *talk* is foolish. For example, they tell students now that to divide a number by zero is impossible. We used to teach that if you divided a number by zero you got infinity. Now, a child can't understand why something is impossible. But he can understand infinity perfectly well."

They waited for the long freight train to pass. Lily thought of her father, as she always did when she saw a train. She felt suddenly happy. No wonder Clare liked Sister Patrick so much, she thought. Of *course* it is easier to understand infinity than it is to understand impossible.

On the trip out I-40, she told Lily in great detail the plot of a novel she had just finished reading. Set in Ireland and Scotland, with some international intrigue Lily forgot to pay attention to, though Sister Patrick kept her meticulously abreast, it was basically about the romance between the good man and the heroine, a cocky young woman lawyer from Edinburgh. The bad man in the book was also in love with her. As Sister Patrick recounted with relish the slow awakening of the independent woman to the love of the right man as they chased people in cars through magnificent Highland scenery or hid together in mountain cabins from murderers, Lily realized that the nun was thoroughly and shamelessly identifying with the young woman lawyer in her convoluted and protracted capitulation to love and passion.

After that, Sister Patrick told jokes. Had Lily heard the one about how the Roman Catholic Church had been built on a rock, but now it was tottering on a Pole? Or about the time the Reverend Mother of a certain convent called all her nuns together and said, "Sisters, I'm afraid we have a problem. We have a case of herpes in the convent." And after a minute of stunned silence, the quavery voice of an old nun piped up: "Well, I don't see that it's such a problem. I was getting tired of drinking all that root beer, anyway."

Then she drew herself up and bunched her lips into a mass of little wrinkles and apologized for her excessive levity as well as for monopolizing the conversation. She loved a long drive into the mountains more than almost anything, she said, and it probably made her a bit wild.

Not at all, Lily said. She was enjoying the way the nun's independent mind flashed out at every turn despite herself; how the musical Irish cadences of her speech gave whatever she was saying a mischievous holiday lilt. But she was right, she was unusually mirthful and loquacious today. Maybe it had something to do with the gorgeous October weather, with the leaves starting to turn, and the air like wine; maybe it was because they were getting to know each other better. After all, they had gone out to lunch more than half a dozen times since the custody hearings. And maybe, also, Sister Patrick didn't enjoy going to restaurants all that much. Now that she thought about it, Lily recalled a tightening in the nun, as though tensing herself for an ordeal, as she swung along beside her hostess, hefting her large pocketbook like a penance, into the frivolous midday tinkle and clatter of whatever fashionable restaurant Lily had chosen.

Or it was possible that Sister Patrick was simply working extra hard to cheer her up because of what day it was.

The nun was asking her about her "work with the old people." It was admirable of Lily to go so regularly to all those nursing homes and give of herself so generously.

"It started off, really, as a sort of 'thank you' to God for not letting my mother waste away slowly—it would have killed her dignity. Then I suppose I got increasingly involved in preserving the dignity of the ones who weren't as lucky as Mother. I can't stand it when they're treated like idiot children or . . . or garbage waiting to be taken out, or something. I get so angry. Every one of them is a unique personality, even though their bodies are in the process of crumbling to dust. Everybody's body crumbles to dust eventually, but no two personalities—*no two*—are ever alike." She had to stop talking for a minute, because she was close to tears. When she recovered, she said with her customary dry nonchalance, "But I certainly don't see myself as a do-gooder or an angel of mercy or anything like that."

"No," said Sister Patrick. "You're not their angel of mercy, you're their angel of dignity. They need both; they need all of their angels. But I'm like you. I believe the personality is important. Otherwise, why did God make everyone unique? And since He did, we should fight any person or institution or system that tries to take away that dignity of uniqueness. Today is the Memorial Day of the Guardian Angels, you know."

"Today?"

"That's right. On this day we offer the intention of the Mass for the guardian angels."

"Does it always fall on this day?"

"Always. October second is always the day of the guardian angels."

They rode in silence for a few minutes, in mutual awareness of all that was not being said. Finally Sister Patrick, unable to repress herself any longer, told the story of how Sister Davis, who was almost blind but who could read a little if she wore special glasses and held the print very close to her eyes, had ordered T-shirts for all her little grandnieces and nephews out of a catalogue. There was a selection of sayings you could have printed on the T-shirts, and Sister Davis had liked one especially, it was so cheerful, and ordered it for all the shirts. Sister Patrick started to laugh. She laughed so hard her fine freckled skin turned scarlet and she had to take her handkerchief out of her pocketbook and wipe her eyes and blow her nose before she could go on. "Well, the weeks went by and after a time Sister began to receive these oddly worded thank-you notes from the children or the parents. She knew something was wrong, but she couldn't figure out what it was. At last, one brave relative had the courage to tell her. You see, what poor Sister Davis *thought* she had seen in the catalogue was 'Smile if You're Happy,' but it was—it was —" Sister Patrick went off into another spasm of laughter. "It was 'Smile if You're Horny.'"

The two women whooped with helpless hilarity. Lily laughed

until the tears ran down her cheeks and she almost drove right past the exit to Maggie Valley.

"We don't want to miss the sign," Sister Patrick, sober and bunching her lips again, kept saying as Lily drove slowly down a road crammed with new motels and restaurants and amusement parks. "It's just a small sign on the right, beside a little wooden bridge. It's easy to go right past it. Sister Lanier did last summer and we had to turn around and go back, and it's harder to spot from the opposite direction." Lily, crawling along at five miles an hour, crouched tensely over the wheel and peered anxiously at the spaces between the glossy motels and their borders of bright asters and marigolds. Just look at the contrast, she thought: ten minutes ago we were hooting like girls over the horny T-shirts; now we're two nervous old ladies afraid we'll miss the turn to our church. Laughter makes you young. I must remember that. Miss Alicia Gallant is always having a hoot over something; maybe that is what attracts Ralph so much.

They found their sign, "St. Margaret's Church," and drove over the wooden bridge and up a steep hill past a motel-like structure, set back from the road among trees, with a large swimming pool. "That's the retreat house where Sister Lanier and I stayed," said Sister Patrick. "Father built that, too. He didn't become a priest until he was eighty. It's quite a story, unique in American church history. When he was almost sixty, he sold all his farmland up in Michigan and moved to Maggie Valley. He bought this entire hill with the intention of building a Catholic church on the top and naming it after his Irish mother. But the Bishop was against it, because there were no Catholics in town. But Father—only he wasn't Father then— persisted, and finally the Bishop gave him permission to build the church with his own money. It took him three years to cut and clear the trees for the road and the site, and three more years to build the church, which he designed himself. And then the Bishop came to see him and said, 'I want you to become a priest and take care of the people in Maggie Valley.' So at the age of seventy-eight, if you please, Father went off to a seminary to become a priest. When the church first opened, only two people showed up for Mass. Now it's packed every Sunday. And members of religious communities come here from all over to make their retreats. Lay people, too, of course."

"It certainly is *up high*," said Lily as the Pontiac labored slowly around alpine curves.

"Ah, yes, but the end result is worth it."

They passed a group of nuns, in short brown habits, climbing the hill on foot. One very obese nun had paused to catch her breath under a tree.

"She needs a scholarship to Weight Watchers," Sister Patrick remarked matter-of-factly.

They reached the top. "Oh, my," said Lily. She pulled into the parking area and switched off the ignition.

"Yes," said Sister Patrick. "Sister Dugan was asking me to describe it. She hasn't been up here yet. I told her your first feeling is 'I will lift up mine eyes unto the hills,' but then you realize that you don't have to lift them up, you're on top of one and you're looking the tops of all the others around you straight in the face."

"And they're all so close. The top of that one over there is actually *lower* than we are. It reminds me of Switzerland. Not that I've ever been to Switzerland. Clare is over there now."

"Is she! Gathering material for a new book, or just having herself a vacation?"

"A little vacation." Lily could never remember whether Sister Patrick was supposed to know about Felix or not, so she edited him out, to be safe. "And she's looking up some of our relatives. My father was Swiss, or, rather, his father was born there. Clare says they're very nice, the relatives. She said she stood on the balcony of her hotel expecting them to drive up in a goat cart, but they came in a large gray Volvo, bearing gifts of Swiss chocolate."

"I can just see Clare," Sister Patrick said, laughing, "up there on the balcony worrying about her relatives driving up in a goat cart."

They got out of the car and the pure, thin air made Lily light-headed. "Heaven must be like this," she said gaily. "Or at least I hope it is." For Theo's sake, she meant. Then realized, perhaps for the first time since his death, that according to the rules of her religion, as well as Sister Patrick's, he might be having to serve some reparation time elsewhere for a little while. Well, that was all right. Father Weir said everyone except outright saints had to stop off in Purgatory for a while, to get cleaned up first. To go straight from this corrupted world to Heaven would be such a change it would blow the ordinary soul into a million pieces, he said.

They went into the church, a small architectural miracle. Its south side was all glass windows looking out at the surrounding mountaintops, and its altar side, facing west towards the one mountain higher than the rest, was made completely of glass except where it was bisected by two huge wooden beams forming the shape of a cross. The vertical beam of the cross was exactly aligned with the center of the high mountain, so that when you knelt in one of the pews your gaze automatically followed the line to the top: you *did* have to lift up your eyes. It was like floating in a glass space capsule among the mountaintops, but still having that one high peak in front of you to aspire to. Kneeling in the pew beside Sister Patrick, who had dropped nimbly to her knees and launched into silent prayer, Lily felt like a spiritual amateur. Ralph would have loved this church. Not the present Ralph, who scowled at her resentfully over the popcorn bowl and wouldn't repair the hole above the tub where the soap dish had fallen out of the wall, but the old Ralph who'd had dreams about how buildings should be built and how people should live in them.

Dear Lord, help me to . . .

While Sister Patrick was telling her jokes, Lily had ransacked her memory for one she could tell in return. But the only one she could remember was that terrible one Freddy Stratton had told her recently in the Fresh Market, when they'd met at the wine shelves. A man went to the doctor, Freddy said, her green eyes twinkling naughtily, and after the doctor examined him, he asked to speak to the man's wife alone. The wife came into the office. Your husband is sick, said the doctor, but there is one way to cure him. What is that? asked the woman. The doctor said, You must cook him three hot meals a day and have sex with him every night. The woman thanked the doctor for his advice and rejoined her husband. As they drove home together, the husband asked his wife what the doctor had said. Well, she replied after a moment, he said that you were very sick . . . and that you were going to die.

And Freddy Stratton had paused, waiting for it to sink in. "But that's awful," Lily had said, when it had, "that's an awful joke, Freddy." "I know," Freddy had said. Then Lily had begun to laugh. The two of them had stood there gripping the handles of their carts and laughed like witches, in bitter, gloating malevolence. Then Freddy had straightened her face demurely and said, "It's a *woman's* joke." "Yes," agreed Lily. And they had picked out their separate wines and parted, each assuring the other how good she looked.

It *was* a woman's joke, but not a nun's joke. Let Sister Patrick keep whatever illusions she had about being a wife, as Lily preferred to keep her ideals about being a nun. Freddy looked awfully good for her age. Better than most of her contemporaries, even Clare. On another trip to the Fresh Market, Lily had noticed a sweet old couple in front of her. A slim, dapper little man in an old Harris tweed jacket with elbow patches was fingering avocados while his round plump wife in her dowdy pantsuit stood patiently and respectfully by, awaiting his finicky decision. Then the woman turned her head slightly, and Lily realized that the old couple were Julia and her father.

Sister Patrick, finished praying, made the sign of the cross over herself. They tiptoed down the aisle, past several kneeling nuns belonging to the group that they had overtaken on the hill. Sister Patrick lingered at the pamphlet stand beside the holy water stoup and examined the choice of postcards: various views of the church, in different seasons. Waiting for her, Lily browsed in a pamphlet, *Aging—A Catholic Perspective:* " . . . our greatest anxiety concerning death is the fear of non-being, loss of identity, personhood. We are afraid we won't exist. . . ."

Hastily Lily replaced the pamphlet and went out into the sunshine, leaving Sister Patrick to make up her mind about the postcards.

"I was hoping we could see Father," said the nun, emerging presently, "but the door to the presbytery was closed. He might be napping. He's ninety-one, you know. We have time to sit on that grassy bank for a little while. I think it's dry enough, don't you? Or we could sit on our jackets. It's warm today."

"We don't have to," said Lily. "I always carry an old bedspread in the trunk of the car for when Jason and I go to the Nature Center together. He likes to take a picnic sometimes, and we sit near the water and watch the otters play."

"How *is* Jason?" asked the nun when they were seated comfortably on Lily's spread (actually an old one of her mother's) in the shade of a hickory tree. At the steep angle at which they were sitting, the surrounding mountaintops seemed to lie about their feet. At this altitude, the colors of the trees were farther along in their turning than they had been in Mountain City. Sister Patrick had not exaggerated: this was a sublime spot. How the late Mr. C.P. Summerall would have loved this view. He would have screwed up his eyes and breathed roughly and then begun to squeeze out his colors, sighing sadly in advance because he knew he could never, ever, quite catch it, though he must go on repeating his efforts till he died.

"Oh, Jason is a little survivor," said Lily, taking out her embroidery. "He has such an affectionate nature, and an empathy far beyond his years. Every day I see more of Theo in him. Theo was always worrying about how other people felt. And Jason is such a little diplomat! Of course, he's had to be, going back and forth between us and the Mullinses, when there are . . . so many differences. I probably shouldn't be telling this, because it puts *me* in a bad light, but last weekend when he was staying with us, I happened to say something a little derogatory about his mother to Ralph. I thought Jason was in the next room playing, and I was so annoyed with Snow, because she had called to say she'd be coming three hours *late* to pick up Jason, which meant Ralph and I both had to rearrange *our* plans, and I said, oh, it wasn't *that* awful, something like 'Well, what can you expect from a laidback hillbilly; at least she did us the favor of *phoning*,' and suddenly we looked around and there stood Jason at the kitchen door, with his arms folded over his chest and a peculiar little smile on his face, and he said, 'Angel, you will apologize for your rudeness.'"

"Did he, now," said Sister Patrick, laughing.

"Yes, he did. And, you know, I did. I did apologize for my rudeness. He made me say it: 'I apologize for my rudeness.' And I *was* sincerely sorry for my carelessness in letting him overhear me as much as anything else. She is his mother, after all. And I admire him for standing up for his mother. I would expect Rafe or . . . Theo to do the same for me, even if they were four years old like Jason."

"Yes, indeed," said Sister Patrick. "And what is Snow doing now? Still living up in Granny Squirrel with all her family?"

"That is exactly what she is doing. That is all she is doing. I suppose one of our biggest points of difference is that she seems to feel that what she is doing is *enough*. Whenever I ask her whether she wouldn't like to train for something or develop an interest, she folds her arms exactly the way Jason did in the kitchen doorway and says . . . well, I'm going to stop imitating her *twang*, that is one of my new resolutions: she says, 'I have a *child*, isn't that an interest? And if I was to go off and train for something, who would be there for Jason when he gets home from Headstart?'"

"She has a point," admitted Sister Patrick.

"Well, not really. There are so many of them huddled together up in that family compound. There's the sister Sue, the one they're sharing the trailer with: Sue and her little boy. And there's the mother, Mrs. Mullins, who's always around, anyway. Do you know, Jason can already make biscuits? Mrs. Mullins has to make them twice a day for the old grandfather—he refuses to eat a warmed-over biscuit—and Jason has helped her so many times that, when he comes to our house, if I stand him on a chair and get out all the ingredients, he can mix them up all by himself. Then I roll them out for him—he's not quite strong enough to do that—and he cuts them out with a jelly glass, and they're the best biscuits I've ever eaten."

"It doen't sound all bad," said Sister Patrick carefully. "He has so many people to love him, to teach him different things."

"You're right," conceded Lily. "That's the way I'm going to have to try and see it. Mrs. Mullins will teach him to dig potatoes and make biscuits, and all his rough little cousins will teach him how to be tough and protect himself, and if I can just teach him to expect the most of himself and help shape his ideals, I will die a happy woman. It's what I care about most, seeing that child grow up strong and intelligent, without being damaged irrevocably by his early bad luck. It's what I am living for now. When Clare called yesterday from Switzerland, to wish me happy birthday, I could tell she was a little disappointed that I didn't get more excited about our relatives in Switzerland. Ten years ago, I might have been. But 'roots' don't matter to me much anymore. Ancestors-in-common are just more antique clutter and old debris. I care about what's here for me to do *now*."

"I know what you mean," agreed Sister Patrick. "I didn't realize your birthday was yesterday. So was my father's. He would have been a hundred and four."

"I wasn't quite that old yesterday, but I'm getting there," said Lily with a dry laugh.

"You know, I —" Sister Patrick began.

"How did you happen to —" Lily began at the same time.

Both women apologized and each begged the other to go first. Sister Patrick said hers could wait and Lily said she was just about to be nosy and hers could wait, too. But the nun blushed and insisted and finally prevailed.

"Well," said Lily, "I was just wondering about the chain of

events in your life that took you from Ireland to Mountain City. How did you come to join a French order, for instance?"

"Because I didn't want to stay at home. Not that I didn't like Ireland, but I wanted to do something difficult for God. For a while I entertained the idea of being a missionary in India, but I didn't have the courage. So I went to talk to the nuns at my school, and they told me about this order. I went to Belgium three days after my eighteenth birthday and entered the noviatiate. The worst part about it was learning French; I have an atrocious accent to this day. I was professed five years later and told I would be going to work in the American South. I remember my first thought was I'd at least get to teach poor black children, which would be *almost* as challenging as being a missionary in India." The nun laughed. "But it was to be nearly thirty years before I taught a single black child, and I can't say to this day I've ever taught a really poor one. Oh, I remember so well the day I arrived in Mountain City. It was spring of 1937, a beautiful spring day. Mother LaForgue and I had travelled down from New York on the train—she and I had sailed from Belgium together; she died a few years ago, of hardening of the arteries, up in Boston at the motherhouse. We had a Pullman, but neither of us had any idea of what we were in for on that train ride. We had no concept of American distances. In Ireland, if you rode the train for two hours, you crossed the entire country. And we hadn't eaten on the train, because we wanted to take Communion when we got to St. Clothilde's. When we arrived at South Mountain City Depot, we were both of us giddy as Dublin barflys, just from hunger and the fresh mountain air. . . ."

My daddy would have been working at the South Depot in 1937, thought Lily; why, he might even have seen the two nuns get off the train. Sister Patrick as a young woman of twenty-three and my father, in the same place at the same time, all those years ago! But she didn't want to interrupt the nun's narrative.

"Mother Duran met us at the Depot. She's dead now, too. I remember she had a hole in one of her gloves, and I was shocked, because in Belgium our novice mistress had been very strict about such things. Whenever we went out, we were to look just so. Odd, isn't it, the things we remember? I can see that hole in Mother Duran's glove as clearly as I can see my shoe in front of me now. Anyway, we got to the school and took Communion, and then we went into the big dining room for breakfast. Suddenly a black hand reached in front of me and set down a bowl of steaming oatmeal. It was the first time in my life I had seen a black hand at that close range. It belonged to Henrietta, the cook. And it was, as it turned out, the closest I was to come to black hands until I went to teach at Mountain City Catholic High in the sixties."

"Where you taught Thalia Thompson's daughter, Claudine," Lily could not resist putting in.

"Claudine Thompson, that young scamp. Always up to some mischief or other. But bright, bright. The bright ones are often the mischief-makers. You have to channel it. What is that you're making? The colors are so wonderfully rich."

"It's going to be a pillow. A belated wedding present. A darling girl I met at the beach last summer, a sort of friend of Clare's. . . ." Editing Felix out again, just to be on the safe side. "She just married into a strict Orthodox Jewish family. Her father was rather upset about it, but she's very happy, apparently."

"That's nice," said Sister Patrick. "What religion was the father?"

"He's Jewish, but not practicing."

"That's not so bad, then, is it? And as long as the girl's happy, as you say."

"Yes. Now, if *Rafe* could just find a nice girlfriend. He's found something he likes to *do,* which is very important; he really loves all this *projecting* about how big companies can make more money investing in real estate—he's had two papers published now, one under his own name and one with his thesis adviser, and he says when he gets his doctorate he can have his pick of business schools anywhere in the country because so many of them have money for just the kind of work he's doing; he'll be one of the first to get a doctorate in real estate, it's a brand-new field in the academic world. So *that's* all right. Now he just needs the right girl. I can imagine just what she would be like, only where is she? Rafe's such an attractive boy; if I were a girl his age—no, a little younger would be best—I'd be falling at his feet. But either he likes girls who aren't suitable, or the girls he aspires to don't seem to aspire to him."

"He's still young," said Sister Patrick. "There's still plenty of time."

"I suppose so. You're right. Better to wait a little longer than to marry someone totally unsuitable —" Lily stopped herself nobly. She stitched on in the companionable silence for a while. Sister Patrick seemed to be appraising her own shoes intently. They were nice shoes, Lily couldn't help noticing. Shoes always looked more elegant when you had long, thin feet. Sister Patrick must wear at least a triple A. Lily cast a disparaging glance at her own $6\frac{1}{2}$ C's. Lily's mother would never let her go barefoot when she was a child. "You don't want your feet to spread any *more*," she would say.

"You know," began Sister Patrick, twisting her nun's flat silver wedding ring around and around her finger nervously and suddenly blushing up to the line of her permanently waved white hair, "I had this dream last night."

Lily's needle halted in the cloth. Good gracious, what sort of dream was the woman to tell her, blushing like that?

"I dreamed of Theo. As soon as I woke up, I knew it had been Theo. The way he looked at the last, when he wore the mustache. You know, he brought his little boy out to the convent to show to Sister Jouret, who'd taught him in first grade. In my dream Theo looked like he did that day. A handsome fellow."

Lily could not speak for a minute. She felt too many things. Astonishment. Pain. Hope. Then plain old-fashioned jealousy: why hadn't Theo come to *her* in a dream last night?

"I would like so much to hear it," she said when she could speak calmly.

In and out went the needle, doing a fish for Lizzie in burning yellow against the blue cloth, as Sister Patrick told her dream in a strange, embarrassed rush compounded with a sort of exaltation. Lily had copied a fish painting of Paul Klee's for Lizzie's pillow, but was adding her own embellishments. ". . . and then he asked if he could come back to the school with me and wash his hands . . . to the old building, you know, the way it used to be . . . and as we walked up the hill together he was explaining something to me very forcefully and energetically, yes, very sure of himself he was, I just now realized that. He was trying to explain himself, probably what had happened with the horse, with Shadow, why she had struck him down. But I couldn't hear without my hearing aids in." The nun laughed ruefully, twisting her ring around and around. "That's a fine how d'you do, isn't it, when you get to the place where you need your hearing aids even in your own dreams."

"Was that the end, then?" asked Lily.

"That was the end. I hope I did right to tell you. Of course, there are so many opinions about dreams. Some would say they're nothing more than a jumbled version of whatever the dreamer is preoccupied with at the time. And, you see, I'd been thinking about my father and, I suppose, Ireland, yesterday on his birthday. And then, there was Theo's name written down right below, in my daybook. I wrote it in last year, on this day, so that I would always pray for him. As for Shadow, well, I dream of her now and then. I always have done, ever since I left Ireland. She was a most unusual horse. The only sad part about last night's dream was that I didn't get to see her. But the rest wasn't sad. Anyhow, I thought I would tell you."

"I find it very hopeful," Lily assured her. "And I believe it implicitly. What I mean is, I believe Theo really did appear in your dream and send a message."

"Well, I don't know . . ." the nun replied uncertainly.

"Oh, *yes*," persisted Lily, growing more emphatic. "So many things make sense. You remember when Theo was just a little boy and Reverend Mother General came over from Paris and he wouldn't shake hands with her until he ran and washed his hands so they'd be clean enough for her?"

"Ah, of course. Sister Jouret still talks about it. Theo was in first grade. As a matter of fact, I think Sister was remembering it just last week. . . ." Sister Patrick bit her lower lip and appeared suddenly thoughtful. "Maybe that's why I dreamed —"

"No, no." Lily cut her off. "It wasn't just your . . . your *jumblings*. The whole thing, well, it's perfectly clear; it's all there!" Having started off by being resentful that Sister Patrick and not she had seen Theo last night, Lily now found herself in the paradoxical position of having to defend the dream against the nun's own skepticism. "It was Theo's way of sending a message that it's all right, don't you see? The details of how he was . . . struck down, exactly what *happened* that day, well, they aren't important, they're just past history. That's why the details aren't important: they're already over, we don't need to know because it won't change anything. That's why you didn't need your hearing aids. But in the realm that matters, the realm where the indestructible personality lives on, the realm mere history can't touch, Theo lives. He lives, and right now he's in the process of climbing that very steep hill to sanctity; he's on the way to wash his hands so that he'll be fit to"—Lizzie's blazing yellow fish swam in the dark waters of her blurred vision, but she kept her voice steady—"to shake hands with God. Oh, I consider it a gift, your dream, Sister Patrick. I really do."

"In that case," the nun answered humbly, "then I do, too."

Lily finished the interior of the fish and broke off the yellow thread. She wondered if there was time to do its red eye and the sizzly red hackles along its back and its red tail. Surely there was no such fish in nature. But that's why Klee was an artist. He trusted the nature of the inner eye. Which was, if you thought about it for a moment, *also* part of nature. "Why was the horse, your Shadow, so unusual?" she asked Sister Patrick, deciding she had time for at least the red eye.

"Ah, well, you see, because she didn't know, for the longest time, that she was a horse." And without any further prompting, Sister Patrick told her in her rich, musical, holiday voice that must have made her such a spellbinding teacher how, when she was twelve years old, her father had brought home a new mare and put her in the stables. Several months later, there was a racket at night that woke the whole family, and when they followed the source of the noise to the mare's stall, they saw this little scrawny shadow backed against the wall, and the mare angry as all blazes. At first they thought someone had put one of the young goats in with mare, as a prank. But then they saw it was a newborn filly. The mare had been pregnant but it had somehow escaped the father's notice. However, now she would have nothing to do with the little horse; she was too young herself to be a mother, was how the father explained it. So they raised the filly themselves. They named her Shadow and she grew up with the dogs and the children. Shadow played like the dogs and she played like the children. Sometimes she thought she was a dog, sometimes a child. She was allowed inside the house, and if you were sitting in a corner reading she would come and put her head in your lap and drool upon your book until you closed it up and stroked her. She was everyone's great favorite. Meanwhile, she was growing, but nobody noticed how much until, one day, when she had reached two hundred and fifty pounds, she "jumped" Sister Patrick as she was running to fetch the mail. "It didn't hurt me, but I guess it could have. That was when Father sent her away to a trainer who would teach her how to be a horse. She didn't come back for a year. And when she did, of course, she was completely changed. I don't really believe she knew us anymore. But after she returned, she became more or less my horse. I felt responsible for her. I always felt, somehow, that I had caused the end of her colthood, or childhood. It was silly, I know; if it hadn't been me, it would have been someone else she would have jumped, sooner or later, and it might have been worse. My baby brother, for instance. But all the same, I felt responsible. We used to go on long rides after she came back in her horse incarnation, and I would talk to her secretly and remind her of the days when she was one of us. And later, when I decided I was going to go so far away and be a nun, she was the first one I told. I tried it out on her, so to speak. Also, to hear myself say it aloud. She sniffed a bit and went right on trotting, as calm as you please, and I had myself a good cry, right there on her back, and that same evening I told my mother and father. They sold her after I went to Belgium and I never saw her again. But after I was professed, I was allowed to go home and tell my family goodbye, because I was going off to America and might never see any of them again. And when my father came to meet me at the station, I could tell he was embarrassed and didn't know how to act towards me, in the habit and all. And I felt awkward myself until it came to me like an inspiration what I could say. 'Well, Father,' I said, 'you see they've made a nun out of me, just like they made a horse out of Shadow.' And he laughed and we hugged and it was fine after that. When we got home, the rest of them were a little awkward at first, but then he repeated what I'd said at the station and it was all fine after that."

They were almost late in getting Sister Patrick back to the convent in time for five o'clock evening prayer. "Don't worry," the nun kept reassuring Lily as they sped back to Mountain City, "if I miss it, I miss it. The great thing about the office is that it's said for you whether you're there or not. When we are traveling alone, or in hospital, or unable for any reason to be there in body, we know that the rest of the community is saying it for us."

"How nice." said Lily wistfully. "I wish we had something like that."

But traffic and traffic lights worked in their favor after all, and Lily's Pontiac, its fuel needle hovering perilously close to Empty, pulled up in front of the convent with three minutes to spare.

"Don't get out, Lily," said the nun, flinging off her seat belt and leaning over to graze Lily's cheek with her dry, warm one. "I'm going to make a run for it. It was such a treat. Thank you so much."

"Thank you, Sister Patrick. For . . . everything. Let's do it again real soon. Let's go back up there again and sit on top of the world."

"I'd love nothing better. And next time maybe we'll see Father; he won't be resting. Oh, and when you talk to Clare again, please give her my love and tell her to write me a letter one of these days."

"I certainly will."

"God bless you, Lily." The nun gave the car door a hefty slam. Her large pocketbook bumping against her hip, Sister Patrick in her smart narrow shoes took the small expanse of lawn in six or seven fluent strides and vanished inside the convent.

Lily tempted fate and braved it as far as the Gulf station on Charlton Street so she could use her credit card. Feeling Clare's diapproval all the way from Switzerland, she nevertheless pulled up beside the full-service island and let a nice man in an overall fill her tank and clean her windshield for her.

She stopped in at Our Lady's and lit a candle for Theo in front of the Blessed Virgin. "Thank you, my darling," she said. "And please keep sending me messages whenever you can, through whatever channels you choose." Then she knelt down in a side pew and said a prayer for each of her other children, and for precious Jason, and for Snow, who after all was his mother and who had sent her a birthday card signed "Love from Jason and Snow." The arrangement of the names, Lily thought, had showed an encouraging delicacy on the girl's part. She also said a prayer for Ralph. If she stopped praying for Ralph, she would be calling thirty-four years of her life into question, and she was not brave enough to do that yet. Unlike Sister Patrick, she was not able to tell her story backwards with such simplicity and assurance. *Could I even begin to step back into those mists of what I wanted, what I thought I was doing, at eighteen or twenty-three or twenty-nine, without thoroughly losing my way?*

As she came out of the church, young Father Devereaux was carrying a stack of neatly folded sheets and towels in from his little Japanese car. He had been to the laundromat. They stopped and exchanged pleasantries. Poor Father Devereaux; it had not been an easy year for him. The wagging tongues of Our

Lady's had taken their toll. Now he never had weekend guests
at the rectory. He had gotten thinner and looked lonely and
rather sad. Oh, the wagging tongues. If Jesus Christ had lived
in Mountain City and invited His disciples for a weekend,
thought Lily, indignant on behalf of the gentle and devout
young Father Devereaux, who reminded her in some ways of
her own Theo, the wagging tongues would probably have billed
it as a gay orgy.

Resolutely she drove home to Quick's Hill. I will be gracious
and receptive, she thought. I will accept a mint julep and tell
about going to the cemetery and maybe about the awful lilies.
No, better not. That might be asking for trouble. But I could
tell Sister Patrick's two jokes. That's what. First the one about
the case of herpes and then the one about Sister Davis and the
T-shirts. Save the longest and funniest for last. With any luck,
that should get us through the popcorn.

In the chapel at St. Clothilde's, the nuns had said their
Magnificat and had the reading and the responsory, and were
now nearing the end of the Intercessions.

"You commanded your angels to watch over your servants in
all their ways," said Sister O'Hare, who was hebdomadary.

"Guide those who are traveling and bring them home safely
in joy and peace," the community responded.

"You gave the angels the mission of announcing peace to
men."

"Inspire counsels of peace in the hearts of leaders and peoples
of all nations," the community answered.

"When you send forth the angels to gather together your
chosen people from every corner of the earth . . ."

"Do not let them pass over any of your children, but bring
them all to the unending gladness of your kingdom."

Then it was time for particular intentions.

"Let us pray very specially for our sister, Jeanne Marvell,
who is unable to come to chapel, that God will help her endure
her infirmity," said Sister O'Hare.

"I would like to ask Our Gracious Lord to grant my niece
Julie good weather for her wedding this coming Saturday," said
Sister Dugan, "if it be Thy will."

"Our old student Stephanie Robbins Starnes telephoned,"
said Sister Lanier, "asking for our special prayers. She and her

husband, Bob, have just found out that their fourteen-year-old son, Paul, has a particularly virulent form of liver cancer. But the doctors are going to try chemotherapy, starting early next week. Heavenly Father, that little family will need all the strength and courage You can give them for their ordeal. And I have one more request, from Jane Reese Cushman, from the class of 'fifty-eight. Her youngest son, Richard, is giving his debut clarinet recital at Little Carnegie Hall in New York this Saturday, the same day as Julie Dugan's wedding, and would like our prayers that he will give the finest performance his talent is capable of."

"Let us pray for all of our departed sisters in the order," said Sister Steinmetz, "and I would like to remember Sister Maria von Blücher in particular, because she was such a comfort to me. I also ask personally for your prayers, as I must go back again to the doctor on Friday."

"On this day a year ago," said Sister Patrick, "our old student Theodore Quick met his violent death, along with a young woman. Dear God, have mercy on their souls. And comfort Lily and Ralph Quick, his parents, and guide and protect his sister, Clare, and his brother Rafe, both of whom were also here with us for many years. And may You and your angels watch over and guide Theo's fatherless little boy, Jason Quick, and bestow wisdom on his mother, Snow, so that she may be able to help him grow up to be a strong and loving man."

"I would like to offer special prayers for the people who are going to die suddenly and alone," said Sister Davis.

"And I, dear Father," said Sister Jouret, "would like to pray for all those persons in the world who are just now most in need of prayers and have nobody to pray for them."

"May the Lord bless us, protect us from all evil, and bring us to everlasting life."

"Amen."